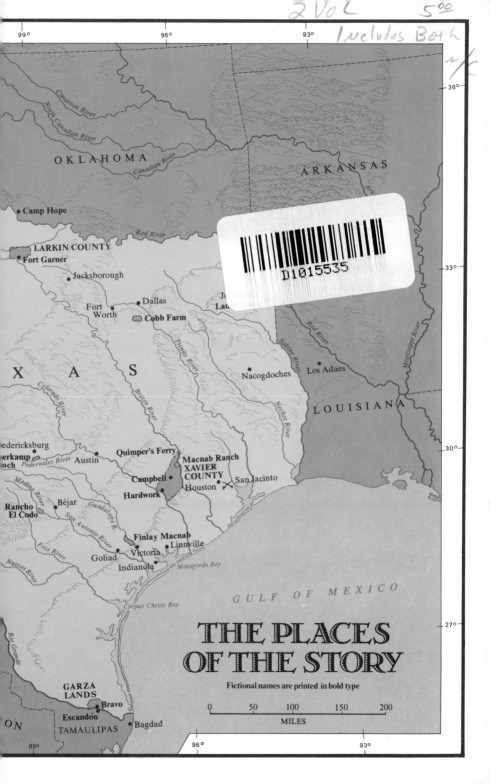

THE PLACES
OF THE STORY

Fictional names are printed in bold type

Camp Hope

LARKIN COUNTY
Fort Garner

Jacksborough

Fort
Worth   Dallas

Cobb Farm

X A   S

Nacogdoches   Los Adaes

LOUISIANA

ederieksburg
erkamp   **Quimper's Ferry**
nch   Austin   **Macnab Ranch**
                XAVIER
         Campbell **COUNTY**
                Houston   San Jacinto
         Hardwork

Rancho
El Codo   Béjar

         Finlay Macnab
                Linnville
      Goliad   Victoria
         Indianola   Matagorda Bay

            GULF   OF   MEXICO

Corpus Christi Bay

GARZA
LANDS   **Bravo**

Escandón
TAMAULIPAS   Bagdad

| 0 | 50 | 100 | 150 | 200 |
MILES

OKLAHOMA   ARKANSAS

Cimarron River
North Canadian River
Canadian River
Red River
Colorado River
Brazos River
Trinity River
Neches River
Sabine River
Red River
Mississippi River
Pedernales River
Medina River
Guadalupe R.
San Antonio River
Frio River
Nueces River
Rio Grande

99°   96°   93°   36°   33°   30°   27°

TEXAS

TEXAS

JAMES A. MICHENER

RANDOM HOUSE   NEW YORK

ACKNOWLEDGMENTS

Arrangements for my thirty-month research work in Texas were made by then-Governor William Clements, who fulfilled every promise he made and to whom I am grateful. My neighbor Margaret Wilson and my landlord Jack Taylor were helpful in arranging several of the meetings listed. I wish to thank the following for enlightening me on many facets of Texas life and history:

Land: Virginia Madison, Hallie Stillwell and Professor Barton Warnock of Sul Ross University on the Alpine area. Horace Goar on the land formations of East Texas. Clayton Williams on West Texas.

Water: Water, not oil, is the lifeblood of Texas, and the Ogallala Aquifer controls the availability of water for West Texas. During many local inspections of aquifer-fed land, the following were helpful: Dr. Idris Traylor of Texas Tech, on the basics; David Underwood of Lubbock and Joe Unfred, on utilization; Derrel Oliver of Muleshoe, on deep wells. Data on rainfall and climatology in general were checked against *Texas Weather,* a new book on the subject by George W. Bomar. Mr. Bomar, of the Texas Department of Water Resources, Weather and Climate Section, personally provided data for the rainfall map. David Murrah, Texas Tech, helped with books.

Animals: R. P. Marshall of the King Ranch spent two fine days with me lecturing on the habits of quail, and V. W. Lehman allowed me to read the manuscript of his masterful research study; it is now a beautifully illustrated book and the authoritative work on quail. Sam Lewis of San Angelo, fastest tongue in the West, introduced me to the armadillo, and Don English, present owner of the historic Appelt Armadillo Farm, allowed me to work with their lively stock. Professor Robin Doughty verified recent scientific data on these controversial little animals. Horace Goar taught me about wild turkeys and took me on a hunt. Bob Ramsey of Hunt showed me how to rattle up a buck and also how to make flint arrowheads in caveman style.

Cotton: Because the cultivation, ginning and utilization of this important fiber would form a leitmotif of the novel, I needed to do intensive work in three different parts of the state. Professors Ray Frisbie and Joe Knox Walker of Texas A&M, on controlling the boll weevil. The Harris Underwood family of Lubbock, on dryland cultivation. Mike McDonald, on preparing cotton for industrial use. Robert Hale of Littlefield, on milling denim.

Ranching: Ranch life is still a salient feature of Texas, and I was privileged to visit some of the best known or most typical. Mary Lewis Kleburg and Tom Kleburg of the vast King Ranch were repeatedly hospitable. B. K. Johnson of La Pryor was instructive; I attended two of his cattle sales. Bill Blakemore showed me his large spread near Alpine; in the same vicinity D. J. Sibley and his wife, Jane, shared their fairy-tale castle atop a mountain, with the six battlement towers, one for each of the Texas flags. The Presnall Cages of Falfurrias not only let me inspect their ranch but also showed me my first mesquite flooring. At Dripping Springs, the H. C. Carters offered friendship and expertise, and the Hardy Bowmans allowed me to participate in a birthday party at their ranch. Nancy Negley of San Antonio and the Palomas Ranch arranged a quail-and-turkey hunt for my instruction, and the Elizio Garcias of Encino showed me one of the oldest ranches in Texas. In Old Mexico, Charlie and Sabela Sellers of Sabinas entertained delightfully. Bill Moody and Violet Jarrett of Del Rio graciously explained their ranches, as did Mac and Eleanor McCollum of Houston. At his ranch near Brownwood, Thomas Cutbirth gave me a fine introduction to old-style barbecuing.

Exotic-game Ranching: I developed a special interest in how Texas ranchers endeavor to preserve certain forms of wildlife that may be disappearing in other parts of the world. The famous YO Ranch of Kerrville allowed me to prowl its pastures. Veterinarian Dr. Stephen Seager of A&M invited me to watch his researches in the field. Thomas Mantzell of Fort Worth had more sable antelope on his ranch than I ever saw in Africa. Lou and Wanda Waters of Utopia had a splendid ranch, and John Mecum, Jr., of Houston invited me to watch the dispersal of his huge exotic-game ranch along the Rio Grande. Dale Priour of Ingram provided technical data.

Longhorns: Charlene and Red McCombs of Johnson City invited me to their ranch for various events and also shared several hours with me on the revival of this historic breed. Jack Montgomery of Yuma, Colorado, read my segments on the Longhorn. Joan and H. C. Carter of Dripping Springs were always helpful, as was Walter Schreiner of the YO Ranch. Don and Linda Wiley of Austin took me to a chain of Longhorn ranches.

Spanish Backgrounds: So much for the land; now for the historical subject matter. On the Spanish heritage, San Antonio Mayor Henry Cisneros was most helpful. Victor Neimeyer of the Institute of Latin American Studies at the University of Texas arranged for valuable contacts in Mexico, where Dr. Israel Cavazos of Monterrey, and Jesus Alfonso Arreola and Javier Guerra Escandón of Saltillo offered perceptive comments. Countless consultants in both Mexico and Texas offered help of basic understandings, and the fact that I had previously written an entire book on Spanish culture speeded the discussions.

Spanish Mission Life: Dr. Felix D. Almaráz, Jr., of San Antonio showed me in detail the great missions of that city. Ben Pingenot of Eagle Pass shared his unrivaled knowledge of San Juan Bautista, the mission which was so important to early settlement in Texas. Charles Long, the lively curator of the Alamo, was repeatedly helpful in sharing with me his knowledge of that historic mission, and Gilbert R. Cruz, National Parks historian, provided additional highlights. Constant visits to the other monuments of San Antonio were necessary, the restored Governor's Palace being especially instructive.

Early American Settlement: Drew McCoy of Brazoria showed me around that crucial area. Officials of the Star of the Republic Museum at Washington-on-the-Brazos were helpful, as were custodians of other valuable collections, especially Dorman Winfrey of the Texas State Library. For a basic understanding of how the early settlers reacted to the land they were occupying, I am indebted to D. W. Meinig's excellent geographical study *Imperial Texas.* Clifton Caldwell generously presented research material.

The Trace: John S. Mohlenrich of the National Park Service was instructive regarding the history of this important road, which I traveled twice. Ranger-actors who portrayed historical characters at stops en route were much appreciated. Rita Stephens of Natchez told me much about the old days on the Mississippi.

Scottish and Scots-Irish Backgrounds: Myra and Gordon Porter of Carnoustie, Scotland, who own much of the land described in Glen Lyon shepherded me around most of northern Scotland. Ailsa and Alfred Fyffe of Cupar, classmates of mine at St. Andrews in 1932, helped and edited the Scottish material.

Three Battles: Anyone writing about the Alamo finds the ground well prepared by two fine books, which do not necessarily coincide in their interpretations: *Thirteen Days to Glory* by Lon Tinkle, and *A Time to Stand* by Walter Lord. I checked with each but obviously did not follow either entirely. I spent many hours inside the Alamo, talking with all the local experts. The Daughters of the Republic of Texas Library staff proved most helpful. For my study of the tragedy at Goliad, I am indebted to Charles Faupel and Mary Jane Plumb, who live in the small town of that name. For basic data of the Battle of San Jacinto, a critical moment in Texas history, I am indebted to Dr. Thomas H. Kreneck, in whose care I toured the site, and to J. P. Bryan of Houston. For Sam Houston's conduct prior to the battle, I followed a recent publication of Dr. Archie P. McDonald, Stephen F. Austin State University.

Germans: Irma Goeth Guenther, granddaughter of a wonderful diarist who came to Texas from Germany in 1845, was a delightful correspondent. Clifford and Sarah Harle of Fredericksburg went far beyond the demands of hospitality to help, and Ella Gold's memories were sharp and lively. Matthew Gouger of Kerrville showed me significant sites; August Faltin of Comfort was repeatedly helpful, and the writings of Glen E. Lich of Schreiner College were most useful.

Texas Rangers: Gaines de Graffenreid, guiding genius of the Texas Ranger Hall of Fame at Waco was constantly helpful, as was his associate Alva Stem. Former Rangers Alfred Alee and Walter Russel were especially informative, the latter giving me a stout walking stick he had used in his ranging days. H. Joaquin Jackson of Uvalde was informative, and some of my best days in Texas were spent with Clayton McKinney of Alpine. For a review of Texas Ranger activities during the Mexican War, I am indebted to Dr. Thomas H. Kreneck, who allowed me to read his manuscript on the subject.

South Carolina: Mary Frampton of Edisto Island was so generous in sharing with me her recollection of Edisto life that she merits special thanks. To Alan Powell of the Charleston Historical Society, I am indebted for an idea which proved most helpful in structuring the novel.

Jefferson: I spent many happy hours in this gracious old town. Mrs. Lucille Bullard was my frequent hostess, and I spent a rewarding day with Wyatt Moore of Karnack, the leading authority of the days when Jefferson was in effect a seaport. Numerous Jeffersonians were helpful, especially Mrs. Lucille Terry. Professor Fred Tarpley of East Texas State University allowed me to read the manuscript of his book *Jefferson: Riverport of the Southwest,* the best book on this area, and arranged several valuable local contacts.

Slavery: I did much work on this painful subject. Randolph B. Campbell of North Texas State University allowed me to read his remarkable manuscript on how slavery operated in the Marshall/Jefferson area. It is now a fine book, *A Southern Community in Crisis.* Doris Pemberton of Houston talked to me at different times. Various librarians drew my attention to important studies. Dr. James Byrd, Commerce, and Traylor Russell, Mt. Pleasant, also offered their insight.

Vicksburg: This great battlefield obviously haunted me. I spent three research trips there, following the experiences of the 2nd Texas Infantry. Katherine C. Garvin provided tour help during one of the trips, and the park staff answered many of my detailed queries.

Frontier Forts: I visited in depth some dozen of these variously preserved sites. At Fort Belknap, Barbara Ledbetter, an enthusiastic local historian, helped. Throughout, Robert Wooster, working toward his Ph.D. in Western military history, provided sensitive guidance. He is writing his own book on the subject. I also had the honor of being thrown out of Fort Davis, a U. S. National Park and perhaps the best restored of the Texas forts. Alas, I never saw it.

Fort Garner-Larkin: To construct this imaginary fort and town, I worked with sites and scholars throughout the entire area. I visited especially all the extant courthouses of that architectural genius James Riely Gordon. At Waxahachie, I met with M. E. Singleton, a man younger than I, whose grandfather, improbable as it seems, fought at San Jacinto.

Oil: Martin Allday of Midland arranged three extensive seminars on Western oilfields, most of which I visited in detail. The following are some of the many who gave generously of their time and knowledge: J. H. Fullinwider, B. J. Pevehouse, Tom Sealy, J. C. Williamson, Ford Chapman, Patsy Yeager, Tom Fowler and Joe Hirman Moore. Don Evans took me on a field trip. John Cox was especially helpful on oil-field financing. Bill Benson of Cheyenne, Wyoming, first put me in touch with the Graham area, about which I would write, and Joe

Benson and Ken Andrews explained in detail how oil-field royalties were distributed. In Livingston, Ben Ogletree arranged a unique experience. At three o'clock one morning I stood with him at a drilling site when a well came in. In appreciation of the good luck which he thought I had brought him, he named this substantial field after me.

Religion: I held many separate discussions about the role of religion in Texas, but the most informative was a three-day seminar with the scholars at Abilene Christian University: Professors Ian Fair, Richard Hughes, Bill Humble and R. L. Roberts. Gary McCaleb, public affairs officer at the university, was especially helpful. At a small rural church in McMahan, I heard the unique Sacred Harp Shaped-Note singing. William N. Stokes, Jr., allowed me to see his rousing account of how his father was 'churched' for allowing members of his Sunday School class in Vernon to dance.

Football: In Abilene, I also conducted a seminar on the second Texas religion, high school football: Wally Bullington, A. E. Wells, W. L. Lawson, David Bourland and particularly Beverly Ball, who told fascinating stories about the role of girl students and women teachers. George Brazeale, high school expert for the *Austin American-Statesman,* was helpful, but my special debt is to Dave Campbell of Waco, publisher of a spectacularly successful magazine about Texas football. On the university level, Coach Darrell Royal, formerly of the University of Texas, was exemplary in his sharing of knowledge of ideas.

Border Problems: On three occasions I worked with the Border Patrol along the Rio Grande. Officers James J. Fulgham, Dennis L. Cogburn, Clifford Green and William Selzer allowed me to accompany them on patrols in the Laredo district. In El Paso, I worked with Alan E. Eliason, William G. Harrington, Dale Cozart and Raymond Reaves.

Mexican Problems: I was meeting with Isidra Vizcaya Canales, a factory manager in Monterrey, when the peso was devalued. I was serving in Mexico City as an official of the United States Government when relations between the two countries deteriorated. I conducted seminars in various parts of Texas to obtain a wide scatter of opinions. Nowhere did I find unanimity as to what might happen by the year 2010. In Corpus Christi, Dr. Hector P. Garcia was most helpful, and in the same city, Tony Bonilla, president of the famous LULAC (League of United Latin American Citizens), was instructive. Yolanda and Mario Ysaguirre of Brownsville were especially gracious and arranged a field trip to Bagdad, and I profited from discussions with Paredes Manzano and Robert Vezzetti of that city.

Texas Business: In the latter chapters of this novel, writing about business and wealth became inescapable. I had the privilege of talking, sometimes at extended length, with the following experts: Trammell Crow, Vester Hughes, John Bucik and Bunker Hunt of Dallas; Gerald Hines, Walter Mischer, Sr., and George Mitchell of Houston; Clayton Williams, Bill Blakemore and John Cox of Midland. David Adickes, an artist friend from the old days in Japan, allowed me to inspect the record of his real estate dabblings, and many others in many locations talked with me about money problems, including John M. Stemmons, Louis Sklar and Larry Budner.

Honky-tonks: I enjoyed extended interviews with the owners of the two premier honky-tonks in Texas, Sherman Cryer of Gilley's in Pasadena, Texas, and Billy Bob Barnett of Billy Bob's in Fort Worth. Each owner was a novel in himself, each of the dance halls was overwhelming.

Rio Grande Valley: I wanted to represent adequately and honestly the unique Mexican-American world of the Valley and its citrus industry: Professor Julian Sauls of the USDA Citrus Laboratory, Les Whitlock of the Citrus Committee, Professor Dick Hoag of the Texas A&I Citrus Center and Clyde White, president of the Texas Cooperative Exchange. Former Governor Allan Shivers and his wife were especially helpful in inviting me to visit their Sharyland home near Mission, where their manager, Blaine H. Holcomb, gave valuable instruction on the citrus industry.

Miscellaneous Interviews: Robert Nesbitt, Galveston; Hayden and Annie Blake, Corpus Christi; Nelson Franklin and Dean Cobb, Austin; Ed and Susan Auler, Tow; Tom Moore, Lajitas. Cactus Pryor and John Henry Faulk, Austin, provided caustic comment.

Airplane Flights: It is obvious from the above listing that I had to visit all of Texas, not only the easy parts, and in doing so, I was dependent upon generous neighbors who allowed me to use their planes: Trammel Crow and John Blanton of Dallas; Mary Lewis Kleberg of the King Ranch; Walter Mischer, Sr., of Houston, H. C. Carter, Joe Hiram Moore and Howell Finch of Austin, the last-named flying me at very low levels over most of the western oil fields; Bill Blakemore and Robert Holt of Midland; Charles C. Butt of Corpus Christi and Presnall Cage of Falfurrias, who flew me over the sandbanks of Padre Island. I also flew with Clayton Williams on several occasions. He lent me his helicopter for two days of wild exploration in far West Texas, and Bob Macy flew me over the cotton farms of Levelland. When I told Clifford Green of Laredo that I wanted to see the Rio Grande close up from the air, he took me on an extended flight in a one-engine plane along the river at an altitude so low that I had to look almost straight up to see the top of the banks above me.

University of Texas: I enjoyed constant cooperation and scholarly assistance from many faculty members of the university. President Peter Flawn was both understanding and helpful; Dean of Graduate Studies William Livingston swiftly resolved any quandaries; Director Don Carleton of the Barker Texas History Center provided both an office and his constant support; his excellent staff found all the books I needed. Dr. Lewis L. Gould, chairman of the History Department, was at all times cooperative, as was Dr. L. Tuffly Ellis, director of the Texas State Historical Association, who put me in touch with many valuable contacts throughout the state. Jack McGuire of the Institute of Texan Cultures in San Antonio offered ethnic research material, and Dorman Winfrey, director of the Texas State Library, was continually helpful. John Wheat, an expert in Spanish Studies, gave valuable help when requested. Since the university has eighteen major libraries, with a total of more than five million volumes, it is a great place to work.

Texas Handbook: Any writer on Texas finds himself indebted to the *Texas Handbook,* a unique three-volume encyclopedia. A treasure trove of historical research, it is now undergoing a monumental expansion to six large volumes that will require ten years of work. It will then be indispensable to any serious student of Texas and will have no equal in any other state.

Assistants: John Kings, who had organized my office and helped on research for *Centennial,* proved once more that he is both an editor and an understanding colleague; Robert Wooster and Frank de la Teja, who are studying for their Ph.D.s in Western history and Latin American Studies, respectively, were delightful to work with; Lisa Kaufman was most skillful in word processing and offered cogent comment; her processor was a valued loan from Kenneth Olson, president of Digital Corporation. Debbie Brothers was most adept in coordinating the final revisions. Anders Saustrup, most knowledgeable in the minutiae of Texas history, carefully vetted the manuscript. In a most generous way, although he lived in San Antonio, T. R. Fehrenbach, author of *Lone Star: A History of Texas and the Texans,* provided special help and original insights when requested.

I would like also to acknowledge those scores of loyal and enthusiastic Texans who sent me letters, diaries, manuscripts, books and documents telling the stories of their ancestors, whose fortitude and resourcefulness contributed to the unique characteristics of this state. Their interest was remarkable, generous, unprecedented in my experience, and most encouraging to a Northerner like me. Thank you all.

This novel is dedicated to three distinguished literary critics

I have been informed that many books of fiction . . . which are unrelated to religion . . . go to the Indies [which would include what later became Texas]; since this is bad practice . . . I commend you, therefore, from this time henceforth neither to permit nor allow any person at all to take any books of fiction there, but only those relating to the Christian religion and morality . . . No other kind is to be allowed.

I, the Queen[1][of Spain]
4 APRIL 1531

Another damned, thick, square book! Always scribble, scribble, scribble! Eh! Mr. Gibbon?

William Henry, Duke of Gloucester,[2]
to the author of
The Decline and Fall of the Roman Empire.
1781

Third. My will is that my sons receive solid and useful education
. . . I wish [them] to be early taught an utter contempt
for novels . . .

Sam Houston,[3]
His Last Will and Testament,
2 APRIL 1863

[1] She issued this order while the King was busy in another country.
[2] He never amounted to much.
[3] He was forced to surrender almost every good job he ever had.

FACT AND FICTION

This novel strives for an honest blend of fiction and historical fact, and the reader is entitled to know which is which.

The Governor's Task Force: The Task Force is wholly fictional, as are all the participants, including the governor. At the end of each chapter the Task Force sessions are imaginary, as are the invited speakers.

I. Land of Many Lands: The three great explorations, and all their incidents, were historical. Only the boy Garcilaço de Garza is fictional. For example, Cárdenas and El Turco were real people.

II. The Mission: Santa Teresa is fictional, but the other five San Antonio missions, which can be visited today, were historical. Of the principal characters, only Juan Leal Goras was real.

III. El Camino Real: Béjar and Saltillo are historical and are accurately reported. All characters are fictional. The Veramendi family of Saltillo and Béjar was real, and very important, but the specific members shown here are fictional.

IV. The Settlers: Only Stephen F. Austin and Sam Houston were historical. Víctor Ripperdá is fictional, but his famous uncle was real. The Quimper family is fictional, as is their ferry. Father Clooney and Reverend Harrison are fictional.

V. The Trace: The Macnabs and all other characters are fictional, but the Glencoe Massacre was historical. The De Leóns of Victoria had a real empresario grant.

VI. Three Men, Three Battles: Jim Bowie, Davy Crockett, William Travis, James Fannin, James Bonham, Galba Fuqua, Mirabeau Lamar and Sam Houston on the Texas side were historical, as were Santa Anna, Cós, Urrea and Filisola on the Mexican. Garza, Ripperdá, Campbell, Marr, Quimper, Harrison and the Macnabs are fictional. Descriptions of the three battles, including the blizzard north of Monclova, strive to depict historical fact. Goliad especially, one of the focal events of Texas history, is accurately portrayed.

VII. The Texians: The Allerkamps are fictional, as is their homeland Grenzler and their ship *Sea Nymph*. The founding of the Texas Rangers was historical, as were their major exploits in this chapter, specifically the expulsion of the Cherokee. Captain Sam Garner is fictional.

VIII. The Ranger: Rangers Macnab, Komax and Garner are fictional. Harry Saxon and Colonel Cobb are fictional. Generals Taylor and Scott were real. Each of the significant actions of the Rangers was historical, but specific sites have sometimes been shifted. The murder of Ranger Allsens was real, as was the retaliation.

CONTENTS

TEXAS

THE
GOVERNOR'S
TASK FORCE

I WAS SURPRISED WHEN SHORTLY AFTER NEW YEAR'S DAY OF 1983, THE GOVERNOR of Texas summoned me to his office, because I hadn't been aware that he knew I was in town. I'd been in Austin for some weeks, preparing a series of five lectures I was to deliver at the Lyndon B. Johnson School of Public Affairs at the University of Texas. The rather grandiloquent title, 'Southwest America in the World Society,' had been chosen by local scholars in a desire to broaden student horizons. The university authorities had left me pretty much to myself; I had paid a courtesy call on the president and had consulted two or three times with the dean of graduate studies, but to hear from the governor himself was something quite unexpected.

I was a native son and legal resident of Texas; however, for the past year I'd been working in Geneva on leave from my job at Boulder's well-regarded think tank, The Institute for Cultural Studies, which I headed. While serving in Boulder, I'd learned the truth of the old statement: 'When good Texans die they go to Colorado.'

I was gratified by my return to the university, for I found its students refreshing, even though some of the brightest seemed to come from up north. The best football players, however, enrolled at Texas, and that's what mattered.

I started in a low key with my students, but won their acceptance by stating in a newspaper interview: 'The students at the University of Texas may not be the best scholars in the world, but they're among the bravest. Anyone who crosses Guadalupe, the main drag by the campus, six times a day without police escort, has to be heroic.' I thought people drove crazy when I lectured at Coimbra University in Portugal, but Portuguese drivers are merely in training for the big time in Texas.

Confused as to why the governor might want to meet me, I left my guest office in the shadow of the main building. When I got outside I glanced up at its tower; the sight of it always set me thinking about the conflicting messages that it sent. After any football university major sports victory, and they came frequently at Texas, it was illuminated gaudily in the school color, burnt orange, but on gray and misty mornings, which came less frequently, I knew that people recalled that horrible August day in 1966 when Charles Whitman, an Eagle Scout, gained a gruesome immortality. After murdering his wife and mother, he filled a footlocker with guns, ammunition and knives and drove to the university. Slaying the receptionist, he took the elevator to the top of the tower, where he unlimbered his arsenal and began shooting at random any students or casual passers-by. In all, he killed sixteen persons before sharpshooters gunned him down. Saluting the handsome tower, I crossed the bustling campus which had so excited me when I first reported there in 1959. The university now had forty-eight thousand students, with some of the most attractive female students in America, a fact which was confirmed every time I stepped outside my office.

I walked south to Martin Luther King Boulevard and saw before me, six blocks down Congress Avenue, that majestic state capitol which had come into being in so strange a manner and with such curious results. In 1882 the state had been broke, but it lusted for the biggest possible capitol building to adorn the biggest state, so it offered three million acres of seemingly worthless western plains to anyone who would finance the project, and some Illinois investors took the bait. Behaving as if they were honorary Texans, they euchered the government out of an extra fifty thousand acres—and everybody was happy.

How wild the turns of history! The land which the legislature gave the Illinois syndicate did seem worthless, but some comparable West Texas land they gave the university—at about the same time—turned out to be dripping with oil, which made it potentially the richest university in the world.

As soon as I entered the familiar old capitol building with its high dome and nineteenth-century dignity, I was as captivated as I had been on that day long ago when I stood in the rotunda with the other children of my grade-school class to honor Sam Houston and the heroes of the Alamo. Today as I passed on my way to the governor's office, a new crop of children listened, eyes aglow.

When I reached the office his secretary, beautiful and leggy, like many Texas women holding such positions of importance, said cheerily: 'So glad to have you with us, Professor. The others are waiting inside.' And with that, she pinned on my left lapel a badge which said 'Dr. Travis Barlow, Institute for Cultural Studies.'

'Who are the others?' I asked, and she said: 'The governor will explain.'

She led me to an anteroom decorated with a buffalo head on the wall and two fine Longhorn hides on the floor, but the real attraction was a group of four citizens, chosen with care, apparently, as if to represent the strength and diversity of Texas. Since we were obviously to form a unit of some kind, I tried to fix in memory each face and its accompanying tag.

The first such pair belonged to a tall, thin, droop-shouldered, scowling man whose appearance alone would attract attention regardless of where he sat, but when I saw his tag I understood his real notoriety. He was Ransom Rusk, designated by both *Fortune* and *Forbes* as one of the richest men in Texas, 'net worth probably exceeding one billion.' He was in his late fifties, and from the way in which he withdrew from others, I judged that he was determined to protect both his wealth and his person from would-be intruders. Although he was dressed expensively he was not neat, and this and his permanent frown indicated that he didn't care what others thought of him.

He was talking with a man of completely different cast, a big, easy, florid fellow, also in his fifties, wearing an expensive whipcord suit of the kind favored by ranchers, high-heeled boots, and about his neck a western bolo string tie fastened with a large turquoise gemstone. When I read his tag, Lorenzo Quimper, I had to smile, for he was a legend, the prototypical Texas wheeler-dealer, owner of nine ranches, friend of presidents, dabbler in oil and everything else, and a rabid supporter of his university athletic teams. He was a handsome man, but there was something too expansive about him; if he were your small-town banker, you would not trust him with your money. Seeing me enter, he turned momentarily in my direction, smiling broadly. 'Hiya, good buddy,' he said, offering his hand. 'My name's Quimper. Welcome to the big time.' He returned instantly to his conversation with Rusk, for in his book I was worth three seconds.

The third person I turned to was a tall patrician woman in her late sixties, beautifully dressed, beautifully groomed. She had a no-nonsense mien and looked as if she was accustomed to serving on boards and making important decisions. Her tag said that she was Miss Lorena Cobb, and I recognized her as the daughter and granddaughter of two remarkable United States senators who in the years following the Civil War had made commendable contributions to Texas and to the nation. She was one of those standard Texas women, overawed in their twenties by the excessive machismo of their men, but emergent in their fifties as some of the most elegant and powerful females on earth. They formed the backbone of Texas cities, persuading their wealthy husbands and friends to build hospitals and museums, then dominating the society which resulted. Women like her made those of Massachusetts and New York seem downright anemic. But the immediate impression she created was one of agreeableness. I admired her manner, even as she sat there with her hands clasped primly in her lap, for she seemed to be saying 'Let's get on with it.'

The most interesting of the four was a small-boned man in his late thirties, about five feet five, weighing not over a hundred and fifty, with a smooth olive skin, black hair and a small, neatly trimmed mustache. His tag said 'Professor Efraín Garza, Texas A&M,' and I concluded from the accent mark in his first name that he might be a visiting scholar from Mexico. But if that was true, what was he doing here? I was about to ask questions when the door to the inner office opened and the governor himself came in to greet us. Red-headed, burly, in his middle fifties, he moved with a restrained energy that seemed to warn: 'Let's go. We haven't much time.'

'Hello! Hello! I hope you've all met.' When we indicated that we had not, he stopped and grabbed Rusk by the arm as if the billionaire was, because of his power, entitled to be introduced first: 'You've surely seen this man in the papers.

Well, here he is, Ransom Rusk.' The tall man smiled bleakly, and the governor moved on.

'This rascal is the state's unofficial ambassador of good will, Lorenzo Quimper.' Newspapers had dubbed him Lorenzo il Magnifico in recollection of the flamboyant Medici prince, and there was a good deal of the Renaissance condottiere about him: lobbyist, oilman, real estate developer, wrecker of the university, builder of the university, principal cheerleader at any university athletic contest, scourge of liberal Jewish professors from the North, he had been a stormy petrel of Texas life for a generation. Hated by many, loved by others with equal intensity, he was the darling of the rough-diamond element in Texas life, their spokesman and defender. At the university baseball games, which he rarely missed, the irreverent bleachers would rise after the visiting team had batted in the fifth inning, and a tuba, a trombone and a trumpet would play a sustained flourish as a huge sign was draped across the railing: 'All Hail, Lorenzo il Magnifico! The Bottom of the Fifth.' And the leader of the undergraduate gang would hoist an immense whiskey bottle filled with some amber liquid and drain it—to the wild applause of an audience who thus toasted Quimper's remarkable capacity for booze. Now when he smiled at me radiantly, in the way a little boy would, I knew I was going to like him. Curse and even despise him at times, yes, but enjoy him.

At this moment he crossed his legs, allowing us to see the full expanse of his remarkable boots. They were light-gray leather adorned in front by large Lone Stars in silver. Above each star, as if to protect it, spread extended greenish-bronze Longhorns, while along the outer flank of each boot appeared a small Colts revolver made of burnished gold. 'Hey!' Professor Garza cried. 'Are you General Quimper?'

'It's one of my companies.'

'You make terrific boots.'

'We go for the muted understatement,' Quimper said, brushing the right Colts with his fingers. 'We call it "Texas refined." '

'And here is the star of our group,' the governor resumed, 'Miss Lorena Cobb.' He kissed her, whereupon Rusk and Quimper did the same. She held out her hand to Garza and smiled warmly. Then she shook my hand with just a little more reserve, for she was not sure who I was.

'The brains of our group, and I say that enviously,' the governor continued as he reached Garza, 'Professor of Sociology, Texas A&M.'

'Did you hear the one about the meeting of the state library board?' Quimper broke in, gripping Dr. Garza by the arm. 'They were doling out funds and this expert from UT said: "Why should we give A&M anything? They already have two books, and one of them isn't even colored yet." ' Dr. Garza, smiling wanly, like a man who had to suffer much, turned and shook my hand. I was pleased to meet him because, unlike Quimper, I had great regard for A&M, in my opinion the top technical school in the Southwest.

Now the governor faced me. 'To head this group of prima donnas, I had to find someone with an international reputation. And here he is, Dr. Travis Barlow, who took a distinguished doctorate at Cambridge in England. And you were an undergraduate here at Texas?'

'I was.'

'And you won a Pulitzer Prize for that book you wrote in Colorado?'

'I did.'

'Well, you're to be chairman of this Task Force.'

'Task Force on what?' Rusk asked, and the governor said: 'That's what we're here to talk about. I did not specify your duties because I wanted none of you to decline.'

When we were seated about the big table in his office he said: 'As a main feature of our Sesquicentennial, I want you to place before our citizens a comprehensive report on two important questions: "How should our schoolchildren and college students learn about Texas history?" And "What should they learn?" '

'First thing they should learn,' broke in Quimper, 'is that the stupid word *sesquicentennial* means one hundred and fifty.'

'Lorenzo!' the governor retorted. 'All Texans except you speak Latin.'

'I would too, if I'd gotten past third grade,' Quimper said in the mock-illiterate style he sometimes affected.

'Is this to be just another study?' Rusk asked.

'Heavens, no!' the governor moaned, and he pointed to a shelf in the corner of his office where a pile of notebooks rested. 'We've studied Texas education up to our armpits. What I seek now are specific, hard-nosed recommendations.'

'On what?' Rusk asked.

'On how to instill in our children a love for the uniqueness of Texas.'

'Doesn't that sound a little pompous?' Miss Cobb asked, and the governor said: 'On the day you become governor of this great state you realize that it really is unique . . . what a priceless heritage we've been given to protect.' I could hear bugles sounding at the Alamo.

'Como Tejas, no hay otro,' Quimper said with a bow toward Garza. 'There's no place like Texas. I tell that to all my ranch hands.'

'That's the point,' the governor said. 'The six of us know how unique we are, but the hordes drifting down from states like Michigan and Ohio, they don't know. And the equal number flooding in from below the Rio Grande, they don't know, either. If we don't take steps to preserve our heritage, we're going to lose it.'

'What exactly are we to do?' Miss Cobb asked.

'Three things. First, define the essentials of our history, the things that have made us rather more significant than the other states.' Now I could hear the band playing at some remote frontier fort in 1869 when Texas fought off the wild Comanche. 'Second, advise our educational leaders as to how they can safeguard this heritage and carry it forward. Third, I want you to hold your Task Force sessions in various parts of the state—to awaken interest, pose challenges, organize displays of Texas history, and above all, allow everyone with a special interest to have his or her say.'

'We could put together a big television show,' Quimper said enthusiastically, but no one supported him.

'As to housekeeping details,' the governor resumed, 'I have ordered that state funds be made available to pay the salaries of three graduate students to assist you. The three I've chosen happen to be relatives of state senators, but even so, I'm assured they're bright. And they're from different parts of the state. Texas Tech, Texas El Paso, and a very talented young publicity woman from SMU. You have them for the duration, researching the facts, helping to organize the report. You'll also have ample funds for travel and for guest speakers. As I said before, I want you to hold each of your meetings in a different city. So that the whole state participates. And of course you'll have access to books, maps, word processors, and central office space here in the capitol building.'

At this point he stepped back to study us admiringly: 'My Task Force! You know, I served in the navy off Vietnam, and even the words thrill me. A task force, sleek ships speeding through the night. Your mission is extremely important.'

'We may be your Task Force,' Quimper said, 'but I'll bet you don't want us to fire any big guns.'

'Let's go in to lunch,' the governor said, and when we were seated he counseled us: 'Lorenzo was right. No gunfire. Make as few people unhappy as possible. Avoid the adverse headline. But snap this state to attention regarding its history.' Then, pointing his finger at Miss Cobb, he said: 'And people like you are the ones who can do it.'

During the luncheon I noticed two peculiarities. Ransom Rusk seemed to speak only to his equals, Quimper and Miss Cobb, ignoring Garza and me. And everyone said 'Miss Cobb,' except Il Magnifico, who invariably addressed her as Miss Lorena, pronouncing it with a courtly 'Miz,' which she seemed to appreciate. After he had done this several times I thought that if I was going to be chairman of the group, I should participate in some of the conversation: 'Lorena's a beautiful name, Miss Cobb,' and she replied with just a touch of restraint: 'It was a cherished song in the War Between the States. Cherished by the Southern troops.'

I detected something else of considerable importance to me personally: Ransom Rusk and Lorenzo Quimper, as two wealthy Texans accustomed to power, expected to dominate this committee. Everything they said and did betrayed this intention, and while they were not stupid, they were in my opinion reactionary and would, if left alone, draft a right-wing document. I vowed right then that I would prevent that from happening, but how, I did not know, because they were formidable men.

Now the governor, wishing to establish our credentials, addressed each of us in turn: 'Rusk, your people arrived in Texas when—1870s? From Pennsylvania? Miss Cobb, your people came from the Carolinas, 1840s, wasn't it? And Quimper, you beat us all, didn't you—1822 or thereabouts, from Tennessee? Wasn't a Quimper the Hero of San Jacinto?' Lorenzo nodded modestly.

When he came to me, it was obvious he had no knowledge of my ancestry: 'When did your people arrive, Barlow?'

But I had a real surprise for him; I smiled and said: 'Moses Barlow. Arrived in Gonzales . . . from nowhere known . . . 24 February 1836. Three days later he volunteered for the Alamo.'

Startled, the governor leaned back, then reached out to grasp my hands: 'That Barlow? We take great pride in men like him.'

I was eager to hear Professor Garza's credentials, but the charming secretary interrupted: 'Governor, please! The deputation's been waiting twenty minutes.'

After apologies for his abrupt departure, he called back: 'Carry on, Task Force! Let's get the ships in the water.'

We spent about an hour going over basics and I was pleasantly surprised at how knowledgeable these people were. Rusk cut directly to the heart of any problem, as billionaires learn to do, which is why they're billionaires, I suppose. Quimper provided us with a constant and I must say welcome barrage of Texas observations such as: 'He jumped on that one like a duck jumpin' on a June bug' and 'They'll be as busy as a cow swatting flies with a bobbed tail.' Like any self-respecting Texan, he was adept in barnyard and ranching similes.

Miss Cobb was, as I had suspected, very bright and well-disciplined, and as always in such circumstances I found myself wondering why she had not married. She was, I learned before the luncheon ended, heiress to the cotton-growing fortune of the two senators, and I was assured by Quimper that 'she could of gone to Washington too, had she wanted to make the fight when Lyndon Johnson pulled that swifty in 1960. He bulldozed a change in Texas election law making it legal for him to run for both the Senate and the vice-presidency on the same day. He won both elections, then surrendered his Senate seat. Neatest trick of his career, because it carried him to the presidency.'

It was she who verbalized our problem: 'We must remind our students and ourselves that Texas is great because it boasts seven different cultural inheritances.'

'Which seven?' Rusk asked.

And now I made an amusing discovery. I had been worrying about the wrong potential dictators, Rusk and Quimper. The real danger was going to be with Miss Cobb, because although she wore the muted gray of a retiring nun, it was really a battleship-gray, and when she spoke it was with steellike authority.

Standing before the big map in a conference room attached to the governor's office, she lectured us as if we were schoolchildren: 'I'm not speaking about regional differences. Anyone can see that Jefferson up here in the swampy northeast bears little resemblance to El Paso down here in the desert, nearly eight hundred miles away. Such physical differences are easy. Even Northern newcomers can see them. But we miss the whole meaning of Texas if we miss the cultural differences.'

'I asked before, which ones?' Rusk did not suffer vagueness, not even from his friends.

'First, Indian. They flourished here centuries before any of us arrived, but in our wisdom we exterminated them, so their influence has been minimal. Second, Spanish-Mexican, which we try to ignore. Third, those stubborn Kentucky-Tennessee settlers, originally from places like New York and Philadelphia, who built their own little Baptist and Methodist world along the Brazos River. Fourth, we latecomers from the Old South, we built a beautiful plantation life of slaves, cotton and secession. Our influence was strong and lasting, as you can hear when Lorenzo calls me "Miz." Fifth, the great secret of Texas history, the blacks, whose history we mute and whose contributions we deny. Sixth, the free-wheeling cowboy on his horse or in his Chevy pickup driving down the highway with his six-pack and gun rack. And seventh, those wonderful Germans who came here in the last century to escape oppression in Europe. Yes, and I add the Czechs and the other Europeans, too. What a wonderful contribution those groups made.'

Quimper said: 'I'd never have placed the Germans in a major category,' and she replied: 'In the early censuses they accounted for about a third of our immigrant population. My father told me: "Always remember, Lorena, it was the Germans who put us Cobbs in Washington and the Mexicans who kept us there." '

Rusk, who had been studying his fingernails during this recital, said in a deep rumble: 'I don't think the Spanish influence amounted to a hill of beans in this state,' whereupon Professor Garza said sharply: 'Then you don't know the first three hundred years of Texas history,' and Rusk was about to respond when I broke in with a conciliatory statement, but the temporary peace I achieved did not hide the fact that sooner or later we were bound to have a Rusk-Garza confrontation.

The incipient fireworks awakened Quimper's interest: 'Professor Garza, the governor was called away before he finished introducing you. How long you been in Texas?' and Garza replied without changing expression: 'About four hundred and fifty years. One of my ancestors started exploring the area in 1539.'

'I'm astounded.'

'My students are, too.'

This information was so striking that Miss Cobb reached over, and without realizing that she was being condescending, touched Garza's arm as if she were a benign Sunday School teacher and he a promising lad from the other side of the tracks: 'Who was that first Garza?'

The professor, looking at her intrusive hand as if he resented it, decided to ignore her patronizing manner and said, with what I thought was obvious pride:

'An illiterate and penniless muleteer on the Vera Cruz-Mexico run. Born 1525. And since I was born in 1945, more than four hundred years separated us. Now, if you allot twenty point six years to a generation, which is not unreasonable, since Garzas usually had sons before the age of twenty-one, that means about twenty-one generations from the original to me.'

Rusk, who had whipped out a pocket calculator, corrected him: 'Twenty point twenty-nine generations,' at which Garza smiled and said: 'There were a lot of very early births. But this first Garza didn't marry till he was thirty-three. We count twenty-one generations.'

'So what's his relation to you?' Quimper asked, and Garza replied: 'My great eighteen-times grandfather.'

As we stared at the handsome young man in the silence that followed, the history of Texas seemed to recede to a shadowy period we had not visualized. But Garza had an additional surprise: 'In his later years our muleteer wrote a few notes about his early adventures—'

'You said he was illiterate,' Quimper broke in, and Garza agreed: 'He was. Never learned to write till he was thirty-three.'

'That's the year he married,' Rusk said, still fidgeting with his calculator. 'His wife teach him?'

'They bought themselves a tutor, a learned black slave. From Cuba.'

'You just said he was penniless,' Quimper said, for apparently nothing was going to go unchallenged in this committee, and again Garza agreed: 'He was. And how he got his wife, his money and his learning is quite a story.'

'Does it exist?' Miss Cobb asked, and Garza replied: 'In family tradition and general legend, substantiated by a few solid references in Mexican colonial history.'

I
LAND OF
MANY LANDS

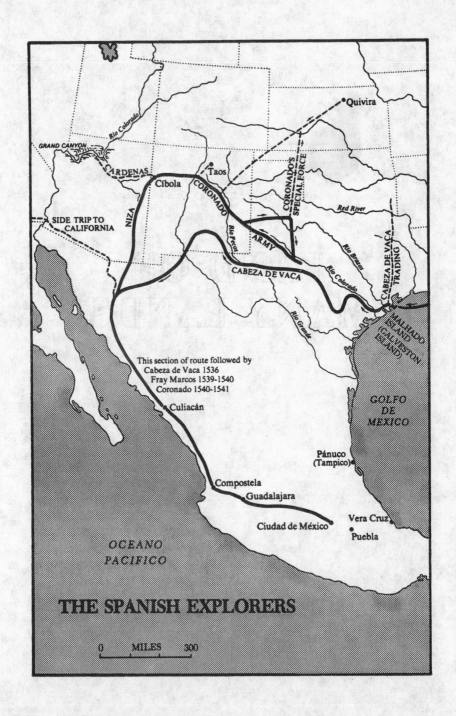

THE SPANISH EXPLORERS

ON A STEAMY NOVEMBER DAY IN 1535 AT THE MEXICAN SEAPORT OF VERA Cruz, a sturdy boy led his mules to and from the shore where barges landed supplies from anchored cargo ships. He was Garcilaço, ten years old 'but soon to be eleven,' as he told anyone who cared to listen.

The illegitimate child of an Indian mother and a rebellious Spanish soldier who was executed before the woman gave birth, he was soon abandoned, placed in a home that was run by the local clergy, and then turned over to a rascally muleteer as soon as he was old enough to work. That occurred at age eight, and he had been working ever since.

On this hot morning he had to labor especially hard, for his master had received instructions that the mules must leave immediately for the capital, Mexico City—La Ciudad de México—more than a hundred leagues distant (one league being 2.86 miles), and whenever heavy work was required in a hurry the ill-tempered man rained blows upon the boy.

From his father, Garcilaço had inherited a build somewhat heftier than that of the average Indian; from his mother, the smooth brown skin and the black hair that cut across his forehead in a straight line reaching down almost over his eyes. And from some mysterious source he had acquired a placid disposition and an incurable optimism.

Now, as he loaded his mules with the last of their cargo and headed them toward that long and tedious trip through the lowland jungles, he consoled himself with the thought that soon he would see the majestic volcanoes of the high plateau and shortly thereafter the exciting streets of the capital. As he left the port city he hummed a song he had learned from other muleteers:

'Klip-klop! Klip-klop!
There in the sky
The great volcanoes of the plain.
Go, mules! Speed, mules!
For here come I
To climb their lovely path again.'

He had memorized a dozen such songs, one for the mules when they were sick, one for dawn over the pyramids, one for a husband and wife tilling their fields of corn. Since he could not read and had no prospect of ever learning, for he was enslaved to his mules, he used his whispered songs as his bible and his dictionary:

'Klip-klop! Klip-klop!
The smoke I see
Marks where the town hides in the vale.
Go, mules! Speed, mules!
Be kind to me,
And you shall find oats in your pail.'

Each trip up from Vera Cruz was a mixture of drudgery and joy, for although traversing the jungle along poorly kept trails was quite difficult, to travel beside the volcanoes and to see the capital looming in the distance was rewarding, especially since he knew that when he reached it he could count upon a few days of rest and better food. So he kept singing.

On this trip, as he approached the capital, he found his mules competing for road space with unaccustomed hordes of travelers, all going in his direction, and when he asked: 'What happens?' he was told: 'An auto-da-fé tomorrow. A great auto.'

This was exciting news, for it meant that the streets would be crowded, and that vendors of sweetmeats and tips of roasted beef would be hawking their wares. He himself would have no money to buy such luxuries, but he could rely upon convivial participants to provide him with morsels here and there. An auto in Mexico City, in the cool month of November, could be a memorable affair.

A formal auto-da-fé, act-of-faith, as conducted in Spain could be a lavish public display of the spiritual glory and temporal power of the Catholic church in its determination to root out any deviation from the True Faith. It consisted of marching soldiers, military bands, a parade of clerics in four or five differently colored robes, the appearance of the bishop himself riding in a palanquin borne by four Negro slaves, and the final appearance of an executioner leading in chains the apostates who were to be burned that day. But in Mexico in these early years an auto was a much simpler affair; on this occasion, as Garcilaço learned on entering the city, two men were to be executed, but as his informant explained, their cases were quite different.

'The first man, from Puebla, has behaved properly. He's recanted his heretical behavior, pleads to die within the arms of the church and will be mercifully strangled by the executioner just before the flames are lighted.'

'Wise man,' Garcilaço said, for he remembered an occasion when an accused had refused to admit his guilt, and his death had been horrible.

'The other man, from this city, is mad with lust for his own interpretation of God's will. Refuses to recant. Says he'll welcome the flames. He'll get them!'

On the morning of the auto, crowds began to gather along the route the procession would take, and as Garcilaço had foreseen, the streets were crowded with vendors, but the greatest crush came at the public square before the cathedral, where stakes had been erected and dry brush piled beneath the little wooden platforms on which the condemned would stand.

Garcilaço found himself an advantageous spot atop a cask, from which he refused to be nudged by latecomers. Doggedly he held his ground, pushing off whoever threatened and once offering to climb down and fight a young man much bigger than he. When this fellow looked up and saw his opponent's grim determination, hair in the eyes, scowl on the brown face, he desisted, left the cask, and elbowed his way to one less vehemently protected.

At noon, with the sun blazing overhead, Indian women sold in wooden cups cool potions of a refreshing drink they made from the sweet limes for which the valleys near the city were famous, and Garcilaço thirsted for his share, but since he had no coins, the women passed him by. However, a Spanish official who had purchased two cupfuls could not finish his second, and sensing the boy's desire, handed him a generous leftover. As Garcilaço gulped the drink while the vendor impatiently tapped her foot, waiting for the return of her cup, the Spaniard asked: 'You're a mestizo?' and Garcilaço, between hurried gulps, said: 'Yes, my father was Spanish.'

'How did he happen to marry . . . ?'

'I never knew him. They tell me he was executed . . . before I was born.'

'Why?'

'Drink!' the vendor admonished him, and Garcilaço drained the cup.

'That was good. Thank you, sir.' The man was about to ask further questions when the boy's master ran along the edge of the crowd in the open space where spectators were not allowed.

'There you are!' he shouted when he spotted his helper, and he was about to pull Garcilaço from his cask when the Spanish gentleman gave the older muleteer a hard shove: 'Leave the boy alone.'

The master hesitated a moment, but when he saw the quality of the man who had pushed him and realized that this stranger was probably from Spain and would have a sword ready for instant use if his honor was in any way infringed, he backed away, but from a safe distance he growled at his assistant: 'Bad news! We must deliver our goods to the army in Guadalajara.' Since that city was more than a hundred and forty leagues to the west, Garcilaço knew that the journey would be a continuation of recent hardships, and that was bad enough, but now his master added: 'You must come with me now.'

This Garcilaço did not want to do, for it would mean missing the auto, but his master was insistent, whereupon the Spaniard said in a low, threatening voice: 'You, sir! Begone or I'll have at you,' and off the master went, indicating by his furious stare that he would punish his refractory helper when the auto ended.

'How lucky you are!' the Spaniard said when the man had gone. 'Guadalajara!

Best city in Mexico.' And when Garcilaço asked why, the man said: 'From there you can move on to the real west, and along the road catch glimpses of the Pacific Ocean. China! The Isles of Spice!'

He had served as a government official on the western frontier and said: 'I'd always enjoy going back. You're a lucky fellow.'

Now the real business of the auto began, with functionaries running here and there to ensure proper observances, and in the hush before the procession appeared, the Spaniard tapped Garcilaço on the shoulder and said: 'Your master, he seems a poor sort.'

'He is.'

'Why don't you run away? I did. From a miserable village in Spain where I was nothing. In Mexico, I'm a man of some importance.'

'I'd have nowhere to run,' Garcilaço said, whereupon the man grasped him by the shoulder: 'You have the world to run to, my boy. You could be the new conquistador, the mestizo who will rule this country one day.' He corrected himself: 'Who will help Spain rule it.'

'Look!' Garcilaço cried, and into the square where the kindling waited to be lit came four black slaves carrying the poles of a palanquin on which sat a prelate, dressed in deep purple and wearing an ornate miter, who stared steadfastly ahead. He was Bishop Zumárraga, most powerful churchman in Mexico and personally responsible for the arrest and sentencing of the two heretics who were to be burned. It was obvious from his stern countenance that he was not going to pardon the wretches.

'They deserve to burn,' the Spaniard muttered as the great procession made a circuit of the square, and when the executioner appeared with the condemned, it was this Spaniard who led the jeering.

The ceremony was swift and awesome. Bishop Zumárraga, from beneath his canopy, accepted the repentance of the man who was to be strangled and ignored the contempt of the man who would be burned alive. Soliciting God's approval of the punishments about to be administered, he turned the prisoners over to the secular arm of the government and left the square, followed dutifully by his priests. It would be the soldiers, not the clergy, who would actually light the fires under the heretics.

At dusk, when the flames had died, Garcilaço walked quietly to the compound where his mules waited, aware as never before of the glory of the religion he professed and of the power of Spain. His mind was confused by a kaleidoscope of images: powerful Bishop Zumárraga's red face as he cried: 'Let the will of God be done'; the soaring chant of the priests as they marched by; imaginary Guadalajara, 'prettier than Mexico City'; and the great Pacific Ocean, 'much more magnificent than what you see at Vera Cruz.'

Most of all he remembered what that unknown Spaniard had said: 'You mestizos can do things. Run away. Accomplish something.' And his own response: 'I'm soon to be eleven,' for he was convinced that when he reached that golden age, things would be better and he would find himself more qualified to reach decisions. With these reassuring thoughts he sang a few verses and went to sleep.

At Guadalajara, which was indeed more attractive than the capital, his master received the unpleasant news that his cargo was needed by the army at Compostela, fifty leagues farther on. He was unhappy, but now Garcilaço was delighted, for the added journey would bring him closer to the Pacific, which he longed to see.

He did not reach the ocean at Compostela, for when he led his mules into that depot new orders awaited: 'Take your goods on to Culiacán, a hundred and forty leagues north. The army waits.' And it was on this leg of the journey that Garcilaço finally saw the Pacific Ocean, that grand, sleeping majesty.

'Oh!' he cried as he gazed westward. 'To sail upon that ocean! To faraway lands!' During the next nights, as he approached the end of his long journey, he could not sleep, for although he had left the ocean, he was aware that it continued to lie just off to the west, and he knew that a daring boy might leave his harsh master, run away, and somehow reach the freedom of the sea.

At Culiacán, the present frontier of the Spanish empire in Mexico, another new order awaited: 'Carry your cargo thirty leagues farther north to our military outpost up there,' and it was on the date Garcilaço had chosen as his birthday that the caravan arrived at that bleak outpost and his Christian zeal was tested, for a soldier came running with astounding news: 'Ghosts!'

Excited at the thought of seeing ghosts in daylight, everyone followed the man to the edge of the settlement, where he kept pointing north and shouting: 'Ghosts! Naked ghosts!'

Down the trail from the mountains, on foot, came four naked men, three white, one black, unlike any Garcilaço had seen before, because they had no bellies. From eating almost nothing for many months, they were perfectly flat from rib to loins. Not a fingernail's thickness of fat showed anywhere. Their feet had soles as thick as leather; their beards were long, except for the black man, who had none; their hair was matted; but their eyes were clear and defiant, with a look that seemed to challenge: 'We have seen everything and know no fear.'

Garcilaço would always remember the first spoken words: 'What is the month and the year?'

'The twentieth day of March, in the Year of Our Lord 1536,' a soldier replied, whereupon the ghosts fell to marveling, and the one who seemed to be their leader repeated: 'March in '36!' and a look of fierce pride came across his face. 'We've been lost for seven years, and missed our calculations by only two weeks!'

When the soldier asked how this could be, he replied: 'The stars were our calendar, and we were only fourteen days in error.'

Now Garcilaço's master growled: 'What are you saying, you ghosts?' and the
leader answered gravely: 'I am Cabeza de Vaca, native of Cádiz, forty-six years of
age, and I have been wandering up there, in El Gran Despoblado [The Great
Unpopulated],' and he pointed over his shoulder.

Clothes were thrown over the four and they were led with great excitement
down to Culiacán, but in the town no one could be found who had ever heard the
name Cabeza de Vaca. However, since the man spoke excellent Spanish, his
interrogators had to pay attention, and he told the commander: 'I sailed from
Sanlúcar de Barrameda at the mouth of the Río Guadalquivir near Sevilla nine
years ago on the seventeenth of June, 1527.'

Still no one could believe him, so a man of knowledge asked: 'On which bank
of the river is Sanlúcar,' and he replied without hesitation: 'On the left bank,
where they make a fine white wine.'

Another man being sent for, this one said: 'When I served in Cuba, I knew all
the sailors who came to New Spain, and there was never a Cabeza de Vaca, and
anyway, that's a very foolish name, Head of a Cow.'

'My name is Alvar Núñez,' the ghost said with noble gravity, 'but I prefer the
name Cabeza de Vaca, given in honor to my ancestor by the king, whose life he
saved. This is my trusted lieutenant Andrés Dorantes, and this is Alonso del
Castillo Maldonado, a very brave man, and this,' he said, touching the tall black
man with affection, 'is Esteban, a doctor of medicine . . . in some ways.'

The two white men bowed low at their introductions, but the black man just
did a little dance on nimble feet, smiling, showing very white teeth.

And that was the beginning of Garcilaço's real life, for these four strangers
from another world traveled with him to Mexico City, and on the journey, which
took many weeks, the boy heard such wondrous things that he swore to write
them down some day, if ever he learned to write.

Garcilaço first experienced the noble quality of Cabeza de Vaca as the result of
error on a cold, wet morning as he led his mules south toward the junction town
of Compostela. The fault was his, as he admitted later, for he was listening so
attentively to any words spoken by the ghosts that he allowed his mules to
wander, whereupon his master started belaboring him about the head. He had
struck four times when Cabeza de Vaca leaped forward, grabbed his arm, and
warned: 'If you strike that lad again, I shall kill you.' From the trembling of his
right hand as he restrained himself, both boy and master knew he meant what he
said.

When the master retreated, Garcilaço made bold to ask his rescuer: 'Why did
you do that for me?' and as they walked together at the head of the column, a
little mestizo boy and a grizzled Spanish veteran, the latter told an amazing story:
'I was a slave for long years. I was beaten, and sent into the thorns to collect

berries. I was abused. At night I wept from my wounds and the loss of hope. I know what slavery is, and I will not permit that man to treat you like his slave.'

'Did pirates capture you?' Garcilaço asked, and the Spaniard replied: 'Worse. Savage Indians. Up there.'

Whenever he uttered the words *up there,* and he used them often in his tales, he did so with a mixture of awe and reverence, as if he feared the vast empty spaces but also loved them.

'I sailed from my home in Spain in 1527, when I was thirty-seven. We stopped at Cuba, then explored Florida. We lost our ships, and in boats made principally from the hides of our horses, which we had eaten, we sailed west to join our friends in Mexico, but on the sixth day of November in 1528 we reached an island which we named Malhado [Galveston], where ninety-three of us beached our boat.

'Through cruel bad luck, we lost all our clothes and the boat, too, when we tried to launch it again, and while we were completely naked the hideous north wind which sometimes blows up there struck at us. Within a few days only sixteen of us were left. For the next seven years, under conditions I prefer to forget, I lived stark naked, and on more than a dozen occasions when that terrible north wind howled at me, I thought I would die, and sometimes hoped that I would.'

(No part of Cabeza de Vaca's story is more difficult to believe than this. He certainly said, repeatedly, that he was *desnudo* for seven years, and that word means *naked.* But was he naked in our sense of the word? Yes, with the qualification that his captors must have allowed him a loincloth and perhaps a deerskin to sleep under during the coldest nights.)

When the pair had become firm walking companions Garcilaço asked how he had acquired such an odd name, Head of a Cow, and he explained: 'In the year 1212 the Spanish Christians were fighting the Moors who had occupied our country for centuries, and as usual, we Spaniards were losing. But my grandfather many times back, a peasant named Alhaja, showed King Sancho how a triumph might be achieved by sneaking along an unguarded path and taking the infidel by surprise. To mark this path for the king, my grandfather crept among the Moors and placed the head of a cow at its secret entrance. Before dawn our men ran to the skull, sped along the unknown path, and won a great victory, which freed our part of Spain. That afternoon the king summoned my grandfather and said: "Kneel, peasant Alhaja. Rise, Cabeza de Vaca, gentleman of my realm." '

He then returned to the tale of his own incredible adventures: 'We few Spaniards who survived the shipwreck and the cold were divided into two groups by the Indians who captured us. Most were moved south, but I was left at the north end of the island with an aggravating man named Oviedo. In our previous travels he had shown himself to be the strongest and in many ways the ablest of our group, but in captivity his will power dissolved. Suddenly he was afraid of everything, and although I begged him each year, from 1529 to 1532, to escape with me, he refused, preferring slavery with the Indians we knew to the risk of worse treatment from others we did not. It became apparent that he was prepared to end his days as a slave, but I was not.'

'You kept hoping?'

'You must always hope. It keeps you alive.'

One part of Cabeza's story the boy found almost unbelievable: 'We lived like this, lad. During the terrible months of winter when useless old men were encouraged to die, we ate only oysters, which were plentiful in the backwaters. During the summer months we ate only blackberries. Best of the year came when we moved inland and gorged on tunas.'

'I love tunas,' Garcilaço interrupted. 'I've eaten them many times when I was hungry. Were yours the same as ours?' Garcilaço asked, and Cabeza said: 'Yes, a cactus flat and round like a dish. And along its edges yellow flowers appear in spring. Then a man's heart leaps with joy, because each flower becomes a prickly fruit, a tuna. When it ripens to a dark red, you peel off the skins, best fruit you ever tasted. We lived on it for months.'

'That's the same,' said Garcilaço, and for a moment he felt that he had been with Cabeza 'up there.'

'In the autumn,' Cabeza continued, 'we ate only nuts of a kind not known in Spain [pecans], a wonderful food. But as the year ended, there was a gap between the end of nuts and the beginning of the oysters.'

'What did you do then?'

'Caught a few fish. Mostly we starved.'

'What did you eat with the oysters and the blackberries?'

'Lad, when I say *we ate only,* I mean just that. While I was a slave, no meat, no fowl, no vegetables, no overlapping the seasons. We ate ourselves sick on whatever we had, maybe a hundred oysters a day . . .' He paused in the middle of the road, recalling those fearful days, then said something which clarified things: 'I would eat nuts until I vomited, and if you placed a bowl before me now, I would once more feel compelled to eat them till I got sick. Because storing their rich oil in our bellies kept us alive through the weeks when there was no food.'

'Which food did you like best?' Garcilaço asked, and he was surprised at the answer: 'The oysters, but not because they were fine eating. When they came, I knew a new year had begun. Stars and oysters, they were my calendar.' Remembering his friend's joy at having his dates confirmed, Garcilaço asked: 'Why was the calendar so important?'

Now Cabeza de Vaca stepped back in amazement: 'Lad, you must always know where you are, in time and space.'

'Why?'

'If your body becomes lost, your soul is lost, and you wither. If we had not fought to keep our calendar and our distances, we would have surrendered, and died.'

'How did you know where you were? You had no maps.'

'Each night as I checked our latitude I would imagine where we would have been on the map of Africa: "Tonight we're the same as Marrakech" or "This night we sleep in Cairo." Lad, I went clear across the continent, Florida to the Pacific, nearly seven hundred and seventy leagues, and always I knew how far we'd come.' (Florida to Culiacán, straight line east to west, about 1,750 miles; their route, about 2,000.)

'How did you tell, what you call it, latitude?'

'The stars told me how far north we were.'

When they reached Guadalajara, Garcilaço turned his mules toward the capital, and one afternoon the boy said: 'The stars seem to have told you everything,' and Cabeza de Vaca replied: 'They did.'

'Would they tell me their secrets? So that I could keep my calendar if the Indians made me their slave?'

'They come out at night, ready to serve anyone. God brings them up in regular order so that we can know when to plant our crops or when, up there, to move inland for the ripening cactus.' It was during those lovely evenings as they rested that the Spanish explorer taught the little mestizo muleteer lessons he would never forget: how the constellations could be identified, the ways a farmer could use them to determine when to plant his seeds, and how a traveler could verify his location.

With each new concept mastered, Garcilaço found his horizons expanding; he had been eager to see the Pacific, but once he saw it, he knew instinctively that discoveries equally great must wait on its western shore, and he began to dream of China. Now as the Spaniard told him about the wonders lying to the north— within his reach if he walked vigorously in that direction—he wanted to explore those regions too. But most of all he felt a burning desire just to know, to experience, to be a heroic man like Cabeza de Vaca. Garcilaço had stumbled upon one of the greatest treasures a boy can find: a man of dignity whom he would like to emulate.

They had reached a point well east of Guadalajara, in the month of June, when Cabeza de Vaca surprised him by speaking of years when he traveled alone as a trader for a different tribe of Indians. 'But, Señor Cabeza,' the boy said, and the proud Spaniard corrected him: 'My name is Cabeza de Vaca, three words, and I prefer to be so addressed.'

'I am sorry, Señor Cabeza. I meant no offense,' and the great traveler smiled: 'Since you have just turned eleven, as you inform me, you may call me Cabeza. Now, what was your question?'

'Well, if you were a slave, how could you also be free to wander about?' and Cabeza said: 'I left Oviedo, escaped from the dreadful Indians on the island and sought refuge with other kinder souls who live inland.'

'But you were still a slave?' Garcilaço asked, and in reply Cabeza de Vaca related an improbable story.

'After I had shown that I was skilled at trading the seashells my tribe collected in exchange for arrowheads made by other tribes, my Indians encouraged me to travel in search of things they needed, and in this way I went far to the north [Oklahoma], where I saw the remarkable cattle of the Indians, much larger than ours, hairy, with a big hump forward. Sometimes I would see a thousand or ten thousand, so numerous were they, and they provided those Indians with robes to wear.

'I also had a chance to taste their meat which surpassed any roasted in Spain. But you know, lad, men are often imprisoned by chains of their own forging. Living with my kind Indians, I was happy with my freedom, but I could not forget that Oviedo was still a captive. I had to go back.'

'Why?'

'Honor.' He strode ahead in silence, then waited for the boy to overtake him. 'Pitiful though Oviedo was, he remained my only link with civilization.'

Two days later, as they neared the capital, Cabeza's spirits brightened and he spoke with animation: 'In 1532, I finally persuaded Oviedo to escape with me from the island, no mean feat, since the big, hulking man could not swim and I had to coax him through the waves. Once ashore, we learned from passing Indians that three other strangers lived with a tribe to the south, and we were overjoyed, but when these Indians turned ugly, tormenting us with sticks, poor Oviedo grew utterly frightened and begged some women to help him swim back to that horrible island. We never heard of him again, the biggest and strongest of our group. He was afraid of his own destiny.'

This mournful memory silenced Cabeza for the rest of that day, but next morning he was eager to talk again: 'You can imagine how excited I was when I found that those three men were my shipmates. We exchanged stories, learning that of the ninety-three who had landed, only we four and poor Oviedo had survived. Urgently we made plans to escape and walk to Mexico, but our Indian masters became engaged in a great fight over a woman, so we Spaniards were separated for the rest of that year, with never a chance of breaking for freedom.'

'You must have been miserable,' Garcilaço said, and Cabeza replied: 'Yes, miserable, but at tuna-time in 1534 we met again among the cactus plants, and everything was now perfect for our escape, so we four set out . . . no clothes, no food, no maps, no shoes.'

'Señor Cabeza, how could you be so brave?'

He did not answer that day, but on the next he sought the boy, as if he were hungry to share his wild experiences: 'In the first days of our escape we encountered disaster. I, always eager to explore, searched widely for anything edible and became hopelessly lost. And because this was the time of year when the great north winds began to blow, the others had to think of protecting themselves. They left me, and since I was now totally alone, it seemed that I must perish.'

'How did you meet the others again?' Garcilaço asked, and Cabeza allowed pride to creep into his voice. Standing taller, his slim body etched against the sky, he said: 'I determined not to die. Moving in great circles, I quartered the barren land until at last I came upon their tracks, and when I overtook them, they said: "We thought that perhaps you'd been bitten by a snake." I said nothing, but I would never have abandoned one of them had they become lost.'

Dorantes and the other two survivors seldom joined in Cabeza de Vaca's discussions with Garcilaço; they were from one group, Cabeza from another, and by habit they maintained that division. So Garcilaço did not see much of Esteban, but when they did talk, he liked him, for the man's dark face glowed when he spoke of his adventures. Once Garcilaço asked: 'Are you a slave like we get from Africa, or are you a Moor, whatever that is?' and he replied: 'I am many things.'

'You seem to have many names, too.'

The slave laughed: 'You noticed? Dorantes calls me Estevan. Castillo calls me Estevánico. Others called me Estebaníco. Cabeza calls me Esteban.'

'What do you call yourself?'

'Doctor of medicine.'

When Garcilaço asked Cabeza about this, the latter chuckled: 'Esteban kept us alive not with his medicine but with his humor. He was a slave, bought and paid for by Dorantes, but on our travels he was free—free to laugh and to be our ambassador to the Indians.'

The amazing thing Cabeza said next explained how these four defenseless men had been able to traverse the vast area later to be called Texas. Indeed, they traveled so widely that they even came into contact with the Teyas, or Tejas, Indians, the Friendly Ones for whom the entire region would one day be named: 'When we were in the country of hills Alonzo del Castillo, who is a cultured gentleman from the university town of Salamanca, discovered that he had magical or religious power. Whatever it was, he could cure sick Indians by touching them and assuring them that God in His mercy would make them well. His first patients must have had simple illnesses, for his gentle care cured them, and his fame quickly spread across this desolate land, inspiring Indians to come to him from far distances.'

Cabeza said that many villagers began to travel with the wonder-workers, sometimes wandering sixty or seventy miles and wailing piteously when they could no longer keep up with the Spaniards. 'Such misguided faith made Castillo afraid that he was trespassing on powers reserved for God, and he refused to treat patients who were obviously dying and for whom he could do no good. Not me, for I realized that our power to heal could prove our passport to freedom.

'One morning as we approached a new village, weeping women took me to a man obviously near death. His eyes were upturned. He had no heartbeat. All signs of life were gone. Thinking to make his last moments as easy as possible, I placed him upon a clean mat and prayed to our Lord to give him peace.

'Late that afternoon the Indian women ran to us, weeping and laughing and cheering, for the dead man had risen from his mat, had walked about and called for food. This caused enormous surprise, and all across the land nothing else was spoken of. In following days Indians came to us from many places, dancing and singing and praising us as true children of the sun.'

Cabeza then said a revealing thing, which at the time Garcilaço could not comprehend: 'When the Indians made a god of me, I behaved like Castillo. I did not want such idolatry, because I knew I was not worthy of it. Any cures I had effected were due to God's intervention, not mine, and I refused to mislead pagan Indians into thinking otherwise. But as captain of our expedition, I needed the assistance our miracles provided, and it was in this cast of mind that we three white men decided that Esteban should be the doctor, since he had no such religious reservations. No man ever accepted promotion with more delight or followed it with finer accomplishment.'

He called for Esteban, who confirmed all that Cabeza had said: 'I started life as a slave in Morocco. I was sold to Dorantes in Spain, and in Cuba and Florida and among the Indians, I was still a slave. I was unhappy, because I knew that with my tricks, I could be a fine doctor.' He smiled at Cabeza as he said this. 'So from the Indians I got myself a pair of rattling gourds, some turkey feathers, woven hair from one of the big humped hides, and announced myself as a healer.'

'He was marvelous,' Cabeza said. 'When we approached a new village, we allowed him to go first, dancing and leaping and singing Indian songs. Shaking his gourds, shouting incantations, his white teeth flashing, he cured old women and won the hearts of sick children with his radiant smile. Since women loved him, he accumulated a harem of first a dozen, then dozens, and finally, more than a hundred who trailed him from one camp to the next.'

Esteban affirmed everything and added: 'I liked the women, indeed I did, but I also knew we needed food. So I would not let them come with me unless they brought us real food, not oysters and blackberries. We four lived on my dancing.'

'Would you show me your dance?' Garcilaço asked, and he said: 'I can't do it without my gourds,' so the boy ran to fetch them, but when his master saw him quit his mules, he struck him sharply across the head. When Esteban saw this, he leaped in the air, then rushed at the master to restrain him: 'He is not your slave!' The master glared at the big black man: 'But you are a slave, you damn Moor,' he said, and spat.

As soon as Garcilaço produced the gourds, Esteban forgot his anger, and with a rattle in each hand he began taking short, mincing steps in the dust, at first shuffling rather than dancing, but quickly becoming more agitated. His eyes flashed. His grin widened. His arms flapped wildly, and soon he was leaping in the air, assuming wild and grotesque contortions. Laughing like a joyous spirit, he danced until all the carters in the cavalcade stopped to watch and then applaud. To see Esteban dance was to see the earth smile.

Always when Cabeza spoke of his adventures in the north, he referred in some manner to the look of the land in which an incident had occurred, and it was during such a narration that he happened to use a phrase which determined the character of Garcilaço's subsequent life.

'Señor Cabeza, you speak of the land, but when you do, you describe many different lands,' and the explorer laughed: 'You're an observant little fellow. I enjoy traveling with you.' He said that, yes, he did speak of many different lands; that was the glory of up there.

'Along the coast where I first stayed, there were beautiful sand dunes and marshes filled with birds. Inland, a waving sea of grass with rarely a tree. Farther to the west where we gathered nuts, rolling crests and clusters of oak more beautiful than any I saw in Spain. Then hills, cut through with little rivers, and after them the vast empty plains, flat as tables and sometimes void even of cactus. Finally more hills, the mountains and the desert.'

He closed his eyes, as if he were praying. 'I can see it all, lad. The years were cruel, of that there can be no doubt, but they were also glorious, and if you ever find a chance to go up there,' and here came the words that fired the boy's imagination, 'you too will see the land of many lands.'

As soon as Garcilaço heard that happy phrase, 'the land of many lands,' he was captured by the lure of the north. The Pacific Ocean was forgotten; anyone could build himself a ship and sail on it, Garcilaço thought, but the challenge of those limitless plains, the ferocious winds, the grandeur of an earth that seemed infinite in its variations—these wonders he wanted to see. From this day on he entertained only one vision: to visit that land of many lands.

When Cabeza resumed his narrative about their travels far to the west (into New Mexico, but not as far north as Santa Fe), he said: 'One night while we three white men talked idly with some of Esteban's women, one of them used a phrase which caught my attention: "Fifteen days to the north, the Seven Cities. My mother saw them when she was a girl." That night I could not sleep, because even as a child I had heard vague talk about holy men who had fled Spain and built the fabled Seven Cities of Cíbola. I knew no more of the legend except that these cities held much gold. So very quietly, using signs and the few words we had, I began asking Indian men about the Seven Cities, and they confirmed what the woman had said: "Yes, yes! That one, he saw the Cities." The Indian thus indicated said he had not actually been to the Cities, but he knew a man who had, and this man had spoken of them with awe: "Very big. One, two, three, four, up, up to the sky."

'I asked if he meant that one level of the house stood upon the other, as in Spain, and the man said eagerly: "Yes! My friend said so. Up to the sky!" whereupon I asked if there had been great wealth there, and this question the Indian did not comprehend, for I carried nothing with which to illustrate what I meant, but the Indian liked us so much that he wanted to please, so he talked with his friends, and even though he did not understand my words, he nodded vigorously: "Yes, just as you say."

' "And what is the name of these Seven Cities?" I asked, but the man did not know, nor did anyone, but I believed there was a chance that I had found those cities of sacred legend.' As Cabeza uttered these provocative words he fell silent, and it was then that Garcilaço enlarged his dream to include the finding of those cities clothed in gold.

When Cabeza next talked with Garcilaço he was serious and almost mystical: 'When it happened, after those years of slavery and wandering and storms, it excited us almost to the point of frenzy. One morning Castillo saw, on the neck of an Indian, a little buckle from a swordbelt, and in it was sewed a horseshoe nail. We took it from the Indian and asked what it was. He said it had come from heaven, but when we asked who had brought it, he answered that some men, with beards like ours, had come from heaven to that river; that they rode on animals like very large deer; carried lances and swords; and that they had lanced two Indians.

'As cautiously as possible, we then inquired what had become of those men, and they replied that they had gone to the sea, putting their lances into the water and moving them, and that afterward they saw men on top of the waves heading toward the sunset. We gave God our Lord many thanks for what we had heard, for we had been despairing to ever hear of Christians again.'

During the last days of the journey, Cabeza took an extraordinary interest in Garcilaço, and one morning he cradled the boy's face in his weathered hands and looked deep into his eyes: 'Lad, you were not meant to be a muleteer. But to accomplish anything, you must learn to read and write.' And with an almost furious determination, he taught the lad, as they walked with the mules, the alphabet, and when they stopped to rest he would draw the letters in the ground with a stick.

Cabeza was also eager to share his specific knowledge of the land he had traversed, as if he were afraid that valuable learning might be lost. He described the many Indian tribes, taught Garcilaço some of the phrases they spoke, said that dog was good to eat, and warned of the many dangers the boy would encounter if he ever went 'up there.'

The night before the two parted company, Cabeza grasped Garcilaço's hands and said: 'Lad, if ever the chance arrives, go up there, because that's where fame and fortune will be found—in the fabled Seven Cities of Cíbola.'

On the day after the arrival of the mule team in the capital, it was reloaded and back on the trail to Vera Cruz, so that Garcilaço saw Cabeza no more, but many years later, when he was hauling freight to Guadalajara, an army captain said: 'I knew Cabeza de Vaca in Paraguay. Yes, when he returned to Spain he sought the governorship of Florida, but learned to his great disappointment that this plum had already been awarded his fellow explorer Hernando de Soto, and he had to settle for a miserable post in Paraguay.'

'Did he succeed in that job?' Garcilaço asked, and the man said: 'Oh, no! They nibbled at him, brought infamous charges against him, and I think he left the country in chains. I know he was in jail for seven years in Spain. My sister-in-law's brother knew him.'

'What happened?' Garcilaço asked, and the captain said: 'I saw him in Africa when I served there. Banished, he was, a man who walked alone, talking with the stars. Years later the emperor came to his senses, brought this honorable man back to court, and paid him a yearly stipend which enabled him to live in relative comfort.'

At age sixty-five, Cabeza de Vaca, the first white man to have journeyed into Texas and across its vast plains, died. Texas, a state which would always honor the brave, had its first true hero.

The miracle of perfect wisdom and sage decision which Garcilaço had expected at age eleven did not materialize; nor at twelve, either. For some days after Cabeza de Vaca's departure the boy wept softly when he went to bed, and for many weeks he recited the alphabet while trudging along with his mules. But one day, when the master caught him looking at the few pages Cabeza had given him, he grabbed them in a rage and tore them up: 'You have no business with learning. Your life is with the mules.' But the master could not take away the boy's knowledge of the stars, and when Orion rose, Garcilaço could see the figure of Cabeza among those brilliant dots of light.

For two long and miserable years he led his mules past the volcanoes, whose charm had fled, and he was supported only by the memory of his brief friendship with Cabeza, foremost of the king's gentlemen, and the hope the latter imparted that day when he took the boy's face in his hands and said: 'Lad, you were not meant to be a muleteer.'

As the hot and sultry summer faded in 1538, Garcilaço, age thirteen, was once more journeying toward Vera Cruz, having accomplished nothing that would release him from his virtual slavery. When the mules reached the outskirts of that teeming seaport where the vessels from Spain waited to be unloaded, he felt sick at heart. All he had achieved was learning the alphabet, but he lacked any prospect of ever owning his own mules.

In this cast of mind he came down the narrow, dirty streets to where the cargo waited, and he was dreaming of Cabeza's clear, open lands 'up there' when he heard a deep-throated cry and felt across his back a blow from a walking stick.

'Watch where your mules go, fellow!' a man called out, and when Garcilaço recovered his senses he saw that the speaker was a friar of more than medium height and well past forty. He spoke with an accent the boy had not heard before, but he was more smiling than angry. When he realized that he had struck a mere lad, he apologized, and for some minutes the two talked in the narrow street.

'I am sorry, boy. Did it hurt?'

'My master gives me worse each day.'

'He must be a cruel man,' and when Garcilaço said that he surely was, the friar became solicitous and asked: 'Are you his son?' Garcilaço replied: 'I never knew my father,' and this became the foundation of their friendship.

He was Fray Marcos, who had recently come to Mexico after service in two lands about which Garcilaço had vaguely heard: Peru, which the friar loved, and Guatemala, which he held in contempt. In Peru he had composed, he claimed, a diatribe against the cruelty with which Spanish conquistadores treated their Indians, and he did not propose to allow such wrong in Mexico. He had arrived only recently and now asked Garcilaço's master if he could accompany the mule train to the capital, from where he would find his way to the great monastery being built at Querétaro, to which he had been assigned. Surly as ever, Garcilaço's master agreed.

As they climbed through the jungles leading to the volcanoes, Garcilaço was impressed by the vigor of the friar's stride; it seemed the mules would tire before Marcos did. His conversation was pleasing, too, for in all he said he displayed enthusiasm: 'Some day a poet will write of our adventures in Peru! Gold everywhere! Majestic mountains! Spanish heroism never before excelled!' He spoke in exclamations, and Garcilaço noticed the way he ended each statement in rising voice, as if eager to get on to the next wonder. When Marcos saw the great volcanoes he fell silent, captured by awe, and it was some moments before he could speak. When he did, a torrent of words leaped from his lips, and Garcilaço could imagine him back in Peru, reporting on what he had seen in Mexico: 'Such towering volcanoes! So perfect in design!'

It took twenty-nine days to drag the cargo from Vera Cruz to the capital, and during that time Garcilaço told Fray Marcos about his friendship with Cabeza, and when the friar learned that the boy knew his letters, he said: 'You must continue. Learn to read well and you can become a friar, like me, and know a life of adventure.'

When Garcilaço asked him where his home had been, he answered: 'My real name is Marcos de Niza, for I was born in that city which some call Nice. It pertained to Savoy, so I was like you, a nothing, perhaps Savoyard, perhaps French, perhaps Italian. But I fell in with the Spaniards and was saved.'

During the concluding days of the journey he showed Garcilaço his Latin Bible, to see if the boy really could pick out his letters, and the speed with which Garcilaço resumed his mastery of the alphabet, even though he could not understand the words, delighted the friar so much that one evening he went to the master and said: 'I should like to buy the boy.' The ugly man said: 'He's not for sale,' but since he was always eager to swing a good bargain, he added: 'How much would you offer?' So for two pieces of gold brought from Peru, Garcilaço became the responsibility of Fray Marcos, who said as he led him away: 'You shall call me Father, both for my religious position and because I love you and will educate you.'

They had been in Mexico City only two days when a detachment of soldiers came to the monastery where they slept: 'You're both to come with us. Bishop Zumárraga wants to interrogate you.' Garcilaço, remembering the austere figure sitting in his palanquin, started to tremble and then to sweat, for in a swift series of images he could see himself being questioned, condemned, and led to the pyre during some tremendous auto-da-fé. Quaking with fear, he asked the friar: 'What have we done?'

To his surprise, Fray Marcos was completely at ease, even smiling: 'In Peru and in Guatemala, I received many such imperative orders. They usually mean some good thing's about to happen. Let's see what it is this time.'

But when they were marched like prisoners through the streets, Garcilaço kept looking at the passers-by and at the patches of sky as if this were the last time he would see either. However, when they were delivered to Bishop Zumárraga they found a kindly man, dressed in the informal working robes of the Franciscan order, who said, as if he were their uncle: 'Sit down. Take refreshment if you wish. We've important matters to discuss.' With that he rang a small silver bell, whereupon Indian servants appeared, bringing with them a man Garcilaço remembered well and loved. It was Esteban, the Moor.

'I have a new master, Little Muleteer.'

'And I have a new father, Big Dancer.'

'What happens here?' the smiling bishop asked, and he was told that Andrés Dorantes, one of the travelers across El Gran Desplobado who had owned the slave Esteban, had sold him to the viceroy for reasons not clearly understood, while Garcilaço's master had sold him to Fray Marcos for reasons left unexplained.

'So you two know each other?' the bishop asked. 'That's good. You can tell your stories to the viceroy.'

But before they were taken to that austere master of Mexico, Bishop Zumárraga wanted to satisfy himself on one point, and to do this he asked Garcilaço to stand before him and submit to questioning: 'Boy, you traveled with Cabeza de Vaca?'

'I did.'

'And he spoke with you constantly, they tell me.'

'Yes.'

'And did he ever speak of the Seven Cities?' At this point the Moor shot Garcilaço a warning side glance, but to what purpose the boy could not determine, so he answered honestly: 'He spoke of them often.'

Before Zumárraga could question further, Esteban broke in with the start of

the great deceit which would engulf many men and color the early history of
Texas: 'Excellency, I saw the Seven Cities. They were glorious, and Cabeza de
Vaca saw them, too.'

When Garcilaço heard this lie he remembered the honest voice of Cabeza as
they had talked on the way to Guadalajara: 'Lad, understand. This Indian woman,
she had never seen the Cities, her mother claimed that *she* saw them. Nor had the
Indian man ever seen them, a friend had reported that *he* had seen them. And
certainly none of us Spaniards had come close to seeing them.'

But it was obvious that Bishop Zumárraga wanted to believe that everyone had
seen them: 'So Cabeza de Vaca, wily man that he was, kept the secret of their
wealth to himself?' As this question was asked, Garcilaço could see Esteban
smelling out the situation and identifying what those in authority wanted to hear,
so in response to sharp questioning, the Moor divulged these supposed facts: 'The
Cities have enormous wealth, the Indians assured us. When I asked about gold
and silver, they cried "Yes!" Jewels, cloth, cows twice as big and fat as ours.
Cabeza himself saw them, didn't he?' When everyone looked at Garcilaço, the boy
had to nod, for this one small part of the statement was true. Cabeza had told him
of the large cows with humps over their shoulders.

'Let us speak with the viceroy,' Zumárraga said as he called for his carriage, and
off they hurried to meet the man who ruled Mexico.

Few men in history have looked more imperial than Don Antonio de Mendoza,
Count of Tendilla, did that day. He was tall and properly lean; his mustache and
beard had been neatly trimmed that morning by the barber who visited him each
day, and when he looked at his visitors he seemed to regard everyone but the
bishop as a peasant. He had sharp eyes which penetrated nonsense and a deep,
resounding voice accustomed to command. He was keenly interested in everything
relating to New Spain, and even before his visitors were seated he plunged into
discussion: 'Tell me, Bishop, what facts do we know about the Seven Cities?' and
Zumárraga replied:

> 'Some say it was in A.D. 714 when Don Rodrigo of Spain lost his king-
> dom to the Muhammadans, but others with better cause say it was in
> 1150, in the reverent Spanish city of Mérida. In either case, seven devout
> bishops, refusing to obey the infidel Moors who had conquered their
> city, fled across the ocean, and each bishop established his own powerful
> city. We've had many reports of the riches those good men accumulated
> and the wonders they performed, but we've not known exactly where
> they went. Many have searched for them, and I've even heard it claimed
> that the Italian Cristóbal Colón was seeking the Seven Cities when he
> discovered our New World. All we know for certain is that the Seven
> Cities are grouped together.'

The viceroy pursed his lips, reflecting on what the clergyman had said. Then he asked bluntly: 'Do you believe the Cities exist?'

'Of a certainty.'

'Ah, but do they? Dorantes left a deposition which I read again only yesterday. He said he had met no one, not a single soul, who had actually seen them or known anyone who had.'

For some moments that November day no one spoke, and finally Bishop Zumárraga uttered words which summarized reasonable thought on the matter: 'God never works accidentally. It stands to Holy reason that if He placed Peru far down here, with its golden treasury, and Mexico here in the middle, with its wealth of silver, he must have balanced these two with some great kingdom up here. The Rule of Three, the rule of Christian balance, requires the Seven Cities to be where Cabeza de Vaca's Indians said they were. Excellency, it is our Christian duty to find them, especially since the seven bishops probably converted the area, which means that Christians may be there awaiting union with the Holy Mother Church in Rome.'

'My view exactly!' Fray Marcos cried, with the enthusiasm he always showed, after he, like Esteban, had decided what his superiors wanted to hear, but the viceroy made a more sober comment: 'If we send a conquistador north to the Seven Cities to bring them back into the fold of the church, who will pay the vast expense? Not the emperor in Madrid. He never risks a maravedí of his own money. I pay, from my own fortune and my wife's, and before I do that I want reasonable assurance of success.'

Suddenly his manner changed, his voice brightened, and he asked: 'What have you heard about this young nobleman Francisco Vásquez de Coronado?' and the bishop said quickly: 'He could lead your expedition. And he could help with the costs.'

'But we must not mount a great expedition—all those men and horses—before the region has been properly scouted.'

'That's why I sought this audience,' Bishop Zumárraga said, and with a bold sweep of his arm he indicated that Marcos, Esteban and Garcilaço were to leave the room.

As soon as only he and Mendoza were together, the bishop said: 'By the greatest good fortune, that friar who just left us is an excellent man with wide experience in the conquest of Peru. I find him a man of prudence and one to be trusted.'

When the viceroy asked if there was aught in the friar's history to be held against him, the bishop replied: 'I would be less than honest with you, Excellency, if I did not also share with you his three weaknesses. First, he has been in Mexico only briefly. Second, he is extremely ambitious, but are not, also, you and I? I cannot hold this a disqualifying fault. Third, he is not a Spaniard, but then, most of our emperor's subjects are Austrians, Lowlanders or Italians. The emperor himself is a German, or, if you wish, an Austrian.'

When the viceroy showed signs of accepting the friar, the bishop seemed eager to disclose even the smallest weakness lest he later be called to account: 'The final point, Excellency, is a delicate one. The boy you saw with him, this Garcilaço, stays by his side constantly, and who he is I cannot say for certain. Some claim he accompanied Marcos from Peru, and these insist that Garcilaço is his son. Others say he was acquired in Guatemala, in which case the boy must have been eight or nine when Marcos got him. Such suppositions are foolish, for we know he was already in Mexico traveling with Cabeza de Vaca. Others, with the better argument, I feel, say that the boy was an alley rat in the sewers of Vera Cruz when Marcos rescued him. You've seen the lad and he seems to show promise.'

'I think we had better question the friar and his boy more closely,' the viceroy said.

Garcilaço would always remember how proud he was of his father that day as the two faced Mendoza and Zumárraga. Marcos wore a voluminous robe made of the heavy fabric favored by the Franciscans, who were often called in the streets of the city 'Christ's little gray chickens,' a phrase he did not find amusing. He was obviously a serious man, and if upon first appearance he had any defect, it was his piercing gaze which revealed him to be a fanatical believer, though what he believed in—the mystery of Christianity or his own destiny—no one could guess.

'Are you a Spaniard?' Mendoza asked bluntly.

'I'm a servant of Christ, and of the emperor, and of you, Viceroy, should you employ me.'

'But you were born in France, they say.'

'No, Excellency. In the city of Nice.'

'So you're a Savoyard?'

'No, Excellency, I'm Spanish. Through service to my church and emperor, I've made myself so.'

'Those are good words, Fray. Now tell me, who exactly is this lad who stands beside you?'

'I was ordered to bring him, Excellency.'

'Indeed you were,' Zumárraga broke in. 'Now explain.'

In the moment of silence which followed this abrupt command, all in the room looked at Garcilaço, and they saw the mystery in the boy. He was one of the first of Mexico's mestizo children, half Spanish, half Indian, that durable breed which even then seemed destined to take over Mexico and remote Spanish territories like the future Texas. In the audience room that day Garcilaço represented the future, a first ripple in the tremendous flood that would one day remake his land.

The boy heard Fray Marcos speaking: 'I have worked in lonely places, Excellencies, and one morning as I stepped off a boat in Vera Cruz, I saw this child here, a lost soul, no parents, no home . . .' He said no more.

'Who were your parents, son?'

Garcilaço shrugged his shoulders, not insolently but in honest ignorance: 'Excellency, here I am, just as I stand.'

For the first time the viceroy smiled. He then turned to Fray Marcos: 'If I gave you Esteban as your guide, could you scout the Seven Cities and then give some would-be conquistador, Coronado for example, instructions as to how to reach them?'

'I would be honored,' Marcos said with no hesitation, and so it was agreed, but after Bishop Zumárraga had taken his charges, and Esteban, from the hall, the viceroy mused:

> Who are these strangers who just left my office? Is the friar a faithful Catholic or has he been corrupted by modern ideas? Why should Spain put its trust in such an unknown? And this Esteban, what is he? Dorantes when he sold him assured me he was a Moor. But what's a Moor? The Moors I knew were not black. They were white men bronzed by the sun. Look at him. He's not black. He's brown. And what religion is he, pray tell me that? He was born a Muslim, like all Moors. When did he become a Christian? And how sincerely? And what of the boy? Is he the first of the mestizos who will be seeking power? Spain! Spain! Our emperor is a German. His Spanish mother who should be reigning is insane. And look at me, sending out an untested friar to find the new Peru, and a man of doubtful allegiance to be his guide. Where will it all end?

In order to ensure that at least one verifiable Spaniard participate in this critical venture, Mendoza asked Bishop Zumárraga to nominate as second-in-command a younger friar with impeccable credentials, and the cleric selected a Franciscan in whom he had great faith, Fray Honorato. Mendoza was delighted: 'The Spaniard can keep an eye on the Frenchman, and both can keep an eye on the Moor.'

But this canny safeguard did not work, because when the entourage was only a few days north of Culiacán, Honorato reported a slight indisposition: 'I don't feel well. Nothing, really, but . . .' With remarkable speed Fray Marcos bundled him up and sent him posting back to the capital. He was now in sole charge and intended to stay so.

But there was in the entourage a man just as ambitious as Marcos and even more flamboyant—Esteban, who, since he was the only one who had ever seen the north, now had to be promoted to second-in-command. Younger than Marcos, he matched him in brain power, and was vastly superior in knowledge of terrain and ability to work with Indians. He could speak in signs with many tribes, but more important, he displayed an exuberance which delighted the people of the villages through which the little army passed, and many who saw him shouted greetings, for they still remembered the magician who could heal.

When it came time to depart a village, more women would insist upon accompanying Esteban, so that his harem increased constantly. He had the capacity of being able to keep his many camp followers happy, and at one time nearly a hundred trailed along, singing with him, hunting food for him, and crowding his tent at night.

Fray Marcos was perplexed. He needed Esteban as guide; he resented him as competitor; and he deplored him for his immorality with women; but he could not even begin to know what to do with him. With no fellow friar to consult, all he could do was brood enviously as he watched Esteban preempt more and more of the leadership. It was becoming Esteban's expedition, and the Spanish soldiers recognized this.

'You must do something about the blackamoor,' they warned, but Marcos could not decide what.

However, sixteen days of this rich fol-de-rol was all he could stand, so on Passion Sunday, 23 March 1539, he proposed that Esteban should push on to scout the country through which the larger body of explorers would later pass. Since the black man could neither read nor write, an extraordinary convention was arranged, as Marcos would explain in the report he sent back to Mexico:

> I agreed with Esteban that if he received any information of a rich, peopled land, he should not go farther, but that he return in person or send me Indians with this signal, which we arranged: that if the thing was of moderate importance, he send me a white cross the size of a hand; if it was something great, he send me a cross of two hands; and if it was something bigger and better than New Spain, he send me a large cross. And so the said Esteban, the black, departed from me on Passion Sunday after dinner, while I stayed on in this settlement.

The plan suited each man, for the white was overjoyed to be rid of the difficult Moor, who was equally pleased to be freed of the white, and he set forth in glory, carrying with him a horde which now totaled nearly three hundred singing and dancing Indian followers.

Garcilaço watched him as he left camp marching at the head of his own little brigade, swinging his rattles, leaping in the air now and then, shouting and exuding the joy he felt in serving as the spearhead of a conquering army.

Just before dancing away, he leaped at Garcilaço and cried enthusiastically: 'Little man, we're conquering a continent. You and I will earn great titles and more gold than we can carry.' And into the dusty sunlight he led his happy band.

Four days after Esteban's departure, Indian messengers ran, gasping, into camp, one of them bearing not a small cross, nor a cross of two hands, nor even a large one, but a cross so huge that he could scarcely carry it. To confirm its significance, he said in broken Spanish: 'The Black One, he has reached Indians who have told him of the greatest thing in the world. The Cities we seek lie just ahead, and they are far richer than Mexico.' One said that this concentration of wealth was known as the Seven Cities of Cíbola, and when he uttered the words—Las Siete Ciudades de Cíbola—they echoed with romance and cast a spell over all who heard them.

The first thing Fray Marcos did in this moment of wild excitement was to kneel beside the big cross and pray, giving thanks that he would have an opportunity to restore to Christianity the thousands of souls whom the Spaniards would soon encounter. His prayer came from the very roots of his being, for although he did seek fame for himself and power for his king, his first and deepest commitment was to the glory of God—that stray souls now in darkness should be brought back to the light of Jesus Christ. It was a solemn moment, but after he had remained on his knees for some time, worldly ambition took over and he began to think of himself. Drawing Garcilaço down beside him, he whispered: 'It's wonderful that you and I should discover this great thing, for when the settlement is completed, I shall be leader of all the priests and monks, guiding them in the salvation of souls, and you shall command a kingdom, like Cortés and Pizarro.'

Now Fray Marcos began his great deception, for after having traveled less than three leagues to the west, he began to speak as if he had reached the Pacific Ocean, a distance of more than a hundred leagues. Why did he do such a thing?

Hope? He desperately wanted to be recognized as a great explorer and he knew that the Pacific lay somewhere to the west. Anxiety? He carried strict orders to determine how far away the Pacific Ocean lay, so that supplies for the impending conquest might be forwarded by sea, but he was so eager to attend the larger task of finding Cíbola that he refused to be deterred by this lesser side trip to the ocean. Envy? He could not stand to have the former slave Esteban reap all the glory. Mental confusion? He had become so intoxicated with dreams that he ignored the requirement of substantiating them with reality. He dealt with soaring hopes, not facts.

But on Wednesday, 21 May, after evening prayers, those hopes received a harsh rebuff, for as he prepared for bed he heard someone shouting: 'Someone's coming!' and through the shadows he saw a bedraggled Indian, his face and body covered with sweat, stumble toward camp, weeping and moaning. When Marcos ran to him he wailed a pitiful story, which the scribe later reported in this manner:

> 'We were one day out of Cíbola, and with due caution Esteban sent ahead a group of messengers bearing a calabash ornamented with cascabels, and two feathers, one white, one red. Something about the calabash infuriated the chief of Cíbola, and he smashed it to the ground, crying: "If you come in to Cíbola, you will be killed."

'When the messengers told this to Esteban, our leader laughed and assured us that this was nothing, and that he had learned from his long travels that when an Indian chief exhibited irritation he proved later to be a good friend. So, ignoring our warnings, he marched boldly to Cíbola, where he was denied entrance and thrown into a house outside the walls.

'All things were taken from him, trade articles and all, and he was allowed no food or drink, and in the morning we who watched saw with horror Esteban running to escape, followed by warriors from the city, and they slew him, and most of those who were with him.'

'Esteban is dead,' the Indians began to wail. 'Esteban's bones lie unburied, unhonored in the sand.' When Garcilaço heard this dreadful news, he wept for his dancing friend, but Marcos comforted him: 'This is but the story of one Indian, and who knows what his motives might be?' However, two days later more messengers from Cíbola arrived, and their news was horrifying:

'Fray Marcos, see our wounds! Of all the warriors who traveled with Esteban to find the Seven Cities, hundreds have been slain, not counting the many women who were with us.'

Marcos and his soldiers now had to admit that Esteban and most of his dancing, riotous followers were dead, and that if they tried to force their way into Cíbola, they, too, would be killed. So they halted where they were, many miles from the golden cities, and in their fear they turned back toward Mexico, and now Marcos concocted a second lie, the really massive one, and reported:

I asked that some of my men should go with me boldly to Cíbola, but I could do nothing with them. In the end, seeing me determined, two chiefs said they would go with me, and I pursued my journey until within sight of Cíbola, which I saw from a hill where I was able to view it. The city is bigger than La Ciudad de México, and at times I was tempted to go to it, because I knew that I ventured only my life, which I had offered to God the day I commenced this journey, but at the end I refrained from doing so, considering the danger that if I died, I would not be able to make a report of this country, which to me appears the greatest and best of the discoveries.

Months later, when Garcilaço stood in the reception hall in the capital, listening as Fray Marcos told of these glories to Viceroy Mendoza, he stood silent and ashamed. He knew that his father had never been close to the Pacific Ocean or to

the Seven Cities of Cíbola, and as for the claim that Cíbola was grander than
Mexico City, that was a preposterous compounding of the lie.

Why did the boy share in this duplicity? Why did he not cry out to Mendoza
'Viceroy, these are lies! There are no Seven Cities! There is no gold!' He was
prevented by three considerations. He loved his father and refused to humiliate
him. Also, despite what he had heard from Cabeza's own lips about his exploration of the region, Garcilaço still hoped that the cities of gold and their lost
Christians existed. But most important was the matter of personal ambition, for
after Marcos had told his infamous lies, the great Mendoza took Garcilaço aside
and said: 'Son, you are one half-Indian who has a fine future in this country.
Because of your good work on the mission, when General Coronado marches
north I want you to accompany him as a guide.'

Like Cabeza de Vaca, like Esteban, like Marcos, and yes, like Viceroy Mendoza
himself, the boy was seduced by the vision of what the land of many lands might
be, and he kept silent.

Garcilaço was proud that the official guide for the Coronado expedition was to be
his father, but he became apprehensive as to what the soldiers might do when they
marched north only to find that the Seven Cities of Gold did not exist. When he
asked Marcos about this, the friar airily dismissed such fears: 'The Cities must be
there. You heard Bishop Zumárraga prove logically that they had to be.'

Garcilaço shrugged and turned his attention to his own affairs. Only fourteen,
but a veteran traveler, he decided to use the great adventure as an opportunity to
build foundations of honor and courage which he had seen exemplified so wor-
thily in Cabeza. He endeavored to seem very military when they reported to the
western town of Compostela, where the huge expedition was about to be reviewed
by Viceroy Mendoza, who had authorized this venture.

First in line was Coronado, a handsome man, lithe, daring and extremely
capable; he believed in God and in the destiny of the Spanish race, and he
contemplated the conquest of a continent. Also, he could laugh easily, and he
enjoyed being with soldiers, parading boldly in the vanguard when on parades like
this one, but prudently sending out trained scouts when danger threatened.

Garcilaço's eyes widened when the first elements passed: two hundred and
twenty-five horsemen, caballeros they were called, young gentlemen unaccustomed to manual work but eager for battle. 'Look!' the boy called to those about
him, for now came a group of horsemen in full armor, some in metal, some in
leather. They were a ferocious lot, and Garcilaço heard an official boast: 'Conquerors of Europe, Peru and Mexico! God help the Indian who makes a wrong
move in their direction.'

Next came the spiritual representation for this great enterprise: five Franciscan
friars, including Fray Marcos, heads high, thirsty to win distant souls to Jesus.

How willingly he and his fellows had volunteered to share all dangers; they were indeed Soldiers of Christ.

Behind them marched sixty-seven foot soldiers—some of whom had campaigned triumphantly through the Lowlands and Austria—displaying the sophisticated weapons which had made them famous: harquebuses, those heavy matchlock pieces that threw devastating round balls at least a hundred feet; crossbows made of ash so strong that some had to be cocked by cranks which drew the cord back to firing position; pikes with hideous three-part jagged ends, fine for disemboweling; and all sorts of swords, daggers, stilettos and maces. And when these foot soldiers of Spain concealed their faces behind vizored helmets or in jet-black pots with slits for seeing, they struck terror in men's hearts.

More than two hundred personal servants followed, some Indian, some black, and eighty stable hands to tend the horses and see that the six cannon were brought forward in good condition.

Garcilaço enjoyed the end of the procession as much as the beginning, for here came more than a thousand Indian helpers, some in war paint, some with feathers, others with decorated clubs gleaming in the sun, all bowing to the viceroy, who nodded gravely as they passed. The next group caused the boy worry, for he could not comprehend how its members would participate in any battle: several hundred women, Indians and a few Spanish soldiers' wives, wearing beautiful flowers in their hair and bright shawls about their shoulders. Clouds of dust hovered in the air as these women went past. After them came the cows and sheep on which the marchers would feed.

At the rear, so valuable that they could be guarded by Spaniards only, came many horses, wonderful chargers of Spanish and Arab ancestry, bred for the most part in Mexico but with a substantial scattering of steeds imported directly from Spain. As animals of war, they had always created terror among the Indians of Mexico, and Coronado expected them to do so again. These precise figures can be cited because on this day of final review, 22 February 1540, the notary Juan de Cuebas of Compostela made careful record of every Spanish caballero or foot soldier present, noting what mounts and arms he brought, and Garcilaço watched as Cavalry-Captain Don García López de Cárdenas stepped forward to have his property listed: 'Twelve horses, three sets of arms of Castilla, two pairs of cuirasses, a coat of mail.'

Late in arriving for the muster was Infantry-Captain Pablo de Melgosa, a doughty little fellow with a perpetual smile, a great gap between his two big front teeth, hair in his eyes and a nose that had been pushed sideways by several fists. He came dustily into camp leading two small donkeys that could scarcely be seen beneath their load of armament. As soon as he stopped the beasts, he shouted for the notary to come and verify his possessions, and when Cuebas had his quills and papers ready, Melgosa began throwing things at his feet and announcing in a loud voice what they were.

'Two harquebuses, both cast in Flanders. Two crossbows, and note that each is worked by gears. Those two donkeys.'

'We don't list donkeys,' Cuebas said haughtily, resting his quill above the paper.

Ignoring this rebuke, the enthusiastic young captain resumed his listing: 'A gallegán of the best Austrian manufacture. This buckskin jacket, this black pot helmet from Toledo.'

After this minor armory had been recorded, Melgosa began divesting himself of things he carried on his body: 'Two swords, also of Toledo. Dagger. Knife with ivory handle. Two knee pieces, which you can see are of the best steel and leather. Gauntlets with brass fittings across the knuckles. And two stilettos.' Any jovial man so accoutered was bound to become Garcilaço's favorite, and in those first days he became Melgosa's part-time page, hoping to learn honor and the arts of war from him.

Garcilaço divided his time between Fray Marcos and his new hero, Infantry-Captain Melgosa, the walking arsenal, who was a joy to be with, for he was an adventurous, rowdy man who never feared to challenge the presumptions of the cavalry.

'Look at them!' he sneered one night as the unwieldy caravan stumbled to a halt. 'Not a man among these dandies knows how to pack a horse. Ten more days of this and those mounts will be dead.' Each gentleman officer had to transport his personal belongings on his own male horses, while the heavy burdens of the expedition were carried by mares and mules. But even the lighter burdens assigned to the horses could be damaging if improperly stowed, and when Garcilaço watched the caballeros, he saw that Melgosa was right; they were killing the creatures on which they depended.

Melgosa was particularly harsh in his condemnation of Cavalry-Captain Cárdenas: 'He ought to know better. Those are excellent horses he has, the best. And he's destroying them.' Now Garcilaço observed the fiery captain, and he could see that Cárdenas had no regard for his beasts' welfare.

One morning as the cavalry was packing, Garcilaço made bold to address the captain: 'Sir, why don't you distribute your loads more evenly?'

'Why is that your concern?'

'Your best horse is getting deep sores.'

'I leave such matters to the Indian slaves.'

'But they're still your animals. Look, you have five that can no longer serve.'

'Could you do better?' he snapped.

'I could,' and when Cárdenas saw how expertly the young muleteer could pack a beast, and care for it when the pack was unloaded, he appointed Garcilaço to mind his string, and the horses mended so quickly that on one unforgettable morning as the expedition approached the northern limits of civilized Mexico, the gruff captain said: 'You can ride that brown mare,' and thus the boy became a member of the cavalry.

But when foot-soldier Melgosa saw him so mounted he became furious: 'Real men fight on foot. Cavalry is for show.' This was the contemptuous attitude which existed in all armies: the disdain of foot soldiers for the cavalry, and the reverse.

Because Garcilaço was now a horseman, his allegiance transferred to Captain Cárdenas, and the more he studied this hot-tempered man the more he thought he understood the nature of honor. Cárdenas was the junior son of a family bearing an exalted title, and this heritage constantly manifested itself, for he was contemptuous of inferiors, punctilious where his vanity was concerned, and eager to challenge anyone who even appeared to affront him. More than Melgosa, more than Coronado himself, Cárdenas loved the brutality of army life, the forced marches, the sudden forays against lurking enemies, the swordplay at close quarters and the military companionship of the field. Much sterner than Fray Marcos, much more combative than Melgosa (who was content to fire his harquebuses from a distance if that would do the job), Cárdenas became to Garcilaço the ideal Spanish fighting man, supplanting Cabeza de Vaca as his idol.

The army had marched some days when Garcilaço had his first opportunity to see how Spanish caballeros were supposed to behave. He was riding in company with Army-Master Lope de Samaniego, second-in-command, when that gallant warrior, much experienced in Indian fighting, was sent to a village to acquire supplies, and in pursuit of his duty, was struck by a stray arrow which penetrated his eye as he lifted the visor of his helmet. He died immediately, which Garcilaço accepted as something to be expected in warfare, but what happened next amazed him.

Following the orders of Cavalry-Officer Diego López, who now assumed Samaniego's command, Spanish soldiers rounded up as many Indians as they could, and a sergeant passed among them, saying: 'This one looks as if he might have come from that village,' and upon this casual identification the suspect was dragged away and hanged. When a long row of corpses swayed in the breeze, the army left, assured that the Indians of this area at least had learned not to shoot arrows at Spaniards.

The incident was important to Garcilaço in that when the esteemed post of army-master fell vacant, Coronado weighed the matter only a few moments before appointing Cárdenas to fill it, and now the boy tended the twelve horses of the second-in-command, the bravest, wildest fighter of them all.

Shortly thereafter, Garcilaço discovered how his attitudes had changed, for a side expedition to what is now California was arranged under the direction of a real fighting man, Melchor Díaz, who was instructed to intercept a Spanish ship sailing up the coast with supplies for Coronado. Once Garcilaço had dreamed only of adventure on the Pacific, but now that he had a new opportunity to visit that great ocean he turned his back, for he wished to stay with Cárdenas on his quest for honor.

As an advance party now entered upon those vast wastelands in what would later be Arizona, Garcilaço's fears for his father increased, because the boy knew that the friar's gross lies must soon be uncovered. And when horses began to die of exhaustion and men to faint from the burdens they bore, the leaders of the expedition began to glare at Marcos, as if to say 'Monk, where is this paradise you told us of?' And Coronado himself came to the rear, where Marcos had hidden: 'Good Friar, how many days to Cíbola? We perish.' And as Garcilaço tended his horses nearby, he heard Marcos swear: 'Three more days, General. I promise.' And the boy shuddered, for he knew that the friar had not the slightest idea where they were.

But once more luck seemed to rescue Marcos from a crisis, for on 7 July 1540, one hundred and thirty-seven days after departing Compostela, a Spanish horseman riding well ahead wheeled his horse and came galloping back: 'Cíbola! The Seven Cities! Yonder!'

All pressed forward, each wanting to be first among his fellows to see the golden cities, but when a group gained a prominence its members fell silent, and a vast sigh rose from the men as they saw the pitiful scene, a shabby collection of dirty houses, a mud-walled nothing.

'Madre de Dios!' Cárdenas whispered.

Captain Melgosa, standing by the general, muttered: 'I've seen single houses in Castilla that were bigger than this . . . and richer, no doubt.'

Finally Coronado spoke: 'Where is Fray Marcos?' and when the trembling friar was dragged forth, the captain-general asked in a very low voice: 'Good Friar, is this what you saw? Is this your Cíbola covered with turquoise and silver? Are these hovels bigger than in Mexico City?' And before Marcos could respond, the various captains began cursing and shouting: 'Send him back.' 'Get rid of this one.' 'He is a great liar and not to be trusted.'

But it was Cárdenas who voiced the true complaint: 'I do not want this one praying over me, telling me what to do,' and Marcos would have been sent back that night except that he was needed for an important ritual without which the army could not proceed.

It was the Requerimiento (Requisition), issued decades earlier by King Ferdinand himself, who had laid down the basic edict that no Spanish army could attack an Indian settlement until this famous statement of religious principle had been recited 'in a loud, clear voice.'

It was a remarkable document, devised by the religious and civil leaders of Spain during the early years of conquest when thoughtful men struggled with the moral problem of how to deal with pagan Indians. Indeed, conquest itself had been halted for three years until agreement could be reached as to whether Indians were human or not. Finally, after much soul-searching, a statement was prepared and verified by churchmen and lawyers; it offered Indians, who were acknowledged as humans the blessings of Christianity and the protection of the crown, but only if acceptance was immediate. If the Indians hesitated, as they always did, conversion by the sword was justified.

Since the army was now within the shadow of Cíbola, Coronado summoned Marcos to read the Requerimiento, but when the friar stepped forward to take the parchment, Cárdenas objected strenuously: 'If he reads it, our enterprise will be cursed!' and he seized the document, handing it to another Franciscan, but Coronado intervened: 'Marcos is still the senior, let him proceed.' So the friar took the parchment, held it close to his face, and read aloud. But no Indian in the distant town could possibly have heard the muffled words, much less understood them even had they been audible.

It was just as well, because the Requerimiento was interminably long, with a jumbled theology which would confuse anyone not an ordained priest. It started by explaining how Adam and Eve launched the human race five thousand years ago and how different nations developed:

> 'Of all these nations God our Lord gave charge to one man, called St. Peter, that he should be Lord and Superior of all the men in the world, that all should obey him, and that he should be head of the whole human race . . . to judge and govern all Christians, Moors, Jews, Gentiles and all other sects.'

The friar read on, explaining to the distant Indians how St. Peter had begun the line of popes who commanded the world, and of how a later pope had asked King Ferdinand and Queen Isabella of Spain for help in ruling certain areas. Then Marcos came to the two parts the soldiers understood: if the Indians immediately accepted the Holy Catholic Faith, great rewards would be forthcoming, but if they stubbornly refused:

> 'I certify to you that, with the help of God, we shall forcibly enter your country and shall make war against you in all ways and manners . . . we shall take your wives and your children, and shall make slaves of them . . . and shall do all the harm and damage that we can . . . and the deaths and losses which shall accrue from this will be your fault . . .'

Fray Marcos rolled up his parchment, returned it, and announced: 'The Requerimiento has been faithfully read. All can testify to that.' The generous offer of peace had been tendered, but there was no response.

'Friar,' Coronado asked, 'are we legally free to attack?' and Marcos replied so that all the captains could hear: 'Jesus Christ commands you to do so!' and battle began.

It was a violent encounter, and Coronado's bright suit of armor flashed in the sun so invitingly that the Indians on the city walls threw down huge chunks of stone that knocked him from his white horse, leaving him defenseless and immobile on the ground.

More rocks came crashing down and would have killed him had not Cárdenas, in an act of spontaneous heroism, thrown himself across the fallen body and absorbed most of the blows. When Garcilaço saw this valiant act, he dropped down and shielded Coronado's head, and was struck by four rocks which otherwise could have brained the commander.

Bruised, cut in three places so badly that his bloody wounds were apparent to all, Garcilaço listened that night to one of the sweetest sounds a man can hear: praise for having behaved well in battle. 'He was as brave as a tested infantryman,' Melgosa cried, but the moment the boy cherished came when Cárdenas, himself badly wounded, took his hand: 'I could not have saved him without you.' When the boy was alone, he whispered to himself: 'Now I know what honor is.'

With Coronado confined to a litter because of his wounds, Cárdenas assumed command, and his first decision was loudly voiced: 'Fray Marcos must leave this army. He contaminates it.' Melgosa wanted him shot, but Cárdenas said contemptuously: 'Let him go. He carries his punishment with him.'

From his sickbed Coronado accepted this recommendation and added: 'Let the boy go with him, whoever he is,' but now Cárdenas became a defender: 'Captain, this boy helped save your life. And he's no liar, like his so-called father,' so it was agreed that Marcos must go but Garcilaço could stay.

This decision caused the boy much confusion, for he loved Fray Marcos and did not want to leave him in his hour of disgrace. 'I cannot fail him now,' he told Coronado, and the captain-general growled: 'Good. Go with him,' for he saw Garcilaço only as part of Fray Marcos and wished him gone, too.

But Cárdenas and Melgosa were disgusted when they heard of the boy's decision, and they took him aside, with Cárdenas saying bluntly: 'Loyalty is a fine thing, lad, but loyalty to a condemned man must be weighed carefully.'

'It must indeed,' Melgosa agreed. 'Admit it. Your father is a fraud. He's led this great army into deep trouble, and it is proper that he be disgraced. But there are still battles to be fought, and Cárdenas needs you for his horses, and perhaps I may need you. Your duty is here.'

To Garcilaço, honor was much simpler: 'I must stay with Marcos,' and he left the two officers, who called after him that he was being a fool. However, when Garcilaço reached his father, who was packing his mule for the long march back to Mexico City, Marcos took him in his arms, eyes wet with tears, and cried: 'I cannot let you damage your life. Stay with the army you have grown to love.'

'Without you I'd have no army. I'm your son, and I shall stay with you.'

At these words Marcos clasped the boy tightly and sobbed: 'I've ruined everything. Did you hear the curses they heaped on me?' He stood clinging to Garcilaço, then said in hushed voice, as if he were seeing a vision: 'But the Cities are there. The walls of gold will be found, just as I said.' And with that he shouted: 'Army-Master Cárdenas! Come take your little soldier!' and thrusting the boy away, he started his mournful exile.

Garcilaço was not given time to brood about Fray Marcos' disgrace, for as soon as Coronado recovered from his wounds he dispatched an elite group of twenty-five to make a swift, galloping exploration of lands to the west, and Cárdenas, in command, took the boy along. Now Garcilaço had an opportunity to see what a masterful soldier Cárdenas was, for he anticipated everything: where to find water, how many deer to kill for food, in what safe place to camp. 'I would like to be a soldier like you,' the boy said, and Cárdenas smiled: 'You could never be an officer like me, but you could serve, and honorably.' When Garcilaço asked why he could not attain command, Cárdenas told him truthfully: 'Command is reserved for those born in Spain.' He did not add 'Of white parentage,' but he intended the boy to catch that nuance of Spanish life.

Twenty hot and thirsty days later Garcilaço was riding ahead of the file when he stopped, gasped, and held up his hand to warn the others.

'Look!' he whispered, and when Cárdenas drew up he said in reverence: 'Dear Jesus, you have worked a miracle.' And one by one the others moved into line, there at the edge of a tremendous depression, and fell silent. It was a moment of overwhelming discovery, a moment that no one could absorb or summarize in speech.

At their feet opened a canyon so grand, they knew of nothing with which to compare it. A mile deep, mile upon mile across, with a tiny ribbon of river wandering at the bottom, its walls were multicolored, shimmering with gold and red and blue and dancing green. Lovely trees, bent from the wind, adorned its rim and sometimes tried to creep down the sides, their tall crowns like tiny tips of fern, so far away they were. And as the afternoon sun moved across the deep gash of the canyon, it threw weird shadows upon pinnacles far below, and new colors emerged as if some great power were redecorating what was already a masterpiece.

'A miracle!' Cárdenas gasped. 'God has prepared this wonder to show us His power.' They had discovered the Grand Canyon of the Colorado, and Garcilaço felt himself growing inches taller when Army-Master Cárdenas said with affection, as he ruffled the boy's hair: 'Remember, this one found it. Let's christen it El Cañon de Garcilaço.' There was cheering, but in the midst of the celebration the boy looked eastward, for he could not forget that the true adventure still waited there, in what Cabeza had described as the land of many lands.

Cárdenas and his swift-marching men required three months for this trip to the canyon, and when they rejoined the main party they found that it had acquired a stranger, to whom Garcilaço took an instant dislike. This man, in his thirties, was a good-looking Indian whose height, facial tattooing and turban headdress identified him as belonging to some tribe far from Cíbola, perhaps a Pawnee from north and east. He had been captured by the Zuñi of Cíbola in a raid years ago and was now a slave, except that he seemed more clever than those who held him. He had a glib manner, a sly, knowing look, and Garcilaço often saw him calculating how to play this white captain off against that Indian chief, and it was clear that he did not propose to stay a slave indefinitely.

He was called El Turco, and nothing else, because the soldiers who found him thought that he looked the way a Turk should, although none had ever seen one, and if the boy intuitively disliked El Turco, the Indian reciprocated with intensity, for he saw in Garcilaço the kind of innocent intelligence which might quickly pierce the lies he was about to tell. El Turco had but one ambition, and everything else was subservient to it: trick Coronado into marching toward the empty east, where his army would perish in the desolate wastelands. When confusion was at its peak, he would escape and travel north to his home village of Quivira, whose valleys and running streams he remembered each night of his captivity.

And the tales he told! He started cautiously, for like Fray Marcos, whom he resembled in certain ways, he always wanted to know first what the Spaniards hoped for; then he tailored his reports to please them. For example, after listening closely to every word the soldiers spoke he learned that coins were of extreme value, but he had never seen one. Cautiously he began: 'We have coins, you know.' When pressed as to what form his coins took, he guessed blindly: 'Colored stones,' and then withdrew into his shell as the Spaniards ridiculed him. To demonstrate how foolish he was, the men showed him coins of silver and gold, and in that instant those two metals became part of his arsenal.

To a different group of soldiers he said casually one day, using signs and grunts and a smattering of Spanish words: 'In my land the great chief has a staff made of something that glistens in the sunlight . . . yellowish . . . very heavy.' He did not at this time mention the word *gold,* nor did he again refer to the chief's staff, but he could almost see his rumors whirling about the camp, so that when Cárdenas came casually by to ask, as if the question were totally unimportant, 'In your land, have you any hard things like this?' as he tapped on his steel sword, the Indian said: 'Oh, yes! But in my tribe only our big chiefs are allowed to own it. Glistens in the sunlight . . . yellowish . . . very heavy.'

At first Cárdenas affected not to have noticed the description, but later he asked in his offhand manner: 'Your big chiefs, do they have much of the . . .' He tapped his steel again.

'Much, much!' And both men left it there.

Two members of the army were aware that Cárdenas had been trapped by this clever manipulator: El Turco knew it, and so did Garcilaço. Reporting to his master after evening meal one night, Garcilaço said: 'Captain, El Turco is a great liar.'

'You should know something about that.'

'I do. My father Marcos lied because he dreamed of doing good. El Turco lies to do something bad.'

'He's told us about gold in his land, and that's what we've come north to find.'

'Captain, he did not tell *us* about gold. We told *him* about it.' And he tried to explain how El Turco never told them anything but what they had already betrayed as their need or interest. But Cárdenas and the others wanted to believe El Turco, and they did.

El Turco also impressed the Spaniards by making shrewd guesses about the past and future, the kind of clever nonsense any reasonably observant person could make, but when some of them proved true, and the Spaniards asked how he had gained this power of clairvoyance, he said slyly: 'Sometimes the devil comes to visit with me, telling me what will happen.'

When Coronado heard about this he became intensely interested, for he had always suspected that the devil hovered near his army, and since it was essential that the Spaniards know what El Turco was up to, Coronado kept close watch on him. One night, as the general was passing where the prisoner was kept, he heard El Turco talking with the devil, who was hiding in a jug.

'Devil, are you in there?' El Turco whispered, tapping on the jug.

'You know I am. What do you want?'

'Where do you want me to lead them?'

'Take them anywhere but Quivira in the east,' the devil said, 'because if they march there, they'll find all that gold I've collected. They must not have it.'

'Where shall I lead them?'

'To the north. Get them lost in that emptiness.'

'I shall do so, Prince of Evil.'

'If you keep them away from the east, I'll reward you.' And with those clever word El Turco tricked Coronado into going east toward nothingness.

Seeking to have his army in the best possible condition for the march, Coronado decided that if his men had to fight in winter, they would require three hundred sturdy cloaks, which he ordered the villages of the area to provide. When this proved impossible, for there was no surplus, the soldiers went on a rampage, stopping any Indian they encountered and ripping from his shoulders the cloak he was wearing. In this rough way they collected their three hundred, and also the enmity of the owners.

During the confusion, a Spanish cavalryman whose name was known but never disclosed because of the great guilt that lay upon him, went to a quiet part of one village, summoned an Indian to hold his horse, went inside the pueblo, climbed to an upper room, and raped the man's wife. In order to avert trouble, Coronado ordered all his mounted soldiers to line up with their horses so that the husband could identify the culprit, and since the husband had held the horse for nearly half an hour, he could easily identify it, but the owner denied that he had been in that part of the village and the wronged husband got no satisfaction.

Next day the enraged Indians assaulted the Spaniards in a most effective way. They stole many of their horses and drove them into an enclosed area where the animals had to run in wild circles. Then the Indians, screaming with delight, proceeded to kill them with arrows.

Furious, Coronado summoned Cárdenas, and ordered: 'Surround the village and teach them a lesson.' After Cárdenas had disposed his troops in a circle that enclosed the pueblos, he directed two captains, Melgosa and López, to perform an extremely hazardous action: 'Break into those tall houses where the lower floors are not defended. Fight your way to the roof, and shoot down into the streets.' As Melgosa started toward his assignment he called: 'Little Fighter, come along,' and with no hesitation Garcilaço did.

When they reached the roof, the captains directed the boy to stand near the ladders: 'Push them down if any Indians try to climb up.' And there he stood through a whole day, a night, and most of the next day as his captains fired into the mob below. But without food or water the Spaniards began to tire and might have been forced to surrender had not one of the soldiers below devised a clever tactic: he built a fire on the ground floor of the pueblo, then sprinkled it with water, making a thick smoke. Soon the choking Indians were forced out, making with their forearms a kind of cross and bowing their heads, a most ancient signal for peaceful surrender. It was not binding, however, until the victors also made a cross and bowed their heads, but this Melgosa, López and Garcilaço gladly did. The ugly siege was over.

But Cárdenas, infuriated by the attack on his horses, was so determined to demonstrate the power of the Spanish army that he ordered his other soldiers to surround these men who had honorably surrendered, and then to cut two hundred wooden stakes, each six feet tall, at which the prisoners would be burned alive.

'No!' Garcilaço shouted as dry brush was piled about the first victim. 'We gave our word.'

Cárdenas in his fury would not listen, so Garcilaço appealed to Melgosa and López, who had accepted the truce, but they too refused to support him.

'Master! No!' he pleaded, but Cárdenas was obdurate, his face a red mask of hatred, and the burning started.

The Indian men, seeing five of their comrades screaming at the stakes, decided to die fighting, and grabbing whatever they could reach—clubs, stones, the still-unused stakes—they began a furious assault upon the Spaniards, whereupon Cárdenas bellowed: 'All Spaniards out!' and after Melgosa and López had rushed Garcilaço to safety, soldiers rimmed the area in which the two hundred had been kept and began pouring shot and arrows into it, killing many.

Those who survived now broke free and began running helter-skelter across open land, whereupon Cárdenas and other cavalry officers spurred their horses, shouting and exulting as they cut down the fleeing Indians, other horsemen lancing them with spears until not one man of that entire group was left alive.

Garcilaço was horrified by what had happened, by the faithlessness of his hero Cárdenas, by the cowardice of his other hero Melgosa, who would not defend the truce he had authorized, and most of all by the burning and chasing and stabbing. He was appalled to find that Coronado did nothing. 'We taught them not to offend Spanish honor' was all he would say, and Garcilaço was left to wonder what honor meant. Fray Marcos, he felt certain, would not have permitted such a slaughter had he been in charge of the army's conscience, and from that moment Garcilaço began to see his father in a much kinder light. Because of his enthusiasm, Marcos may have told many lies, but he was a man who had at least known what honor was. Cárdenas did not.

But for a boy of fourteen to pass moral judgment upon adults is a perilous undertaking, for now that Coronado was injured and confused, Garcilaço saw that it was Cárdenas who proved to be the true leader. It was he who supervised the killing of animals for meat to feed his men. Marching across deserts blazing with heat or swirling in storm, it was Cárdenas who buoyed the spirits of the army, and when brief, explosive battles with Indians became unavoidable, his horse was always in the lead. Like his general, he was driven by a lust for gold and fame, those terrible taskmasters, but in discharging his duty like a true soldier, he recaptured Garcilaço's reluctant respect.

But now he did a most unsoldierly thing. He broke his arm, and when it refused to mend and the army set forth to conquer the opulent city of Quivira, he had to stay behind.

On the morning that Coronado started his triumphal march east—toward disaster in the drylands if he persisted—he summoned Garcilaço: 'Son, can you count?'

'Yes, sir. And I know my letters.'

'Good. Start now, and count every step you take. When we strike camp, tell me how many. I'll measure your stride and know how far we've come.'

So the boy walked in dust behind the horses, counting 'Uno, dos, tres, cuatro,' and whenever he reached a thousand he made a mark on a paper the Franciscans had given him. At the end of that first day it showed twenty-three such marks, and when he presented the paper to Coronado, the general thanked him: 'Nearly four leagues. Good for a first day.' And next morning the counting resumed.

After many such days, continuing to count even in his sleep, Garcilaço calculated correctly that considering the distance east from Cíbola, the expedition must have entered the lands traversed by Cabeza de Vaca. He was at last in Tejas, the fabled land of many lands.

What a massive disappointment it was, for Coronado, always obedient to the urging of El Turco, had entered those bleak lands at the headwaters of what would later be called, in Spanish, El Río Colorado de Tejas. Distraught by the lack of any sign of civilization, he then angrily turned north, only to find himself locked in a series of deep canyons of a river of some size, El Río de Los Brazos de Dios, The River of the Arms of God. Here, surrounded by dark cliffs, the Spaniards had to face the fact that they had been led not to gold-encrusted Quivira but into a barren wilderness where they stood a good chance of dying. Sensible men would have abandoned the enterprise right there, but Coronado and his captains were Spanish gentlemen, and a tougher breed was never born. 'We'll go on to the real Quivira,' Coronado said. 'Wherever it is.'

In this extremity, on 26 May 1541, the expedition had been campaigning for more than four hundred and fifty strenuous days without capturing one item of value or finding any kingdom worthy of conquest, so the leaders knew that their venture would be judged by what they accomplished at Quivira, and this powerful obligation made them believe that gold still waited. In a council there in the ravines, Coronado decided that he, with thirty of his ablest horsemen, six sturdy foot soldiers and the Franciscans, would make a last-ditch sortie to the north, relying on the gold they would surely find there to salvage the reputation of his expedition. The bulk of the army would return to familiar territory and there await the triumphant return of the adventurers.

But now the Spaniards were confronted by a quandary best expressed by Captain Melgosa: 'Where in hell is Quivira?' Fortunately, Coronado's group contained two scouts of the Tejas tribe, and they spoke the truth: 'General, Quivira lies there' —and they indicated true north—'but when you reach it you will find nothing.'

'How can you say that?' Coronado thundered, and they replied: 'Because we have hunted at Quivira. Nothing.' Such discouraging information Coronado refused to accept, so the frenzied search for gold continued.

About this time an extraordinary act of Garcilaço's caused much amusement. Late one summer afternoon, when he saw the northern horizon turn blue and felt the temperature begin to drop, he supposed he was about to experience what Cabeza had so often spoken of with fear and respect. 'It may soon be winter!' he warned the Spaniards, but they laughed: 'Lad, it's July!' However, within the hour a bitter wind was roaring across the empty spaces, and in the midst of this sudden storm, while others were huddling inside their blankets, Garcilaço threw off his clothes to stand naked in the wind.

'What are you doing?' Melgosa shouted from his tent, and when he ran to the boy with his blanket, all Garcilaço could answer was: 'Cabeza told me he lived for seven years attacked by such winds, and he was naked. I wanted to test him.'

'Cabeza de Vaca was a liar. Everyone knows that. Come inside.' When Garcilaço sat crouched by the fire, with the others thinking he had drifted toward insanity, he thought of Cabeza: He must have been a liar, for no man could survive such a norther, yet he did. We know he did.

On a blistering July day in 1541, Coronado and his small band lined up at the southern bank of a miserable arroyo and stared across at Quivira (in what is now

Kansas). They saw an indiscriminate collection of low mud huts surrounded by arid fields with few trees and no rich meadowlands. Smoke curled lazily from a few chopped openings in roofs, but there were no chimneys, no doors and no visible furniture. Such men and women as did appear were a scrawny lot, dressed not in expensive furs but in untanned skins. Of pearls and gold and turquoises and silver, there was not a sign. The Spaniards had wandered nearly three thousand miles, squandering two fortunes, Mendoza's and Coronado's, and had found nothing.

Garcilaço noted how the leaders reacted to this final disappointment. Coronado was overcome, unable to comprehend it and powerless to issue new orders. One captain raged, then started to prepare his men for the long homeward journey. Melgosa looked at the supposed city of riches and showed his gapped teeth in a disgusted smile: 'I've seen pigsties in Toledo look better than that.'

It was Melgosa who issued the first order: 'Double the watch on El Turco,' and during the dreadful blazing days the slave who had been the agent of this disaster —but not its cause, for that lay within the cupidity of the captains—sat unconcerned in his chains, humming ancient chants used by his forebears when they knew that all was lost and death was at hand.

Garcilaço himself was anguished by the magnitude of the defeat, even though he had known it was coming, and he several times spoke with El Turco: 'Why did you deceive us?'

'You deceived yourselves.'

'But you lied, always you lied about the gold.'

'I never put gold in your hearts. You put it there.'

The dark-skinned man laughed, that easy, ingratiating laugh which had so charmed and blinded the Spaniards: 'As a boy, I had a fine life, chasing buffalo. As a young man, I had two good wives, there by the northern rivers. When we were captured by the Zuñi, the others were treated badly but I protected myself by talking quickly with the leaders in the pueblos. And with the Spaniards, I had my own horse.' He shook his chains, laughing at the rattling noise they made. Then he ridiculed his captors: 'The Spaniards were such fools. It was so easy for me.' And once more he became the insatiable plotter: 'You're an Indian like me. Help me to escape. I know a city to the north. Much gold.'

One night Captain Melgosa said to Garcilaço: 'Come, lad. Work to do,' and he took him into El Turco's tent, where they were joined by a huge butcher from Mexico, one Francisco Martín, who kept his hands behind his back.

'Turco,' Melgosa began, 'each word you've said has been a lie. You led us here to perish.' The Indian smiled. 'And yesterday you tried to persuade the Indians here to massacre us.' Still the great liar showed no remorse, so Melgosa flashed a sign, whereupon Martín brought forward his powerful hands, threw a looped rope about El Turco's neck, and with a twisting stick, drew the noose tighter and tighter until the Indian strangled.

With Martín's help, Garcilaço dug a grave into which the corpse of this infuriating man was thrown. Had he but once told the truth, he could have become a trusted guide. As it was, he deceived everybody, including himself.

Coronado, head bowed and gilded armor discarded because of the sweltering heat, started his shameful retreat, unaware that history would record him as one of the greatest explorers. Under his guidance, Spanish troops had reached far lands: California, Arizona, New Mexico, Texas, Oklahoma, Kansas. His men had described a hundred Indian settlements, worked with and fought with a score of different tribes, and identified the difficulties to be faced by later settlers. But because he did not find treasure, he was judged a failure.

One member of the expedition did find success, although of a temporary nature. One morning a messenger posted north from Mexico with an exciting letter drafted by the emperor, Carlos Quinto, in Madrid:

> Captain-General Coronado, Greetings and God's Blessing. You have in your command a Captain of Cavalry, Don García López de Cárdenas of the noble family of that name. Inform the Captain that his brother in Spain who inherited the noble title and all wealth and properties pertaining to it has unfortunately died. Said Captain Cárdenas is to return by fastest route to Madrid, where he will be invested with the title now belonging to him and be handed the substantial properties to which he is entitled. By order of His Majesty the King.

When Infantry-Captain Melgosa heard this news he grinned, spat through his gapped teeth, and told Garcilaço: 'See! It always happens this way. It's cavalry officers who get messages from the emperor.' Then he burst into gusts of laughter, clapping Cárdenas on the back: 'Infuriating! The only man in the whole army who gets any gold is this damned cavalry officer.' And they got drunk on wine Melgosa had saved in expectation of celebrating the capture of Quivira's gold.

How ironic it seemed to Garcilaço that of all who set forth on this glorious expedition, the only one who profited when it ended in disaster was the badly flawed Cárdenas. The rest earned only bitterness.

But the boy need not have envied the apparent good fortune of Cárdenas, for although the army-master was awarded both the title and fortune when he reached Spain, he was then accused of having burned Indians alive. He was in and out of jail for seven years, fined eight hundred gold ducats and sentenced to serve the king without pay for thirty-three months at the dismal post of Oran in North Africa. But because the king liked him, this was reduced to two hundred ducats and twelve months' service at the kindlier post of Vélez Málaga, where he prepared for further adventures in new lands.

Coronado's heroic aspirations ended in confusion, for when he issued his reluctant order 'March south!' some sixty of his braver underlings announced that they intended to remain permanently among the pueblos of what would become New Mexico. Coronado flew into a rage to think that they were willing to chance a new life in a new land while he had the doleful task of returning to Mexico to report his failure.

One of the would-be settlers wrote some years later: 'He said we had to go back with him, and he threatened to have us hanged if we refused or said anything more about it.' So the settlement which could have justified the expedition was aborted.

However, three other members of a much different type also asked to remain behind, and they posed a more difficult problem. They were Franciscan friars— Fray Padilla, an ordained priest, and two who had taken only minor orders. In robes already tattered, they came before Coronado to say: 'We will stay here.'

'Why?' the general asked, almost pleading with them to drop their foolishness, and they said: 'Because we must bring Jesus into pagan hearts.'

Officers, common soldiers, even some of the Mexican Indians tried to dissuade them from what appeared to be certain martyrdom, but the advisers were powerless, for God had whispered to the three, and finally Coronado had to give them permission to remain.

One of the minor friars set up his mission near Cíbola, while the other sought to convert the local Indians along the Río Pecos, and they marched off to their extraordinary duties.

As for Fray Padilla, Garcilaço would remember always that final morning when the friar started his long walk back to Quivira, whose Indians he dreamed of bringing into the Holy Faith. He did not go alone or lacking goods, for when Coronado accepted the fact that the friar could not be dissuaded, he provided him with so many people and so much goods that Padilla looked as if he were heading a minor expedition: a Portuguese soldier, two Indian oblate brothers who had taken no orders but whose lives were dedicated to religious service, a mestizo workman, a black translator, a train of mules well laden, a horse, a substantial flock of sheep, a full set of instruments for the Mass, and the six young Quivira Indians who had guided Coronado back from that settlement.

It was a fumbling attempt to Christianize a vast new land, and when Garcilaço, still avid to learn what honor was, watched the little procession depart, he asked himself: 'Why would men volunteer for such a fatal assignment?' But as the words hung in the air he realized that honor included not only physical and moral courage but also a daring commitment to central beliefs, and for a moment he wished that he might one day march in the footsteps of that friar.

As Padilla moved off toward sure death he grew smaller and smaller in the eyes of Garcilaço, but larger and larger in the eyes of God.

Years later a Franciscan gathered reports from all who had known the friar and wrote: 'The Portuguese soldier and the two oblate brothers were traveling with Fray Padilla one day when hostile Indians attacked. Insisting that his friends escape with the only horse, he knelt in prayer and was transfixed by arrows.'

Imperial Spain was neither generous nor understanding with her unsuccessful conquistadores. When Coronado returned with no gold, he was charged with numerous malfeasances and crimes. The great explorer was for many years abused by officials dispatched from Spain with portfolios of charges made by his suspicious king. When Coronado's case ground to a halt, Viceroy Mendoza was similarly charged and harassed. Captain Melgosa received nothing for his many acts of heroism, and the mestizo Garcilaço was treated worst of all.

Even though of the meanest birth, he had striven throughout this long and dangerous expedition to conduct himself according to his understanding of honor. He had been first to sight the deep canyon, but he did not shout: 'See what I have found!' He had saved his commander's life when the stones fell, but he did not cry: 'How brave I am!' And he had fought for two days on the roof, an incident whose aftermath he tried to forgive, because he felt that no man of honor would kill so wantonly.

But at the end of his journey he was dismissed with no pay, no job and no honors, for he was judged to be 'merely another Indian.'

He was mustered out in 1542, and lacking funds with which to buy enough animals to work the profitable Vera Cruz–Mexico City route, he had to be content with that portion of El Camino Real, the Royal Road, which ran from Guadalajara to Culiacán, with an occasional side trip delivering mining gear to the new silver mines at Zacatecas. Occasionally he would come upon a cargo destined for Mexico City, and one day in 1558, overworked and disheartened, he was engaged on such a trip when he was accosted on the streets of the capital by a tonsured monk who asked: 'Are you the Garcilaço who once knew Fray Marcos?' When he nodded, the monk said: 'You must come with me,' and he led the way to a small Franciscan monastery, where a very old cleric came unsteadily forward to say in a weak voice: 'My son, why have you not come to me for help?'

It was Fray Marcos, and in succeeding days this frail old man spoke often with Garcilaço, reviewing the evil things that had happened to him and complaining of how his enemies never allowed the world to forget that it had been his misleading information which had tricked Coronado's army into its disasters. 'Son, it's impossible to determine what is truth and what falsehood. I cannot now remember whether I saw the Seven Cities in reality or in a dream . . . but that's no matter, for I did see them.'

Garcilaço was now a grown man of thirty-three, who worked hard and to whom a crust of bread was either firmly in hand or was not, and he was not disposed to tolerate philosophical niceties: 'You were never on the hill. And if you had been, you couldn't have seen the Cities. Not from where we were.'

'The hill has nothing to do with it. You do not judge a man by whether he climbed a hill or not. I saw the Cities. When I preach about the City of God that awaits us in its glory, do I climb some hill to see it? No, it exists because God wants it to exist. And the Seven Cities of Cíbola exist in the same way. They will be found one day because men like Esteban and me will always seek them.'

At this mention of the dancing black man, Marcos fell to weeping, and after some moments, said softly: 'I was not generous with him, Garcilaço. I deplored his way with women. But in the long view of history, what are a few women, more or less?'

This rhetorical question brought a most unexpected consequence: 'Garcilaço, my son, I have been most eager to find you. I sent that friar to seek you out. When the last viceroy took his Spanish soldiers home with him, one of them left behind a daughter. Ten years old . . . we could find no mother.' He fell to coughing, then said: 'I took her in. She works in our kitchen . . . María Victoria. But she's getting old enough now that people are beginning to talk, to say ugly things about me—the usual charges you heard when you were her age.' He brought his hands together under his chin and stared at his son: 'It's time that girl found a husband.'

He led the way into the kitchen, where María Victoria, a golden-skinned mestizo girl of fifteen, proved so attractive that Garcilaço asked in honest bewilderment: 'Why would she be interested in me?' and Marcos said: 'Because I've been telling her all these years how brave you were in the north, how you proved yourself to be a man of honor.'

He grasped María Victoria's right hand and placed it in Garcilaço's: 'I give you my daughter.' He kissed them both, then said: 'My children, in this life honor is everything. It is the soul of Spain. Some caballeros have it, most do not. You Indians can earn it too, and if you do, it adorns life.' Tears came to his eyes as he added: 'I've always tried to preserve my honor, and have done nothing of which I am ashamed.'

He himself conducted the wedding ceremony, and shortly thereafter, died. For some years chroniclers, when summarizing his life, belabored the infamous role he had played in lying about Cíbola, but now his scandals have been forgiven and forgotten.

María Victoria and Garcilaço did not forget him, and for good reason. Fray Marcos had been a Franciscan pledged to poverty, but as a prudent man he had always managed to sequester his share of the gold coins which passed his way in either governmental or religious activity. 'It wasn't really stealing, children,' he assured them two days before he died. 'A man of honor never steals, but he can put a few coins aside.'

When Garcilaço asked: 'Where's the gold hidden?' Marcos merely smiled, but some days after the friar's funeral María took her husband to where she used to sleep, and hidden in a wall behind her cot he found a substantial hoard. 'Fray Marcos knew that the father-provincial liked to make surprise visits,' she whispered, 'to make sure his friars kept obedient to their vows of poverty. Father could always guess when the old inspector was coming, and then he gave me his gold to hide.'

The windfall enabled the newlyweds to purchase land, build a house, hire Indians to drive the family mules down to Vera Cruz, and buy a black tutor from Cuba to educate them. Many years later, when it became customary for well-to-do mestizos to take surnames, the viceroy bestowed *Garza* upon them, and it became a tradition in the family that their progenitor had been a Spanish sailor of that name.

. . . TASK FORCE

At our organizing meeting in January we had agreed that our young assistants would assume responsibility for inviting to each of our formal sessions some respected scholar who would address us for about forty minutes on whatever aspect of Texas history we might be concentrating upon at that time. Their first offering provided a lucky coincidence.

In conformance with the governor's desire that we hold our meetings in various cities across the state so as to attract maximum attention to our work, our February meeting, which would emphasize Hispanic factors in Texas history, was to be held in Corpus Christi, that beautiful, civilized town on the Gulf. It was appropriate that we meet there, because Corpus was already more than sixty-percent Hispanic, with every indication that the percentage would increase.

When I started to make plans as to how we would get there, I learned how convenient it was to work with really rich Texans, for Rusk had three airplanes to whisk him to and from his oil and banking ventures, while Quimper had two for his distant ranches. Since each had a Lear Jet for longer distances and a King Air for shorter, we had our choice, and in this time-saving way we covered much of Texas, for as Quimper told us: 'When you have interests in a nation as big as Texas, stands to reason you got to have planes.'

When we landed at the airport in Corpus, we were met by Dr. Plácido Navarro Padilla, an elderly Mexican scholar from the cathedral city of Saltillo, which lay two hundred and sixty miles south of the Rio Grande. During the hectic decade 1824–1833, Saltillo had served as the capital of Coahuila-y-Tejas, so that a natural affinity existed between it and Austin, our present capital.

He was a dapper man, with neatly trimmed gray mustache and silver-rimmed eyeglasses, and had the easy grace which marks so many Spanish scholars. He could disarm those with whom he argued by flashing a congenial smile and an apologetic bow of his head, but in debate he could be fierce. When our staff member from SMU introduced him, she explained: 'Dr. Padilla has specialized in Mexican-Texan relations . . .'

'Excuse me,' the doctor interrupted in excellent English. 'My name is Navarro.'

'But it says in our report,' Ransom Rusk countered, 'that your name is Padilla.'

'That is my mother's name. It comes last, Spanish style. My father's name . . . my name . . . is Navarro.'

'We're proud to have you with us,' Rusk said with an attempt at warmth. 'Proceed.'

'Your Republic of Texas fell under United States rule during the final days of 1845, actual admission coming in 1846. Since this is 1983, you have been American for a hundred and thirty-seven years. But you must remember that Spanish interest in your area started with Alonso Alvarez de Piñeda in 1519. Serious settlement started in El Paso in 1581, and Mexican control did not end until 1836, so that you were under Spanish-Mexican hegemony for three hundred and seventeen years. In other words, Texas was Spanish more than twice as long as it has been American, and this must never be forgotten.'

He proceeded with a forceful analysis of the Spanish heritage in Texas, a subject on which he was well qualified, since he had taught it during seven summer sessions as visiting professor at the University of Texas: 'Your land is surveyed in leagues and labors, according to Spanish custom. Many of the laws governing your use of rivers are Spanish in origin. The religion in large parts of your terrain is Roman Catholicism. The names of your towns and counties are often Spanish. Your best architecture is Spanish Colonial, as are many of your rural customs. Texas is indelibly dyed in Hispanic colors, and the inheritance is a good one.'

Rusk, always a defender of Anglo-Saxon superiority, was not prepared to accept this emphasis on things Spanish: 'Suppose we grant that in the beginning your impact was impressive. But it has been the relatively few years of English-speaking domination which have given Texas its character.'

'For the moment it might seem that way,' Dr. Navarro conceded, 'but during the passage of centuries cultural influences have a stubborn way of persisting, and I would suppose that with every passing decade the power of your Spanish inheritance will become more evident.'

'Are you equating Mexican with Spanish?'

'I am.'

'Now wait. If I see five hundred Mexicans on Texas streets, Dr. Navarro, I see never a hint of Spanish influence, barring their language and religion.'

'What do you see?'

'Indians. You can't find a drop of Spanish blood.'

Dr. Navarro smiled disarmingly: 'In odd corners of Mexico you will find people like me. Pure Spanish through unbroken generations.'

I was rather irritated with Rusk because of the surly way in which he heckled our speaker, and I had about concluded that I must rebuke him for his incivility when he smiled bleakly and told Navarro: 'I accept your correction. You've been around here a lot longer than I have.'

It turned out to be a stimulating meeting, for which our young assistants were much relieved. Navarro threw off sparks like a busy grindstone on a frosty morning, especially when he spoke of those first three Spaniards who were associated, if only peripherally, with Texas.

'I understand there's a movement afoot among your historians to play down the importance of Cabeza de Vaca, Fray Marcos and Coronado in the beginnings of Texas, and this I can understand. Cabeza de Vaca never knew he was in Texas; Fray Marcos never came near the place; and if Coronado entered your state, which many doubt, it could only have been in the bleakest part of the Panhandle.

'But our concerns extend far beyond the geographical boundaries of Texas. This state has an imperial significance. Its natural sphere of influence includes all the areas explored by these three men, even those areas in northern Mexico. If we think regionally, we see that every step Cabeza de Vaca, Fray Marcos and Coronado took had implications for Texas and its imperium. These men remain important factors in your history.

'But I am more interested in their psychological reverberations, and here you must indulge me if I wax poetic, for I visualize myself as a poet striving to write the *Odyssey* and the *Lusiads* of Spain in Mexico.

'Cabeza de Vaca established the ideal pattern for a Texan: bold, daring, persistent, observant, optimistic even when disaster hovered. He is the stubborn Texan, the gallant, the unconquered, and I cherish his memory.

'Fray Marcos had an apocalyptic vision of what the Texas imperium might become, and just as he fired the vision of his contemporaries, he ignites ours today. He is the patron saint of the great liars in Texas history, the braggadocios, the adventurers whose tales exceed their adventures. Every Texan land-seeker who assured his wife "The good location for us lies just over that hill," every wildcatter who traced a streambed to the sure oil site, every builder in Houston right now who is convinced he will find tenants for his condominium if only some investor will finance the next six months—they're all descendants of Fray Marcos, the confidence man, and Texas would not be the same without them.

'When I hear the name Coronado, my heart salutes. A great dreamer who in your Texas vernacular "put his money where his mouth was," he risked all and lost all, but in doing so, gained immortality. The history of Texas is filled with his kind, the great gamblers, the men whose eyes were fixed beyond the horizon. Like him they try, they fail, but do not complain. I would like to fail the way Francisco Vásquez de Coronado failed.'

After recommending that we not drop these noble Spaniards from our curriculum, he came to the heart of his challenging talk, which I will abbreviate, using only his words:

'I beg you, as you work at laying the foundations of historical education in Texas, not to fall prey to The Black Legend. This is a historical aberration promulgated by devout Dutch and English Protestants in the sixteenth century. It is a distortion of history, but it has taken root, I am sorry to say, in many quarters of American historical writing. Its main tenets are clearly defined and easily spotted. Do please try to avoid their errors.'

'What are they?' Quimper asked, and Navarro gave a concise summary.

'The Black Legend claims that everything bad which happened in Spanish history was due to the Spanish Catholic church. The phrase seems to have originated from the black cloth worn by Phillip II and his priests. It claims that insidious popes from Rome dominated Spanish civil government. That priests tyrannized Spanish society. That the Inquisition ran rampant through Spanish society. That Catholic domination caused the end of Spanish culture and inhibited Spanish learning. That priestly domination caused the weakening and decline of Spanish power, both at home and in the colonies.'

In our meetings Ransom Rusk always struggled for clarification of ideas, and now, even though he had a strong bias against Mexicans, he labored to understand the point Navarro was trying to make: 'I was taught in college that Spain was backward because of its religion. Where's the error?'

For the moment, Dr. Navarro ignored this interruption, for he wished to nail down an important point: 'So long as The Black Legend muddied only theological waters it could be tolerated, but when it began to influence international relations, it became a menace, for then it claimed that Catholicism, under the baleful guidance of its black-robed priests, sought to undermine and destroy Protestant governments as well as Protestant churches.'

'I've always believed that,' Rusk said, whereupon Navarro looked at him with a forgiving smile: 'I almost believed it, too, when I was a student at Harvard, because that was all they taught. So you can be forgiven, Mr. Rusk.'

'Thank you. Now I'd certainly like to hear your whitewash of the situation.'

'That is what I am noted for in Mexican intellectual circles. Whitewashing The Black Legend.'

He proceeded with an insightful analysis of the baleful influences of The Black Legend: 'It obstructed serious American study of Spain's influence because it offered such a ready-made explanation for anything that went wrong. Did Spanish power in Europe and the New World wane? "See? The Black Legend was right!" Did Spain mismanage her colonies in America, much as England mismanaged hers? "The malignant influence of the Catholic church!" Did things go contrary to the way Protestants wanted? "Blame it on The Black Legend." '

Quimper interrupted: 'But Spain did decline. It did fall behind. We all know that.'

Navarro surprised me by agreeing heartily with what Lorenzo had said: 'Of course Spain declined. So has France declined. And certainly England has. But they all declined for the same reasons that the United States will one day decline. The inevitable movement of history, the inescapable consequences of change. Not because either England or Spain was nefarious, or unusually cruel, or blinded by religion.'

This was too much for Rusk's stalwart Baptist heart: 'But damn it all, your Inquisition did burn people!' to which Navarro replied without even pausing for breath: 'Let us say about the same number that English Protestants hanged or burned for being witches. And some fanatics argue that your killings were more reprehensible because they came so late, after a social conscience had been formed.' I seemed to remember that the last auto-da-fé in Mexico occurred in 1815, when the great revolutionary leader Father José María Morelos was condemned by the Inquisition and shot by soldiers. But Navarro's obvious skill at polemics so intimidated me that I remained silent.

But now he changed tactics, becoming even eager to acknowledge each weakness of Spain or her church, and he even conceded that The Black Legend might have contributed some good in that it had driven Spanish historians to a more careful analysis of their culture in their determination to defend it. In the end we respected him for his unrelenting defense of things Spanish.

'You must never let prejudice blind you to the fact that in the years when Spain first explored and took possession of Texas, it was the foremost empire on earth, excelling even China. It dominated the continent of Europe, much of the Americas, trade and the exchange of ideas. It was majestic in its power and glorious in its culture. It controlled far more completely then than either the United States or Russia does today. Its influence permeated what would become the future Texas, and to teach students otherwise would be to turn one's back upon the spiritual history of Texas.'

Just as I began to fear that he was trying to make too strong a case for Spanish and Catholic influence, he broke into a wide, conciliatory smile: 'You must remember one fundamental fact about your great state of Texas. If we date its beginning in 1519 with the Piñeda exploration, or 1528 with the marooning of Cabeza de Vaca on Galveston Island, it was about two hundred and fifty years before the first Protestant stepped foot on Texas soil. Of course, Mr. Rusk, when the rascal finally appeared his boots made a deep impression.'

He then turned to one of the most difficult problems: 'The glory and the power! You simply must believe that when Coronado ventured into what is now the Texas Panhandle in 1540 he was impelled by two forces of precisely equal importance, spiritual desire to spread Christianity and temporal hunger for gold and the power it would bring. I have read a hundred accounts of those stirring days, and I have done everything possible to discount the bombast and the speeches made for public consumption, but in the end I stand convinced that men like Coronado really did believe they were doing God's work when they proposed to subdue heathen lands in northern New Spain. I can cite a score of instances in which the conquistadores placed the rights of the church above those of the state, and they did so because they saw themselves first as God's servants, discharging His commands. Gold and power the conquistadores did not find in Texas, but they did find human hearts into which they could instill the saving knowledge of Jesus Christ. I have always felt that Texas started as a God-fearing state and that from the first moment it was Christian.'

In a more subdued tone he proceeded to discuss the matter of Spanish power in Texas, and his analyses were refreshingly sophisticated: 'Texas was so far from Mexico City and so infinitely far from Madrid that power was never transmitted effectively. To tell the truth, when I study those two hundred and fifty years of rather futile Spanish dominance I find myself wondering: Why did not Spain send fifty men like Escandón to settle Texas? They'd have altered the entire picture.'

'Who was Escandón?' Quimper asked, and Navarro replied: 'José de Escandón? The wisest and perhaps the best man Spain ever sent to the Rio Grande. Arrived in 1747. Please teach your children about him.' He broke into a disarming chuckle. 'Mr. Rusk, with five hundred like Escandón we might have worked our way clear to the Canadian border. We came this close'—and he pinched two fingers together—'to making you speak Spanish.'

The scholarly chuckle turned into a laugh. 'But history and the moral will power of commanders determine outcomes. It was destined, perhaps from the start, that Texas would not be adequately settled by the Spaniards. The men like Escandón were never forthcoming. They could not be found . . . they had no one in Madrid pressing their cause. Spain edged up to the immortal challenge, then turned aside.'

Now our speaker became a true professor: 'I trust that in any published materials for school or college you will, out of respect for your heritage, use proper Spanish spelling. Avoid rude barbarisms like Mexico City. It's La Ciudad de México. It's not the Rio Grande, it's El Río Bravo del Norte. And because in Mexican Spanish *j* and *x* are so often interchangeable, please differentiate between Béxar, the original name for what you now call San Antonio, and Béjar, its later name. Same with Texas, then Tejas. And do keep the accents.'

Rusk and Quimper looked aghast at this pedantry and I was afraid they were going to protest, but Professor Garza saved the day: 'Of course, in our scholarly publications we are meticulous in respecting Spanish usage. I'm especially demanding of my students. But in general writing for our newspapers and schools, custom requires Mexico City, the Rio Grande and Bexar. Up here, most accents have vanished.'

'Ah! But I notice from your nameplate that you keep Efraín.'

Garza smiled and said: 'I do that to please my father,' whereupon Navarro asked with an almost childish sweetness: 'Could you not do the same with La Ciudad de México? To honor those of Spanish heritage?' and Garza said: 'Texas honors its Spanish heritage in a thousand ways.'

Navarro bowed politely, then addressed us as a committee: 'When you draft your recommendations you are not required to alter a single item in the American portion of your history. It is sacred. All national histories are. But in the long run, I am convinced that the Spanish heritage of Texas will manifest itself in powerful ways. It will produce results you and I cannot envisage, perhaps a whole new civilization here along the Rio Grande.'

Approaching the end of his presentation, he continued: 'Do not, I beg you, teach your children that Spain was a devil. It was merely one more European country trying to do its best. Do not castigate the processes of exploration and settlement available to it as inferior or negative. They were the best that could have happened in the middle of the sixteenth century as Spain started her unfortunate decline.'

Smiling at us in that ingratiating way Spanish-speaking scholars sometimes command, he concluded: 'Some centuries from now, say in 2424, scholars like you and me sitting in Mongolia may argue that in the later years of the twentieth century, North America started its decline. One hopes that those scholars will be generous in their assessment of what you Americans and we Mexicans tried to accomplish.'

II
THE
MISSION

Misión Santa Teresa
de Casafuerte

To
Rancho El Codo

Fray Damian's
canal

Río San Antonio

The first
canal

Villa
San Fernando de Béjar

Misión
San Antonio de Valero
(The Alamo)

Presidio
San Antonio de Béjar

SAN ANTONIO
DE BEJAR
1730s

Misión
Purísima Concepción

TO THE OTHER MISSIONS

WHEN CHRISTIANITY WAS ABOUT TWELVE HUNDRED YEARS OLD, RELIGIOUS leaders sought a tighter structuring of holy orders, and in 1209 the Italian Francis of Assisi started what became the Franciscans, an order of subtle appeal. It stressed celibacy, poverty, profound devotion and a love of humanity. Its members, like all members of the mendicant orders, were known as *friars* and they did not live in fixed abodes or monasteries; they traveled endlessly, built missions, performed good deeds, and provided examples of humility.

The Franciscans found Mexico a dramatic theater for their operations, and if the Indians of that country escaped formal slavery, it was due in great part to the humanitarian efforts of the Franciscans; if the Indians acquired certain limited blessings of Spanish civilization, it was because brave Franciscans established missions on the remote frontier. They were teachers, hospital attendants, farmers and understanding friends, but primarily they were servants of Jesus Christ.

In 1707 the silver-mining town of Zacatecas, which lay near the center of Mexico, was excited by an announcement that would convert their drowsy rural place into a city of some importance.

'The Franciscans are finally going to build a college here!' ran the rumors. 'We're to be headquarters for all the north.' 'They've started to dig!'

And when men wandered from the central plaza out to the edge of town they saw workmen, Indians mostly, patiently cutting through the rocky earth to provide foundations for a building that would be of surprising size. The gray-clad cleric in charge verified the news: 'It's to stand here . . . just as you see it forming.'

'How many monks?'

'Only friars.'

'But if it's a monastery . . .'

'It's not a monastery, nor is it a proper university like the one in Mexico City.'

'What is it?'

'A teaching center. With some administration on the side.'

The Zacatecans could not comprehend, so he put down his shovel and explained, pointing once more to the north: 'Here we study to prepare ourselves. Up north we do God's work.'

'Then you won't live here?'

'Here while we study. Later wherever God sends us.'

Throughout that first year the many idlers of Zacatecas watched as the Franciscans built the college. More precisely, the friars supervised its building, for the hard work was done either by Indians who were practically slaves or by paid mestizo artisans who had worked on similar structures elsewhere in Mexico.

Among the mestizos on the site in 1716, when the interior decoration of the college was in progress, was a skilled worker in wood, Simón Garza, who had been born in the mining town of San Luis Potosí, where his father had followed the family's tradition of carting materials to and from the silver mines. Since the Garzas had had five sons but only twenty mules, Simón, the youngest boy, came too late to inherit any animals. Instead, he apprenticed himself to a carpenter, and after a year of supervising Indians who worked in pits sawing planks from felled trees, he became an expert in fitting together these planks so as to make a solid wall with no chinks. Later, the Franciscans were delighted to find him, and he worked diligently at their building, perfecting his trade.

At age twenty-six Simón was undergoing an experience in this northern town which disturbed and at the same time delighted him. In the past his occupation had kept him on the move and a lack of money had prevented him from paying court to the young women in those towns where he worked, but in Zacatecas he had steady employment, so six nights a week when work was done he found himself in the spacious public square before the cathedral, watching as the young unmarrieds of good family walked about from seven till nine.

They did not walk aimlessly. The men strolled unhurriedly in a counterclockwise direction, keeping toward the outside of the tree-lined square, and as they went they looked always toward the center of the square, where, inside the large circle they had formed, walked the young women of the town in a clockwise mode. About every ten minutes a young man would meet head-on, almost eye to eye, a particular young woman, twice in each circuit of the plaza, and in this practical, time-honored Spanish manner the unmarrieds conducted their courtships. Over a period of three weeks, any young man could pass his preferred young woman more than a hundred times, during which he could notice with the precision of a scholar the degree to which her smiles had softened.

The traditions of this paseo, as it was called, were rigorously observed. Girls of the purest white skin paraded, their mothers protecting them from the advances of any man of lesser standing; these families were the elite of Zacatecas, the peninsulares, born in Spain itself and dreaming always of a return to that splendid land. Almost as exalted were the criollos, of pure Spanish blood but born in Mexico, and these protected their heritage even more carefully, for they realized that they had little chance of ever getting to Spain; their families occupied positions within Mexican society which did not allow the accumulation of enough funds to permit that. Such criollos lived cut off from Spain, especially when their duties sent them to a distant town like Zacatecas, but they were the inheritors and protectors of Spanish civilization, and they never allowed their neighbors to forget it: 'My child is pure Spanish . . . eleven generations . . . unsullied. We came from Extremadura Province, just like Cortés and Pizzaro . . . same family. If you look closely, you'll see she has the Pizzaro eyes.'

Entrance to the paseo was restricted, with Indians being forbidden to participate; Spanish and criollo families did not want to run the risk that their children might strike alliances with the aborigines, no matter how beautiful the girls or manly the young fellows. A few mestizo girls were in the parade, but only as servants who walked well behind their white mistresses, serving as a kind of protecting influence should one of the young men prove too bold. Mestizo men were absolutely excluded, but well-behaved young fellows of good character like Simón Garza were allowed to stand along the periphery and watch.

However, as the sun went down on Sunday nights, the mestizos of Zacatecas held their own paseo in a nearby plaza, and here young people of the most exciting character paraded. Girls with jet-black tresses and delicate olive complexions smiled at young men dressed in freshly laundered trousers and white shirts. Flowers abounded, and occasionally some girl wore about her neck a disk of pure silver, smelted from the ore of the Zacatecan mines. This rural paseo was apt to be far more colorful than the one conducted by the Spaniards.

It might be assumed that Simón Garza, eager for a wife, would participate boldly in this lovely courtship ritual, but he did not. Inordinately shy, he came each Sunday night to this lesser square, watching enviously as young men braver than himself made the rounds and identified the women with whom they might fall in love. Afraid to enter the paseo that he was eligible to join, he spent hours daydreaming about what kind of woman he might ultimately find, and ended by lamenting: I'm growing older and nothing's happening.

One Thursday evening in 1719 when Garza finished work he wandered back to his cramped room, and when he saw the bare walls he was overcome with loneliness: God! I must do something! Splashing water carelessly over his face to wash away the sawdust, he grabbed a crust of bread and some cheese and almost ran to the main plaza, where the young Spaniards and criollos of good breeding were already forming their circles. Trembling, as if he were about to undertake some dangerous adventure, he edged close to where the marchers would pass, maneuvering so that he could view the oncoming girls directly.

During the first three circuits of the parade Simón received only vague impressions of the graceful women as they went by him. They seemed like the sailing ships he had seen at Vera Cruz, proud, beautiful, moving forward, then passing slowly out of sight. But on the fourth round he found himself staring into the face of a mestiza walking sedately behind her mistress. She was somewhat older than the others, and her graceful deportment caused him to gasp. She seemed to be about twenty-two or -three, slightly taller than average and with a mature, gracious smile. When she walked, her long skirts appeared to move of themselves, poetically and barely touching the ground. Her shoulders were heavy-set, as if accustomed to hard work, but her most conspicuous characteristic was the manner in which she leaned forward when strolling, as if prepared to meet life head-on, regardless of its threats.

She was Juana Muñoz, daughter of a farmer whose fields lay to the north of town, and like other such girls, she had worked in various large houses in Zacatecas at whatever jobs were available: maid, cook, governess. Some years back she had been courted intermittently by a soldier, but he had moved on to another post, and now she realized that at twenty-two she was perilously close to an age when chances for marriage would diminish. Therefore, when she became aware that the carpenter from the Franciscan center had begun to notice her, she watched for the moment when she would pass where he stood and sent a carefully orchestrated series of signals, each time a little bolder than before, until he had good reason to think that his intentions were known and reciprocated.

When this subtle communication was repeated on Friday and Saturday at the Spanish paseo, Simón felt with some justification that the time had come for him to make some overt step, but what kind he did not know. A more enterprising man would simply have joined the mestizo paseo on Sunday night, smiled knowingly at the young woman, and when the marching ended, reached for her hand, introduced himself properly, and walked her sedately to where some member of her family waited to take her home. But Simón was not equal to this; he blushed furiously even at the thought, so on Sunday, even though he went to the paseo, he stood mutely at the edge, staring his heart out at the winsome girl but unable to read in her eyes the panic signal: 'Young man, if you wish to speak with me, for God's sake, speak!' When the paseo ended and it looked as if she might come and talk to him, he fled.

On Monday, in considerable confusion, he began seriously to evaluate the friars working at his building and he concluded that Fray Damián, a quiet fellow with a gentle manner, would best understand his plight. So that afternoon he tugged at the friar's sleeve and whispered: 'Could I please to speak with you?' and he was relieved when the cleric, only four years older than himself, smiled paternally.

It was a strained consultation, for Simón was ill-qualified to reveal his problem, and through bad luck he had chosen as his confidant the one cleric in Zacatecas least fitted to help. From an early age Fray Damián de Saldaña had known that he would become a servant of God, and his devotion was so concentrated that he passed through puberty hardly realizing that girls existed. He was fully aware that courtship, marriage and parenthood were not for him, and during his assignment at Zacatecas he had not once witnessed the paseo, for he had catalogued it as 'something the others did.' Therefore, he did not understand when Simón said hesitantly: 'At the paseo . . . there's a woman . . . I want you to speak to her for me. I need a wife, and she seems fine, quite fine.'

'Who is she?'

'You must find out for me.' As soon as Simón uttered these words he was overcome with confusion, and with his hands pressed close to his legs he bowed low and whispered: 'I have reason to think . . .'

'Of course I'll help.'

And it was in this way that Fray Damián de Saldaña, thirty-three years old and born in Spain, first went to the Spanish paseo in the great plaza fronting the cathedral of Zacatecas. It was a June evening, not yet summer-hot, with a quiet breeze coming in from the uplands. At sunset, when he took his place near the church with the carpenter at his side, a golden glow suffused the town and a pale quarter-moon hung in the starless sky. Flowers, shade trees, fruit trees along the irrigation canals, all prospered in these rich early days of summer, and the loveliest flowers of all were the young women of the town as they casually entered the plaza to begin their promenade.

'Which one is she?' Fray Damián asked, and with the greatest embarrassment Simón had to reply: 'She hasn't appeared yet. She might not come tonight.' But a short while later he tugged at the friar's arm. 'There she is!' he said with almost boyish delight, but Damián did not hear.

Four places ahead of Garza's mestizo housemaid came three Spanish girls, their insolent swaying and noisy chatter youthful and superior. The girl in the middle position was the housemaid's mistress, an especially attractive lass, with an impish face and long braids, wearing clothes which seemed more perfectly fitted to her fifteen-year-old body than did those of the other girls. She was more frank, too, in greeting the glances of the young men who passed, slowing down so that pleasantries could be exchanged. At such times she almost stopped, so that her friends had to drag her along, slapping her on the back as they might have chastised a wayward child. Then she would giggle, throw her hands over her face, and remove them so quickly that she could still toss a farewell smile at the men.

'Is she not handsome?' Simón asked, but again Damián did not hear, for he was watching with the most intense interest the girl's progress.

She was Benita Liñán, daughter of an official sent from Spain to supervise the agriculture in this part of Mexico. She had been born in Avila, one of the fine walled cities of Castile, and since her family intended returning there as soon as her father's work in New Spain was completed, she had been warned not to express any serious interest in the many young men who sought to woo her, for she was to be married in Spain, but this did not prevent her from flirting with them. Indeed, the older woman who served as her dueña, and who watched carefully from the Liñán balcony, sometimes doubted whether she would ever get their headstrong child back to Spain, for Benita showed a strong inclination toward becoming involved here in Mexico.

Fray Damián felt a tugging at his sleeve, and heard: 'That's the one. Walking alone. I think I ought to let her know I'm here.'

'What?' He had forgotten his carpenter's mission.

When Simón explained his plot, that he would arrange to be near the woman when the bell rang, Fray Damián said: 'That's sensible. That's very sensible.' He coughed. 'I'll join you when the bell rings.'

In fact, he moved much earlier in order to gaze more directly at the lively child who had so attracted him, and when he had eased himself unobtrusively into the crowd of watchers, working his way to the front row, he felt his heart thumping whenever she came swinging along, whispering words both to her friends and to the passing young men. He was startled by her beauty, and well he might be, for she was the epitome of all the dark-eyed, laughing women who graced the cathedral towns of Spain, and who gave his homeland so much of its remarkable character.

And then his heart missed a beat, for he realized that Simón's young woman was in the company of his girl, and that in attending to the courtship of his carpenter, he was abetting his own interest: How remarkable! It's almost as if someone had arranged this curious thing.

The bell rang, the paseo ended, and the crowds dispersed, but Fray Damián did not intercept the carpenter's woman and make the introduction, for he was preoccupied with the girl. 'I'm sorry, Simón. I think it'll be much better if we speak to her tomorrow.' And on the next night, after again hovering by the cathedral to watch Benita, he did intercept the woman in whom the carpenter had evidenced such interest: 'I am Fray Damián from the college, and I wish to present Simón Garza.' The carpenter bowed, Juana smiled modestly, and the formalities were honored.

'I am Juana Muñoz, of this parish.'

'And your parents?' Damián asked.

'Farmers, of the parish to the north.'

'I introduce a man of good repute,' Damián said, and then he excused himself and hurried off to see where the saucy girl's dueña had taken her, and he saw with uncharacteristic satisfaction that she was being led into the house of a family of some standing. He asked a passer-by whose house it was, and the man said: 'Anselmo Liñán, official from Avila in Spain.'

Even though he was aware that he was becoming enmeshed in a very dangerous game, Fray Damián sought a dozen excuses for being in the plaza during the Spanish paseo: It's as if the gears of a huge grinding machine were working to sort out the persons whom God intended to be married. That poor fellow over there will never find a wife. That lively girl by the cart had better find her husband soon, or she'll be in trouble. And somehow, by God's grace, it works.

He kept a close watch on Benita, whose name he now knew, and was pleased to see that she had formed no attachment of any kind, but he was worried about her flippancy and her predilection for flirting with almost any fellow who happened to catch her eye in the paseo.

He had not yet spoken to the girl, and she was unaware of his presence, but one night an unusually perceptive friend whispered to Benita as they passed under the church towers: 'I think that one is watching you,' and she snapped: 'A priest? Nonsense!' But upon careful inspection of the friar's behavior, she had to conclude that he was watching her, and no others. The idea intrigued her.

In late July, Fray Damián finally had a logical excuse for appearing at the paseo, for his carpenter had asked him to speak formally to the servant girl Juana Muñoz, and Damián added, with grave propriety: 'Your young man Simón would like me to conduct the wedding. Do you agree?'

'I would be honored. My parents will come in from the country.'

So a wedding was announced. It would take place after the turn of the year, and as a gesture of good will toward Garza, Fray Damián sought permission for it to be held in one of the church's chapels. He was directed to consult with Anselmo Liñán, who as a Spanish official helped direct the social affairs of the church, and when details were clarified, Liñán said: 'Fray Damián, the colonel tells me he would like to talk with you about reinforcing the Franciscan presence in the northern areas.'

'I'm ready to go, I assure you.'

'Could you dine with us? This week?'

'Oh, yes!'

Fray Damián was a tall man, very thin, with a sharp nose and beetling eyebrows, who had never paid much attention to his appearance. But on the day of the dinner he tried to make himself presentable. Using much water in an attempt to hold down his unruly hair, he also brushed his sandals and beat out his frock to remove the dust which had accumlated at the building site. Looking somewhat better than usual, he went to the Liñán home, and was delighted to find that Benita, now posing as a demure and well-behaved young lady, would attend the dinner with her mother. His seat was opposite hers, and although he tried his best to avoid her eyes, lest he betray his surging emotions, he could not prevent this from happening. When it did, he blushed so painfully that he was certain everyone at table must see it, but Benita seemed unconcerned, smiling at him as she might have smiled at some elderly uncle whom the family favored.

The talk this evening was mostly about the empty lands north of that river which the Spanish called variously El Río de las Palmas, El Río Bravo, or some other arbitrary name. Lately they had begun to call it El Río Grande del Norte, or simply El Río Grande. 'The problem lies not with the lands themselves,' an enthusiastic lieutenant was saying, 'but the fact that they join us to the French in Louisiana. Mark my words and mark them well, one of these days we'll be at war with the French over those border lands.'

His colonel, an imperious man, smiled condescendingly and said: 'You're a clever lad, Tovar. I received word yesterday that the French have already threatened our settlement at Los Adaes.'

'Why would the French want to invade us?' Liñán asked, but the colonel ignored the question, turning abruptly to Fray Damián: 'Tell me, what plans do you Franciscans have for strengthening the north?' But before Damián could respond, he banged on the table till the glasses rattled: 'Best thing Spain's ever done, the union of the friars at the mission and the army at the presidio.'

'Why do you say that?' Liñán asked.

'Most effective way ever devised for settling and holding a virgin territory. It was originally used as a way of resettling Spain after the defeat of the Moorish invaders, you know.'

'I would have thought bringing in farmers was the telling circumstance,' Liñán argued.

'Men like you will be welcomed in Tejas only when the friar here, and the soldier here'—and he slapped himself on his chest—'only when we've pacified the place.'

The colonel jabbed a finger at Damián and asked: 'What plans do you Franciscans have for helping your compatriots in the north of Tejas?' and the friar responded: 'We're eager to send men forth tomorrow.'

'I hear the missions you used to have up there accomplished little.'

'Our early missions did falter,' Damián conceded. 'Founded 1690, abandoned 1693. That's why I'd like to explore the north. To find a better site. To do a better job.'

'You'd better take me along,' the colonel joked, 'or those Indians'll eat you in a minute.'

'It is the salvation of those Indians which will take us north,' Damián said firmly, and as the discussion continued, with a good wine from Andalucía flowing, the three-pronged mission of Spain in the New World was made clear: Fray Damián to Christianize; the colonel to civilize; and Anselmo Liñán, the farmer-businessman, to utilize.

When the discussion reached this level the colonel proved a most sensible man, appreciative of the contributions his two colleagues could make, and willing to concede that he could not operate well without them: 'How do you gentlemen assess the relative contributions of our three arms? I mean, in the problem of settling an area like Tejas?'

To his own surprise Fray Damián was the first to respond, and he did so vigorously: 'The commission we are given by His Majesty the King is so clearly stated that none can confuse it. Spain's responsibility is to save souls, to bring new lands into the embrace of Jesus Christ.'

'That's always said first,' the colonel agreed, 'but let's remember that our fundamental purpose is to find ourselves a new Mexico, a new Peru, and to conquer it and hold it for the empire.'

'In the early stages, yes,' Liñán acquiesced, 'but after the first ten years the goal must be to use the pacified Indians in commerce, as we've done here—to make things, dig ore out of the ground, to farm, if you will, so that Spain can have the profits of trade.'

'You'll produce damned little without an army,' the colonel said, and it was Damián who voiced the sensible approach: 'We serve the king best when we serve Jesus Christ first. But my Franciscans would be powerless in Tejas without the support of you two.'

'You'll have it,' the colonel said. 'As soon as you're ready to move out.'

'I was ready at the age of ten,' Damián said, and this encouraged the other two to ask where his family had lived, and he said: 'In a lovely village named after our family—Saldaña—halfway between Burgos and León in the north of Spain.'

Anselmo Liñán, as the father of a marriageable daughter, was preoccupied with questions of heritage and could not help asking: 'Were you of the nobility?' and when Damián blushed furiously, those at the table concluded that he was not.

But his embarrassment stemmed from a much different cause, which he endeavored to explain as delicately as possible: 'My father had seven sons in a row. I was the fifth. And by country custom dating back a thousand years, he was entitled to the dignified name Hidalgo de Bragueta.' As soon as he uttered these words, the colonel and his lieutenant guffawed, but Don Anselmo blushed as deeply as the friar, and when Benita asked almost petulantly: 'What's he saying, Father?' he hushed her with a stern 'I'll tell you later.'

Hidalgo de Bragueta, a most honorable appellation, could best be translated as *Sir Knight of the Codpiece,* for it proclaimed to the countryside that this prepotent gentleman had sired seven sons in a row without the intrusion or, as Damián's father liked to put it, 'the contamination' of a single daughter.

'You were the fifth son?' Liñán asked, and Damián explained: 'From time long past our family honored the custom of Mayorazgo. First son inherited all the land. Second son married a rich daughter of our neighbors. Third and fourth into the army, fifth and sixth into the church. Seventh son? Who knows?'

'Then one could say that you are of the nobility?' Liñán probed. 'Sort of?'

'My grandfather thought he was king, at least of Asturias. My father had more sense.'

'Will you go back to Saldaña?'

'I'm a Franciscan. I roam the world. My home is in heaven.'

At this profession of faith the local Spaniards sighed, for it was understood that every man in Zacatecas who had been born in Spain yearned to return there at the earliest opportunity; they might work diligently in far outposts like this, or along the real frontier in Tejas, but they certainly planned to take their savings back to some Spanish town as soon as practical, even the clergy.

'I have a place at Málaga,' the colonel said. 'A vineyard . . . a few oranges. Nothing much, you understand.' Turning to Liñán, he asked: 'Where?'

'Avila.' He had to say no more, for his listeners could imagine that fair city perched upon its little hill, the heavy stone walls that enclosed it wandering up and down the slopes.

No one spoke, for everyone in the dining hall loved his or her corner of Spain, that fortunate land which God had created to prove that life on earth could be almost as favorable as life in heaven: Fray Damián could see his father's shepherds bringing in their flocks at night; the colonel could see his silvery city nestled beside the Mediterranean, its streets crowded with revelers at bullfight time; and Liñán could see not only sanctified Avila but also the rich fields that lay beyond her walls.

'To Spain!' the colonel proposed, and the wine was passed, with even young Benita lifting her glass, for she, too, remembered Avila.

'To Tejas!' Fray Damián suggested, and they drank to this also, because the subjugation and settlement of that farthest frontier was their immediate concern; not until it was pacified and producing wealth could they sail back to Spain.

In the nights that followed this dinner Fray Damián began to acknowledge the emotional danger into which he had fallen, but he was powerless to protect himself. He continued to contrive excuses for going to the plaza at sunset so that he might see Benita again, swinging along, joking with her girl friends, trying to escape the surveillance of her dueña. Each night she became more haunting, and when he lay on his crude straw-and-hay mattress, he could not sleep, for she appeared in his cell, smiling and biting her lip, as she did so enchantingly when she sensed that older people were watching. When he rolled over and punched his pillow he fell into the habit of whispering her name: 'Benita,' and then looking about in terror lest some wakeful friar had heard.

He realized the wrong he was committing, but he could not drive her from his mind, and when there were marriages to be conducted in the town—mahogany-skinned farmers taking brides with nut-brown complexions—he fell to wondering whether any of these men felt the same emotions as he, and for how long into the marriage. Tormenting visions assailed him as he tried to imagine what marriage was, and he recalled the easy, robust relationship that had existed between his no-nonsense father and his strongly opinionated mother. 'My dowry gave you the fields your peasants plow,' she would shout at her husband, 'and don't you ever forget it.'

Whenever she said this his father would explode in laughter: 'Have you ever seen those damned fields? A crop of rocks.'

'You Saldañas!' She never spelled out what she meant by this, but she did tell her seven sons: 'Remember, you're only half Saldaña. The good half comes from the Bermejos.' His name was really Damián Vicente Ignacio de Saldaña y Bermejo, and he was proud of both halves.

He would die rather than prove false to the vow of chastity he had voluntarily taken, and he could never bring dishonor upon his family name, so he withdrew from any direct contact with Benita Liñán. But neither of these honorable restraints could drive the vision of Benita from his mind, and one night when the anguish was heavy he confessed to himself in his quiet cell: I am a miserable human being. I am as low as a man can fall.

The temptations were exacerbated in 1720 when the time arrived for the carpenter Simón Garza to marry the maid Juana Muñoz, for when Damián saw the couple standing before him he grew faint. Behind the bride stood Benita, and as he began to recite the words of the marriage rite the two women became intermingled, and he believed he was officiating at two marriages: Garza and Juana, himself and Benita.

Clearing his head, he mustered courage and stumbled through the ceremony, and seeing at last only the two good peasants, he fervently wished them well in their great adventure: 'Simón and Juana, God Himself smiles on you this day. Know love with one another. Rear your children in the love and knowledge of Jesus Christ.' And he lowered both his voice and his head, for he acknowledged how unqualified he was to speak on behalf of the Deity.

Fray Damián's infatuation with Benita was solved, or rather alleviated, in a manner which he could never have foreseen. In the autumn of 1721 the young military officer Alvaro de Saldaña arrived at Vera Cruz, through which almost everything coming into Mexico must pass. Five years before, in the town of Saldaña, perched among hills in northern Spain, his practical-minded father had told Alvaro, his seventh son: 'There's no land left for you. Ildefonso will have it all. And I doubt if you would be a proper recruit for the church. What's left but the army?' Using his few remaining connections, Don Vicente had arranged for Alvaro to become an officer and had then pulled strings to have him sent to Mexico, where brother Damián could watch over him. Alvaro was twenty-six, unmarried, afire with ambition, and the bearer of a letter of commendation addressed to a former commander of his father: the estimable viceroy, the Marqués de Valero, considered by many to be the finest man in that office since the days of the great Mendoza, to whom he was distantly related.

The letter begged the viceroy to give consideration to a father's request that Alvaro be permitted to serve in somewhat the same region as Damián, 'it being a distinct honor for one family to provide two such manly sons to the service of our noble King and in a land so far from home.'

When the letter was placed before him, Viceroy Valero regarded it carefully; he had often hunted with the Saldañas; he knew the honorable history of that family; and he had been vaguely aware that one of its sons had been conducting himself favorably as a Franciscan in Zacatecas. But he had an entire country to look after, a job he had performed commendably for nearly six years, and now he rose from his ornate desk to study the large map which dominated so much of this thinking; it showed that impressive network of roads which fanned out across Mexico, binding the various scattered parts together. It was called in its entirety Los Caminos Reales (The Royal Road System), and now Valero inspected the critical segment running from Vera Cruz to Mexico City to San Luis Potosí to Saltillo to the miraculous ford across the Rio Grande at San Juan Bautista, then straight through Tejas to a tiny spot at the extreme northeast called Los Adaes. It was a route of conquest, a highway of poetic names, but once the traveler passed Saltillo, it was not a road at all, merely a poorly marked trail through empty land.

Not exactly empty, the viceroy thought. Apache Indians sometimes raid Saltillo, and everywhere in the north they lurk to slaughter my men.

Then he began to laugh, sardonic, bitter chuckles, when he thought of the final destination of El Camino Real: Los Adaes—soon to be the capital, and perched at the farthest edge of the region. Turning away in disgust, he growled: 'Damn the French!'

In three words he had summarized Spanish policy in Tejas: when peace reigned between France and Spain, Tejas could go to hell, not one gold piece would be spent; but when trouble threatened, Tejas became 'our noble bastion in the north, where heroic Spaniards defend our outpost of empire against the evil plans of the French.' Tejas policy was determined not by the viceroy in Mexico City but by the acts of Frenchmen in Louisiana, and since 1719 their behavior had been ominous.

I'll send young Saldaña to our northern frontier, Valero decided, and when the eager young officer was brought into his presence, he said affably: 'Your father, who fought well for me, asks if you might serve near your brother. I grant his wish. You shall join him in Zacatecas.'

'My father will bless you, sir, as I do now.'

When Alvaro reached the mining town he was disturbed to see how much older-looking and leaner his brother had become, but as they talked he found Damián as compelling as ever, for the friar's religious dedication had obviously deepened, causing him to speak with a gravity he had not shown before. The brothers spent two days exchanging information, and they did so enthusiastically, for they had always been friends, sharing secrets they did not share even with their other brothers.

Next morning the colonel told Alvaro: 'The pouch you brought from the viceroy brings a message that you and your brother are to accompany me on a tour of inspection. All of Tejas up to Los Adaes.'

'Excellent!' The young man's enthusiasm was so genuine that the colonel invited him to dinner that night, where he sat facing the provocative daughter of Anselmo Liñán.

The Saldaña brothers formed an interesting pair in the candlelight, Damián in his somber gray habit, Alvaro in his bright uniform, the former thin and moody, the latter robust and smiling. Damián spoke little, nervously; Alvaro, with fluency and confidence: 'The ship that brought us to Vera Cruz was a disgrace, but we had as a fellow passenger a man who could sing like a lark, and he kept us forgetful.' He said also that in the capital the viceroy had explained how important Tejas was and that he, Alvaro, was most eager to see it, to which the colonel replied: 'You'll see enough before we're through.'

As Alvaro continued, Damián became aware, with a mixture of pain and interest, that Benita, seated directly across from his brother, was listening to him with undisguised attention and that whenever he seemed about to stop, she encouraged him with further questions. During the course of the dinner he fairly well presented the outline of his life and his ambitions, with Benita nodding approval.

After dinner she came boldly to Fray Damián and said, in his brother's hearing: 'You must be proud to have Alvaro in your family. We're certainly proud to have him as a visitor.' Given this incentive, Alvaro interrupted: 'Could I take you riding tomorrow?' to which she replied modestly: 'My dueña does not ride, but perhaps my father . . .'

The colonel, overhearing the exchange, asked: 'Liñán, is it permissible for me to take these young people for a canter tomorrow?' This posed a difficult problem for Benita's parents, for they still dreamed of seeing their daughter married in Spain, but slowly they were awakening to the fact that families in their modest position usually spent their lives in Mexico, with never enough money saved to enable them to return to the homeland. Therefore, incoming officers of undoubted Spanish blood like this Saldaña were becoming more attractive.

'She can join you,' Liñán said.

No one thought to invite Fray Damián, who spent the hours of their excursion in the grip of a confusion which would engulf him increasingly. He was pleased that his brother had made such a favorable impression on Zacatecas, but he was disturbed that it had to be Benita who translated that favor into action. On the other hand, he realized that she was each day growing closer to that age when she must marry, and since she could never marry him, he was gratified to think that she might choose his brother, for then she would remain within his circle, a part of him, however complex and ill-defined. Now, as he abstractedly placed bricks in a line for the Indian workmen to handle, he awakened to the fact that a tremendous change had overtaken him, as if the normal experiences of a youth which he had avoided were now roaring back in all their tumultuous confusions: 'Dear God! Am I jealous of my brother? Do I wish it was I riding with Benita?' And as he spoke thus to the bricks he was lifting, he visualized the two young people riding ahead of the colonel or falling cleverly behind, and leaning across their horses' necks and kissing.

In the days before the expedition to the north departed, Alvaro and Benita saw a great deal of each other, and often the austere friar was present, watching them as if he were an uncle. And although Alvaro remained unconscious of the meaning of his presence, Benita understood.

On the morning of departure, 11 December 1721, the colonel produced three fine horses for himself and the Saldaña brothers, but what happened when Fray Damián saw his caused a great commotion, because he said: 'As a Franciscan, I'm forbidden ever to ride a horse.'

The colonel looked at him askance: 'What foolishness have we here?'

'Our vow of poverty. Caballos are for caballeros. Mules and donkeys are for the poor.'

The colonel scoffed at such an idea, but when Damián absolutely refused to accept his horse, the animal was led away and a mule brought forward. It was a criminally inclined beast, one eye lower than the other, one ear cocked, the other flat, and it did not propose to have on its back a friar with a floppy habit, for as soon as Damián tried to mount, it shied away and landed two solid kicks on his right leg.

In no way did this daunt Damián, for looking about, he found a small stick with which he began to hit the mule lightly about the head. The blows did not hurt, but the animal did not like them and drew back in small mincing steps, whereupon Damián danced after him. In time he tamed the animal enough so that he could mount, but the caravan had not even started when the mule leaned forward, planted its two front feet like stone pillars, and tossed Damián over its head.

Again Damián showed no anger; instead, he stood facing the mule, saying: 'I shall have to ride you and you shall have to behave.' At this the mule backed off, and the dancing continued, causing a country poet to begin composing in his head a rather naughty ballad, which would soon be widely recited: 'El Fraile y el Baile' (The Friar and the Dance, or, more colloquially, The Dancing Friar).

At last the mule surrendered, Damián mounted, and the forward scouts started north. As the main body prepared to follow, with seventeen soldiers and handlers, Benita ran to Alvaro and kissed him. There were gasps from some of the older people, but the colonel approved: 'That's the proper way to send soldiers on a journey.'

'Colonel, bring him back safely! Please bring him back.'

Early December was one of the best times of year in the arid area between Zacatecas and Saltillo, for the intense heat of summer had dissipated. And since this year the fall rains had come late, there was still such a profusion of wildflowers that what would otherwise have been a desert looked like a veritable spring garden. In the invigorating coolness they rode easily, noting the deer on the horizon and the tardy rattlesnake preparing for this winter's hibernation, and often they could see in the distance bands of Indians, who vanished among the gentle hills as the expedition drew near.

Saltillo was a beautiful settlement of stone houses intermixed with low buildings of adobe and a central plaza as charming as any in Mexico. It was so protected on all sides by hills that the colonel said: 'Even a big enemy army would have a difficult time capturing this town if it was properly defended. I'd preempt the high ground and cut the foe to pieces if they tried to come up that valley.'

In Saltillo they witnessed Spain's fundamental attitude toward colonization. This remarkably attractive town contained only two men from the homeland, the commander and the priest, while much rougher Zacatecas had eleven. 'What accounts for this?' Damián asked his brother, and Alvaro offered a shrewd explanation: 'As you say, Saltillo is beautiful, but what is its function? To guard the border in case the French attack. But Zacatecas! Ah! It has those silver mines, and they've got to be protected.'

'Is money everything?' Damián asked, and his brother replied: 'In Madrid, yes.'

One night the Saltillo commander complained: 'We really must have more honest-to-goodness Spaniards. Those born in Mexico can be fine people—my sister's married to one—but they can't be relied upon to preserve the true Spanish culture. And the mestizos they send us?' He spat.

'It's the same in Zacatecas,' the colonel said consolingly. 'Young Saldaña here—the lieutenant, that is—he's the first honest Spaniard we've had assigned there in two years.' He looked approvingly at Alvaro, and then tapped Damián on the shoulder: 'We don't get friars like this one, either, not from the locals they send us.'

'Will the day come,' the Saltillo commander asked, 'when all of Mexico will be governed by mestizos? They'd get their orders from Madrid, of course. They can be very clever, you know. I've had some mestizos on this frontier I'd put up against any of your men from Spain.' He reflected on this, then added: 'But they could never claim to be gentlemen. There's always something missing.'

'I would deplore the day,' the colonel said, tapping a finger as he spoke each word, 'when any part of our empire is governed by locals. We must never allow that to happen.'

'To the north it's already happening,' the commander said. Waving his arm brusquely to indicate all of Tejas, he said: 'You'll find few Spaniards up there, you may be sure.' He summoned an aide: 'Pánfilo, can you think of anyone north of the river who was born in Spain?'

Pánfilo laughed and said: 'There are very few of anything north of the river, regardless of classification. Almost none born in Spain.'

'The missions? Surely, some of our missionaries . . .'

'I don't count them,' the aide said.

They dined that night on roast lamb, sweet potatoes, tortillas made fresh from the best corn and a marvelously cool beverage from crushed pomegranate fruit.

They toasted the king in Madrid and the viceroy in Mexico City, and when the commander asked if the Saldañas knew any songs from their area in Spain, the brothers offered several with graceful harmony. In response, the two old campaigners offered songs of their own. The formal part of the evening concluded with the opening of a bottle of wine that the commander had been saving for such an occasion.

As the Saldañas walked back under the stars, Alvaro, emboldened by the wine, confided: 'When we return to Zacatecas, I think Benita and I . . .' He hesitated. 'I think we shall be married.'

He looked toward Damián, expecting congratulations, but his brother had turned his head upward toward the sky to contemplate the heavens. As the friar studied the intricate patterns made by the stars, he imagined the three of them, himself, Benita, Alvaro, existing together in some kind of agreed-upon arrangement. He could not yet envisage what its design might be, but only that it must ensure that he not be deprived of their friendship. 'Father would approve, I know,' he said quietly.

Even the colonel, not a sentimental man, was astounded by the rugged beauty of the trail north from Saltillo, for it penetrated interlocking ranges of mountains that twisted through quiet valleys; these contained no houses or farms, for the Indians in this region could be ferocious. 'This must be the most beautiful empty land in the world,' Alvaro cried, and the colonel replied: 'It's our job to see that it doesn't stay empty.'

The Saldañas received important indoctrination regarding their assignment when they reached the Rio Grande, which had on its south bank a remarkable collection of buildings forming the Franciscan center of San Juan Bautista. It contained three different missions staffed by two friars each; nearby stood a solidly built presidio where the soldiers protecting the area lived. Travelers who stayed at the missions heard from the friars how difficult it was to share a settlement with soldiers who had no love of God or respect for Jesus and who made the work of salvation almost impossible. But those who lodged at the presidio heard whining complaints against the feckless friars who did not work, obeyed no civil law, and converted one dying Indian every two or three years . . . at best.

At the dinner in Zacatecas they had agreed that the Spanish system of settlement was ideal, but when they saw it in actual practice on the frontier, they had to admit that it was painfully disorganized. When soldiers mingled with friars, all kinds of animosities erupted. Soldiers seduced Indian girls in the missions, while the friars carelessly allowed Indians access to restricted areas, where they stole precious supplies needed by the soldiers.

If a friar of outstanding Christian humility governed the mission while a soldier of exemplary character headed the presidio, the system had a chance of functioning, and sometimes it did, but more often a situation developed, like the one in San Juan Bautista, in which overt hostility was avoided but petty antagonisms were inescapable. The colonel, suspecting this, assigned Fray Damián to one of the missions, while he and Alvaro lodged at the presidio, so that the young soldier could experience frontier life at its most typical.

'You'll excuse me, Lieutenant Saldaña, because I know your brother is a friar, and I suppose one of the best,' said the captain in charge of the presidio, 'but these damned friars . . .' He shrugged his shoulders as if to say that mere words could not describe their duplicity.

'Anything I should report to Zacatecas?' the colonel asked.

'Nothing, and everything,' the captain said, and with that summation he began listing the malfeasances of the clergy, and a sorry portrait he painted of frontier clericalism, for he charged the friars with theft, willful contravention of the king's ordinances and general insubordination: 'And one particular charge which I do hope you'll mention in your report. By agreement they are obligated to share with us the fruits of their labor—corn, a good goat now and then, a portion of any steer that is slaughtered. And they have green vegetables in their gardens, I know it, I've seen them. But we get none. They use their food to feed their Indians.' The only charge he did not bring against the friars was one which did surface at other posts: 'I must admit, Colonel, that unsavory as they are, they do not meddle with the Indian women. In their religious duties they're true Christians, anyone would admit that, but in the management of the mission as a part of our system, they're no better than a bunch of lying, lazy thieves.'

At the mission that night charges which did involve Indian women were laid before Fray Damián, with urgent requests that he convey them to the authorities in Zacatecas. 'We cannot prevent those devilish soldiers, whom God has never known, from consorting with our Indian converts. Well, to speak truthfully, they're not really converts, not yet, but we have high hopes. As soon as a girl of that certain age comes to our compound, the soldiers get after her, and before long she's pregnant. At times it seems that our major function on the frontier is the production of mestizo bastards.'

There was one serious complaint which both the friar and the colonel felt must be presented to the authorities, and it was voiced in noninflammatory tones by the friars: 'The order clearly states that we shall have in each mission two friars, which we have provided, and three armed soldiers, which the presidio is to provide. But we never get the soldiers.'

To this justifiable complaint the military officials had solid response: 'We originally placed three soldiers in each mission, as required by the king, but when we did we heard much fault-finding from the friars—"The soldiers did this." "Your soldiers did that." "The soldiers molest the girls." Well, I told them frankly: "If you don't want our soldiers for your work, we can sure as hell use them in ours," so we took them back.'

The colonel suggested that perhaps the presidio could screen its men carefully and find one each for the three missions, but the friars protested: 'That is not what the order provides.' On the night before the expedition departed, the colonel finally put his finger on the sore spot: 'I take my military orders from Mexico City, you know,' and the friars replied: 'And we take our orders from Guadalajara.' It was obvious that the rupture would remain unhealed.

Crossing the Rio Grande was physically trivial—water up to the ankle on a stone riverbed as smooth as a table—but emotionally exciting, for now the Spaniards entered a potential battleground: real Apache ready to attack from the west, shadowy Frenchmen lurking in the north. The terrain was inviting to horsemen, great stretches of waving grassland punctuated occasionally by clumps of mesquite bushes, those low, thorny, jagged miniature trees which had always populated the river courses of Tejas but which, in recent years, had begun to invade the grassland wherever the grand balance of nature had been disturbed by the grazing of cattle or the scraping of a hoe. For a friar who hoped to establish here his mission and a presidio, with a town following in due course, this was forbidding land, for it contained little visible water.

But after eight days of such travel, with crossing of two rivers, the Nueces and the Medina, the Spaniards entered Tejas, where they found sights which gladdened their hearts. A small stream, the San Antonio de Padua, ran with spring-fed water, and on its far bank earlier Franciscans had erected two missions of obvious stability, while on the near bank, a short distance away, a sturdy presidio housed the soldiers guarding the area. Close to the barracks an informal little village consisting of two adobe houses had begun to germinate, and here lived the four mestizo families who endeavored to farm the good fields along the river.

In all ways the settlement was minimal: at the missions, two friars, three soldiers in each and fifty-one Indians, two of whom had converted; in the presidio, a captain, a sergeant and fifty-two soldiers; in the two-hut village, seven adults and three children.

These Franciscan efforts had been named Misíon San José and Misión San Antonio de Valero, after the popular saint of Padua and the equally popular viceroy who had authorized its founding. The viceroy carried a formidable appellation: Baltazar Manuel de Zúñiga (this could be considered his name) y Guzmán-Sotomayor (his mother's name) y Mendoza y Sarmiento (historic names adhering to his family). And as if this were not sufficient, he was also Marqués de Valero y Duque de Arión (his hereditary titles).

San Antonio de Valero would have been a proper name for this settlement, short and musical, but some busybody remembered that the Marqués de Valero had a renowned half brother, the Duque de Béjar, who had given his life in defense of Christian Budapest during battle with the infidel Turks, and this intruder thought it might please the viceroy if the new settlement was named after the hero, so it became San Antonio de Béjar. But as in the case of Mejico and

Mexico, local Spanish was cavalier in its interchange of *j* and *x*, so it quickly became San Antonio de Béxar, which the locals promptly abbreviated to Béxar.

Here the internecine struggles which had been so prevalent at the Rio Grande missions were avoided, allowing Spanish colonial rule to flourish at its best. Sensible friars at the mission and strong-minded military men in the presidio forced the intricate system to work, riding down any incipient troubles. Into a strange and alien land populated by passive Indians who feared the fierce, untamed Apache to the west, had come a handful of devout Spaniards to build their low-roofed buildings and dig their irrigation ditches.

As soon as Fray Damián saw Béxar he loved it: 'Oh, I would like to work here!' and he asked the colonel: 'Could I not start my mission . . . off to the north, where I wouldn't interfere with San Antonio de Valero? There is so much work to be done.' But the soldier had specific orders: 'Our job is to inspect and protect the real frontier, the area of the Nacogdoches mission,' and so with profound regrets Fray Damián left a place which had excited his imagination and started the long march to the bleak northern extremity of Tejas.

'The journey from Béxar to Los Adaes,' explained a soldier who had fought in Europe's mercenary armies, 'is as long as marching up from Paris, across Flanders, across the Netherlands, and into the Germany. Tejas is big.'

As they kept bearing to the northeast, the brothers noticed radical changes in the scenery. They started across flat grassland and mesquite, then encountered rolling country with many trees, and next were in a completely different terrain, with trees but also with real prairies suitable for farming. Finally they came to what they thought was best of all, fine woodlands with promising soil: 'Here a man could cut down the trees and make himself a farm that would feed a village.'

As they traveled through this magnificent and almost pristine region, so totally different from the land around Béxar, Damián reflected on an oddity which perplexed him: 'Why is the capital of Tejas so far north? On the borders of Louisiana?' He pondered this, but could find no rational justification: 'By all reason the capital should be at Béxar, for it is central and the source of leadership in Tejas, but since no one at the Council of the Indies in Madrid has ever been to Tejas or seen an accurate map, the capital is kept far to the north, from where it will be almost impossible to provide good government.'

Alvaro offered a clear explanation: 'France. They control Louisiana a few leagues to the east. Our father fought against them three times, and even though we have a kind of peace now, would you like to gamble on what the situation will be next year? Madrid's clever: "Keep the capital on the frontier. Keep your eye on those damned Frenchmen." '

In late January they reached the west bank of the Neches, a stream one could jump, and although military practice required that a military force cross over at dusk so that it would be prepared to march on in the morning, regardless of any change that might have occurred to the river, the western bank was so hospitable that the men had unpacked the mules and pitched camp before the colonel could stop them. That night a winter storm of huge dimension struck, and by morning the Neches was a torrent which raged for seven days, to the colonel's disgust with himself for having ignored a basic rule.

However, since the Saldaña brothers were an enterprising pair, they utilized the forced delay to inspect one of the saddest sights in Tejas, the abandoned ruins of a cluster of missions that had once served the region. They had flourished briefly in the 1690s, giving promise of becoming a focus of some importance, but the hostility of the Indians and the fluctuating attitudes of the nearby French had doomed the effort. Worthy Franciscans had lost their enthusiasm and sometimes their lives in these ruins. Their efforts had marked the high tide of Spain's colonizing effort, and they had not succeeded.

Soldier and friar looked upon the ruins from vastly different perspectives, and it was Alvaro who voiced the no-nonsense interpretation sponsored by the Spanish government in Madrid: 'No cause for grief, Damián. Missions are thrust into locations to establish a foothold, no more. Pacify the Indians, start a community, and when things are stable, invite the civil government to take over. The mission closes, job done. The buildings gradually fall apart. And you friars move along to your next obligation.' He saw the deserted ruins simply as proof that in this instance the procedure had failed.

But Damián saw in the rotting timbers the tragedy of crushed aspirations, the death of plans which once must have seemed so promising, and he could hear the early friars assuring one another: 'We'll establish our mission here, and bring the word of God to the Indians, and watch as families from Spain move in to build a city.' Now only the pines whispered over the graves.

'This could have been a major settlement,' Damián said. 'Families should be living here. Children in the shadow of the church. This is heartbreaking.' He asked his brother to kneel as he said prayers for the departed souls who had struggled so diligently to accomplish so little. For Damián, a mission was not some temporary agency that appeared casually and slipped away when its work was done; it was intended to serve as the everlasting soul of a community, and any abrupt demise was tragic.

When they finally negotiated the swollen Neches, they came upon rude buildings in which new missions were being attempted, but their success seemed doubtful, and as Damián bade these Franciscans goodbye, it was with a sense of futility. Spain was not impressive in these remote corners of its empire.

The ninety-odd miles to Los Adaes were some of the most mournful Alvaro would ever travel, for they proved that the expedition was leaving the Tejas sphere of influence and entering a world in which Spaniards played no significant role: 'It's all wrong, Damián. We should be back in Béxar, building a city.'

The new capital was a pitiful sham, a few wooden buildings at the farthest end of a supply line along which Madrid rarely sent anything usable. Spanish officials confided: 'The French over at Natchitoches arrange things so that we can buy goods smuggled in from the former French capital at Mobile, and for every honest man in the area, there must be a dozen cutthroats who have escaped down the Mississippi River.' The chapel had barely the equipment for a proper Mass, and Damián thought that if this was the best Spain could do with its empire, that empire was doomed.

The captain acting as governor was always sickly, the foul air from the marshes having affected his lungs so that he coughed continuously. After he read the instructions sent him from Mexico City, he informed Damián: 'You are to come back with settlers and attempt a new mission in these parts,' an assignment which the friar accepted without comment.

'Am I to man the presidio?' Alvaro asked, and the governor tapped the letter: 'No mention of it.' But the colonel interrupted: 'These are good men, Captain. I shall recommend that they work as a team, and I pray that you will second it.' Without giving the suggestion even a moment's study, the weary governor coughed several times, then said: 'Very well. It can do no harm, I should think.'

When the garrison troops were lined up to see the visitors off, Alvaro saw to his disgust that no two men had the same uniform and that most had none. They were a ragtag disgrace to the army, and the governor confided: 'These are my best. The worst run off to New Orleans once they see this place.' And this ineffectual man, governor of all Tejas, wiped his nose on his sleeve.

Joyous news awaited the brothers when they returned to Béxar, for a letter from Benita Liñán informed Alvaro that she was eager to marry him as soon as he returned home. It sounded as if she had wedding plans under way, even though the young officer had not yet spoken to her father, as custom required.

When they reached Zacatecas, Benita told Damián that they wanted him to officiate, and as he was preparing for a day which he knew would bring him confusion, he received good news of his own. The administrator of the district summoned him and his Franciscan superior to headquarters, and told them: 'The new viceroy arrived in Mexico while you were in the north, Fray Damián, and he believes that the French menace has subsided. He doesn't want to build a mission near Los Adaes. But he does command the Franciscans to establish one more strengthening mission at Béxar. And the father-principal and I have decided that you're the one to go. We'll provide you with an escort directly after the wedding.'

Damián, contrasting the fraternity he had experienced at Béxar with the mournful emptiness of the Louisiana border, was delighted with what he held to be a promotion. But when it occurred to him that he might be rejoicing over something which represented a reversal of God's plans for him—perhaps He meant for me to do His work in Los Adaes; perhaps those ruined missions were left along the Neches to inspire me—he was ashamed of himself for having found joy in a lesser task while escaping the greater to which heaven might have assigned him. This was a real concern, and one which agitated him for some weeks, so that as the wedding approached he found himself beset by doubled turmoil: he was in love with his brother's bride, there could be no other word for it, and he was ashamed of himself for exulting over his escape from unpleasant or even dangerous duty. He fell into that anguish of self-doubt which would characterize his early years as a missionary: I'm a poor example. I have sin upon me and I cannot cleanse myself. I'm unworthy to be a shepherd and am amazed that God does not strike me.

He was diverted from such self-chastisement when he met the young friar who was to share the duties at the new mission, for Fray Domingo Pacheco, fourteen years younger, was a round-faced, happy brown-skinned mestizo. His father, a Spanish soldier in charge of a ranch belonging to the viceroy, had been so beset by loneliness that he had taken to wife a comely Indian woman, who had been given the name María and who had raised their son Domingo with songs and slaps, kisses and chastisements.

Fray Domingo looked upon the world as a place of contradiction and insanity which could be managed only with a grin, a shrug of the shoulders and the avoidance of as much unpleasantness as possible, and by unpleasantness he meant work. When assigned a job, he nodded, said it was easy to perform, assured the man in command that it would be done promptly, then worked as little and as slowly as possible, smiling warmly whenever a supervisor stopped by to inspect his progress. With Domingo things were always going well, tomorrow was sure to see the task finished, and for each time an observer saw him frown, he saw him smile a score of times.

He was not a stupid fellow, for in his twenty-two years he had accumulated a world of practical knowledge, so that his instructors at the college were often surprised by the astuteness of his answers and reassured by his obvious devotion to his calling. Though he had been characteristically satisfied with taking only minor orders, he was a still a full-fledged friar, and he could perform marriages and baptisms but he could not sing the Mass or engage in certain other restricted rituals. Fray Domingo was a servant of God who believed that with all the sour-faced monks and friars and priests in the world, there must be a place for someone who smiled.

He had what Fray Damián would never attain: an absolute faith in the benevolence of God and a comforting assurance that whatever he, Domingo, did was in accordance with God's will. This supreme confidence came from his mother, who had belonged to a primitive tribe of Indians far south of Oaxaca; this group held women in low regard, and when she first learned of Christianity and the exalted role played by the Virgin Mary, she placed her entire confidence in the new religion. It was a beautiful religion, consoling, rich in its promises and realistic in its earthly performance. If the Spanish conversion of Mexico had accomplished nothing but the reorganization of women's lives, as in the case of María Pacheco, it would have achieved great triumphs, for she accepted the new faith joyously and taught her son to do the same.

Although he shunned work, Domingo was in no way a coward. He knew that the frontier was a dangerous place, for he had seen those plaques shaped like hearts that adorned the walls of the refectory at the college: SACRED TO THE MEMORY OF FRIAR LUÍS GALINDO, MARTYRED AT SANTA FE, 1680. There were memorials to the Franciscans who had accompanied Coronado on his expedition and who had remained behind in the wilderness to find their martyrdom, and he had heard of how the missionaries in Tejas, north and south, had had to defend themselves against the very Indians they had been sent to save. But none of this information daunted his resolve to be the finest servant of God ever sent north; he was willing to die, even if he was not willing to work unnecessarily in the years prior to his martyrdom.

'I will be your faithful companion,' he assured Fray Damián, who, in a gesture of gratitude, invited him to participate in the forthcoming nuptials.

The wedding was held in the cathedral, and it seemed that everybody of prominence in Zacatecas and surrounding villages participated in the happy occasion. Women of various hues wept when sprightly Benita Liñán half walked, half danced down the narrow nave to where her future brother-in-law waited to perform the ceremony. Dressed in a fine black habit, he stood very tall as he received the bride, but he did not create an imposing impression, for he trembled and his face grew quite red, as if he had forgotten his lines. When the time came for him to take the hand of the bride and place it in the hand of the groom, he shook so noticeably that those in front feared he might be ill, but he regained control and finished the ceremony in clear voice, giving a benediction which all who heard it would remember:

> 'My brother, my sister, may you live within the arms of Jesus Christ, may you create a home which radiates love, may your children prosper in their dedication to God, and may all who see you proclaim: "This is a Christian marriage." Brother Alvaro, sister Benita, this is a day of great joy for me as it is for you, and may the Grace of God descend upon us all who have solemnized this act of Holy Matrimony.'

Damián spent a restless night, rising three times to kneel and pray that his mission in Tejas might reflect in all its operations the will of God. He asked for a blessing upon his companion, that good man Fray Domingo, and he asked special blessings for the couple who were starting their marriage that night, Alvaro and Benita de Saldaña. At the third prayer, when he came to this last name, he dropped his hands from the praying position, allowed his head to fall upon the bed, and wept.

In a thoughtful gesture that gave great pleasure in Mexico City and at the same time ensured financial support in Béxar, the Franciscans decided to name their new mission after the favorite saint of the incoming viceroy, and then add his title so there could be no misunderstanding as to who in heaven and on earth was being honored: Santísima Misión Santa Teresa de Casafuerte. And then, to make clear who in Mexico was running the place, they added: del Colegio de Propaganda Fide de Nuestra Señora de Guadalupe de Zacatecas.

When this grandiose name was first pronounced the mission consisted of some sixty acres of virgin soil containing not even a shed, but it was favorably located on the west bank of the Río San Antonio, about two miles north of Misión San Antonio de Valero, where the Saldaña brothers had once stayed. The new mission had a promising site and nothing more, except grazing rights to some five leagues of range land, twenty-two thousand acres, fifteen miles to the southwest.

To make the place function, the two friars would have to build, with whatever help they could persuade the nearby Indians to lend, all the structures of a substantial establishment. A church would be needed, domiciles for the two friars, quarters for the three soldiers assigned to protect the place, housing for the converted Indians who would live there, and either barns or sheds for the cattle, with several small buildings for the care of such tools as the mission might accumulate. It would require boundless energy to accomplish all this and yet win the watching Indians to Christianity.

In the days when the two friars were getting started they were grudgingly accommodated at Misión San Antonio, which did not welcome their competition and made it clear that this accommodation could not continue indefinitely, so the opening argument at Santa Teresa concerned which building should be erected first. Fray Domingo was all for concentrating on a house for himself and his superior, but Fray Damián believed that their first obligation was to build a church: 'How else can we win the Indians to Christianity?'

'Brother,' Domingo argued persuasively, 'how can we preach to anyone if we ourselves lack a place to sleep?' He punched himself in the belly: 'Feed yourself, sleep well, then worry about the souls of others.'

This advice Fray Damián had to accept, for Fray Domingo refused to work on the church until he had a place in which to live. So with the aid of two Indians he constructed an amazing hut: in front it was composed of rough adobe bricks, unevenly made and haphazardly piled around a big open door. The three other sides were poles stuck upright in the ground, interlaced with grapevines and plastered with mud. The roof was an untidy mixture of logs, thatch, saplings, mud and grass. The whole looked like the lodge of a careless beaver, dragged onto dry land, with projections everywhere and dirt universal. This was the jacal common throughout northern Mexico, and when Fray Damián's mission was finished, it would contain two score of them.

But even after this ramshackle cell-like structure was built, Fray Domingo showed little inclination to do construction work at the church; his strength lay in his ability to talk Indians into becoming members of the mission so that they would do the work. At the end of the first two months, whereas Damián had performed wonders in getting the foundation footings dug and filled with rock, he had not brought in a single Indian, while Fray Domingo, whistling and singing in the fields, had lured more than a dozen into the system. Demanding of them only three or four hours' work a day, 'in the service of the Lord,' he had his Indians cut the timbers for the roof of the adobe church in one-tenth the time Fray Damián had been taking.

The first confrontation between the two friars concerned this matter of adobes, for the making of these sun-dried clay bricks was a messy affair, and Fray Domingo flatly refused to step into the mixing trough himself and tread into the muddy clay the straw that bond the bricks together. 'I won't do it, and I can't trust my Indians to do it,' he wailed, so Damián, desperately needing a steady supply of the adobes for his walls, tucked his robes about his middle, kicked off his sandals, and entered the mixing trough, treading the clay and straw until it was ready for pouring into the wooden molds, where it would drain until firm enough to stack in the sun. All this he did himself.

Sometimes at night, when he lay exhausted from his arduous labors, he would listen as Fray Domingo explained about the Indians, whose languages he was learning: 'The governor at Chihuahua had one of his scribes make a list of all the Indian tribes in the northern Spanish lands. And how many completely different tribes do you suppose there were? Hundreds of them. And they speak more languages than I could ever learn. Tell me, Damián, how many tribes in the two missions here at Béxar?'

Damián listened drowsily to the recitation: 'Pampopa, Postito, Tacame, a few Borrado, Payaya, Orejone. And remember, Brother, each group has its own interests, its own animosities toward all the others.' Damián did not hear this warning, for he had fallen asleep.

The first significant problem at Santa Teresa arose one day when Domingo rushed over to where Damián was laboring with roof beams: 'Brother! Joyous news! My converts Lucas and Mariá wish to be married in the church, roof or no roof.'

This was a portentous development and the friars knew it, the first visible proof that they were making some headway with the Indians: 'I'm so delighted, Brother Domingo, that you have accomplished this.'

'And he's one of our best workers! He helps make our adobes.'

'I shall prepare for the wedding immediately,' Damián said. 'I'll put that big beam in place so that we can have at least part of a roof to stand under,' but as he talked he realized that Domingo had drawn away, almost imperceptibly but definitely away, and when he met with the couple to be married he understood why, for in such Spanish as Domingo had taught them, they said: 'We like this one . . . laughing . . . to say the prayers.'

Damián's face betrayed no emotion, for he recognized the validity of this request; Domingo had converted them, had shown them the radiance of God's love, had demonstrated the brotherhood of all who live in Christ. To them he was the shepherd; Damián, the taskmaster. Gravely the disappointed friar bowed to the request of these first converts; as founder of Misión Santa Teresa de Casafuerte, he had aspired to conduct the first marriage, the first baptism, the first prayers for a soul going to heaven, but it was not to be. At the Indian wedding held beneath the protection of the partial roof he had spurred into being, it was laughing, joking, singing Fray Domingo who performed the ceremony and blessed the couple.

The two friars did not allow this first contretemps to disrupt their relationship, for Domingo did not use his personal triumph at the wedding to color in any way his basic subordination to Damián, whom he acknowledged in all things as his superior; and Damián, although hurt, did not seek any petty revenge upon his assistant. The two men remained amiable and friendly, with Damián laboring each day more sturdily at the building of the church, and Domingo at building good relations with the Indians, who saw his darker skin as proof that he was one of them, partly at least.

But when the tasks of building became more arduous and difficult than even Damián's exceptional energy could manage, he did feel it necessary to draft a careful letter to his superior back in Zacatecas:

> Esteemed Father-Guardian. It is my pleasure to inform you that so far affairs at the Misión Santa Teresa de Casafuerte are progressing according to the schedule you proposed and in obedience to God's will. We have baptized several Indians of the Orejone and Yuta tribes and arranged Christian marriages for two couples who are now living within God's grace.

> Fray Domingo Pacheco accomplishes wonders with his charges and is already talking about establishing a large ranch some leagues to the west. I encourage him in this because he has exceptional skill in working with Indians, who seem to love his friendly ways.

> The building of the mission is left largely to me, since Fray Domingo must attend to other matters, and I am afraid that I shall soon fall behind schedule. But you have with you in Zacatecas an excellent carpenter, name of Simón Garza, who is married to the woman Juana

Muñoz, and I wonder if you would send him to help me in the building of this mission? I sorely need a carpenter, and Garza is one of the best.

Please give this request your prayerful consideration.

S.S.Q.B.L.M. de V.R.
P.A. Dios G. a V.R.M. Añs.

The formalized signature was to be read: 'Su servidor que besa la mano de Vuestra Reverencia. Pido a Dios guarde a Vuestra Reverencia muchos años.' (Your servant who kisses the hand of Your Reverence. Pray to God that Your Reverence may have many years.)

The forthrightness of Fray Damián's plea and the double touch of formalized humility at the closing apparently impressed the authorities at Zacatecas, because when the next caravan from Saltillo approached the mission two small horses moved forward, bringing into Tejas a pair of the hardest-working citizens that state would ever know, the carpenter Simón Garza and his wife, Juana.

They were given a corner of the mission compound, in which they built themselves a small jacal, and it was here that Juana had her first child. Her husband worked many hours a day on the mission buildings, and told his wife one night: 'Strange. I was sent here to be an assistant to Fray Damián, but it turns out that he is my assistant.'

'What do you mean?'

'I lay out the work. Where the beams should go and how they should be fastened. But he does all the lifting, the really hard work.'

Garza was correct. Fray Damián, thirty-nine years old, labored like a man possessed: first, dwelling places for his charges, then a dwelling place for the Lord, then a warmer, dryer jacal for Fray Domingo, who worked so diligently among the heathen, then a better barn for the cattle, then a stockade around the entire to protect it from the fierce Apache who fought the mission's intrusion, seeing it as an encroachment on their territory, and now his most important project of all, the one that would ensure the prosperity and safety of the fledgling settlement.

Bringing Fray Domingo and Garza together one evening when that day's work was done, Damián said: 'We shall never prosper until we bring a little canal from the river, across our fields, where we need water, and directly into our compound, leading it along this depression and out through that part of the wooden fence. Can we do this?'

Garza deferred to Fray Domingo, who disappointed him by saying: 'It would require far too much work and we don't have enough shovels.' When Damián looked at the carpenter, Garza said: 'Domingo's right. Huge effort. And we have only two shovels. But I can make some. For without secure water we can't live.'

So Damián and Garza laid plans for the building of a canal that would eventually run almost a mile, five feet wide and three feet deep, meaning that an immense amount of earth would have to be moved. But like many of the great accomplishments of the world—the building of a pyramid or the digging of a tunnel—it was a measurable job in that one started it, worked for a couple of years, edged it along as best one could, and realized one happy day that it could be finished. The digging of this canal, which would vitalize the mission, was not a gargantuan task that staggered the imagination of those obligated to build it; it was a day-to-day job of moving earth, and the two planners with their Indian helpers attacked it with that understanding.

Garza, forging all the spare bits of metal he could find, and using oak limbs for handles, fashioned two extra shovels, which were converted into badges of honor to be conferred on particular Indians who worked well: 'Juan Diego, you can have a shovel today. Esteban can keep the one he had yesterday. But only if he digs well.'

Invariably Fray Damián assigned himself the most difficult tasks, such as lifting the loosened earth from the trench, but he actually reveled in the hard work, believing that it made him more definitely a servant of God. On Sundays, when all others rested, he rose before dawn, prepared to sing the Mass, cleared his mind of mundane matters and reflected on the majesty of heaven. When the entire community had gathered in the rude church, with soldiers from the presidio often in attendance, he preached his simple message of salvation:

> 'God willed that a mission be established here, and He did so for three reasons. First, he wanted His word brought to you Indians so that you might gain salvation. Second, He wanted a settlement erected in the wilderness where Christian families could establish themselves, as Corporal Valdez and his Elena have done with His blessing. And third, I think He wanted us to build our canal so that His children could have better gardens and more sheep and a secure fortress against the enemy.
>
> 'In all these ambitions we prosper. Fray Domingo's choir never sang more sweetly than it did this morning. The soldiers at the presidio eat better than last year. And soon our canal will deliver water right to the edge of our gardens. Faithful women to whom we owe so much, no longer will you have to haul the water from our wells. It will come gushing right into our furrows and we shall have more beans than we ourselves can eat. Then we can even share our prosperity with Misión Valero.'

In the latter months of 1726 he worked so strenuously on the canal that even when he was dead tired, his bones tingling pleasantly, he would be unable to fall asleep, and one night as he lay awake he recalled a special plea which Fray Domingo had pressed with unusual vigor: 'Fray Damián, you're the master here, no question about that, but I do think that you and I deserve better vestments than they allow us. We're representatives of the church, of the king himself, and we should have proper dress in which to conduct prayers. You know that as well as I.'

It was a persuasive argument. If men at the farthest frontier, men on the battle line of civilization, represented the forces of civilization, they should be properly accoutered, which meant the friars who conducted church services ought to have blue robes of decent quality. But a decision to spend the money required for such robes, a considerable sum, could be made only in Madrid, and Damián could think of no reasonable process whereby he might force his petition all the way to the king, and so as he worked he pondered this problem.

Domingo was persistent: 'Damián, I work six days a week out on the ranch we're building so that our Indians can herd our cattle safely, and I don't mind looking like a peasant when I'm building the little jacales my families will stay in . . .' This was a silly petition, and Damián knew it as well as Domingo, for the latter did almost no work at the ranch; he sat astride his mule and directed his Indians to do it, but he was supervising the construction of a small settlement of four jacales in which the shepherds could take shelter when they guarded the remote pasturelands.

Through Domingo's careful husbandry, Santa Teresa had accumulated a herd of more than a thousand long-horned cattle, for which he had paid nothing: 'Any morning four good riders can go out on the range and collect a hundred good bulls and cows, free.' But he had used mission funds to purchase from breeders in Saltillo a starting flock of sheep, a hundred goats and ninety horses, all of which were reproducing well. He had also acquired through ingenious stratagems a mixed complement of donkeys, mules and oxen, so that he was responsible for a substantial investment. It was he who traded the surplus to the army for services only the military could supply, and it was also he who arranged that some of the best horses be herded back to Saltillo and sold for coins which could be spent in Zacatecas for those things like tobacco, chocolate and sugar candies which helped make life bearable. He had a just claim on the Spanish government, for he served it well, and now he wanted a proper blue vestment for Sundays.

Fray Damián could not in clear conscience claim such a garment for himself; he visualized himself as a mere friar obligated to build a mission, and the kind of garment in which he appeared was of no consequence, for he could not believe that Peter or Matthew or Luke had bothered much about his dress when he served Christ. But if he himself lacked pretensions, he realized that other men were differently motivated. He had watched the subtle effect on the Indian Juan Diego when he was allowed to use a shovel—he became a better man when confidence was reposed in him. Domingo was the same; he had resigned himself to secondary orders, but within the limitations of his position, he served well and was entitled to perquisites. Accordingly, one morning Fray Damián drafted a letter intended for the very highest authorities, whether in Mexico or Spain.

But submitting such a request was not a simple procedure. First, the petition had to be written on stamped paper, printed and distributed by the government; no request or report of any kind could be official unless at its head appeared the stamp of the Spanish government, a system comparable to the one which England would introduce into its colonies facing the Atlantic. Since such paper was jealously guarded and distributed in a niggardly fashion, careless requests rarely surfaced. Fray Damián could get his stamped paper only at the presidio, where the commanding officer had a low opinion of missionaries. For two months the latter refused to issue the paper, but Fray Domingo handled this by quietly suggesting to the commander that if the paper was not immediately forthcoming, there would be no more chickens from the mission farm.

Fray Damián wrote his petition on 21 January 1727:

> Since my faithful assistant Fray Domingo Pacheco of excellent reputation represents the majesty of the Spanish Crown in Tejas, it would be proper for him to have a vestment of blue linen-and-wool, highest quality, and I beseech the authorities to allow him to have it. And since I labor constantly to finish the canal upon which the welfare of this mission depends, I ask for three shovels of first-class iron with handles of oak from Spain to match. If the oak cannot be spared, I can fashion handles here, but do prefer Spanish oak, for it is best.

The petition, properly folded, was sent down to San Juan Bautista on 29 January, and there it languished until a courier was sent to Monclova on 25 February. From there it went at a leisurely pace to Saltillo, arriving in mid-March in time to catch a messenger headed for Zacatecas, which it reached on the tenth of April.

The authorities at the Franciscan offices realized that they had no jurisdiction over such a special request, and they had learned through harsh experience not to take such matters into their own hands, not in the Spanish system, so they forwarded the petition to Mexico City, but they were bold enough to add an endorsement: 'These are two good men, so perhaps they might have two vestments, one tall, one short.'

Franciscan headquarters in the capital received the document on 19 May and refused even to study it, referring it to the viceroy's office. This authority kept it on file till the fifteenth of July, when it was forwarded to Vera Cruz for shipment to Spain with a second endorsement: 'Fray Damián de Saldaña is the son of Don Miguel de Saldaña of Saldaña, a man to be trusted.'

A Spanish trading ship sailed from Vera Cruz at the end of July, but it stopped in both Cuba and Española, laying over in the latter port for two months and not sailing for Spain until the third of October. No officials in these two ports were allowed to touch the pouch from Mexico, so Damián's letter was delivered at the port of Sanlúcar at the end of a four-week crossing. From there it was sent to a section of the Council of the Indies holding session in Sevilla, where clerks studied the unusual request for three weeks. It was finally decided what should have been clear at the start, that this was a unique problem which could be solved only by the king, so belatedly a mounted messenger took the letter to Madrid. He arrived on the twenty-ninth of November, and at dawn on the next day the King of Spain eagerly reached for official messages from his dominions in the New World, reading each one meticulously and making upon it such advisory notes as he deemed fit.

In the afternoon he came upon Fray Damián's stamped and endorsed paper: 'A blue habit for Sundays and three iron shovels.'

The king leaned back, rubbed his tired eyes, and tried to visualize Mexico, a part of the empire for the last two centuries. It was difficult, for he was a newcomer to the throne of Spain. When the powerful Austrian Habsburg line—Charles V, Philip II and their successors—died out in 1700, the French Bourbons supplied the next king, Phillip V, a boy of seventeen.

Although no member of his royal family had ever visited Mexico, he had seen enough drawings and read enough reports to know fairly accurately what it was like; Mexico City, Oaxaca, Guadalajara and even Zacatecas were familiar locations, but when he tried to picture Tejas, his imagination failed, for it was the loneliest and least important of his frontiers.

'How many Spaniards in Tejas?' he asked the courtiers who brought him his belated lunch.

'Born in Spain, sixteen, maybe twenty. Born in Mexico itself, perhaps two hundred, counting mestizos. Indians, of course.'

'Sixteen Spaniards in the entire territory, and he wants a blue vestment. Notice that he is bold enough to ask for the best linen-and-wool. Who is this man?'

One of the aides looked at the petition and particularly at the endorsement from the viceroy: 'Son of Don Miguel de Saldaña, of the village of Saldaña. He supported you vigorously when Europe wanted to put someone else on our throne.'

'Good man,' the king said, and as he ate, another aide pointed to a peculiarity in the petition: 'Did you notice, Sire, that he asks for the habit not for himself but for his assistant? What he seeks are the shovels.'

The king pushed back his meal, lifted the petition once more, and asked: 'Am I thinking of the same Saldaña? The one who served us so well in Portugal?'

'The same.' Once more the king hesitated: 'Have any of you ever been to Tejas?' No one had, in either the meeting room or the entire court, so the king asked: 'Isn't that where they have the buffalo?' and while the courtiers argued whether these great animals—several of which had been imported to Spain for the amazement of the citizenry—inhabited Tejas or Santa Fe, the king impulsively took the petition and not only signed it but even added a notation of his own. The paper was then returned to the Council of the Indies, which endorsed it and started it upon its slow journey back to Sanlúcar, to Cuba, to Mexico City, to Saltillo, to San Juan Bautista and finally to Misión Santa Teresa de Casafuerte. It arrived on 19 July 1728, eighteen months after posting, and with it came a package.

It was so heavy when Fray Damián lifted it in his tired, calloused hands that he cried out thoughtlessly: 'Be praised, Garza. We have our shovels,' forgetting that Fray Domingo, who was eying the package jealously, hoped for something much different. And indeed, when he and Garza ripped open the sea-stained crate they found their three shovels, with handles of Spanish oak, best in the world.

'Look!' cried Domingo, and from a corner of a small package inside the larger peeked a swatch of blue cloth, and when he opened his prize with trembling fingers he led up for all to see a most beautiful blue habit with hood and belt and flowing folds. He could not restrain himself from throwing the precious garment about his shoulders, but as he started to parade in the sunlight so that his Indians could applaud, he chanced to look back at the package, and there beneath the first robe lay a second. Stooping to take it in his hands, he allowed its full length to fall free, and he saw that it was a larger robe of much finer cloth than the first, and it was apparent to him that this had been sent by the king as a personal gift to his superior.

'This must be for you,' he said, but Fray Damián pushed it back, and then took the first robe from the shoulders of his assistant: 'This one will do for me.'

'Do you think so?' Domingo asked, and Damián said: 'I'm certain.'

Now that Fray Domingo had appropriated the habit intended for Damián, he took doubled interest in his work, riding out to the ranch southwest of the mission each Monday and working there throughout the week. The Santa Teresa ranch was a reach of unlimited definition, with no roads or fences, nor any houses in which anyone of even the slightest importance would wish to stay. It did contain a rude corral but had no barns or sheds or tool cribs, nothing but an endless expanse of grassland suitable for the untended grazing of cattle. Its effective area was about five leagues, but this meant nothing because if no other owner in the region gained title to adjacent lands, it could just as well have been five hundred.

Its chief asset was that it lay within a sharp turn of the Medina, whence its name, Rancho El Codo (Elbow Ranch). Indeed, the Medina surrounded it on three sides, guaranteeing the cattle all the water they needed.

Within a compound it had four miserable adobe-and-wattle jacales in which the Indian families who tended the cattle lived; two of the hovels were occupied by married men who had brought their wives and children with them, the other two housed unmarried men, and sometimes when Fray Domingo studied the six adults who worked for him he speculated as to why they so willingly submitted themselves to this arduous labor, for neither he nor Fray Damián had the authority to force them to work.

He was pondering this question one August afternoon as the Indians were sweating over the branding of young stock while he rested in the shade. The branding was necessary because the rule from Madrid was stern: 'In settled areas, any cattle unbranded promptly after birth remain the property of the king.' The ranch at El Codo could have twenty thousand cattle if it wanted them, but it had to round them up and brand them, and that work was dusty and dirty and arduous, since each animal had to be wrestled to the ground before the red-hot brand could be applied.

Why do they consent to such toil? Domingo asked himself as he watched the Indians. And for that matter, why does Fray Damián work so hard? And how about me? I could be in Mexico City enjoying myself.

And it occurred to him that he and Damián were much like the Indians: We work because it's the will of God. We build the mission because Jesus Christ wants it. This is honorable work, because my father and mother and the priest in Saltillo told me it was. The Bible says so, too. The Indians obey us because deep inside they know it's right. They're living better lives than their fathers, and they know it.

Wherever he worked with Indians, Fray Domingo organized a choir, and the one at El Codo was among his finest, because three of the men had deep voices, Domingo a lilting tenor, and the fourth Indian man a strong voice which maintained a strict monotone in the middle, never moving up or down no matter how carefully the friar coached him. He was like a cello that could strike only one powerful note around which the other singers had to organize theirs, and when this choir sang on Sundays or in the evenings at prayer, the music glorified the countryside.

It was a tradition of the Franciscans that 'we never discipline the Indians except for their own good,' and Domingo believed that his own rules were just and lenient. If his Indians lagged in their field work, he reproved them. If anyone persisted, he lectured that person severely, and if the error continued, he beat him or her with a leather strap reserved for that use. But as soon as the punishment was administered, he invited the culprit back to the choir, and after a few resentful moments the reproof was forgotten, except by a few who left, never to return.

It was Domingo's love for music which projected Misión Santa Teresa into a storm that nearly destroyed it. An enthusiastic friar newly arrived from the more traditional Franciscan center at Querétaro northwest of Mexico City, took vigorous exception to the fiery dances enjoyed by the Indians of Béxar, for he categorized these exhibitions as 'licentious debauchery of the worst sort, calculated to induce venery and the most debased forms of sexual extravagance.' With written approval from the authorities at Saltillo, who had never seen these dances, he proceeded to stamp them out.

But when he eliminated them at Misión San José, they erupted at Misión San Antonio de Valero, and so on. However, with extraordinary vigor he succeeded for a while in halting them all except for those at Santa Teresa, where Fray Domingo's lyric choir would start a celebration with hymns, move on to Spanish ballads he had taught them, and progress to some lively Indian chants, until they reached the point where all the listeners were stomping their feet and clapping their hands, and even dancing. Sometimes the noise grew so vigorous that the two friars deemed it best to retire.

Fray Damián saw nothing intrinsically evil in such dancing, but the new friar thought differently, and backed by an official paper from the religious authorities in Guadalajara, he marched in to the officer in charge of the presidio at Béxar and demanded that he stop the dancing at Santa Teresa: 'It's an affront to God, who wants it stopped at once.'

The officer had been searching for some excuse to discipline the two friars at Santa Teresa, for he found the senior man, Fray Damián, too aloof, and the junior, Fray Domingo, much too niggardly with the food his Indians grew. So he issued an edict: 'No more dancing at Santa Teresa.'

He expected Fray Domingo, who started his music with proper gravity but allowed it to deteriorate quickly, to object, but to his surprise it was tall, thin Fray Damián who came quietly to the presidio, speaking softly and with obvious deference: 'Captain, the Indians have always danced, and while I admit it sometimes leads to excesses, as the new friar claims, I have found no great wrong in it and much good.'

'But I've issued an order.'

'I think you might want to reconsider your order,' Damián said gently.

'Where Indians are concerned, I never reconsider.'

Damián did not wish to argue, but he did voice an important judgment: 'Captain, when we move in upon the Indians with our missions and our presidios we ask them to surrender a great many things they love, traditions which have kept them strong . . . in a most inhospitable land, I may point out. They've been gracious here in Tejas in making such surrender. Don't ask them to sacrifice everything.'

'But the dances are against the will of God. The new friar said so.'

'I think our laughing Domingo represents the will of God, too.' Before the captain could destroy that specious argument, Damián said: 'I sometimes fear his singing accomplishes more than my prayers.'

'There will be no more dancing.'

'Very well,' Damián said obediently. And when he returned to the mission he waited till his companion returned from the ranch, herding along several steers that were to be slaughtered there.

'The dancing . . .' Damián fumbled.

'What about it?'

'The captain has ordered it stopped.'

'He has no authority . . .'

'He has.'

'The captain is an ass.'

'That we know,' Damián conceded. 'We've known it for better than a year. But he has the civil authority to preserve the peace.'

'Our hearts beat faster . . . with delight. I'll not stop it.'

'You shall. It's my order, too.' And Damián spoke with such unprecedented force that Domingo gasped, and the dancing was halted.

The three soldiers watched very carefully, on orders from the captain, and sometimes the new friar himself stopped by to check on the observance of the edict, and all had to agree that Fray Damián had restored order to the mission.

But one day some weeks later, when gaiety had been stilled in Misión Santa Teresa, the captain and a retinue of soldiers were inspecting the lands west of Béxar to see for themselves how much of the range the mission had expropriated for its cattle, and as they approached the four shacks where the Indian herdsmen lived, they heard much revelry. When they followed the noise they saw that in one of the jacales six Indian adults, three children and a Franciscan friar in a long, dusty habit were dancing in a circle, clapping hands and singing at the top of their voices.

'Look!' shouted a child, and the dancers halted, one by one, and looked toward the outraged captain and his men.

The legal papers were filed next day, a formal complaint signed by the captain of the presidio charging Fray Domingo Pacheco with insubordination, misuse of royal lands, venery and conduct unbecoming a member of the clergy. All the animosity of the presidio versus the mission exploded in this diatribe, and it was expressed so forcefully and in such proper terminology that Mexico City had to respond.

Since ancient Spanish legal tradition provided that members of the clergy could be tried only in courts staffed by fellow clerics, a solemn priest, born in Spain, was dispatched to Béxar, and he started his investigation not by examining the accused friar at Santa Teresa but by moving through the little community and listening to whatever gossip the soldiers and the friars from the other missions wished to reveal. When he was finished he had accumulated enough petty accusations against both friars to charge them with almost anything, and grimly he announced: 'Tomorrow I shall examine the culprits.'

When the two friars stood before him they made a poor impression, for they were not the neat, well-shaved clerics he was accustomed to on the streets of Zacatecas; Damián appeared in a faded, dusty blue habit, and Domingo's unkempt beard wandered over his chubby face. Ill-matched—Damián tall, thin and fiery-eyed; Domingo short, fat and marked by a silly grin—they should have stood in silence as he abused them, but to his astonishment, they showed every inclination to defend their actions.

Fray Damián was particularly vigorous in his self-defense: 'I have labored day and night to build this mission . . . to make it self-sufficient, to bring Indians into our fold. Some men might have accomplished more, but none could have worked more diligently in the service of our Lord and our king.'

'But you did allow the dancing?' the judge asked.

'I did. I worked my Indians from dawn to dusk, and I thank God that Brother Domingo taught them to sing, for it made them better workers in God's cause.'

'Were you not ordered by the civil authority to stop the dancing?'

'I was. And I did.'

'But was there not continued dancing at the mission's ranch?'

'I'm told there was.'

'And did not your Fray Domingo join in the dancing?'

'I'm told that he did.'

'Are you not responsible for what your friars do?'

Fray Damián considered this probing question for some moments, standing erect, his eyes staring straight ahead, his hands clasped at his chest. It would be both easy and correct for him to claim that what happened at the distant ranch was beyond his control, but to deny his long-time companion would be worse than craven; it would be against the rule of the Franciscans.

'I'm responsible.'

'If I were a vengeful man,' the priest said, 'I would add you to this indictment. You have failed miserably in your duty.'

'I demand that you include me,' Damián said, and he took a step forward.

'Stand where you are!' the inquisitor ordered, his face reddening. But Damián kept moving forward until he reached the desk behind which his judge sat. Once there, he reached for a quill and would have inscribed his name on the indictment had not the priest knocked the quill away and bellowed: 'Soldiers, arrest this man!'

So what had been intended as an orderly hearing ended in a general debacle, for as soon as Fray Domingo saw his protector dragged toward the exit door, he leaped at the guards and began pummeling them. A general melee ensued, in the midst of which the enraged priest shouted: 'Chain them both!'

In a tiny cell behind the presidio, no beds, no water, food only once a day, the two friars remained in manacles for three days, and when released, they had to promise both the priest and the captain that they would henceforth permit no Indian dancing.

They had resumed their now somber duties when a convoy arrived from Saltillo with an unexpected member, a young officer bringing a commission that installed him as the new commander of the Presidio de Béxar and retired the former incumbent.

As Damián came from the mission to greet the officer he saw from a distance that the new man was Alvaro, and ran forward to embrace him: 'Dearest brother! You are needed here.' But before Alvaro could respond, Damián asked: 'How is Benita?'

'Fine. If permission is given, she could be coming here.'

Fired by this hope, and supported by an understanding commander, Fray Damián launched what could be called the golden years of Santa Teresa, for with assistance from the soldiers, the walls of the mission were completed, its canal and, most important, its adobe church; and at the ranch Fray Domingo increased his herds until they taxed the ability of his Indians to control them; and the dancing resumed.

If Fray Domingo had been required to pacify only the relatively amenable Indians at the ranch near Béxar, he would have succeeded, but the Franciscans had had the bad luck to place their missions on land which was more or less claimed by Indians of a much different type.

The Apachería was not a specific land area, nor was it a highly organized brotherhood of tribes. The word represented a mystical concept, *the region and union of the Apache.* The imprecision was twofold: the specific territory was never defined and membership was so elastic that any Apache tribe could be included or excluded, as it preferred. One thing was certain: in recent decades the Apache had come to consider the lands around Béxar as part of their Apachería, and evicting the white intruders became an obligation.

Even so, a kind of truce might have been negotiable—Spaniards to the east, Apache to the west—had not another warrior tribe of Indians invaded the western plains at about this time. The newcomers were the dreaded Comanche, horse Indians from the Rocky Mountain areas, who considered all other humans their enemies. Apache and Comanche, what a sadly mismatched pair: the former somewhat sedentary, the latter constantly roving; the former without many horses, the latter the finest horsemen of the plains; the former a loose confederation of many differing tribes, the latter fearfully concentrated; and both wanting to occupy the same lands.

No Comanche had yet been seen at Béxar; they would not appear in force for nearly fifty years, but their unrelenting pressure on the western reaches of the Apachería meant that the Apache were forced to move eastward, and this brought them into conflict with the Spanish at Béxar. But for the time being, a kind of rude accommodation did exist, as proved by an enthusiastic report on conditions at the mission submitted at this time.

In 1729 an investigative priest from Zacatecas, whose name Espejo fortuitously meant *glass* or, as some said, *spyglass,* visited all parts of Tejas on an inspection tour. After dismal experiences in Nacogdoches and the coastal areas, he reached

Béxar in an uncompromising mood, but here he saw how ably the Saldaña brothers cooperated in governing the place:

> At the end of September 1729, I came at last to Misión Santa Teresa de Casafuerte del Colegio de Propaganda Fide de Nuestra Señora de Guadalupe de Zacatecas, and all the unpleasantness of preceding days vanished as if God had set down in the wilderness a great shining lantern.
>
> The mission was guarded by two exemplary friars, Damián de Saldaña of good family and superior orders who manages all, and Domingo Pacheco, a mestizo of lower orders who performs wonders with his Indians, of whom 234 Pampopa, Postito and Tacame reside in the mission. About three Indians per year have been formally converted, the rest behaving as Christians but not belonging to the church.
>
> The order of the day reflects the piety of Fray Damián. Church bell at sunrise, when all attend Mass. Copious breakfast for forty-five minutes, then everyone to work on the building projects supervised by Fray Damián, who is an outstanding builder.
>
> Lunch at noon, again well provided, and siesta for all. At two in the afternoon return to work, and at five the church bell again, whereupon the entire population reports to the church to recite the Doctrina Cristiana, which includes: Way of the Cross, Lord's Prayer, Hail Mary, Apostle's Creed, Confiteor, Precepts of the Church, Seven Sacraments, seasonal points of faith, and concluding with the Four Last Things. It is heartening to hear these Indians who only a few years ago followed pagan beliefs about rocks and rivers recite in unison the holy words that mean they are now approaching salvation.
>
> At meals Fray Domingo served us with beef, mutton, cabrito and chickens. He also provided squash, potatoes, watermelons and lentils. From the carefully tended orchard he had all the fruits of the season, including peaches, pears and plums, with dried cherries. In obedience to the strict prohibition issued by our King in order to protect the industries of Spain, the mission grows no grapes or olives, although I believe each would prosper here were they allowed.

Then Father Espejo listed in detail some sixty valuable items owned by the mission, divided into five categories, and samples from each will indicate the material progress Fray Damián had made:

FOR THE WOMEN	FOR THE MEN
1 loom	5 plowshares
3 spinning wheels	7 hoes

4 scissors	5 scythes
17 needles	1 pair tongs
7 candle molds	7 shovels

FOR PROTECTION	FOR THE BUILDERS
3 harquebuses	2 planes
5 pistols	2 iron wedges
20 bullet molds	5 sledgehammers
6 swords	67 iron nails

FOR GOD

2 incense burners
3 small bells
5 sets of altar cloths

The report ended with two footnotes, the first displaying pride, the second confusion:

This mission owns several treasures, a statue of San Antonio de Padua, carved in Zacatecas, and a set of fourteen Stations of the Cross, painted on canvas in Spain. It also has two fine blue habits of linen-and-wool, plus three iron shovels, gifts from His Majesty the King.

As to the charge so often voiced that 'the only Indians who ever convert are old people about to die,' I confess that this is justified. Young braves refuse to give up their dancing and other favored abominations, but older warriors as they approach death listen attentively to Fray Damián's preaching. Soldiers at the presidio sneer: 'The friars catch only falling leaves,' but I told them: 'Three souls saved, even in extremis, are still three brands saved from the burning, and you should rejoice in their salvation,' but the soldiers laughed, as young men will.

In his summary paragraphs he delivered his judgment as to this mission, saying in part:

Santa Teresa de Casafuerte, in its exemplary conduct and its fruitful relationship with its presidio, justifies in unmatched perfection the accepted Spanish theory of governing new provinces: to Christianize, to civilize, to utilize. I can foresee only continued blessings for Béxar, and as soon as I return to Zacatecas, I shall recommend to the Council of the

Indies that civilian settlers from Spain be brought here to establish the city which shall complement this fine venture.

In a separate memorandum, which he discussed with neither of the Saldañas, Espejo proposed an idea that would bring great happiness to each of the brothers:

> Béxar is now so firmly established, even though its population is minimal, that the time has come when more wives ought to be encouraged to join their husbands at the presidio. This will give the Indians and mestizos a taste of true Spanish civilization, which can only edify them. I therefore propose that Benita Liñán de Saldaña be allowed and encouraged to move with her three sons to Béxar immediately. I know this lady. She is a splendid example of Spanish womanhood at its best and will add honor to the presidio.

The proposal was quickly adopted by the military in Zacatecas, and one morning in December 1729 a soldier posting in from the Rio Grande shouted at the gates of the presidio: 'We come bringing great treasure!' and he caused so much excitement that Fray Damián was summoned from his mission labors and was present when a mule train came up to the presidio bearing Benita. When she stepped down, dust-covered, Damián gasped, for at twenty-five and the mother of three rambunctious sons, she was far more beautiful than before. Throwing her arms wide, as if to embrace the entire wilderness, she cried: 'I am so glad to be here!'

Brushing aside the soldiers who tried to help with her children, she ran first to her husband, kissing him ardently and displaying their sons. Then she turned, saw Damián waiting beside the wall, and ran to him, throwing her arms about him and kissing him on the cheek: 'Brother Damián, I am honored of God to be allowed to share in your work. These are your nephews.'

The next year was a period of some confusion for Fray Damián: he dined frequently at the presidio, once such an alien and unfriendly place, and there he saw how well Benita had raised her sons; he found many other excuses for visiting, and was invariably heartened by her continued liveliness, though he would never admit even to himself why he kept going there. In his quiet, austere way he was in love, and sometimes when he labored on some new mission structure he felt a deep hunger to see her again, to satisfy himself that she was there, and to appreciate the fact that she was a woman, totally different from himself and wonderful in her unique way. Seeing her, listening to her charming manner with her sons was enough, he thought, and in a subtle act of self-deception he began to convince himself that he visited only to help her with her eldest boy, Ramón, now seven: 'That one, Benita, he'd make a fine priest.'

'How foolish! He's a rowdy little boy who hates to sit still while you say prayers. He has no sense of vocation and little likelihood of ever attaining one.' Damián ignored this sensible assessment and continued visiting the boy, but with no constructive results.

When Alvaro said one day: 'I do not like the idea of your Fray Domingo spending so much time at the ranch,' Damián assured his brother that much good work was being done there with cattle and goats and sheep. But Alvaro's apprehension focused on other matters: 'It's the Apache. They keep moving closer, and sooner or later I fear they'll try to attack the ranch.' Again Damián protested: 'Domingo has the touch of God. He saves souls, and given time, he'll bring peace even to the Apache.'

Alvaro grew quite serious: 'You don't seem to understand. With three walled missions here at Béxar, with this stout presidio, with the armed huts in the village, I'm still afraid the Apache will attack one night. Imagine what they might do at an unprotected ranch.'

'God ordered us to establish that ranch,' Damián said. 'He will protect it.'

'I hope so, because I won't be able to.'

Some days later, when Domingo had returned to the mission, Damián accompanied him to the presidio, where the three leaders consulted, the fat little friar trying to convince Captain Alvaro that life at the ranch was safe: 'Each week the Apache understand a little better what Christianity means, and the salvation it will bring them.'

'Are they living at the ranch? Real converts, I mean?'

'No, but they do come in now and then, and I talk with them.'

Alvaro stood up and saluted: 'You're a brave man, Domingo. Much braver than I, and may God protect you.'

'I dance with them. I sing with them. I pray with them. And that's the pathway to salvation.'

Faithful to his promise, Father Espejo did forward his urgent appeal to the king, begging him to send civilian settlers to Béxar, but before any response was possible, the growing town was tripled in size by an extraordinary event. In early 1731 three faltering missions wasting away in the north were transferred to San Antonio de Béxar, where they joined the three already in operation. Of course, the buildings themselves were not transported; they were so forlorn and storm-shattered, they could not have been moved, but the six friars and the best of their Indian helpers made long treks through Tejas, expressing robust satisfaction when they saw the vastly improved site they were to occupy.

How beautiful their names are, Fray Damián thought, as he helped the three new missions select their locations: Nuestra Señora de la Purísima Concepción, San Juan Capistrano, San Francisco de la Espada. Like shining beads on a rosary.

When they were in place—the first two on the eastern bank of the river, like the earliest mission, San Antonio de Valero; the third on the western bank, like Santa Teresa and San José—Damián warned the new friars: 'Your success will depend on two things. Prayers to help you do better at converting Indians than we've done. And securing an assured water supply for the fields that will feed you and your Indians.'

The incoming friars encouraged Fray Damián to tell them more about bringing water onto their land, and they were so persistent in seeking his advice that he ended by laying out the three additional ditches which would in future years account for much of Béxar's growth. Having shown the newcomers how to survey so as to avoid costly aqueducts unless they were inescapable, he continued to counsel the friars until work actually started, then found himself once more with a shovel, demonstrating how the digging should be done.

Fray Damián was forty-five years old when the new missions started functioning, rather tired and increasingly emaciated in appearance, but he was so eager to help these servants of God get started correctly that he labored on their ditches as if he were a member of their missions, and when at last the precious water began to flow, he felt as if he had helped write a small addition to the Acts of the Apostles.

There was at San Juan Capistrano, the mission which honored a saintly man who had worked among the Bulgarians in much the way that Damián worked with the Indians, a young mestizo friar named Eusebio who, because of his extreme sanctity, had been allowed to take major orders, and he was so awed by this privilege that he honored with extra seriousness each precept of the Franciscans. Particularly, he wore about his waist the long heavily knotted cord that served a double purpose: it was a belt holding the blue habit close to the body, but also a flagellum, a scourge to be applied whenever one felt he was indulging in vainglory. Sometimes when Damián paused in his work, he would see Eusebio walking under the trees, beating himself with his knots and crying 'Mea culpa, mea culpa.'

One morning as Damián dug in the ditch at one of the new missions he noticed Eusebio sitting on a log, striking himself. 'Really, you're not required to punish yourself that way.'

'I'm vain,' the young friar mumbled. 'Far too proud of the high position to which God has promoted me.' And he struck himself again.

'Stop it! If God did the promoting . . .'

'Are you never vainglorious?'

'I have little to be vain about. At this mission Fray Domingo saves the souls. I dig the ditches.'

'But is your mind never troubled?'

'On the night I was assigned to Béxar, I cried: "I have sin upon me. I'm unworthy to be a shepherd."'

'What changed your mind?'

'Work.'

'But the great battles of faith?'

This last word seemed to animate Damián, for he put down his shovel and climbed from the irrigation ditch to take his place beside the young friar. 'I take great solace from the Epistle of James,' he said, quoting haphazardly as his memory allowed from the startling second chapter which gave Protestant rigorists so much trouble:

'What does it profit if a man say he has faith, but has not works? Can faith save him?

'Faith, if it has not works, is dead, being alone.

'You see then that by works a man is justified, and not by faith only.

'For as the body without the spirit is dead, so faith without works is dead also.'

The young man stared at him, but Damián merely kicked at the earth as he said: 'I know that I am lesser than Domingo, who does the work of God, but I find comfort in doing the work of man. Domingo builds castles in heaven, I build adobe huts here on earth. And I do believe that God sometimes wants both.'

'You never lash yourself?'

'In the morning I'm too hopeful that on this day I shall be permitted to accomplish something good. At night I'm too conscious of another failure.'

'Is Domingo really a holy man?'

'He's a good man, and sometimes that's better.'

'His goodness, what does it consist of?'

'He brings happiness in his sack . . . wherever he goes.'

'Was he not rebuked for lewd dancing?'

Damián ignored this painful charge, shifting the emphasis: 'From our ranch he attempts to bring peace to the Apache . . .'

'I'd be terrified to move anywhere near them.'

'Have you converted any Indians, Eusebio?'

'One. A very old man about to die. He sent his wife running for me, and when I reached him he said with a smile: "Now!" and five minutes later he was dead, still smiling.'

'With your prayers, Eusebio, you saved one man. With his songs and his courage Domingo may save an entire tribe, thousands of Apache living at last in peace . . . a glory to the goodness of God.'

'I would be afraid to try,' Eusebio said, rising and whipping himself again, while Fray Damián climbed back into the ditch, determined to help bring water to Misión San Juan Capistrano.

Hernando Cortés had completed his conquest of the Valley of Mexico in 1521, which meant that by 1730 the Spaniards had controlled the country for two hundred and nine years, and while it is true that they had constructed on Indian foundations a chain of glowing cities like Puebla, Oaxaca, Guanajuato, Zacatecas and the charming settlement at Saltillo, they had not accomplished much in remote areas like Tejas. In 1730, Béxar, the leading town, contained a population of some two hundred, Spaniards and Mexicans, only fourteen of which were civilians not associated with either the military or the friars at the missions.

But now the letter which Father Espejo had sent to Spain requesting that true-born Spanish settlers be dispatched to Tejas to build a civilian community reached the king, who had for some years been contemplating just such a solution to his problems in northern Mexico:

> In my opinion we can never secure a frontier province like Tejas until we populate it with trusted men and women of pure Spanish blood, preferably those born in Spain or the Canaries. I advocate sending over a large number of farmers direct from Spain or such persons already in Cuba.

But even though he was an absolute monarch with exceptional powers, he had been unable to move his conservative bureaucracy from their cautious ways, so that the intervening years had seen nothing accomplished in the populating of Tejas. Now, with this new proposal before him, he confronted his ministers and said: 'The time has come. How about those recalcitrants in the Canaries?' And thus he initiated an intricate series of movements which would eventually bring to Tejas its earliest formal colony of civilian settlers.

The Canary Islands lay in the Atlantic Ocean, far removed from Spain and opposite the coastline of Morocco. The islands had been populated centuries earlier by a dark-skinned people from the mainland of Africa, but in time they were conquered by Spain and brought into the bosom of Spanish religion and culture. They were Spaniards, but of a different cast.

The Canaries consisted of seven major islands, none large, and of these, the poorest in material goods but the most stubborn in resisting authority was Lanzarote, the one nearest Africa. By a curious chance it rested on approximately the same parallel of latitude as Béxar (29°/30'), so that in making the move to Tejas, these Canary Islanders would be leaping, as it were, some five thousand eight hundred miles due west to a somewhat comparable climate. The king, in suggesting that the Tejas settlers be drawn from the Canaries, had Lanzarote specifically in mind, for he had recently received a confidential report regarding these unfortunate Islanders:

> I know the people of Lanzarote occupy an island with miserably poor soil, but they have never shown the slightest interest in farming or even in properly tending their scrawny sheep and goats. While we all know that the people of the Canaries are generally illiterate, those of Lanzarote are by far the most ignorant. And although our government gives them royal aid, they consistently eat more than they produce. Never have they contributed in any way to the social or economic advancement of our Kingdom and I see no hope for improvement in the future. I recommend that the Crown transplant a number of Lanzarote families to Tejas, where under changed conditions they might under pressure learn to become useful citizens. At least we should give my recommendation a trial.

To this proposal the king gave hearty approval, and steps were taken to deposit a group of Lanzarote families at the doorstep of the Misión Santa Teresa in Béxar.

For the king's command to take effect, his officials had to convince the political leader of Lanzarote that the idea was prudent, and now they were thrown up against one of the wiliest, most contentious, arrogant, conniving and headstrong men of that time.

He was Juan Leal Goras, and according to traditional Spanish custom, he should have been called Leal, his father's name, but he stubbornly insisted that his name was Goras, and so he was known. Now in his fifties, he had five children and one eye, having lost the other in an argument with a mule. Obstinately, he refused to wear a patch over the missing eye, and with moisture trickling down his cheek, pointed the gaping hole offensively at anyone with whom he spoke. He was illiterate, a deficiency which did not prevent him from becoming the most litigious man in the Canaries; he initiated lawsuits against everyone—priest, king's official, neighbor with a goat, the sea captain of a little ship plying between the islands—and even when he won, he enjoyed prolonging the hearings in hopes of gaining a mite more advantage.

Even before he and the other fifty-three Islanders boarded the ship that would carry them to Mexico, Goras was shouting suggestions as to how their accommodations might be improved, and when the captain snarled 'Go to hell!' Goras threatened a lawsuit. But on 20 March 1730 the rickety craft set sail, and next morning, after a rough passage, his people landed at Santa Cruz on the main island of Teneriffe, where they picked up a few additional emigrants. With inadequate food supplies, they then sailed for Cuba, a difficult crossing of forty-five days of heat and seasickness. At one point the captain, driven almost crazy by the torrent of suggestions from Goras, cried: 'Put that man in chains!' And the would-be admiral crossed the Atlantic bound to two huge grinding stones intended for the first grain mill in Tejas.

The settlers wasted two months in Cuba, then spent ten steamy days sailing to Vera Cruz, where on 19 July a horrendous epidemic of el vómito prostrated most of them and killed several.

They left Vera Cruz joyously on 1 August, headed for the great volcanoes that marked the backbone of Mexico, and they were grateful to reach higher land where el vómito did not flourish, but now they had an equally grave problem.

The two huge millstones were gifts to the Islanders from the king himself: 'The Crown will support you with your every need, clothes, food, utensils, money, until your first crop comes in.' So the stones had sentimental as well as practical value, but they were so large that the oxen drawing them began to die. By the time the Islanders reached the foothills of the volcano at Orizaba, it was obvious that hauling the stupendous things was no longer practical; nevertheless Goras bellowed: 'If the king gave us the stones, we keep them with us.' But when more oxen died, even Goras had to agree that the stones should be abandoned until officials in Vera Cruz could recover them.

After twenty-seven painful days the Islanders entered that majestic valley of Mexico, one of the wonders of the world, guarded by the volcanoes Popocatépetl and Ixtaccíhuatl, garlanded in flowers and protected by one of heaven's bluest skies. There at the center stood the splendid capital itself, with its university, its printing houses, its grand eating places and stately mansions. To see Mexico City after the bucolic simplicity of the Canaries was an adventure in empire, and Goras told his people: 'We'll make Tejas like this, an example to the world,' but a muleteer who had once led his animals to Saltillo warned: 'I doubt it will be the same.'

For almost three months Goras and his Islanders languished in the environs of the great city. A few of them, including his own wife, died; young people contracted marriages; worn-out horses were exchanged at the king's expense, as promised; and some of the Islanders, including Goras, began to think that they should remain in these pleasant surroundings rather than head for Tejas.

But the king's orders were that they must move on to Béxar, and so, on 15 November 1730, they resumed their pilgrimage, reaching Saltillo in mid-December and resting in that lovely town with its salubrious breezes and good food until the end of January 1731.

More people died; children were born; more horses collapsed from exhaustion; and on 7 March the surviving Islanders reached the Medina, some distance east of where Fray Domingo had his profitable ranch. Looking across its narrow waters into Tejas, they were appalled by what they saw: a continuation of the sea of grass, more mesquite, never a hill, not a single habitation, only an occasional wild horse or a strayed cow with enormous horns.

'Oh God!' Goras cried when he saw their new home through his one good eye. 'Is this Tejas?'

He was encouraged, however, by a soldier accompanying the group, who assured him: 'At Béxar, where the missions are, everything is better. They have gardens there and food enough to share.'

On 9 March 1731, Goras led his Islanders to the gates of the Misión Santa Teresa, where they were rapturously greeted by a tall, thin friar: 'Settlers at last. My name is Fray Damián, and everything within this mission is at your service, for God has delivered you safely to this destination.'

The friar embraced Juan Leal and the other men, pressed the women's hands, and fought back tears when he saw the emaciated children. 'Fray Domingo!' he called. 'Do bring these children some sugar squares!' Then he turned to the group and said in a strong, quiet voice: 'Let us kneel and give thanks that your long journey is completed.' As the little congregation knelt inside the mission gates, he prayed, but Goras, counting the days by the system he kept in his mind, did not, for he was thinking: 20 March last year to 9 March this. That's three hundred and fifty-five days, and for this?

If Fray Damián had previously thought he'd known trouble with his Indians and soldiers, he was forced to come up with a new definition of that word where the Islanders were concerned, because within a few weeks Goras was threatening to bring lawsuits against Damián for failing to provide a suitable place for the Lanzarote people, against Fray Domingo for not carrying out the king's promise that they would be taken care of in these early days, and against Captain Saldaña for malfeasances too numerous to specify. Since none of the Islanders could write, and since he knew the complaints had to be made on the proper stamped paper, he badgered Damián de Saldaña to document the charges against his brother Alvaro de Saldaña, and vice versa. In fact, so many garbled reports reached Zacatecas that the commandant there roared one morning: 'What in hell is going on up there in Béxar?' and he organized an inspection tour which he himself led.

He learned that the major grievance was one that had surfaced in all parts of northern Mexico: Who controlled the water? The six missions, including Fray Damián's, argued with some reason that since they had established irrigation rights on the San Antonio, a limited stream at best, it would be illegal and against the interests of the crown for the Canary Islanders to build their own dam and siphon off an undue share of the river. But Goras argued brilliantly: 'Surely the king did not intend that his loyal servants be brought here and set down in a wilderness with no water.' And he pointed out that the six missions, even with the presidio thrown in, housed fewer Spaniards, real Spaniards, that is, than his new village of San Fernando.

At this, one of the soldiers asked: 'And when have Canary Islanders been considered real Spaniards?' Goras challenged him on the spot: 'A duel. Any weapons you like. Our honor has been abused.'

He was now engaged in five distinct lawsuits, but the Islanders still had no stone houses, no garden plots, no horses and, worst of all, no water. This was an intolerable situation and Fray Damián knew it. One night after the most acrimonious confrontation, in which the Islanders charged the Saldaña brothers with treason to begin with and thievery and lechery as tempers grew, Damián consulted with Fray Domingo: 'Surely, in the interests of God, we must do something to resolve this bitterness.'

Domingo started to laugh. 'Do you remember, Damián, how we sat here one night, just like this, and you told me in your solemn way: "Domingo, Tejas will never function properly until we import real Spaniards here to establish standards?" Well, now you have your Spaniards. Are you happy about it?'

'I had not expected such Spaniards,' Damián replied, but the two friars decided on their own to take those Christian steps which any man of good conscience would feel forced to take, regardless of what course the presidio or the other missions might follow. 'We must share our water,' Damián said. 'And the richness of our land.'

Before dawn Domingo and three Indians drove out to the ranch with wagons to be filled with produce and spare tools. Cows, goats and sheep were rounded up, and then the men slept for a few hours, but at sunset they started back to where the Canary Islanders needed help.

In the meantime Damián and Garza, working by starlight, traced out a route whereby an irrigation ditch could be led along the crest of hills in such a way that water could be brought from the San Antonio directly onto the fields of the Islanders, avoiding the necessity for a costly aqueduct like the one another of the missions would be required to build. But when Goras saw the run of the proposed ditch, he objected strenuously: 'My fields are over there. The ditch should run here, and if it doesn't, I shall bring a lawsuit to alter it.'

Just as the Saltillo men were sure all problems relating to the Islanders' community had been resolved, Goras, supported by two cronies, marched to the presidio with yet another startling demand: 'We were promised that if we left our secure homes and ventured into this wilderness, we would henceforth be called, because of our bravery, *hidalgos,* with right to the title *Don.* I am to be called Don Juan, he is Don Manuel de Niz, and that one is Don Antonio Rodríguez.'

In Spanish society, the word *hidalgo* carried significant connotations. It was composed of three small words: *hijo-de-algo,* which meant literally *son-of-something* or, by extension, *son-of-someone-important,* and it was impossible for even a minor member of the nobility like Don Alvaro de Saldaña to dream of calling men like Goras and his illiterate peasants Don.

The soldiers and most of the friars flatly refused to do so, but Goras and his Islanders threatened new lawsuits if they were denied their honorific. Since they had already flooded Guadalajara and Zacatecas with petitions, they fired this one at Mexico City itself, demanding that the commandant draft their protest on his own stamped paper.

This was too much: 'Goras, if you give me any more trouble . . .'

Before he could complete his threat the one-eyed Islander demanded in a loud, offensive voice: 'And where are those grinding stones the king gave us? I suspect you stole them, and I'm starting a lawsuit to recover them.' The commandant had never heard of the promised grinders, but some months later they were delivered to Saltillo with a specific message from the king that they were to be sent on to his loyal subjects at Béxar, with this added instruction:

> In accordance with promises made on my behalf, all male heads of families who left Lanzarote for this dangerous undertaking are to be known henceforth as hidalgos and are to be addressed as Don.

In this manner the civil settlement of Tejas was launched, with the Canary Islanders becoming aristocratic hidalgos at a stroke of the king's pen.

Fray Damián was a saintly man, but he was no saint. No sooner had he championed the Canary Islanders in their demand for an irrigation ditch and helped them start it than he summoned his carpenter Simón Garza and their two best Indians to an emergency meeting: 'Before the Islanders dig their ditch and draw off their water, let us deepen ours, all along the way.'

As the work progressed, he found to his surprise that Simón Garza was frequently absent from the ditch, and Damián began to believe that the carpenter, always so faithful, was scamping his duties. Such unlikely behavior was so agitating that Damián began watching Garza more closely. One morning when the carpenter had sneaked away, Damián followed him to the larger of the two mission barns, where he expected to find him sleeping while the others worked. Entering quietly by the main door, he adjusted his eyes to the darkness and moved to where a shaft of sunlight illuminated a cleared corner, and there Damián saw what amounted to a miracle, a true miracle brought down to earth and given form.

Working in secret, Garza had hewn and bonded together three oaken planks, scraping and smoothing one side of the resulting board until it was quite even. From the long board thus created, he had sawed off seven large squares of wood and had begun to bond three other oak boards together to form a second long board from which he could saw off seven more squares.

Suspended from a nail above his work space hung a painting, done in Spain, of one of the fourteen Stations of the Cross, those panels displayed in all churches showing scenes of Christ struggling through the streets of Jerusalem on the way to

His crucifixion. Garza had taken this sample from the mission church; below it on a kind of horizontal easel rested one of his first seven squares. With such tools as he had been able to improvise, Simón had nearly completed his carving of the Third Station, in which the solitary figure of Christ falls to the cobbled pavement of the Via Dolorosa, weighed down by the heavy cross he must bear. Below the figure rose from the wood the words JESÚS CAE POR PRIMERA VEZ (Jesus falls for the first time).

With an innate appreciation of what oak could represent and of the mystery of Christ's Passion, this unlettered carpenter was creating a masterpiece, for the figure of Christ seemed not only to rise living from the oaken surface but also to proclaim its religious significance.

And there was the mystery! The Christ that Garza had carved was indeed living, but not in any realistic way. If, for artistic purpose, the arm holding the cross required lengthening, he carved it so, and if the head needed to be cocked at an impossible angle, he cocked it. Indeed, as he studied that painting in the darkness of the barn he had intuitively corrected each wrong thing; he had held to the good basics and discarded all that was meretricious. Simón's Third Station was not Indian art or primitive art or any other kind of art capable of being designated by an adjective; it was art itself, simple and pure, and Fray Damián could only gape in awed respect.

Bowing his head in reverence, he could visualize the fourteen completed carvings on the walls of his church, and he knew that they must become the chief treasure of Béxar.

Humbly he faced his carpenter and said: 'Surely God is working through you, Simón, to give us this miracle. Henceforth I shall dig your ditches and you shall complete your carvings in this barn.'

In many ways the year 1733 represented the apex at Misión Santa Teresa, for the peaceful Indians near Béxar had learned to live within the compound and to listen to sermons even though they showed no inclination toward becoming Christians. At the ranch Fray Domingo had achieved great success with his cattle and a limited one with his Apache; indeed, he had two of them singing in his informal choir on those occasions when they wandered by the corrals to inspect the Spanish horses they hoped to steal on their next night raid.

Relations between the mission and the presidio, always a measure of how things were progressing, had never been better; the Saldaña brothers had seen to that. Surprisingly, the religious contacts with Zacatecas and the governmental with Mexico City were also unruffled. It was a time of peace, especially with the French to the north, and Fray Damián could have been forgiven had he taken pride in his custodianship of the most important mission in Tejas.

He did not. His innate self-depreciation prevented him from accepting praise for what he deemed his ordinary duty, and on some days he almost castigated himself for not achieving more of God's work. However, his relationships with his brother and sister-in-law had never been better, for these three sensible adults— Damián, aged forty-seven; Alvaro, thirty-eight, and Benita, twenty-nine—had evolved a routine which produced great satisfactions.

On two or three days each week Damián took his evening meal with his brother's family, bringing with him such produce from the mission farm adjacent to the church as he felt he could spare, plus cuts of meat from the animals that Domingo had brought in from the ranch for slaughter. Benita, on her part, would have her Indian servants bake bread and occasionally a fruit tart, if the mission orchards had provided plums.

The three would bow their heads as Damián asked blessing, and then engage in chatter about the doings in Béxar and Saltillo as the platters of food circulated and the bottle of wine was opened. Whenever a problem of management arose, regarding either the mission or the presidio, the brothers would consult, but often it was Benita who offered the practical and equitable solution.

She had developed into one of those extraordinary women who find in the rearing of a family and the organization of her husband's day-to-day life a key to her own happiness; she had never been overly religious and saw no reason to depend upon the rewards of an afterlife to compensate for disappointments in this. She had been reared by her Spanish parents to believe that the greatest thing that could happen to a woman in Mexico was to marry some incoming Spaniard, make him a good wife, and in later years go first to Spain and then to heaven. In the wilds of Tejas she had begun to doubt whether she would ever return to Spain, and she had long ago decided to leave heaven to God's dispensation.

Sensible as she was, she had always known why Damián wanted to stay close to his brother and why he now brought gifts rather more lavish than conditions warranted. She knew that Damián, thinking of her as his spiritual wife, was joined to her with bonds so powerful that neither imagination nor death could dissolve them, and she felt obligated to him. He was her responsibility, and by her acquiescence she knew she had accepted the pleasant burden of his emotional life. When he was ill, she tended him. When his robe required mending, she sewed it. When he told little jokes about the mission Indians, she laughed. And whenever he appeared at her house or departed, she showed her pleasure at his arrival or her sadness at his going. In Benita he had a wife without the responsibility of one.

Was Alvaro aware of this unusual triangle of which he was a silent part? He never alluded to it. He welcomed his brother with more than brotherly affection and saw no unpleasant consequences from what might have been a dangerous arrangement.

Partly this was because Damián was so helpful, not only with his food contributions but also with his attention to the three Saldaña boys; he played games with them and taught them their letters, and often took them to the mission when Fray

Domingo was in attendance so they could learn to sing. Invariably, when he visited their home at the presidio he brought them little presents, sometimes so trivial they could scarcely be called presents, but so thoughtful that they proved his continuing love.

He had always been especially fond of Ramón, a bright, eager lad now eleven and thirsty for knowledge of the world. Damián had long ago surrendered his silly hope that Ramón would one day become a priest: 'That boy would last in a Franciscan college one week, Benita, or maybe one day. Take my advice. Make a pirate of him.'

On Sundays, and high holidays, everything changed, for now the presidio Saldañas entered Damián's world, and they were properly reverent, for no one could live at the edge of the wilderness without speculating upon the nature of the good life, and orderly religion was seen as one of the abiding consolations. When Damián prayed, Alvaro listened, and when his brother preached, the commander followed his arguments. At communion, which carried special weight when one seemed so far from civilization, Alvaro, Benita and their eldest son accepted their wafers solemnly, knowing that by so doing, they were somehow in contact not only with Jesus Christ but with fellow Catholics in Mexico City, Madrid and all other respectable nations of the earth.

On those occasions when Fray Domingo came in from the ranch to lead his Indian choir, Alvaro sang with them in his strong baritone voice, and at such times the three adult Saldañas often looked at one another, assured that a bond of friendship and love held them together.

They would never see Spain again, none of them, but in Tejas they had discovered the joy of lives decently led and work well done.

On 5 September 1734, a day that would be remembered with horror, a little Indian boy half ran, half staggered up to the gates of Santa Teresa with a story that only a child could tell without retching.

To the ranch belonging to the mission, Apache had come, scores of them, and with systematic barbarity had burned every building and driven off every animal. The mission Indians who had tried to defend the place had been slain; the children, all nine of them, had been taken captive; and the five women . . . The little boy had not the words to describe what had happened to them: 'The Apache undressed them . . . then, you know . . . then they cut them apart.'

Fray Damián clutched at the back of a chair: 'They what?'

'They cut them apart,' and the boy showed how first a finger had been cut away, then another, then a hand and a foot and a breast, until the final rip of the gut, deep and powerful from left to right.

'Mother of God!' Damián cried, and immediately sent Garza to fetch Captain

Saldaña, and when the brothers faced the boy, they asked: 'What happened to Fray Domingo?' and now the child burst into tears.

'When they were not looking,' he said in his Yuta dialect, 'I ran to the bushes by the river. I hid there all day, and when night came . . . I am sleepy.'

'Of course you are,' Damián said gently, taking the boy onto his lap. 'But what happened to Fray Domingo?'

'Upside down, by the fire. His feet tied to a limb. No clothes on. They built a fire under his head. Each woman puts a stick on the fire to make it blaze, then cuts away a finger or a toe. He screamed . . .' The boy shuddered and would say no more.

The Saldaña brothers knew they had to organize an expedition to punish the Apache and, if possible, retrieve the captured children and any young women who might have survived. A force of thirty soldiers, sixteen Spanish and mestizo laymen, two dozen Indians and four friars set out for the Santa Teresa ranch, where the smoldering buildings bespoke the ruin that the Apache had wrought. Not even halting to bury the corpse of Fray Domingo, still hanging from a tree, the infuriated men picked up the trail of the Apache and spurred ahead. For three days they sought to overtake them, but failed; however, just as they were about to turn back in frustration they heard a whimpering in some bushes and found the seven-year-old sister of the boy who had escaped. When it became apparent what indecencies the Apache had visited upon her, several of the fort soldiers began to vomit.

That was the nature of Béxar's endless struggle with the Apache. The familiar Indians of this part of Tejas—the Pampopa, the Postito, the Orejone, the Tacame, the dozens of other tribes—were semi-civilized, like the more amenable Indians the French and the English were meeting along the Mississippi and the Atlantic seaboard; Europeans could reach agreements with Indians like the Mohawk, the Pawnee and the Sioux, for those tribes understood orderly behavior, but the Apache did not. Their rule was to strike and burn, torture and kill in the cruelest ways imaginable. No persuasion touched them, no enticement tempted them to live harmoniously with anyone else, white or Indian.

They were a handsome people physically, lithe, quick, remarkably at home in their environment, and capable of withstanding the greatest duress. They could go days without food or water; they could withstand burning heat or sleeted trails; and if they were horribly cruel to their captives, they could themselves accept torture with insolent defiance. They were the scourge of the lower plains, ravaging Tejas and venturing frequently all the way to Saltillo in the south, a city they loved to plunder.

Sometimes they traveled four hundred miles in order to steal an especially fine string of horses, but they liked mules too, for these they slaughtered and ate. But even when there was no prospect of capturing horses, they raided white settlements just for the pleasure of killing people they knew to be their enemies, and when a district held no white people, as most of Tejas did not, they raided the camps of Indians weaker than themselves, slaying them indiscriminately.

When Fray Damián rode back to Rancho El Codo to bury his longtime associate and dear friend, he was well aware of the serious undertaking he was about to launch. Directing Simón Garza to climb the tree and cut the cord that kept the charred remains of Fray Domingo swinging by its ankles, he caught the body as it fell, and staggered with his burden to a proper spot, where a grave was dug. As the body was deposited he uttered a prayer and made a promise:

> 'Brother Domingo, friend of years and warmth to my heart, you died in an effort which brought joy to God. I promise you that I shall take up the burden that you have put down. I shall not rest until the peace you sought is brought to the Apache and they are safe in the arms of Jesus Christ.'

He proceeded in an orderly manner to fulfill his oath: 'Simón, halt your work on the Stations and carve a fine plaque showing the martyrdom of Domingo, and this we will send to our colleagues in Zacatecas.' To his Indian helpers: 'Cándido, I must leave to you the completion of our ditch, and speed it. Ignacio, I can't ask you to live at the ranch, for that's too dangerous now that the Apache have struck, but you must move through the countryside and rebuild our herds.'

For himself, he must quit the mission walls and move out among the Apache to bring them God's word, but before he could leave he must find someone to guide Misión Santa Teresa temporarily, and he recalled the devout Fray Eusebio who castigated himself so severely. After gaining approval from the head of Eusebio's mission, he installed him, and smiled as the young dreamer lashed himself with his flagellum, crying: 'I am not worthy of such high promotion.'

In the months that followed, Fray Damián was sometimes seen by military expeditions headed north or south from Béxar, and scouts reported back to Captain Alvaro: 'There we were, loneliest stretch we'd ever seen, Béxar two days distant, and out of nowhere comes this gaunt, long-legged friar on a mule. "You must be careful of the Apache at night," he told us. "They'll steal your animals." We asked him where he was going and he said: "To the Apachería." '

And that was where he went, and because he moved alone, on a mule and unarmed, a man approaching fifty, they gave him entry to their camps. When he had learned enough of their language, they talked with him and explained that it was impossible for Indians and white men to live together. They acknowledged that he personally commanded powerful magic, but they also pointed out that they were no longer powerless: 'Those you call the French. Beyond the rivers. They sell us guns. Soon we shoot. Better hunters, you never catch us.'

He was so astonished to find that the French were supplying arms that he told the tribe with whom he had been living and to whom in the evenings he had been preaching: 'I must leave you now and tell my brother at the fort that peace with the Apache must come before everyone has guns.'

They not only let him return to Béxar but they sent a trusted squaw with him, and on the way she confided: 'That other camp. Two days south. They have two of the children taken in the big raid.'

They detoured, and Damián found that what the woman said was true; a boy of ten and a girl of eight were in the tents, and Damián persuaded the Apache to release the latter so that she could return to her people, but the child refused to leave. Her people were dead; she had seen them die; and now she had found other parents in the camp.

'But God wants you to live a decent life, within the church,' Damián argued.

'Leave her alone,' the boy snarled, grabbing her away.

'My son, it is proper that she—'

'Get away.' In some curious fashion the children were blaming the friar for the terrible things that had happened to them, and this Damián could not accept. Reaching for the girl, he drew her to him and with a trembling forefinger traced the scars across her face, put there not in the heat of battle but by Apache braves who tortured their captives, even the children.

'What is your name, Child of Heaven?'

'Let her go!' the boy cried again, and this time he wrenched the girl away, struck her violently, and shoved her along to some older women, who began to beat her.

Regardless of his own safety, Damián lunged toward the little girl to rescue her from such abuse, but he was halted by a tall, powerful Apache warrior whose garb caused the friar to stop in horror. With the hand that had traced the girl's scars, he reached out and touched the man's garment, realizing that it was the robe Fray Domingo had been wearing prior to his horrible death.

Holding on to the robe, he said quietly in Apache: 'This is the garment of my friend. I must have it for his grave.'

The Indian understood and respected the emotion represented: 'Your friend, very brave.'

Still clinging to the robe, Damián said: 'You must let me take it.'

'What will you give me?'

Damián had nothing to offer but his mule, and this the Apache took gladly, for it would make a feast. So Fray Damián de Saldaña returned to his mission, on foot, trailing an Apache woman astride a donkey, and clutching to his bosom the robe in which his dearest friend and companion of many years had approached his martyrdom.

His efforts to bring peace and Christianity to the Apache not only failed, they ended in repeated embarrassment. At the conclusion of his first venture into alien territory, after the Apache woman led him into Béxar, he persuaded Alvaro that the Apache were of sincere intent when they suddenly changed face and discussed the possibility of permanent truce, and he pointed out that with the Indians receiving French guns, it was imperative that a peaceful understanding be reached. So against his better judgment, Captain Saldaña agreed that Damián, with a new mule, should return with the woman and arrange for a plenary between Apache chiefs and presidio soldiers.

Damián, heartened by the possibility that he might be the agent for ending the raids and retaliations, returned to the western lands and persuaded his Apache to send for those who controlled the south. With delight he listened as the newcomers consented: 'We'll go and talk, and if he's like you, a man of bravery, perhaps . . .'

A party of sixteen, led by Damián and the squaw who had made the earlier trip, rode east one March morning in 1736, arriving at Béxar four days later. When the six missions were in sight, Damián and the woman rode on ahead, sounding signals that brought many men to the walls. Captain Alvaro, not at all certain that truce was possible, cautioned his men to remain alert, then nervously admitted the Apache into the presidio.

In sign language the Apache talked incessantly for two days, consuming a vast amount of food as they did, and at dusk on the second day, at a signal from their chief, they suddenly raised a war cry, slew the two guards, and ran outside to join some ninety more of their men who had crept close during the preceding days.

They were a force powerful enough to have assaulted the presidio itself had they so decided; instead, they drove off more than a hundred and twenty Béxar horses, galloping westward into the shadows, whooping and screaming and firing their French guns in the air.

Fray Damián was so distraught after this debacle, which he had unwittingly engineered, that he fell into a kind of trance, not insensible to those about him but quite unable to talk or act. He lay on his straw paillasse staring at the ceiling, indifferent to food, and from time to time calling out the word *Domingo,* but when attendants hurried to see what he wanted, they found him weeping and unable to speak further.

His health deteriorated rapidly, and it was only the care of Benita, sent to the mission by Alvaro, that saved him. She was a woman of thirty-two now, and as lively in spirit as when Damián had first seen her promenading around the square at Zacatecas. Her eyes still glowed mischievously and her skin remained unblemished, as if time were loath to touch something so flawless. Most surprising of all, under these deplorable circumstances, she still retained a cheerfulness that prevented her from taking troubles too seriously.

'Come now, Damián! We need you in Béxar,' she said teasingly. Disregarding mission rules, she propped open the door to his cell, brought in flowers, and personally cooked nourishing meals for him. When he seemed to revive, with senses clarified so that he could understand what she was saying, she assured him that her husband did not blame him for the disaster with the Apache: 'They're savage brutes, and what could anyone expect?'

'I expected peace,' Damián said.

'No one should have been so easily deceived.' she said.

'Were you?'

She reflected on this for some moments, then said the right thing: 'No, but I love you for being such a dear, good man and I prayed that you might be right.' As soon as she said this she realized that her words stressed the fact that he had been wrong, so she added quickly: 'It's always good to try, Damián. Maybe another time . . .'

As he watched her move about his cell he appreciated anew the miracle that even though he was forbidden by church law to have her for himself, she was nevertheless a part of his being, a mystical wife in another world whose conventions he could not fathom. She was the woman he had loved from that first moment when he saw her laughing with the other girls, and that she should now be so close to him, and mending his broken spirit, was a joy he could share with no one, not even with Jesus Christ in his prayers.

When Damián finally rose from his cot, a most pleasing honor awaited him: Simón Garza had finished his fourteen Stations of the Cross, but their installation had been deferred until Damián could supervise it. Actually, all he did was stand in his adobe church and tell the workmen how to hang the carvings, but when the light fell across them, showing the marvelous detail Garza had achieved with his rude chisels, tears came to his eyes and he fell to his knees and prayed. It seemed that God Himself must have bent down and guided Garza's hand, for Damián could not conceive how an illiterate mestizo carpenter could otherwise have accomplished such a work.

When the carvings were in place, Captain Alvaro, supported by friars from the other missions, told Damián: 'We must have a celebration to dedicate your Stations,' and it was arranged that a cloth covering would be draped over each carving, and that Garza would move from one location to the next, pulling aside the cloth to reveal the beauty beneath. Damián would expound the religious significance while the choir trained by Fray Domingo sang holy verses he had taught them. Fray Eusebio, still protesting that he was not worthy of such high honor, would represent the other missions.

It was the culmination of Damián's custodianship. Indian women filled the rude church with flowers, and as the veils fell away and sunlight illuminated the carvings, Damián thought that Jesus Christ Himself had come to Béxar to relive those tragic, hallowed moments when he moved painfully along the road to Golgotha.

Damián's exultation was short-lived, because when word of the episode with the Apache reached Mexico City, the viceroy cast about for a new governor of Tejas who would bring stricter order to the region. Unfortunately, he had no one available to send, but a conniving assistant who wanted to rid himself of a real incompetent whispered: 'Excellency, why not send Franquis? He's a Canary Islander and he'll know how to handle things.'

What a sad miscalculation! If one searched the archives to find an example of Spanish colonial policy at its worst, one would surely select Don Carlos Benites Franquis de Lugo, a vain, arrogant, opinionated fop who never displayed a shred of either courage or discernment but who did distinguish himself as one of the most inept and vengeful Spaniards ever to function overseas. In fact, he was too obtuse even to realize that his assignment to Tejas was a demotion, for he boasted to his friends: 'I'm to restore Spanish dignity in an area which has forgotten what discipline means.'

The character of his administration was defined when he reached San Luis Potosí, where he raged at the local garrison for not having fired enough salutes to honor a dignitary of his exalted stripe: 'I am, after all, Governor of Tejas!' At Saltillo he abused the entire establishment because not all the officials were lined up to meet him as he entered town, but he reserved his most ridiculous behavior for San Juan Bautista, a hard-working post with limited amenities. He was so incensed by the lack of spit-and-polish in the presidio that he dismissed everyone on the spot, and then had to hire them back when he learned that no replacements could reach the forlorn outpost in less than a year.

In Tejas he took immediate dislike to the Saldaña brothers, accusing Fray Damián of being tardy in asking Zacatecas for a replacement for Fray Domingo, and of deepening the Santa Teresa ditch without written authority. But his special scorn was reserved for Captain Alvaro, whom he denigrated as follows:

> Through arrant cowardice he failed to protect the ranch of Misión Santa Teresa against the Apache, causing the Blessed Fray Domingo, may God smile upon his martyrdom, to lose his life most horribly. Later, acting without reason or military competence, he allowed the very Apache who killed Fray Domingo, may God smile upon his martyrdom . . .

He became so indignant as he composed this report, he ended by convincing himself that Alvaro was a cowardly incompetent: 'Handcuff the recreant and throw him in jail, being sure that his legs are tightly chained.'

To demonstrate his own heroism, he organized a hastily put-together expedition to subdue the Apache—about fifty Spaniards and their poorly armed helpers against ten thousand scattered Apache—and his troops would have been annihilated had not Simón Garza and two Yuta scouts detected a concentration of warriors hiding in a mountain pass and prevailed upon the governor to beat a disorganized retreat. As it was, the Apache overtook three stragglers and tortured them viciously.

In this sad year of 1736, Tejas saw Spanish occupancy at its worst. Travel between Béxar and the distant capital at Los Adaes was interdicted by the Apache; food was scarce because the irrigation ditches, without Damián's supervision, were not functioning properly; and all else was in disarray because so many of the able administrators languished in jail with chains about their legs.

It was in this ugly setting that Fray Damián proved what a quintessential Spaniard he was; the first responsibility of any man, even before his duty to God, was to protect his own family. Lands for his son, a husband for his daughter, a job for his nephew, an appointment for his brother-in-law—these were the obligations of a Spanish man.

He was so outraged by the arrest of his brother, and so distraught by what might happen to Benita and her three sons, who were, after all, like his own, that he devised a procedure that would have delighted Machiavelli, for he used stamped paper stolen from the presidio on which to press it:

> Respected Archbishop Vizarrón. Congratulations on your great success as Viceroy of all Mexico. The King could have chosen no one better fitted for that exalted position, and I stand ready as a humble friar to assist you in all you do.
>
> My brother, Captain Alvaro de Saldaña of the Saldañas of Saldaña, has served bravely on the frontier, and I believe there is a law which states that an officer who has seen active duty in any new territory is entitled to six leagues of Crown lands upon retirement. On behalf of my brother, now occupied with other matters, I beg you to make this award.
>
> There is, a few miles west of here in a bend of the Medina, a stretch of land called Rancho El Codo, once occupied by the ranch of this mission. It has now been abandoned because of Apache raids and is of no practical use to anyone until the Apache are subdued. My brother and his wife, in years to come, can tame this land if you will cede it to them now in reward for the hard work they have completed on the frontier of your dominion.

In composing this seditious letter, Damián was aware of three crimes he was committing: The ranch belongs to the church, and I'm stealing it for my family. I'm drafting letters when Governor Franquis has forbidden anyone to do so. And I'm trying to slip my letters past the officials at San Juan Bautista, who have orders to prevent the entry into Mexico proper of clandestine letters. But then he thought of Benita and her children: I must take the chances.

In one of the other missions he found a Franciscan who was heading back to

Zacatecas, and since this friar also hated Franquis, he volunteered to take the risk. The letter reached the archbishop, who was now viceroy, and when he inquired about the reputation of the Saldañas he found it to be exemplary, whereupon he signed a grant awarding former Captain Saldaña more than nine thousand leagues, twenty-five thousand acres, along the Medina.

Later, when he learned of Damián's insubordination, he bore no resentment, for by this time it was evident even to Madrid that Governor Franquis was a horrendous mistake, and he was deposed after little more than a year of his reckless despotism. The unfortunate man had been correct, however, in some of his charges against Damián: he had been so preoccupied with building the mission that he had not attended to the winning of souls, and repeatedly he had left the mission without permission to go wandering through the Apachería. When it became apparent that he was to be removed from Santa Teresa, Damián recommended that Fray Eusebio be given permanent charge of the mission, but Eusebio protested that he was far too humble to warrant such an exalted position. Instead, Zacatecas sent up the trail to Béxar two young friars to assume control at Santa Teresa, one with major orders, to replace Fray Damián, and one with minor, to take over the work done by Fray Domingo.

Damián greeted the two with the warmest brotherhood and even relief, for he knew that his effectiveness had waned. He was fifty-one now, and extremely tired, so that rest in some quiet corner of the Franciscan empire seemed highly desirable, but as the father-principal in Zacatecas had proposed, he would stay on at Santa Teresa until the transition had been smoothly made.

The new friars were enthusiastic young men prepared to repair the situation in Béxar, as they phrased it, and their eagerness to take command provided Damián time to evaluate what he had accomplished on the frontier.

'Nothing,' he told Alvaro and Benita. 'I feel my life's been a waste.' When they asked why, he replied: 'Conversions to Jesus? I haven't brought two dozen souls to salvation.'

'That was Domingo's task,' Benita said consolingly.

'But I've done so little.' He felt old, and futile, and superseded.

'Let's look at what you and I have accomplished,' Alvaro proposed, and he recited their litany of constructive deeds: 'We brought order to a region which knew it not. And we've established regular mail connections with Saltillo.' On he went, naming those simple deeds which taken together represented the quiet triumph of civilization.

But this was not enough for Benita, because she better than either of the brothers thought she knew the cause of Damián's malaise: He sees his life running out, and without a wife or children to represent him when he's gone, he fears it might have been in vain. So she began to tick off his particular achievements: 'You built the irrigation systems, and when Misión Espada needed an aqueduct for its water supply, you showed them how to build one.' Stopping, she formed an arch with her fingers and said: 'Building an arch that will stand is something, believe me.'

She spoke of the compound walls he had erected, of the church, of the houses for the Indians. And then she mentioned the one thing of which she knew he was truly proud: 'You encouraged Simón to finish his Stations of the Cross. Yes, when we three die we shall leave in Béxar an enduring memory.'

When she uttered the word *die*, applying it even to herself, Damián shuddered, and in the silence that followed he acknowledged for the first time that his mournfulness stemmed from growing awareness of his own approaching death: 'Life is so brief. We should have accomplished so much and we did so little.'

'My three sons!' Benita snapped. 'I call them something. And Alvaro's promotion to colonel, I call that something, too.'

Damián could not accept this reprieve: 'Once we had Santa Teresa firmly planted, I should have gone to Nacogdoches and brought order to the frontier. And after Alvaro established order here, he should have gone on to Los Adaes and done the same there. We do a little and claim it was a lot.'

Benita rose from her chair, walked to where Damián sat, and placed her hand on his shoulder: 'We can be proud of the Béxar we built. It will stand here for a long time . . . a long time.' She bit her lip and pressed Damián's shoulder: 'And you can be proud, Damián. Two hundred years from now, when the work of your mission is long completed, your church of Santa Teresa will still stand, and people will applaud it. Yes, I saw that last report of the inspectors from Querétaro: "No mission north of Saltillo, neither in Sonora nor in Tejas, excels what Friar Damián has achieved in Béxar." ' She bent down and kissed him.

Cherishing her touch, he looked up and whispered: 'I suppose it's important that Indians have food if they're to work at Christian duties. And it's very important they have decent houses. And a mission needs walls to keep goodness in and evil out. But I merely built walls. Domingo built souls.'

As the long evening ended he tried to summarize: 'I've one regret I can't erase. I failed to convince Madrid to send us enough real Spanish settlers—farmers who would farm, knitters who would knit.' When he fell silent, Alvaro nodded: 'That was our great failure.'

'I don't discount the Mexican mestizo. All things considered, Simón Garza is one of the best human beings I've ever known, and there must be others like him, but what does the government in Mexico City send us? Rabble, rubbish, and they expect to build a province with such people?'

As he uttered these harsh and true indictments of Spanish policy he did concede that the Council of the Indies had made one serious effort to settle the north, and when he thought of those contentious Canary Islanders calling themselves hidalgos, he had to chuckle: 'They're the best Spaniards we have, and if the king had sent us fifty more boatloads, we could have settled Tejas and conquered Louisiana, too.' He was in this frame of mind one afternoon when the inescapable

Juan Leal Goras, his long beard unkempt, appeared at the mission, his devious mind busily at work.

'Fray Damián, I do not come with pleasant news. Your men here at the mission are drawing down more water than we agreed upon, and I'm starting a lawsuit against you before you escape from Tejas.'

'How many suits have you and I had before, Don Juan?'

'Five, and each one essential for the protection of our interests.'

'And how many have you won?'

'None, but that's not the point. Each suit brought to your attention some grievous wrong which you then had the sense to correct.'

'Why didn't you just come and complain without the lawsuits?'

'Because you damned friars will never listen to mere words. But when I start a suit you clean out your ears.' Pushing his face close to Damián's, he added: 'And don't be fooled by the score, five suits, five losses. How could it be otherwise when the judges are all corrupt? All in the pockets of you friars.'

'All the judges?'

'I've conducted lawsuits in all parts of the world . . .'

'You mean the Canaries and Tejas?'

'It's the same the world over. Judges are corrupt.'

'Suppose that when you do engage your suit, Don Juan, that I bring witnesses to prove that you've dug a branch of your canal for which you have no permit? Which was not in our agreement? And I prove that it is you who are breaking the law, not I?'

'That's the kind of argument corrupt judges listen to.'

At this point Don Juan shifted the discussion dramatically: 'Fray Damián, we couldn't have had a better missionary in Béxar than you. Nor a better captain than your brother. I want him to stay on as a civilian. Why don't you stay, too, as our parish priest?'

The suggestion was so improper to make to a Franciscan, whose mission in life was to wander, not to tend a specific church, that Damián remained mute, but it was also flattering, coming as it did from Goras, who pressed on, interpreting the friar's hesitancy as indecision: 'Our whole community wants to have you stay. You're a man we've learned to trust.' Goras could see the friar thinking intensely, but not even his conniving mind could have guessed what Damián was thinking: I could stay here with Alvaro and Benita and watch their sons grow. My home would not be broken.

Slowly and in some confusion he told Goras: 'I'm a Franciscan. I go where God sends me.' And as soon as Goras left, Damián started making his own secret plans to go on a mission which he felt that God had authorized: once more among the Apache, hoping that this time his example of fearlessness and brotherhood would encourage them to consider peace.

One afternoon, when his preparations were almost complete, he went quietly into his little church, and in the quiet shadows he studied once more Simón Garza's Stations of the Cross, contemplating both their beauty and the religious mystery they represented: How fortunate I was to work with men like Simón and Domingo. They made the things I tried to do doubly effective. And how wonderful that I should have done my work in companionship with Jesus Christ. As he looked at Garza's depiction of the crucifixion he could feel the nails in Christ's hands, the thorns digging into His brow: He was such a good man on earth, such a kind man in heaven.

As he prayed before the last Station he noticed that the two young friars now responsible for Santa Teresa had also entered the church, and unaware that Fray Damián was there, they were talking like young enthusiasts.

'I've found this quarry. Rock so soft you cut it with a saw. But when it's sun-dried in place, it hardens like granite. Tufa they call it.'

'With such stones we could replace the adobe. Make this a real church.'

'Better yet, we could replace everything.'

At this Damián gasped, for he could not imagine sacrificing Simón's glorious Stations. The young friars now discovered him, and realizing that he must have heard their plans, were eager to apologize: 'We didn't know you were here. We're so sorry.'

'No, no! I assure you, it's time to build a new church.'

'Do you really approve?'

'Yes!' he cried vehemently. 'Each man builds only for his generation. Everything he does ought to be restudied . . . improved by those who follow.' He waved his hand deprecatingly. 'I built so poorly. They told me in Zacatecas: "You need build only in wood, for temporary use." ' His voice dropped to a whisper: 'But the heart yearns to build in stone . . . for eternity.'

As he moved his right arm across the spread of the little church his eyes were directed to the Stations of the Cross, and almost as if he were a parent defending his children, he stepped before the carvings and lifted his arms to cover one of them. 'I would not want you to replace these . . . not destroy them, that is.' And his plea was so profound that one of the young friars stooped and kissed his hand.

'We would never have damaged them, Brother Damián. We planned to have them as the heart of our new church.'

'Did you?' he asked in great excitement, and as the two moved about the church, explaining to each other how the roof could be taken off and the walls replaced with minimum confusion, he stayed with them, encouraging them and talking far more than was necessary.

On 21 September 1737, when day and night stood even across the world, Damián left his mission riding a mule, with a donkey in tow. He rode westward toward Rancho El Codo, which Alvaro, Benita and their sons now owned, and here he stopped to utter a long prayer for the soul of Domingo Pacheco as it made its way through purgatory to heaven. He spent his first night at the ranch, and rose refreshed and eager for the serious part of his journey.

Not till three days later did he make contact with any Apache; then he came upon a good-sized band which did not include either the squaw or any of the chiefs who had known him earlier, although there were members who had heard of the decent manner in which he had treated other Apache. They made him as welcome as Apache ever did, but he was aware that some of the younger braves resented him and were advising their fellows against any contact with a Spaniard.

In the two days he spent in the Apachería he found some leaders who were willing to listen when he explained about the advantages of Christianity and an orderly life within the Spanish empire. 'Like me,' he told them, 'you will enjoy the full protection of the king.' He was convinced that the conversion of the Apache was at hand and that God had sent him to be the agent.

But on the third day, in the midst of the most serious explanation of how God and His son Jesus Christ shared responsibilities in heaven, three impatient young braves kicked aside a buffalo skin before which Damián sat, seized him and dragged him to an oak tree, from which they hung him by his thumbs. Then, before the older chiefs could protest, which they showed little inclination to do, the young men stripped the dangling body and began making little cuts across it with their flint scrapers.

They were not deep, just a slash on the arm, or on the leg, but the young men kept darting back and forth, now away from Damián, now toward him, always making another small cut, until his body was red-stained in all its parts.

The young men now called upon the women of the tribe, and with obvious delight the squaws joined them, dancing around and making deeper cuts in parts of the body hitherto untouched. One woman, hair falling across her dark face, evil-smelling, was lifted up to cut at the base of his left thumb, not severing it but nearly so; she and her sisters wanted to see how long it took for the weight of the body to pull the damaged thumb apart, and when this happened, and the body swung sideways, suspended only by the right thumb and twirling in a tight circle, the women shrieked with pleasure, and ran back to stab at the body that now gushed blood from various deep wounds.

Damián, still conscious, for no cuts had yet been made in a vital place, held to his belief that this hideous affair was merely a ritual torture, but now two of the women rushed up and made such deep slashes in the lower part of his stomach that a great shudder ran through all his body, visible to his tormentors.

'He dies! He dies!' they screamed, and this encouraged other women to dance in and stab at him. One was even lifted high enough so that she could cut at his throat, but this terrible pain Damián ignored, for when he stared at her hawklike face he saw not an Apache woman but Benita Liñán. She smiled at him as she had on that first evening in the paseo, and as his blood spurted she leaned forward to cradle him in her arms.

. . . TASK FORCE

San Antonio! Loveliest city in Texas, Venice of the Drylands, its river runs right through the heart of town, providing a colorful waterway for festive barges and an exotic riverside walk along which one could promenade forever. How glad I was to be coming back to a city I had cherished as a boy, for this had been my family's preferred vacation spot.

I remembered well the Buckhorn Saloon, that relic of the Old West, with its fantastic guns and cattle horns. I sneaked my first beer there, my mother watching from a distance, then teasing when I spat it out. Later, when I returned from Europe to find the Buckhorn moved, I felt as if my youth had officially ended.

San Antonio! Conservative, always lagging behind more daring towns like Houston and Dallas, it had long been the largest city in Texas but had now given way to those two giants. Recently it had stunned the state by electing as mayor a man of Spanish heritage, and in decades to come it might once more become a leading city because of the spectacular development of its Spanish-speaking population.

For our April meeting there our staff had enlisted a Franciscan friar who served in one of the city's famous missions, Friar Clarence Cummings, born in Albany, New York. He was respected as an expert on the five surviving missions that line the river like a string of jewels on a necklace, but even before he appeared he caused animosity in our Task Force.

Rusk complained: 'I didn't join this committee to get a course in Catholic theology,' and Quimper chimed in: 'If this keeps up, next meeting will be a public baptism.'

This was too much for Professor Garza, a wise and prudent Catholic: 'What makes you think the friar will try to proselytize you?' and Rusk growled: 'He better not try!'

In two minutes Friar Clarence won the skeptics over, or at least neutralized them. He was a tall, good-looking, robust fellow in his late thirties, clad in a brown robe, bare feet in rugged leather sandals. After the briefest introduction he said in no-nonsense style: 'I hope you'll join me in a cell we use as a projection room, because it's important that you see the slides I've prepared,' and when we were seated with our staff in the cell in the Misión San José, he surprised us with the title of his talk: 'Form and Legacy.'

'Now, what does that mean?' Quimper asked, and he replied: 'That's what I've come to explain.'

With carefully organized notes accompanying a set of excellent colored slides he had prepared from his own drawings and photographs, he began his talk with a promise: 'I propose to concentrate on two subjects only, the physical form of the Spanish mission in its heyday and its legacy for us today. No theology, no moralizing. We begin with this simple question, which must have preoccupied those in charge at the time: "If your mission is to fulfill its purpose, what form should it take?"'

At that he darkened the cell, and with the heavy stone walls enclosing us, we had little difficulty in imagining ourselves back in 1720: 'This drawing—I studied architecture at Cornell before joining the Franciscans at a rather advanced age— shows the landscape you will have to work with. The wandering river. The loop where the horses pasture. The flat land where your mission will ultimately stand.'

With seven choice slides he showed us the terrain of San Antonio as it must have been in 1717, with no mission visible: 'Since you are Spaniards imbued with the traditions of your homeland, you will insist upon centralization, with civilian settlers and their activities clustered closely together. A main difference between Catholic Spain and Protestant America, I've always thought, is that Spain likes to collect its citizens in villages dominated by the church. There they find mutual protection during the night. During the day, when conditions are safer, they can march out to their distant fields. Americans, fed up with clerical control both in Europe and New England, want their homes and farms as far apart as possible. I grew up in rural New York, with the nearest farm half a mile away, and you cannot imagine my amazement when I first saw the crowded little villages of Spain and Italy, one house abutting the other. How do they breathe? I thought. And how do they get to their distant fields each morning?'

He warned us not to attribute this spatial difference to social factors: 'The attacks of Apache and Comanche in Texas were just as severe as the attacks of marauding armies in Europe, but the Americans refused to cluster for protection, while the Spaniards did. In San Antonio your civilians will cluster.'

Under his guidance we did imagine ourselves about to build a mission in 1719, and while we were in this frame of mind he flashed onto the screen a majestic slide of the Alamo, that sacred mission, heavily rebuilt, around which the soul of Texas rallies. This time it had been photographed at dusk, with an ominous cloud to the east, and after it had been on the screen for a few moments, Miss Cobb wiped her eyes with a handkerchief, and I noticed that the staff, then even Quimper, and finally Rusk, followed with similar reactions. Here was a photograph that would affect the heart of any Texan who saw it unexpectedly. Within those walls brave men had died defending a principle in which they believed; on those parapets my ancestor, illiterate Moses Barlow, had given his life for a cause with which he had been associated for less than two weeks.

Rapidly, in a series of beautiful slides, the friar now gave us a swift review of the four other surviving missions, those heavy structures with such delicate names: San José y San Miguel, Nuestra Señora de la Purísima Concepción, San Francisco de la Espada and, the one I preferred, San Juan Capistrano.

He showed them in storm, in sunlight, at evening with birds nesting, and at the break of day with a golden sun exploding over their walls. He showed us architectural fragments, and stretches of reconstructed walls, and windows glowing with majesty, and fonts where the friars washed their feet, and after a while we became so much a part of those missions that we were prepared to listen to what he had to say about us.

'Our five San Antonio missions cannot compare in raw beauty with the handsomely preserved and reconstructed missions of California. We have no one superb example of architecture like Santa Barbara, no outstanding summary of mission life like Fray Junípero Serra's San Carlos Borromeo, and the reason is simple. Since the Spanish missionaries in California were not required to face extremely hostile Indians, they did not have to fortify their buildings. They could enjoy the luxury of graceful architecture and widely spaced structures. But our poor friars in Tejas had to build both a church and a fortress to protect it. Most experts agree that if you want to understand mission life, you must come to San Antonio, because our rude buildings, constructed without guile, represent what the mission experience was all about, and now, at the halfway point in my talk, we're going to leave this cell and move out to see the structures themselves.'

To visit the five missions of San Antonio was like walking slowly and with deep passion into the beginnings of Texas history. Each was different. The Alamo had been massively added to; it was really a museum as well as a sacred gathering place, always cluttered with visitors. San José had also been rebuilt, most faithfully, and best represented what mission life had been like within its spacious walls and its little cubicles for Indians. But the mission that clutched at my heart from the time I first saw it as a boy, giving me insight into those early days, was Capistrano, with its simpler lines, its lovely three-part bell tower and especially that long severe wall with the five cemented archways. It spoke to me with such force that even now I fell silent when I saw it.

The Alamo had awed me; San José had delighted me; but Capistrano, when I stood before its simplicity, invited me to become a member of its congregation, concerned about its canal and the gathering of its crops.

As we gazed at this noble relic, Friar Clarence altered the tenor of his talk: 'So much for the past. You've seen what form these missions took, and a very good one it was. But what concerns us now is the legacy of these missions in the life of modern Texas. So as we stand here I want you to focus on the acequia, the little canal that brought water to the mission. It ran over there, we think, and today when Texas needs water so badly that it dreams up all kinds of tricks to find and save it, it's interesting to remember that our first irrigation ditches were dug by the friars of these San Antonio missions. An unusual Franciscan worked here in the 1720s, Fray Damián de Saldaña, born in Spain, who had great skill in laying out irrigation systems. He could be called the Father of Texan Water Conservation, and the work he did back then is as functional as anything we attempt today. I've often thought that the farmers and ranchers and citrus growers who lead water onto their lands should contribute a mite of their profit for a statue to that far-seeing friar.'

'Was he that important?' Rusk asked, and Quimper jumped in: 'Any man who can show Texas how to use its water is a certified Lone Star hero.'

When we returned to the projection room we were eager to hear how Friar Clarence would link the missions to modern Texas: 'If Spain had given us nothing but these five missions, the legacy would have been monumental. Because they had a fine solid form, they stand today as treasures of the first order. So even though they do reach us in damaged or altered state, we can still thank the prudence of our predecessors that they exist at all, because in such buildings the spiritual history of Texas is preserved.'

But whenever he approached such religious matters, he remembered his promise: 'But we're talking about form and function, not theology, and I would like to close with a reminder of how creatively the mission discharged its obligations in the early 1700s and how, its job done, it made itself obsolete by the end of the century. San Juan Capistrano, which seems to have affected our chairman so deeply, is a case in point. Founded near Nacogdoches in 1716, it died there and its functions were moved to a spot near Austin. Dying again, it was brought to San Antonio, where it enjoyed some success. As many as two hundred and fifty Indian residents. Five thousand head of cattle. Its own cotton fields and woolen manufacturing. But by 1793, when it had to be secularized, only a dozen Christianized Indians, less than twenty cattle, and the looms in disrepair.'

'What does *secularize* mean?' Rusk asked, and I was impressed by the manner in which this extremely capable man was always willing to reveal his ignorance when an unusual word was introduced whose exact meaning he wished to learn.

Instead of replying in words, Friar Clarence flashed onto the wall a series of photographs showing the five missions as they had existed at various times in the nineteenth and twentieth centuries, before restoration began. We were shocked at their pitiful condition: walls down, garbage piled high, roofs fallen in, and ruin in each little church. 'Strictly speaking,' Friar Clarence explained, *'to secularize* means *to convert from religious ownership and use to civil.* Like today when an urban congregation finds that its members have moved to the suburbs and it sells the church building to some little-theater group. In Texas the word carries a special meaning, for when the missions finished trying to tame the frontier and Christianize the Indians, in both of which they had limited success, the system had no further utility. So the church turned the missions back to the civil government. Hungry fingers grabbed for the valuable land, but nobody could see any use for the buildings, so they were allowed to fall into ruin or removed for other construction.' On that mournful note the slides concluded.

When the lights came up I saw that he kept his head bowed, and for some moments he remained that way. Then he smiled and said softly: 'How beautiful a concept! And how suddenly it was outmoded.'

'Why?' Miss Cobb asked, and he turned to her: 'I believe that many meritorious ideas are allowed a life span of about thirty years. Liberalism in France flourished briefly before World War II, made its contribution and vanished. Dr. Spock's theories of child rearing set a generation free, then collapsed in excess. The Erie Canal in my home state. And the mission concept as applied to Texas. All made great contributions, then perished.'

'Railroads outmoded your Erie Canal after its allotted life,' Miss Cobb said. 'And airplanes killed many railroads and almost all the ocean liners. What killed your missions?'

He reflected on this, then chuckled: 'Texas.'

'Now, what does that mean?' Miss Cobb pursued.

'From its start, any Texas mission was destined for a short life. Distances were so great. The Indians were so intractable. So often, when its work failed in one place, it moved on to some other challenge.'

'If that's true, why do I see five stone buildings?'

'Ah!' he cried, a light burning in his eyes. 'You can never convince a man like the Fray Damián of whom I spoke that what he's doing is temporary. Once he positions that first adobe, he begins to build for eternity.'

'But you say his mission has disappeared?'

'Others killed it, not he. Damián succeeded beyond imagination. His form vanished. Completely destroyed. But the legacy survives.'

As he said this his face assumed a radiance which warmed us: 'I promised you at the beginning: no theology, no moralizing; just form and legacy. But you must have deduced from what I've said that the Texas missions would provide us with only a limited legacy if they were mere architecture. Their grandeur is twofold: art plus the spiritual force which evoked that art. The friars could not have survived in this wilderness without some guiding principle, and it was Christianity. There were drunkards among the friars, and some who chased after Indian girls, and others who had never known vocation, but there were also men of supreme devotion, and upon their efforts the future city of San Antonio and the state of Texas were founded. That is their legacy.'

His words had an astonishing result. 'Friar Clarence,' Rusk said in his deep and rumbling voice, 'you ought to change your name. It doesn't sound appropriate here in a nest of missions.'

'What would you advise?'

'Friar Ignacio. Friar Bernardo. Something Spanish.'

'I suppose we're all stuck with the names we were given. Rusk seems totally inappropriate for a man of your power.'

'What had you in mind?'

'Midas. Croesus. Maybe Carnegie.'

'You gave us a terrific explanation, Friar Clarence. Now tell me, how much would it cost to print your lecture in a book? To be given free to all the schools in Texas?'

I was surprised that a Texas billionaire would concern himself with pennies, but he addressed the problem scientifically, as if it involved great sums: 'Barlow, call a printing house and find out.' When I reported: 'They say that they can give you a black-and-white edition for about sixty cents a copy,' he gave one of his rare smiles, and said: 'That seems reasonable. Friar Clarence, I'd like to print such a book. Give young people the real story of the missions, just as you gave it to us. You're a very solid young man and your ideas merit circulation.'

Friar Clarence said tentatively that he would be honored, but I could see from his hesitation that he expected some catch, and Rusk revealed it: 'Of course, I'd want to eliminate that last part on the religious bit.'

Instantly the young scholar said: 'Then I wouldn't be interested, because obviously you've missed the whole point of my talk. Form and function were the outer manifestations of the mission. The heart and core was the religious conviction, and don't you forget it. Publish a book about missions and ignore their religious base? Oh, no!'

But Rusk was a clever man, and he said something now which absolutely stunned me in its simplicity and moral deviousness: 'I mean a booklet with illustrations—your excellent drawings, your photographs in color.' You could see that Friar Clarence was startled by this new dimension, but you could also see the poison of vanity working in him; Ransom Rusk was the serpent in paradise, tempting not Eve with an apple but a Franciscan friar with an image of a fine book in which his words would be distributed to Texas schools.

Very slowly he said: 'I would like to see that done, Mr. Rusk,' and Rusk rose and clapped him on the shoulder, whereupon Friar Clarence added: 'But I would insist upon that last section, for it would be the soul of my book.' And in that simple statement the book became his and not Rusk's.

Now Rusk had to think. He certainly did not want to subsidize Catholic propaganda, and he temporized by asking our staff: 'How much would the cost be elevated if we used color? Maybe sixteen full pages of his best photos and drawings?' The young people consulted on this, recalling projects of a similar nature on which they had been engaged, and they suggested: 'Total cost, about two and a half dollars a copy, but only if you print in large batches.'

'That would be possible. Now, Friar Clarence, here's what I propose. That you and I will agree that Miss Cobb here, a good Protestant, and Professor Garza, an equally good Catholic, will study those last remarks to see if they're acceptable. I mean, not rank proselytizing. Agreed?'

The young friar considered this for some moments, then extended his hand, but as Rusk reached to grasp it, Friar Clarence said to Garza: 'I'll depend on you to see that the vital material stays in,' and Rusk responded as he accepted the hand: 'I'll depend on you, Miss Lorena, to see that the truth of The Black Legend is not completely whitewashed.'

III
EL CAMINO
REAL

NUEVA ESPAÑA Y EL CAMINO REAL
1788-1792

All public roadways in the Spanish Empire were Caminos Reales, royal highways, but those segments connecting Vera Cruz and Los Adaes became a principal avenue of empire

0   MILES   200

Santa Fé

COMANCHERIA

Red River

Rio Brazos

Rio Sabine

Natchitoches

El Paso del Norte

APACHERIA

Nacogdoches

Los Adaes

Rio Pecos

Rio Colorado

TEJAS

Rio Grande del Norte

Rio Medina

Rancho El Codo

Béjar

Rio San Antonio

Chihuahua

San Juan Bautista

Rio Nueces

COAHUILA

Laredo

Monclova

Saltillo

Culiacán

GOLFO
DE
MEXICO

OCEANO PACIFICO

Zacatecas

San Luis Potosí

Compostela

Guadalajara

Jalapa

Ciudad de México

Vera Cruz

DON RAMÓN DE SALDAÑA, ELDEST SON OF COMMANDANT ALVARO AND BENITA, was sixty-six years of age and sprightly in mind and limb. Often he reflected upon the three great joys in his life and the two inconsolable tragedies.

He was sole owner of the vast Rancho El Codo, twenty-five thousand acres named after an elbow of the Medina, that river which marked the boundary between the two provinces of Coahuila and Tejas. It was a rich and varied parcel, well watered, and stocked with thousands of cattle, sheep and goats. Most important, it bordered a segment of Los Caminos Reales, that system of royal highways which reached out like spokes from Mexico City, the hub of New Spain. This portion reached from Vera Cruz through Mexico City to San Antonio de Béjar, as the town was now called, to the former capital of Tejas at Los Adaes, and its presence along the ranch meant that Don Ramón could sell provisions to the royal troops that patrolled the vital route; Rancho El Codo was an inheritance of which he was justly proud.

He was also inordinately pleased that he had, like his grandfather in Spain, sired seven sons in a row without, as he boasted, 'the contaminating intrusion of a single daughter.' The humorous honorific, Hidalgo de Bragueta, Sir Knight of the Codpiece, was not customarily used in Mexico, but Don Ramón liked to apply it to himself.

His third and chief pride in these declining years of a long frontier life was his granddaughter Trinidad, thirteen years old and as charming a child as could be found in the northern provinces. Petite and dark-haired, she was a lively young lady with a wonderfully free and outgoing nature better suited to a canter over the mesquite range than to an afternoon of sipping hot chocolate with the mission friars, and although she was not a vain girl, preferring at this stage in her life a good horse to a pretty dress, she did like to look trim and paid attention to her appearance.

The thing that strangers noticed most about Trinidad was her curious face, for although it was beautiful, with a flawless light complexion bespeaking her unsullied Spanish blood, her mouth was strangely tilted, creating the impression of a timeless smile. Her lower teeth had grown in most unevenly, preventing her jaws from meeting naturally, and this made the left corner of her mouth dip down while the right turned up. Had her other features been less than perfect, this defect might have marred her looks; instead, it created a kind of additional interest, for when she came up ready to curtsy to a stranger, her unusual mouth seemed to be smiling inquisitively as if to say 'Hello, what have we here?' And when she did speak, a very slight lisp, or unevenness, added to her air of mystery and to her attractiveness.

She was a clever child; her doting grandfather had taught her to read Cervantes, stories from the Bible, and even the less salacious of the romances being published in Mexico City; and a French cleric who had served some years earlier in one of Béjar's five missions had taught her his native language. She also had a marked talent for drawing, and so skillful were her rough sketches of people in the town that everyone who saw them could recognize this pompous priest or that officious occupant of the governor's residence. She was at her best, however, on horseback, for she was at that age when young girls are almost reluctant to face maidenhood and an interest in boys, and seek intuitively to cling to girlhood, lavishing their considerable affection on horses. In Trinidad de Saldaña's case it was one particular horse, a spirited brown gelding called Relampaguito, Little Lightningbolt. She would allow no one to abbreviate this rather long proper name or to give her horse a nickname; he was Relampaguito, a horse of importance, and she cared for him as if he were a much-loved younger brother.

It was Don Ramón's pleasure to ride forth in the early morning with Trinidad at his side, leave the town of Béjar where the Saldañas had their town house, and ride toward the Misión Santa Teresa. From the presidio he would pick up an armed guard and continue on to the edges of his ranch, whose new pastures, acquired from one of the Canary Island families, now reached eastward to those belonging to the mission.

Grandfather and granddaughter rode easily, side by side, admiring the good work begun by Uncle Damián in building this mission and later reveling in the splendid ranch the family had acquired through the energy and the agility of the Saldaña brothers. At such times Trinidad liked to ride on ahead, act as if she were a military scout and call back 'I see Apache!' Then both grandfather and grand-daughter would race their horses toward some spot on the horizon and rein in as if they saw Apache campfires, although once in a while Don Ramón would warn: 'You must never joke about the Apache. At a place like that down there my uncle Damián was martyred and your father killed,' and then the past became painfully real for the little girl.

The great tragedy of Don Ramón's life was that although he had sired seven sons, all had died during his own lifetime: four in service to the king—two in Spain, two in Mexico; one of cholera, which swept the northern provinces periodically; and two tortured and scalped by the Apache. All were dead, and Don Ramón sometimes recalled bitterly the words of that wise ancient who said: 'In peace, sons bury their fathers; in war, fathers bury their sons.' In Tejas it had always been war, threat of war against the French, real war against the Apache, comic war against the pirates who tried to infiltrate from the Caribbean, unending war against nature itself. And what made the slaughter of his sons so difficult to accept was that often the wars in which they engaged were later proved to have been unjustified. His fourth son, Bartolomé, had been slain during a skirmish with the Austrians, and shortly thereafter a solid peace with Austria came into effect. Same with the French. From his earliest days Don Ramón had been taught to fear them, but now all the territories along the Mississippi River which had once been French were Spanish, and to make things even more bewildering, just a few years ago a Paris-born Frenchman living in Natchitoches, had he but lived a little while longer, would actually have served as governor of Tejas.

All his sons dead! Don Ramón, more than most, had witnessed the fearful price paid by those Spaniards who had sought to bring civilization to Tejas: the loneliness of the first missions, the years of unrewarded drudgery in the presidios, the martyrs among the friars, the slain heroes like his sons, the anguish of the governors who tried to rule without funds or adequate police facilities, and the backbreaking efforts of the good women like his late wife who supported their men, making each new house just a little more civilized, just slightly more removed from the roughness of the frontier.

Once when his sorrows seemed almost unbearable, he clasped his granddaughter to him and cried: 'Trinidad, if this forsaken place ever becomes habitable, remember your fathers and your mothers who strove to make it so.' She was ten at the time, and said: 'I have only one mother. I had only one father.' And he swept his arms grandly over the entire town and cried with passion: 'All the good Spaniards here are your fathers and mothers. They have all lived so that you might live. And you shall live so that those who come after . . . when this is a great city . . .' He kissed her head. 'They will all be your children, Trinidad, yours and mine and Fray Damián's.'

'Even the Canary Islanders?' she asked, for relations with those proud and arrogant people had never been good.

'Today even they are my brothers,' Don Ramón said, but he had not really intended going that far.

Don Ramón, his granddaughter Trinidad and her mother Engracia, widow of Agustín de Saldaña slain by the Apache, lived in a beautiful rambling adobe-walled house facing the Military Plaza that stretched westward from the still-unfinished church of San Fernando. Passers-by were charmed by the Saldaña home: 'Its walls are always so neatly whitewashed, and the seven wooden beams which jut out from the front wall are always hung with pots of flowers or with golden gourds or strings of corn and chilies drying in the sun. Don Ramón's house looks as if happy people live inside.'

Behind this inviting wall hid a nest of eleven interconnected small rooms forming a large horseshoe, the center of which was a lovely patio opening onto an even more beautiful garden where stone benches faced a fountain that gushed cool water whenever Indian servants worked the foot pumps. No one who stepped inside this house or into the garden for even two minutes could deceive himself into thinking that it was a French house or English, and certainly it wasn't German. This was an evocation of Spain set down in the wilderness of New Spain, and as such it epitomized the ancient Spanish preoccupation with protecting families; stout walls safeguarded them from outside terrors, and a tiny chapel enabled them to hold private religious services. And just as the house protected the family, so the family jealously guarded its prerogatives, prepared to do almost anything, including murder, to defend them. The Saldaña family was fighting to avoid submersion in a sea of mestizo and Indian faces, determined to resist intruders coming down El Camino Real from the new Spanish possession of Louisiana or from the uncivilized Yankee lands farther east and north.

And therein lay the second tragedy in Don Ramón's life, festering, causing him nagging grief: his blood was pure Spanish, nobody could challenge that, but it was of diminished quality because he had not been born in Spain. He was a criollo, not a peninsular; that honored name was reserved for those actually born in the Iberian peninsula. Criollos could have pride; peninsulares had glory.

Since the only chance the Saldañas of Béjar had to reestablish their honor was to marry Trinidad to some gentleman of Spain, this became almost an obsession with Don Ramón, and one afternoon in 1788 he said to Engracia: 'Each day our little girl looks more like a woman. Please tell me how we can find her a suitable husband . . . a real Spaniard . . . from Spain.'

Engracia Sarmiento de Saldaña, having been born in central Spain to a minor branch of the notable Sarmiento family and brought to Mexico, where her father served as governor of a province to the south, appreciated the wisdom of getting the Mexican Saldañas back into the mainstream of Spanish life: 'I never forget, Don Ramón, that your father Alvaro and your saintly uncle Damián, may God bless his soul in heaven, were true-born Spaniards. You, unfortunately, were not, through no fault of your own or your father's.'

Don Ramón took no offense at this sharp reminder of his deficiency; he was always ready to lament, even in public, that he was not a peninsular, and he had witnessed too many instances in which families of distinction from the best parts of Spain had slowly deteriorated in Mexico: 'You've seen what happens, Engracia. They come here as proud peninsulares, and first they allow their sons and daughters to marry locals. Good families and all that, but born like me here in Mexico. With that relaxation to begin with, it isn't long before someone marries a mestizo. I've seen it a dozen times. Beautiful girls. Some sing like angels, sew well, keep a good house, tend their babies. But they *are* half Indian. And look what happens to *their* children. Look at young Alenón. He finally did it, married an Indian girl.'

He sighed at the incalculable loss. 'The famous Alençón blood, lost in a desert of Indian adobes.'

'Is there any way we could send Trinidad to Spain?' her mother asked.

'If Ignacio or Lorenzo had survived when they went to Spain . . . but they died. I suppose we have family, somewhere. How about the Sarmientos?'

'My family would be very contemptuous of any girl born in Mexico . . .' She said this without rancor or self-pity, but the manner in which her voice trailed off betrayed the enormous damage she had incurred by marrying a criollo.

'I knew our former governor. Not well, but I did know him.'

'You know what he said when he sailed home. "May the Indian dust of this forsaken land never dirty my boots again." I doubt that he would welcome her.'

'I've been thinking, Engracia, that perhaps you and I ought to travel down to Mexico City. If we started next year in February, Trinidad would be fourteen. She's an extremely attractive girl, you know that. Her quizzical little smile, it tears my heart, and there must be many young officers from Spain . . .'

'I would travel a great distance, Father, to find my daughter a proper husband.'

'Let me speak to Veramendi about it.'

And so the serious discussions started, with Don Ramón walking sedately the three blocks that separated the Béjar residences of these two leading families.

On Calle Soledad, for many years the only real street in town, the Béjar branch of the powerful Veramendis of Saltillo owned two elegant many-roomed houses, facing a common patio which was itself a work of art: seven old trees for shade and graveled walks graced with statues carved by Indian workmen who had copied Italian engravings of religious figures. Half a dozen niches in the adobe walls contained flowerpots holding vines whose creeping ends flowed down across the wall, forming beautiful patterns when the sun shone through them.

In the larger house lived the head of the local Veramendis, an austere man who kept to himself, supervising the education of his many children. His very able son Juan Martín, now ten, could already speak three languages—Spanish, French and English—because the wise old man could foresee that these latter tongues were bound to become important in Tejas.

Don Ramón did not go to the big house, but to the smaller one in which lived his good friend Don Lázaro Veramendi, of the lesser branch, who had grand-daughters of his own and therefore the same problems as the Saldañas.

'Good day, dear friend!' Don Ramón called out as he entered the patio and saw Veramendi reading under one of the gnarled trees. 'I remember the day that tree was planted . . . how many years ago?'

The two men, each approaching seventy, discussed the origin of this garden and agreed that it must have been planted either just before or just after the arrival of the Canary Islanders, sixty years earlier. 'Those were exciting days,' Don Lázaro said.

'And so are these. Do you feel the changes that overtake us?'

'I do.' He was about to specify what changes concerned him when two of his granddaughters, girls of eleven and fourteen, ran onto the patio from one door of their home, past the flower beds and through a door of the larger house. As they ran the two old men studied their untrammeled movement.

'It's them I've been thinking of,' Don Ramón said, and when Veramendi looked up in surprise, Saldaña added: 'I mean all the girls of our families. Our Trinidad especially. Where will she find a husband?' Before Don Lázaro could respond, he clarified his remark: 'I mean, of course, a respectable Spanish husband? Where?'

Veramendi, proud of his family's distinctions, astonished his friend by saying judiciously: 'I no longer worry about that, Don Ramón. We're Spanish, yes, and proud to be, but neither you nor I was born in Spain, and we do well in Béjar. I think our children will do the same.'

'But maintaining the Spanish blood, things Spanish, a sense of Castile and Aragon—how can we ensure that if our granddaughters . . .'

'They'll marry as events dictate, and do you know one thing, Don Ramón? I doubt if any of them will ever see Spain. This is the new land. This is our homeland now.'

'Wouldn't you prefer . . . ? How many granddaughters have you—four, five?'

'I have six, thanks to God's bounty,' Veramendi said, 'and five of them will need husbands. María's to be a nun, by the grace of the Virgin, so we need only five young men.'

'And you'll be just as happy if they've been born in Mexico?'

'I was born in Mexico and I yield to no man . . .'

'I mean, wouldn't you be just a bit prouder—more secure, I mean—if your girls were married to men born in Spain? Men with honest Spanish roots?'

Don Lázaro clapped his hands and laughed at his friend: 'You have roots in Spain—the town of Saldaña, if my memory serves me. And what the devil good has it ever done you?'

Don Ramón pondered this difficult question a long time, his brow deeply wrinkled. But then a benign smile appeared: 'I often think of those dark centuries when Spain writhed under the heel of Muhammadanism. There was every reason for my ancestors to marry with the infidels. Power, money, an appointment at the Moorish court. But they protected their Spanish blood with their lives. No Moors in our family. No Jews. We starved, lived in caves, and in the end we triumphed.'

'Do you feel about mestizos the way your ancestors felt about Moors?'

'I do. To be the carrier of pure Spanish blood fortifies the spirit. On that awful day when messengers galloped in to inform my father that his brother, Fray Damián, had been tortured to death by the Apache, our family found courage in the fact that we were Spaniards, untouched by Mexico, and that as Spaniards we had to behave in a certain way . . . to preserve our honor.'

'So what did your Spanish father do?'

'He handed me a gun, although I was barely fifteen, called for volunteers, and set forth to punish the Apache. We killed sixty-seven.'

'And what did that prove? Forty years later the Lipan Apache were still there, and they killed two of your sons not ten miles from where they killed your uncle.'

'Finally we drove them back. In the end, Spain always conquers.'

'So in their place we got the Comanche, and they're worse.'

Don Ramón fell silent, put his left thumbnail against his teeth and studied this amazing Veramendi, who had from boyhood been so willing to accept Béjar as it was, never cursing the Indians, never brawling with the Canary Islanders, never arguing with the friars about the allocation of river water to the irrigation ditches. He had always whistled a lot, and now he whistled easily as if any problems really worth serious worry lay far in the distance.

'Don Lázaro, I don't think you'd worry even if one of your granddaughters married a mestizo!'

Veramendi pondered this, and said: 'It seems highly likely, what with the dilution of our Spanish blood, that two or three of my girls might have to find their husbands among the locals.' When Saldaña gasped, Veramendi added an interesting speculation: 'Let's be perfectly reasonable, Don Ramón. The Spanish army doesn't send many peninsulares to Mexico any more, only a scattering of officers now and then, and damned few of them ever get north to this little town. We don't even get any peninsular priests any more. Saltillo's no better. I looked last time I was down there. And in Mexico City the grand families pick off the young Spaniards as soon as they arrive from Vera Cruz. So true Spaniards are gone. No hope at all.

'That leaves young men like you and me as we were half a century ago. Spanish, but born in Mexico. And there's a limited number of us, believe me. I saw it in Saltillo. So what does that leave our granddaughters, yours and mine? It leaves a crop of fine young men half Spanish, half Indian, and you have some of the best on your own ranch.'

Saldaña was shocked: 'Would you allow a mestizo ranch hand to marry one of your granddaughters?'

Veramendi, not willing to confess that he had been preparing himself for just such an eventuality, changed the conversation dramatically: 'Do you want to know what I really think, old friend?' When Don Ramón said: 'I'm afraid to listen, the way you've been raving,' the old man said firmly: 'I suspect that you and I are looking in the wrong direction. Right now we face south, looking always at Mexico City, from where God in His merciful bounty sends us all the good things we enjoy. Right now we look south along El Camino Real as our blessed lifeline. Dear friend, let's face realities. Let's change our position and look north. The good things of this life henceforth will not come up El Camino Real, they will come down it—from Louisiana, or from los Estados Unidos.'

When Don Ramón failed to respond, his friend said, as he gazed north: 'So what I really suppose is that my granddaughters will marry Frenchmen posing as Spaniards. Or even worse, one of those rough norteamericanos.'

'But aren't all americanos Protestants?'

'Men can change, especially where a beautiful girl's involved . . . and free land.' Again Don Ramón was flabbergasted, whereupon Don Lázaro clapped him on the knee: 'Since your little Trinidad is about the prettiest in town, you may find yourself completely surprised at whom she marries.'

At last Don Ramón found his voice: 'By God, Don Lázaro, you sound as if you wouldn't even stop at Indians.'

'I don't want them for these girls,' Don Lázaro snapped instantly, 'because the Indians are not yet civilized. But the granddaughters of these girls, they might be very proud to marry the type of Indian who's going to come along.'

'When I was a boy, if the viceroy heard a Spaniard utter such a statement . . . off to the dungeons at San Juan de Ulúa.'

At this, Veramendi leaped from the stone bench, danced about the garden, and chuckled with delight. Then he took a position staring down at Saldaña and reminded him of a few important facts:

'Two years ago I was sent by our viceroy to New Orleans to help our Spanish Governor Miró bring that French city into our system, and I never worked with a better man. Judicious, far-seeing, patriotic. I wish we had a governor like that in Tejas. He preached constantly to those below him that our new province of Louisiana was to be a haven for people of all kinds, French in the majority, norteamericanos next in number, Spaniards of the better sort ruling fairly and running the businesses, with many, many blacks and Indians doing the work. All nations and yes, unwisely, all religions. Governor Miró accepted everyone as his brother.

'Well, you can guess that his liberal attitude toward religion got him into immediate trouble, because officials in Mexico supported the Inquisition, which is a fine institution, if properly run. But Madrid sent out a wild-eyed, savage-spirited Spanish priest named Father Sadella to head our Inquisition. Yes, Father Sadella came out to New Orleans to establish religious courts, religious jails and religious gibbets from which he was going to hang every damned Protestant or free-thinker like me and maybe even Governor Miró himself. And when Louisiana was sanctified he was going to hang all the Protestants in Tejas. He had lists of names.

'He was a terrifying man, Don Ramón, and had he come down here, in due course you would have found yourself entangled in his webs. For what? I don't know, but he would have found something you had done or hadn't done. He was tall and very thin and had deep-set eyes which darted from side to side as if he constantly expected a dagger. Imagine, jails and gibbets established in Tejas!

'Governor Miró assembled eight of us he could trust and asked us bluntly: "What can we do to save ourselves from this dreadful man?" and I said: "Murder him, tonight," but Miró warned against such action: "If we did that, Madrid would have to respond, and all of us would be hanged." A Spanish officer from Valencia, a pious man I believe, for I saw him always in church, made the best proposal: "Let us arrest him right now, and throw him onto the *Princesa Luisa,* which is ready to sail, and then hope that the ship sinks." A very wise priest born in Mexico City added the good touch: "We'll march him aboard at ten in the morning with the whole town at the docks to jeer at him and laugh. We'll make a holiday of it as if all Louisiana approved what we're doing. And that will draw Father Sadella's ugly teeth."

'So we had a festival, even the firing of a cannon. I arranged for that. And that's how we saved Tejas from the leg irons and gallows of the Holy Inquisition.'

Don Ramón studied his knuckles, which had grown taut as the tale unfolded: 'Why do you tell me something for which you could still be thrown in jail?'

'Because it represents the new truth, as I see it. Mexico City would never have dared oppose the Inquisition. New Orleans did. Down El Camino Real, from our new holdings in Louisiana, will come new interpretations of old customs. And along the same road, from los Estados Unidos, will come new ways of doing things, a new sense of government, and lusty, energetic young men who will marry our girls.'

'Will you permit that?'

'Who can stop it?'

'Is the old Spain dead?'

'It's been dead for fifty years. I could have built a great city here. All it needed was two thousand Spaniards of the better sort ruling fairly, supervising things and running the businesses. But they were never forthcoming. Spain had its chance, but passed it by.'

The two men, debris from a flood of empire which had receded with terrible swiftness, sat gloomily for some minutes, seeing in imagination the royal road along which the promised help should have come but never did. Then, as if by malignant design, a bugle sounded from the presidio and the army contingent marched out for one of its weekly parades, seeking to prove that Spain still had the power to defend its farthest outpost.

Two aspects of the march impressed them when they went to the gate to watch: the slovenliness of the drill and the incredibility of the uniforms. Only the two officers, Captain Moncado and Lieutenant Marcelino, were properly outfitted. In gold trousers and smartly polished boots they made a stiff and handsome pair, very military in appearance except that Marcelino had no proper hat. He marched bareheaded, which made him seem two feet shorter than his commander and somewhat ridiculous.

The enlisted complement for Béjar was ninety-four, but of these, only sixty-four had bothered to show up, and of those, only two groups of three each wore uniforms, but no one outfit was complete. The front rank wore fine blue uniforms, but here again hats were missing. The second group, marching immediately behind, wore green uniforms that had been popular thirty years earlier; this time only one hat was missing.

The eight men in the next two ranks also had uniforms, each one completely different, and behind them came twenty men dressed in either leather jackets or army trousers, but never both. And whichever half they did have was preposterously patched with cloth of another match.

The next ranks wore no uniforms at all, only the floppy white garments of the countryside, and of these men, half had no shoes; they marched barefoot. Unbelievably, the last fifteen in the parade had no hats, no shirts, no shoes; they marched in trousers only and these of every possible length and style.

At the front, Captain Moncado and Lieutenant Marcelino moved smartly and in step as if they were on duty in Spain, as did the six enlisted men who had matching uniforms. But the rest straggled along, kicking dust, out of step, neither neat nor erect, for all the world more like field hands returning to town at the end of a wearing day than soldiers representing Spanish dominion overseas.

Two-thirds of the troops had guns, but of every imaginable make and age; surely, if the poorest dozen were fired, they could not be reloaded in less than ten minutes. Some of the remaining men carried lances, shields or swords, and many had no formal weapon whatever except a club hacked from some tree. And this was the military might which was supposed to protect Béjar and its six missions, safeguard the roads, and defend the outlying farms from the skilled attacks of some four thousand Comanche, those dreaded horse Indians from the north who had captured a few Spanish steeds, bred them, and galloped south to lay waste all Spanish settlements. This was the grandeur of Spain in the year 1788.

Don Ramón, remembering how meticulous his father had been about maintaining the dignity of Spain when he occupied the Béjar presidio, stalked over to the ramshackle building after the parade ended to rebuke Lieutenant Marcelino: 'You could at least wear a proper hat.'

'The government provides us with no hats,' the young man snapped. 'We get damned little of anything, really.'

'If you had any self-respect, you'd buy your own.'

'We're supposed to, but we get no money.'

'And your men! Shocking. Can't you discipline them?'

'If I say one unkind word, make one threat, they desert.'

'You should be ashamed of yourself, young man,' and from that day Don Ramón avoided the presidio and its unruly complement, for he remembered when Spain was Spain.

When Veramendi learned of his friend's unfortunate run-in with the military, he said: 'Old friend, you aren't going to like this, but the two thousand real men who never arrived didn't have to be notable Spaniards like your ancestors and mine. They could very nicely have been Canary Islanders, if they'd had the courage of that fellow who gave your father and uncle so much trouble.' He whistled for one of his granddaughters, and when the girl Amalia appeared, a saucy child of fourteen with bright eyes and big white teeth, he asked her to fetch a book from his desk. As she disappeared Don Ramón asked: 'Would you really let her marry a mestizo?' and Veramendi said with a smile: 'Who else will be left?'

When the girl returned, Don Lázaro caught her by the hand: 'Stay! I want you to hear this. I want you to hear how you should speak to little men who assume authority.' Then, turning to Saldaña, he explained: 'This is a copy of the letter which our famous Canary Islander, Juan Leal Goras, sent to the viceroy in Mexico City, demanding, not begging, for some additional right he was entitled to. Listen to how he begins his respectful plea:

> 'Juan Leal Goras, Español y Colonizador a las Ordenes de Su Majestad, Quien Dios Protege, en Su Presidio de San Antonio de Véxar y Villa de San Fernando, Provincia de Tejas también llamada Nuevas Filipinas, y Señor Regidor de esta Villa. Agricultor.'

Slapping his granddaughter lovingly on the shoulder, he said: 'That's the kind of man we need in Tejas. Give your full credentials, like some dignitary, then sign yourself 'Farmer.' When the girl laughed, not understanding the force of what her grandfather was saying, he drew her to him, kissed her, and said: 'And that's the kind of man I want you to marry, Amalia. Someone with spunk.'

When Trinidad learned that she would be traveling to Mexico City she wanted to kiss her mother and her grandfather for their generosity, but she was so overcome by love that she stood in the white-walled room where they took chocolate in the afternoons and lowered her head for fear she might cry. Then a most winsome smile took possession of her curiously tilted mouth, and she gave a childlike leap in the air and shouted: 'Olé! How wonderful!'

She maintained this level of excitement for several days as the great trip was planned. Since it was over a thousand miles to the capital, any citizen of Béjar would be fortunate to make the journey once in a lifetime. Trinidad, supposing that she would see the grand city once and no more, packed her two trunks with the greatest of care.

Béjar at this time was not large, less than two thousand inhabitants, but since the old capital of Los Adaes had been abandoned, it had become the principal Spanish establishment north of Monclova. And because of a startling change in viceregal administration, it now had additional responsibility. A vast collection of provinces, including California, New Mexico and Tejas in the north, along with six huge provinces like Coahuila and Sonora to the south, had been united to form the Provincias Internas with their capital at Chihuahua, but since this city was five hundred miles to the west and connected only by Indian trails to Béjar, most local decisions had to be made in the Tejas capital. For extended periods, Béjar was left on its own.

The town was in a fine setting. Four waterways now ran in parallel courses from north to south, lending color and charm with their shade trees: to the east, the original canal servicing the missions; next, the lively San Antonio; to the west, the irrigation ditch that Fray Damián had laid out for the Canary Islanders in 1732; and farther to the west, a little creek whose water serviced expanding agricultural fields. These waterways created four clearly defined available land areas, and by 1788 each was beginning to fill up with the houses of permanent settlers.

Well to the east, on the far side of the river, stood the unfinished buildings of the dying mission that would one day be named the Alamo, and around it clustered a few mean houses occupied by Indians. On the west bank, within the big loop where the horses pastured, stood eleven well-constructed houses belonging to leading mestizos, and along the rest of the river rose twenty-six other houses of a mixed population. The finest area was that between the westernmost irrigation ditches, and on it stood fifty-four homes clustered about the center of the town; the Saldañas and the Veramendis lived here. West of all the ditches were the scattered homes of farmers.

The carefully recorded census showed: Spaniards (peninsular and criollo) 862; mestizos 203; Indians 505; other colored (Indian-Black, oriental) 275; blacks (all slaves) 37; total 1,882. These citizens performed a rich assortment of duties: ten merchants, each with his own shop; ten tailors; six shoemakers; four river fishermen; four carpenters; two blacksmiths; one barber and one digger of sewers. Lawyers: none.

There were also more than six hundred Indians living in or near the six missions, but the fortunes of these once-valuable institutions had begun to decline so badly that there was talk of closing them down; indeed, a Father Ybarra had recently been sent north to report on that advisability. He was working now on his recommendations, and since he was a gloomy, unpleasant man, the citizens assumed that his document would be, too.

The town was dominated by the presidio, with its ninety-four military misfits, and the large church started in 1738 by the Canary Islanders. Age had softened this building into an object of some beauty, if one appreciated the harsh desert style adopted by its Franciscan architects.

Trinidad loved Béjar and made each of its corners her own, begging her mother to take her first to some site across the river, then to the lovely missions to the south. The best part of town, she thought, was the two plazas facing the church: a smaller one to the east toward the river, a larger to the west toward the hill country beyond. In these plazas she and her friends had whiled away many hours of childhood. But lately Trinidad enjoyed even more the family journeys to what she called 'our family's mission,' Santa Teresa, where the handsome carvings by Simón Garza depicted the Stations of the Cross. She preferred the one in which Santa Veronica wiped Christ's face with her cloth, and the other in which the man stooped to help Jesus carry his cross, for these showed the kindness of humanity; the others showed only aspects of its brutality. The jamming down upon Christ's head of the crown of thorns made her feel the thorns piercing her own forehead, while the actual crucifixion was too painful to contemplate.

After one of these journeys, she asked her grandfather about the carvings: 'Is it true that the man who made them was an Indian?'

'Half Indian. His Spanish blood enabled him to be an artist.'

'Is it true that he was the grandfather, or something like that, of Domingo, who works at the ranch?'

'How do you know Domingo?'

'We played together. I taught him to read. He taught me to ride.'

'You stay away from Domingo.'

'Why?'

'Because I tell you to.'

That night Don Ramón had only a broken sleep, for he was tormented by visions of his granddaughter marrying some savage Indian from the mountains of Mexico, and he knew he must prevent this. Early next morning, before the women were up, he called for his best horse, but before he could leave for the ranch, Trinidad, who had heard the clatter of hooves, bounded into the stables in her nightdress.

'Where are you going?' she called.

'Where you're not welcome. Go back to bed,' and before she could protest, for he had always allowed her to accompany him on his travels, he had spurred his horse and headed for the gates of the presidio. There he rounded up a company of armed men to protect him, and together they rode westward over the plains in the early morning sun.

He rode for several hours, until he came to the cluster of buildings from where his men worked the vast, unfenced ranch of El Codo with its thousands of cattle that fed the little town of Béjar. There was a house for the Garza family, whose men had been supervisors for decades, a barn for storing feed, three different sets of corrals, a line of low shacks for the Indians and a good stable for the horses. There was also a large lean-to under which the awkward carts with their creaking solid wheels were kept. It was a handsome assembly of adobe buildings, none pretentious and all well fitted to the terrain in the Spanish manner. Don Ramón was proud of this ranch and not pleased with the job he had to do on reaching it, but he was so determined to protect his granddaughter from the kind of talk Don Lázaro Veramendi had been engaging in that his mind was firm, and as soon as he saw Domingo's father he began.

'Teodoro, you and your family have worked so well for us . . .'

'Only our duty, señor.'

'We want to reward you.'

'You already have, many times.'

'In 1749, when I helped the great Escandón explore the valley of the Rio Grande, he liked my work so much that he awarded me four leagues of land along the river.'

'That could be good land, señor, from what the soldiers say.'

'I'm going to give you that land, Teodoro. We'll never make good use of it, I fear.'

'Señor, I wouldn't want to leave El Codo . . .'

'You must,' Don Ramón said firmly. 'You've earned our gratitude.'

'Magdalena might not wish to travel.'

'Wives do what their husbands say, so let's hear no more about it. You have the four leagues. I've brought the papers, signed by Viceroy Güemes.' From his saddlebag he produced the valuable parchment authorized by King Fernando VI, signed by the viceroy and notarized by the current governor of Nuevo Santander, Melchor Vidal de Lorca. The nearly eighteen thousand acres were worth at that time about one cent an acre; in years to come, six thousand dollars an acre, and after that, much more, for they lay on the rich north bank of the Rio Grande, where, according to legend, a walking stick fifty years old would flower and grow fruit if stuck in the loam and watered.

When Garza rode with Don Ramón to the ranch house, he informed his wife Magdalena of the extraordinary proposal, and although neither he nor she could read, he showed her the impressive document heavy with wax seals. They discussed the offer for several minutes while Don Ramón inspected his shoes, his fingernails and his knuckles; then they came to stand before him, holding hands, and Magdalena, delighted to get land, any land, said: 'Don Ramón, we kiss the soles of your shoes. Land of our own after these many years. God will bless you, and we will too. Teodoro and I will go down to the river and take the land'—and here she tapped the precious parchment—'but because we love you and your family, we'll leave our son Domingo here to care for the ranch, as before.'

'No, no!' Don Ramón said. 'Your son must go with you!'

Now Teodoro began to argue that in simple fairness they must leave Domingo behind, but when this was said a second time, Don Ramón became angry: 'He will go with you. To build the corrals, the barns.'

So it was settled, and Don Ramón slept at the ranch for three nights until the Garzas were packed and lesser hands instructed as to the care of the cattle. He gave the departing family four good horses, a fine bull, six cows and the loan of seven armed men to protect the exodus as it crossed the hundred leagues of Indian lands separating it from the place where the Rio Grande approached the Gulf of Mexico. As they pulled away from El Codo, Don Ramón rode with them for several hours to make sure that they were really on their way; then he embraced Teodoro and his wife, wished them luck in their new home, and shook hands formally with Domingo, seventeen years old, handsome, clever, honest. 'You're a good lad, son. Build your own ranch, and make it prosper.' He reined in his horse, told the armed men protecting him to wait, and watched as the little caravan headed toward the southern horizon. By this time next month they'll reach the place, he thought. I remember it that first night when Escandón and I were riding ahead. Rich land, plenty of water, even some trees, as I recall. Escandón advised me to choose my land on the south side of the river. When I said I liked the look of the north, he said: 'It's yours, if you think something can be done with it.' And now it's Garza's. He reflected on this for many minutes, finally muttering to himself: 'Their son could make his fortune on good land like that. That's why I chose it, for its richness.' As he recalled the capable youth he had sent into exile, other thoughts surged into his mind, but he repressed them, for he did not wish to consider such possibilities: He's a mestizo. He has his own place, and it's not here.

Signaling to his escort, he headed back to town.

The cumbersome entourage which Don Ramón assembled in February 1789 for the long trip to Mexico City would be able to cover about four leagues a day (roughly ten and a half miles), and since the distance was about four hundred leagues, the trip would require a good hundred-odd days of unrelieved travel, plus time for repairs, for rest on Sundays, when Doña Engracia refused to allow the horses to be worked, for the forced halts at swollen rivers, and for much-needed recuperation periods in the provincial cities like Saltillo. The journey would thus require about half a year, then a six-month visit in the capital, plus another half year for the return. No family initiated a trip like this without prayers and solemn adieus, for everyone knew that sickness or flood or the Apache and bandits who prowled the lonely stretches might take the lives of all. When the Saldañas bade farewell to the Veramendis, there were tears aplenty, especially when the dear friends Trinidad and Amalia embraced.

The Saldañas knew that the bleakest part of the journey came at the start, for once they crossed their own river, the Medina, they left Tejas and entered upon those empty, barren plains reaching down to the Rio Grande; it was proper, they thought, that these wastes not be a part of Tejas, for they were El Desplobado, totally unoccupied, and could best be understood as the desert which constituted the northern part of Coahuila.

The Saldañas would traverse almost three hundred miles of this desert before they reached partial civilization at Monclova and real settlement at the entrancing city of Saltillo, so they wrapped damp cloths about their nostrils and lips to keep out the dust and plunged into the forbidding lands. After nineteen wearing days they reached the Rio Grande and the excellent hospitality of the missions at San Juan Bautista, where they lingered for two weeks. The friars were glad to welcome them, for they brought news of Tejas, and the Saldañas were pleased to stay because the missions had fresh vegetables.

Almost regretfully Trinidad bade the friars farewell, and now started the dangerous part of the journey, eighteen days across the desolate, exposed stretch to Monclova, for it was here that the Apache often struck, wiping out whole convoys. Eleven mounted soldiers accompanied the travelers, for the Saldañas were personages and risks could not be taken. Day after day the wagon in which Engracia de Saldaña rode creaked over the forlorn pathway, this royal road, with never a house to be seen nor even a wandering shepherd. Once Don Ramón told his granddaughter: 'When they ask in the plaza at Béjar "Why aren't there more settlers here?" this is the reason,' and with a sweep of his arm he indicated that terrifying emptiness, that mix of sand and stunted trees and washed gullies down which torrents cascaded when the rains came, pinning travelers inside their tents for days at a time.

South of Monclova everything became more interesting, for now the Saldañas entered one of the most enchanting areas in all of Mexico: beautiful barren fields sweeping upward to become graceful hills, then low mountains and, finally, crests of considerable size. El Camino Real now became truly royal, providing grand vistas and magnificent enfolding mountains, so that one had the impression of piercing into the very heart of the hills. Repeatedly Don Ramón halted the troop to say: 'I remember this spot when I was a boy. Captain Alvaro, my father of blessed memory, brought me and my brothers here and we took our meal by that waterfall. How long ago it seems.' He told Trinidad that she, too, must remember this spot: 'Let's see. You were fourteen last month. If you marry at sixteen, as a girl should . . . babies . . . then the babies marry . . . and they have babies.' He stopped to count. 'You could be traveling down this road in 1843 with your own grandchildren. And when you do, halt here and have your merienda and lift a cup to me, as I now do to my father, may God rest his soul.'

It was from such conversations that Trinidad had acquired for a child so young an unusual sense of the passing of time. She perceived that a human being was born into a certain bundle of years, and that it did not matter whether she liked those years or not; they were her years and she must live her life within them. If they turned out to be good years, fine. If they were bad, so be it, for they were the years in which she must find her husband and have her children and perhaps take her grandchildren to a merienda in the mountains like this, at spots where her grandfather and his father had enjoyed their rest stops and the tumbling waters.

When the picnic ended she ran to Don Ramón and kissed him, and he said: 'There will be even better moments than this, Trinidad, you mark your old grandfather's words.'

The first of them came in the gracious town of Saltillo, for here Trinidad saw her first community of any size, and she was awed by its magnificence: 'It is so big! There are so many shops! A person could find anything in the world here!'

For the first two eye-opening days she savored Saltillo, especially the new church, so large and so majestic, its ornate façade exquisitely adorned with intricate carving and crowned by a beautiful shell above the entrance. To the right rose a stern tower topped by three tiers of pillars, behind which hid a carillon that echoed long after the last peal was struck. It is overwhelming, like God Himself, Trinidad thought. One side of Him is all gentleness and beauty. The other is almost frightening, so big, so powerful. But the more she studied this uncompromising structure the more she accepted both halves.

Four times she returned in daylight hours, captivated by its mystery, and when Don Ramón teased her for wasting her time, she explained: 'I've never seen anything so grand before. In Tejas . . .' He went to a store and purchased pen and paper for her, and with these she sketched the church, rather effectively, Don Ramón told Engracia, and he pleased Trinidad by asking solemnly if she would sign it for him, and she did: '*Trinidad de Saldaña, Dibujado en Saltillo, 16 de Mayo de 1789.*'

It was not until the evening of the third day that Trinidad discovered another wonder of a city, for then her elders took her to the church plaza, where she saw for the first time not the aimless wandering about of young people in a rural village like Béjar, but the formal Spanish paseo of a major town like Saltillo. She and her family reached the plaza when the paseo was in full swing, and for some minutes she watched, open-mouthed, as handsome young men and alluring girls swung past, talking always to someone of their own sex, pretending to be indifferent to the other. Finally she brought her clasped hands up to her lips and sighed: 'Mother, this is so beautiful!'

It was, and there Trinidad stayed till the last promenaders left the plaza. She had seen something which touched on the rhythms of life, its uncertainties, its mysteries. She could not get to sleep that night, for in her mind rose the awkward

towers of the church and in their timeless shadow walked the young people of
Saltillo, pursuing their unstated passions in the ancient Spanish way.

It was obvious to Engracia that on the next night her daughter was going to
plead for permission to join the paseo, and this posed a problem, which she took
to her father-in-law: 'I'm certainly too old to parade with her holding my hand.
And she knows no one with whom she can walk.'

'Let her walk alone.'

'Never.'

'I seem to remember girls walking alone, when I was younger.'

'Not girls of good family.'

Don Ramón, recognizing that he must assume responsibility in the matter,
went to the manager of the inn at which they were stopping, and said forthrightly: 'Don Ignacio, our fourteen-year-old granddaughter wants to join the
paseo. Do you know a girl of impeccable family with whom she could walk?'

'I have a granddaughter, excellent family, her mother born in Spain.'

'Don Ignacio, I would be honored.'

'To the contrary. We've all heard of your martyred uncle, Fray Damián. The
honor would fall upon our family.'

So it was arranged that Trinidad would make the paseo with fifteen-year-old
Dorotéa Galíndez. When the evening bells rang, the nervous girls asked their
elders how they looked, and Don Ramón replied: 'If I were twins, I'd fall in love
with each of you.' Then, nodding very low to Dorotéa, he added: 'If there's a
cavalier out there tonight, he'll ride away with you.'

Señoras Saldaña and Galíndez waited about an hour before taking their daughters to the plaza, for they wished to introduce them into the parade unostenta-
tiously, but as soon as the two girls entered the plaza the young men meeting
them in the paseo grew attentive, and for the first time in her life Trinidad
realized that she had more than an ordinary appearance. Her warm smile and
uncalculated approach so tantalized the passing young men that one young fellow
said to the friend with whom he was walking: 'That's the kind of face you
remember at midnight when you can't get to sleep.'

Dorotéa, a year older, warned Trinidad that girls must never look directly at the
boys; they must appear to be engrossed in each other. Dorotéa played this game to
perfection, finding in the country girl from Tejas a person of unlimited curiosity,
and the two chattered happily as the young men passed. But Trinidad was not
interested in games; she was noticing attractive young men for the first time in her
life, and she was bewitched, her pretty face turned brazenly toward them, her
unforgettable smile greeting them with joy.

That night Dorotéa told her mother about Trinidad's forward behavior, and
Señora Galíndez spoke to Engracia: 'You must warn your pretty daughter against
an unbecoming boldness.' So the next afternoon Trinidad's mother and grandfather explained that it was most unladylike for a young woman to demonstrate too

much interest in young men. 'You are to smile, of course,' Don Ramón said, 'but only to yourself. That adds mystery.' Inviting Engracia to walk the narrow room with him, he explained: 'Your mother is Dorotéa. I'm you.' And he minced along, talking with great animation to Engracia, who smiled back at him. 'This is how proper girls make the paseo,' and on he pranced.

'You look so funny!' Trinidad cried.

Don Ramón stopped, and reprimanded her: 'If a girl of good family like you smiles openly at young men, it's very forward. And if you actually encourage them, you're brazen, as Señora Galíndez warned.'

'She's a busybody.'

'Without her approval you cannot walk with her daughter,' Engracia said, and when Trinidad started to reply, her mother pressed a hand against her lips. 'Child, remember that three days from now we go on to San Luis Potosí. Dorotéa stays here, and if her reputation is damaged by some foolish thing you do, she suffers, not you.' She cuffed her daughter lightly on the ear and said: 'Now you behave yourself.'

Trinidad did behave herself for the first half of that night's paseo, but as the girls rounded a corner by the church steps Dorotéa gasped 'Oh!' and Trinidad looked forward. Then she, too, gasped.

Joining the men's circle in an easy, indifferent manner came the most engaging young man either girl had ever seen. He would have been spectacular even had his face not been so pleasing, for he was an outstanding blond among all the dark-haired Saltillo youths, and so graceful that he seemed to move without his feet actually touching the ground. He was one of those fortunate men who would always be slim, and he would retain that air of youthful excitement, that devastating smile, those bright eyes filled with wonder. Age would not wither him nor years increase his girth. He was now nineteen, a mere five feet five inches tall, weighing no more than a hundred and forty pounds, and so he would remain.

When the young man came abreast, Trinidad threw caution away and smiled directly at him. To her dismay, she realized that he was smiling at Dorotéa, and she at him.

Although Señorita Dorotéa Galíndez had been a very proper young lady when none of the passing men interested her particularly, she became a very skilled young temptress when someone as intriguing as this newcomer came her way. She now lost all interest in Trinidad, and since she would encounter the stranger twice in each complete turn of the circle, as soon as she completed one pass she began preparing for the next, so that although the young man would be meeting many girls in his round, he would meet none more obviously affected or more eager to make his acquaintance than Dorotéa. She saw to that.

So the enchanted evening progressed, one of the most compelling and confusing that Trinidad would ever know: the beauty of Saltillo, the grandeur of the new church, moonlight filling the plaza, the smell of flowers, this handsome stranger, but most of all, watching a determined young woman of fifteen planning her moves to entrap a devastating young man of nineteen who was making his own plans to entrap her. Trinidad was by no means watching this as one detached; she wished desperately that the young fellow had saved his smiles for her, and the more often she saw him the more she liked him, but she was sensible enough to know that Dorotéa had stepped in before her, so she contented herself with watching Dorotéa's skill.

Bells sounded in the dark tower. Annoyed pigeons flew over the plaza briefly and returned to their roost above the bells. A watchman started his rounds, nodding to the citizens as they made their way home. The flowers of Saltillo dozed and Trinidad de Saldaña, agitated as never before, clasped her grandfather's hand with unwonted emotion and whispered as he led her back to the inn: 'Saltillo is so wonderful, Grandfather, and Tejas seems so bleak.'

Dorotéa, up betimes and asking a thousand questions, had much to report when the Saldañas came down for eleven o'clock chocolate: 'He's French. He comes from New Orleans. His family owns large vineyards in France, but his father manufactures mining things and ships them to Vera Cruz for the capital.'

'What's he doing in Saltillo?' Don Ramón asked, and Dorotéa said brightly: 'Oh, he's looking to see if we have any mines in places like Béjar and Monclova.' Then she winked at Trinidad: 'And he's going to San Luis Potosí to see if he can sell a marvelous new machine to the people there. His name is René-Claude d'Ambreuze. He speaks fine Spanish, and he's stopping at the other inn.'

'So he's in business?' Don Ramón said huffily, but Engracia, gazing in wonder at the self-satisfied girl, asked: 'How did you learn where he's staying?'

'I know people. I asked the porters in the plaza.'

'When is he going to Potosí?' Don Ramón asked, and Trinidad's heart almost stopped, for she immediately visualized this godlike young man joining their party for the three hundred miles to the mining capital, and before anyone could speak further she saw herself and René-Claude—what a heavenly name!—cantering across the high plains of Mexico, she in the lead, he avidly in pursuit.

'He'll be here soon,' she heard Dorotéa say, at which Engracia asked sternly: 'You didn't speak to him? Without an introduction?'

'No,' Dorotéa said pertly, arranging her dress. 'I told his innkeeper to suggest that he stop by.'

'My dear child,' Engracia protested, 'that was indeed forward. It was even brazen.'

'Look!' And down the narrow street that joined the two inns came the young Frenchman, threading his way through the rubble that had collected overnight, sunlight on his pale hair, that smile on his lips.

'Is this the inn of Señor Galíndez?' he asked, his slight accent betraying the fact that he was not Spanish. He had barely asked the question when he saw Dorotéa;

recognizing her, he bowed low and said with great charm and no sense of extravagance: 'The young princess I saw last night.'

Trinidad noticed all this and also that he stood at attention, waiting to be asked properly to join their party. Don Ramón rose, brought his heels together, and bowed like the grandee he was: 'Young sir, my family and I would be most honored if you would sit with us and tell us what's happening in that strange city of New Orleans.'

The young man bowed with equal gravity and said in a voice so low that Trinidad could barely hear: 'I am René-Claude d'Ambreuze, and I would be most honored to join you and your two daughters.'

'I'm of the Galíndez family,' Dorotéa said boldly as he took his seat beside her. 'These are the Saldañas of Béjar in Tejas. And this is my dear friend Trinidad de Saldaña.'

René-Claude scarcely acknowledged the introduction, for little Trinidad seemed quite youthful compared to the dazzling Dorotéa. 'I passed through Béjar some weeks ago. Very small. But this Saltillo! Ah, this is a little Paris.'

'Have you been to Paris?' Trinidad found herself blurting out.

'I was born in Paris.'

'Oh, what is it like?' For the first time young D'Ambreuze looked directly at Trinidad, saw her brilliant eyes, her strangely formed mouth, and thought what a pleasing sister she'd make.

'I know little of Paris,' he said honestly. 'They took me away when I was a child.' Then, turning as was proper to Don Ramón, he said: 'New Orleans, on the other hand! Ah! Queen of the Mississippi.'

'Is the Mississippi really so big?' Trinidad asked.

He turned once more to face her inquisitive eyes: 'Saltillo could be tossed between its banks and we'd all be lost.'

It was a splendid day in that spring of 1789, with René-Claude paying great attention to Don Ramón, much courtesy to Señora Engracia, and distinct respect to the Galíndez elders; he had been well reared by loving aunts and governesses, and he showed it. At four-thirty in the afternoon he took lunch, Mexican style, with the Saldañas, again sitting with Dorotéa, and at eight in the evening he helped Engracia escort the two girls to the paseo, where he saluted them graciously each time he passed.

On the next day two things happened to disturb Trinidad: through unladylike questioning she learned that whereas the Saldañas were going to leave Saltillo three days hence, René-Claude's business interests would hold him here for two more weeks, which meant that she would be leaving the young Frenchman entirely to Dorotéa. And swinging around a corner of the inn late that afternoon, she came upon him and Dorotéa eagerly kissing and clinging to each other. They did not see her, and she drew back, flushed and trembling, as if she herself had participated in this embrace. While she did not begrudge Dorotéa her good fortune, she was chagrined that she had not been the girl in René-Claude's arms.

When she joined her grandfather for lunch, which was served at five, she found that her mother was staying in bed to rest for the next leg of the journey. Alone with Don Ramón, she felt immeasurably old, as if she were coeval with him, and she spoke in that way: 'I doubt that New Orleans will ever be a Spanish city.'

'It is now, silly girl.'

'But I mean truly. French ways, they seem to be very strong wherever the French go.'

'Now, what do you know about French ways, young lady?'

She did not say so, but she felt that she knew an enormous amount, really, an enormous amount. Then she heard her grandfather speaking.

'I've always thought that God placed Spain where He did to keep things organized.' Don Ramón arranged dishes and rolls to represent Europe. 'Lesser nations all around her. Portugal here, and what a sorry land that is. France up here, a bunch of troublemakers. England over here, accch!' The harsh guttural showed what he thought of England. 'And down here the despicable Moors, enemies of God and man.' In the center of this maelstrom of failed nations and infidels he placed a bright orange: 'Spain: God's bastion of reason, and stability, and all the things that represent goodness in this life.'

'Then why has England grown so strong?' Trinidad asked like a philosopher. 'From what we hear, that is?'

'God is preparing them for a fall. They strayed from the true religion, and it's impossible that Protestants should ever triumph. That's why los Estados del Norte . . .'

The table now became North America: 'Up here the French used to be, but they could never govern themselves, as we've seen in New Orleans. Over here godless americanos, who are doomed.'

'They won their freedom from England,' Trinidad said.

'With French help. Two godless nations fighting it out. And here . . .' Now the orange became Tejas: 'In the middle of this mess, Tejas, Spanish to the core, God's bastion, just as in Europe.' He patted the orange, reveling in its security, and said: 'God arranges these things according to His grand design. Believe me, Trinidad, Tejas is not where it is by accident. And you're not in Tejas by accident. Your destiny is to rear Spanish sons who will build there cities much finer than New Orleans.'

But three days south of Saltillo, during the long ride to Potosí, even Don Ramón had to wonder whether God did not sometimes forget His assignment in Tejas, for the Saldaña caravan, traveling with three other families heading for the capital, came upon a detachment of soldiers marching north, bringing with them the latest gang of conscripts destined for duty in Béjar. And what a sickening lot they were.

'My God!' Don Ramón cried. 'You're not taking them to Tejas?'

'We are,' the commander of the troops said. 'I chain them only when we stop at night.'

And well he might! For he had in his charge a sweeping of Mexican jails: a group of seven who were spared hanging if they would serve in the north, sixteen younger men whose families had abandoned them shortly after birth, and a score who had proven themselves to be worthless workers. Behind them trailed a scruffy collection of women, young and old, whose lives were somehow entangled with those of the prisoners. They were indeed prisoners, and to call them settlers or soldiers was preposterous.

'You're turning them loose in Tejas?' Don Ramón cried in disbelief.

'No great worry. Two-thirds of them will run away and get back to the capital before I do.'

Don Ramón studied the sorry detachment and whispered a suggestion to the commander: 'Couldn't you march them into a swamp? Or just shoot them?'

The commander chuckled: 'The really bad ones we send to Yucatán. These are what we call the hopefuls.'

Don Ramón had to laugh, but the experience fortified his resolve to find for his granddaughter a respectable Spanish husband.

On the nineteenth day after their departure from Saltillo two of the soldiers bringing up the rear galloped forward. 'Party overtaking us from the rear,' one reported.

Everyone turned around, and saw that the soldiers were right; a column of some kind was approaching at a worrisome speed, and a hasty consultation took place. The commander asked: 'Am I right? No unit is supposed to be on this road?'

'None that we know of, sir.'

'Comanche?'

'I think so.'

Men instinctively fingered their guns.

'Women to the front! Immediate!' The captain hesitated: 'I mean to the rear, as we face them.'

The approaching column, which appeared to be some fifteen or sixteen Indians, must have seen the soldiers halt and take up defensive positions, but on they came, and as the dust rose, Don Ramón, his white hair unprotected by any hat, rode back to take position in front of the women: 'You are not to cry panic. You are not to run. I will hold them off.' He saluted his two women, but the effect of his words was lost when Trinidad cried joyously: 'It's René-Claude!' And deftly she spurred her horse and dashed out to meet the Frenchman, whose party had left

Saltillo almost two weeks later than the Saldañas but had been able, by means of long rides each day, to overtake them.

It was a lively meeting there in the great empty upland of Mexico, with blue mountains in the distance and spring flowers covering the swales. Soldiers from both groups swapped stories, and the two other merchants who had been invited by young D'Ambreuze to join his entourage talked with Don Ramón about conditions in both Coahuila and Tejas.

But the two who reveled most in the fortunate meeting were Trinidad and René-Claude, for without the distracting presence of Dorotéa Galíndez, the young Frenchman was free to discover what a delightful young woman Trinidad was. They rode their horses ahead of the line, or off to one side, chattering easily and endlessly. One morning Trinidad thought: Today I wish he would try to kiss me, and when they were off toward the mountains he did just that. She encouraged him at first, then pushed him away and said: 'I saw you kissing Dorotéa,' and he explained: 'Sometimes that happens, but this is forever.'

'Did you enjoy kissing her?' she asked, and he said: 'Of course, but it was your funny little smile I saw at night when I was alone.'

'You may kiss me,' she said, leaning across her horse's neck.

When they were in the presence of the elders they had to be more circumspect; then they sat and talked, and one evening Trinidad asked him to explain his name.

'Many French boys have two names, like mine. And the little *d'* is your *de*. Means the same, the place where your family came from, an honorable designation.' He tried to teach her how to pronounce his last name with a French twirl, and when her tongue could not master it he accused her of being dull-witted.

'How about you?' And she mimicked him by saying *Trinidad* the way he did, with heavy accent on the last syllable as if it really were *dod*, rhyming with *nod*. 'It's not that way at all,' she protested. 'It's *dthodth*. Soft . . . a whispering song.'

Now it was he whose tongue became twisted, but at last, with her gentle coaching, he mastered this beautiful name: *'Tree-nee-dthodth!* It really is a song!' And so they continued, two young people in love, finding music in each other's names, respect for each other's traditions.

In fact, the pair became so open in their affection that Don Ramón told Engracia: 'Well or sick, you must go out and act as dueña for your child.' Then, in some confusion but with his jaw set, he ordered Trinidad to get into the wagon and sit with Engracia while he rode ahead to talk with the young Frenchman.

'There is always the matter of honor, young man. Surely you will agree to that?'

D'Ambreuze, bewildered that Trinidad had left him and that Don Ramón had taken her place, mumbled something about men always being beholden to the demands of honor: 'Duels, and things like that.' He spoke as if he certainly did not expect to be challenged to a duel.

'I mean,' Don Ramón said, turning sideways on his horse, 'those ancient rules which have always governed the behavior of gentlemen.'

'Oh, that! Yes. Women first into the carriage. Men to hold the horses lest they bolt. Oh, yes!' He spoke with such enthusiasm that one might have thought he was Europe's champion of the ancient rules, that he would lay down his life in furtherance of them.

'I mean the subtler kind, young man.'

'Well . . .' René-Claude's voice trailed off, for now he was truly bewildered.

'It has always been a rule among gentlemen, rigorously observed by all who presume to call themselves that . . .' Now Don Ramón hesitated. 'Are you a gentleman?' Before René-Claude could respond, he added: 'I mean, your father *is* in trade, isn't he?' He spat out the words distastefully.

The young man drew to attention: 'The D'Ambreuze family own large vineyards near Beaune, and do you know where Beaune is? Burgundy, its own principality. No one owns large vineyards there unless they're gentlemen. Nobility, really.'

'But in New Orleans, your father is in trade?'

'My father's an inventor. He devises machines used in mines. I'm a gentleman, so educated and trained, as were my great-grandfather before me and his great-grandfather before him. But more important, I'm a Burgundian.'

'Well, yes,' Don Ramón said, shifting his weight to bring his face closer to D'Ambreuze. 'What I mean, there's a rule among gentlemen that no one can come into another man's castle and seduce his daughter. Not while the visitor is a guest in the castle.'

D'Ambreuze said nothing, for now he knew the burden of the old man's warning. By joining the Saldaña party without an invitation, he had assumed the role of guest whether he intended so or not, and he was bound by the most ancient code not to take advantage of the daughter of the house, not while he was in this privileged position. In the fluid life of San Luis Potosí or on the wide avenues of the capital he might feel free to seduce her, if his charms and stratagems prevailed, but not while he was a guest in the home, as it were, of Don Ramón.

'It would never have occurred to me to take advantage,' he said.

'It occurred to me,' Don Ramón replied. 'Now shall we stop for our morning rest?'

It was this unnecessary halt which made up the minds of the two guest merchants: 'We do not like to say this, but this dallying . . . these picnics . . . we're wasting valuable time. Our soldiers too, they want to move ahead.'

'We shall. I've been inconsiderate of you gentlemen, and I'm sorry,' and René-Claude announced to the group resting by the side of the road—a rather good highway now, since it had been in use two centuries longer than the miserable roads in Tejas—that he and his company must, reluctantly, forge ahead. He went to Trinidad, and taking her by the hands, he drew her to him and embraced her in front of the others, then bowed low as if wearing a plumed hat in the old days: 'Mademoiselle, we shall meet again in Potosí, or Mexico, or New Orleans, but wherever it is, it will be heaven.' Saluting Don Ramón and the soldiers who would be staying with the slower party, he went to the head of his column and led his entourage across the beautiful spaces of upland Mexico.

Days later, as the Saldañas approached Potosí, Trinidad rode with her grandfather and confided: 'I shall pray tonight that René-Claude's negotiations have kept him here longer than he intended.'

'I doubt, dearest child, that you could ever marry a Frenchman. They're not dependable. I've never believed that they're serious Catholics.' He poured forth a century of Spanish apprehensions about their northern neighbors, ending with a prophetic warning: 'I even doubt that New Orleans will remain Spanish till the end of the century.'

'What possibly could happen?' Trinidad asked. 'René-Claude himself told me they have no armies in America.'

'With the French something always happens. Do not count on young D'Ambreuze.'

'Don't you like him?'

'Too much,' her grandfather confessed. 'And I see that you like him too much, also. Be careful, Trinidad. He comes with the wind. He goes with the sunrise.'

But his granddaughter's ardent hopes were realized. By one device and another, René-Claude had managed to linger on in the mining town, attending to business which he did not have and wasting so much time that his two companions had proceeded to Mexico City without him.

Each day he had watched El Camino Real for signs of travelers coming down from the north, and on a bright July day two men, traveling without military guard, rode into town with the exciting news that Don Ramón Saldaña from the distant town of Béjar in Tejas would be arriving, if his current slow speed held, on the morrow.

Upon receipt of this news René-Claude saddled his horse, hired three companions, and rode north to escort the travelers properly. Trinidad had supposed that this might happen, for she had paid the two men to seek out the young Frenchman and inform him of her coming. She was therefore at the head of her column when she spied the four horsemen, and without waiting for confirmation she dashed ahead, waved vigorously when she saw René-Claude, and brought her horse close to his so that she could kiss him.

When the two groups met formally, Don Ramón said brusquely: 'I had hoped you were in Mexico City.'

'I should be, but I had to see you and your daughter again.'

'Let us not deter you. You've made your welcome. You will show us to our inn, I feel sure, and then you will hurry on.'

'That I shall, Don Ramón, but first I must speak seriously with you.'

'That can wait till we've cleaned up,' he said, and he would speak no more until he had seen his women properly ensconced in their quarters at the inn. It was a place of thick walls and many rooms, in one of which the two men met over drinks of cool pomegranate juice.

'Don Ramón, I seek your permission to pay serious court to your granddaughter.'

'She's not fifteen.'

'She will be when you've returned to Béjar and I stop by to claim her.'

'What are your prospects?'

'The best, Don Ramón, as you will find when you inquire about me in the capital. I am a younger son, it's true, and my older brothers have the vineyards. But I've done well in New Orleans. And in Saltillo. And Potosí. And I'm sure I'll do even better in the capital. For that you need have no concern.'

'In Saltillo you seemed quite enamored of the innkeeper's daughter.'

'In spring the birds inspect many trees before they build their nests.'

'They do, they do,' Don Ramón said, recalling his own casual courtships. But then he spoke forcefully: 'I'm a Spaniard, and I'm taking my granddaughter to the capital so that she can meet Spaniards. French and Spanish, it's never been any good.'

'You've had Frenchmen as your kings.'

'And that's been worst of all!'

There in Potosí the battle lines were drawn: it was obvious that the young Frenchman would continue to pay ardent suit to Trinidad, while the old Spaniard would do all he could to keep the young lovers separated, or at least under close surveillance. Don Ramón, accepting the challenge, said: 'I doubt that a granddaughter of mine would ever want to marry a Frenchman.'

'With all respect, Don Ramón, I disagree.'

'I doubt that I could ever give my consent.' But he liked the young man's spirit and did not try to prevent him from taking rooms at the same inn.

Now began a clever game of cat and mouse, with the Frenchman testing every gambit to place himself alone with Trinidad, and her grandfather using his talents to outwit him. Alas, Don Ramón's own grandchild sided with the enemy, exchanging surreptitious messages of love and stolen kisses. But with Engracia's determined help, Saldaña did succeed in protecting his child's honor.

After four days of this he suggested bluntly that D'Ambreuze move on: 'Your business waits,' and to his surprise the brash young fellow said: 'It does indeed. But I also shall wait . . . in the capital.' And he was off, this time without escort, for south of Potosí, El Camino Real became a major road in the silver trade, and soldiers guarded it on a permanent basis.

Two weeks later the Saldañas started their own hundred-and-twenty-league trip south, which they took at a pace more leisurely than before, so that it was early August before they entered upon that splendid final plateau on which stood the marvel of the New World.

If Trinidad had been impressed by Saltillo as a major center, she was dumfounded by the capital, for it exceeded even the stories that soldiers had recited during the long journey. The cathedral was three times the size of the lovely church in Saltillo, the plaza fifteen or twenty times larger, and if the shops in the northern town had been lavish, the ones in Mexico City were true cornucopias, crowded with elegant wares from all over Europe: brocades and silks and intricately woven cottons and hammered gold for women; guns and silver-handled swords and burnished leatherware from Toledo and fine suitings for the men.

What made the capital even more exciting was that on the second morning René-Claude appeared at the Saldañas' inn, prepared to escort Trinidad and her mother to various parts of the metropolis: the bullring, where masters from Spain performed; the concert halls, where fine singers from all over Europe entertained; and those unique taverns which started serving delectable dinners at eleven o'clock at night. Here Trinidad could listen to the wandering Negro poets recite impudent impromptu verses cataloguing the scandals of the day. Standing before her table one night, the best of the black poets cried with obvious joy:

> 'Little girl with the laughing smile,
> Please stay among us for a while.
> Mexico is criminal, it's true,
> That's why we need a pretty little . . .
> That's why we need a witty little . . .
> That's why we need a lovely little girl like you.'

The poetry wasn't very good, but it was delivered with great enthusiasm and considerable boldness. To Don Ramón, the poet declaimed:

> 'While you spend money wildly in the city,
> The clerks back home are checking on your books.
> They scratch their heads and say "The pity:
> These figures prove that you're the chief of crooks." '

At this sally the crowded tavern applauded, and other diners pointed their fingers at Don Ramón and chided him for being a thief. He was required to nod and smile and tip the insulting poet handsomely, for if he failed to do any of these things, the black man would remain there shouting really damaging verses. However, on this occasion the minstrel achieved his greatest success with the lines he launched at René-Claude:

'My fine young lad with eyes of blue,
I see you come from France.
But our police are on to you,
So do not take a chance.

'For if you try to steal our girl
This entire town will rise,
And knock your head into a whirl
And boot you to the skies.

'Take my advice, young man of France,
Forget the old man's threats.
Lead forth your lady to the dance
And you will cash your bets.'

With this, he threw his arms wide, reached down and kissed Trinidad, embraced René-Claude, and after gathering coins from the latter, danced his way through the restaurant, a figure of whirling grace, black as the night and free to exercise privileges no one else in that room would have dared. At the exit he leaped, turned in midair, and threw the entire assembly kisses with his long, agile fingers.

There was nothing in Tejas like this black poet, nor was there anything like the grandeur of Mexico City or its university more than two centuries old, and as Trinidad came to know the metropolis in which she would remain for half a year, she also came to understand something of Spain's glory. She knew now why her grandfather was so proud of his heritage and wanted her to share it with a Spanish husband who might even take her back to the homeland. One night, after they had attended one of the city's dozen theaters for a program of one-act plays and singing, she confided: 'It seems so old and so learned and the buildings so important . . . It's not at all like our poor Tejas,' and Don Ramón said: 'Spain itself is even better.'

But his search for a Spanish son-in-law was not going well, and he was relieved when D'Ambreuze announced that he must go down to Vera Cruz to supervise the arrival of mining equipment from France, but was appalled when the young man suggested that the Saldañas accompany him, for it would be a distance of some seventy leagues through fever-ridden jungle. However, Trinidad made such an outcry about wishing to visit Puebla, one of the most gracious cities in the entire Spanish empire, that he did agree to lead his family that far. There, in what was called the City of the Angels, with the great volcanoes looming over the myriad churches—three hundred and sixty-five in outlying Cholula alone—they said farewell to D'Ambreuze. Don Ramón saluted him, Engracia allowed him to kiss her, and Trinidad clung to him as the horses were brought up for the dangerous journey down to where the ships from Europe arrived almost every week.

Back in the capital, Don Ramón made serious inquiry concerning D'Ambreuze, and learned from officials who had served in both Spain and New Orleans that he did indeed come from an excellent family and that his people in Louisiana had been among the first to accept Spanish rule back in the 1760s.

One diplomat said: 'We had to hang a dozen French leaders, you know. They were stubborn, would accept nothing Spanish, so we strung them up. But the D'Ambreuze clan were different. Good Frenchmen. Good Catholics. And now they're good Spaniards. There's been talk that René-Claude's father, or perhaps René-Claude himself, in due course, might be our Spanish governor in New Orleans. So the young man is not a nobody, of that you can be sure, Don Ramón.'

Over the weeks Saldaña pondered his problem, and one afternoon when Trinidad was out with friends visiting the architectural masterpieces of the capital, he said to her mother: 'By sixteen our precious little lady ought to be married. I'm afraid my dream of Spain was fruitless. I have the sad feeling that our good friend Veramendi was correct when he predicted that the real power would be coming down El Camino Real from the north and not up from the south.'

'Are you saying . . . ?'

'I'm saying that when I study the decline of Spain in the New World, our young French friend begins to look better every day.'

'Oh dear.' Engracia was not prepared for a French son-in-law, nor for the French to have a foothold of any kind in Mexico, especially Tejas. 'In the old days things were so much simpler.'

When D'Ambreuze returned from Vera Cruz, bronzed and temporarily underweight because of fever, so that he seemed almost a wraith, he insisted that everyone accompany him on an expedition to the ruins of some pyramids north of the city. A field trip involving many horses and servants was arranged, and when the Saldañas stood at the base of the major pyramid, its sides encrusted with growing trees and small shrubs, they marveled at the building talents of the ancients. For the first time Don Ramón contemplated the fact that before the Spanish came to Mexico, Indians of great ability must have lived here, capable of building edifices ten times more grand than anything yet seen in Tejas. It was a disturbing thought to a man who had always scorned Indians, but the impact of the pyramids was even greater on Trinidad, for she could not believe that these wonders looming out of the wasteland could have been built by the ancestors of the Indians she had known, and a most strange thought occurred to her, which she shared with her parents: 'They must have been different Indians from the ones we see. That Indian maiden who married the Spanish soldier Garza, she must have been quite different.' And when she returned to the city she began looking into the faces of the Indians, staring at them impolitely, trying to find in them any indication of the master-builders who had constructed those pyramids.

When the Saldañas returned to the capital from this excursion, Don Ramón

umped in a chair and told Engracia: 'I don't think we're going to find a proper
usband for Trinidad.'

'Not here,' she agreed. 'It looks as if Spain has already surrendered Mexico.
he's surely not sending any young officers here.'

Therefore, Don Ramón did not immediately reject René-Claude's impertinent
uggestion that he accompany the Saldaña expedition back to Béjar, but some-
hing the young man said alerted the old man to the fact that the young couple
ere rather more deeply in love than he had anticipated: 'I had planned to sail
ack to France, report to my uncles, and return to my job in New Orleans.'

'Why did you change your plans?'

'I wrote my uncles that I had found in Mexico the girl I wanted to marry, and
hat I would seek to go home your way.'

'You may join us,' Don Ramón conceded, without enthusiasm, but the young
man realized that to win Trinidad, he must please her grandfather, so he said
rightly: 'In Vera Cruz a man at the port told me to ask when I next saw you
. . .' And here he took out a worn slip of paper: 'Are you really an Hidalgo de
ragueta?'

Don Ramón straightened as if he were about to salute the king: 'I am indeed.'
Then he chuckled: 'Self-appointed, you might say.'

'And what is it? The banker wouldn't tell me.'

'It means that the king himself would have granted me the right to use the title
Don, if I lived in Spain.'

'For what?'

'For siring seven sons in a row. No daughters.' But as soon as he said this he
dded: 'I did have seven sons, and all died, but not one of them gave me the
xtreme joy my granddaughter does.'

D'Ambreuze rose, stood at attention, and said: 'Don Ramón, I salute you, and I
ope that I shall be allowed to give you seven great-grandchildren.'

But Ramón de Saldaña was no fool, and he knew well that young men often
voo young girls with faithless promises, then leave them in despair, and both he
nd Engracia began telling Trinidad, when they had her alone, of that endless
hain of tragedies in which unsuspecting girls were betrayed: 'There was the
scobár girl in Zacatecas when I was young. This high official of the court in
Madrid came out to try a case of thievery from the silver mines . . .' It mattered
ot who was doing the preaching, the histories were all the same: 'Shortly after
ny father took command at the presidio in Béjar . . . I was just a boy, but I
emember this girl Eufemia, sent up from Potosí to stay with her brother, who
vas our lieutenant, while she had her baby. It was a baby boy, and after Uncle
Damián christened him, with her brother attending . . . Well, the lieutenant
sked for leave. My father granted it and three months later the young man
eturned to Béjar with the simple announcement "I killed him," and we were all
appy that his honor and that of his sister had been restored.'

In conjunction with his moralizing stories Don Ramón kept a severe watch upon his granddaughter, and this was effective in San Luis Potosí and during the long march north of there. But now, as the young people approached Saltillo, a magical city even if one were not in love, it was obvious that the lovers had reached a point of commitment; they were determined to marry and they wanted that mutual promise publicly announced, so Don Ramón watched with extra diligence.

As they entered the city and Trinidad saw once more the plaza where she had met René-Claude, a frightening thought overtook her, for she remembered that it had been Dorotéa Galíndez whom he had kissed in Saltillo, and she wondered what might happen when the two met again. But when they reached the inn she heard Dorotéa's hearty cry: 'My dearest friend Trinidad! Meet my husband!' So that danger dissolved.

It had been a long day's ride, this final stage to Saltillo, and at midnight Don Ramón was truly fatigued; he slept so soundly that he did not hear Trinidad slip down the tiled hall and out through a window where D'Ambreuze was waiting. They walked back to the plaza where they had met and saw two beggars, their clothes in tatters, sleeping in a doorway. They saw the verger swing shut the gates of the church and wend his way home. They heard the nightwatchman, who would query them if he found them in the streets, and then they discovered an alleyway leading to a sheltered garden, and when they were under the trees René-Claude put cupped hands to his mouth as if he were going to shout. Instead he whispered: 'Don Ramón, heaven is my witness that we are not in your castle!' Then he told Trinidad: 'I am free to make you my wife,' and there they sealed their love.

One day south of Béjar, when Don Ramón had about decided that he must soon discuss with René-Claude the size of Trinidad's dowry, most of the soldiers galloped ahead to inform the town of the Saldañas' return, and while the reduced caravan was in the process of fording the Medina prior to reentering Tejas, the Apache struck. There were more than two dozen warriors, and Trinidad would have been carried off had not Don Ramón defended her valiantly, but the Apache, having seen how young she was, stopped fighting the soldiers and tried again to capture her, for she would be a prize among the campfires.

But now René-Claude, only twenty years old, galloped directly at them, drove them back, and took three arrows through his chest. His horse ran blindly on, taking him closer to the Indians, who sought to take him alive for the protracted tortures they enjoyed, but with his dying strength he struck at them until they had to cut his throat to subdue him.

When the Saldañas brought Trinidad to their house in the church plaza, she passed into a kind of coma, unwilling to believe that her chivalric, loving young man had somehow vanished from the earth, as dead as those shadowy figures who had built the pyramids, and she remained in this condition for several days. Fray Ildefonso from Santa Teresa came to talk with her, but she stared right past him and would say nothing. Finally, on the fifth day, he shook her and said sternly: 'Each morning the rooster crows, and you've lost five of his days. Now get up and get dressed.' And he stayed right there in the low-ceilinged room until she left her bed.

When her mother's nourishing meals had restored her strength she ventured into the plaza, but seeing the church at one end and a bed of flowers beside the governor's residence at the other, she imagined that she was back in Saltillo, and sorrow overcame her and she fled back to her room, where she would have returned to her bed had not Fray Ildefonso given strict orders that this must not be permitted.

So she walked like a forlorn ghost through the beautiful rooms of her home and gradually regained control of herself. René-Claude was dead, and a large part of her heart was dead, too. But Fray Ildefonso's sagacious counsel helped her to see her inescapable situation: 'You're fifteen years old. Four times that many years lie ahead, and you must use them wisely. God intended you to be the guiding spirit of a Christian household, the mother of children who will help build His world. That is your proud destiny, and you must work toward it. Sew, cook for the poor, help at the mission.'

It was repugnant to contemplate the full resumption of life after so grievous a loss, and the idea that she should in the future encounter someone whom she might want to marry was inconceivable, but her common sense affirmed Ildefonso's basic counsel that she must reintroduce herself into the mainstream of life. Few girls of fifteen in northern Mexico had ever seen so clearly the grand design of life, so she squared her shoulders and prepared to take her place within it.

What appealed to her most, after her profound experience at the pyramids, was to work at Misión Santa Teresa, for there she could help the Indian mothers care for their babies. But the new priest in town, this Father Ybarra, who had come north to see if the missions should be closed down, absolutely forbade her to step foot inside Santa Teresa: 'This place is not for women. If God had intended you to enter these precincts, he would have made women friars.'

When Fray Ildefonso explained that this poor child of God needed such work in order to protect her sanity, Father Ybarra, a member of the secular clergy who had never liked Franciscans to begin with, told the gentle friar to mind his own business, and within a week Fray Ildefonso was on his way back to the college in Zacatecas. In his absence Father Ybarra was even harsher with Trinidad: 'Stay where you belong. Pray. Strive to regain God's grace.'

Such orders Trinidad refused to obey, and with obvious distaste Father Ybarra watched her moving about the village as if she were a married woman, and for no specific reason he conceived a great dislike for this girl with the twisted mouth who always seemed to be smirking sardonically at what he said. In church on Wednesdays and Sundays he tried not to look at her, for he was obsessed with the idea that she was somehow allied with the devil. When one of the Saldaña servants informed him that in Saltillo on the way north 'some funny business happened on several nights when the young one slipped past the sleeping Don Ramón,' he began to watch her closely, hoping that she was pregnant. He practiced the anathema he would hurl at her from his pulpit when her shame was known—*hussy, slut, harlot* and *wanton* featured heavily—and he was disappointed when it became obvious that she was not with child.

As he went about his duties, those assigned him by the viceroy, who had long suspected that expenses of the northern missions were unjustified when compared with the meager results they produced, he also developed an intense hatred for Misión Santa Teresa, whose saintly founder Fray Damián he saw as a charlatan: 'Got himself killed by the Apache . . . in their camp . . . fooling around with their women, no doubt.' He convinced himself, because of his extreme dislike for Trinidad, that he must somehow unmask the chicanery of her great-uncle Damián, and he spent much of his energy trying to do just that.

He also convinced himself that Trinidad herself, a loose girl with an irreverent attitude, would come to no good, and several times he considered excommunicating her until she showed proper humility, but he was afraid to do so because of the importance of the Saldañas and their obvious friendship with the Veramendis.

He was in the plaza one morning, watching attentively as Trinidad left her house to meddle in some improper affair or other, when he saw her run across the square and throw her arms about Amalia Veramendi, Don Lázaro's daughter, as if they were old friends. The girls talked animatedly for some minutes, then walked off arm in arm. He wondered what secrets they had.

It was easily explained. Since the day of the Apache attack Trinidad had been unable to mention René-Claude's name, but desperately she had wanted to, and perhaps it was this cruel blockage that had driven her into a depression; now, with a sympathetic young woman about her own age available and interested, she was at last free to talk: 'You can't imagine, Amalia, how wonderful he was.' This was an unfortunate beginning, because Amalia looked sideways at her friend and thought: You'd be amazed at what I can imagine.

Trinidad, unaware of the envy she was creating, burbled on: 'Grandfather did everything possible to humiliate him . . . drive him away . . . said no child of his would ever marry a damned Frenchman. René-Claude just smiled, gave Grandfather all the courtesies, and melted him the way the sun melts snow in the Alps.'

Amalia, suspecting that her friend had enjoyed experiences denied her, wanted to explore more deeply, but refrained. With feigned girlish modesty she asked:

'Was it . . . well, is loving a man . . . do you have to surrender as much as it seems?'

'Not with René-Claude. He said we would be equals. And he behaved that way. Of course, he'd take care of the money and make all the big decisions, and maybe we'd live in Saltillo or maybe New Orleans. He'd decide that. But he asked me always what I wanted, which horse I preferred.'

The girls, each so eager to confide, still shied away from honest questions and answers. 'Is loving a man,' Amalia began, 'well, is it . . . does it . . . ?'

This should have encouraged Trinidad to speak her feelings. Instead, she reflected, smiled at Amalia, and said: 'It's all right.'

'This new priest, Father Ybarra. He condemns it. He seems very afraid of love.'

'Father Ybarra is a fool.' It was unfortunate that Trinidad said this, even to her trusted friend, because although Amalia was of the same opinion, when she criticized Ybarra to others she repeated not her own judgment but Trinidad's, and when word of this reached the priest's ears, his mind became set: he would settle with the Saldañas, important though they might be.

Things were in this state when a lone stranger came down El Camino Real from the north. No soldier protected him, no Indian guides, no companions. Just a tall spare man in his late twenties, with a head of heavy dark hair, a tooth missing in front, and an apparent willingness to challenge the world. He announced himself as Mordecai Marr, trader out of Mobile with important connections in New Orleans. He led a horse that had gone lame two days out and three overburdened mules laden with goods of considerable value which he proposed trading from Béjar, or perhaps from the new capital at Chihuahua if a decent road could be routed to that distant city.

Before he had located a place to stay, and there was only a pitiful half-inn run by some Canary Islanders, he asked for the residence of Don Ramón Saldaña, and when this was pointed out he walked directly there, tied his horse to a tree and allowed his mules to stand free. Banging on the door in a most un-Spanish way, he demanded of black Natán, who opened it: 'Yo deseo ver Don Ramón de Saldaña. Yo tengo letras para él.' He spoke painstaking Spanish but with a barbarous accent, and used the word *letras* instead of the proper *cartas*.

When Don Ramón appeared, it was obvious that Mr. Marr expected to be invited in, for he placed his foot against the door so that it could not be closed against him: 'I have letters to you from the D'Ambreuze family in New Orleans. They heard I was coming.'

Don Ramón was not a man to be forced into extending an invitation, and especially not to anyone like this bold americano, so he spread himself sideways, as it were, until he occupied the entire doorway, then said graciously: 'I am pleased to accept a communication from the distinguished family I had expected to be allied with mine.' He took the letters and was about to shut the door when Marr grabbed his left sleeve.

'Is it true what they said? The Frenchman was killed by the Apache?'

'Yes.'

'I saw them trailing me, two days ago, so I laid low and shot two of them. It's good to carry two guns . . . loaded.'

He made another move to enter the house, but this time Don Ramón pressed the door shut and left him standing in the street.

After the most careful calculation, Don Ramón decided against showing Trinidad the letters, for he felt they would only exacerbate her already tense emotions, but when he read them a second time and felt the warmth revealed in them, the obvious sincerity of a family that had gone to great lengths to have them translated into good Spanish by some official in New Orleans, he felt obliged to share them with her. So, though fearful that such reawakening of her interest in D'Ambreuze throw her again into depression, he decided to give them to her when she arrived home, but Trinidad did not *arrive* home in the ordinary sense of that word; she roared home like a child of eight at the end of a successful game, shouting: 'Grandfather! Amalia told me that letters from René-Claude have arrived!'

Don Ramón did not know what to say, for he had too many things he wanted to say: 'Your Amalia is a busybody.'

'The man stopped there first, asking about rooms and saying he had letters from René-Claude.'

'From his family.'

'It's all the same,' and she jumped up and down, hands out, begging for the letters.

'Stop that! You're a young woman now, not a child. And besides, the letters are for me, not you.'

'It's all the same,' she repeated, and she meant it. René-Claude and his parents, she and hers, all were united by love, so that a letter from his father was indeed a letter from René-Claude to her.

When she sensed that her grandfather was prepared to surrender the letters her boisterousness stopped; she moved away from him and began to weep, her lovable little face doubly distorted, and in total desolation of spirit she fell dejectedly onto a heavy wooden settee. 'Oh, Grandfather, I loved him so much. Life is so empty when I think of what it could have been.'

Her grandfather sat down beside her, placing his arms about her trembling shoulders: 'I've lost seven sons and a loving wife. I know how terrible pain can be.' They sat there for some time, each unable to speak further; then, with a tightening of her shoulders which Don Ramón could feel, she asked, as if she were a child again: 'May I see the letters, Grandfather, please?'

'Of course,' he said gently, and before she began to read them he rose and wandered into another room.

She had the same reactions that he had had, for the D'Ambreuze parents had written with such obvious pride in their son and such hopes that he had found a good wife that she felt as if they were standing there in the flower-filled room, on the dark-red tiles, and after a long while she sought her grandfather and returned the letters: 'You and I lost a good second family. I'll write in your office.'

'Write what?'

'I want to send them our love. Tell them what good people you and my mother are.' Her voice shook, but she finished her thought: 'They must want to hear as much as I did.' And she wrote a long detailed letter, telling them first of her experiences with their son in Saltillo, which she described lovingly so that they might hear the bells and see the movement of people in the plaza, and ending with what René-Claude's business companions had reported about his strong reputation. It was her hope that the letter conveyed a sense of Béjar and Saltillo and the Spanish family of which their son had been for a brief few weeks a member.

Later, when she went to see Amalia, a year older and two inches taller, she felt as if she, Trinidad, were the more mature, and she spoke like some adult addressing an eager child: 'I'm so glad you told me about the letters. Because I think perhaps Grandfather was going to hide them from me. Afraid they might upset me.' She laughed nervously.

'Can you still see him? I mean . . . in your mind?'

'He's standing behind every corner. I expect to see him in your kitchen when we go in.'

'Will you always feel that way?'

'Forever.'

'But you'll marry, won't you?'

'Grandfather says I'll have to. When he dies I'll own the house, the ranch.' She became very serious and asked Amalia to sit with her under the trees in the Veramendi garden. 'I've been thinking about becoming a nun.'

'That would be wonderful! A bride of Christ!'

'And I have a very serious disposition toward it, really I do.'

'You would be wonderful as a nun, and some day, with your brains, Mother Superior Trinidad.'

Later, when things had gone terribly wrong, Trinidad would remember this conversation and particularly this sentence. Amalia had said 'with your brains,' and her tone had betrayed how envious she had become of her good friend.

Even now, perplexed by this change in Amalia, Trinidad went to her mother to discuss it, and Doña Engracia sat her down beside the silent fountain and clarified the situation: 'Don't you see? She's jealous of you. You've been to Mexico City, and she hasn't. You've known a fine young man, and she hasn't. You read many books, and this makes her fear that you're more clever. And I suppose, Trinidad, that she thinks you're prettier.'

'But that's all suppose,' the bewildered girl protested. 'Why would that make her change?'

'Because that's the way of the world,' her mother replied. 'You be careful what you tell that young lady.'

But Trinidad had to confide in someone, and in subsequent meetings with Amalia she returned to the possibility of becoming a nun, and she would picture the entire progression from novice to head of some great religious establishment in Spain, or maybe Peru. 'But the other night when I was thinking quite seriously about this, it occurred to me that to become a nun, I would have to gain approval from Father Ybarra, or from someone like him . . .'

Both girls shuddered, and Amalia said: 'Father Ybarra drives people away from religion. Who could ask his approval for anything?' When the dour priest heard this comment repeated he attributed it to Trinidad, and his antipathy toward her deepened.

On several occasions the two young women pondered why the church would promote such a vain, self-centered man to a position of power, and Trinidad drew the sensible conclusion: 'I suppose all towns get some man like Father Ybarra, sooner or later. The only good thing about him is, he's finishing his report on the missions and will soon be leaving.' She kicked the dust. 'Good riddance, too.'

Now Amalia opened the important topic: 'I was home when he arrived.'

'Father Ybarra?'

'No. The americano. I didn't actually open the door when he knocked, but I could have, and there he was.'

'What did he look like?'

'I'd never seen an americano, of course.'

'Nor I.'

'But he was just what we'd been told. He was taller than usual. White. No mestizo. Lot of matted hair on his head. Blue-eyed. A tooth missing in front. A deep voice. To tell you the truth, Trinidad, he was really rather frightening.'

'How did you speak to him? I mean, if he didn't know Spanish?'

'Oh, but he did! He spoke it hesitatingly and very slowly, like a little boy just learning big words.' Amalia went on: 'He smelled. Yes, like a horse after a hard ride in the sun, and he must have known it because he asked Don Lázaro where he might find lodging and a bath.'

'Where is he now?'

'You know the Canary Islanders beyond the plaza, that nice family with the large house? Grandfather sent him over there, and I believe they took him in.'

The two young women left the Veramendi garden, casually walked south to the big church, past the Saldaña house and the low, handsome governor's palace, and there on the western edge of town they studied from a safe distance the adobe house of one of the capable Canary Island families, but they could detect no sign of the stranger.

Two days later, however, Trinidad and her grandfather were surprised to see that Mr. Marr had somehow got hold of a small building on the opposite side of the plaza, right in the shadow of the church. 'What does he intend doing there?' citizens asked. 'Is this to be a store?'

No, it was a warehouse for the holding of his trade goods prior to shipment onward to Saltillo or distant Chihuahua, but when the goods were stowed and the people of Béjar learned about their excellent quality, they began to pester the americano for a right to buy, and slowly, almost surreptitiously, he sold a copper kettle here, a swatch of fine cloth there, until he was operating a kind of informal shop.

'I wonder if he has a permit?' Don Ramón asked as he observed operations from across the plaza, and apparently others had raised the same question, for when the quasi-store had been in operation only four days, the captain from the presidio and the town's judge appeared at the warehouse to inquire as to Mr. Marr's papers.

Without hesitation he produced them, documents signed in both New Orleans and Mexico City granting Mordecai Marr the right to trade in the provinces of Tejas and Coahuila. 'We'll take these and study them,' the judge said, but with a quick motion Mr. Marr recovered his papers and said: 'These do not leave my possession.' The fact that he spoke slowly and in a deep voice intensified the gravity of his declaration, and the visitors acceded.

But he was not rude, for as soon as he was satisfied that the papers would remain with him he became almost subservient, asking the good captain and the respected judge whether they would consider taking to their ladies a trivial sample of his wares as thanks for the courtesies their husbands had extended. And he cut off generous lengths of cloth from his best bolt.

When the men had their gifts under their arms and were out on the plaza, he followed them and asked almost conspiratorily, as if they were his business partners: 'Where do you think I might find a house to buy in your town? It's so very pleasant, I need go no farther.'

They thought there might be one available at the far end of the plaza, and with that, they exchanged the most cordial goodbyes, but the two officials did not return to their places of business; they walked across the plaza and knocked on the door of Don Ramón de Saldaña, an elder in such matters, and asked him to send his slave Natán to fetch Don Lázaro de Veramendi, and when the four were assembled in Don Ramón's most pleasant garden, Trinidad, passing to and fro with drinks and sweetmeats, overheard bits of the discussion.

'His papers said he came from Philadelphia. What do we know about Philadelphia?' The four men had considerable if sometimes garbled knowledge on most topics likely to be discussed, for all could read, and their pooled information was that Philadelphia was reported to be the largest city in the new nation to the north. It had been the principal site of the recent revolution against England. It had an excellent seaport, but not directly on the sea. And it had once been the capital but had lost that distinction to New York, another fine seaport but also not on the sea.

'In fact, what do we know about los Estados Unidos, which seem to be pressing so hard upon us?' They knew that there were thirteen states, maybe more in recent years; one man said he was almost certain that there was also a new state called Kentucky. Another claimed to have special information: 'I've been told that they're Protestants, with many states forbidding Catholics to enter.' One good thing about Los Estados Unidos, some years back, when they were still English, they had fought France and won, but that was in Canada. It was a trading nation, but already showing signs of belligerence. The four men deemed it quite probable that sooner or later Spain would have to teach the americanos a military lesson.

'And most important of all, what do we know about this Mr. Marr?' He was a big man who had just shown in the matter of the papers his willingness to fight. He spoke Spanish, but in a way that indicated he had learned it in a hurry, as if he wished to use it for some specific purpose. He was armed. He had come down El Camino Real by himself, a daring feat, and he seemed to be in good funds, as witnessed by the gifts he had just made. But he was not a pleasant man, on this all four agreed.

'He is our first breath of los Estados Unidos,' the judge said, 'and not a reassuring one.'

'I think we must conclude he is a spy,' the captain said.

'For what? To what purpose?' Don Ramón asked.

'For the general intelligence that all armies need,' the captain replied. 'Else, why was he spying out all the streets of our town?'

'He was looking for a place to lodge,' Don Lázaro explained, and it was strange that though the two older men were willing to accept the newcomer, the two younger ones were prepared to throw him out of town. The difference was that the older men had fought their battles long ago and were now free to agitate for new ones, assured that they would not have to do the fighting, while the younger men knew that if trouble came in this stranger's wake, they would be the ones to bear the brunt.

'I think,' said the judge, 'that we have a very dangerous man amongst us,' and he was about to propose certain protective steps when Father Ybarra burst into the room, flushed and obviously distressed at not having been summoned to a meeting of such importance.

'Why was I not told?' he demanded, and after Trinidad had brought him a glass of wine, which he took contemptuously, he added: 'At a meeting like this I must be represented. After all, it is I who shall be reporting to the viceroy on affairs up here.'

'We met by accident,' the captain lied. 'The judge and I were inspecting his papers, as our duty required, and we assembled quite by chance.'

'What papers has he?'

'Impeccable. Authorized by Mexico City to trade in our province. Customs duties properly paid.'

'How could they be?' Ybarra snapped. 'He came in overland.'

'Nacogdoches,' the judge replied almost wearily, and in that moment the four original members of this meeting combined against the priest in defending the American. For half a year they had watched Ybarra and had recognized him as one of those petty, officious tyrants, adrift in all lands and in all religions, who assumed mantles of superiority in whatever affairs they touched. He was an impossible man, and if he opposed the American, they had to support the stranger.

'Will he become Catholic?' Ybarra asked. 'The law says he should.'

'If he wants land, I suppose he must,' the judge said evasively. 'But as a mere trader . . . I'm not sure how the law stands on that.'

'But surely he must become a Spanish citizen,' Ybarra pressed.

'I'm not sure on that either. Did his papers refer to that, Captain?'

'They said nothing specific.'

'You know what I think?' the priest asked. 'I think he's a spy, sent down by the americanos to see where they can attack us.'

The judge looked at the captain, who said slyly: 'We think you're right. We must all watch him . . . very carefully.'

Father Ybarra, thinking that he had the support of these officials, gloated: 'The minute he applies for land, he falls within my reach. Because we do not grant land rights to non-Catholics, is that not right?'

'Absolutely correct,' the judge said, but then he added: 'We have the law, but it's easily evaded.'

'How?'

'Foreign men marry our women and acquire their land.'

'A man like Marr will never settle down,' the priest said. 'No matter how much he wants land.'

How wrong he was! Within a week Mr. Marr was asking in his slow, patient Spanish: 'If the government allowed me to buy my shop, will it also allow me to buy land?' and he confided to five different customers at his informal store how highly he regarded the Béjar district, and as the months passed, Béjar began to accept him as pretty much the man he said he was: 'I did well in Philadelphia. Never much money, but always had a job. Never married, but I liked an Irish girl, except that my parents weren't prepared to welcome a Catholic into the family. That and other things, they drove us apart. I tried Pittsburgh and then Kentucky and then down the river to New Orleans. And then I heard of Texas, as we call it up north.'

'How did you lose your tooth?'

'I never allow a man to call me Mordy more than once. But if you travel long enough, you're bound to meet somebody bigger than you are.' He grinned at his questioner, showing the gaping hole, and said: 'But I won a lot more fights than I lost.'

And always he came back to the matter of land: 'A man travels as much as I have . . .'

'How old are you?'

'My papers say twenty-eight. I guess that's about right. One thing for certain, I'm old enough to want to settle down.'

'Why Béjar?'

The man who asked this probing question one afternoon when the store was empty, except for him and Marr, had traveled a good deal in the army and by ship to Cuba, and he knew precisely the value of his town, as he explained to the americano: 'You know, this isn't Vera Cruz, where the ships come in each week. This isn't Zacatecas, with its silver mines. And it certainly isn't Saltillo . . . Why don't you go on to that town if your papers say you can? There's action and beautiful girls and real shops down there.'

'I've never been to Saltillo, which must be a fine town from what you say. But it's a far piece down the road, and I doubt it will ever have much contact with America. But Béjar! I tell you, when trade starts with the north, which it must, this town will grow like a mushroom in morning dew. I want to be here when that happens.'

'How soon can it happen?'

'Next year if cities like New Orleans prosper. Fifty years if things lag.'

'And you want to own land when it does happen?'

'I do.'

This questioner, a Canary Islander with all the tough shrewdness and character of that group, began taking Mr. Marr about the countryside, explaining who owned what: 'As far as you can see and then twice that, Gertrudis Rodríguez.' On another journey, which covered two days with camping out at night: 'This great holding, Rivas family, one of the best.' The man later remembered that at this point Marr asked: 'Is that the Rivas with the two pretty daughters?' It was.

But the trip which Marr seemed to appreciate most was one that took them along the wandering Medina: 'Pérez ranch here, Ruiz up here, Navarro at the turn.' And then on the second day he was told: 'Here in the big bend of the river, Rancho El Codo. The Saldañas'. It once belonged to the Misión Santa Teresa, but somehow it got transferred to the family of the mission's saintly founder.'

'How many leagues?'

'Vast. Who has counted?'

'The Veramendis. Where's their ranch?'

'Bigger than any of these, but down in Saltillo, owned by a different branch of the family.'

They spent that night at El Codo, where the lack of supervision once provided by the Garza family was painfully obvious; Don Ramón had moved in other families, but all they seemed to do was build stronger walls to protect themselves against possible Comanche attacks, and that very night, toward four in the morning when a moon just past full threw a brilliant light, the Indians did strike, about thirty of them. They did not try to attack the biggest of the adobe houses, in which the travelers were sleeping along with the family, but they did surround a smaller house, where they killed two mestizo men and one of the wives, and galloped away with the other wife and two of her little girls.

The camp was in futile uproar when Mordecai Marr shouted for order: 'I want your best horses. All your guns. Juan here will ride with me. Who else?'

He apportioned the guns sensibly; some to the people who would stay behind in case the Comanche tried to attack again while the posse was gone, but most to the five who would ride with him. One man, terribly frightened by the disaster, tried to dissuade Marr from chasing the Indians, but the big American growled: 'We'll catch and kill them and bring back those young ones.'

And he did just that. After a bold two-day run far to the west, he doubled back and took the Comanche by surprise as they came carelessly over a hill with their captives. After an opening fusillade that killed several Indians, Marr grabbed another gun and shot several more. Then, disregarding his own safety in the confusion that resulted and using his gun like a club, he dashed to the two children, dragged them to safety behind a hillock, and returned to the battle, which the Comanche were abandoning.

The other five white men had taken one Indian, and when Marr learned from the weeping children that their mother had been tortured and slain soon after their capture, he went berserk and leaped upon the Comanche, bore him to the ground, and smashed his head with a large rock. He kept pounding at the man's chest until Juan and the other men pulled him away from the bloody mess.

'Come back!' he screamed into the emptiness, his hands dripping. 'Come back any time, you goddamn savages!' With great solicitation he started consoling the little girls, but when he saw their bruises and learned what they had suffered, he burst into tears and had to move away.

Word of his heroic rescue sped through Béjar prior to his return, carried by a workman from the ranch who said nothing to diminish the bravery of this americano who had been willing to fight the whole Comanche nation. Marr's rescue of the two children was marveled at, for only rarely did a captive of the Comanche ever return to civilized life; they were either kept in perpetual slavery or hacked to pieces over a slow fire. Dread of the Comanche permeated Béjar, and for good reason, for there had never been enemies like these fearful creatures of the western plains, and any man brave enough to chase them down, his six against thirty, and rip away their captives too, was indeed a hero.

People crowded his warehouse and helped him unpack when a fresh convoy of mules arrived from New Orleans with treble the goods he had had before. He stood beside his bales and recounted his exploit: 'I was a damned fool, understand that. I'd never do it again, of that you can be sure. I went crazy, I suppose. The woman and her children . . . And I could never have done it without Juan and the others. What shots those men were.'

'But you did it!' admiring women said.

'Once, but never again.'

The people of Béjar did not believe this, because on several occasions Mr. Marr gave clear proof of his hot temper. One day a stranger from Saltillo protested that the price of cloth was too high, and Marr patiently tried to explain that he had to import his goods by land from New Orleans rather than by ship via Vera Cruz. When the buyer pointed out that the distance from Vera Cruz to Béjar was much longer, Marr politely agreed: 'Longer, yes. But from Vera Cruz you have organized roads. From New Orleans, mostly trails.'

'Even so . . .'

At this point, Mr. Marr, according to people who were there, lifted the Saltillo man by his ears, dragged him to the door, the American's face getting redder each moment, and tossed him out into the plaza, bellowing in an echoing voice: 'Then buy your damned cloth in Vera Cruz.'

Unwisely, the stranger reached for his knife, whereupon Marr leaped upon him, knocked the knife away, and pummeled him until the captain of the presidio ran up to halt the fray. After that, people did not argue with nice-mannered Mr. Marr about prices.

After Trinidad had listened to three or four similar examples of Marr's mercurial behavior, she concluded that he was nothing but an americano bully, and she decided to have nothing to do with him. Next morning when he crossed the plaza to speak with her, she rebuffed him. But that afternoon Amalia came running to the Saldaña house with news that led her to change her mind: 'Have you heard about the wonderful thing Mr. Marr's doing?' And when Trinidad went to his warehouse she found on the counter a small wooden box with his hand-lettered sign: POR LAS NIÑAS HUÉRFANAS. In it were three silver pieces, his own contribution to the two children orphaned by the Comanche. Soon he would have a substantial number of coins, which he intended giving to the Canary Island family that had assumed care of the little girls, who were slowly recovering.

It was because of this sign that Trinidad found occasion to speak with the americano, for later when she returned to add her contribution she noticed that someone, not the one who made the sign, had changed the word *por* to *para*. Both words meant *for*, but in specialized contexts and to use one where the other was appropriate was almost humorous. When she commented on the editorial change, he laughed: '*Para* and *por, ser* and *estar*. No foreigner can ever learn the difference.'

She was impressed that he understood the difficulty and spent some time trying to explain the inexplicable, how *ser* and *estar* both meant exactly *to be,* but, again, in minutely specialized applications. She said: 'It's very complicated. *Yo soy* means that I am, that I exist. *Yo estoy* means that I am somewhere.' And he said: 'I solve it easily. I use *ser* on three days of the week, *estar* on the other three, so I'm always half right.' And she asked: 'What about the seventh day?' And he said: 'Like God, on the seventh day I rest. I use neither.'

Instinctively she was repelled by this big, rough man with the missing tooth, for she was finding him to be just what Don Ramón had predicted the americanos would be: arrogant and uncivilized, Protestant and menacing. But he was also intriguing, so despite her apprehensions she began to stop by his warehouse to chat, and one day she startled her grandfather with an extraordinary bit of information: 'Mr. Marr is becoming a Catholic.'

Yes, he had gone to Father Ybarra and said with proper humility: 'I wish to convert,' and the priest, eager to bring such a spectacular man into the church, forgot his earlier animosity and started giving religious instruction. It was a case of the brutal converting the brute, and one Sunday at service the dour priest was able to announce, while pointing with satisfaction to where Marr sat: 'Today the last unbeliever in our town has joined the Holy Church, and we welcome him. Jesus Christ is pleased this day, Don Mordecai.' And from that time on he was no longer referred to as Mister, but as Don.

On Monday morning after his conversion was solemnized, Don Mordecai visited the local government offices and started turning over four maps of the area while asking numerous questions of the custodian: 'Who owns this stretch of land?' 'On this map it refers to Rancho de Las Hermanas. Who are the sisters?' 'Who is this man Rivas?' On another day he spread four maps on the floor and pointed to an anomaly: 'The map of 1752 spells our town Véxar. Menchacha's map of 1764 calls it Béxar. This map of 1779 calls it Véjar. And the one three years ago calls it Béjar. What is our name?'

The clerk noticed with both pride and confusion that Don Mordecai was now calling it 'our town,' as if his conversion to Catholicism had also conferred citizenship: 'You can spell it however you please, but it's always something soft and beautiful.'

Marr said he did not think of Béjar as soft and beautiful, but the clerk assured him: 'You will when you've found yourself a plot, built your own house, taken a wife, and settled down with us.'

'All those things I should like to do,' Marr said, and by nightfall every one of the Spanish citizens knew what he had said, as did many of the Indians.

But Marr soon found that it was not a simple matter for a foreigner to acquire land in a frontier province, and his attempts to do so met with frustration. Either none of the good land was for sale, or he found himself ineligible to buy any of the marginal fields. Returning to the maps, he identified hundreds of thousands of acres of unclaimed land, but invariably some constraint prevented him from acquiring any. It was the same with purchasing a house in Béjar itself. There were none for sale, even though half a dozen changed hands while he watched.

It was then, in the summer of 1792, that he seriously analyzed his situation: Spain is finished in this part of the world. Within ten years Louisiana will break away. Then Mexico will break away, too. But an independent Mexico will never be strong enough to hold Tejas. And when Tejas breaks loose, everything will be in confusion.

He pondered how he could profitably fish in these troubled waters, and was guided by the folk wisdom his grandfather had often recited: 'Mordecai, I seen it so clear in England. Them as had land, had money. Them as didn't, didn't.' At the conclusion of this silent session, Mordecai summarized his strategy: I'll settle in Béjar, find me a wife, and grab hold of some land.

Before noon next morning he began paying serious attention to Trinidad de Saldaña, for the maps showed that the vast acreage her grandfather owned at El Codo stood right where El Camino Real turned to approach Béjar. Any future road leading to the west toward Chihuahua would have to cross the established camino on this land, and he could foresee settlements there and the exchange of goods and the development of real farms, not just empty land called loosely a ranch, with no fences, few buildings and very little control.

The old man can't live forever, he told himself as he studied the ranch from a hillock to the east. When he dies, it goes to his granddaughter, and a man could do lots worse than her.

He began intercepting her when she crossed the plaza, or speaking to her when she sat under the trees with her friend Amalia. He took great effort to obtain invitations to dinners where she and her grandfather were to be, and when Engracia de Saldaña died of the fever that raged north of the Rio Grande—'virulent, pulmonary and strangling,' the doctor called it—he paid a formal visit to the house across the plaza with a large package of sweetmeats imported from New Orleans as his contribution to the funeral feast. He spoke with Trinidad for some minutes, consoling her for her grievous loss: 'I liked to see Doña Engracia crossing the plaza, for then I knew happiness was on the way.'

Trinidad, caught up in her new lamentations, perceived nothing of Don Mordecai's plan to acquire her land through his quiet courtship, but Don Ramón smelled him out in a minute, and now began the protracted, painful duel between the elderly Spaniard and the brash newcomer.

'I don't want you to speak any further with Marr,' Don Ramón warned his granddaughter. 'The man does not have decent intentions.'

If Trinidad had accepted her grandfather's accurate assessment, much trouble would have been avoided, but she was beginning to stare down the corridor of years and see only loneliness ahead. The man she loved was dead. Her mother was dead. Her grandfather was obviously failing, and when he died, she would have to manage El Codo by herself. So although she was not actively seeking a potential husband, she was aware that Mordecai Marr was a vigorous fellow who could solve many of her problems. Her next defense of Marr revealed her increasingly muddled thinking, for she cited the opinion of a man she detested: 'But Father Ybarra has welcomed him into the community.'

'A worse recommendation a man could not have. Stay clear of them both.'

Trinidad certainly had no desire to engage in any close friendship with the americano, but she did recognize him as a man of character, and he certainly represented a vitality which was lacking in her life and in the life of this town. She did not like Marr, but she was stirred by what he represented, and when she compared his stern and unmistakable masculinity with the rather colorless character of the few unmarried Spanish and mestizo men in the region, she had to prefer Marr.

She had not yet begun to consider him as a possible husband, especially since her emotions were now dominated by her grief over the death of her mother, but she was neither surprised nor displeased when one day he caught her in a passageway where none could see and kissed her rather vigorously.

'I'm sorry,' he said immediately. 'Please forgive me.' Before she could respond, he kissed her again, forcefully. When she recalled the scene later, she had to compare the delicate, almost unfolding caresses of René-Claude with the elemental love-making of this americano, and although she much preferred the former and was grateful that her first experience had been so reassuring, she did sometimes suspect that it had been the courtship of children, whereas Marr's more assertive approach was that of a mature man for a rapidly maturing woman. In other words, she did not automatically reject his advances, for she sensed without putting her thoughts into specific words that it was understandable for him to come along when he did and how he did.

There was, however, among the soldiers assigned to the presidio that young lieutenant whom Don Ramón had rebuked for sloppiness some years before. He was named Marcelino, born of a distinguished Spanish father and a Mexican woman who was one eighth mestizo, and that eighth dated far back, so that of the young man's sixteen great-great-grandparents, only one had been Indian, and only five of the remainder had been born in Mexico. He was about as Spanish as one could be in the Mexico of this time, but by no stretch of generosity could he be *called* either Spanish or peninsular. At best he might try to pass as criollo.

In both the presidio and in Father Ybarra's headquarters there was a ridiculous list of names, compiled by clerks with nothing better to do, which purported to designate the particular mix of blood for any citizen in the Spanish dominion. This extraordinary list, which no sensible person took seriously, contained eighty-five different categories, for narrow-minded men deemed it important to indicate precisely what percentage of the four major strains each citizen contained: Spanish, Indian, Negro, Chinese, the latter having slipped into Mexico via the Acapulco-Manila trading galleons that crossed the Pacific each year. Also, it was important to know the father's derivation and the mother's; in the samples given here from the preposterous list, the father, of course, comes first:

peninsular (gachupín)	Spanish-Spanish, both parents born in Spain
criollo (Español)	Spanish-Spanish, but of lower status because at least one parent born in Mexico
limpio (clean) de origen	both parents probably Spanish, but cannot prove it
mestizo	Spanish-Indian
mulato	Spanish-Negro
coyote	mulatto-Indian
calpamulato	Indian-mulatto
zambo grifo	mulatto-Negro
galfarro	Negro-mulatto
zambaigo	Indian-Chinese
cambujo	Chinese-Indian

In this way the purity of the Spanish race was protected and the infiltrations of lesser strains identified, and many of the designations carried derogatory overtones to demonstrate what the superior groups really thought of such mixing:

lobo (wolf)	Indian and Negro
zambo (lascivious monkey)	Negro and Indian

Marcelino carried the designation *limpio de origen,* meaning that he was almost acceptable, but to Don Ramón he was not acceptable, for the latter, with each passing year, took more seriously the responsibility of finding for his granddaughter a husband of proper category.

Therefore, when the attractive young officer began paying court to Trinidad, Don Ramón moved to protect his granddaughter, unaware that Marr, the americano, posed a much more serious threat. After Lieutenant Marcelino had thrust himself three times upon the Saldañas, obviously enamored of the household's young lady, Don Ramón stifled his pride and went to the presidio, which he had been avoiding.

'Lieutenant, you've become a credit to the army.'

'I try to be.'

'Of that incredible rabble you brought here two years ago, half ran away, one committed murder, and three raped the little Indian girls in the mission.'

'A sorry lot. Not a credit to Spain at all.'

'That's what I've been thinking of these days, Lieutenant. Spain. I want my granddaughter to marry a man of Spain.'

'I am a man of Spain. For many generations.'

'Not exactly.'

Marcelino, who had always been aware of his classification and was not disturbed by it, laughed easily, and this irritated Don Ramón: 'I'd prefer if you did not present yourself at our house or sit in church staring at Trinidad.'

'Don Ramón, when a man has a very pretty granddaughter, all men stare at her.'

'You're to stop.'

'As you command, sir,' the arrogant young fellow said with a low bow, 'but if I were you, I'd worry far more about an americano suitor than one like me.'

Saldaña reached out to grasp the insolent officer, but the latter merely pushed his hand away, and the interview ended dismally, with Don Ramón embarrassed and Lieutenant Marcelino disgusted with such frontier snobbery. But that afternoon the old man returned: 'Is what you said true, young man? Is the americano paying serious court to my girl, behind my back?'

At the very moment that Don Ramón was asking this question, feeling that as his granddaughter's guardian, he was obligated to know the answer, Trinidad, now lacking a mother or a proper dueña, was slipping across the plaza and into Marr's warehouse. With the door barred, she and the americano were talking in a far corner when he suddenly grabbed her. She tried to scream, but he silenced her with furious kisses, and when she tried to break away, he forcefully prevented her escape. Soon she was upon the floor with him on top of her, but after moments of enormous confusion she stopped struggling and lay in awful turmoil as he made wild love.

When it ended she was appalled by its force, by Marr's uncontrollable passion, and could not comprehend her own inability to fight back; she had submitted against her will, of that she was certain, yet she could not believe that she had stumbled into such a confusing situation without anticipating its outcome.

In the days that followed she and Marr tried, each in separate ways, to reach some understanding regarding the assault and its consequences. He decided, during long lonely walks beside the river, that he must brave Don Ramón's objections and propose to Trinidad, winning himself a good wife and a splendid spread of land. He could foresee years of happiness and wealth in Béjar, and as a man of twenty-eight the time to begin his enjoyment of them was now. As for Trinidad, he liked her and felt sure he could have a good life with her. He failed completely to realize that his violent behavior might have alienated her, but he did tell himself: When we meet, I'll offer an apology, if it looks like she wants one.

Trinidad faced problems that were more complex, for in addition to the big ranch at El Codo, she would, at her grandfather's death, inherit all plots of land in town belonging to the Saldañas, and she wondered whether any young woman of seventeen could handle such responsibilities. She was aware that stalwart women among the Canary Islanders had operated businesses when their husbands died, and she supposed that she could do as well as they, but none of them had had entire ranches to control, and most of them had had sons to help.

She had great respect for the Canary Islanders, who amusingly called themselves Don This and Don That, as if they were real gentry, and she would have been happy had she found some young Islander of promise, but she had not. She liked the young lieutenant at the presidio, but her grandfather had already told her of their quarrel and his dismissal of the man.

That left Mordecai Marr, who had so much to commend him in the way of valor, daring, imaginativeness and masculine ardor, but just as much to condemn him: vile temper, harsh manners, a lack of sensitivity, and the fact that he was an americano of uncertain lineage and unproved character. However, his willingness to convert to the true religion was in his favor, and his obvious love of land made her think that he would be a good custodian of her properties.

Some days later she returned to the warehouse, and when Marr interpreted this as a signal that she had not been unhappy with his behavior, she told him sternly: 'You behaved like an animal, Señor Marr, and I'll have no more of that.' Honestly surprised by her reaction, he promised: 'I'll never offend you. Believe me, a man who wanders about like me . . . he doesn't learn how to act with girls.' And this time when they made love he was a different man, even displaying tenderness when they parted.

These bewildering experiences made her hungry to talk with someone, and since no member of her family was available, she turned once again to Amalia Veramendi, in whose garden they conversed.

'Would you ever consider marrying an americano?' Trinidad asked. 'Don Mordecai is attractive. And he works hard.'

'Have you been visiting with him?'

'Well, he has kissed me.'

'What's he like? How does he compare with your Frenchman?'

'They're very different, Amalia.' She hesitated: 'But I suppose all men are different.'

'Do you think he'll stay here . . . permanently, I mean?'

'Oh, yes!' Trinidad said with confidence. 'He wants to buy his own land and settle. He said so.'

'I heard him tell Father he might move his headquarters to Saltillo.'

'He did?' Trinidad was startled by this information, for Marr had never spoken to her of such a possibility.

'Well, he discussed the possibility of buying some of our land in Saltillo. Our relatives must have three thousand leagues down there.'

'Did your father say he'd sell?'

'The Veramendis never sell.' Amalia laughed apologetically when she uttered these pretentious words, for she was not an arrogant girl. 'Would you marry an americano?' she asked.

'I wanted to marry a Frenchman.'

'I'm afraid, Trinidad. I really am. I don't mean about husbands. I mean about everything.'

'What's happening?'

'My dear grandfather talks so much about the death of Spain. The loss of all things good and gentle.'

Trinidad looked up at the trees, and then, as if relieved to escape from talking honestly about Mordecai Marr, she spoke not about her confusion but Spain's: 'I know what he means. When we went south on our wonderful expedition to the capital, we met a file of prisoners marching north, some of them in chains . . . and where were they going? Right here to Béjar. To serve as soldiers, if you will. Dreadful men, to be the new leaders of Tejas. It was sickening to see them. It's sickening to learn how they behaved when they got here. I had a clear vision that this was the end of Spain. Don Mordecai says it can't hold on another twenty years.'

'He'd better be careful what he says.'

'Oh, he didn't mean that americanos would come down. He meant that the people of Mexico would throw the Spaniards out.'

'He'd better be just as careful about that.'

And then Trinidad returned to the real problem: 'You didn't answer my question. Would you marry an americano?'

'No! I wouldn't be allowed, for one thing. And for another, I wouldn't want to.'

The problem the young women were discussing became academic when Don Mordecai, accompanied by Father Ybarra, came formally to the Saldaña house on the plaza and asked Don Ramón for permission to marry his granddaughter Trinidad. To the old man's amazement, Marr presented him with translations into Spanish of three documents from Philadelphia signed by clergymen and a judge, testifying to the good character of Mordecai Marr and to the fine reputation of his family.

Don Ramón left the two men in the large entrance salon and sought his granddaughter, smiling at her bleakly and confessing: 'It's not what I wanted, and I'm sure it's not what you wanted, but . . .'

'There could be only one René-Claude,' Trinidad whispered.

'We should have accepted that Lieutenant Marcelino,' the old man said, 'but I

drove him off.' He shook his head and stared at his granddaughter, prepared to
terminate this loveless match if she spoke, but she did not.

'Do you accept him?' he asked, and she nodded.

There was no formal announcement of the proposed wedding, but rumors
quickly spread through Béjar and even out to the ranch, so that when Don
Mordecai rode there with two soldiers to inspect his future holdings he was
greeted with congratulations and a jug of strong wine, which he shared with the
Mexican and Indian families who would soon be working for him. The ranch
men talked about needed improvements and Marr assured them that work would
soon start. It was a happy meeting, with much discussion of Indians: 'Don
Mordecai, we think that when you rode out and killed the Comanche and took
back the children, you scared them away. We've seen none.'

'We'll make this ranch safe, and keep it safe,' he promised.

In all parts of Béjar he delivered the same message: 'We shall build permanently. We shall make this town important.' To the amazement of the townsfolk,
he initiated trade with Zacatecas, and what was more important, went to the area
capital at Chihuahua over a trail that could scarcely be called a road: 'Béjar will be
the major point for trade to the west. Within our lifetime this will be the center of
a new empire, the empire of trade.'

But when the town was satisfied that it had obtained in Don Mordecai a new
resident with powerful vision and great managerial capacity, it was shattered by
the announcement that he was not, after all, going to marry Trinidad de Saldaña,
but Amalia Veramendi!

Yes, the more powerful family had approached him with the tempting proposal
that if he married their daughter, the couple would be dowered with some forty
thousand acres of the choicest land around Saltillo. Banns for the marriage were
posted on the church door; congratulations flowed; and because his proposed
marriage to Trinidad had remained only an informal arrangement, the community
forgave Don Mordecai his impetuous behavior.

Trinidad learned of the astonishing news from the casual conversation of a
maid: 'I promised the Veramendi cooks that I would help them bake goods for the
wedding.'

'And who's getting married over there?' Trinidad asked, and the maid replied:
'Amalia, to Don Mordecai.'

Trinidad did not weep; she did not even become angry. She walked quietly into
her garden and leaned against a tree, endeavoring to understand the various facets
of Don Mordecai's behavior: his arrogant arrival, his brutal love-making; his
honest attempt to make amends; his obvious hunger for land; the temptation of
the Veramendi lands. And she concluded that she'd had the misfortune to encounter a new type of man, with no morals and no honor. Bewildered and deeply hurt,
she went to her grandfather and asked him quietly to ascertain the facts, and it
was he who became violently angry, and when he returned he was grim-faced:

'The scoundrel has proposed to Amalia and been accepted. I told them frankly of his earlier interest in you, and assured them that if . . .' He could not finish, for he was trembling with an icy rage.

He remained in this torment for two days, then realized what the honor of his family required. Striding across the plaza in the shadow of the church, he banged his way into Marr's warehouse, slapped him stingingly across the face, and challenged him to a duel.

He then reported to the presidio and asked young Lieutenant Marcelino to serve as his second, and the officer said stiffly: 'Duels are illegal, as you know. But I cannot refuse, Don Ramón, for you have been dealt a great blow, and I shall be proud to act as your second.'

Marcelino found the captain of the presidio, José Moncado, and together they went to Marr's: 'Sir, you have been challenged by a gentleman of distinction. He is an old man with a trembling hand. To duel him would be an outrage. Please, please, go to him and apologize.'

'Nothing of the sort,' Marr said in slow, careful Spanish. 'He's done little but insult me since I came here, and I want to finish with him.'

'It would be murder for an excellent shot like you to accept this old man's challenge.'

'His insults started on the first day . . . when he barred his door . . . refused me entrance.'

'You insist?'

'I do. Amalia's brother will be my second.'

The two then went across the plaza to dissuade Don Ramón from his folly, and they pointed out the dreadful danger he faced: 'Several times the americano has proved what an expert shot he is. You must withdraw your challenge.'

Don Ramón looked at his visitors as if he were an innocent child being reproved for something he did not understand and which he had not done: 'He has dishonored my granddaughter. What else can I do?'

'But at the Comanche fight, he never missed.'

'What has that to do with me? I fire. He fires. It's a matter of honor.'

When they found that they could not deter him, they enlisted the support of Don Lázaro, a curious choice, since he was grandfather to the Veramendi girl whose acceptance of Marr had caused this trouble; he tried, however, to be persuasive: 'My dear old friend, he will kill you for certain.'

'Not if I kill him first.'

'You can scarcely lift a heavy pistol, let alone fire it.'

'I'll hold it in two hands. It's a matter of honor.'

Don Lázaro considered this for a moment and agreed. 'You have no choice, that is true. May God protect you.' Then he said: 'I had nothing to do with Amalia's agreement to marry him. My son did that. I was ready for an americano, but not this one,' and with that he bowed to Don Ramón and returned home.

So on a June morning in 1792, two parties left town and walked to a slight rise overlooking the river south of town, where three of the missions lay like a string of pearls. A level space was marked off, a line drawn, and starting places for the duelists indicated. Captain Moncado said stiffly: 'I shall count to fifteen. At each count, you will take a pace away. As soon as I cry "Fifteen" you may turn and fire.' Then he changed the tone of his voice and asked passionately: 'Gentlemen, will you reconsider? There is no justification for this duel.' When neither contestant spoke, he said with near-disgust: 'So be it. I shall start counting.'

With each numeral sounding in the crisp morning air, the two men, so pathetically ill-matched—a Spanish gentleman at the end of his days protecting his conception of honor, an American invader with his own rough ideas of justice—moved apart.

'Fourteen!' Moncado cried. 'Fifteen!'

Don Ramón whirled, fired with trembling arms, and sent his bullet far to the right, kicking up dust at the foot of a wayward tree.

'Don Mordecai!' Moncado shouted. 'Show mercy!'

But Marr, who had anticipated this wild shot and who had postponed firing until it took place, drew steady aim, kept his pistol motionless, and fired a bullet straight into the old man's heart.

When the burial of Don Ramón had been solemnized, by a friar from Santa Teresa and not by Father Ybarra, the heavy consequences of the duel began to emerge, for it was now that the priest saw fit to announce the results of his investigations into ancient malfeasances at Misión Santa Teresa. Had Marr proceeded with his proposed marriage to Trinidad, Ybarra would have buried his accusations out of deference to his prize convert, but with Marr marrying the Veramendi girl, the priest felt free to indulge his vengeance upon a young woman he disdained:

> Even the most cursory inquiries at San Antonio de Béjar would satisfy a judge that the so-called saint Fray Damián de Saldaña, founder of Misión Santa Teresa, committed acts of the gravest impropriety in tricking the then viceroy into approving a devious plan whereby Damián's brother, Captain Alvaro de Saldaña of the presidio, obtained possession of lands pertaining to the mission. Some, commenting on the trickery whereby this exchange took place, call it ordinary family protection; others call it more accurately plain theft.
>
> I recommend that even though Misión Santa Teresa may soon be secularized and its possessions redistributed as the court in Madrid decides, it is imperative that lands stolen from it be returned immediately, so that a just disposition of them can be made. I recommend that the ranch

known as El Codo in the bend of the Medina west of Béjar be taken from the Saldaña family and restored to its rightful owner, Misión Santa Teresa.

When the order approving this reached Béjar, Captain Moncado sorrowfully and Father Ybarra joyfully served notice on Trinidad that she must surrender the twenty-five thousand choice acres, along with any buildings situated on them and all cattle grazing there. She would be left the house in town and the few plots of land scattered about Béjar, but nothing more.

With her customary nobility, she acquiesced, without showing any rancor toward Father Ybarra, who had persecuted her in so many ways; on the Sunday following her dispossession she even went to church for solace, enduring one of his last sermons prior to his return to the capital. He used as his text the parable of the faithful servant, pointing out how Fray Damián had proved faithless to his trust, whereas he, Ybarra, had come north as a faithful servant to rectify that wrong.

When he was gone, Trinidad discovered that although the court trials and paper work relating to the formal transfer of El Codo would take years, the friars at Misión Santa Teresa retained possession only four days before turning it over to the Veramendis, who gave it to their daughter Amalia as a wedding present. This, when added to Rancho San Marcos, which adjoined it and which was also given to the newlyweds, meant that Don Mordecai, in town barely two years, now controlled forty-three thousand acres: ten miles along the river, seven miles wide.

The happy couple saw Trinidad occasionally, and when they did a miracle of human behavior occurred: they forgave her. As often happens when a crime of grave dimension has been perpetrated, the guilty made a great show of forgiving the innocent, so that when the Mordecai Marrs met Trinidad in the narrow streets or in the plaza, they smiled generously. One afternoon Amalia actually came to visit, a young, gracious, condescending matron, and she explained that since Mordecai had obtained land near Béjar, he now saw no necessity to move on to Saltillo, which had been his original intention when he learned that the Veramendis had huge estates there: 'We shall be very happy here in Béjar, I'm sure. Mordecai's trade with Chihuahua increases monthly.'

These social scandals of Béjar were forgotten when the Comanche went on another rampage. After slaying scores of isolated countrymen to the west they tried to overrun El Codo, but its fortifications held. So they raged on to Béjar itself, mounting such a furious assault that all men and women, and even children, had to be mustered by Captain Moncado to hold them off.

They struck the town with fury, breaking down barricades, killing many but failing to reach the houses about the central plaza. Repulsed by the bravery of Moncado and his stout right arm Mordecai Marr, who fired four different guns as fast as women could reload them, the Comanche turned abruptly, struck at unprotected Misión Santa Teresa, and overwhelmed it. Two young friars there were pierced with a score of arrows. The older domesticated Indians were slain by fierce stabs and slashes; the younger were kept alive for prolonged torture, the children to serve as slaves. Infuriated by the resistance, the Comanche set all buildings ablaze, battered down the wooden doors of the stone church, and took savage, howling delight in throwing upon the fire Simón Garza's great carvings of the Fourteen Stations.

In flames the patient work of Fray Damián disappeared. The Indian houses so carefully built by Fray Domingo in 1723 vanished; the barns where the cows had given birth and the cribs in which their feed had been stored, the school where children had learned to sing, and the cell in which Damián had prayed for guidance—none survived the rage of the Comanche.

Loss of the northernmost mission caused Father Ybarra to speed his report on the remaining five, and in his careful recommendations to Zacatecas, Mexico City and Madrid, he summarized the criticisms of Spain's mission effort:

> In advising you to halt the operations of the Franciscans in Béjar and throughout the rest of Tejas, with the two exceptions already noted, I act in pain and sorrow, but the facts can support no other conclusion.

> The first important mission of which I have knowledge was San Francisco de los Tejas in the Nacogdoches region, established in 1690. Others so numerous that I cannot name them followed, including the six at Béjar starting in 1718. At the end of a hundred years of concentrated and costly attempts to Christianize the Indians, I find after a most careful count that Tejas contains exactly four hundred and seventeen Christian Indians, and not one of them is an Apache or a Comanche. Captain Moncado at the presidio in Béjar estimates that it requires three and one half soldiers to protect each Indian convert, yet the converts perform no tasks beneficial to the general society.

> I am most suspicious of the conversions that do occur. Most of the converts are old women who have lived lives of great licentiousness and deem it prudent to have their sins remitted before they die. The young, the hardy and those who could do strong work for Jesus are little touched by the missions; as a matter of fact, if we secularized them all immediately, the young Indians might well be inclined to join our established churches at one-tenth the cost and ten times the results.

> I do not speak disparagingly of the friars who attempted to do God's work in these remote and depressing areas. Those serving now are exemplary Christians, and some have striven mightily, but they have accom-

plished little. I am told that in the earliest days, when the missions first opened, results were better, but the numbers of Indians converted to the True Religion were always minimal, and to continue this fruitless effort would be financially and religiously unjustified.

Close the missions. Send the friars back to Zacatecas, where they can do some good. Use the emptied buildings as fortresses in time of siege. Sell the mission ranches with their cattle to local men who can make better use of them. And do it now.

What Father Ybarra overlooked in his harsh and overall accurate summary of the mission experience in Tejas—so much bleaker than that in California and New Mexico—was the civilizing effect of men like Fray Damián and especially Fray Domingo in the 1720s and 1730s, when they lit brave candles in the wilderness, demonstrated Spain's sincere interest in the souls of its Indians, and helped establish little centers of safety and learning capable of maturing into fine towns and cities.

Also, the Franciscans did succeed in civilizing the smaller Indian tribes that clustered about the missions, but their failure to domesticate first the fierce Apache and then the terrible Comanche, now the dominant tribe, created the impression that they had failed in all. This was unfortunate, a historic misinterpretation which implanted in Tejas lore the fiction that 'nothing can be done with the Indian.' Father Ybarra's 1792 report summarized what many Spaniards had concluded, and this legend grew and festered until Tejas, once an area teeming with Indians of many tribes, some most civilized, became Texas, a state with almost no Indians, for it preferred to operate under the slogan attributed to a Northern general serving in Texas: 'The only good Indian is a dead Indian.' In due course, the Indians of Texas would be either expelled or dead.

But the greatest injustice in Father Ybarra's judgment on the missions was that he did not take into account the nature of God or the workings of His will. God had not come to Tejas in white robes attended by choirs of angels; He came as a toilworn Franciscan friar, a confused captain trying to do his best in some remote presidio. He came as a mestizo woman lugging two bawling babies who would grow into stalwart men; He came sweating Himself over the vast amount of work to be done before the place could be called civilized; and God knew, if Father Ybarra did not, that fat Fray Domingo dancing at sunset in what his detractors called 'a near state of tipsiness and shouting at the top of his voice' was closer to heaven than Ybarra would ever be.

After the destruction of Santa Teresa, Trinidad spent two agonizing weeks surveying her deplorable situation, but could reach no sensible conclusions. She felt such confusion that during the third week she kept entirely to herself in the beautiful house with the low-ceilinged rooms, tended only by Natán. She applied these hours to an unemotional evaluation of all that had happened to her since she first began to confide in her dear friend Amalia Veramendi. Through the shadows of her darkened room passed ghosts of the two dead men she had loved so dearly, René-Claude and Don Ramón, and images of the two living ones she despised, Don Mordecai and Father Ybarra, and she had to conclude that not only had those two men abused her, but that Amalia had betrayed her. Despite constant review, she could not find herself at fault. She had responded as any spirited young woman would to the courtship of René-Claude, and even though the Galíndez and Saldaña families had rebuked her for unladylike enthusiasm in the Saltillo paseo, she could not think of a single action she would reverse. She had loved him; she still loved him; and she would love him until she died.

Her relations with Don Mordecai were more difficult to evaluate, for she had actively speculated about her need for a husband, and although she had not sought Marr out or overtly encouraged him, she had wanted to know what kind of man he was, and even what kind of husband he might prove to be. What else could I have done? she asked herself in the darkness of her room. That Marr turned out to be unprincipled was her bad luck, not her fault.

Gradually, as sensitive young women had done throughout history, she tried to construct a realistic portrait of herself: I've done nothing wrong. I regret nothing. And I will not allow them to submerge me in some swamp.

But her moral courage did not solve her personal problems. As she moved about her little town she could feel disapproval directed toward her, but she bit her lip and grappled with specifics: The loss of El Codo? Of course our saintly Fray Damián was less than honest when he maneuvered its transfer to his brother. Away it goes.

Once she had conceded this, she no longer grieved about this loss, but she did realize that she must leave Béjar, though to go where, she did not know. That decision she would postpone until she resolved a matter that was perplexing many thoughtful Mexicans these days. Summoning Natán, she told him: 'It would be painful for me to hold another human being in bondage,' and with exquisite attention to legal detail she gave him his freedom. She also took care of an old Indian nurse, then left funds to the church for perpetual novenas for the soul of Don Ramón. As she delivered the silver she looked up at a crucifix, and without kneeling she stared into the eyes of Christ and whispered: 'You died to save me, and Don Ramón died to protect my honor. I will strive to be worthy of your love.'

Consoled but still uncertain as to what she must do, she returned to her garden and sat alone, allowing tears to flow: I'm lost. Oh God, I am so alone. Then slowly, from some deep reservoir, an idea began to germinate, and with her eyes still wet, she moved inside to find pen and paper, and drafted a letter:

Esteemed Domingo Garza,

I write from the dark valley of the human soul. A beautiful Frenchman
who was to marry me was slain by Comanche. My mother has died. A
strong americano I was to marry has married another, then killed my
grandfather in a duel. The ranch at which you worked has been taken
from us. Misión Santa Teresa, where your great-grandfather carved those
wonderful Stations, has been burned and his work lost.

In these tragic days I remember when my grandfather made me learn
my letters and I taught you, and I remember how your grandfather
taught you to ride, and you taught me. I remember how you were always
kind and thoughtful, and how you obeyed the harsh rules my grandfather sometimes laid down. I remember you as a young man of goodness,
and now I pray with tears welling from my eyes that in your goodness,
and if you are free to do so, you will come and rescue me from the terror
in which I live.

> San Antonio de Béjar
> Provincia de Tejas
> 1792
>
> Trinidad de Saldaña

She posted the letter to the growing town of Laredo, from where it would go
downriver to the settlements established by the great Escandón in the 1740s, and
in time to the lands once held by the Saldañas. There it would be delivered to
Domingo Garza, son of the couple that now owned these lands on the north bank
of the river.

It would require, Trinidad judged, about three months for the letter to reach
Domingo and three months more before she could receive a reply. In the meantime she moved about the paths of Béjar as if she intended remaining there the
rest of her life, heiress no more, sought after no more. She attended church; she
asked about new laws at the presidio; she watched as Amalia and her husband
reinforced their foothold in the community. She never spoke against them to the
acquaintances she met, and she counseled with no one.

At the end of two months and two weeks she was startled by an importunate
banging on her door, and when she opened it she found standing before her, his
clothes covered with dust from his long ride, Domingo Garza. When he faced her
and saw once more that twisted smile and those luminous eyes, he was transfixed,
unable to move, for he was a mestizo and she was a daughter of Spain, but as he
hesitated she looked directly into his eyes and whispered: 'You have saved me,' and
thus set free, he swept her into his arms and buried his head against her neck to
hide the tears he could not control.

He stayed in Béjar one week, visiting the burned mission and riding out to see the ranch which he had once supposed he would some day manage for the Saldañas, as his ancestors had done for so long. Later, when Don Mordecai heard that he was in town, he sought him out to make a generous offer: 'You know the ranch. I need a manager I can trust. I'll give you a good job and a good wage.' Then he added with a sly wink: 'And if in due course you should care to marry the Saldaña girl . . . '

Domingo said promptly: 'Now that's a good idea. I need a job.'

So the two men, protected by troops from the presidio, rode out to the ranch, and when they arrived they dismissed the soldiers, telling them to wait within the walled area. Without dismounting, they moved about the ranch, with Marr explaining what Domingo's duties would be, and when they were far from the others, with Marr pointing to a fence that Domingo would have to mend, Domingo drew back, leaned forward from his left stirrup, and landed a mighty blow on Marr's chin that toppled him clean out of his saddle.

With never a sound, Domingo leaped onto the prostrate Marr and began hammering him as hard as he could with both fists.

Bigger and stronger, Marr was not defenseless, but overwhelmed by Garza's sudden move, he could not easily apply his superior force. When he struggled to his feet, lashing out with his powerful arms, Garza danced and dodged, landing such severe blows that before long Marr was winded and sorely hurt.

But still he defended himself, and when Garza saw that his opponent was tiring, he smashed in with a series of wild punches, kicks, jabs and belts, until Marr fell to the ground. As he lay there, clearly defeated, Garza did not grant him the honors of war. Not at all. With his first outcry in the battle he leaped upon the fallen man and smashed him so furiously about the face that blood spurted; the remaining big front tooth popped out, and Don Mordecai fainted.

Wiping his hands on the grass, Domingo tied Marr's horse to his own, then rode slowly back to where the soldiers waited. 'You'd better go out and find him,' he said. Surrendering Marr's horse to them, he started the long ride back to Béjar, asking for no protection.

He arrived at sunset, well speckled with blood, and before the moon was up he and Trinidad de Saldaña, protected by four riders he had hired, were on their way to Laredo, but they had barely left town when she cried: 'Oh! I must go back!' He feared she was reconsidering her decision, but when they reached the beautiful old house on the plaza, all she wanted was that sketch she had made of the church at Saltillo, which Don Ramón had framed. It was one of the memories of her past life which she would never surrender.

She moves on, a mature woman of seventeen, granddaughter of a man of honor who had proved with his life that he was entitled to that claim. He had made himself an Hidalgo de Bragueta, siring seven sons in a row without, as he said, 'the contaminating intrusion of a single daughter.' Yet before he marched into the morning darkness to fight his final duel he had embraced his granddaughter, telling her: 'You are the best son I ever had.'

Across the bleak and dusty wasteland she walks, hoping to spare her splendid horse and oldest friend, Relampaguito. She fords the Medina, that stream which had defined her family's ranch, then the Atascosa of the meager water, then the Nueces, on whose bloody banks her grandsons will die, striving to protect it. Still on foot, she crosses the Nueces Strip, which entire armies will contest in future years, and finally she reaches those fertile fields along the Rio Grande, where citrus and murder and big families and corruption and untold wealth will flourish.

From her womb will spring nine Garzas, like her, prolific, until it would seem that she had populated the entire river valley. Some Garzas will go to the Congress of the United States, others to distinguished service in the Mexican army to face their cousins fighting against them in the American. A few will become agricultural millionaires; many will die unremembered paupers; but in each generation some Garza men will exhibit the courage shown by Domingo when he rode alone through Comanche country to claim his bride and punish her betrayer; and with reassuring frequency some Garza woman will display that quizzical half-smile which had distinguished the founder of her family, Trinidad de Saldaña. And like her, she will be memorable and much loved by men.

. . . TASK FORCE

A week before the June meeting in El Paso the three members of our staff asked to see me privately: 'Dr. Barlow, you're playing this too low key. We think you should take command of the formal sessions, knock some heads together, keep Rusk from running everything, with Quimper's help.'

I sat for some moments, contemplating their unhappiness, then asked: 'Have you ever heard of the principle which guides many of our best organizations? *Primus inter pares?*' Apparently no one had, so I interpreted: '*First among equals*, the best possible definition of a chairman.'

'What's it mean?' the young man from Texas Tech asked, and I said: 'The chairman must never think he's the hottest thing on the block. Banging the gavel and all that,' and the young woman from SMU warned: 'You'd better do some gavel banging or those tigers are going to eat you up.'

I assured her that when the time came to write our report, Professor Garza and I would form a dependable team in defense of liberal proposals, while Rusk and

Quimper, as announced conservatives, should be expected to oppose: 'That'll leave Miss Cobb with the swing vote, and remember, her ancestors were liberal senators. If our ideas are any good, she'll side with us.'

'You work on that principle,' the young woman said, 'you're going to lose every contest. Those three old-timers will hang together in defense of old principles. They're tough.'

'The governor appointed them for that very reason. And if they weren't tough, I wouldn't want them.'

The young people also warned that Professor Garza's talents were not being properly utilized, and the young man from El Paso said: 'If I was in his place and Lorenzo Quimper made one more joke about Texas A&M, I'd quit. Just quit.' But I said: 'That goes with the territory. You stay around Garza long enough, you'll find he needs no protection.'

And when we met to plan for the meeting, Il Magnifico started right out with his latest joke: 'You hear the one about the Aggie who . . .' and Garza, after winking at me, moved directly up to him, made a tight fist of his right hand, and shoved it two inches from Quimper's nose.

'You know what that is, Lorenzo?' and when Quimper said he did not, Garza explained: 'It's an Aggie-joke stopper,' and Rusk asked: 'How's it work?' and Garza said: 'It moves forcefully against the nose, and Aggie jokes stop.'

For just a moment, Quimper turned pale, but then he saw me laughing and swiftly recovered. Like a big, friendly teddy bear he embraced Garza, assuring him: 'Some of my best friends are Aggies.' The young woman from SMU watched this, and whispered: 'See! I told you measures were needed,' and I whispered back: 'Garza took them.'

The staff informed us that they were finding the chore of locating a speaker for the June meeting so difficult that they suggested we postpone it till July. The problem was: why has an apparently insurmountable animosity traditionally existed between longtime Spanish-speaking residents and English-speaking newcomers.

This was a topic fraught with danger, both historical and current, and although the staff had already located several scholars well qualified to lead our discussion, they all happened to be native speakers of Spanish, and to this both Rusk and Quimper objected. 'I do not care to listen to any more apologists for Spain and the Catholic church,' Rusk said firmly, and before I could defend our past meetings, Quimper jumped in: 'Texas is a Protestant state. At least, the people who run it are Protestants, and we don't need any further indoctrination to the contrary.'

This was too unfair to let pass, and since it reflected on my leadership, I had to intervene: 'Gentlemen, could we have had more ecumenical speakers than Dr. Navarro and Friar Clarence? Did they not anticipate the very points you're making? I heard no misrepresentation or proselytizing. And I'm sure that if—'

Rusk cut me down: 'Barlow, just a minute. Didn't I give those men the respect

ue them? Didn't I take steps to have the friar's talk published? I think that
uimper, Miss Cobb and I have behaved damned well, and now we say "No more
ologists. Let's hear some straight facts." '

When I looked to Miss Cobb for support, she disappointed me: 'The men are
ght, Travis. We must have a quite different kind of speaker for our meeting in El
aso.'

I didn't know what to do. Every scholar I knew who was qualified to guide us
rough the tricky mazes of our topic was either from Mexico or someone who
as an apologist for Spanish history, and it looked as if we'd reached an impasse.
ut then Dr. Garza saved the day.

'There's this excellent older man at Michigan State. A Dr. Carver, if I have his
ame right.'

'What does he specialize in?' Rusk asked, for he obviously was not going to
low me to make this important choice.

'That's the interesting part. I've heard him speak. Excellent. And his field is
ench-English turmoil in Canada, with special emphasis on Quebec Province.'

'Is he a Catholic camp follower?' Quimper broke in.

'His religion I don't know. But I heard him give a paper at a conference at
rizona State and again at San Diego State. I did not know him personally, which
why I can't remember his exact name. But everyone had the feeling that he was
e of the best.'

When our staff had an opportunity to check him out they found that his name
as Carter, that his field was minority relations in Canada, and that he had also
gun in recent years to specialize in problems along the Mexico-United States
rder from San Diego to Brownsville.

'What's his religion?' Rusk asked, and when a staff member said: 'Jehovah's
itness,' he replied: 'Jesus Christ!'

For the El Paso meeting Quimper drove from his ranch into Austin, where
usk's jet picked us up for the short flight to Love Field in Dallas. There Rusk
mself climbed aboard, and as soon as we were airborne I reassured my fellow
embers: 'I've checked Carter out, read some of his papers, and he's just what
e've been searching for.' Before either man could respond, I added: 'We must
ve a couple of clowns on our staff. Carter's a Baptist.'

By the time we landed at El Paso—after a flight longer than from New York to
incinnati—Rusk and Quimper were in a relaxed mood, and in the long and
easant evening prior to our meeting they invited us all, including the staff, across
e Rio Grande to a festive meal in Ciudad Juárez. But before the waiter could
ke our order Rusk stared at the three staff members and growled: 'Which one of
ou comedians told me that tomorrow's speaker was a Jehovah's Witness?' When
e girl from SMU said: 'I did,' and Rusk asked: 'Why?' she said: 'Because you
ere making such a fuss about it.'

Rusk pointed his finger at her: 'He'd better be good, or you're fired,' and she replied: 'If this is the condemned woman's last meal, it'll be the best,' and she ordered extravagantly, at Rusk's expense.

Her position was secure, as we quickly realized when we met our speaker next morning on what must be one of the more distinctive of the American campuses —early Tibetan architecture—with one of the more unfortunate names: UTEP (University of Texas at El Paso). Herman Carter, in his sixties, was the kind of scholar young Ph.D. students aspire to be: knowledgeable, with a constantly growing reputation and an increasing interest in the world as he grew older. He seemed at first to have no sense of humor, and certainly the three publications he distributed to us revealed none, but when pressed on some vital point he was able to come up with just the right witticism to relax tensions. He produced one Ph.D. student every three years, and saw to it that she or he found a good position, for anyone he trained was employable.

'You could have assigned me no topic more difficult than the one you did, but also none more significant to your purpose. Let's see what generalizations we can establish before the discussion begins, because it would be painful to waste your time and mine in belaboring the obvious.' With that excellent preamble, to which we assented, he launched into his subject, drawing heavily upon his experiences in Quebec, in Belgium and in Cyprus, each of which was engaged in internecine struggles.

'It would not be easy to find two groups of people less qualified by history and temperament to share a land like Texas in the early 1800s, than the old Spanish-Mexican to the south and the new Kentucky-Tennessee man to the north. God reached deep into His grab bag when He asked those two dynamite caps to share the land between San Antonio and Louisiana. The older group was Catholic, of Spanish descent, family oriented, careless about on-the-spot administration, town oriented, ranchers if they could afford the land and the cattle, obedient to authority up to the moment of revolution, and extremely proud, punctilious as well. The intruding group was Protestant, British, individually oriented, insistent upon good local administration, farmers with a positive passion for the soil, suspicious of cities, disrespectful of any national authority, especially religious, but just as eager for a duel as any hidalgo. Dear God, what an unlikely mix!'

For an entire day this elderly man threw off ideas like a summer electrical storm over the prairie: sharp flashes of lightning followed by distant and impressive thunder. He had no personal involvement in what was happening along our Rio Grande or along the desert borders between Arizona and California, so he could speak freely and allow his imagination to roam; but he did have an acute concern about the demographics of the Mexican-American confrontation and was vitally involved in the guessing game as to what was going to happen.

At one point I had to break in: 'Dr. Carter, you speak as if our problem nothing but the Quebec-Canada problem clad in serape and sombrero,' and he said: 'Precisely. When cultures are in conflict, certain inevitables result.' I must indicate some of the specific ideas and challenges he asked us to consider as observable in Texas.

Knives versus guns: 'You so often find in Texas newspapers a story which appalls white society. Some agitated Mexican immigrant has found life intolerable and has grabbed his knife to carve up five or six of his friends, sometimes even including his wife. Horror! Indignation! But the same paper will carry a story about some decent white anglo who has shot the same number of people when drunk, and this is condoned because of the stress the man was under or because he was such a good fellow when sober.'

Music: 'I'm distraught when I live along your border to realize that whereas Mexico and her sister nations have produced some of the most wonderful, joyous songs in the world, things like "Guadalajara," "Cu-cu-ru-cu-cu," "La Bamba," and "La Golondrina," your popular music stations play only the most cacophonous noise. This gap is so wide, it can apparently never be bridged.'

Games: 'The difference between a poetic bullfight and a brutal American-style football game is so vast that words cannot resolve the difference. And it's symbolic, I think, that each culture looks with real distaste at the brutality of the other. I've heard sensible anglo women along the border inveigh against the savagery of the bullfight, but make no comment about their own young men who are killed each autumn playing football or about the scores who become paraplegics for the rest of their lives. I don't particularly like bullfighting, but I sometimes think that it's better to kill a bull than to maim a man . . . especially a young man.'

Toward the end of an exciting day he threw at us, as if we were performers in a circus having to catch the Indian clubs he tossed through the air, three ideas of such fresh and startling dimension that they became subjects for repeated discussion in the months to come. In this respect he carried out one of the best functions a learned man can perform: he stirred up the minds of his listeners, who could if they wished reject his conclusions but who still had to grapple with his data, hoping to form generalizations of their own.

A name: 'One of the tragedies of Texas history has been a failure to devise an acceptable name for citizens of Mexican heritage who have lived in the state much longer than newcomers of Anglo-Saxon heritage. We call these distinguished men and women *Mexicans,* ignoring their centuries-old citizenship on our soil, their education and their often superior moral condition and manners. But we also call the illiterate peon from Chihuahua who crawled across the dry riverbed last night a *Mexican,* and the tragedy of it is that we do not differentiate between the two. The most ancient citizens are grouped indiscriminately with the most recent infiltrators, and everyone suffers. One day in California, I asked my Hispanic students: "What do you want to be called?" and they said: "Persons of Spanish name and heritage." How could you fit that into a newspaper story? What we seek is a single word which is short and without adverse coloring. *Chicano* is liked by some, deplored by others. It won't work. Many younger students prefer the contentious *La Raza*. Too militaristic. In fact, nothing works, and Texas is stuck with an abominable situation. It uses old words to stigmatize new situations, a classic example of how society so often fails to produce words which define the real problems of our society. We need a verbal invention which acknowledges the grandeur of the Mexican contribution, but we can't find one.'

At this point he stopped, looked at Professor Garza, and asked: 'How do you like being called a Mexican, after the centuries your family has been in Texas?'

'I don't like it, especially when the person doing the categorizing is some newcomer from Detroit. Appropriates the name *Texan*. Then castigates me as a foreigner.'

'You see any solution?'

'None. It's as you say, a cultural crime that cannot be corrected.'

'What do you call yourself?'

'A Texan of Spanish heritage.'

'That's a hell of a name. By the way, how far do you have to go back to find unmixed Spanish blood in your family?'

'Twenty-one generations, a Spanish soldier in Vera Cruz.'

'So you really are Mexican?'

'Except that in 1792 a wonderful woman of pure Spanish blood married into the family and had nine children.'

'In Texas?'

'Where else?'

Now Miss Cobb surprised us: 'Professor Carter, when you referred to your Mexican students in California you called them Hispanics,' and he asked: 'I did?' and she said: 'You certainly did.'

He laughed and said: 'That may be the solution. Garza, what do you think?' and Efraín said: 'I've never found it offensive,' and we agreed unanimously that our report would use that term.

Government: 'A salient fact about Texas, and one often forgotten, is that in 1824 the Mexican government provided one of the best constitutions our hemisphere has seen. Had this been put into effect, honestly and with respect for its provisions, Mexico and Texas would have enjoyed one of the world's good governments and separation would not have become necessary. But there's the overpowering difference. Mexicans had the intelligence and the mental agility to form a splendid document, one of the best. But they never began to have the managerial ability to implement it. So separatism became inescapable, because American settlers, no matter where they went—Oregon, Utah, California—insisted upon a stable government. Today when I read that Constitution of 1824, I could cry. So noble a document to have so ignoble an end. It could have saved Texas for the Mexicans, but no one could be found to operate it.'

The future: 'Because the people of the Spanish-speaking nations to the south have such a high birth rate . . . Did you know that Mexico's population in 1920 was a mere fourteen million and now it's seventy, with no upper limit in sight? And the explosion in Central America is even more startling. Same situation in Canada, the French outbreed the British at a relentless rate. "The Victory of the Crib," they call it. Well, we must suppose that this will continue into the indefinite future, and if it does, we must also expect to see an unconquerable movement of Spanish-speaking people up from the south and the eventual Hispanicization of California, Arizona, New Mexico, Colorado, Texas and no doubt Florida. Let me tell you exactly what I envisage for Texas. I think that along the Rio Grande there is already developing a kind of ipso facto third nation, reaching from Monterrey and Chihuahua in the south to San Antonio and Albuquerque in the north. I'm not sure that this new nation will require any modification in governmental forms. It could still be Mexico and the United States. But the interchange of people, language, money, jobs, education, traditions, food habits, religion and entertainment will be complete and free. And it will be untrammeled because no one will be able to halt it.'

He stopped, rose from his chair, and walked to a window from which he could see much of El Paso, that bustling city, but even more of Ciudad Juárez, that larger city on the other bank of the river. From Juárez rose a huge cloud of dust thrown off by one of the Mexican cement plants, and the winds were such that the heavy dust fell not upon Juárez but upon El Paso.

'The course of history cannot be stopped at will,' Carter said. 'Last night, as I understand, you passed freely into Mexico and freely out. I believe it will always be that way.' Then he offered his final judgment. Turning away from the window, he hummed a few notes of 'La Adelita' and said: 'The ultimate mix could be a very good one. The soft beauty of Saltillo and the hard integrity of Kentucky. A new world along a new kind of frontier.'

IV
THE
SETTLERS

EARLY AMERICAN
SETTLEMENT

0   MILES   50

ON A WINTRY DAY IN 1823 A TALL BEEFY WANDERER WITH A BLAND, OPEN face like a rising sun stood with his scrawny wife, pudgy eleven-year-old son and three mongrel hunting dogs at the edge of a rain-filled bayou in the western reaches of the new state of Louisiana. A straggler from Tennessee, who had fled to avoid bankruptcy and jail, he was not pleased with what faced him.

'Don't mind the water, we can wade through it. Done so many times on our exploration. But I do worry about this next stretch between here and Texas.'

'We'll get through,' his red-headed wife mumbled. Reaching for her rather unpleasant son, she warned: 'You're to stay close, Yancey. Help us load the guns if they attack.'

The three were dressed in buckskin garments, laboriously cut and sewn by the mother, who appeared to be responsible for all vital decisions while her pompous husband thrashed about deciding issues which never seemed to matter. The conspicuous thing about the family was the incredible amount of gear each member carried: guns, an ax, pots, extra articles of clothing and bundles of dried food. From every angle of their bodies useful items protruded, so that they looked like three porcupines waddling through the woods; they were so impeded that they could cover only about nine miles a day when better-organized travelers would have completed fifteen. 'We'll head due west,' the father said as if he were a general, 'make the shortest transit possible, and be safe in Texas before they know we're about.'

His introduction of words like *exploration* and *transit* betrayed the fact that he had at some earlier time known life within a respectable Tennessee family, but a love of petty gambling and a positive addiction to idleness had led to a sad decline in his fortunes. His fall had not been spectacular, just a slow erosion of holdings and a series of disastrous lawsuits over land titles. When his family lost interest in his welfare because of his marriage to the daughter of a shiftless frontiersman, he had no recourse but to leave home, a man with no land, no prospects, and very little hope of improving his lot.

'Will there be Indians ahead?' the boy asked.

'Worse. Renegades. White men turned sour.'

This man, thirty-three years old, had decided in the fall of 1822 that his condition in Gallatin, Tennessee, was so deplorable that he could escape only by taking to the road: Nashville to Memphis to Little Rock to the southwest corner of the Arkansas Territory. He and his family had struggled to reach the banks of the Red River, which he had followed into Louisiana. There they had cut west toward the Mexican frontier state of Tejas, known along the Mississippi as Texas, refuge for any American who wanted to start his life over in a new and burgeoning area.

But to reach this reported paradise from Louisiana entailed great risk, for when travelers came to these final bayous separating the civilization of New Orleans and its outriders from the wilderness of Texas, they faced, as the Jubal Quimpers did now, about thirty miles of one of the most dangerous territories in the Americas. 'Listen,' they were told, 'and listen close! In the old days they called it the Neutral Ground, meanin' it didn't belong to neither Louisiana nor Texas. They hoped that settin' it up like that, they'd be able to avoid conflict between Americans and Spaniards. But what did they attract? Pirates, murderers, smugglers, women who deserted their families, runaway slaves who stabbed their masters, forgers. Finally they gave it to Louisiana, but it's still scum of the earth. Hell hides in that Strip acrost the water.'

'I don't want to go,' Yancey said, but his mother caught him by the arm and moved him toward the bayou: 'We were pushed out of Tennessee. Got nothin' left but Texas.' Then, touching a sack she had protected since starting their exodus: 'We get this corn planted before May, or we starve.'

Jubal was about to plunge into the muddy water when a voice from the east halted him: 'Hey there! Tejas, mebbe?'

The family turned to see a remarkable sight, a roundish, white-haired, ruddy-faced Irishman in the habit of a Catholic priest, holding his hat in his left hand and puffing heavily as he anxiously endeavored to catch up, for like the others, he was frightened of the Strip.

When he overtook the Quimpers they saw that he carried very little baggage: a small knapsack made from untanned deerskin, a simple bedroll of sorts and a battered book, apparently a Spanish Bible, for its spine carried in faded gold lettering the words *Santa Biblia*. From its ragged leaves protruded ends and bits of paper, for it served as his file. 'I am Father Clooney'—puff-puff—'of County Clare'—gasp-gasp—'servant of God and the government of Mexico.' He uttered the first syllable of his name and of his native county in a beautiful Irish singsong, which made his round face break into radiant smiles as he proudly said the words.

'I'm Jubal Quimper, Methodist, Gallatin, Tennessee, on my way to Texas, and what are you doin' in these parts?'

The priest told a most improbable yarn: 'When the wine was red, I told my bishop in Ireland to go to the devil, and before firing me he advised: "Francis Xavier Clooney, you may think that your bishop should go to eternal damnation but you must never express it." I could find no assignment in Ireland. Bishops have evil memories.

'So I emigrated to New Orleans and could find no parish there. Bishops have long arms. When the Spanish government, some years back, announced that they wanted priests to serve in Tejas, few Spaniards being willing to work there, I sailed to Mexico and volunteered. I was about to take charge of all Tejas north of San Antonio, when the Mexicans threw the Spaniards out, and me job was gone again. The new rulers in Mexico City told me: "We're sending our own people to Tejas. We need no strangers." So back I sailed to New Orleans. But they soon found that Mexican priests were just as reluctant to move into Tejas as Spaniards had been. So back they came running: "Father Clooney, we need you!"'

'Did you learn Spanish?' Quimper asked, and the priest, still puffing from his run, said: 'Some. I can conduct prayers . . . in Latin . . . much like Spanish. And you?'

'You wander through these parts, you pick up words here and there. Did you say you're an official of the Mexican government?'

'In north Tejas, I'll be the Catholic church. I'm to conduct the baptisms, the marriages, the conversions.'

'Conversions?'

'Yes! You told me you were Methodist, a respectable religion I'm sure, but not the right one. Unless you convert to my religion, you'll get no land in Tejas and you may even be thrown out.'

'I can't believe that,' Quimper said, but it was his wife who made the stronger statement: 'We'll stay Methodists.'

'Then go no farther,' the priest said, and from his ragged Bible he produced a paper, printed in Mexico City and delivered to the Mexican consul in New Orleans, which laid down the rules. Spreading it in the rain, he and Quimper, with their fractured Spanish, deciphered the explicit law:

> No immigrant will be allowed to take residence in Tejas or acquire land there unless he brings with him documents proving that he is of law-abiding character. And if he is not already a member of the Roman Catholic Church, he must convert.

Quimper showed the document to his wife, and then asked Father Clooney how the law could be evaded, if one was of reasonably good character but not a Catholic.

'Impossible,' the priest said. 'And I'm surprised you'd ask me such a question, since I'm sent here to uphold the law.'

'What can I do?' Quimper asked, his big, undisciplined body betraying his agitation.

'You can become a good Catholic, like the law stipulates.' Father Clooney had a singing vocabulary acquired in the Catholic schools of Ireland and was always introducing words like *stipulate* into his conversation. 'I'm being sent into Tejas to convert men just like you, Quimper, so that you can legally take up your league-and-a-labor.'

'What's that?'

'The Mexican government is considering a new law. Every Catholic immigrant will get free land. Much more if he's married.' Consulting his document again, he said: 'A league is four thousand four hundred and twenty-eight American acres, a labor is a hundred seventy-seven. The rule is that you get a labor of free land if you intend to farm it, plus an entire league if you run cattle.' He coughed, folded the document, returned it to his Bible, and wiped the rain from his round face: 'If I were you, I'd claim I intended running cattle.'

'We have no cattle.'

'We have no sunshine,' said Father Clooney, 'but we expect to have some soon.'

'I must become a Catholic?'

'There's no other way.'

'And you can make me one?'

'That's me duty. That's why I'm here.'

'What do I do?' Lest he seem too eager to reject his inherited religion, Quimper added: 'I'm a good Methodist, you understand, but I must have land.'

'You kneel, and your wife and your son kneel, and I ask you a few simple questions.'

The three Quimpers moved apart, the big, fleshy father of weak character, the thin, tense wife of tremendous moral force, and the flabby son who understood little and cared less and who now said: 'This paper says just what he said it did.'

'I will not accept land on such terms,' Mattie Quimper said, and from the stern tone of her voice Jubal realized that once more he was going to have difficulty with his headstrong wife: 'You take the oath, or you go back to Tennessee. I'm bound for Texas.'

'I will swear to no such blasphemy,' she said, and since nothing he could say persuaded her otherwise, it looked as if the Quimpers would end their escape to Texas at this bleak frontier.

But now Father Clooney exercised that gentle logic for which he had been famous among his friends in Ireland. He did not have a superior mind, no one ever claimed that, but a friend at the seminary once said: 'He's highly flexible. Finds solutions which you and I would never discover.' Brushing Jubal aside, he took Mattie by the arm and asked in that sweet voice: 'Me daughter, it's land you crave, is it not?' When she nodded, he continued: 'They told me in Mexico there were parcels along certain rivers in Tejas which exceeded that of Jerusalem or Ireland. Now, me girl, if you want to share in that land . . .' He stopped, smiled, and shrugged his shoulders.

'Must I?' she asked, and he replied: 'You must.' She then asked: 'But does swearin' mean I give up my own religion?' and he said, smiling at her benignly:

'Well, yes and no,' and she said: 'I believe you, Father,' and she allowed him to lead her back to her family.

So the three Quimpers knelt in the Louisiana mud, their faces turned west toward Texas. It was a solemn moment both for them and for the priest, for they were formally rejecting a religion which had nurtured them and he was performing his first official act as an agent of his new government. All were nervous as he whispered through the pattering rain, probing at his converts with a series of significant questions: 'Do you accept the Body of Christ? Do you acknowledge in your hearts that the Holy Roman Catholic church is the ordination of Jesus Christ Himself? Do you accept without reservation the supremacy of our Worldly Father, the Pope? Are you willing to announce yourselves publicly as members of the Roman Catholic church?'

When the three supplicants replied in whispers more muted than his own, Father Clooney administered the oath, but young Yancey noticed something that the white-haired priest could not see: his mother, holding her hands behind her back, kept her fingers crossed. His father did not, and as soon as the final blessing was given, making them good Catholics, Jubal leaped to his feet and said: 'Now, can we have this in writin'?' and gladly Father Clooney drew from his untidy Bible a printed document which he now filled in, attesting to the fact that Jubal Quimper *et uxor et filius* were good Catholics.

But this did not satisfy Quimper: 'You must write down that we're entitled to our league-and-a-labor.'

'I have no authority to issue such a statement,' Father Clooney said, whereupon Jubal grabbed the certificate and was about to shred it: 'Then I'm not a convert.'

'Wait!' the priest said. 'Is it so important to you?' and Quimper replied: 'I'm willin' to abide by the laws of any land I live in. But I demand that my new country put in writin' its promises to me.'

'My words would carry little weight,' Father Clooney protested, but Quimper said: 'I've found that words on documents carry terrifyin' weight. I'm here in this swamp because of words on documents. And I want your words on this one.' So the priest rummaged through his bedroll until he found a pen and a vial of ink.

The paper he signed still exists in the archives of Texas. It is rain-spotted and not legally binding but its import is unquestioned, and was the foundation of everything good that was to happen to the Quimpers in Texas:

This document testifies to the legal conversion into the true Holy Roman Catholic Church of Jubal Quimper, his wife Mattie and their son Yancey aged eleven. By the laws of México this entitles them to take up free and without hinder a league-and-a-labor of the best land, as he may identify it.

The paper was signed boldly by Father Clooney, formerly of Ballyclooney, County Clare, now an ecclesiastical representative of the Mexican government. Since these were his first conversions in his new assignment, he carefully dated the paper '3 Enero 1823, Provincia de Tejas, México,' and when Quimper pointed out that they were not yet in Texas, Clooney said with that elasticity which would always characterize him: 'In spirit we are. So let's make speedy tracks to take up our inheritance.'

Father Clooney, who had watched many struggling people trying to survive in a harsh world, was always concerned with the physical welfare of those he counseled, and now he gave the Quimpers solid advice: 'You've got to buy a mule. You can't lug all that gear into Texas.' But Jubal asked: 'Who can afford a mule?' and Clooney replied: 'We'll find a way.'

It was providential for both the Quimpers and the priest that they had joined forces at the bayou, for the transit of the Neutral Ground where law did not prevail proved more dangerous than even Jubal had anticipated. 'I want all guns to be loaded,' Quimper said as they entered the Strip, and when Father Clooney warned: 'The powder may get wet if we load now,' Jubal said: 'That's the risk we take.'

They were less than six miles inside the area when three Kentucky ruffians, fugitives from murder charges, accosted them and demanded tribute. When Father Clooney refused to surrender the few dollars and Spanish coins he had collected, they threatened to kill him as a conniving priest: 'We don't want your kind in Texas.' And they might have slain the four travelers had not one of the robbers dropped dead with a bullet through his head.

Mattie Quimper, off to one side, had listened to the threats and had quietly reached for her husband's gun. Holding her breath to steady her arm, biting her lip to still her nerves, she had aimed not at the biggest Kentuckian's chest but at his head, and when he dropped, she threw Father Clooney one gun and her husband another, and these two men happened to fire at the same survivor, killing him too. The third renegade escaped through brush, and for the next two days the four immigrants kept a round-the-clock watch lest the escapee return with others to seek revenge.

As they were about to leave the Strip they came upon a small settlement perched on the left bank of the Sabine River, the boundary line between American Louisiana and Mexican Tejas, and here they were accosted by an extraordinary man, sour of face, lean of body and profane of speech: 'Ran me out of xxxxx Alabama, printin' xxxxx dollar bills better'n the xxxxx gov'mint. Now, if you have any xxxxx Spanish coins, I can earn you a tidy xxxxx profit.'

He had been a blacksmith by trade and might have made a good living almost anywhere in America, or Texas, had he applied himself to his calling, but he had an insatiable habit of manipulating coinage, and now he offered his services to the Quimpers: 'What I do, I take a Spanish coin, pure silver, and I smash it so fartin' flat and in such a clever way'—into even a simple statement like that he was able to introduce three horrendous expletives—'that I can cut it into quarters.'

'Everybody does that,' Quimper said, and he was right, for coinage was so scarce throughout America that the fracturing of dollars into four quarters or sometimes even eight bits was common.

'Of course ever'body does it,' the forger acknowledged. 'But they cut a dollar into four quarters. I cut mine into five.'

And he did. Taking a Spanish coin provided by the priest, he hammered it in such a way that in the end, with the identifying marks preserved, he produced five pieces. Quimper was afraid to risk his own money in this criminal activity, but Father Clooney approved the inventiveness, and from his voluminous robes produced a handful of coins, which the forger quickly cut into fives, keeping for himself one-tenth of the gain.

As the priest was pocketing his profit, a dirty, ill-kempt boy of nine or ten ran up, shouting: 'Black Abe done killed his woman!' and everyone ran to see what new tragedy had struck an area accustomed to disaster.

Black Abe, a white man from Missouri with an infamous reputation even among his evil companions, had tired of his woman's nagging and had stabbed her many times with a long knife. When the priest reached her she was still breathing, but the flow of blood was so copious that she obviously could not survive. 'Do you seek peace with your Maker?' Clooney asked softly. 'No filthy papist touches me!' she managed to whisper, and with that farewell to an ugly world she died, whereupon Father Clooney knelt by her bed and pleaded with God to accept the soul of this bewildered woman.

The sanctity and emotion of the scene was broken by shrill yelling from outside, where the young boy who had brought the message to the forger's shop had taken a severe dislike to Yancey Quimper, much older and heavier than he. For no good reason but with lethal skill the little ragamuffin was belaboring Yancey, bringing blood to the nose and blackening to the eyes.

'Stop it!' young Quimper pleaded, and when his assailant continued pummeling him, he dropped to the ground, protecting his face with his hands. He had assumed, from having watched grown men fight in Tennessee, that when he fell to earth the fight would end, but in the Neutral Strip such a fall merely encouraged the attacker to finish off the job, and now, to the approving yells of the watchers, the fierce little tiger kicked at Yancey's head, then leaped upon him, boxing him about the ears with both fists.

'Finish him!' some of the men shouted, and the boy might have done so had not Father Clooney come out from the house where the dead woman lay. Striding into the middle of the cheering men, he drove off the boy and raised Yancey to his feet, brushing away the dirt and helping to stop the tears.

Deprived of this amusement, the men roiled about for some minutes, after which one of them cried: 'You can't do nothin' with Black Abe. Let's hang him.' So a posse was organized and Abe was soon apprehended trying to escape through the canebrakes.

Dragged back to the informal village on the Sabine, he was reminded of his many crimes and castigated for having slain one of the few women in the area: 'Abe, you gonna die. You want a prayer from this here priest passin' through?' When Abe said that he did, Father Clooney stepped to the tree from which the rope dangled: 'Son, despite your wicked ways, the Lord Jesus Christ intercedes for you at the throne of God. Your repentance is marked. Your immortal soul is saved and you shall die in peace and in the perpetual love of Jesus Christ.'

When the rope was hauled up by four big men, one of them the smith, and Black Abe's kicking stopped, Clooney said: 'I pronounce him dead. Bury him.' As an afterthought he said: 'Bury her too. Side by side, as they lived in this turbulent vale of tears.'

That night the Quimpers observed for the first time that their priest, in times of stress, as after this hanging, would search about for alcohol in which to drown his emotional insecurities. Tippling at first, he would progress quickly to real gulps, and when he was comfortably drunk he would wander among whatever groups were sharing the whiskey, introducing himself with a benign smile: 'Me name's Father Clooney of Ballyclooney on Clooney Bay in County Clare, servant of God and the government of Mexico.' He would sing the words, continuing for about an hour, after which he would calmly lie on the floor wherever he was and fall asleep.

When morning broke, the four immigrants were so eager to enter Texas that the priest prevailed upon the forger, who operated a small ferry, to load them into his water-logged craft and pole them across the muddy Sabine. As they reached the midpoint Jubal happened to say the name of the river, whereupon the forger proved that he'd had a fair education: 'Ever' newcomer says it like you just did. *Say-bine,* no accent, rhymes with *wine.* Ancient Greek. Us locals call it *Suh-bean,* heavy accent last syllable, rhymes with *queen.'*

He deposited them on the slippery western bank just as a true deluge broke, inundating everything and especially the unprotected ferry, whose profane operator cursed God, the storm and the crazy Catholic priest who had lured him into this predicament.

Father Clooney paid no attention to either outburst. Shepherding his new flock as if they were a thousand devout souls passionately addicted to his church, he asked them to kneel in the storm, and with water cascading down their faces and soaking their bodies in a kind of heavenly baptism, the Quimpers entered Tejas, and when Jubal rose he proclaimed rather sententiously: 'We wanted to come. God brought us acrost the Strip. And now we enter our inheritance.'

Mattie did not immediately rise from her kneeling; fingering the mud, she delivered an important judgment: 'This earth can grow things. Let's find our land and get the seed in.'

'We have time,' her amiable husband assured her, but she said: 'Even in paradise, if we miss the growin' season, we run into trouble,' and it was she who led the way south.

Father Clooney, now fifty-eight and engaged in what would surely be his final assignment, felt himself fortunate to have found the Quimpers, whom he discussed with God in his prayers: The boy's not much. He needs Your help. The mother could build Rome in a week, and I hope You'll bless her. Did You see her gun down that bandit and then throw me the other rifle? The father? Now there You have a problem. Big, likable, in some ways younger than his son. But he's a good shot and he does keep us in food. Tighten him up a bit.

Together the ill-assorted troop headed south and west into Mexican Tejas toward the new Stephen Austin colony earmarked for American settlers. As they went they lived off the land, and now Quimper was delighted to have Father Clooney as a hunting companion, for as a boy in Ireland the priest had learned the mystique of firearms and enjoyed the ritual of stalking almost as much as the satisfaction of bringing home game. Clooney was a voracious eater, almost a glutton, so he felt a vested interest in killing a deer or a bear with regularity, and he was good at butchering, so that during their journey the Quimpers and their spiritual leader fared well.

Mattie did not entirely trust this Irish priest who claimed he worked for the Mexican government, but she was growing grateful to him for the work he did in their caravan. Always he was first to volunteer for any task, something her husband never did except where hunting or eating was concerned; she must make the fire, and do the cooking, and form the lead bullets, and tend the clothing, and at times seem to carry everything but the guns. With the arrival of this smiling priest always eager to help if food was in the offing, she had a chance to breathe and to be a woman rather than a beast of burden. In fact, after their fifth day together, she found herself liking him, but her stern Protestantism prevented her from showing it.

Two of his weaknesses disturbed her. The Methodist clergymen she had known stormed against drink and gambling, but Clooney engaged in both, for while she labored at cooking or sewing, he and Jubal would play at cards, using awkward pebbles as counters. The betting would become quite furious, and she would hear Clooney cry: 'Aha, Quimper! You tried to hide that ace, and now you'll eat it.'

One night when they were well into Texas, the two men sat playing cards as Mattie inspected the precious corn seed to see if the two wads of smelly plug tobacco were still keeping away the weevils which would otherwise infest it. Clooney, seeing the colorful, easily handled kernels, cried: 'I say, Mattie. Lend us a handful for our game.' She demurred, for to her the corn was sacred, the agency of all that was to follow, but in the end Jubal supported the priest: 'Come on, Matt! We'll guard the corn with our lives. Aren't we using it like money?'

So now the two noisy gamblers fought for kernels of corn, and the competition could not have been more keen had they been using Spanish pieces, but at the close of each session there stood Mattie, reaching out to reclaim and count her corn, which she put safely back into the canvas bag, with the tobacco.

When they were some thirty miles inside Texas they came to their first settlement, a fragile collection of houses on Ayish Bayou, and the comparison of this bayou with the one they had known in Louisiana was so favorable that Jubal had to comment: 'This here is civilization. A man could choose his land right here and be happy.'

The citizens at Ayish Bayou were so proud of their settlement that they suggested to the Quimpers: 'Stay here. This land was made for farmers.' But their real joy came when they learned that Father Clooney was a properly ordained priest, for they had seen no clergyman for many years, and early on the first morning a family that had moved down from Kentucky approached him with a compelling problem. Their daughter, seven months pregnant, and her young man, a farmer also skilled in building log houses, had entered into a bond two years before, which they now presented to the priest as they were by honor required to do. Clooney had heard of such agreements and had been instructed in how to handle them, but he had not yet seen one, and he inspected the paper with a solemnity which the Quimpers had not previously observed:

Know all men by these presents, that with the public knowledge of this community the maid Rachel King and the bachelor Harry Burdine do undertake to live together as Man and Wife without benefit of clergy, there being none in these parts. We hold them to be truly married in the Eyes of God, and on their part they undertake a solemn pact to marry legally as soon as a Priest of the Holy Roman Catholic Church shall pass this way. In furtherance of this Vow they promise to pay a fine of $10,000 each if they fail to present themselves to said Priest at first opportunity.

We do this thing, all of us, because we are lost in the wilderness without church or clergy but secure in the knowledge that Jesus Christ Himself knew marriage to be a Holy Communion blessed by God Himself. Rachel and Harry are duly married, and promise they will confirm when the Priest passes by.

'This is a precious document,' Father Clooney said as he returned it to the couple. 'If the others will join in a circle, we shall ask God's blessing on this marriage.' So the Quimpers and all from the Bayou who were available formed a tight circle about the priest and the young couple, and in the simplest words the Irishman conducted a wedding and then gave a blessing. Recovering the paper for a moment, he scratched upon it the notation: 'Rachel and Harry were duly and properly married on 10 January 1823 at Ayish Bayou, Provincia de Tejas. Father Francis X. Clooney, cleric of the Mexican Government.'

As he was about to hand back the certificate, Jubal stopped him: 'Write that the couple, as good Catholics, are now entitled to their league-and-a-labor.'

'We already have it,' Harry Burdine said, but Quimper told him: 'It's good to have it in writin'.' And Father Clooney made the notation.

At the wedding feast—real bread made from hoarded flour and real whiskey made from corn, with venison and bear abundant—four couples asked Father Clooney if he would convert them to his religion and give them certificates of proof, and Quimper noted the offhand manner in which the priest did this. 'It's as if he took the marriage seriously,' he told his wife, 'and the conversions as a kind of necessary joke.'

'Priests don't make jokes,' Mattie protested.

'I think this one does. He knows we're doing this just to get some land, and he doesn't mind. But a marriage . . . that's forever, whether it's Catholic or whatever.'

This speculation ended when citizens of the Bayou warned the newcomers as to what confronted them in their new homeland: 'Have all your papers in order when you get to Nacogdoches. You, too, Father. Because in Nacogdoches they're very strict.'

The way this difficult Indian name was pronounced reminded the Quimpers that they were now in a new country, for the sister town in Louisiana, Natchitoches, had been pronounced French style, NAK-uh-tush, while only a few miles to the west its sister town was called in the Spanish manner Na-ku-DOE-chess, and whenever the locals uttered it they betrayed the fear and respect in which they held it. One old Mexican who had lived most of his life along the Bayou, explained why: 'Long ago we had a big, important settlement across the Sabine in Louisiana. Los Adaes it was called, capital of all Texas. So one day what happens? This Barón de Ripperdá from Spain arrives, finds that the people at Los Adaes were tradin' with the French in New Orleans, and why not? There were no Spaniards in the area to trade with. And he becomes so angry that he finished Los Adaes. Just wiped it out. Five hundred settlers were given five days to gather all their goods and march down to San Antonio, four hundred miles through forest and over swollen streams. They pleaded with him. No avail. Off they had to go, and one in three died on the way. Starvation . . . Indians . . . fever.'

The old man rocked back and forth, then pointed at Father Clooney: 'The priests did nothin' to help. Everyone was afraid of Barón de Ripperdá. And do you know what? Tell them what, Christopher.'

Christopher, a talkative farmer who ran a meager general store and lodging house, was quick to share bad news: 'When you reach Nacogdoches, who do you suppose you'll find in charge? The nephew of Barón de Ripperdá. Same kind of man. Same kind of ideas. Says he wants to shut down Ayish Bayou the way his uncle closed down Los Adaes.' He spat.

'Yes,' the old Mexican resumed, 'you'll find this new Ripperdá in control, and just as mean.'

'You're still here,' Quimper said, and the old man explained: 'The expulsion happened fifty years ago, and when we reached this spot my father knew his family couldn't complete the journey. We'd all die. So he broke away. Wife . . . three children . . . me just ten weeks old. And he said: "Barón de Ripperdá can go to hell." Father built us a log cabin—you can see it acrost that little stream—and there he raised corn and children and added rooms to the cabin.'

'What you must do with this new Ripperdá,' the settlers advised, 'is agree with everything he says.'

'He won't issue you any land, of course,' one of the women warned. 'He refuses to honor promises or contracts. Says we American Protestants are creeping in to steal Texas.'

'I have papers,' Quimper said. 'I'm a good Catholic.'

Several people laughed: 'We're all good Catholics. We're all entitled by law. But Ripperdá gives us no land.'

'You seem to have yours.'

'We've been here a while. Most of us came during the worst days of the Neutral Ground. Just crept in, as Ripperdá says.'

'How do you get title?'

'We don't. What we do is hope that Ripperdá dies . . . or goes away . . . or somebody shoots him.'

When the four travelers reached Nacogdoches they found two surprises: the little settlement was a real town with a store and a lodging house, and to Father Clooney, Víctor Ripperdá was not at all as he had been described by the dissidents at Ayish Bayou. When the priest reported to him, he found a young man, thin as the noontime shadow of a reed, with a small mustache and a winning smile that displayed teeth of extreme whiteness. He was polite, deferential to any visitor, and meticulous where governmental detail was involved: 'You must understand from the start, I'm not the alcalde. I'm an army major guarding the frontier while the real alcalde is absent.' Almost distastefully he handed Clooney an order issued by that vanished official: 'Behold your alcalde!'

> Sittazins of Nakadochy. I shal be abbsint sevvin weaks. You must obbay Majer Riperdee til I git bak.
> Sined,
>
> James Dill, yore alcaldy.

'He's one of your norteamericanos,' Ripperdá explained. 'From Pennsylvania.'

'How did he become alcalde of an important post?' Clooney asked, and Ripperdá laughed: 'How did an Irishman become our priest?' He then offered Clooney a drink and asked: 'What did they tell you about me when you entered Tejas?'

Clooney did not want to reply, but when Ripperdá insisted, he said: 'They spoke of your uncle . . . the expulsion.'

Ripperdá shrugged: 'What lies they tell in their cabins. You know, he had little to do with that sad affair. The Marqués de Rubí, he made the decision, told my uncle to enforce it.'

'Did five hundred leave? Did a hundred die?'

'Yes, and my uncle did everything possible to help the survivors regain their old homes. He was a gentleman.'

Waving his hand before his face as if to expunge recollections of the tragedy, he said: 'Father Clooney, we're so glad to see you. We haven't had a priest for some time, so you come to a land which hungers for your care!'

'I'm proud to have so large a parish . . . so important a parish.'

'Sit down, please. Manuel, fetch us more wine. Now tell me, how did an Irishman who speaks such halting Spanish become priest of this vast area?'

Father Clooney took a copious draft of wine, savored it, wiped his forehead with the back of his hand, and smiled at his new superior: 'Francis X. Clooney, of Clooney Bay in County Clare, Ireland. I told my bishop to go to hell—'

'You never did!'

'And he told me where I could go. New Orleans. Your Mexican consul found me there, hired me to work in Tejas. Told me to report to you and bring Christianity to this wilderness.'

'You must not tell me to go to hell,' Ripperdá said with an easy laugh.

'I have learned that superiors have powers which . . .' He stopped. 'If I did, where would you send me?'

Without hesitation Ripperdá said: 'Yucatán. That's where we send our bad boys . . . and our bad priests. It's a dreadful place.'

'I'm here to help, as you command,' Clooney said, but Ripperdá corrected him: 'I'm your superior, yes. But years may pass without my seeing you.' And he pointed to a rude map of what the Mexican government assumed settled Tejas to be—a thin sliver running from northeast to southwest—and Father Clooney saw that his territory extended from the Red River on the north almost to San Antonio on the south, a distance of more than three hundred and fifty wilderness miles, and at least a hundred miles from east to west, a staggering total of thirty-five thousand square miles.

'In Ireland I had a parish of three villages. Of a Sunday I could walk from one to the other.'

'Here you'll have a parish bigger than all of Ireland.'

'My word, I do wish me old bishop could hear you say that.'

'To walk this one will take six or seven years. Marriages, baptisms, burials, they all await you.' The serious official leaned back, stared at the priest, and said frankly: 'I would have expected a younger man,' and Clooney replied: 'I've spent my life preparing to do some great work. Tejas is it.'

'And who are those hapless three you brought with you?' Ripperdá asked, and Clooney corrected him: 'Quimper is the best hunter I've ever seen. Tennessee man.'

At the mention of this state, Ripperdá groaned: 'Tennessee and Kentucky, they'll be the ruin of Tejas. Mind, I prophesied this. Up there they must teach boys to be animals.'

And when the Quimpers appeared before him, documents in hand, he refused to look at the papers or issue them land: 'You have no claim. I have no authority. I advise you in your own best interests, go home.'

'But the law says—'

'My instructions tell me what the law is.'

In their six meetings with Ripperdá he never once claimed that he was the law. Meticulous in his observation of the proprieties, he referred always to some mystical body of law promulgated in Mexico City, just as his famous uncle had depended upon laws passed in Madrid for the closing down of the ancient capital across the Sabine. 'This is not my action,' the baron had protested in 1773. 'It's the king, in Madrid, who views your town as useless. It's the king who has proclaimed: "Close down that wasteful place." '

Víctor Ripperdá had no baronial title to protect him, and no king in Madrid to offer him a job when his tour on the Mexican frontier ended; he had to rely upon the good will of the administrators in Mexico City, whose whims were many. He had learned that if in a post like Nacogdoches he did nothing, made no specific decisions, he could not find himself in trouble, so prudently he refused to issue land titles, build a church for the new priest, or authorize the settlement of any of the Americans who were beginning to stream across the Sabine. Mexico's frontier policy, as Americans in Tejas saw it, was 'Do nothing, and nothing bad can happen to you. Make one mistake, and you may be shot.'

This was not a fair assessment. When American settlers probed west they were supported by stable government in Washington and the state capitals. They were backed by a growing economy. They faced Indians who more often than not could be reasoned with. They were pushed along by a constantly growing population of Englishmen, Scots and Germans eager to test themselves against the wilderness. And most important, they carried with them ideas of education, freedom and self-government ideally suited to the establishment of new governments in new areas.

Mexico had an opposite experience, especially in Tejas, where it faced the most intractable Indians in the Americas. It had to rely upon an inadequate number of

Hispanic settlers, with no fresh replacements streaming in. Its productive base was limited and its military disorganized by constant rebellion. The preoccupation of Mexicans was, properly, the founding of a stable government, and in their search they experimented repeatedly with imperialism, republicanism and liberal democracy, leaving them little energy for the development of distant territories.

Most important of all, whereas Spanish culture had proved itself capable, in both Aztec Mexico and Inca Peru, of overthrowing established civilizations centered upon cities, it was not well adapted to the settling of vast open spaces. Its religion was communal rather than individual; its educational theories did not apply to the frontier; and the preference of its people for the small, clustered settlement rather than the remote farm proved ill-suited to Tejas.

Individual Mexicans like Víctor Ripperdá were as capable as any Americans, and if their Tejas had consisted of well-defined settlements waiting to be taken over, they would have succeeded, as they did at Santa Fe, but to throw such men into an empty wilderness without adequate support was imprudent, as the Quimper family was discovering.

Despite the fact that their papers were in order, they were forced to remain in Nacogdoches for tedious weeks, pestering Ripperdá to make up his mind about their land, but he found it expedient to ignore them, to delay making any decision regarding their immigration, and when in desperation they begged him at least to tell them what their prospects were, he laughed: 'Me? I have no control over immigration policy. The law says one thing, my superiors say another. Who am I to cut that Gordian knot?'

No appeal, no steady decline in the family's funds could move this slim, dapper official, and it became apparent to the Quimpers, especially Mattie, who despised the man, that he was capable of keeping them in suspension not just for weeks, but for months or years: 'Gettin' a decision out of him? Impossible,' and she began agitating for the family to move south toward San Antonio, where some official might be met who would make decisions.

Her husband warned that if they left Nacogdoches without permission, Ripperdá might dispatch his militia to overtake them, and then they would languish in jail, as many American trespassers did.

Mattie was all for taking the risk; she yearned to get her seeds planted in land which she could call her own, and she pestered her husband to make the move, but he was afraid. The situation became more complicated one morning when young Yancey came running with exciting news: 'Many Americans! Coming from the Bayou!' And when his parents ran out they saw that a substantial contingent of immigrants had arrived from the Neutral Ground, quite different from the customary stragglers who kept drifting in, to Ripperdá's disgust; these men and women had legal documents attaching them to the settlement plans of a man from Missouri whose name the Quimpers already knew but whose reputation for honest dealing they could not yet assess.

'The empresario Stephen F. Austin has called for us,' the spokesman of the group said. 'He has title to vast lands along the Brazos River, and he offers a league-and-a-labor to every family of good reputation.'

'Do you buy the land?' Quimper asked, and the man said: 'No. Surveyor's fee only, if I understand correctly.'

Jubal showed the man his own papers, especially the form signed by Father Clooney proving that the Quimpers were good Catholics and as such were entitled to their land. The newcomer said: 'It's not like the papers we have, an authorization from Austin, but I'm sure it would be acknowledged if you wanted to come along with us.'

As soon as this suggestion—it was not a promise—was made, the Quimpers unanimously sought to join the Austin group, but when they applied to Ripperdá for permission to leave Nacogdoches, he balked: 'Stephen F. Austin I'm aware of. He has empresario rights. His people are free to move south. But you have no rights.' And he was adamant. The Quimpers could not leave the north to acquire land, nor could they obtain other land in the north. It was infuriating, but it was standard Mexican procedure.

When the new contingent of settlers started south, the Quimpers grew desperate, and Mattie wanted to join the procession whether she was entitled to do so or not, but her husband was afraid to take the risk, and the three immigrants watched with longing as the caravan moved on.

The next days were painful, with Mattie even suggesting that they shoot Ripperdá and get going; her husband hid the three guns and went for the last time to see the administrator. For years he would remember that meeting: Ripperdá wore a new outfit imported from New Orleans, fawn-gray in color, neatly stitched, with new boots to match. He wore one small medal bestowed by a previous administration, and an ingratiating smile: 'My dear friend Quimper, I would gladly help you if it lay in my power to do so.' Whenever he said something like this he twisted the left side of his mustache, then raised his hands in a gesture of helplessness. 'But I am powerless, as you know.' He would issue no permissions, make no promises. In fact, he would do nothing at all, and as Jubal's fury rose, Ripperdá's benign calm increased, but as the two men faced each other, Quimper suddenly realized: If we leave for the south, he won't do anything, either. He will never do anything about anything.

That night he told his wife and son: 'Gather what things we have. At dawn we head south.'

Before the sun was risen the three Quimpers were once again laden like oxen, with additional acquisitions from Nacogdoches—among them a stout hoe jutting out from Mattie's back—and they were about to sneak away when Father Clooney, awake for his prayers, heard their commotion and ran to intercept them: 'Dear children! You must not attempt this.'

'Ripperdá won't have the courage to stop us. You know that.'

'But I was thinking of the long trail ahead. You cannot travel it bearing such heavy burdens,' and while they protested in whispers that they must reach their destination in time to plant their corn, he left abruptly, but soon came back with a gift he had purchased to help these good people on their way . . . if they ever gained permission to go.

It was a handcart such as peasants throughout the world used for pilgrimages: two tall wheels shod in iron, a large bed with sides, a canvas cover to guard against rain, two stubby handles with which to guide it. As the priest pushed it forward he praised the wheels: 'Big ones pass easily over bumps. Little ones move faster, but they do catch.'

Mattie, who carried most of the family gear, appreciated what such a cart would mean, and with a glance of thanks, went to it ceremoniously, depositing on its oaken bed her new hoe, her cache of food, her sewing kit, her hand-shovel and a dozen other items, some surprisingly heavy. But her sack of corn seed she kept tied to her waist.

When the cart had accepted comfortably the family gear, Father Clooney said: 'Now we must add the things that will make life more bearable,' and he left them again, returning with more gifts, items he knew they would need: another ax, a strong hammer, a hatchet, another spade, a big crosscut saw, more salt. 'And you'd better take this augur to bore holes for the legs of your stools.'

But by the time all these things were stowed, the sun was well up, and Father Clooney warned his new Catholics: 'If you start now, Ripperdá will surely know, and he'll have to arrest you.'

'But we must go!' Mattie cried, and he said: 'So you shall. For I must move along the rivers to perform marriages and baptisms, and I'm asking for you as my guide and hunter. To provide me with food and protection. I have reason to think that Ripperdá will approve, because otherwise he'll have to send soldiers, and he wouldn't like to do that.'

So the morning escape was delayed, but by noon, after Father Clooney had met with Commandant Ripperdá and it was agreed that the Quimpers would accompany him on his journey, they started off. As they left Nacogdoches, Víctor Ripperdá bade them goodbye with such warm smiles that one might have thought he had arranged the expedition: 'Go, and may God speed you in your great work,' to which Mattie Quimper retorted under her breath: 'Stay, and may the devil take you on his next visit.'

The excursion was a joyful experience, for it was March, and the air was warming and the forests of Texas were threatening to break into leaf. The rivers ran with new vigor, and birds and flowers returned in abundance.

To Father Clooney, who recognized this as his last abode on earth, each day was a new delight, and constantly he said to the others: 'Imagine having a parish like this! Forty miles to the next cottage, with warmth and love awaiting you when you arrive.' He never doubted, not even when he found himself surrounded by Methodists, that when he sat down at dusk he would be greeted with respect and in time with affection.

At lonely cabins he performed weddings and baptisms, usually on the same day. He went to the most forsaken graves, a pile of stone, no more, and said prayers with those who had lost babies and grandfathers. He blessed people. He converted those whose claim to land would otherwise be denied, and he ate voraciously of whatever food the people offered: 'My father always told me, eat beef while you still have teeth. For a long time you'll drink nothin' but broth.'

Few clergymen have ever reported to a new assignment with more abounding love and gratitude than Francis X. Clooney, this exile from Ballyclooney: God has given me a second chance, and I will show my thanks.

To Mattie the trip was equally exciting. Landless in Tennessee, the daughter of a wretched man who had to crop on shares without ever receiving his legal allowance, she had married Jubal Quimper because he did have land, and she had watched helplessly as men more clever than he stole that land with spurious documentation and protracted lawsuits. Landless once more, she had traveled across Tennessee and through Arkansas, seeing people far less able than she enjoying fields and farms and stretches of their own forest, and always before her, as she trudged along, glowed a vision of land which she and her family would one day own: Ever' damned thing we do on it will make it better and our children will make it better still.

'Land hunger' it would be called in later years when scholars tried to explain why so many people like Mattie poured into Texas, and no better description could be fashioned. She was tired, dead tired of being pushed around, and when she picked up that rifle in the Neutral Ground and killed the renegade, she felt that she was protecting her right to acquire land when she crossed over into Texas. The vacillations in Nacogdoches had driven her to such desperation that she might indeed have slain Ripperdá had not her husband restrained her, and now to be freed of those restraints, to be on the way to great expanses of empty land— this was an exploration toward paradise, and she knew it.

Despite the relief the handcart provided from beastlike burdens, Mattie still did most of the work about the nightly camps: she cooked, she laundered in the rivers, she looked after the priest when rain soaked him and he ran the risk of a cold, she molded the bullets and saved the deerskins for later tanning. She hoarded her supply of salt, dispensing it in niggardly fashion when her husband brought in a portion of some bear he had slain, for then she knew that her crew would eat well. But most important of all she kept the fires burning when they sputtered, hauling in the fallen timbers herself.

For Jubal the long trip was merely an extended hunting party: deer, an occasional turkey, pigeon, wild pig or bear. One day he came rushing back to the camp, shouting like an excited boy: 'Mattie! Mattie! What I seen off to the west!' And at her feet he threw a huge chunk of meat and an animal's tongue five times larger than a deer's.

'What is it?' she asked, and he said: 'I went further than ordinary, that's why I didn't get back last night. Far to the west, I saw this movement, huge, like a movin' carpet. Know what it was? Buffalo. Yep, out there we got buffalo.'

'What are they like?' she asked, and he said simply: 'Mattie, they're so big! So much hair. And they come in such endless numbers!'

On some days when he was certain where Father Clooney and the others were headed, so that they could be easily overtaken, he would trek to the west, sit on some mound, and watch the herds moving slowly across an open space where the forest ended and the plains began, and he would wonder if the great beasts could be domesticated: They'd make wonderful cows! They must give milk, elsen how could they feed their young? But I wouldn't want that bull over there to come chargin' at me. When he killed one and cut off only the most succulent parts, leaving the rest to rot, he often mused: We never ate so well. No potatoes or flour, but meat like no man ever saw before.

He would have been content for the trip to continue endlessly, for he had never before enjoyed such hunting, but when Mattie warned him that their supplies of powder and lead were perilously low, he realized that they must soon strike civilization or find themselves in trouble, and he began to ask at lonely cabins along the ancient forest trail: 'How far to Austin's Colony?' and invariably the settlers spoke well of the empresario: 'You can trust that one. He charges for his land, but it's worth it. May move down myself one of these days.'

'He charges? I thought all you paid was the surveyor.'

'Yes, you pay him, but it ain't much. Then you also pay Austin, maybe twelve and a half cents an acre, maybe twenty-five, I've heered both.'

Quimper stopped, calculating in his head: How much was a league-and-a-labor? Nearly five thousand acres. Even at twelve and a half cents, that would be . . . Jesus Christ! It was then that he developed his suspicions about Stephen F. Austin: He's nothin' but a Tennessee banker moved south.

He asked Father Clooney about this startling development, and the priest said: 'As I understand it, the way they told me in New Orleans when they gave me the parish, Austin's the only man the Mexican government trusts. He's the only one the American settlers trust. When you get your land from him you get a clear, sound title. Otherwise, real trouble.'

Quimper would confide in no one, not even his wife, how much money he was bringing, but Father Clooney gained the impression that he had enough to pay for his acreage if he so desired but that it galled him to think that he must do so. 'Jubal, if payin' out a little money ensures a proper beginnin', pay it. You'll be happier and so will your woman.'

'It don't matter about Mattie, she'll do what I tell her.'

'Jubal, that woman dreams of havin' her own land. Why else would she work so hard? Get it for her in the right way.'

For Yancey Quimper, eleven years old, growing shrewder each day, the trip was a kind of grand awakening: 'You told me we would be traveling the Camino Real. Don't look very royal to me.' He was a whining kind of boy, noticing everything and complaining about it: 'They ought to build some bridges like we saw in Arkansas.' He also thought the scattered settlers should build better cabins: 'If they fitted the logs closer, the wind wouldn't blow through.'

Astutely he analyzed the elders he was traveling with: Pop don't like work. But everybody seems to like him. When the men play cards at night, they all like Pop. Father Clooney likes whiskey too much. And Mom bites her lip to keep from givin' them both hell. He grew to think of his mother as a workhorse, not masculine like the two men, but not feminine either, and then one day as they approached a well-built cabin by a stream and Mattie saw from a distance a woman in a neat dress, Yancey watched as his mother withdrew from the convoy and stepped behind some bushes, where she slipped out of her dirty buckskins, washed herself in the stream, and then unpacked the gray-blue woolen dress she had brought from Tennessee. When she rejoined the men, her hair drawn neatly behind her ears and fastened with a cord, she appeared as a tall, handsome woman in her early thirties, and for the first time her son realized that under different circumstances she could have been beautiful.

When they reached the cabin, she assumed command of the travelers, introducing her husband and the priest, and when the settlers, a family named Seaver, wanted their two children baptized in order to protect their inheritance, she arranged the informal ceremony, even though it had to be Catholic. Father Clooney performed graciously, assuring the Seavers that they were bringing their children into the family of God and praising them for the loving care they had obviously bestowed upon their offspring. Yancey noticed, during the prayer, that upon any likely occasion Father Clooney spoke of love, and one morning he asked about this, and was told gently: 'Son, we're forced by circumstance to lead harsh and sometimes cruel lives. We're driven from our villages. We live in exile along El Camino Real. We lose our health, and sanity seems not to abide with us. What really is left?' At this point Yancey realized the old fellow was describing his own condition. 'The love that God bestows upon us,' Clooney said. 'And the love that we share with one another, that's all we have.'

'Who do you love?' Yancey asked, and the priest replied in dreamlike sentences: 'I love the bishop who sent me into this exile, because it was his duty to do so. I love Víctor Ripperdá, who treated us so poorly because he bears great burdens. I love the Seavers, who watch over their children in this wilderness. And I love you Quimpers for the bold way in which you face life.'

After the Quimpers and Father Clooney crossed the Trinity River, they followed its right bank eastward for some days until they intercepted a minor but well-defined road leading to the old Spanish mission complex at La Bahia, later to be known by its more famous name of Goliad. Had they remained on El Camino Real they would have reached San Antonio; this new road would carry them southwest into the empresario lands of Stephen F. Austin.

At the spot where the Goliad Road crossed the Trinity River they came to a small settlement, and in its cabins were six couples who had married without the sanctification of clergy. They warmly welcomed the arrival of Father Clooney, whose prayers and written certificates would regularize their unions. Yancey, unaware of the insecurities which could gnaw at families in the wilderness, could not appreciate the joy with which the couples greeted the priest: 'Why are they so excited about getting a piece of paper?' His mother tried to explain that not only was legal possession of land involved but also a secure place within society, but he asked: 'They have their cabins. They have their guns. What more do they need?' and his mother explained: 'No man or woman is ever safe until they have their land. So they can pass it along to their children.' He said: 'But with all this empty land, anybody can have anything,' and she warned: 'You can have it for a while, as long as it's still empty. But when people start pressin' in, the sheriff comes around some day and asks: "Where's your paper . . . provin' that this land is yours?" and on that day, if you don't have the paper, other men can move in and take your land away.' She said this solemnly, and added: 'That's what happened to your father in Tennessee. He had made the land his, done everything, but he had no papers, so they took it away.'

Demanding that her son sit down and pay full attention, she said: 'It's the duty of a man to find his land, take possession, and protect it. Because without land, a man ain't nothin'.' And from such admonitions young Yancey began to erect the emotional framework which would structure his life: Get land, like Mom says. Be a good fellow, like Pop.

His attention was diverted by the festive preparations under way for the celebration of the six marriages, and he accompanied his father and three villagers on a hunting expedition to secure meat for the barbecues that would follow the ceremonies. They went far afield, shot two buffalo, six deer and two wild pigs, providing enough food for days of gorging, but Jubal wished to do more: 'You got any turkeys around here?' and when the men said that some roosted in the dead trees along the Trinity, he told them: 'Carry the meat back to the cabins. Yancey and me, we're goin' to get ourself a couple of turkeys.'

This was a dangerous boast, and Jubal knew it, for the shooting of a wild turkey demanded great skill and patience; killing a buffalo was ten times easier. He began his sortie by heading for the river, then trailing along it in search of the kind of exposed tree in which the great birds liked to roost at sunset. The moon was not going to rise till about midnight, and its help would be needed if he was going to see the turkeys perched on the bare limbs. 'Why don't we shoot them in daylight?' Yancey asked, and his father said: 'Nothin' in this world harder to shoot on the ground than a turkey. They got nine extra senses and a bell which rings if an enemy steps close: "Trouble out there!" I've shot me many a turkey, but never on the ground.'

When they found a promising tree, with signs beneath it indicating that birds might have roosted, they took a position from which they would be able to see the turkeys in silhouette, and as they waited for the birds to arrive, Yancey asked: 'Is what Mom says true? Do you have to have land?' and Jubal replied: 'Your mother's very strong-minded on some things, and usually she's right. But on this I'm beginnin' to have doubts. A man needs a woman. He needs children. He needs faith in God. But often he don't need a settled cabin and a hunk of land to which he's tied. He can do very well just movin' about.'

'Do you want land?'

Jubal considered this, sucked his teeth, and said: 'For your mother? Yes. To put her heart at ease. For me? No.' Without endeavoring to explain this decision, he added: 'In Tennessee I had a bad time. I wish I had nothin' to do with documents and lawyers and courts. I'm a better man than any of them, Yancey, and you're to be the same.'

He was not at ease about his son, for he detected in the lad a lack of firm character. Yancey had not mastered the gun. He could not track an animal. And at the slightest inconvenience he tended to whimper, as he was doing now: 'Why do we have to stay here in the dark?'

'Listen! That's turkeys comin' in to roost.' And in the darkness the watchers could hear the movement of heavy wings as the huge birds, barely able to fly, made massive efforts to lift themselves high enough in the air to glide onto the waiting limbs.

'When the moon moves behind them, we get turkeys.' He instructed his son how to pass him the gun when the firing began: 'There'll be time for two shots. We must make them count. So as soon as I fire the first gun, hand me the other, like this. No other way but this: push . . . slap . . . stand back.' After they had practiced several times while the turkeys made soft noises in the tree, he said: 'I think you have it right, Yance.'

There came a moment of great beauty when the moon first edged above the horizon, bathing the river bottom in a radiant light, and even Jubal gasped when he saw the silhouettes of turkeys perched in the farthest trees: 'All day they root about the ground for food. All night they sleep in trees. Waitin' for us, Yance.'

Finally the moon was right, and Jubal whispered: 'No better time than now.' Checking to be sure his son was properly positioned, he took careful aim with his first gun, held his breath, and fired its precious bullet at the big birds. Almost before the sound could be heard, a turkey dropped from the tree, and with a speed that startled his son, Jubal reached for his second gun. But the noise and the unexpected speed startled the boy, who did not deliver as promised. There was confusion and enough delay to allow the turkeys time to scatter, so that when Jubal finally did bring his gun into position the trees were bare.

For a moment Jubal was tempted to berate his son for the maladroit way he had allowed the birds to escape, but he restrained himself, for this incident, coming after many others like it, merely confirmed Jubal's suspicion that his son was never going to be a hunter. He could be something else, for he was intelligent, but the hard, stony character that made a reliable hunter was lacking.

The marriage ceremony for the seven couples—another having come many miles to join the festivities—was both a triumph and a disaster, for the food which the hunters had provided enabled the women to build a feast that would be long remembered, and with a very good fiddler on hand, the dancing would be lively and prolonged. The social success of the affair was assured; it was the spiritual that provided the trouble, because on the afternoon of the day when the weddings were to be solemnized at dusk, with the baptisms of the couples' children to follow, one of the men grew chicken-hearted: 'Hell, I been livin' with Emily for six years, always knowin' that if things went wrong . . . ppphhhttt . . . no trouble. Now she's tyin' a knot about my neck—no, thank you.' And off he went into the woods.

It was the general opinion that Lafe Harcomb had merely suffered an attack of gun-shy and that within a day his friends could lure him back to the ceremony, so the weddings were postponed, and the men were correct in their guess, because about noon on the next day Lafe came straggling back to town: 'She ain't half bad, my woman. We been through a lot together. Flood . . . attacks by them Karankawa raidin' north. I doubt I could do much better.'

So the multiple ceremony was rescheduled for that afternoon, but now a more serious problem arose, and it was the women who circulated the distressing news: 'Father Clooney is too drunk to officiate.' When the men investigated, they found that after the preceding day's disappointment, Father Clooney had found a rather large jug of whiskey. He was immobilized, unable to speak coherently, and just as belligerent as when he had told his bishop to go to the devil.

Since the Quimpers were more or less in charge of the priest, the settlers looked to them for a solution, but they had none. 'He's blind drunk, quite unable to stand, let alone conduct a weddin',' Mattie told the women. 'He's in there singin' old songs and he's wet his drawers.'

For a second time the wedding had to be postponed, and the couples converged on the Quimpers: 'Get him sober and keep him sober till tomorrow mornin'. Husbands runnin' away. Priests dead drunk. Let's get this thing finished.' So a watch was set over Father Clooney, and slowly through the night the tremendous cargo of alcohol he had absorbed drained from his system, and at dawn Mattie assured the others: 'I think he'll be able to stand up after breakfast.'

But during the night a much different problem surfaced at this crossroads, for a tall, acidulous man who introduced himself as Joel Job Harrison came to the cabin where the Quimpers were tending their drunken priest and said in conspiratorial tones: 'I suppose you know. I'm sure they must have told you.'

'What?' Mattie asked.

Harrison glanced about, then stared contemptuously at the inert priest: 'I'm a Methodist minister. I do what I can to keep the true faith alive in this papist land.'

'Doesn't the government . . . ?'

'It must never know. I work in secret . . . to keep the true faith alive.'

'And if they catch you?'

'All the people in these cabins, they all support me.'

'Then why don't *you* marry them?'

'I have. Secretly, at night.'

'Why do they marry a second time with the priest?'

'To ensure their land.' Bitterly, without compassion, he looked down at the prostrate Catholic: 'Look at him! God's vicar! Guide to lost souls, and himself more lost than any.'

Jubal said: 'What's going to happen to you if . . . I mean in the years ahead?'

Reverend Harrison, for he was indeed an ordained Methodist missionary, looked about the cabin, drew close to the older Quimpers, and said: 'Surely, Texas will soon be flooded with trustworthy Protestants. When that happens, we'll break away from Mexico. What will happen to me in the years ahead? I'll build a strong church in a free Texas.'

'You could be shot for such talk,' Jubal said, drawing away.

'Jesus was crucified for His talk, but everything He said came to pass.'

'What do you expect of us?' Mattie asked, and the tall man said: 'Food when I pass your way. Help when I organize meetings in your region.' Again he looked down at the unconscious priest: 'There lies the enemy. As helpless as the Mexico he represents.' And like a ghost he vanished.

On the third try, the seven marriages were solemnized in accordance with Mexican law; Father Clooney was unsteady on his feet and somewhat cotton-mouthed in his speech, but after the vows were exchanged and the paper-marriages brought into the family of the Lord, he surprised the audience by bending his head back and sending to heaven a prayer that might have come from all their hearts:

> 'Almighty Father, we are Your smallest children. We have no cathedral here in the wilderness. We have no choir to sing Your praises, no trumpets to proclaim Your glory. We are drunk when we should be sober, and we run away when we should stand firm. But we do our best. We join hands in love and have children to bless us. We help the poor and care for the infirm. We pay our lawful taxes.

'God in heaven, we beseech You to look after us. We are not a mighty force and there are no generals or cardinals among us. But we occupy the frontier and establish new footholds for Your law, and in our humility we ask for Your blessing. Amen.'

On the third day south along the Goliad Road, Yancey had a chance to see what his family and Father Clooney meant when they spoke of love, for when they approached a cabin on the western side of the road a bedraggled young woman so weak she could scarcely stand called to them: 'We are dying. We've had no food for days.' And when they entered the cabin they found that it was so

'My man, a deep fever. He cannot move.' There on the hut's lone cot lay a man near death, shaking with fever, and in a corner, his two daughters, three and five, huddled like skeletons.

'I cannot leave and hunt,' the woman said, and as she saw Mattie, another wife in the wilderness, she ran to her, fell into her arms, and collapsed weeping. Then, slipping from Mattie's grasp, she fell to the floor.

Yancey was astonished by the speed with which his parents and the priest responded to this cry for help: Father Clooney took charge of the children and started feeding them from his store; Mattie prepared a paillasse on the floor and placed the wife upon it, whispering as she did: 'It's goin' to be all right. Your children are bein' fed.'

Jubal said crisply: 'Son, fetch the rifles!' They hunted all morning, killing enough game to feed the family for weeks, then they butchered the best parts and dragged them back to the cabin, where they camped for nine days until the health of the family was restored. As soon as the husband was strong enough to sit up, Jubal and the priest engaged him in gambling for Mattie's corn, and the lonely cabin was filled with jollity as the women did the work and Yancey looked on.

'You can make do, now,' Jubal assured the family. 'We'll kill a couple more deer or somethin', and things'll be all right.'

As they prepared to leave, Mattie asked: 'Have you papers stating that the land is yours?' and when they replied yes, she told them: 'Half the battle's won. You'll surely be all right.'

When they had the cart loaded, the man showed them a trick which would make its progress even more expeditious, for he drove one of his precious iron nails deep into the wood at the front, forcing the nail back upon itself to form a loop through which he passed a rope: 'One pushes from behind, one pulls from the front,' and automatically Mattie fitted herself into the rope and prepared to start pulling, but before she did so the settlers offered advice which they thought might prove vital: 'As you move into Austin's land, keep careful watch for the Karankawa,' and Mattie asked: 'What are they?' and they explained: 'Big Indians, powerful. They live along the Gulf but they been raidin' north. Taller than those we see around here. And they eat people.'

'But that's impossible!' Father Clooney protested, whereupon the wife said sharply: 'It may be impossible in Ireland, but not here. The Kronks, they do eat people.'

'Not in my parish!' Rumpling through his papers, he found a report, and said, almost like a protesting little boy: 'They told me the Indians would be found only along the seacoast.'

'That was last year. But so many white people movin' in, they've had to come inland. We heard they ate a family on the Brazos.'

'I'll put a stop to that,' Clooney said, and the woman warned: 'You'd make a tidy morsel, Father.'

They had been on their way only two days, heading for the Brazos River, when Yancey saw an alligator, huge and menacing, lurking on the bank of a small stream. Its ugly jaws, locked but with teeth showing, seemed capable of biting a man in half; its bumpy hide glistened menacingly in the sun.

'Shoot him!' the boy shouted, but his father said: 'Let him go. If you don't bother him, he don't bother you.' And with a well-aimed stone he nicked the alligator's tail, so that the beast snapped his jaws and disappeared into the muddy water.

One morning Jubal said: 'More trees ever' day. Must be approachin' the Brazos,' and other signs appeared, confirming their nearness to that spinal column of Texas. But Mattie, always alert to messages from their proposed home, saw more ominous signs: 'Someone's out there. Behind the trees. Followin' us.'

Her husband said deprecatingly: 'Nothin' out there, Matt, old girl,' and on they plodded.

But Mattie was not satisfied, so on her own she left the trail to inspect the trees, and when she reached them she found herself suddenly facing nine or ten of the tallest, fiercest Indians in North America. They were immense, powerful of arm and leg, and she knew they were the cannibals. They were supposed to be on the seacoast, but here they were, in the forest.

Before they could grab her, she uttered a wild scream: 'Kronks!' and as the echo ricocheted through the trees, she started running to rejoin her men.

'Over here!' Jubal yelled as he and Father Clooney sprinted with their guns to a smaller grove of oaks which he hoped they could defend. For one pitiful moment young Yancey stood riveted by fright; then, urged by a shout from the priest, he found courage and ran to the trees, arriving there at the same time as his terrified mother.

Wisely, Jubal formed his three helpers in a circle about the base of a tall oak, from where they fended off the Indians with carefully aimed shots. Yancey reloaded for his father, and Mattie was supposed to do the same for Father Clooney, but after the first round of shots she yelled at the priest: 'Load for yourself!' and she began firing on her own, hitting one of the Karankawa in the leg.

Realizing that the white travelers were going to keep on fighting, the huge Indians fired their two dilapidated muskets a few more times, missing even the oak tree, then withdrew, dragging their wounded companions behind them. 'My God, they were big!' Jubal cried as they disappeared. 'If we'd had only one gun, they'd have killed us all.' Turning to his wife, he kissed her: 'You know how to use a gun, old girl.'

Now came the glorious days! With moccasins, alligators and giant Karankawa safely passed, the travelers approached the outer limits of the Austin Colony, and as they neared the left bank of the Brazos they saw land that compared favorably with any in the world. Slight rolling hills created lovely valleys and gentle glades. Little streams wandered aimlessly, providing scenes so inviting that Father Clooney cried several times: 'Build your cabin here!' but always Mattie pushed ahead, for she had in mind a picture of the land she wanted, and it featured spacious meadowlands beside a big river, not some picturesque refuge close to a little stream.

Each mile down the Goliad Road brought new surprises, but the miraculously placed clumps of oak trees on the otherwise open land pleased Mattie most: tall and straight, the fifteen or twenty oaks would be arranged in rude circles that resembled Greek temples, with a carpet of grass beneath the lower branches and reaching across many yards to where the next group of oaks stood. The result was a kind of majestic park, stretching forever, and when they had traveled through such splendid regions for two days Father Clooney said: 'We've come to a paradise right here on earth. You can build your home anywhere and live like kings.' And Mattie nodded.

She was also relieved to detect in her son a slight change for the better, because on two occasions the boy had halted the procession to stand in wonder before some miracle of nature, and she thought as she watched him: Any boy who appreciates growin' things ain't all weakness.

The first amazement was a tree called *bodark,* a wonderful, thorny thing which would produce enormous orangelike fruit of thick skin and of absolutely no use to men or their cattle. The proper name, of course, was *bois-d'arc,* later to be known as Osage orange, and what made this particular tree memorable was that on its branches devoid of leaves clustered not less than forty huge round balls of green plant life with no detectable means of sustenance. 'Mistletoe?' Jubal asked, but when Yancey pulled down a cluster for study, the family saw that it was merely a leafy parasite.

The second encounter was more dramatic, for as the family turned a corner in the rude footpath they came face to face with a large live oak from whose many branches tumbled a cascade of the most beautiful gray-green tracery, with delicate lacy tips that drooped nearly to the ground. 'Spanish moss,' Mattie said. 'Heard about it but never seen it.' Yancey, encountering this lovely wonder for the first time, stood silent.

Jubal had to be concerned with more practical matters, for one morning while Mattie and the priest were admiring the varied landscape, he chanced to see at some distance from the trail a sight which caused his heart to skip several beats: 'My God! It's a bee tree!' And when he dragged Yancey to the half-dead tree Jubal thumped the hollow part of the tree with practiced knuckles. 'Crammed with honey!' he assured his son. 'With this tree we could feed a village.'

But when he started to show Yancey how to protect his head with his shirt, his belly exposed, the boy began to whimper: 'I don't want to be stung by no bees,' and he ran back to the others, whining: 'Pop wants me to stick my hand in a bee tree.'

Father Clooney, excited by the prospect of finding honey, took the Quimpers' two blankets, ran to the tree and, wrapping himself and Jubal in as much protection as possible, proceeded to break off dead limbs to provide entrance to the tree, and when they had done this they found, as Jubal had expected, the edges of a hoard so rich that it would have supplied a family of three for half a year.

Battling the bees that attacked any naked spot they could find, the two men used oak leaves on which to pile the rich comb they were extracting, and when they had accumulated all they could carry, they started back to the road, with bees following in savage assault. Laughing and running with hands loaded, the two ignored the stings they were receiving and reached Mattie, who slapped away the bees and provided pots in which the seeping comb could be stored.

'Any land that has bee trees is goin' to be a fine place to settle,' Jubal said, and as the days passed he found, to his delight, that in this region such trees abounded. But as they approached what seemed to be the bottom land of some river, they discovered another bounty which promised equal pleasure: very tall trees up which climbed thick vines reaching to the very crown. 'Those look like muscadine vines,' Jubal cried excitedly. 'We had them in Tennessee. Great for jam, better for wine.'

'That's nice to hear,' Father Clooney said, but on that same day they came to other trees, not so tall but holding vines twice as thick and ominous. 'These must be mustangs!' Jubal said. 'I've heard about them. Skin so thick you can't bite it, and if you try, it'll burn your mouth out. But the fruit inside? Delicious. Sweet and acid at the same time. They could make fine jelly.'

'But could they make good wine?' Clooney asked, and when Quimper said they couldn't, the priest said: 'We'll stay with the muscadines.'

And then, as they reached the left bank of the Brazos, thirty feet higher than the bed of the river, they saw on the opposite bank something which gave Mattie such reassurance that she wanted to plant her seeds immediately. 'Look!' she shouted to the others, and when they did they saw fields of wild oats and rye, sown by no one, harvested never, just the bounty of the earth and a promise that if here one planted wheat and corn and nurtured it, crops would grow abundantly. In late March this grain, which had ripened the summer before, had been well beaten down by rain or fed upon by birds, but even so, there remained a remembrance of the oats and the rye, wild and tough and scant, but veritable food. Mattie looked at the priest, then at the grain, and said: 'Father, give us a prayer of thanksgivin'. This is land we can use.'

The three men were willing to halt where they were, for this was satisfactory, but Mattie clung to her vision of the perfect site, and forcefully she led the way to a rise from which they could look across the Brazos to land of wondrous beauty: groves of oak trees, swinging paths through rich grass, open areas for the building of homes, and the reassuring calm of a blue sky overhead. 'That's what we want,' Mattie said.

But how to get the cart across the river? Each of the men had suggestions: 'Swim across and leave the cart here.' Or 'Cut two logs, wedge them under the wheels, and float it across.' Even Yancey chimed in: 'Cut grapevines and we'll pull it across.' Mattie listened respectfully to each proposal, and rejected them all: 'We'll build a raft, and after it has carried us across, we'll use it as a ferry for others who come this way.' And she would accept no alternative.

With the tools acquired in Nacogdoches the two men and Yancey felled enough trees to form a substantial platform in the muddy water, and when Mattie bound the logs together with long lengths of vine, the cart was gingerly wheeled upon it, and cheers sounded when the raft held firm. With a long pole Mattie shoved the raft and its precious cargo into the middle of the river and across to the other bank.

As soon as the raft touched land she rushed ashore, dropped her bag of seed, and began pacing off the dimensions of her proposed cabin, and when she stood where the door would be, she spread her arms and cried: 'This is it.'

She had chosen a superior site, for here the wandering river formed a large S. At the first turn the current had eaten away the bank, leaving a huge red cliff thirty-two feet high, and then, as if bouncing back from that effort, it had done the same a little farther along but on the opposite shore, so that when Mattie stood on the spot she had selected for her home, she could see a most pleasing domain: the two red cliffs, the tangled woodland along the river, clusters of oaks on the higher ground, deer watching from a distance, soft hills adding movement, and over all, the bluest sky any of them had ever seen. 'We'll build the cabin here,' she said, whereupon her husband broke into rude laughter: 'Build it here and swim to safety when the floods come.'

He took her to a grove of oaks that towered more than thirty feet above the stream below, and stood with his hands on his hips, staring at the trees: 'Don't you see nothin'?' When she asked what she was supposed to see, he pointed to a mass of grass and driftwood caught in the branches ten feet above her head. 'What is that?' she asked, and he said: 'Can't you see? That's where the flood came last time.'

And when she looked more closely, both at the trees on her side of the Brazos and those opposite, she saw that along a line as clearly defined as if some giant had drawn it with his pen, remnants of a great flood were visible; at that tumultuous time the water had stood more than forty feet higher than it did now, and when she moved back to study other trees on the upland plain, she realized that the river must have been two or three miles wide. The awesome size appalled her, and she asked: 'When did this happen?' and her husband said: 'Last year. Ten years ago. You can't tell by the flotsam, because it's dead. But do you doubt it happened?'

'I do not,' she said, and forthwith she moved inland, studying the trees and their trapped refuse, until she reached a high mound to which no flood had crept: 'This will be safe.' And while the men watched, she moved beyond the mound to an open space, where she began to grub the ground with her hoe. When it was well broken, she took from her canvas bag handfuls of corn. 'The place is right,' she said. 'The moon is right and the soil is right. I've come a long, long way for this blessed moment.' Inspecting each kernel to be sure the tobacco had kept it weevil-free, she planted her first crop, and only when each grain had been safely embedded in the rich soil did she look for a place to sleep.

The time had now come for Father Clooney to continue his pastoral way down the Brazos to those settlements whose spiritual life he would be supervising, but before he departed he felt he must help the Quimpers erect their cabin. And now he asked: 'How will you inform Stephen Austin that you've settled on his land?'

'When you see him, you must tell him what land we've taken. I'll write a letter askin' that surveyors be sent.' And when the three adults had calculated roughly what a league-and-a-labor would be—4,605 acres, or about 2.5 miles long on a side—the men began cutting stakes to indicate their corners, but as soon as the riverside square was determined, Mattie quietly began to move the stakes in order to form a long, slim fronting on the river. 'This gives us a lot more land along the water.'

Satisfied with her little kingdom, she now began to plan her house, but she had not gone far when Jubal interrupted: 'Stop where you are! We're not cuttin' logs for no big cabin. That can come later.'

'What are we doin'?' Mattie asked, and Jubal pointed to the mound that had attracted her to this site: 'We're goin' to dig us a deep hole in the face of that mound, build us a log front out here, and short side walls to close off the rooms.'

'A cave-house?' Mattie cried. 'Not for me!'

'Matt, old girl. Us men got to do the cuttin' of them trees, and doin' it this way . . . Figure it out. Only one wall and two halves instead of four walls. Half a roof instead of a whole one.'

'But we'll be livin' in a cave,' she protested, and her husband said: 'Many do. And I promise you this, once I find the time, I'll cut the rest of the logs and build you a real house.'

But it took him and Father Clooney so much time and effort to cut and notch two big logs for the base of the front wall that they simplified their plan. They used the two finished logs as corner posts, sunk deep into the ground and strongly braced, and joined them together by a palisade made of saplings dug into the earth side by side.

'Now we tie all together,' Jubal said as the outside portion of the cave-house was formed. 'Yancey, Mattie, start tearin' down grapevines!' And when these were dragged in abundance to the site, everyone worked at weaving them through the saplings, which were then plastered with a heavy red clay dredged from the bottom of the river, forming a solid wall.

The roof they wove of heavier vines, covering it with sod so that grass would grow and keep it impervious. When all was done, Jubal said: 'We got us a house half in the air, half in the cave. Warm in winter, cool in summer,' but Mattie added: 'And dark all the time. And filled with smoke.'

'Don't you worry, Matt, you'll have better one day.' So the Quimpers moved into their house, with its dirt floor, hastily carpentered benches and stools, two wooden beds, a trestle table, and pegs on which to hang things. It was not what Mattie had wanted, but as she stepped inside she muttered to herself: 'We'll get out of this cave. We'll have a house with proper sides. I don't know when or how, but this ain't a proper home.'

Father Clooney, admiring the handiwork in which he had shared so vigorously, said: 'I think I should bless this home,' and he gathered the Quimpers for a prayer:

'We have come to Tejas seeking freedom and a better life. May this house which we have built with our own hands be a perpetual center of love. May the fields prosper. May the animals multiply. And may the owners find that joy which the Israelites found in their new home. Amen.'

As soon as the Irishman departed, carrying in his pocket Jubal Quimper's claim for the land where the Goliad Road intersected the Brazos River, Jubal launched the project that would provide a meager and uncertain income in the new land; he started felling trees with which their raft could be enlarged, and after weeks of the most painful labor, for his hands grew raw, he had himself a serviceable ferry for lifting travelers back and forth across the Brazos. 'Quimper's Ferry' it was called, and as such it would find an honorable place in Texas history, for across it would move men of distinction, and their cattle, and their armies.

But what most travelers remembered about Quimper's Ferry was not the husband's ferry but the hospitality which the wife dispatched, for she ran a kind of inn or stopping place, and hundreds who straggled down the Goliad Road would testify in their memoirs that the difficult travel from the Sabine River to the Brazos almost discouraged them:

> We was attacked by Indians and threatened by panthers in the woods, and our food was low and we seen alligators, and one man died from rattlesnake, and we would of turned back, sick in spirit, but then we come to Quimper's Ferry on the Brazos and Mrs. Quimper welcomed us to her cave-house, and we didn't have no money at the time to pay her but she said no mind, and she fed us and give the children honey for their bread. And it was in those days we first thought Texas might be a decent place to settle.

In the autumn of that first difficult year Jubal discovered just how rewarding a place this was, for as he tramped the woods he came upon a tallish tree with fine green leaves and some husks about its trunk, carry-overs from the preceding fall: 'This is a nut tree! Look up there!' And scattered profusely through the heavy branches he saw clusters of long, plump nuts in a profusion he had not seen in Tennessee.

They were pecans, still protected by a greenish husk, and in the colder days that followed he saw that the husks curled back toward the stem which attached them to the tree. Reaching up to pick one, he inadvertently shook the tree, whereupon a waterfall of nuts fell about his shoulders as the pecan tree willingly divested itself of that year's crop.

In great excitement he gathered the unexpected harvest, stuffing his clothes with the rich food and running toward the hut, shouting: 'Matt, old girl! God sent us food for the winter!' Just as Cabeza de Vaca in 1529 had survived autumn and early winter only on pecans, so the Quimpers, nearly three hundred years later, relished the same remarkable bounty.

Now the pattern of Quimper living became clear. On bright autumn days Jubal and Yancey would search out the pecan trees, shake the branches and garner the fallen nuts so rich in foodstuff. Hauling them home like conquering heroes who had risked much to catch their prey, they would toss the nuts toward where Mattie waited. 'Matt, old girl! We did it again!' Jubal would shout, and then retire, highly pleased with himself, while his wife built a fire, heated water and dipped the pecans to soften the shell and moisten the nutmeat to make it easier to extract.

While her husband watched approvingly, she cracked the shells, sharpened a fine-pointed stick and made Yancey use it to dig out the meats, which she dried on a flat stone beside the fire. When he had extracted huge quantities, warned constantly by Jubal: 'Don't break them, Yancey,' Mattie prepared her hoard in one of three ways: 'Folks like 'em just toasted, or better if we can find a smidgen of salt, or best of all, if I coat 'em in honey real thick with just a touch of salt.'

Often when travelers stopped, the men would gorge on handfuls of Mattie's pecans as they played cards, almost fighting for the toasted nuts if they were the honeyed version. Jubal always explained the trouble he'd had in finding the trees, watching them through the ripening seasons and dragging home the garnered hoard. 'Yancey breaks a lot of the halves,' he apologized. 'It's a pity, but Mattie's real good at toastin' them and addin' the honey.' The Quimpers were proving that properly handled, this nut provided one of the world's complete sources of food. Yancey was not fond of pecans: 'Too much work. Now, if a family had slaves to do the pickin', that would be somethin'.'

Management of the ferry was arranged slowly and without conscious decision. Jubal had built it, and in the early days had operated it, not effectively—he did nothing effective but hunt, play cards and find pecans—but with enough skill to earn a few coins. However, when more travelers began coming their way, he found himself occupied with gathering meat during the day and gaming with the visitors at night, which meant that he was often too busy to man the ferry: 'Mattie, old girl, I hear a stranger callin'. Can you go fetch him?'

So she would interrupt whatever she was doing, go down the steep incline to where the ferry waited, and with increasing ability, pole it across the Brazos to pick up the traveler. In time she began to think of it as her ferry and to resent it if either her husband or her son, each stronger than she, interfered with her operation, for from it she accumulated small sums of money which she set aside to speed the day when she could have a real house.

The Quimpers had occupied their dwelling about seven months when the owner of their land, Stephen Austin, came up the Brazos to regularize their holding, and as soon as they saw him they liked him. He was an intense smallish man in his late twenties, with a sharp face and gentle eyes. He spoke softly, was greatly interested in the progress of the ferry, and amused by the way the Quimpers had marked out their land. When he saw their corner stakes he burst into laughter: 'You rascals! Stretching your land along the river, preempting the good frontage! Don't you know the law of all nations?'

'What are you talkin' about?' Quimper asked, almost belligerently. He was four years older than Austin and much heftier.

Austin laughed and clapped him on the shoulder. 'Let's have a drink,' he said, and when Mattie came with a weak but sweet wine they had made from their muscadines, he explained: 'From the time of Hammurabi, in all orderly societies, governments have told their people: "Sure you want land. But at the river the frontage on the water can be only a small percentage of the depth of the field. You cannot own a long, narrow strip which prevents others from reaching the river." '

'What percentage?' Jubal asked, and he said: 'The customary Spanish grant along the Rio Grande has been nine-thirteenths of a mile facing the river, eleven to thirteen miles back from the river.'

'Outrageous!' Mattie exploded. 'That's a sliver, not a field.'

'I agree,' Austin said. 'Up here we allow a square,' and using a stick in the dust, he sketched a more legal claim.

He was also amused to find that the Quimpers had staked out a rather large chunk of land on the opposite side of the Brazos, where their ferry landed, and he told them: 'My father taught me to oppose that. "No man shall own both sides of a river." If Mexico City ever lets us have our own legislature, I'll sponsor a law saying so.'

'Our ferry has to land somewhere.'

'But you can't own both sides of the river. That would tempt you, in time of trouble, to close down the river.'

'What can we do?'

'Keep your dock over there. Keep your road up to higher ground. And even build a small warehouse, if you wish. I'll certify to the Mexican government it was necessary . . . for public convenience.'

Austin stayed with them for two weeks, paying liberally for his lodging, and in this time they had an opportunity to assess his character: he was straightforward, pedantic, stern in protection of what he viewed as his rights, and a loyal Mexican citizen: 'I have surrendered all thoughts of ever returning to the United States. We have an honorable government in Tejas, and under its protection we can live in dignity and security.'

They did not learn then, or ever, whether Austin was a true convert to Catholicism or not; some travelers insisted that he had been a stout Catholic back in Missouri, others that they knew people there who had seen him attending a Protestant church. It was definite that he had claimed Catholic membership when seeking permission to assume the huge grant which his father had acquired shortly before his death, and certainly the Mexican government considered him a loyal Catholic.

This interpretation was strengthened when Austin spoke highly of Father Clooney: 'When sober, he's a devout man of God, and we're lucky to have him in our colony.'

But the religious problem became more complicated in the early months of 1824 when Joel Job Harrison came south from his cabin on the Trinity to organize his clandestine Methodist services. He took lodging with the Quimpers and convened his first study group at their makeshift inn, a gathering of nine families who had converted in order to get land, but whose secret sympathies were still strongly Protestant. At their first meeting up north, Quimper had not liked Harrison, for he had recognized the tall, angular man as the kind of fanatic who plunged his friends into trouble, and the man's frenzied words had strengthened this adverse impression. But now when he saw Harrison engaged in his pastoral work and watched the compassion with which the Methodist greeted these lonely souls along the frontier, he had to admit that the gawky preacher was a man of God, as simple and honorable in his way as Father Clooney was in his, and as eloquent:

'It is our holy mission here in the remote woods of Texas to keep alive the sacred fire of Protestant vision. Surely it is the destiny of this great land of Texas to be like the rest of the United States, a haven of Protestant decency and security. We are Methodists and it is our duty to preserve our faith and keep it strong for those who follow. How shameful they will see us to have been if we allow our sacred faith, the noblest possession a man can have, to wither. Friends, I implore you, be of stout heart and soon we shall see our churches flourish openly in this wilderness. We are the beginners, the sowers of seed, the keepers of the sacred flame.'

He made the simple act of gathering for quiet worship away from the watchful eyes of the Mexican authorities an affirmation of religious and political principle, and he implied that any who did not participate were morally defunct and not worthy of the exalted name of Protestant or Texan, for he identified one with the other. He was incapable of believing that a real Texan could be a Catholic, and although he never preached his treason openly, he also doubted that a Texan could be a true citizen of Mexico.

When Quimper asked him about this, Harrison explained: 'I'm sure that what you say is true. Of course Austin pays homage to Mexico. He must. Otherwise he loses his land. And I'm sure he wants the public to consider him a Catholic, for this confirms his ownership. But in his heart, what is he? I'll give you my right hand, up to the elbow, if Austin is not an American patriot waiting to take Texas into the Union, and a loyal Protestant just waiting to open our churches in this colony and in the rest of Texas.'

The two men left it there, with Harrison convinced that the Quimpers were still faithful Methodists prepared to summon their fellow religionists to prayer sessions whenever he had an opportunity to visit his Brazos territory. 'I suppose in my heart I'll always be a Methodist,' Jubal told his wife when Harrison returned north, 'but I don't like worshipin' in secret, especially when it could get us into trouble.' One evening as the pair sat and watched deer graze beneath the far oaks, Jubal asked: 'Mattie, do you consider yourself a Mexican citizen?' She pondered this, then said: 'I never considered myself a Tennessee citizen. I get up in the morning, do my work, and go to bed.'

'But could you be a Mexican? Are you goin' to learn Spanish?'

'Enough people come through here speakin' it, I'll have to.'

'Well, are you a Catholic?'

She evaded a direct answer: 'Two of the best men I've met are Father Clooney and Reverend Harrison. I like them both.'

'But you have to choose sides.'

'Why?' And she displayed no interest in which side he had chosen.

The question of Mexican citizenship became more pressing when a guest reached the ferry to stay at the cave-house while trying to round up extra mules to drove overland to New Orleans. In halting English he gave his name as Benito Garza, said he was eighteen years old and a native of the little town of Bravo down on the Rio Grande: 'I cross river'—he called it *reevair*—'and catch the mule. You know what it is, the mule? Father a jackass, mother a horse. The mule all gunpowder and fury. But I, I tame the mule—'

'We know all about mules in Tennessee,' Jubal interrupted. 'But you're not going to take those seventeen mules all the way to New Orleans? Alone?'

'Oh, no! At the Trinity, I meet Mister Ford. He got fifty mules, sixty, from San Antonio. We take them together.'

The Quimpers liked Garza, for the young man was so enthusiastic that his ebullience became infectious: 'Mr. Ford, fine man. He give me money, I get him mules in Mexico. Maybe I buy four, five more right here?'

The Quimpers knew of no farmers in the vicinity who might have bred mules, but they promised young Garza to watch his while he scouted the river, and on the next day the irrepressible young man reappeared with four good animals: 'I always find them somewhere.'

During the young muleteer's last night at the inn, Mattie could not control her curiosity: 'Your mother? What's she think about such a trip? To New Orleans?'

'She's dead. But I go on trail first time, twelve years old.'

'Twelve?'

'She tell me: "You got to learn when you young." '

'Where's your home?'

'Rio Grande. Lots of land. Lots of children, too. Brothers get land. I get mules.'

Despite her inclination to be impartial in most things, she could not help comparing this adventurous Mexican with her timorous son: 'Weren't you afraid? Twelve years old?'

'No,' he said brightly. 'Men all alike, Mexican, Texican. You quick, you got a little money, is all right.'

'What was your mother like?' Mattie asked as she passed her salted pecans.

'Most beautiful girl in San Antonio. Everybody said so. Frenchman wanted to marry her. American, too. But she walk to Rio Grande to marry my father. Nine children. Wonderful love story.'

'And what will you do?'

'Make much money, New Orleans. Then help my sisters find husbands.'

When the young fellow headed up the trail with his twenty-one mules, Jubal said: 'He's the best visitor we've had since Father Clooney left.' Then he added: 'I think I'll learn Spanish, serious.' When he caught the rhythm of that beautiful language, probably the easiest on earth for a stranger to learn, he told his wife: 'When I had to argue with that Ripperdá at Nacogdoches, I wanted nothin' to do with Mexicans. But now that I see this land, and a fine young man like Garza, I'm beginnin' to think that Mexico is where we'll spend our years.' She replied: 'Texas, Tennessee, they all seem the same. Catholic, Protestant, likewise.'

'But you said you respected Reverend Harrison?'

'I respect Father Clooney, but that don't make me a Catholic.'

At times Jubal could not understand his thin, secretive wife. Her indifference to some things mystified him. She could work interminably without complaint. She ran the ferry, and certainly it was she who kept the inn functioning. But she always came back to her two obsessions: 'Jubal, I won't live in this cave-house much longer' and 'Jubal, we got to get hold of that land on the other end of the ferry.'

To the first demand her husband temporized: 'As soon as we get ahead, I'll build you a real house,' and to the second he reasoned: 'You heard Austin say you can't control land on both sides of the river,' and she asked bluntly: 'Does Austin need to know?' and sometimes when the ferry was waiting on the far side of the river, Jubal would see his wife marching about the land, driving stakes to mark what she wanted.

She was doing this one day when the Karankawa struck, and only by rushing down to the river and jumping onto the raft as it slid away from the shore did she escape being killed. The Indians raged along the bank, then disappeared into the wood on that side, rampaging far toward isolated cabins, where they killed the inhabitants.

The response was powerful. A contingent of thirty well-armed men marched down to the new headquarters settlement of San Felipe, where they joined with settlers from the coast in a ten-day campaign against the Kronks. When the Brazos River men straggled back to the ferry, they told Mattie wondrous tales about their battles: 'We overtook them in their camp. Ten of us up here. Ten over here. Ten makin' the attack. Cross-fired them till they had to accept a truce.'

'Was Yancey in the fight?' Mattie asked.

'No, he watched the horses.'

'Not right for a boy to be killin' folks.'

'He better kill Indians or they're gonna kill him.'

There was a strange outcome to this inconclusive battle. One morning when Mattie had guided the ferry to the far bank, depositing two travelers headed for Nacogdoches, she heard a rustling in the woods and saw to her horror that a very tall Karankawa was hiding there, armed with an old-fashioned gun. Unable to reach the ferry as before, she reached for some stick with which to defend herself, but the big Indian put down his weapon and came forward with hands outstretched. Because Mattie had always been willing to accept as her brother any honest man she encountered, she felt no hesitancy in dropping her stick and holding forth her hands, and thus began a strange friendship with a brave the Quimpers called The Kronk.

He lived in a self-made hut beside the inn, and when he had learned a few words of English he explained, with the help of vigorous signs, that the men of his family had led the sortie against the Brazos cabins and had been practically eliminated in the retaliation: 'Sun goes down. Karankawa no more.' He spoke with great sorrow of the deplorable time in which he lived: 'White man too strong. He break us.' He made a snapping sound with his fingers, like twigs being shattered. He was capable of real grief, as when he spoke of his women slain in the last battle: 'Babies, they best. Always hope, babies grow.' He liked Yancey, who was terrified of him, and longed to teach the boy those things fathers teach their sons, but young Quimper drew away, and one night Mattie was appalled when her son said: 'If a new battle starts, the men will kill Kronk for sure.'

When Mattie upbraided him for the insensitivity she perceived, Yancey replied: 'He's an Indian, ain't he?' and the conversation ended.

The Kronk was so helpful around the cave-house that Jubal said one morning: 'Mattie, I think that with Kronk's help we might could build you a set of real outside walls for this dugout,' but she snapped: 'I don't want no improvements. I want a real house with four walls around,' and he laughed: 'We ain't that ambitious.'

With great effort Jubal, The Kronk and Yancey chopped out some stout lengths to substitute for the vertical poles that had framed their cabin, and slowly, finishing one side after another, they inserted the heavy logs, converting their flimsy-walled cave-house into a sturdy one. Travelers familiar with the former stopping place congratulated them on the improvement, but invariably the Quimpers confessed: 'We couldn't of done it without The Kronk.'

Strangers who had often been required to fight the Indians were sometimes startled to find a real Karankawa living at the ferry, but those who settled in the area grew accustomed to the bronzed giant with the flashing white teeth. They often found him sitting with Mattie, talking in his strange way with words which only she seemed to understand. She was not afraid to ask him anything, and one afternoon she said bluntly: 'Why did you Kronks eat people?' and he explained with grunts and gestures and the few words he knew that it was not done from hunger but as a ritual, confirming victory in battle or as a source of valor, as when warriors ate the heart, liver and tongue of a gallant adversary.

'But you did eat them?' she asked and he replied: 'Good. Like turkey.'

He became a kind of unpaid servant at the inn, but in return for his help he did receive food and such clothing as he wanted and the Quimpers were able to provide. His chief contribution was as a hunter, and under Jubal's tutelage he learned to be as parsimonious with his powder and lead as Quimper himself. With a fine hunter like The Kronk available, Jubal no longer took Yancey with him, for the boy was useless in the field; The Kronk was a skilled shot, and with his gun, which his tribe had purchased from French traders in the early years of the century, he could knock down a buffalo or trail a deer almost as well as Jubal himself. As a pair they were formidable, and travelers grew accustomed to having copious helpings of meat when they visited Quimper's inn.

Once when he returned with three slain deer, Mattie asked: 'Why do you shoot so many deer? So few turkey?' And he explained: 'Deer easy, turkey damn hard.' When she asked the difference, he said: 'Kronk sneak up, deer see. They think "Is Kronk or tree stump?" and they stand there, I shoot. But when Kronk sneak up on turkey, leader cry "By God, Kronk comin'!" and off they go. Kronk never see 'em again.'

Often in the long months of that first year before Mattie's corn had ripened or the crops matured, meat was all they had had. Months would pass without flour for the making of bread; salt was scarce; vegetables did not yet exist; and men would say: 'Last night I dreamed of fresh bread, covered with butter and sprinkled with salt. God, how I hate venison.' But when they had Jubal's honey to flavor the great chunks of roasted meat, the frontiersmen stopped complaining. 'It's uncanny how Jubal can smell out a honey tree three miles away,' they said, but others said: 'He's just as good at trackin' bear. When Mattie smokes it properly, you cain't tell it from Pennsylvania bacon.' But what Jubal really enjoyed was stalking the wild turkey, for as he told the others: 'Salt or no salt, bread or no bread, that bird is delicious.'

Once a wandering Irishman named Mulrooney brought the Quimpers a bundle containing real flour, about three pounds, which he had acquired at great cost from an incoming vessel at the mouth of the Brazos: 'Could you make me some bread? I'm starvin' for bread.'

Mattie said that she could, if he'd let her keep some slices: 'Because I'm starvin' for bread, too.' But when he saw that she was preparing to mix a dough using most of his flour, he protested: 'No, ma'am! No!' and he told her that in backwoods Tejas they used half flour, half acorn, and he proceeded to take Yancey with him to gather the latter.

'No, not that kind,' Mulrooney said. 'Them's red oaks. Very high in tannic acid. Burn your gut.' What he sought were the fat, beautiful acorns of the live oak, a variety whose nuts were reassuringly deficient in tannin. The numerous but tiny acorns of the post oak he ignored completely: 'Waste of time. Not enough meat.'

When he and Yancey had a bag full of the rich-looking nuts, he peeled them and asked for a bucket of scalding water, in which he boiled them for three hours: 'We're drivin' out the acid. Now, when that's done, we boil them again for three hours in very salty water. Sweetens 'em up.'

The two boilings took most of a day, but that night he spread the blanched acorns before the fire so that they might be crushed and pulverized at dawn. When this was done he had a fine white flour almost indistinguishable from the bought variety, and from this mix Mattie made her bread.

'By God, that's good!' Mulrooney exclaimed when his first piece was smeared with honey. 'You know, Miss Mattie, you and me could make a fortune with this here bread,' and the Quimpers agreed that it was palatable. It was more than that. 'It's damned good,' Jubal said, and he told Mattie: 'Remember how he did it. Stay away from them red oaks.'

On a summer day in 1824, as Mattie poled her ferry across the Brazos, she saw well to the west a phenomenon which did not startle her but which did attract her attention. As she explained later: 'I thought nothin' of it, at first. Dark clouds along the horizon, but after a while I realized they were darker than any I'd seen before. And they didn't move like an ordinary storm. Just hung there, like a distant curtain.'

While the darkness intensified without any visible motion, she deposited her passenger on the far shore: 'Mister, somethin' strange. I'd watch for cover.'

'What do you think it is?' the man asked, and she said: 'I don't rightly know, but some place back there is catchin' rain. And if they're gettin' it now, we'll get it soon.'

When she returned to her own side of the river she called for Jubal, but he was off tracking honey bees, so she spent a few minutes outside, studying the storm: 'Yancey! Come here and see this cloud.'

When the boy stood with her, she repeated: 'Somebody upriver's catchin' a lot of rain,' and soon thereafter Jubal came running home with news that the river was rising.

For most of that long summer day the tremendous black clouds remained motionless along the northwestern horizon, depositing enormous quantities of rain, so that as dusk approached, the Brazos showed a sullen rise of nearly a foot. Jubal said: 'If it starts to rain here, Mattie, that river could really run wild.'

When the first drops did come splattering down, just at nightfall, Mattie told her men: 'I think I'll stay with the ferry . . . in case,' and by the time she poled it across the river to the more protected anchoring place on the opposite shore, the rain was falling not in drops but in torrents, and she realized that it was bound to lift the river level so drastically that she would have to remain there through the night and away from the turbulent center of the rampaging river. She was drenched. Hair, eyes, clothes, hands, all were soaked in the lashing rain. From time to time as she poled away from the uncontrolled flood she became aware that great trees, uprooted from the northwest, were moving down the current, and these she must avoid.

Will the cabin survive? she asked herself toward dawn when it became apparent that this was to be a historic flood, far in excess of any whose remnants Jubal had pointed out to her on that first day. Pray God it doesn't reach our hill.

In its outer reaches, of course, the great flood was not a swift-moving body of water; it was a quiet intrusion, sometimes hardly moving at all, but remorselessly it submerged everything; only at the center of the riverbed did the waters form a foaming, rampaging, irresistible torrent. Fifty miles to the south, where the distance between the Brazos and the Colorado narrowed to a corridor, the flood became so tremendous that the back waters from the two rivers actually joined in a great sweeping ocean. At Quimper's Ferry the flood rose so high, it drove Mattie three miles inland before she managed to tie her craft to the branches of an oak whose trunk was seven feet under water.

There she remained for two cold days until she saw that the waters were beginning to recede, whereupon she poled across fields to where the ferry was customarily tied, and as the waters swiftly dropped, she crossed the Brazos and brought her craft home. 'We thought you was dead,' her husband said matter-of-factly as she climbed up to her rain-soaked cabin, and she told him: 'I thought I was, too, but God helped with the pole.' She looked at their undamaged home, then kissed her husband: 'Thank God, Jubal, you made us build up here.'

Yancey broke in: 'When the flood came three feet up the wall we thought we was done. But The Kronk led Pop and me to that grove of oaks and tied ourself in a tree.' Jubal hushed him: 'We was all lucky. And for that we can thank God. I wish Father Clooney was here to lead us in prayer.' And for the next hundred years people along the Brazos would remember it as 'the year the Brazos ran wild' or 'the year the rivers joined.' Mattie recalled it as 'the year I lost my corn.'

The Quimpers were less lucky with another event caused by the flood, and this too would be remembered. The excessive waters disturbed many animals, causing them to venture into new areas and adopt new habits, and one of those most seriously displaced was a huge rattlesnake eight feet three inches long from the tip of his rattle and as big around as a small tree. He was really a monstrous creature, with a head as big as a soup plate and fangs so huge and powerful, they could discharge a dreadful injection. Veteran of many struggles, master of the sudden ambush, he had subdued baby pigs and fawns and rabbits and a multitude of rats and mice. His traditional home had been sixteen miles up the Brazos in a rocky ledge that gave him excellent protection and a steady supply of victims, but the floods had dislodged him and sent him tumbling down the river along with deer and alligators and javelinas. During the height of the flood each animal was so preoccupied with its own salvation that it ignored friends and enemies alike, but as the waters receded, each resumed its habits, and the snake found itself far downstream, lodged in unfamiliar rocks and with a most uncertain food supply.

The rattler now had to be more venturesome than usual, and began foraging far from its crevice. Sometimes it went down close to the river, exploring the rocks there, and on other days it slithered inland, watching always to be sure that it had adequate cover to protect it from the blazing sun whose unimpeded heat would kill it. Mice, rabbits, squirrels, birds—the great reptile devoured them all, stunning them first with sharp jabs of its fangs, then swallowing them slowly and constricting its belly muscles to break down the bones and digest the food.

The rattler was a fearsome beast, made more so by frontier legend, most of it spurious: 'It cain't strike at you elsen it's coiled. Needs the springin' power of its coils. Then it can reach out twice its length.' Coiled, it could strike with remarkable accuracy; uncoiled, less so, and never more than half its length. This monster could strike four feet, a menacing distance.

'The snake, he cain't never strike you elsen he warns you first with a shake of his rattles. "God's recompense," we call it.' Most of the time when hunting small animals it struck with no warning, but often at the approach of a man or a large animal, it activated its rattles furiously to scare away the intruder.

'A rattler is thrifty, carries just enough venom to kill a man.' Later experts would demonstrate that whereas twenty-five milligrams would kill a child, and one hundred a man, a grown rattler could deliver two hundred fifty milligrams, enough to kill two men, while a really big snake could inject a thousand milligrams in one shot.

'One drop of rattlesnake venom in yore bloodstream, you're dead.' Many frontiersmen had been struck by medium-sized rattlers and survived, but to be injected with a full charge of venom by a snake as large as this one would be fatal.

'No man ain't never been struck by a full-sized rattler and lived.' A rattler carried only a limited supply of venom in its sacs, and if it had recently discharged this in killing some animal, it could strike its next victim with the full force of its fangs and inflict only a small wound that would quickly heal. Certain boastful men had survived as a result of this phenomenon.

This great beast at Quimper's Ferry, longer than any hitherto seen along the Brazos, did not seek contact with human beings; it did its best to avoid them, but if any threatened the quiet of its domain, it could strike with terrifying force. It would not have come into contact with the Quimpers had not Yancey gone probing along the farther bank, not doing any serious work or accomplishing much, but merely poking into holes with a stick to see what might be happening. As he approached where the snake lay hidden, he heard but did not recognize the warning rattle. Thinking it to be a bird or some noisy insect, he probed further, and found himself staring at the huge coiled snake not ten feet away.

'Mom!' he screamed, and Mattie, working at the ferry, grabbed the gun she kept aboard for protection against wandering Karankawa, and ran to help, but when she reached Yancey she found him immobilized, pointing at the coiled snake whose rattles echoed. 'Do something!' he pleaded.

Infuriated by his craven behavior and terrified of the snake, she pushed her son aside, and with her heart beating at a rate which must soon cause her to faint, she raised the gun. Not firing blindly, because she knew she had only one chance, she took aim as the snake prepared for its deadly thrust, and pulled the trigger. She felt the shock against her shoulder; she felt the snake brush against her knee; and she fainted.

Yancey, seeing only that the rattler had struck at his mother and that she had fallen, concluded that the snake had killed her, despite the gun blast, and ran screaming up the river to the ferry landing: 'Pop! A big rattler killed Mom.'

Jubal and The Kronk waded and swam across the Brazos and ran trembling to where Mattie still lay beside the dreadful snake, and when they saw her they supposed that each had killed the other: 'Snake hit her just as she pulled the trigger. Oh Jesus!' But then the Indian saw her right hand twitch, and when he stepped gingerly past the snake and lifted her head, he saw that she was still breathing. Inspecting her throat and face, he called: 'No dead. Scared. Scared.'

Jubal and Yancey, taking over from the Indian, satisfied themselves that Mattie was indeed alive, and with a love they had not shown before, they carried her upriver to the ferry, where they placed her tenderly aboard, but before they pushed off, The Kronk ran up carrying the enormous snake, whose head had been blown apart. 'We keep,' he said, and the men knew that he intended eating at least part of the fearful enemy out of respect and envy for the courage it had shown.

When Jubal tanned the skin he stretched it to maximum length, extending the accordionlike scales until he had an awesome object that climbed the entire wall of the cabin and back four feet along the ceiling, ten feet, five inches in majestic length. Recovering the skull from The Kronk, he attached it so that it appeared to be striking at the diners seated below, and strangers seeing it for the first time said: 'They warn't never a snake that big,' but Jubal said proudly: 'Finger them rattlers yourself. They're real, and my little wife's the one who killed it.'

Whenever Mattie looked at the fearful object she thought not of her own heroism in battling the monster but of her son's behavior. She never spoke of this to the boy's father, and certainly not to the boy himself, but she did often recall her own father's stern admonition to his children when they were living in a Tennessee hovel and subsisting on beans with an occasional slab of pork: 'You don't have to fight the world, and you don't have to be the bravest in the village, but by God, if you're my kids, you got to do what's right when you face danger. I don't care if the other man is twice your size. Go at his throat.' Mattie had gone at the great serpent's throat; her son had not.

Mattie kept her small collection of coins gained from running the ferry in the canvas bag which had once protected her corn, and one morning when she felt satisfied that she had saved enough, she asked a farmer who was heading downriver to the rude store at Austin's headquarters at San Felipe to perform a commission for her; and two months later a man on horseback arrived bearing a small keg of nails and a long package. It was a pit saw with two big handles, and when it was assembled she told her husband: 'We'll rip us some planks and build us a real house. I'll live underground no more.'

The Kronk was essential to her plans, for she needed his strength to dig a pit deep enough for a man to stand in: 'And now cut the tallest, thickest tree trunk you can move to the pit.' And when it was hauled across the pit, she climbed down with instructions to her men: 'I'll do the dirty work. You do the strong.'

Grasping the lower handle, she pushed the saw up, while one of the men standing astride the log topside pulled it into cutting position. Then the men bore down while Mattie pulled, and in this laborious way, with sawdust in her face day after day, she supervised the cutting of the planks needed for her house. She never complained, for she kept before her the vision of the home that was to be, and when she felt she had enough planks, she climbed out of her pit, dragooned two travelers to stay as helpers, and started building her house.

At various places in Texas she had seen the type of house she wanted; it had come west from South Carolina and Georgia and provided an excellent device for surviving in a hot or humid climate. 'It's called a dog-run,' Mattie explained to The Kronk, who did much of the heavy work. 'We build a little square house here. Leave seventeen feet open space, then build another, same size, over here.'

'Why here, here?' the Indian asked, and she said: 'One house sleeping. One house living,' and he said: 'Work too damn much.'

Then she explained that the two squares would not remain separated: 'Up there, one long roof over everything. Down here, one long porch, end to end.'

'In between, what?' The Kronk asked, and she said: 'Place for cool breezes. Place for dogs to run in the day, sleep at night.' He then wanted to know what the porch was for, and she said: 'Work done, we watch sunset. Travelers come, they sleep on porch,' and he said approvingly: 'Damn good.'

When it was completed, with liberal use of improvised wattle-and-vine walls that would serve until more planks could be cut, Mattie waited till Reverend Harrison came by on his way to Stephen Austin's headquarters: 'Will you bless this house, Reverend?' He did, praying that the Quimpers would enjoy years of happiness and prosperity in it, but some weeks later, when Harrison was returning from his talk with Austin, he appeared at the door of the house unannounced, to find Jubal and two travelers playing cards and swigging from a jug of muscadine wine. Mattie saw the flare of disgust that crossed his face as he said: 'Do you allow gaming in a house I dedicated to the Lord?'

'I do,' she said. 'Jesus drank wine.'

Coming close to pronouncing anathema upon her, he cried: 'You and your husband and all of them stand in danger of being rejected of God. Gaming and drinking, they'll be the ruin of Texas.'

Jubal had always known it was bound to happen, and now it was upon him: Reverend Harrison and Father Clooney had arrived at the same time, and some kind of ugly confrontation seemed inescapable.

The Protestant clergyman came first, on a surreptitious round of Methodist prayer meetings at which he delivered agitating news about events in Mexico City, the capital of the country: 'They threw out the Spanish, as we know. But before long they invited that fool Iturbide to make himself emperor, and what American would want to live under the dictates of an emperor?'

A man who had traveled in Mexico said dryly: 'They shot him last year,' but this did not alter Harrison's diatribe: 'Each day men like Iturbide remain in control, the yoke of Rome is fastened ever more tightly about our necks. Each day we do not resist, we become more surely the vassals of the Pope, and I can feel in my bones the constant loss of freedom we're undergoing. We're in peril, and we must bind ourselves ever closer or we shall lose our freedom, our church and our understanding of God.'

Night after night he conducted his frenzied meetings, until he had many of the farmers almost prepared to take up arms to defend their rights, and he was equally persuasive with women, for he spoke eloquently of what would happen if their children never learned the beneficent lessons of Protestantism: 'Do you want your daughters to become nuns, locked away in some convent, the prey of priests, never to know the blessings of a true Christian home?' He also frightened them with graphic descriptions of what it meant to worship regularly in the Catholic mode, and he nailed down his preaching with a plea which came from the heart: 'The Protestant church is the true church of Jesus Christ. He called it forth. He ordained us to do His great work on earth. And we must remain faithful to His precepts.'

He was effective because his listeners, hungry for moral guidance, always knew where he stood. He was for the New Testament, morality and Methodism; he was against Rome, alcohol, sexual indulgence, dancing and any kind of irreverence. But in this summer of 1825 he added a bold new dimension to his preaching: 'I cannot believe that the good Christians who came to Texas from Kentucky and Tennessee will long continue under the tyranny of Mexico and Rome.' And once he said this, he realized its implications: 'When that joyous day comes, we'll join the United States.' He justified this treasonous behavior as 'faith plus patriotism.'

He was conducting a secret meeting for elders at the Quimpers' inn late one afternoon, with some twenty farmers surrounding him, when a watcher, posted to detect any approach of Mexican soldiers, ran in: 'Father Clooney comin' on his mule.' And when the conspirators peered out they saw the familiar figure of the Irish priest, older now and thinner, riding up to the porch.

They had no opportunity to disperse before he dismounted, brushed the dust from his black vestments, and entered. One glance at the unusual number of guests and the tall minister who commanded them satisfied him as to what was happening, but he affected not to know. Greeting Reverend Harrison warmly, as if he were no more than some farmer he had met on the Trinity, he smiled at the others he had known before and said to the strangers: 'I don't believe I know you. Father Clooney, of Ballyclooney, County Clare in Ireland, appointed by the Mexican government to be vicar of this parish.'

Having put the conspirators at ease, he then offended their leaders by asking Mattie Quimper: 'Could a perishing pilgrim have a wee nip?' and when she provided one, Reverend Harrison glared at the disgraceful cup as if he wished to turn its contents into vitriol.

Father Clooney was filled with news acquired at the assembly of the Catholic clergy recently convened in San Antonio, and although his personal recollections of that meeting were not altogether pleasant, he was eager to share the substantial news which came from it. His unhappiness stemmed from the way he had been treated—as an interloping Irishman who spoke abominable Spanish—by the more austere Spanish priests who had been trained in Spain and the older Mexican fathers with their education in Mexico City and Querétaro. They had scorned him as a village nothing, a cactus-priest of the bayous, not really one of them and not to be trusted. They had heard of his excessive drinking and of his casual approach to conversion, and many suspected that he was a secret agent sent by the American government to prepare the way for a Yankee takeover. But since none of them would have dreamed of moving one step north from San Antonio or of serving in wilderness areas like the banks of the Trinity, they were content to let this renegade Irishman do their pastoral work for them. His latest experience with these arrogant superiors had not been pleasant but it had been instructive, and now he gushed forth the resounding news:

'As you've surely heard, there was a wonderful revolution in Mexico last year. Emperor Iturbide was overthrown by a group of sterling patriots, and the old viciousness has been cleansed away. A new Mexico, a new life for all of us.

'The hero of the change is a most splendid man, devout, loyal, brave. General Antonio López de Santa Anna. You'll hear much of him in the glorious days ahead, for he brings freedom and distinction to the word *patriot.*

'But the excelling news is that Santa Anna and his associates have given us a new constitution, and I promise you that in Mexican history the date 1824 will become as famous as 1776 is in your America. Because the Constitution of 1824 is a noble document, assuring us the freedoms we've sought. It gives Coahuila-y-Tejas its own state government. It protects us. It guarantees a permanent republic. And it erases all memories of Emperor Iturbide and his follies. What a glorious day for Mexico!'

His listeners soon caught the infection of his enthusiasm, for if what he said about the new constitution was true, most frictions with the central government would be eliminated, and Tejas, under its own regional government, would have a chance to forge ahead. But Reverend Harrison had a pertinent question: 'What does the new rule say about religion?' and Father Clooney answered forthrightly: 'It says that the official religion of Mexico must forever be Roman Catholicism.'

'And will the official church be supported by our tax money?' Harrison asked, and again the round-faced priest gave a straight answer: 'The church will be supported, as before, by the public treasury.'

'If that is so, men who love freedom must oppose your new constitution.'

It was now dusk, and in the crowded dog-run two men of radically opposing views faced each other: Reverend Harrison, tall, austere, dreaming always of a greater Texas, and touched by God but unable because of the law to stand forth as the minister he was; and Father Clooney, the sometimes wavering Roman Catholic priest who was not wholly accepted by his own church but who stumbled along, fortified by his love of Jesus Christ and his compassion for souls wandering in the Tejas wilderness.

They were ill-matched. Harrison had more vigor and a much deeper conviction that what he was doing represented the drift of history and the will of Jesus Christ; Father Clooney was older, wiser, better educated, and fortified by a church that had existed for eighteen hundred years. One important characteristic was shared in common: both clerics aspired to do what was best for Texas, which they saw as one of the brightest hopes in North America or in the world.

Very carefully the priest asked Harrison: 'You say you cannot accept this excellent new law?'

'Not if it makes me pay for the support of a religion I cannot trust.'

Clooney did not flinch at this harsh dismissal: 'Reverend Harrison? Yes, I've known since the day you started holding these secret meetings who you were and what your interests were. Have I tried to interrupt your preaching? Have I put the soldiers to arresting you, which by law I should have done? Have you and I not survived amiably, and are we not friends this evening? If we trusted each other under that bad old constitution, surely we can do so under this good new one.'

Harrison and some of his people were stunned by the fact that Father Clooney had knowledge of their affairs, for they realized that they were subject to arrest, and one man asked: 'What are you going to do, now that you know?' and Clooney replied: 'Nothing. I would much rather have in Catholic Tejas people who were good Methodists than rascals who were poor Catholics and poor everything else. Friends'—and here his voice broke—'we are striving to build in Tejas a new society, a strong one, a decent one. We cannot accomplish this if we are at each other's throat. And you cannot find the security you yearn for if you reject this new constitution.'

His urgent words struck a deep chord in Jubal Quimper's heart: 'If the new law gives us everything we want except religious freedom, I say let's accept it, because in the long run the press of people moving into Tejas will make it Protestant.' Unwisely he looked at Father Clooney, expecting the priest to confirm this probability, but this the old man could not do: 'The new law says that Mexico is a

Catholic nation. Up here, at the edge of government, it doesn't seem that way. But from San Antonio south, you will travel many days before you find a Protestant. Of course Mexico is Catholic, and of course it must remain so. But the good Catholics of that nation will continue to govern Texas much as they do now. You will enjoy respect and the ordinary freedoms.'

'I do not believe it,' Reverend Harrison snapped. 'Mark my words, we shall see Mexican troops along this river, coming here to enforce Catholicism and to put down Christianity.'

'What a terrible error in words!' Father Clooney said instantly. 'No religion monopolizes Christianity.'

'Catholicism tries to,' Harrison snapped, and the meeting ended. Many participants, in later years when some of the issues thus raised had been settled, wrote accounts of this famous confrontation, and one almost illiterate farmer summarized it best:

> We had met at Queemper's Ferry to pray and bad luck trayled us, for Father Cloony the Papist found us out and threttened to arrest us for our unlawful prayrs. Rev. Harison debated with him and we went home hopeful for the days ahed becaws the new laws of Mexico sounded good, but feerful of the yeers ahed becaws we beleeved that Rev. Harison was right and that Texas would soon have to fite for her verry existance.

Promulgation of the reassuring Constitution of 1824 had a curious aftermath. Hopeful newcomers like Jubal Quimper were now encouraged to think of themselves as Mexicans, citizens of a liberal democracy not unlike that in the United States, and then began to refer to themselves as Texicans, a fortunate verbal invention. 'Stands to reason,' Jubal told Mattie, 'if they're Mexicans south of the Rio Grande, we ought to be Texicans north of it.' And it was by this strong, musical name that they knew themselves.

Bathed in euphoria, the Texicans forgot Reverend Harrison's prediction that they would soon be fighting for their existence, but in 1825 that prophecy came true. The enemy, however, was not Mexico. The remaining Karankawa decided they had no chance of living as they had in the past unless they exterminated the white men who had intruded upon their historic territory. Intent upon defending themselves, they launched a series of raids so savage, so cruel in their extermination of lonely cabins and unprotected women that the settlers had no alternative but to fight back. 'Kill them now, or perish later!' was the mood at San Felipe as the settlers prepared for what they prayed would be the final battle.

One group of volunteers assembled at Quimper's Ferry, then marched south, where it would join men gathering along the coast. Since boys above the age of ten were expected to join the expedition with their own guns, Yancey, now aged thirteen, reported, and as the avengers approached the coast he felt his excitement mounting, for he was eager to perform well. But when they had sneaked close to one Karankawa settlement—a cluster of movable ba-acks, or tepees—and the time came for battle action, he froze as he had when confronted by the rattlesnake, and while those about him decimated this first contingent of Indians with a surprise volley, then exterminated them in the wild follow-up, he stood transfixed at the bloody killing.

'We wiped them out!' the volunteers shouted as scouts advised them where to head in order to trap the next group of Kronks. Two men who had seen Yancey's craven behavior walked with him, offering advice: 'When the firin' starts, don't listen to the noise and never look at the Indians as human bein's. You're shootin' squirrels, that's all. You've shot squirrels, ain't you?' When Yancey said he had not, the men said: 'Well, you're goin' to shoot somethin' much better than squirrels tomorrow. You keep with us. We'll show you.'

That night the Quimper's Ferry people were overtaken by a late contingent from the Trinity, and foremost in that group was Reverend Harrison, who conducted services in the darkness, assuring the avengers that they were doing God's work in removing the Indian menace from this part of Texas: 'We shall always face an Indian enemy, wherever we move in Texas. And we shall enjoy no peace till we exterminate him.' When two men from the ferry region who had not known the minister before asked: 'You think the battle against them will go on forever?' he replied: 'The fight for goodness never ceases. Our grandchildren will be fighting Indians.'

On the next day, at about noon, the last great battle against the Karankawa took place, and these proud Indians, for centuries the lords of the three rivers and the scourge of those lesser tribes who tried to infiltrate, realized that their sunset was upon them, and they fought with terrible valor, one brave driving alone at the heart of the white army, coming on and on until he arrived at the mouth of the guns with only a broken stave in his hand.

'Urrk! Arrgh!' he shouted in meaningless syllables, trying to grasp with his bare hand the rifle barrels whose fiery discharges tore him apart.

In terrible struggle the mighty Karankawa died. Braves . . . old men . . . women . . . little girls . . . boys defying the rifles. A notable tribe endeavored to protect its homeland, and failed. Toward evening a pitiful remnant fighting on the far edge of the encounter rallied under the leadership of two heroic warriors to break through the encircling ranks of white men. Signaling to other survivors, women and children alike, these few started a long retreat south toward refuge across the Rio Grande, and after harrowing days without food or water they vanished, except for a few stragglers, from the soil of Texas, to be known no more except in fabled stories about 'them Kronks who ate people.'

They went in sorrow and defeat, the first of more than four-score Indian tribes who would be banished from Texas until the triumphant whites could boast: 'We ain't got no Indians in Texas. We couldn't abide 'em.' Sister American states would devise ways whereby the Indian and the white man could live together—not wholesome ways, nor sensible—but the citizens of Texas could not. The antipathies were too strong.

Yancey did not distinguish himself in this final battle, for, as before, the sound of gunfire immobilized him, and he could only watch as the struggle evolved. At one point in the battle a Karankawa dashed right past him, not fifteen feet away, and one of Yancey's counselors bellowed: 'Fire, goddamnit, fire!' But Yancey was unable to do so.

However, on the way home, when he marched with other men, he began to talk about his heroics among the Karankawa, so that by the time he reached the ferry he had convinced himself that he had behaved with more than average bravery, and when he was close to the family dog-run he told his companions: 'You know, there's a Kronk who moves about here, now and then,' and this so excited the victorious Texicans that when they suddenly saw before them The Kronk, they unhesitatingly slew him, the last Karankawa the Brazos would ever see.

Mattie was appalled by this gratuitous slaughter, but when she confronted the killers, they said honestly: 'Yance never told us he was tame,' and she deduced the criminal part her son had played in this assassination. She did not chastise him for this terrible act, but on succeeding days as she sat on her porch at dusk, exhausted by the multiple tasks she was required to perform while Jubal was out hunting meat or searching for honey trees, she realized how severe her loss was in the death of The Kronk. He had been a member of the family, their custodian, their watchman, the one who stepped forward when there was work to do, the one with whom she talked when the men were away and she faced long days of work. Painfully, this savage Indian had made the transition to civilization, and in the end that civilization had destroyed him for no reason except that he was an Indian.

On the third evening, when she appreciated most clearly the dreadful loss she had sustained, and the reasons for it, she began to weep, not for The Kronk, whose days of confusion were over, but for all those who ventured into a strange land or encountered strange responsibilities, and the sorrow of civilization was almost more than she could bear. She wanted no more of war, no more of argument between Catholic and Protestant, no more confrontation between Mexico and the American states. She wanted only to operate her ferry, run her inn, feed the traveler, and save enough money to buy a new dress at the store in San Felipe or perhaps some extra forks and spoons.

But most of all, she prayed in her desolation that her son would somehow or other grow into manhood, with the capacity to meet a man's obligations.

No American settlers since the Revolution of 1776 had faced the nagging moral problems encountered by those citizens of the republic who moved into Texas in the period of 1820–1835. And none faced the confusions with more vacillating reactions than Jubal Quimper.

Even those later settlers who would cross an entire continent to build new homes in California or Oregon would have the reassurance that in moving from one part of the United States to another, they would carry their religion, their language and their customary law with them. But when people like the Quimpers emigrated to Texas they surrendered such assurances, placing themselves under the constraints of a new religion, a new language and a much different system of law.

Facing these complexities, Mattie and Jubal followed one simple rule: 'Whatever Stephen F. Austin decides is probably right.' Like many others, they revered the strange little man, forgiving him his arbitrary manner. Mattie especially realized that there was a good deal wrong with Austin: Why has he never married? Is he afraid of women? And why does he stare at you with those fixed eyes, like a hawk? All he can think of is his colony.

But despite his faults, and they were many, she saw him as the reliable guide, and whenever he stopped at her inn during his travels throughout the colony, she nodded approval to what he told the visitors who dropped by to talk politics with him: 'Gentlemen, Tejas will not only live under this new Mexican Constitution of 1824; it will prosper.'

'Aren't there weaknesses in it?' a farmer asked, and Austin snapped: 'There are weaknesses in every document drawn by the human mind. Our new law has certain peculiarities reflecting Mexican custom, but they will not impinge upon our freedom. Tejas is to be a Catholic state, but we've seen how easily we live under that constraint. And, yes, priests and soldiers will be tried in courts manned only by their own people, but that's always been the case and we haven't suffered.'

'Are you satisfied,' a settler from Alabama asked bluntly, 'to live under Mexican law for the rest of your life?' and Austin answered: 'I am.'

Jubal Quimper, usually agreeing with whoever spoke to him last, grasped Austin's hands and said: 'Mr. Austin, I'll stand beside you as a Mexican citizen . . . permanent.'

But some days after Austin departed with this pledge of allegiance from the people at Quimper's Ferry, a copy of the new constitution arrived and the man from Alabama who had interrogated Austin rushed to the inn, waving the paper in the air: 'Good God! Listen to what this document says!' And he asked Quimper to read the offending passage: 'With the adoption of this constitution, slavery is forbidden throughout Tejas, and six months from this date, even the importation of slaves already on their way to Tejas will be outlawed.'

Neighbors quickly gathered, and thus began one of the insoluble contradictions of Texas history: of a hundred families like the Quimpers, not more than fifteen owned slaves, which meant that the vast majority could have had no financial interest in preserving slavery, yet most of those without slaves defended the institution and seemed ready to battle Saltillo to preserve it.

Jubal and Mattie were representative: 'We never had no slaves in Tennessee and didn't know many people who did. Lord knows, we don't have any to share our work here in Texas. But it stands to reason, it says right in the Bible that the sons of Ham shall be hewers of wood and drawers of water, and that's the way it's got to be.'

Mattie, who befriended everyone, even Karankawa, was especially strong in her condemnation of the proposed law: 'Niggers ain't really human. I don't yearn to own none, but those good folks who bring 'em here ought to be protected in their property.'

This question so agitated the settlers that a delegation of three planters, led by Jubal Quimper, went resolutely down to Austin's headquarters and told him bluntly: 'Our liberties must be preserved.' And with that simple statement arose the tantalizing ethical issue which would plague Texas for decades, because goodhearted men like Jubal Quimper honestly believed that their freedom could be ensured only by the right to enslave others.

Austin, perceiving the moral wrong in this position, laid bare his honest feelings: 'Gentlemen, I tell you frankly that I oppose slavery with every fiber of my body, now and forever. I condemn it four times. It's bad for society in general. It's bad for commerce. And bad for both master and slave. Never have I departed from this belief and never shall I. The wise men in Saltillo who framed our constitution knew what they were doing, and they did it well. Slavery should be outlawed.'

There could have been no statement of principle more unequivocal than that, and it persuaded Quimper, who spoke for the others: 'You're right, Stephen. What we need is a whole new start. No masters. No slaves.'

But no sooner had Quimper renewed his support than an extraordinary reversal occurred, for that night Austin began to review the problem, not according to his personal convictions but according to his role as leader of a tentative colony not yet securely based, and the more he studied reality the more convinced he became that Tejas had little chance of survival if it failed to attract hundreds or even thousands of established Southern gentlemen who would bring with them prosperity and culture. In an open meeting next morning he attacked the philosophical problem first.

'Gentlemen, order, order. I do not derogate the great states of Kentucky and Tennessee from which many of our finest settlers have come, nor do I speak against any man standing here. But I have become painfully aware that our colony can progress only if we attract in large numbers families of wealth, high cultural attainment and sound moral training from our educated Southern states like Virginia, Carolina, Georgia, Alabama and Mississippi. When they join us with their books, their wealth and their long experience in trade, they will make Tejas a state of which we shall be proud.'

There was a long silence while the inescapable truth of what he had said was judged, and then Quimper cried: 'You're right, Stephen. We need schoolteachers and men who know the Bible.'

While many nodded and some whispered, Austin waited, almost afraid to point out the consequences of what he had just said, but finally he summoned courage and spoke: 'Such men will not join us if they cannot bring their slaves. What white man could grow sugar cane in our steaming river bottoms? What white man from Alabama could toil under our blazing sun chopping cotton? Then pick it? Then haul it to the gin? Only Negroes can do such work, and slavery seems to be the pattern ordained by God for handling them. It is clear that Tejas must have slavery or perish.'

So Jubal Quimper, in a committee of seven, only one of whom owned slaves, helped Austin draft an appeal to the state government in Saltillo and the national government in Mexico City, explaining that whereas the abolishment of slavery was unquestionably right for the rest of the nation, it was not appropriate, at this time, in a frontier region like Tejas: 'We cannot work our fields without slaves, and we cannot populate our empty spaces unless men of property from the Southern states of America are permitted to bring their slaves with them.' Austin, a man who hated slavery, had become its champion.

During the trip back home Quimper reviewed the sudden shifts of their leader: 'First he was stern morality: "Slavery must be abolished." Then he was all for the South: "They must be allowed to bring in their slaves." I wonder where he really stands? Matter of fact, I wonder where I stand.'

This moral confusion on the part of Austin and his adherents would continue, for when Austin concocted a dream for enticing thousands of German and Swiss settlers, he became an ardent opponent of slavery, in deference to their known dislike for keeping anyone in bondage:

> 'The possibility of such a country as Tejas being overrun by a slave population almost makes me weep. Slavery is an injustice and a demoralizing agent in society. When I started this colony I was forced to tolerate it for a while, because I had to draw upon the slave states for my emigrants. But slavery is now most positively prohibited by our Mexican constitution and I hope it may always be so, for it is a curse of the curses and one of the worst reproaches of civilized man.'

But later he would be forced once more to consider the realities of settlement, and again he would reverse himself completely:

'I used to oppose slavery, but during the last six months I have had to restudy the matter and now conclude that Texas *must* be a slave country. Circumstances and unavoidable necessity compel it. It is the wish of the people, and I shall do all I can, prudently, in favor of it. I will do so.'

Quimper, listening to this speech, noticed that Austin had dropped the Spanish *Tejas* in favor of the English *Texas,* indicating serious doubt that his colony could long remain with Mexico, which he also now pronounced in the American fashion. Never again would his friends hear him use the Spanish names which he had tried so faithfully to defend but which he now abandoned forever.

Jubal's attention to such heady political matters was diverted in late 1828 by an exciting letter from his former lawyer in Gallatin, Tennessee:

> Jubal, I send you great news! Your persecutor, Hammond Carver, was killed in a duel, and this legally terminates his case against you. I have ascertained from his survivors that they have no intention of resurrecting the suit, and they have acknowledged in writing that the contested land is yours, along with all the buildings on it. You find yourself not a rich man but one with ample fields and some money, which you can claim only by coming here in person. Do so immediately, for you and Mattie have many friends in these parts who are eager to see you resume your life among them.

This heaven-sent opportunity to escape the tensions of a frontier Texas made Jubal realize how much he longed for the stability of a settled Tennessee, and he was ready to depart immediately: 'Mattie! We're free to go home!'

She deflated his enthusiasm by saying with bulldog stubbornness: 'I have no wish to see Tennessee again,' and he began placing before her all the reasons why they should return to the pleasant life that they could now have in Gallatin: 'Arthur says we won't be really rich, but we'll have enough to buy us a couple of slaves. You won't have to worry about the ferry, and we won't have strangers traipsin' into our home. More important, we can have real walls and windows.'

He threw at her an impressive summary of the differences between civilized Tennessee and barbarian Texas, but in the end she countered with an incontestable reply: 'I like it here.' And in fragmentary comments she let him and Yancey know how deeply Texas had infected her: 'Nothin' I saw in Tennessee is better than that clump of oak trees in the meadow.' During another debate she said: 'I like the Brazos, the way it rises and falls, like it had a will of its own.' On a different day she said: 'My heart beats faster when a stranger comes to the door at night, needin' food—and we have it.' And finally: 'Like a rock gatherin' moss, I've allowed Texas to grow over me, and I admire the feel.'

Guarding each word, she said: 'You and Yancey can go back and settle the claim, and if you're so minded, you can stay. I'll give you your freedom, in the courts if you wish, but this is now my home and I expect to end my days runnin' my ferry.'

The force of her statement made Jubal pause. Twice he started to speak but could find no words, then abruptly he turned away and went to walk beneath the oak trees that Mattie loved so deeply, and as he tried to see their new home through her eyes he began to appreciate why she loved Texas and was so unwilling to leave it. After more than an hour of walking along the Brazos he returned to his wife and took her in his arms: 'Mattie, old girl, if this is your home, it'll be mine, too. I could never leave you, because I know how often it was you held me upright.'

She cherished his embrace but did not wish to impede him: 'If your heart's set on Tennessee . . .'

'Hush! I'll go back, sell the land, and buy some lumber in New Orleans. I'm goin' to build you a proper house.' With this commitment, from which he would never deviate, Jubal Quimper became a Texican.

That day Mattie, with a song trembling on her lips, started to pack the goods her two men would require for their long trip, but her work was interrupted by Yancey, who came whispering: 'I don't want to go. Indians and that Strip and all,' and she could guess that what really held him back was his memory of that fistfight with the smaller boy. What will happen to him? she asked herself. A boy who refuses a journey up the Mississippi?

She had finished packing when a cloud of dust appeared from the south; Benito Garza was on his way to New Orleans with another convoy of mules for the American army. He was twenty-two now, a slim, neat fellow with a small mustache, an ingratiating smile and a fair command of English: 'This time I take the mules myself. I do not need guide of trader from San Antonio.'

He had brought with him a Mexican boy, no more than fourteen, and a large remuda of some three dozen mules, which he hoped to augment as he moved north: 'I like to buy any mules you might have, Señor Quimper?' When Jubal said he had none, Garza asked: 'Is it true, señor? You're going to Tennessee?'

'I must.'

'A town on the Mississippi?'

'It's a state. Like Coahuila-y-Tejas.'

'But it is on the Mississippi?' When Quimper nodded, the ebullient young man slapped himself on the knee and cried: 'Then you must come with us! Save time, save money. Catch a steamboat up the river!' And he worked his arms like the pistons of a riverboat, spouting imaginary steam with his mouth and sounding a whistle. Mattie was enthusiastic about such a plan and tried to persuade her son, now sixteen, to go along: 'You can help manage the mules, and you'll see the steamboat,' but he still refused to go, not wishing to take such risks.

The two men left in October and wandered up the Goliad Road with some fifty mules, adding to them at the Trinity and then keeping to the southernmost route along the Gulf till they crossed the Sabine into Louisiana. There they found tolerable roads leading to New Orleans, where Jubal stayed in Mexican lodgings with his two companions. He told Garza as the latter dickered with the American authorities over the prices of his mules: 'Benito, I'd enjoy travelin' with you some time again. You know how to move about.' And Garza said: 'You'd be welcome. I need to practice English if so many of you are coming to Tejas.'

'You must. Because I'm tellin' you . . . I'm warnin' you, really, Texas won't be Mexican forever.'

'I think it will be,' Garza said, and when they were back in their mean quarters he asked Quimper: 'How long, señor, have you been in Tejas?' and Quimper thought a moment, then said: 'Six years,' and Garza laughed: 'Señor! And you're telling me who is to run Tejas! My people explored Tejas three hundred years ago.'

Quimper considered this, then said with no rancor: 'Amigo, that may have ensured you a foothold in what you call Tejas. But in the Texas that's comin' you better speak like an American and think like one, or you're goin' to be homeless,' and the young man snapped: 'Garzas will be living here when you've run back to Tennessee.'

The only thing about Garza that Quimper did not like was this quickness at resenting whatever the young man interpreted as an insult to his Hispanic heritage: 'If you're goin' to live in a white man's state, Benito, you mustn't be so touchy.'

'But I am a white man, and Tejas is my state.' Quimper let the matter drop, for he no longer tried to understand how the Hispanic mind worked.

When Quimper left the Mississippi riverboat at Memphis and started overland to Nashville, he experienced several moments of solemn discovery: Tennessee is so cramped compared to Texas . . . A man can hardly breathe, hemmed in by all these trees. He did enjoy the snug little towns and the orderly plantations manned by slaves, but repeatedly he caught himself longing for the Brazos and the great, open freedom of Texas: I'll sell the land and get back home.

He spent his first two weeks in Nashville listening to talk about those events which had occurred since his hasty departure in 1822: 'We got ourself a great new governor, Sam Houston, him as fought with Andy Jackson against the Indians at Horseshoe Bend. Strong man, strong ideas, outstandin' patriot. Goin' to be President of the United States one of these days.'

Wherever he moved he heard good reports of Houston: 'Big man, you know.

Brave, too. Lived among the Indians. Speaks their language, I'm told. Taller than that post, I'd judge.'

'How did he become governor?'

'Oh, he was a military hero! General Jackson thought very highly of him, and that helped him get elected to the Congress, in Washington. How many terms did he serve, Jake? Three?'

'Two,' Jake said. 'Could of been elected permanent, or senator, either. But we wanted him for governor, and with Andy Jackson's help, we got him.'

Quimper had no opportunity to see Houston in Nashville, for men explained that the governor had business to the east: 'You know, he's standin' for reelection this year. Foolish for anyone to run against him, most popular man in the state.'

By the time Quimper left Nashville for the short trip to Gallatin he had heard so much about Houston that he said, on his last night in town: 'He's the kind of man we could use in Texas,' but his fellow diners dismissed the idea: 'His home's in Tennessee. Hell, he *is* Tennessee.'

When Quimper arrived in his old hometown of Gallatin he heard only one topic of conversation: 'Little Eliza Allen of our town! She's goin' to marry the governor! Tomorrow!' Since the Allens were among the leading citizens in Gallatin, Jubal did not know them socially, but he was pleased to think that if the wedding was public, he would have a chance to see and perhaps even meet Sam Houston.

The celebrations took place in January 1829, and they were a sumptuous affair, for not often did a small town like Gallatin find one of its daughters marrying the governor of a state, a man certain to be reelected, and after a term or two in the federal Senate, perhaps be elected to the presidency. Several score of guests rode out from Nashville and others came long distances from the eastern part of the state, where Houston had once lived. He was a rising star with whom politicians of all stripes wished to be associated, and when Quimper saw him, a giant of a man, and holding on to his arm a delicate little woman dressed in white with just a touch of pink in her ribbons, he was awed: He looks like a governor! He looks like a Texican! I was right when I said we could use him.

When the wedding was solemnized in high form, Quimper found himself thinking: Not much like the mass unions that Father Clooney celebrates, and he felt a longing for that simpler life: I know what Mattie meant. I couldn't live here in Gallatin after that free life on the rivers.

But such thoughts were expelled that night when, at about ten, the men of town were nicely inebriated and someone shouted: 'Let's give the governor and his lady a real shivaree!' Nearly a hundred drunks assembled outside the tavern with horns and drums and washboards and bugles and tin pots. Led by one of Eliza's cousins, the crowd surged along the streets, gathering recruits, until it reached the small house in which the governor and Eliza were spending their first night together.

There a noise was generated which had not been matched since the explosion of a powder depot some years before. Horns blared, men bellowed, drums were banged, and the night was made raucous with a serenade whose tradition dated back two thousand years. A marriage was being launched, and the community wished to mark this mystical occasion not only with prayers but also with riotous celebration, and when two men came up with a barrel of whiskey on wheels, the noise really began.

It was a shivaree honoring a great and much-loved man, a man of dignity and power, and all who shattered the night did so in hopes that somehow their destiny would be matched to his. But it was also a serenade to a gentlewoman whom the town loved, and after a while the men started a chant:

> 'Eliza! Eliza! The world's fairest flower.
> Eliza! Eliza! Pray come to my bower.'

It was well after two in the morning before the barrel was empty and the tin pots beaten beyond recognition. Then off to their beds straggled the celebrants, except those who returned to the taverns, banging on the doors and demanding admittance. Quimper, remaining in the streets through the night, judged that he had never participated in a better shivaree and he doubted that anyone else had, either.

A few days later, Jubal found an opportunity to talk with Houston: 'Governor, I've cast my lot with Texas, and I can see that you're the kind of man we need down there. To pull things together before we join the Union.'

Houston, afraid that this might be a trap seducing him into some impropriety, said easily: 'Now, sir, I can tell you that I've always thought well of that part of Mexico. In 18 and 22 I applied for a land grant down there. Can't remember whether I ever received the papers or not, but I know it's a splendid territory.'

'You have a dazzlin' future, Governor, Texas or wherever.'

The big man appreciated such flattery and accepted it gracefully: 'My future's twofold. To build a proper house for my wife and to get reelected governor of this great state. That's enough to keep me busy.'

The next day Quimper was startled to see Governor Houston striding through town in his favorite costume: Indian garb, sandals, buckskin britches, with a bright red shawl draped about his shoulders. 'What's he doin'?' Jubal asked a bystander, and the man snorted: 'Keep watchin'. You'll see wonders.' And on subsequent days Houston appeared in three radically different costumes, none appropriate to his high office. Finally Jubal had to comment: 'Governor, you seem to like unusual dress,' to which Houston replied: 'I dress like the land, different seasons, different colors.'

And then, on the sixteenth of April in that first year of marriage, Gallatin and all of Tennessee were stunned by the news that the delicate and lovely Eliza Allen

Houston had for some mysterious reason never to be revealed left the governor's bed and board, telling her family that she could never return.

'Impossible!' the men in the taverns cried, while their wives at home met secretly to explore in hushed conversation the devastating possibilities. That Eliza's abrupt behavior must have had some dark, sexual cause, there could be no doubt, and since specifically what it had been would never be disclosed, speculation was not only invited but also inventive.

The scandal was intensified when the governor announced that he must, out of respect to his constituency, refuse to stand for reelection, and when his friends implored him not to take such drastic action, he shocked them completely by resigning the balance of the term to which he was already entitled. While they fumed, he boarded a steamer and sailed into lonely exile among the Indians he had known previously. Rarely in American history had a man who had risen so high fallen so low.

His precipitate departure raised far more questions than it answered, for in the silence surrounding the case his partisans launched an explanation, totally unauthorized, which cleared his name. But this could be circulated only at the expense of Eliza Allen, whose irate family had no intention of allowing her to shoulder the blame for this destruction of Houston's career, so in self-defense the male members of the Allen family engineered a solution unique in American political life.

They nominated a panel of twelve sober citizens of impeccable repute to hold a series of public meetings, the more salacious details kept private, to apportion blame in this affair. At the conclusion a vote would be taken and a determination made as to whether Eliza Allen, of Gallatin, was or was not guilty in even the slightest degree in the scandalous affair of Governor Sam Houston.

When eleven solons had been selected—military heroes, lawyers, clergymen, bankers—one Leonidas Allen, a relative of the abused wife, suggested: 'I'm glad to see this fellow Quimper back among us. He's become a man of sober judgment, reputation restored by the courts. I'd like to see him stay here. Let's signify our acceptance by inviting him to serve on our jury.' No member of the committee listened to the evidence with closer attention than Quimper, and when the time came for the first crucial vote, he experienced no uncertainty. The question was clearly stated: 'Was Eliza Allen, at the time of her marriage to Governor Houston, a virgin?' The vote was eleven-to-one affirmative, and as soon as the man who voted nay was known, one of the colonels challenged him to a duel on the grounds that he had impugned the reputation of a gentlewoman, but the voter justified himself by explaining that he was a lawyer from Virginia who felt that the question as stated could not be answered, since substantive evidence had not been provided. The colonel accepted the apology; the challenge was withdrawn; and the ashen-faced Virginian, aware of how close he had come to being shot, begged permission to alter his vote to affirmative, and when the balloting was announced, Eliza was unanimously found to have been a virgin.

Each of the other possible charges against her was analyzed similarly, and in vote after vote the correctness of her behavior was sustained. When the final tally was made, it was clear that Eliza's reputation had been not only cleared but also burnished; by the twelve ablest men in Gallatin she was found to have been immaculate in both behavior and spirit.

At the conclusion of the investigation two members of the panel composed a stirring document in which Eliza's purity was extolled and the governor's lack of it deplored; it covered all the debatable points and indicated the jury's vote on each, and it ended with an exhortation to the journals of Tennessee and surrounding states that they give the fullest possible coverage to the voting. But the Virginia lawyer, already frightened by what might have happened as a consequence of that first vote, now advised the committee that whereas the report accurately summarized their debate, and while its decisions were irrefutable, it might be wise to delay publication until the jury could be sure that Sam Houston had left the state.

After prudent delay the report was circulated, and interested newspapers did publish it, but by then Houston was lost in the wilds of Arkansas, living among his beloved Indians and remaining drunk most of the time. A traveler told Quimper: 'Shortly after Houston arrived in Arkansas, I saw him drunk in a saloon, where a local braggart challenged him to a duel. I was standin' with Houston when he accepted. Asked me to be his second, so in the mornin' haze, lengths were stepped off. The two duelists, obviously unsteady, marched, turned, aimed and fired. Nobody got hit for the good reason that me and the other man's second, realizin' that our men were drunk and without any sensible basis for a duel, had loaded the pistols with blanks!'

While Jubal was still chuckling over this portrait of the former governor, he was confronted by a great temptation. Leonidas Allen, the man who had sponsored his membership on the Houston jury, invited him twice to dinner in the Allens' spacious mansion, and only the most attractive Southern hospitality prevailed, but on a third visit Leonidas took Jubal aside and said in a low voice: 'Surely you've noticed that my older sister, Clara, is quite taken with you.'

Jubal had not noticed, but when he returned to the company of the ladies he could not avoid Clara's ardent glances. As he left the mansion, Leonidas whispered: 'We would be most honored, Clara and me, that is, if you'd dine with us tomorrow.'

'Sir, I'm married. I have a wife in Texas.'

'Things can always be arranged.'

He spent a feverish night, for with the funds he had received from the settlement, plus those which would accrue to him if he married Miss Clara, who was not at all repulsive, he could own one of the Gallatin mansions. Also, he could hear Mattie saying: 'I'll give you your freedom.' But as he tossed on his straw mattress he thought of the Brazos, and Stephen Austin trying to build a state, and of Texas reaching empty to the horizon, and of Mattie poling her ferry.

Early next morning he went to a bank, arranged for his new wealth to be posted to a New Orleans agent against whom he could draw when he returned home, and headed for the Mississippi without bidding either Leonidas or Clara farewell.

When his boat put in to an Arkansas levee, one of the hands cried: 'There comes Sam Houston. Meets us every trip.' And up the gangway came the former governor, already drunk but looking to the steamboat's bar for replenishment. Jubal, fearing that Houston might have learned about the jury report, hid among the passengers but stayed close enough to hear Houston haranguing the travelers: 'Let's all get off the boat and head cross country to Oregon. I'm goin' there as soon as practical.' When Houston was safely off the boat and lying immobile beside some cotton bales, Jubal said to a passenger: 'Look at him! Governor of a state! We don't need his kind in Texas.'

New Orleans, Nachitoches in Louisiana, Nacogdoches in Texas, El Camino Real and south along the banks of the Trinity to the Goliad Road, this was the pathway of empire, except that other things besides immigrants traveled it. This autumn, cholera made the journey too, meeting up with Jubal Quimper just before he reached the village on the Trinity in which Reverend Harrison hid and from which he conducted his forbidden prayer meetings.

The two men were glad to see each other, and Harrison sat fascinated as Jubal reported upon the doings in Tennessee; it was Harrison's opinion, delivered from afar, that Governor Houston, a giant of a man, as Quimper reported, must have outraged his gentle wife in some grotesque sexual manner: 'Your jury rendered the judgment he deserved. You did the work of the Lord.'

On the second day of the visit, Quimper fell into a fit of such violent shaking that the preacher cried: 'Dear God, Jubal, you must have the plague!' And as soon as these dire words were spoken they were flashed throughout the small community, and the minister's house was quarantined.

It was a useless gesture, because by that night four other cases of extreme ague had been identified, and by morning it was clear that the Trinity River had received from some mysterious source, perhaps from Jubal Quimper himself via New Orleans, its latest attack of this dread disease. Called alternately *the plague,* or *cholera,* or *the vomiting shakes,* or simply *the fever,* it assaulted the human body so furiously and with such total destruction that the victim rarely survived three full days, and that was the case with Quimper.

Reverend Harrison, ignoring the pleas of his secret parishioners that he dissociate himself from the stricken man, said: 'If Jesus Christ could medicine the lepers,

I can medicine Quimper,' and he remained with Jubal, cooling his fevered face with damp towels until convulsive seizures showed that death was imminent.

'Beloved brother in Christ, Jesus awaits thee in heaven. May the merciful God stay this plague and may the earth be made whole again.' In the last minutes he bathed the dying man's face once more, praying frantically, as if to finish his beseeching before his friend died: 'Dear God, take into Your bosom this traveler. On earth he tried to do Your bidding. In heaven he will grace Your throne.'

When Quimper died, Harrison closed the eyelids and arranged the sweat-drenched bedclothes. Then he left his house, but others in the village were afraid to move near him.

Quimper's clothes had to be burned, of course, but a few durable possessions like coins remained, and these the minister gathered, proposing to carry them the sixty miles to Quimper's Ferry, for he felt that it would be improper for Mattie to learn of her husband's sudden death from strangers. He was delayed, however, by the necessity of burying four others who had fallen to the plague, and when this was finished he wondered whether it was proper for him to move into another community, lest he carry the cholera with him.

Waiting six days, he concluded that he was not going to be stricken, so down the Goliad Road he went on his mission of compassion. As he neared the ferry he wondered how he should speak to Mattie, for her husband had been far too young to die, but even when he stood at the pole that carried the flag travelers were instructed by a signboard to raise if they wanted the ferry to fetch them, he was undecided. He heard young Yancey shouting: 'Mom! The ferry!' and he wondered why this growing boy did not himself come across to get him, but since Yancey did not, Mattie appeared, wiping her hands on her apron and heading for the heavy pole.

With the skill acquired from many crossings, she brought the raft to its landing and shouted: 'Welcome, Pastor! Jubal will be coming home any time now.'

When he climbed into the ferry he sat silent for so long that Mattie asked abruptly: 'What is it, Reverend? Bad news?' and he said simply: 'Jubal died. Cholera.'

She did not interrupt her poling. Pushing the heavy post into the bottom mud, she walked along the edge of her craft, shoving the ferry forward, then dragging the pole in the water as she strode forward to push once more. Working and keeping her eyes upon the swirling water, she said nothing till she brought her craft home safely to its resting place. Then, helping the minister to negotiate the steep bank, she said: 'Father Clooney's here. Six weddings set for this afternoon.'

They walked to the dog-run, where the priest was sitting in the shade at the far end of the porch. 'Hello, Reverend,' he said, and Harrison replied: 'I bring heavy news. Jubal . . . the plague.'

Father Clooney had helped bury many plague victims, but never could he adjust to the incredible swiftness with which this terrible malady struck, and to have it take a man to whom he, Clooney, was so much indebted was a burden trebly heavy.

'Let us not tell the others,' he suggested. 'It's their wedding.' So the three agreed that not even Yancey would be told until after the ceremony.

'I'll move along,' Harrison said. 'I couldn't attend the wedding.'

'You could if you wished,' Father Clooney said. He wanted to add, so that Harrison would join, that such weddings were formalities demanded by the Mexican government, but he could not frame the words. No wedding was a formality, not any, not under any conceivable circumstances.

Harrison, unwilling to participate in or bear witness to such an improper mixture of politics and faith, moved sullenly away, but Clooney, on the other hand, became more excited and devout as the holy moments approached. Taking a nip now and then to encourage himself, he was feeling at the height of his power by the time the six couples had gathered, and he surprised them by saying with deep solemnity: 'Let us gather at the river,' and he led them to a plateau adorned by oak trees where the couples could look down forty feet to the Brazos as it carried mud to the sea. He had not chosen this spot by accident, for when the farmers stood with their brides and their children, he cried in a kind of chant:

'When storms strike far inland, that little stream down there can rise in fury and sweep across this land which seems so safe up here. Forty feet of sudden turbulence, and who can believe that? It will be the same with your marriages, an unexpected storm can overwhelm you, and who would believe that?

'Wise men and women, when they enter into marriage, do so with some religious blessing, with God's most precious sanction, for they know they need that extra help. If the families of the Brazos did not protect their homes up here, the stormy river would sweep them away. And if you do not call upon God to consecrate your marriages, they too can be swept away.

'In this solemn moment when you start your new lives I give you the balm of God's love. I anoint you. I bless you. I give you the gentle kiss of Jesus. Above all, I give you protection against the great storms of life. In life and in death . . .'

Here he chanced to look across the fields to the house so recently struck by untimely death, and his throat began to close up and his eyes to fill with tears. He lost track of what he was saying and almost began to blubber, so great was his anguish over the fate of Mattie Quimper, and he became so incoherent that the wiser men among the grooms winked at one another: 'The old man's drunk again.'

He wasn't, not then, but when he returned to sit with Mattie on the porch, endeavoring to console her, he did start to drink heavily, so that when Reverend Harrison returned, eligible to rejoin them now that the Romish ceremony was ended, Clooney was ready to embrace him as a brother: 'Harrison, we must both give consolation to this good Christian woman.'

As evening approached he became quite drunk, and at one point he said to Harrison, as if he had never seen him before: 'Me name's Father Clooney, of Ballyclooney on Clooney Bay, in County Clare,' but when the stiff Protestant ignored him, he realized his foolishness and said hastily: 'You're Reverend Harrison! You and I must look after Yancey now. He'll need a father,' and he began calling: 'Yancey, Yancey!' When there was no answer, he looked hazily at Harrison, lay down upon the porch, and passed easily into a deep sleep that would last through the night.

'God blessed me in one thing,' Mattie said as darkness fell. 'He allowed me to know four good men. You. That one down there. Stephen Austin. And Jubal. Many women never know none.'

Harrison said boldly: 'You must take a new husband, Mattie. You'll need help to run the inn and the ferry.'

At this moment, on the far shore, a late traveler hallooed: 'Can you fetch me? I have no food, no blankets.'

She left the porch, went down to the Brazos, and poled sturdily across the narrow river to where the pilgrim waited. When the boat was loaded she shoved off, and in the moonlight brought him to the warmth of her inn.

. . . TASK FORCE

We experienced the first open break in our Task Force when we met in October 1983 to plan our impending meeting in Tyler, where the topic was to be 'Religion in Texas.' We found it difficult to agree upon an appropriate speaker, for although none of us had strong convictions regarding specific theologies, and certainly we did not want to intrude on clerical matters, we were aware that sectarianism had played a recurrent role in forming Texas attitudes. But we did not know whom to invite, and because there were differences among us we postponed our meeting till November.

The blowup involved not religion but the successful American invasion of the little Caribbean island of Grenada. Rusk and Quimper, as gung-ho Texans, applauded the action. 'We should of done it years ago,' Quimper said. 'And since we have a running start, let's move on to Nicaragua and Cuba.'

Miss Cobb, descendant of Democratic senators, voiced a much different view: 'President Reagan, having seen how much the invasion of the Falklands helped Maggie Thatcher win reelection in Great Britain, is pulling the same trick in the United States.'

'And succeeding,' Rusk snapped, and she agreed: 'He is. Brilliantly. If the election were held tomorrow, he'd win in a landslide. America does love its successful little wars, but tires quickly of its big unsuccessful ones.'

'That's communist talk,' Rusk said, and Quimper agreed: 'If you got strength, you got to show it, or they don't believe you have it.'

Dr. Garza tried to slow down the animosities by advancing a more sober theory: 'America must proceed very carefully. In every Latin country there's latent memory of Marines invading at will. If we run rampant in the Caribbean, we'll engender a profound revulsion. We must go slow.'

Rusk spoke like a letter-to-the-editor of a Texas newspaper when he said: 'We shouldn't give a damn what they think about us. We should discipline Cuba, right now. And if Nicaragua is in the Cuban camp, we should knock it out too. We've had enough liberal shilly-shallying.'

'Do you want to nuke Nicaragua?' Miss Cobb asked, and Rusk replied: 'If necessary,' to which Garza asked: 'And risk Armageddon?'

With the battle lines thus firmly drawn—Rusk and Quimper versus Cobb and Garza—the members looked to me, and I could not escape revealing my opinion: 'I side with the popular opinion in Texas. I believe the invasion of Grenada was justified. I think it forestalled Cuban action. And I'm sure it's reelected Ronald Reagan.'

Miss Cobb was disappointed with me: 'Do you know how big Grenada is? Smaller than the tiniest Texas county. Does America gain glory by subduing such a target?'

'Wake Island was lots smaller,' I retorted quickly, 'and we gained a lot of glory there. You excise a cancer when it's small, or you lose a life.'

Garza groaned at this forced analogy, and there would have been further debate had not our staff insisted that we reach a decision concerning the program for our meeting on religion, so we turned from one heated battleground to another.

Dr. Garza suggested a professor from a Catholic college in New Mexico, believing that this would provide continuity from the very first days to the present, but Quimper objected vigorously, and with reason: 'I thought we settled that at our El Paso meeting. No more Catholics. Texas is a Protestant state, whose moral attitudes were determined by Protestants.'

'You're right,' Garza conceded with no rancor. 'I was just trying to advance the interests of my boys.'

'Don't blame you,' Rusk interrupted. 'But now I want to advance the interests of my boys. My grandparents were Quaker and Baptist. Very few Quakers in Texas, thank God, because the two religions—'

'What two religions?' Miss Cobb interrupted.

'Quaker and Texas, they don't mix. I recommend we invite a Baptist minister.'

'Now wait, Rance,' Quimper protested. 'Texas was settled primarily by Methodists. And I'd like to hear an honest Methodist interpretation.' After the two men wrestled over this without reaching a solution, Rusk asked: 'Lorena, what are you?' and Miss Cobb said: 'What the Southern gentlefolk always were, Episcopalian, but in Texas we've carried little weight.'

The four now turned to me, and Quimper asked: 'Barlow, you've never said what religion you are,' and I replied: 'Home Lutheran,' and they all asked: 'What's that?' and I explained: 'When I taught school in a small town in the Panhandle the board was very nosy about their teachers' religion, and my crusty old principal told me: "Tell 'em you're a Home Lutheran. Very devout, but you conduct your services in the privacy of your home." I did, and got away with it.'

Rusk took me up on this: 'Since we can't agree among the four of us, and since Texas has almost no Home Lutherans, whom would you suggest?'

After making a chain of phone calls I came up with an almost perfect solution, and at our November meeting in Tyler, where a few late roses were still in bloom, I presented him, a tall, thin man in his fifties, wise of countenance and witty of eye. He looked like a clergyman, even in mufti, for you could see that he had been trained to speak in a certain way and to enforce his words with effective gestures. What was equally important to our purpose, for he was to outline a weighty and sometimes contentious topic, he had a sense of humor.

I allowed him to introduce himself, which he did gracefully: 'I'm an ordained minister, professor in the Bible department, Abilene Christian College. The Roman numerals after my name indicate how many generations of my family have served in Texas. I'm Joel Job Harrison VI.' He asked our forbearance as he explained the religious history of his family, for he said that if we understood it, we would better appreciate the religious tempests which had from time to time swept Texas:

'The first Joel Job Harrison came to the Trinity River in the early 1820s, as a secret Methodist circuit rider sent down to infiltrate Catholic Mexico. Devout religionists in Kentucky gave him explicit instructions: "Combat the papists." He seems to have been a violent defender of his faith, conducting secret meetings up and down the rivers, and as you know, he helped ignite the sparks that led to open warfare against Santa Anna. Faithful to his own preachings, he led one of the critical charges at San Jacinto, then roamed across Texas during the republic, building the Methodist churches that had not been permitted under Mexican rule. He was not a likable man, if we can believe the diarists of that time, for some of them dismiss him with contempt. But he was a warrior, and Texas Methodism owes him many debts.

'Joel Job III was one of those titanic clergymen who sweep across Texas from time to time. Reading his Bible one day, he made the discovery that projected him into endless battles against the Baptists, the Presbyterians and all other infidel sects. It was a curious thing. He came to believe that whereas John the Baptist had clearly baptized Jesus Christ in the Jordan River by a process which could only be called total immersion, so that there was Biblical justification for the rite as performed by the Baptists, there was no holy obligation to keep on using it, and he began to preach strong and beautifully reasoned sermons against the Baptists, and especially against the sect called the Campbellites.

'Well, the Baptists weren't going to sit by and allow this to happen, so they threw three of their ablest men against him, one after another, and great public debates were held across North Texas. A tent would be raised or a building rented, and J. J. Harrison III, in heavy black suit and red string tie, his white hair flowing, would take on the current Baptist champion. For five successive days they would debate each afternoon, two o'clock to five, and thousands would lean forward to catch their words. Joel Job III had a majestic voice, a gift for scorn and an unrelenting sense for the theological jugular; both he and his adversary believed they were fighting for immortal souls. Their debates became famous, and the men were fondly referred to as "our peerless ecclesiastical pugilists." You can find in old bookstores printed versions of their battles: "The Harrison-Brand Debates," "The Harrison-Cleaver Debates" or "The Famous Harrison-Harper Debates." Harrison's name always came first because he was the more famous arguer and the one who attracted the crowds, but he confessed in a letter to a fellow Methodist clergyman:

'I always felt that I had defended Our Cause ably, but I rarely felt that I had won, because those Baptists threw against me some of the most tenacious debaters I had ever faced. They were men of learning, devotion and infinite skill in the nasty tricks of argument.

'Lanning Harper was the ablest man I ever battled, and in our four series in 1890 to 1893, I fear that he bested me on several occasions. Looking back on those days, I think of him as a Lion of Judah and I would not care to face him again tomorrow. He had a wry sense of humor, and several times, after we had lambasted each other on Monday, Tuesday and Wednesday, we would unite on Thursday against the Presbyterians, whose doctrine of fatal predestination we simply could not comprehend, and it was Harper who introduced the doggerel which summarized our contempt. I can still hear the audiences laughing when he recited:

'We are the sweet selected few,
The rest of you be damned;
There's room enough in hell for you,
We don't want heaven crammed.'

He was smiling as he finished these lines, but abruptly he turned grave, for now he must share with us a somber incident in his family history, one which produced both anguish and theological glory:

'Throughout the lives of I, II and III, my ancestors were aware, vaguely at times, of a powerful, primitive force gathering strength on the horizon. It centered upon a man named Alexander Campbell, born a good Presbyterian in County Antrim, Ireland, in 1788. The birth of a child forced Campbell to decide what he thought about baptism, and the more he studied the Bible the more convinced he became that Presbyterians were out of step with the New Testament when they merely sprinkled a baby and called that baptism, while the Baptists were correct to insist upon total immersion. To the scandal of his time, he left the Presbyterians with loud renunciation and became a Baptist.

'He didn't stay long, for although he granted that his new church was right on baptism, he found it wrong on almost everything else. He especially rejected the vainglorious church structure it had erected to govern what in Christ's day had been free, individual churches, each master of its own destiny. Fulminating against synods, regional associations and presbyteries, he was extremely harsh on professional clergymen who set themselves above ordinary laymen. "Protestant priests," he called them scornfully. In every aspect of religious life Campbell yearned to get back to the simplicity of that first glorious century of the Christian era.

'His theories swept across the American South like a firestorm, with converts announcing themselves as Campbellites. And from what established churches did these converts come? From the Methodists and Baptists. The infection grew malignant, with entire congregations quitting the known churches and moving en masse into Campbell's arms.

'Well, Joel Job III as a faithful Methodist realized that something must be done to stanch this hemorrhaging, so during the great debates, after lambasting the Presbyterians on Thursday, he and his Baptist adversary would unite on Friday to excoriate the Campbellites, who did not like that pejorative name. They called themselves the Churches in Christ, for they believed that they preserved the simplicity that Jesus would have approved. I have several pamphlets which preserve Joel Job's attacks on the Campbellites, and they are rather sulphurous. Again and again he warned: "Do not lure good Methodists into your infamous trap." '

Our speaker paused to reflect upon those tempestuous days, then squared his shoulders and revealed an astonishing fact: 'In 1894 the religious world of Texas was shocked when this tower of Methodism, this peerless debater, went into seclusion, studied his Bible, and emerged with a startling revelation: "I can no longer support the Methodist church as it now exists. I am departing from it to become a minister in the Church of Christ." This was trebly scandalous, since he was in effect joining forces with his ancient foes, the Campbellites, against whom he had so furiously inveighed.'

Harrison shook his head, even now startled by his ancestor's apostasy, but then he smiled like a little boy: 'I warned you that we took religion seriously, and as you might expect, in his new reincarnation Joel Job III became a conservative terror. Apparently he hungered for a simpler, stabler form of worship, so before six months had passed he found himself joyously in the middle of the great fight which tore his new religion apart.

'You may smile when I tell you what four innovations he fought against. Missionary societies and organizations, because they were not specifically designated in the Bible. Sunday School, because he could find no justification in the Bible. Rebaptism of Baptists, Methodists and Presbyterians who wanted to join the new church: "If one baptism was good enough for John and Jesus, it's good enough for Farmer Jones of Waco." And his most violent hatred: instrumental music inside the church, for he could not find it mentioned as such in the New Testament. He particularly despised organs, which he felt to be an Italian-French contamination and therefore probably Catholic.

'Have you ever read an account of what happened when he learned that members of his own congregation had collected funds for the purchase of an organ? He found that they had got the money by conducting an entertainment of singing at which punch was served. The punch contained no alcohol, but when he shouted about it from his pulpit you'd have thought it was hundred-and-fifty-proof rum.

'When the organ was brought within the church, he threatened to burn the place down, and was halted only by the liberals, who threw eggs at him while newspaper reporters watched.'

Our speaker shivered, recalling the shock of those fevered days, but soon the inevitable smile returned: 'As you probably know, I am myself Church of Christ and happy with the way my ecclesiastical life has developed. Believe me, I burn no churches.'

'Would you object,' Rusk asked, 'if I called you a modern-day Campbellite?' and he replied: 'Yes, I would. My church is much bigger in concept than the doctrine of one man. Why not just call me a Christian?'

He waved his hands as if to brush away the great schism of which Joel Job III had been so conspicuous a part. 'With his son, J.J. IV, our family got involved in Prohibition, which racked Texas politics. He stormed the state with his old Methodist evangelism resurgent. He gloried in hauling onto his stage mothers and children made destitute by the drunkenness of their men, and if some sad bank teller absconded with three thousand dollars, he trumpeted the case in forty counties, proving that alcohol had done the man in. He smashed his way into saloons, offered to wrestle peddlers of booze, and harried Texas into voting for Prohibition. On the day it became national law he cried at a great mass meeting in Dallas: "The soul of America has been saved."

'Now he stepped forward as a watchdog of enforcement, riding with sheriffs as they raided speakeasies and testifying in court repeatedly. Those favoring the free movement of contraband up from Mexico or down from Oklahoma said of my grandfather: "Nothing wrong with Joel Job IV that a couple of cold beers wouldn't fix," but he attained his greatest fame, and I think power, in the election of 1928 when he opposed the candidacy of Al Smith, partly because Smith was Catholic but even more because Al favored demon rum.

'When Smith was nominated in Houston my grandfather shouted from a dozen pulpits: "Darkest day in Texas history. Defames the sacred memory of the Alamo." And from that moment on he toured the state relentlessly, preaching against Smith and the Democrats who proposed to lead the nation astray. Like all Harrisons, Number IV was a Democrat, but Al Smith was more than he could stomach, and after the votes were counted, the Republican National Committee sent him a telegram of gratitude for having moved Texas into their column: "You have done a masterful job for Texas and the entire nation." Grandfather believed this, and one of my earliest memories is watching as he took this telegram from his portfolio to let me read it. Tears streamed down his face as he said: "In 1928 we fought the good fight. But in 1932 the forces of evil struck back." He was speaking of repeal. He died believing that America was sliding to perdition because of its tolerance of drink.'

Quimper, a heavy drinker, interrupted: 'But, Reverend Harrison, didn't you recently lead the fight against alcohol? In those three western counties which held a referendum on saloons?'

'I did, and I'm proud to say we kept those counties dry. I consider alcohol an abiding evil.'

'Thank you,' Quimper said, bowing as if to a debating adversary.

Then Harrison said: 'I share these things with you to remind you that in Texas, we take religion seriously. It can even be, as I shall demonstrate in a moment, a matter of life and death.' He then launched into his formal paper, which I shall summarize in his words:

'Except during the republic, when secularism ran rampant, religion has always been a major force in Texas life, and often *the* major force. No state in the Union pays greater deference to religion or supports it more vigorously. The founding fathers were unequivocal. Stephen F. Austin sought for his colony only devout Christians. Even a somewhat suspect hero like William Travis of Alamo fame, who dealt in slaves and deserted his family, could in 1835 write to the leaders of his church:

> We are very destitute of religious instruction in this extensive fine coun-
> try . . . About five educated and talented young preachers would find
> employment in Texas, and no doubt would produce much good in this
> benighted land. Texas is composed of the shrewdest and most intelligent
> population of any new country on earth, therefore a preacher to do good
> must be respectable and talented. Remember Texas.

'Texas became a state partly because loyal Protestants from the North and the South refused to accept Catholicism or any established church as the state religion, and much of the animosity anglos in the new nation of Texas felt toward their Mexican citizens along the border stemmed from the fact that those loyal Catholics adhered to customs which were morally offensive to the puritanic Protestant majority in the northern parts of the state. Even today you less traditionally devout members of this Task Force cannot comprehend how embittered we Protestants can become when we hear that churches along the border permit the drinking of alcohol and the gambling of Bingo on church property. We cannot understand such profanation.

'The religious impulse influences Texas life at every level and in the most unexpected ways. To this day it keeps most stores closed on Sunday. It determined that Texas would lead the nation in the fight for Prohibition. It dominates school boards. It accounts for great universities like Southern Methodist, which Joel Job III helped found, and Texas Christian and Abilene Christian, which J.J. V was so instrumental in financing. In today's world it explains why so many radio and television stations allocate much of their time to media ministers, who collect more funds from Texas listeners than from any other state.

'Indeed, if one studied only the outward manifestations of religion, one would be justified in concluding that Texas is now and always has been the most Christian of nations, and it is understandable that many Texans, and perhaps most, believe this to be the case. We love our churches and defend them vociferously.

'But if one steps back dispassionately and assesses with cold eye the actual conditions in Texas, one must wonder how deep this religious conviction runs. You are more likely to be murdered in Odessa than in any other city in the nation. It and Grand Forks, North Dakota, are of comparable size, but Odessa produces twenty-nine point eight murders per thousand; Grand Forks, one. Dallas gunmen shoot more police officers in a year than do the citizens of Philadelphia, Detroit, San Diego, Phoenix, Baltimore, St. Louis, San Francisco and Boston combined. Such amazing figures can be explained only by some inherent Texas differential. Our state officials go regularly to jail for blatant offenses which do not occur with such frequency in states like Iowa and South Dakota. Each autumn three or four Texas high schools watch their football teams forfeit all their games because they broke the rules, knowingly. Deaths on Texas highways from drunk driving are shattering in their regularity.

'And one has to be amused at the famous bass-fishing contest held at the Lake O' The Pines near Jefferson. Total prize money, one hundred and five thousand dollars. Created an open scandal because Texas sportsmen were caught fastening onto their hooks twelve-pound frozen bass flown down from Minnesota, allowing them to thaw in the warm water, then reeling them in with delighted cries: "Hey! Look what I caught!" When this was detected, other contestants hired scuba divers to swim to the bottom with live bass from Wisconsin to fix to their lines. Solution? Give every fisherman a lie-detector test. When sixty percent of the winners failed, loyal Texans cried: "Understandable. They were all from Oklahoma."

'Historically, Texas Christians, good church members all, have been loath to face up to the moral problems of their time. Joel Job I was a stout defender of slavery, and both Harrison II and III leaped into Confederate uniform during the War Between the States to serve as chaplains, for they believed that slavery was ordained by God and must be prolonged. Harrison IV, who led the fight against drink and Al Smith, also led the fight for the revival of the Ku Klux Klan and preached two notable sermons explaining why it was doing God's work in Texas.'

At this point he coughed, rather nervously I thought, and fumbled among his papers for a small document, whose nature I could not determine from where I sat, before continuing: 'Nothing exemplifies better the complexities of the moral order in Texas than this well-edited little publication: *The Blue Book for Visitors, Tourists and Those Seeking a Good Time While in San Antonio, Texas, 1911–1912.* It defines the red-light district, Via Dolorosa to Matamoras, and lists the more luxurious houses of prostitution therein. Lillian Revere seems to have run an attractive place at 514 Matamoras Street—Old Phone:1357, New Phone:1888, Private Phone:2056. To get there, her advertisement said, you took the San Fernando streetcar, got off at South Pecos and Matamoras, and there you were. The book divides the women into three classes—twenty-two A's, twenty B's, sixty-two C's—and gives addresses and phone numbers. It also lists thirty-three cabdrivers who can be trusted. Among the names, several attract attention. Beatrice Benedict, Class A, apparently ran three houses, but how she did this is not explained. One of the Class B girls was named El Toro, one of the Class C's was Japanese. One of the cabdrivers was John Ashton (English Jack). And on page seventeen is something I rather liked, the complete baseball schedule for San Antonio's games in the Texas League.'

Reverend Harrison told us that he had often pondered these apparent contradictions and had decided that they did not really represent moral confusion: 'The Texan who guns down his neighbor does not visualize himself as committing a crime. He is merely settling an argument within the accepted Texas tradition. The Texas billionaire who has three wives, three households and three families of children at the same time cannot conceive of himself as doing anything wrong. He is merely perpetuating the free life of the frontier, and he sees himself as being a better Texan for so doing. With no apologies he supports his church, helping to finance its attack on immorality and loose living.

'Every example of social disorganization which the Northern critic might cite in an attack upon Texas can be explained away by the Texan apologist with the statement: "But that's the way we've always done it in Texas." If any item of behavior is accepted by the majority, then it becomes part of the Texas theology, serving as its own justification. The good people who published *The Blue Book* were satisfied that they were providing a constructive service.

'In no instance is this more clearly demonstrated than in the case of wetbacks along the Rio Grande. For generations, Texas planters, first in cotton then in citrus, utilized those people under living conditions which were appalling at best and tragic at worst. Good church members who sent their sons and daughters to SMU or TCU saw nothing wrong in treating their Mexican workers worse than they did their animals, and their justification was: "They're better off here than they would be back in Saltillo."

'In the early 1900s the fiery Baptist minister John Franklyn Norris led a noisy crusade against horse racing, gambling and alcohol. Distressed by the perfidy of women, he launched fevered sermons against short skirts, bobbed hair and dancing. But his fiercest ire was reserved for any professors at Baylor, the Baptist university, who veered even one inch from what he felt was the literal truth of the Bible, and he succeeded in getting several fired. Idolized by Texans as their revealed prophet, he startled some of his weak-kneed supporters in 1926 by winning an argument with a gentleman and winning it by the simple expedient of whipping out a revolver and shooting the man dead with three well-placed bullets. The jury found him innocent on the grounds, I suppose, that he was a member of the cloth, and therefore incapable of doing wrong.

'How tragic these Texas religious debates could become was illustrated in the case of W. C. Brann, the Voltaire of Waco, who in the 1890s published a famous muckraking journal, *The Iconoclast,* which delighted in castigating Baptist for their spiritual and moral deficiencies. Unable to bear his gibes, which circulated about the world, religious fanatics took stern measures: once they thrashed him in public; then they kidnapped him; they came close to lynching him; and finally they killed him with a shot in the back, "right where the suspenders crossed," and later they desecrated his grave.

'The contradictions have survived into our time, for recently Brother Lester Roloff, another powerful evangelist, ran children's homes in the Corpus Christi area which broke every rule in the book, yet the state excused him on the grounds that he was a God-fearing clergyman and therefore exempt from normal restraints.'

'What should we, in fairness, say in our report?' Miss Cobb asked, and Joel Job VI was prompt in his response: 'That Texas really is a state which honors religion far more than most. Basic to everything we do is a reverence for religion, but we insist upon constructing our own theology.'

V
THE TRACE

THE NATCHEZ TRACE

0   MILES   200

OF THE VARIOUS NATIONAL GROUPS THAT SETTLED IN TEXAS, AND THERE WERE more than twenty—Germans, Czechs, Poles, Wends—the one which gave the area its basic character came from Ireland. They arrived in great numbers, filtering down the famed Natchez Trace from Pennsylvania, Ohio, Kentucky and Tennessee.

They were a resolute, courageous, self-driven, arrogant lot. Often surprisingly well educated, the vast majority had been raised as Presbyterians, although many in recent years had become Methodists or Baptists. To appreciate their unique qualities, it will be instructive to follow one stubborn fellow as he makes his way slowly, accidentally toward Texas.

To do this it will be necessary to jump backward in time to the blustery winter of 1802 and to a long, beautiful glen that ran west to east at the center of Scotland. At its far end, Glen Lyon was marked by a small mountain-girt loch, from which tumbled a sparkling river that bred trout and provided water for the sturdy Highland cattle grazing along its banks.

On the shore of the loch, so positioned that a man could survey the protecting mountains and also see any enemies who might be climbing the glen, stood a dwelling, low and dark, of but three rooms. Its foundation was of solid boulders; its sides were of heavy half-worked stone; and its thatch-and-turf roof was held down by a network of thick heather ropes from whose ends dangled large rocks to offset the lifting power of the winds which often howled down the mountains.

This dwelling, Dunessan by name, was occupied by the family of a redoubtable man in his seventies whose forebears generations earlier had fled into the remote fastnesses of Glen Lyon after being harried and driven from their ancestral lands. A stubborn clan, they had persistently backed the wrong side in wars and had paid the penalty.

The old man was Macnab of Dunessan, patriarchal head of the local branch of the Macnabs, one of the most contentious clans in Scotland. He was a big man, veteran of a dozen Highland battles, and he looked especially formidable when clad in the crimson-green-red tartan of the Macnabs, with dirk and claymore at the ready. He wore white mutton-chop whiskers and a Highland bonnet, and seemed always ready to take up arms for some new battlefield, but recently an old bullet wound in his left leg had begun to impede him, forcing him to stay close to his house, from which he still roared orders to his kinsmen.

On this morning he was in a gentler mood, for he rested with his grandson Finlay on a wooden bench outside the door, trying to catch whatever heat the wintry sun provided. 'Have you ever wondered,' he asked the boy, 'why we Macnabs always cling to the Macdonalds and guard against the treacherous Campbells?'

'Glencoe,' the lad said promptly.

'But why Glencoe?'

When the boy, only ten years old, displayed an imperfect understanding of that tragic name, the old man drew him closer: 'In the long run of human history no event surpasses the villainy of the Campbells at Glencoe.' And he proceeded to summarize that Highland horror in which the Campbells, seeking to curry favor with an English king, insinuated themselves into the good graces of the rebellious Macdonalds. Appearing suddenly in the remote and gloomy fastness of Glencoe, they passed themselves off as friendly travelers, but after more than a week of feasting and singing and wooing the Macdonald lassies, the Campbells, in dead of night, fell upon their hosts and slaughtered them.

'It wasn't the killing, mind you,' the old man said, his hands trembling with rage as he recalled this ancient wrong. 'Our glens have seen murder before. It was the perfidy. To sup with a man for ten days in a row, and on the eleventh, when your belly is filled with his bread, to slay him in the dead of night, befouling his own home . . .'

'Why didn't the Macdonalds fight back?' young Finlay asked.

'Those trapped in their own homes had no chance. But those clans outside who pertain to the Macdonalds have never stopped seeking revenge.' Taking his grandson's hands, he said solemnly: 'Laddie, wherever, whenever you meet a Campbell, expect treachery. Never forget that your father died fighting them.'

The next two years in Glen Lyon were marked by the arrival of a tall, gawky man who intended to bring piety and learning to this embattled area.

He was Ninian Gow, Master of Arts from the University of St. Andrews in eastern Scotland and ordained as a minister in the Presbyterian church founded by John Knox. He was deep-visaged and had large dark hairs which grew out from his Adam's apple and moved in the air when he preached; he was incontestably a man of God and a fearless champion of decency. He loved his church and had made great sacrifices to serve it, but he loved mankind more. His two abiding convictions were that Scotland could not be truly saved until its young people, boys and girls alike, learned to read, and that it was doomed unless it combated the evils of popery.

'The Campbells are Catholics, you know,' he roared during his first sermon in the glen. 'The glorious Reformation which brought us the true religion, Presbyterianism in its moral grandeur, never reached the blighted glens in which the craven Campbells lurked. They remained unconverted, as they do to this day, ensnared in the web of popery.' At this point he halted his sermon and stared out at the small gathering of Macnabs and Macdonalds, asking finally in a hushed voice: 'Is it any wonder that they saw no evil in worming their way into the affections of the Macdonalds and then slaughtering them?'

Silence filled the tiny kirk, broken only by Gow's deep voice crying: 'Let us pray.' This was an ominous invitation, for a prayer by Ninian Gow was apt to last a good twenty minutes, and on those sulphurous Sundays when he paid full attention to the papist menace, it could consume twice that time.

He had not been in Glen Lyon long when he began to recognize that Finlay Macnab, grandson of the clan's patriarch, had unusual prospects, and when he consulted the local dominie he was pleased to hear: 'The lad masters his numbers quickly and learns to read more ably than others older than himself.' The teacher said that Finlay had also acquired a fine, open style of lettering, and this obviously pleased him, for he said: 'Clear handwriting is proof of a clear conscience.'

When Ninian Gow made his first report to old Macnab on the boy's progress, he broached the subject of the University of St. Andrews as a likely target for the lad's ambitions. Finlay's grandfather had never considered sending his grandson to college, but he had such a high regard for the good sense of the new minister that after he heard him out, he said he would think about it, then asked: 'And where is this St. Andrews?'

That simple question was all Master Gow needed: 'It lies on the coast of Fife, an old city of gray stone hard by the Northern Sea. It is marked by ancient ruins and fine new college buildings. It's the foundation of Presbyterianism in Scotland, and it is not by accident that its once Catholic cathedral is now in ruins. God struck it down. And along its hallowed streets, set deep within the cobbled stones, stand memorials to the founders of our religion whom the papists burned to death for refusing to abjure their new Presbyterianism.'

'It sounds like a holy place,' said Macnab, and his wife nodded silent agreement.

'It's more!' the minister said, revealing a hitherto hidden side of his character. 'For a small town it has an unusual number of taverns, twenty-three in all, it's said, where the scholars gather after their studies, and of course it has the gowf.'

'The what?' Macnab asked.

'The gowf. A links of fair green stretching beside the sea. A wee ball stuffed with feathers. Three clubs to smash it with, and four happy hours in the windy sunlight.'

'Surely it's not a game you're speaking of?' the dour Highlander asked.

'Aye, the grandest game of them all. All the scholars at St. Andrews play at the gowf, I more than most.'

'Do you still play?' Macnab asked.

'Aye, that I do. We have no links, that's true, but I have my clubs and I brought with me three wee balls, and in the evening I like to hit them far and away down the meadows, making believe that I am once more at St. Andrews, studying the Bible at St. Mary's College and playing along the links at the seaside.'

On many occasions he returned to the subject of St. Andrews and the feasibility of young Macnab's reporting there for schooling, but finally the old man told him why he opposed the idea: 'I have no mind to seeing a grandson of mine take up the ministry.'

'Oh, sir! Only a few who attend St. Andrews elect the ministry. It's for everyone. The merchant. The laird. The man who sends his ships to Holland.'

'But what would a grandson of mine profit from such a place if he was to come back to this glen and live as I have lived?'

'The learning, man, think of the learning!' And he spoke with such reverence for the simple act of knowing that Macnab began to consider this curious possibility: that a son of the glen could attend the university and become a better man for having done so, regardless of what occupation he followed thereafter.

The practicability of such a move became so challenging to Macnab that one afternoon he walked down to the kirk and asked the minister: 'Tell me one thing. What boy in a crofter's glen needs Latin?' and Gow said softly: 'The boy who is destined to leave the crofter's glen.'

The answer was so perceptive that after supper Macnab held a quiet discussion with his wife and their clever grandson. 'Would you like to go to St. Andrews, as the minister says?' he asked the boy, and Finlay replied: 'I'm good at books. First in Euclid and Cicero.'

'To what purpose?' the old warrior asked in real perplexity.

'I don't know,' Finlay said honestly. 'I like to play about with figures and words.'

'What say you, Mhairi?' Macnab asked his wife.

'I have always thought he was a lad of promise.'

'That means he would make a good drover.'

'I would,' Finlay said eagerly. 'I could drove the cattle to Falkirk for the Tryst this year.'

'You?' the old man asked in wonder, for he had not perceived his grandson as ready for such responsibility. 'How old are you, lad?'

'Twelve.'

'At twelve I had not left the glen,' the chieftain said.

'But you had fought the Campbells . . . three times,' his wife reminded him.

'So you would like to go to the college?' the old man asked.

'I am so minded.'

As the summer progressed, Macnab ruefully conceded that he would never again trudge over the far hills to Falkirk, and that it was time for his grandson to do so: 'Besides, there will be older friends to help when it comes time to bargain with those clever buyers from the south,' and once this big question was settled, the old man agreed that Finlay should keep some of the money from the cattle sale and proceed to the University of St. Andrews. By July all was settled, and Ninian Gow was writing letters to a friend of his in the old gray city:

> I am sending you a fine wee laddie, Finlay Macnab of Glen Lyon, age thirteen when he arrives. Take him under your wing and tutor him for the University, which he should be ready to enter at age fourteen. He has completed Euclid, is knowledgeable in Sallust and is capable in all ways.
>
> Nina Gow
>
> Post scriptum: I am converting heathen Highlanders into good Christians at such a rate that John Knox must be smiling.

The last half of July and all of August were spent in preparing Finlay for the arduous task of droving his cattle to the great market at Falkirk, nearly eighty long miles to the southeast over steep mountain crests and down beautiful glens. The boy practiced with Rob, the deerhound-collie who would do most of the work; whistled signals would direct the dog to round up strays and keep the herd moving forward, but at times it would seem as if the dog was directing the boy and not the other way around, so quick and intelligent was this remarkable animal.

Meanwhile, the boy's grandmother had been gathering the things she must supply: the strong cheese, the beef strips dried in the sun, the oatcakes hardened on the windowsill, and particularly the great kilt in which her grandson would live for many weeks. It was not one of those townsman's kilts, little more than a pleated skirt tied at the waist; this was a Highlander's fighting-droving kilt, a huge spread of patterned fabric—crimson-green-red for the Macnabs—which covered the body from head to heel, with much left over to form a cape in case of storms.

When his grandmother had it trimmed to her taste, she threw it on the ground, spread it out, and commanded her grandson: 'Lie down.' And when he placed himself prone upon it, so that it reached from his ankles to well beyond his head, she showed him how to roll about and dress himself in it, not rising to his knees until it was properly fitted, and then to a full standing position so that he could fasten the overage about his waist, to be unwound when needed. A Scots Highlander dressed in such a kilt carried twenty pounds of tartan, a kind of ambulatory tent, which kept him safe in all weathers.

When he stood before her, wrapped in this cloak of honor, she thought: What a handsome lad he is, with the flashing blue eyes of his clan. And his youthful eyes did have that fire, for in the eighth and ninth centuries the Vikings of Norway had guided their longships to the fjords of western Scotland, raiding and ravishing, and many Highlanders carried the strain of those heroic days: stalwart bodies, placid dispositions until aroused, and always, scintillating eyes like those of the Macnabs.

'You're ready,' his grandmother said.

Toward the end of August the first drovers appeared in the glen, and all stopped by the home of Macnab of Dunessan to exchange greetings and information. They were from the Outer Islands mostly, men from Lewis and Harris and the Uists who had shipped their cattle by boat across the Minch to the Isle of Skye, and then through the perilous open fjord which separated Skye from the mainland. Any drover from the Outer Isles who reached Glen Lyon with his herd intact was already a hero.

These Islanders were an uncouth band, speaking Gaelic with just enough words of mainland Scots to enable them to function. Short, dark, somber in mien and rude in manner, they terrified the normal mainland Scot, who said: 'Two Skye men passing through a glen are worse than three floods or four thunderstorms. And a Uist man is worse.' They stole cattle, robbed cottages, terrorized daughters, and left scars wherever they touched. They were the scourge of Scotland, the Island drovers who knew not God.

But in Glen Lyon they met their match, for the various Macnabs, long inured to battle, were themselves some of the most polished cattle thieves in Scottish history. It was said of the present Macnab, that sanctimonious, churchgoing scoundrel, that 'he loves animals so tenderly that he feels it his responsibility to take into his care any strays that wander his way.' Many a Skye drover entering Glen Lyon with one hundred and twenty-one animals departed with only one hundred and eighteen, and it was frequently remarked at how good a cowman Macnab was, since his own herd increased so steadily.

'A good dog and a quick eye make the drover,' Macnab often said, and he had both, plus an ingredient he did not specify: he was fearless in the prosecution of his trade and took great risks in augmenting his herd. On the cattle trails he had lived with two dirks hidden in the folds of his kilt, and he had never been afraid to use them. He now quietly handed a pair to his grandson, with the admonition: 'If you ever touch your dirk in a fight, be prepared to use it all the way.'

He would be placing eighty-one head of cattle in his grandson's care, perhaps more if things went well before departure, and since it would have been idiotic to trust so much of value to so young a lad, even though he was a husky fellow well able to care for himself, he was sending along a helper, Macnab of Corrie, who, with his two dogs, had made the trip many times before. They would be twelve days on the trail, up hill and down, and they would expect to deliver to Falkirk Tryst a full eighty-one head, plus such others as they might casually acquire en route.

In the meantime, Ninian Gow instructed young Finlay as to what he must do when the cattle had been delivered and sold: 'You are to leave Falkirk and walk directly to Dunfermline, keeping your money well hidden in your kilt without mentioning it to anyone. From Dunfermline, head straight to Glenrothes and then to Cupar, from which it will be an easy walk to St. Andrews and the university, where you will inquire for Eoghann McRae, with whom you will live and who will tutor you for entrance to the university. Above all, lad, be prudent, for this is your entry into the world of learning. Make it a good one.'

That was the miracle of Scotland. From the most impoverished hovels, from the farthest glen, dedicated ministers and schoolteachers identified boys of promise and goaded them into getting an education at the universities in Aberdeen, Glasgow, Edinburgh and, above all, St. Andrews, those centers of learning whose scholars down through the centuries have done so much to alter and improve the English-speaking world. Unable to find employment in Scotland, they emigrated to London and Dublin and New York. They made Canada and Jamaica and Pennsylvania civilized places in which to live; they started colleges in America and universities in Canada. A thousand enterprises in England would have failed without the assistance of the bright lads from Glen Lyon and the Moor of Rannoch and lone shielings on Skye. They would govern India and South Africa and New Hampshire, and wherever they went they would leave schools and hospitals and libraries, for they were the seeds of greatness and of civilization.

There was no sensible reason in the world why a grandson of Macnab of Dunessan, drover and cattle thief extraordinary, should aspire to St. Andrews to study Latin, except that for two thousand years the men who governed the world, making it in each century just a little better, had known Latin. And from the moment Gow had first seen young Finlay he had suspected that here was a lad with the potential to become such an individual.

At about this time various women in the glen remarked that the minister had come to them begging for curious ingredients: 'He asked for raisins. Wanted to know who had currants. Was especially eager for some orange peel, and who has such in Glen Lyon?' He borrowed also, with no promise ever to pay back, spices, flour, suet, a dozen eggs, a healthy dram of whiskey and two pounds of butter. When all was assembled he went to a young Widow Macnab whose husband had recently died fighting the Campbells and asked her help in sewing a heavy cloth bag, and when this was done he sought permission to use her kitchen: 'But first we must find some treacle, for without treacle it would be nothing.' Then he was ready.

'In my home near the Grampian Hills we called it a clootie dumplin', a dumpling made within a cloth,' and when the ingredients were properly mixed and spiced, he and the widow stuffed them into this cloth, sewed it up, and pitched it into a pot of boiling water, where it seethed for six hours, no less. When it was done, heavy as stone, Ninian Gow told her: 'My mother boiled me one when I set out for college. It will keep twelve days, maybe sixteen, and give the parting lad a kiss of love as he eats each morsel.'

Finlay celebrated his thirteenth birthday at the end of August. Next morning he rose early, eager to head south with his eighty-four cattle, his grandfather having acquired by usual means three additional head. While Rob barked at his heels, his grandmother, with tears in her eyes, gave him his bundle of dried beef, his grandfather handed him a stout walking stave, and Reverend Gow appeared with a heavy gift which he described as a clootie dumplin': 'Eat it sparingly, lad. It should keep you in good health to St. Andrews.' And the dominie, a man who always stood at the edge of poverty, offered the only present he could afford: a notebook he had used in his schooling from which a third of the pages had been torn.

'Keep healthy, lad,' his grandmother called, for she might not see her grandson again for a dozen years.

'Keep mindful, son,' his grandfather shouted, tapping his own waist where his dirks were kept.

'Keep honest,' the minister said.

'Keep to your books' was the dominie's admonition, and the boy was on his way.

His route was eastward down Glen Lyon, a marvelously quiet beginning with hills lining the way, but he was soon joined by a rough Skye man coming across the hills from the dark Moor of Rannoch to the north. Finlay, afraid there might be trouble, drew close to Macnab of Corrie, then said boldly to the Skye man: 'These are the cattle of Macnab of Dunessan,' and when the Skye man finally led his cattle off on their own route, he left behind, unknowingly, a fine animal that Finlay had taken under his protection. His herd was now eighty-five.

At midpoint in the glen Macnab of Corrie said: 'It's best we go boldly over the hills,' so they forded the little stream that defined the glen, their cattle lowing in protest, and climbed steeply into what Corrie warned was dangerous ground: 'This is Campbell country, and when a man droves cattle across such land he does so at his peril, for Campbells will sweep down at any moment and steal half his herd.'

This theft and countertheft among the Highland clans was not judged in the harsh manner it would have been in England, where misappropriation of another man's horse or cow could mean a hanging. Highlanders stole each other's cattle in a kind of game, a test of gallantry and intelligence, with always the chance that one clan might rise up in desperation and launch a general slaughter—not of the other clan's cattle but of the clan itself. It was heroic competition, and none were more cruel at it than the Campbells, or more sly and self-protective than the Macnabs. There was a saying among the drovers from Skye: 'To avoid the Macnabs in Glen Lyon takes twenty more miles, but it could save you twenty animals.'

When the Macnabs dropped down to beautiful Loch Tay they traveled eastward along its northern shore for many miles, then entered with considerable nervousness the narrow glens leading to Campbell lands, and after they had reached a spot where it was necessary to bring the cattle into an orderly ring for the night's rest, both Finlay and Corrie felt uneasy. They slept fitfully while their three dogs watched the cattle, and as they had feared, at dawn a loud, ferocious man challenged them: 'This is Campbell land, and who might you be, trespassing upon it?'

Finlay was about to say proudly that these were cattle of Macnab of Dunessan, but Corrie, mindful of the fact that the Macnabs had always sided with the Macdonalds in wars with the Campbells, said deceitfully: 'We drove for Menzies of that Ilk.'

'A good man,' the Campbell henchman grunted, 'but the fee for passing here is two of your beasts,' and when Finlay started to protest, he growled: 'No beasts, no passage.'

Corrie, sweatingly eager to maintain peace, said quickly: 'I'll find you two,' but the Campbell said: 'I'll do the picking,' and he sorted out two of the best.

When the huge guardian started to leave with the animals, Finlay was so outraged that he reached for his dirks, and although he was only a lad and pitifully smaller than the Campbell, he would have tried to stab him from behind had not Corrie restrained him: 'Laddie, sheath your dirks. There's a better way.' And the big man departed, not realizing how close he had been to death.

The two Macnabs made as if they were leaving the glen, but that night, in the silvery glow that passed for darkness in these high summer latitudes, Corrie, Finlay and the dog Rob circled back to where the Campbell cattle rested, and there, with the subtlest whispers, Corrie instructed the boy as to what his dog must do: 'Send him to the far end. Tell him to fetch us three. But make no noise.'

To one not acquainted with the Highland sheepdog, it might seem preposterous to expect Rob to understand such a thieving mission, but the dog was an enthusiastic conspirator and something of a thief himself, so quietly he ran to the grazing beasts, separated five, then turned two loose when Finlay whistled softly in the darkness.

Edging the cattle southward to where his master waited, Rob delivered them without a sound to the boy, who swiftly joined them to the Macnab herd and even more swiftly spirited the whole group out of the Campbell domain.

When all were safe, Corrie, not a demonstrative man, leaped in the air, and in the light of the newly risen moon, grasped Finlay's hands and cried: 'The Campbells stole two of ours but we rescued three of theirs!'

To celebrate, Finlay cut open his clootie dumplin', and he had never before tasted anything so good as this grainy mixture of wheat, fruit, spices and honey, nor had he ever before feasted with such mixed emotions: to have outsmarted a Campbell, to have watched his dog steal the cattle so skillfully, and now to eat in remembrance of his kind minister and mentor Ninian Gow . . . This was a day not to be forgotten, and at its close, when he and Corrie spread their tartans on the bare earth, when Rob and his two helping dogs circled the Glen Lyon cattle, he somehow passed from boyhood to young manhood. With his claymore at his belt and his herd now augmented to eighty-six, he felt ready for the great Falkirk Tryst. He had become an accomplished drover on the route and he would become an equally accomplished trader when the throng of English buyers pressed down upon him, seeking to stampede him into an early sale to their advantage, not his.

But he could not sleep. This day had been too eventful, especially that dreadful moment when he thought he might have to leap at the Campbell with his dirk. As the August night waned and the stars wheeled overhead, Rob became aware that his master was uneasy, so the dog left the care of the cattle to the other two dogs and came to lie with Finlay, and when dawn broke they were still lying there, both asleep, both exhausted from the previous day's excitements.

Why had Falkirk been chosen, years ago, as the center for this great cattle exchange? No one knew, except that Scottish drovers had learned that this was about as far south as their animals could travel without beginning to lose weight, and the English buyers knew that this was about as far north as they cared to adventure into a land that was, in their opinion, still uncivilized. Falkirk formed a reasonable compromise, and a happy one, for in this year 1805, with peace in the land and the great Scottish rebellions of 1715 and 1745 only memories, a horde of wanderers not directly associated with the cattle trade had pitched their tents along the edges of the cattle field, and here they offered revelry of a wild and often bawdy nature.

There were mountebanks from Lowland Scotland, magicians from England, actors and singers from Edinburgh, women who cooked warm and delightful dishes and their husbands or companions who sold tots of whiskey under the trees. It was a traveling carnival, policed by dour watchmen who sprang into action only when some Highlander threatened to cut out the gizzard of the Englishman with whom he had been trading: 'Now, now, laddies! Stop that foolishness!' And often the drover, the Englishman and the constable, friends again, would repair to one of the trees and get seasonably drunk.

Falkirk Tryst lasted about two weeks, during which the cautious Highlanders tried every trick known to their ancestors, a canny lot to begin with, to lure the Lowlanders into paying a more than favorable price for the cattle, while the Lowlanders hesitated, delayed, and even threatened to leave Falkirk altogether, trying to scare the drovers into sacrificing their beasts at a loss lest they fail to find a buyer.

The two Macnabs had improved their chances considerably by the traditional Glen Lyon process of stealing unwatched cattle from their neighbors, and now

their herd numbered ninety-one, and since every beast added to their original lot
had been a choice animal, they now had a rather fine selection to offer, and Finlay
intended making the most of it.

Seven different English buyers had sought to frighten him into disposing of his
animals cheaply, and at the close of the second day Corrie warned: 'Laddie, you
know we canna take these beasties home wi' us,' and he replied with a mature
wisdom which startled the older man: 'Aye, and these buyers cannot come so far
and return home empty-handed.'

As Corrie watched his young charge he discovered that the boy had a positive
affinity for sharp dealing. He actually enjoyed the danger of holding his cattle
back despite the risk of being left with no buyers. He relished contact with the
shrewd English experts, and although he did not himself drink whiskey at the
trees, he found pleasure in joining the men who did. But what surprised Corrie
most, this young fellow of his stood wide-eyed when the dancing girls with their
many petticoats pranced about.

'Come away from there,' the caretaker warned, but Finlay remained, enchanted
by the pirouetting.

Now the Tryst became a thrilling test of wills, and on each of those first seven
nights Finlay and Corrie sat beside their valuable herd, arguing and eating a little
more of that delicious clootie dumpling', until the once-plump cloth bag became
as wrinkled as a hag, and on the eighth night, when the dumpling disappeared
altogether, Macnab of Corrie said: 'Laddie, I think tomorrow we must sell,' and at
last Finlay agreed.

The seven potential buyers had dwindled to three, and the one who needed the
cattle most noticed that whereas the herd had contained ninety-one beasts at the
start of the Tryst, it now numbered ninety-four, and they were choice. Said the
would-be buyer to the helper who would drove his purchases south: 'I've always
liked doing business with Macnabs. They care for their cattle.'

'And for other people's,' his drover said admiringly.

A deal was struck, and with some regret Finlay watched his precious animals
herded south; they had been fine cattle and on the trail they had behaved themselves and grown plump on the good Highland grasses. But now came the painful
moment when the Falkirk Tryst drew toward a close. Tents were taken down and
the music stopped. Mountebanks joked no more and the dancing ceased. Macnab
of Corrie showed Finlay how to tie his coins into a corner of his kilt, then said: 'I
shall take my two dogs and move westward toward Argyll, for I have business in
Glen Orchy. You trend eastward toward St. Andrews, and Rob can fend for
himself. He's able.'

So the older Macnab left, with a heavy weight of coins sewn into a corner of his
kilt, and his dogs went with him. Now young Finlay was left with a mournful
task which certain drovers had been performing at the closing of the Falkirk Tryst
for decades. He led Rob to the northern edge of the fairgrounds, and there he tied

about his neck a small cloth bag into which had been placed the notation: 'This is Rob belonging to Macnab of Dunessan in Glen Lyon. Cost of his food guaranteed. Finlay Macnab of Glen Lyon.'

When the bag was secured, Finlay felt his throat choking up, so for some moments he looked away, but then he moved close to the faithful dog and talked with him: 'Rob, I may never see you again. You were the best, the very best of all.'

He could speak no more, so he knelt with his dog, embracing him, and finally he patted him lovingly and said: 'Rob, go home!'

Obediently, the red-brown dog left his master and started on the long, long journey back to the head of Glen Lyon. He would be nine days on the trail, and would from time to time come pleadingly to some inn or crofter's cottage, where he would be fed, for the note about his neck assured the owner of that place that next year when the Macnab cattle came south to Falkirk, honest pay for the dog's feed would be delivered.

Rob had gone about a quarter mile on this remarkable journey when he stopped for one last look at his young master, and it was only with the sternest discipline that dog and boy refrained from dashing madly toward each other, but the time for parting had come, and each looked with love at the other and went his way.

It was self-reliant lads like this who walked over the hills from all parts of Scotland to the ancient Kingdom of Fife where, at the eastern edge beside the North Sea, the premier university of Scotland stood. Glasgow's was bigger, Edinburgh's more notable, Aberdeen's the most scholarly, but St. Andrews was the peer, the heart and soul of both Scottish history and the Presbyterian faith. It was a noble university, gray and quiet in outward appearance, vital and throbbing with intellectual intensity. Sometimes it seemed as if the preachers of half the Protestant world had come from this devoted town by the bitterly cold sea, where the warmth of theological disputation often compensated for the rawness of the climate.

During his thirteenth year Finlay Macnab studied with Eoghann McRae, the tutor to whom Ninian Gow had recommended him; he lived with this penurious man and shared his meager table, at which, after the so-called meals had ended, he would pore over his Greek, his moral philosophy and his figures. But in the early mornings, when he and his tutor took their walk before breakfast, he would observe the glory of St. Andrews, for in obedience to a very ancient tradition, its students wore bright red gowns, never black until they had acquired degrees, so that the town seemed filled with brightly moving flowers, hurrying this way and that, a blaze of red gowns darting into doorways.

At age fourteen, Finlay was incorporated to the Leonardine College of the university, and the principal of the college asked the young man to meet with him: 'Macnab, I've good reports of your seriousness. I do hope you'll be studying for the ministry.'

'I have no call to the pulpit,' Finlay said honestly.

'Then avoid it, by all means. But make yourself a scholar.'

'With help, I shall,' Finlay said.

During his entire stay at the university he would not see his grandparents or his dog or the lovely shadows of Glen Lyon. He continued to live with his first tutor and to share the miserable meals, but now he was entitled to wear the famous red gown and cherish this badge of scholarly fellowship.

But at the beginning of his third year a totally unexpected transformation took place, as he explained to his tutor: 'I find I am not suited for the higher learning.'

'You're a true scholar.'

'I no longer like the university. My mind runs to the moors—to action, to trading cattle at the Falkirk Tryst.'

'I must summon the medics. You're sick.'

He was not. His mind was clear and it was delivering a masterful image of the kind of man he was intended to be: one who acted, one who dared to take risks, one who loved the hurly-burly of the Tryst. Firmly he told his tutor: 'I am ill-fitted to be a scholar. I shall go home.'

At this moment of confusion he was visited by a man he had not expected to see again, Ninian Gow, who had been summoned back to the university to occupy a chair of some importance. Unaware of the agitation which had beset his young friend, he resumed conversation as if no change had taken place: 'Well, Finlay, what shall you do, now that you're on your way to becoming a verified scholar?'

'The world has gone topsy-turvy, Master Gow.'

'What could you mean?' the new professor asked, and in a burst of words Finlay revealed recent developments. Gow, sensitive to such matters, allowed the torrent to flood along, then said quietly: 'God has instituted this confusion because He has extraordinary plans for you.'

'What?'

'He wants you to do His work in Ireland.'

'I know nothing of Ireland.'

'God wants you to remain here at St. Andrews three more years, make yourself into a devout clergyman, then sail across the Irish Sea and save that benighted country.'

'That I cannot do.' At age seventeen, Finlay was a well-organized, stubborn-minded young man, able beyond his years and of firm convictions. He was devout, convinced that John Knox had been correct in leading the way to Protestantism, and totally satisfied that Presbyterianism was the Lord's chosen instrument for the salvation of the human race, especially the Scottish. But he did not want to become a clergyman, for substantial reasons which he now revealed: 'I could never

be a saintly man. When one of the Campbells took away two of my cattle, I
wanted to kill him. And would have, had I not been stopped.'

'Campbells deserve punishment,' Gow said, 'but not killing.'

'And when I walk through the shops, I like to stare at the pretty girls.'

'Clergymen do the same. They marry.'

'But I have not the inner calling.'

Gow studied this solemn declaration for some moments, then said with that
generosity of spirit which would make him a notable professor, next at Glasgow
and finally at Oxford: 'God summons us in different ways. He doesn't require you
to become one of his ministers, or even to finish university. Come with me, and
remind yourself as to what service is.'

They walked to that sacred spot where Patrick Hamilton, born a Catholic but
inspired by the reform teachings of John Knox, had been burned at the stake by
the local Catholics: 'Finlay, he refused to recant even when they piled more
faggots at his feet. He was an enemy of popery, and so must you be.'

And beside the reddish stones which marked where Hamilton had died, Gow
told of Ireland's problems: 'We have planted, successfully I'm sure, a mustard seed
in the northern counties. Trusted Scotsmen by the score cross the Irish Sea to
protect the land we've won and to advance Presbyterianism against the onslaughts
of popery.'

'What could I do?' Finlay asked, and Gow said: 'There is a need for husband-
men, for fine merchants, for anyone who will help strengthen Protestant roots in
that ill-fated land.'

'That's the kind of work I'd be fitted for,' Finlay said, and some days later,
when Gow brought him the news that a Scottish landowner in Northern Ireland,
a trusted Presbyterian, was seeking a man who understood cattle and horses to
serve as factor on his estates, Finlay volunteered for the job. After submitting
glowing testificates penned by Gow, by his longtime tutor McRae and by the
principal of St. Andrews, he received from across the Irish Sea the exciting news
that he had been selected.

When he bade farewell to Professor Gow, he said apologetically: 'My life was
changed at Falkirk Tryst. I discovered that I belong with the sweating merchants,
the mountebanks.' When Gow indicated that he understood, the young man
added: 'And the swirling petticoats of the dancing girls.'

'When a man once has the Latin, he can never be completely lost. God will find
you proper work to do.'

With little regret, Finlay Macnab laid aside forever the good red gown of St.
Andrews, unmatched in all the universities of the world, and set forth like many
another Scottish young man before him to walk across Scotland and say farewell
to the lone cottage at the head of his glen, but when he reached it he found it
occupied by a different set of Macnabs, for his grandfather and grandmother were
recently dead, and even his dog Rob was missing.

'Did you ever know a dog named Rob?' Finlay asked, and when the new Macnabs said no, he stood mournfully by the rough-walled cottage, tested the ropes that kept the thatched roof intact, and lamented the passage of the simple glories he had known here and would know no more. Adjusting his kilt, he started for that exquisite chain of western glens which would take him down to Glasgow, where he would be looking for a boat to Ireland.

As he began the journey that would ultimately lead him to Texas, Finlay was eighteen, of average height, weighing eleven stone, four. He came from a line of men who had defended their rights in battle; he was himself a skilled cattle thief, a good man with the claymore, and one who loved the conviviality of his fellows. He had three fundamental characteristics which determined his behavior: he was a fierce Protestant whose ancestors had defended this religion with their lives; he had a stubborn sense of honor which lay quiescent when respected but flared into the wildest self-defense when insulted or transgressed; and he had a passionate love of freedom, which his people in the glen had sustained against Campbells and the English kings. Everything he had experienced—the lessons of Greek and Roman history, the accounts of his own clan, the records of his Scottish church, the works of the great philosophers—had instilled in him an almost fanatical dedication to liberty, which he would not surrender easily.

He was, in short, one of the finest young men his world was then producing, and there were other freedom-seekers like him arising in France, in England and in Germany. But the most able pool of emigrating talent was developing within that intrusive Presbyterian enclave in Northern Ireland, where, in obedience to the thrust of history, many young people were trending toward Texas without ever realizing they were headed that way. When they arrived, they would prove a most difficult group to discipline, especially when the center of political control lay far distant in Mexico City, manned by persons of a different culture contemptuous of their aspirations.

Finlay's employer in Ireland was a big, rugged man with the reassuring Scottish name of Angus MacGregor, whose ancestors had received assistance from the crown in London in putting together halfway between the towns of Lurgan and Portadown, southwest of Belfast, a tremendous holding of spacious fields reaching all the way to Loch Neagh. It was on this estate that Finlay entered upon his duties: 'Young man, you're to make my herds prosper, trade my horses profitably, and keep the damned papists in line.'

When the first MacGregor had come as a stranger to these lands, the population had been ninety-two-percent Catholic; by the time he died, it was down to half. When the present MacGregor inherited, his occupying farmers were about forty-percent Catholic, and now they were no more than eighteen-percent. In this orderly, irresistible manner the lush green fields of Northern Ireland were being rescued from popery, and after Finlay Macnab had been factor for a while, he could boast: 'All my drovers are now trusted men from Scotland, loyal Highlanders who speak our tongue.'

These invaders became known as the 'Scots-Irish,' which signified that in heritage, religion and firmness of character they were Scots, while in terrain and culture they were Irish. It was a powerful mix, this blending of two disparate Celtic strains, and they might more properly have been called Celts, for that is what they were: dreamers, wild talkers, men of dour concentration when needed, and great colonizers.

The free-living local Celts exerted a powerful negative influence on young Finlay, for they taught him the pleasures of good Irish whiskey and the joy of teasing the local lassies, two occupations which delighted him but which also plunged him into serious trouble. One morning, after being unable to remember how the preceding night had ended, he looked at himself ruefully and mumbled: 'I've made a far journey from St. Andrews,' and he was pleased that Professor Gow could not see him now.

In 1810, at the age of eighteen, he found himself involved in two situations from which there could be only one escape. He had fallen in love with the daughter of a Lurgan squire, and he coveted the jet-black mare of a Portadown butcher. The squire would not surrender his daughter to a lad who seemed bent on becoming a rascal, and the butcher would not sell his mare to a young fellow unable to pay a decent price. Young Finlay resolved the dilemma neatly: he stole both the girl and the mare, and after placing the former astride the latter, he led a merry chase over the fields and roads of Northern Ireland. In the end he abandoned both the girl and the mare, who were restored to their rightful owners, while he, always a jump ahead of his pursuers, made his way secretly to Dublin, where he caught a freight boat to Bristol in England, on the safe side of the Irish Sea.

Unable to find work, he resorted to his traditional occupation of cattle stealing, only to discover that in England this had never been a game. When he returned to his lodgings one evening with a fine cow, his landlord whispered: 'They're after you, Finlay, and if they catch you, it's the gibbet.' Finlay suspected that this might be an evil trick whereby the landlord hoped to get the cow for nothing, but he hid in a grove of trees just in case the constables really did come, and when he saw three of them snooping about he scurried down lanes and through alleyways till he reached the Bristol docks. Leaping aboard the first ship available, he found himself, by ironic chance, headed for America's most Catholic city, Baltimore.

In 1812, at the age of twenty, he arrived in America just in time to become involved in the war starting that year, but after trying to decide whether he was an American patriot or a British partisan, he concluded that he was neither and offered himself to both sides, providing each with horses, cows, pigs, sheep and goats.

By 1820, when he was well established in Baltimore, whose German citizens liked to do business with him, his careless dalliance with Berthe Keller, daughter of a Munich baker, obligated him to marry much sooner than he had intended. Berthe was a hefty blond young woman he would never normally have chosen, but when his father-in-law died in 1824, Macnab found himself proprietor of a flourishing bakery, which he quickly enlarged into a ships' chandlery of impressive dimensions.

He liked working on the beautiful Baltimore waterfront and was on his way to becoming a man of some importance, with a stodgy wife and three flaxen-haired children, when the inherited Macnab tendency surfaced, for in 1827 he was detected in a most nefarious transaction involving cattle owned by neighboring Germans. With no alternative but a term in jail, he decided to leave town.

When his complaining wife, disgusted with his irresponsible behavior, refused to accompany him on his flight, he was rather relieved, for she had proved an irritable woman and he was glad to be shed of her. Leaving his two daughters with their mother, he kept his son, Otto, slipped out of Baltimore before the enraged cattle owners could pounce upon him, and headed for the National Road leading west.

They were nearly eighty miles out of Baltimore, approaching Hagerstown, when young Otto gained his first insight into the nature of this trip, and indeed his first childish glimpse into the structure of life itself. Although not yet six, he was a precocious lad who suspected that he and his father were leaving his mother for good, and this caused pain. He knew that where his father was involved, his mother had been a bossy woman, but with Otto she had been a loving protector, standing always as his principal support, and he missed her. Often in the morning he expected to see her coming toward him with a bowl of porridge, or at night with hot sausages.

He was so confused in his loneliness that sometimes he wanted to cry, but his stern heritage—half dour Scot, half stubborn German—plus a warning look from his father forced him to bite his lip and march resolutely ahead. But at dusk, when he crawled beneath his blanket, he did not try to hide the fact that he was miserable.

But he felt no uncertainty about traveling with his father, and even though he did not fully understand why Finlay had fled Baltimore in such a hurry, he was sure that no blame fell on his father. A perplexed little boy, he stepped forth boldly each morning as they probed into the wilderness.

One evening as they plodded along the ill-kept road, trying to decide where to spread their thin blankets for the night, Otto saw through the growing darkness a light that shone from the window of some cabin situated well off the road, and the little hut seemed so established, so different from the wandering life he was leading that an overwhelming hunger assailed him.

'Poppa, let's stop here!'

'No, we'll find a valley before real darkness.'

'But, Poppa, the light!'

'On ahead.'

They kept to the road, this stubborn father and his son nearing six, and it was then that the little boy fixed in his mind the image which would live with him for the rest of his life: a cabin secure in the wilderness, a light shining from the window, refuge from the lonely, shadow-filled road. And it was also then, because of the way in which his father urged him to move on, that he first suspected that he would not be allowed to share in that forbidden warmth, at least never for long. And whenever afterward he saw such lights at night his heart hesitated, for he knew what they symbolized.

Twenty-five miles west of Hagerstown the Macnabs had to make a crucial decision, for there a path deviated to the north, heading over the hills to Pittsburgh, an enticing target.

'Is it true?' Finlay asked a traveler as they stood at the junction. 'Do boats with steam engines leave Pittsburgh and run all the way to New Orleans?'

'They do,' the stranger assured him. 'But you'd be wise to beware of them.'

'Why?'

'For three solid reasons,' he said. 'They're very expensive and would eat up your savings. They're very dangerous, for they blow up constantly. And the criminals who sail them will steal what money you have left, cut your throat, and toss you overboard. Stay clear of those boats at Pittsburgh.'

Finlay accepted this advice, but the more young Otto thought about the mysterious boats of steam that wandered down a thousand miles of river, the more obsessed he became with them, and he pestered his father: 'Let's go to Pittsburgh. Let's take a boat. I'm tired of walking.' And when Finlay reminded him of the dangers the traveler had pointed out, Otto said pleadingly: 'But you would know how to fight those bad men.'

'There's the money, too. We'll need all we have when we get to Cincinnati.'

With a melancholy the boy would never forget, the Macnabs rejected the steamboats and continued their way to Morgantown and on to Parkersburg, where at last they would join the Ohio River, along whose grassy banks they would walk the last three hundred miles to Cincinnati.

Otto was a thin, wiry lad who looked as if he might not grow into a tall or robust man. But he displayed, even at this untested age, a cool efficiency and a stubborn determination. He intended one day to sail down the river aboard a steam vessel, and as he walked he remained constantly aware that off to his right, somewhere, lay the great river, and he could imagine himself breaking away from his father, heading north and finding it. He was satisfied that if he ever did so, some boat would see him, stop, and pick him off the bank.

He was lost in such romantic thoughts one morning, when he let out a gasp which seemed to come from deep within, as if his heart had been touched: 'Oh, Poppa!'

For there, in full majesty, rode the Ohio River, highway of the nation, bringer of good things to alien parts. Much bigger than he had imagined, more sinisterly dark, in its motion it bespoke its power and the fact that anyone who ventured upon it would be carried to strange and magnificent places like Cincinnati, Louisville and Paducah.

'Poppa, look!'

From the opposite shore a small craft had set out, obviously intending to cross to where the Macnabs waited, and Finlay told his son: 'That's a ferry. It'll come to our side and carry us across.'

'We ride on it?' the boy cried with delight, and when another traveler said: 'We sure do, sonny,' Otto kept his eyes riveted to this reassuring sight.

But as he waited for the little ferry to cross the river, he became aware that something of magnitude was approaching from the right, and just in time he turned to catch the majestic approach of a large river steamer. Belching smoke, its great paddles churning the water, it was a thrilling sight. Well-to-do passengers lined its two tiers, their fine clothes enhancing its magnificence.

It was the *Climax* out of Paducah, one of that grand, adventurous fleet which had started under the imaginative command of Nicholas Roosevelt in 1811 to bring steam navigation to the network of great rivers that bound the central areas of America together. 'Oh, Poppa!' Otto cried as the lovely boat passed, for he had seen his first riverboat and it had captured him.

On the ferry they crossed into Ohio, then followed country roads along the right bank of the river as it wound its way from Parkersburg through the empty wastes of southernmost Ohio and on to Portsmouth, where the Scioto River joins the Ohio. It was a journey of compelling beauty; the vistas changed constantly; at night solitary lights glowed on the opposite shore, indicating where some adventurous soul from settled Virginia had decided to test the wilderness in Kentucky.

Deer accompanied the travelers; and one evening a small bear approached their sleeping place when Finlay was absent, gathering sticks for a fire. Otto, who had never faced such an adversary before, hesitated for one frightened moment. Then, realizing instinctively that he must protect their belongings, he grabbed the nearest piece of wood and made right for the beast. Thrashing about with his little club, he bewildered the bear, but not for long. With a sweep of its paw the animal pushed the boy away, nudging him into a thicket.

Astonished at the insolence of the beast, Otto first shook his head, then glared at the animal. With a grunt to give him courage, he fought his way out of the brush, uttered a furious yell, and charged back at the little bear, who was now rummaging among the Macnab possessions.

Otto was prepared to do battle by himself, but his father, hearing the commotion, hurried back: 'Otto, no!'

The warning was ineffective, for Otto was outraged by the brusque treatment the bear had handed him and was determined to drive the creature away, but before he could resume his assault, Finlay rushed up and with a much larger stick belabored the animal, who growled, studied his adversaries, and rumbled off.

Trembling, Finlay sat with his son beside the river, and there they remained as the long twilight waned. 'You were very brave,' Finlay said. 'I'm proud of you.'

'He was stealing our food.'

'Never tangle with a bear.'

'But it was only a little one.'

'A bear's a bear, son. Don't ever tangle with one.'

'But you did, Poppa.'

Finlay could think of a dozen appropriate, fatherly warnings: 'Yes, but I'm a grown man.' Or, 'You were lucky it was a little bear.' Or, 'If you have to fight a bear, don't use a stick. Get a gun.' He stifled such admonition, for he believed that his son's action had been proper. Once allow a boy to run away from a serious challenge, he could continue to do so through life.

Softly he said, as if Otto were his own age: 'You were right, son. If you start to do something, keep going and finish the job.'

They followed the good road along the Ohio right in to Cincinnati, a growing town of more than twenty thousand where a few resolute Germans were already establishing firms to serve the various needs of the steamboats plying up and down the river. Three ferries crossed the river to service the citizens in Kentucky, and after several exciting days Otto told his father: 'This is better than Baltimore.'

In many ways the little boy talked and acted like a grown man; as frontier boys did, he was skipping a whole decade of his growing up; he was already a mature young fellow who had walked six hundred miles through the wilderness and fought his bear. He knew what loneliness was, and how a great river served people.

Because of his waterfront experience in Baltimore, Finlay had no trouble finding a job with a German merchant who needed his expertise in buying cattle and hogs for the river traffic, and in pursuit of this work, he often visited the glamorous steamboats that docked at Cincinnati. Aboard these craft he heard for the first time about the real wonders of the river: 'New Orleans! Finest city in America! Them Creole girls. Them great eatin' houses.'

At the age of seven Otto began running errands for his father, learning the names of the steamboats and their home ports, and in doing so, he fell under the spell of a river town much different from New Orleans. He first heard of it from a tall bearded boatman with a poetic touch: 'Tell you what, sonny, when you ship down the Mississip, as you surely will, the place you want to see is not New Orleans. The real spot is Natchez-under-the-Hill.'

'That's a funny name.'

'It's a golden name, like out of one of the Greek fables, like maybe the gods put it there to test men.'

He spoke with such music and strength that Otto leaned forward to catch his words, and as the man continued he became not an ordinary roustabout but a chronicler: 'To make things flower perfect, the gods built Natchez-atop-the-Hill, with gleamin' white houses and pillared porches and a score of slaves to keep things clean. That's rich-folks country, and river folks like you and me, we ain't allowed up there. For us the gods built Natchez-under-the-Hill, about the finest little spot in America.'

Aware that he had caught Otto's attention, he moved his hands in ominous gestures to indicate knives and daggers and pistols and gallows-rope: 'A man don't watch out, they knife him. At night you hear screams, somebody's bein' murdered. You hear a splash! There goes a corpse into the Mississip. Men walk bent over, they're smugglers. In the saloons you can get Tennessee whiskey, rots your gut, or a bullet, ends your gut. And there are girls, and dancin' through the night.'

Otto missed not a word of this report, but the riverman would have been astounded had he known the impact his words were having on this flaxen-haired lad. But in succeeding days, when Otto heard more about Under-the-Hill, and when he had time to weigh exactly what had been said, discarding the poetry, he was wise enough, even as a boy, to conclude that the lower Natchez was a sorry place frequented by men and women of a low degree. He could not have explained why he was reaching this conclusion, or what it signified, but he was developing a powerful rejection of goings-on; he was becoming a youthful conservative, in the best sense of that word, who deplored gambling, knifing, girls who danced all night . . . and general irresponsibility. He opposed them all.

His father was also hearing a new word, one that would exert an equal influence on his life. Because Cincinnati specialized in butchering hogs, it was known as Porkopolis, and one of Finlay's duties was to provision riverboats with ham, bacon and sausage. One day after Finlay had loaded a boat bound for New Orleans with seventy salted carcasses, the satisfied captain paid him, then uttered a name Finlay had not heard before: 'We find ourselves with extra cargo space, Macnab. Could you scurry about and find us some bolts of cloth? Doesn't have to be fancy stuff, because it'll be transshipped to Texas.'

'Where's that?'

'Surely you've heard of Texas? Garden spot of the continent.'

'Where is it?'

'Part of Mexico now, but not for long.'

'What do you mean?'

'Texas is the ass end of Mexico, which don't give a damn for it. Each trip I make down the Mississippi, I carry men from Kentucky and Tennessee who's goin' to Texas. Stands to reason that with their long rifles, they ain't gonna be Mexicans for very long. They's gonna bring Texas into the Union, and the sooner the better, I say.'

'Why do people go there?' Finlay asked.

'To get rich! You plant cotton, it explodes in your face. You plant corn, you get two crops a year. Cows have twins in Texas, it's the law. And you get a league-and-a-labor, that's why.'

'What are they?'

'A league is four thousand four hundred and twenty-eight acres of pastureland, you get it free for cattle. A labor is a hundred and seventy-seven acres of better land you get for farming, also free.'

'I can't believe it.'

'You get it the minute you step acrost the border and say— What's your name? Finlay Macnab? When you step up and say "Here I am, Finlay Macnab" you get all those acres of the best land in America.'

'You said it was Mexico.'

'It'll soon be America, you can count on that.'

Macnab asked so many questions about Texas that he became known along the waterfront as a prospective settler, and one day a Mr. Clendenning invited him to lunch aboard one of the steamboats docked at the wharves. 'Can I bring my son?' Finlay asked. 'He dreams about steamboats.'

'To be sure,' Clendenning said expansively, and when they were seated in the spacious dining salon with its gold and silver ornamentation, the stranger told Otto: 'This is how we live on the great boats, sonny.'

'Do you live here?'

'Up and down.'

'You live on the river?'

'For the time being.'

'How long?'

'Until I've visited all the ports of call.' He now explained to Finlay that he was the traveling representative of the Texas Land and Improvement Company, head-quartered in Boston, and his pleasant task was to sell future immigrants to Texas the best bargain this weary old world had ever seen. Pushing away the dinner plates, he spread an interesting series of documents on the table and said: 'This is scrip, authorized by the Mexican government and fully backed by the Texas Land and Improvement Company of Boston, Massachusetts. Each unit of scrip you buy entitles you to one acre of the choicest land in North America. Buy yourself three or four thousand units, and you're set for life.'

'Did you say *buy?*'

'Yes. You deliver this scrip to the Mexican officials, and presto—they invite you to go out and survey your three or four thousand acres.'

'I was told I would get a league-and-a-labor free, something like four thousand acres.'

'No, no! You're *entitled* to the league-and-a-labor, and it's there waiting for you. But you have to bring the scrip to prove your legality. My firm vouches for you, says you're of good character, and you get the land.'

Macnab felt deflated. For some days now he had been visualizing his four thousand acres of choice land, his for the asking, and now to find that he must buy something in order to qualify was disheartening. He supposed the cost per acre would be something like a dollar or two, and so large a debt he would not be able to manage: 'How much is this scrip?'

'Five cents an acre.' Clendenning, noticing the relief in his prospect's face, said heartily: 'That's what I said. That's what I meant. Five cents an acre, just to make it legal.' While Finlay was congratulating himself on such a bargain, Clendenning added encouragingly: 'So what our more responsible customers do, they put up one thousand dollars and get title to twenty thousand acres. Then they are really in business.'

'Can I get so much?'

'Dear friend! Mexico wants you to come. They want you to settle their vast empty spaces. You can have forty thousand acres if you wish, but I've been recommending only twenty. More manageable.'

'Have you been there? Have you seen the land?'

'Macnab, do you know the passage in the Holy Book, "A land flowing with milk and honey"? Some day we'll find that a man from Texas wrote the Bible, for that describes the land precisely. One day I was walking beside the Trinity River —marvelous stream—and what did I see? A shattered old tree whose insides were filled with honey bees, millions of them. There was enough honey in there to feed a regiment. And right beside that tree one of the sturdiest cows ever you saw, aching to give milk. A land flowing with honey and milk, just like the Bible says.'

'How many acres would you go for, if you were me?'

The salesman did not answer. Instead, he turned to Otto, and with a benign look suffusing his face, said: 'I would think only of my son. If I could get twenty thousand acres securely in my hands, and improve it, when I died I would leave this lad'—and here he stroked Otto's head—'a fortune of incalculable wealth.' In the pause which followed this sensible advice, he smiled at Otto, then added: 'Can you imagine your son at age twenty, with his bride at his side, taking command of a farm of twenty thousand acres? The cattle? The fields of corn? The faithful slaves working the cotton? And you sitting on the porch, surveying it all like a proud patriarch in the Old Testament?'

Mr. Clendenning did not press Macnab to make a decision that day, but as the three left the boat Finlay did furnish a useful bit of information: 'I could handle the thousand dollars, if your company guaranteed that I'd get the land.'

'Guarantee?' Clendenning cried as if his integrity had been impugned. 'Look at these guarantees! These ironclad papers.' He made no attempt to close the deal, but when the boat sailed next day for New Orleans, he did leave behind a set of handsomely printed papers which specifically ensured the legality of any sale which might develop.

Being a cautious Scot, Finlay carried them next morning to the office of a German lawyer with whom his employer did business to seek an opinion, but before the lawyer, a man with a high collar and long-tailed coat, would give it he handed Finlay a card on which was printed:

ALL A LAWYER HAS TO SELL
IS HIS TIME AND HIS JUDGMENT
THEY'RE AS VALUABLE TO HIM
AS THE BANKER'S GOLD COINS ARE TO HIM

'How much?'

'Two dollars.'

'Good.'

The lawyer studied the documents left by the representative of the Texas Land and Improvement Company, then shrewdly pointed out: 'This is a Boston company presuming to do business in Mexico. I find nothing that binds the Mexican government to honor the promises made here. I'd be very reluctant to hand my good money over to such an agent, with so little to back his claims.'

'I wondered.'

'How much is he charging for the land?'

'Five cents an acre.'

The lawyer was dumfounded, and showed it. Land touching Cincinnati was selling for two hundred dollars an acre, and he had during the past week supervised the sale of some four hundred acres. Five cents was meaningless.

'How many acres . . . ?'

'Twenty thousand,' Finlay said.

Again the lawyer gasped: 'I can't imagine such a piece of land.' Taking a pen, he multiplied some figures and said: 'One thousand dollars. I could find you some wonderful land here, out in the country to be sure. But one thousand dollars is a lot of money.'

'Twenty thousand acres is a lot of land.'

'And Texas is nowhere.' The lawyer rose and placed his arm about Macnab's shoulder: 'It's Mexico, remember, and from what we hear up here, that's a most unstable country. It's not like Prussia, even England . . . and God knows it's not like the United States.'

'They tell me it soon will be part of us.'

'But you do not buy land on such a fragile expectation. Very dangerous, Macnab. Now, if you seek a farm, I know some excellent ones, but if you want full value for the two dollars you paid me, take my advice and buy several plots I know which abut on the river. Growth there is unavoidable.' He even quit his office to show Finlay the land he had in mind, and it was a splendid pair of lots that fronted on the river, so for some days Finlay's dreams deserted Texas and focused upon a chandler's shop on the Ohio.

He never saw Mr. Clendenning again, but toward the end of January 1829, another salesman from the Boston firm came ashore from an upriver boat, and where Clendenning had been persuasive, this man was brutally forceful: 'Macnab, the land's selling like icicles in hell. You'd better grab your twenty thousand.'

'I've heard bad reports about the influx of criminals. Men who've been there say it's a madhouse.'

'One or two men fleeing their wives, a handful escaping unjust debts, and that's about it. I'd judge Texas to be one of the most moral states in Christendom.'

When Finlay demurred, the salesman grew angry, a tactic which worked along the frontier, where men appreciated harsh opinions firmly stated: 'Damn it all, Macnab, if you're so lily-livered, write to Stephen Austin hisself and ask him,' and he wrote out for Finlay directions as to how to address the founder of the American settlements in Texas. That night Macnab drafted his letter:

> Bell's Tavern
> Cincinnati, Ohio
> 27 January 1829

> Dear Mr. Austin,

> My son Otto, aged seven, and I are contemplating a permanent remove to Texas and feel great solicitude about the nature of the population which will inhabit your country. We have been informed that you permit no one to settle within the limits of your colony unless able to produce vouchers of good moral character. This we can do, from Ireland of the north, from Baltimore and from this town, and we should like to live among other settlers of equal repute.

> We are, however, much disturbed by rumors current here that only the worst venture into Texas and that our prisons are filled with persons of low character who swear that as soon as they are turned out they will head for Texas, for they say that it is a territory in which a man with ideas and courage can make a go of it, by which they mean that criminals thrive in your colony.

> My son and I are part of a responsible crowd gathered here willing to try our fortune in Texas, and we are awaiting the return of a Mr. Kane who

left us last September to explore your country. If he gives a good report, we shall want to join you, but in a letter from the east bank of the Sabine River dispatched in October he warned us: 'Tomorrow I shall cross over into Texas. Pray for me, because I am told that no man is safe west of the Sabine.' What are the facts?

We are also apprehensive about becoming citizens of Mexico, for we hear that it is a country ruled by brigands who have a revolution twice a year. Again, Sir, we are desirous of true information.

Respectfully yours,

Finlay Macnab
Presbyterian

Remembering the lawyer's warning that the scrip carried no guarantee that Mexico was bound to honor it, Finlay wanted to ask Austin for clarification, but the salesman protested: 'You wouldn't want to worry an important man with a trivial matter like that!' So the question was not posed.

In the weeks following the posting of this letter Macnab interrogated many travelers regarding Texas and received conflicting reports. Said a Georgia man: 'A noble land. More salubrious than either Alabama or Mississippi. Ideal for the propagation of slaves, and high-spirited. I've never had a regretful thought since establishing my plantation there.'

But an Arkansas woman who had fled the colony for the civilization of Cincinnati groaned: 'Texas no more! They call where me and my man lived a town. No stores, no schools, no church with a steeple, and no cloth for sewin'. My old man and me had a race to see who could get out the fastest, and I won.'

But then came a response from Stephen Austin himself:

San Felipe de Austin,
Coahuila-y-Tejas
20 April 1829

Dear Mr. Macnab,

Your letter of 27 January reached me yesterday and I now put aside all other occupations to answer the sensible enquiries you make relative to this country.

You express an understandable solicitude as to the kind of settler who will inhabit Texas. In 1823 when I returned from Mexico City to proceed with settlement of my colony, I found that certain criminals had infiltrated and I immediately adopted measures to drive them away.

I forced them to cross back over the Sabine River, but from sanctuary in Louisiana they conducted raids into Texas, and what was worse, they lied about our colony, circulating every species of falsehood their ingenuity could invent. They were joined by others of their kind who had come to the Sabine, hoping to invade our colony, and there they sit in their bitterness, circulating lies about us.

I can assure you, Mr. Macnab, that the citizens of Texas are just as responsible and law-abiding as those of New Orleans or Cincinnati, and that ruffians will never be allowed in this colony. The settlers already here are greatly superior to those of any new country or frontier that I have ever seen and would lose nothing in comparison with those of any southern or western state. They are, in my judgment, the best men and women who have ever settled a frontier.

You say you are apprehensive about living under the Government of Mexico. Let me assure you that the policy which Mexico has uniformly pursued toward us has been that of a kind, liberal and indulgent parent. Favors and privileges have been showered upon us to such an extent that some among us have doubted their reality, so generous have they been. The present ruler of Mexico is a man to be trusted, and the Constitution of 1824, under which he rules, is just and liberal, and in no way inferior to the constitutions of your various states. I can foresee no possible trouble that you might have with the Government of Mexico, which is now stable and far-sighted, and of which I am proud to be a citizen.

The minor disturbances which do sometimes arise down in Mexico never affect us here. We stay clear and have nothing to do with them. All that is required in Texas is to work hard and maintain harmony among ourselves. This is a gentle, law-abiding, Christian society and we would be most pleased to have you join us.

Stephen F. Austin

When Macnab received these warm assurances he surrendered all doubts about Texas, telling his son: 'It may have a few rascals, but so did Ireland, and I can name several in this town.' He began to collect all debts owed him and to set aside those few and precious things he and his son would carry with them to Texas, but now two problems arose. Austin's letter had been so reassuring that Finlay, despite being a cautious Scot, had buried his uneasiness about the validity of scrip; he was eager to buy some, but found no one at hand to sell him any. And he had developed a real fear of riverboats. Four different steamboats, which he himself had provisioned, had blown up, with heavy loss of life, and he became apprehensive lest the one he chose for passage to Texas become the fifth.

Otto, of course, was eager to board anything that floated, and each day he kept his father informed as to what boats were at the wharf. When one sailed south without the Macnabs, Otto would list its replacement: '*Climax* left, but *River Queen* tied up.' To Macnab's surprise, this particular newcomer brought him an urgent letter:

> Finlay Macnab
> Bell's Tavern
>
> I shall be in Cincinnati shortly. Make no move till I arrive.
>
> > Cabot Wellington
> > Texas Land and Improvement
> > Boston, Massachusetts

Now Macnab had to consider seriously his passage to New Orleans, and as he was talking with experienced men at the tavern, one chanced to mention an alternative to boats: 'Have you ever thought of walkin' down to Nashville and pickin' up the Natchez Trace?'

'What's that?' Finlay asked, and several men crowded in, eager to explain. They said that in old times, before the advent of steam, carpenters along the Ohio used to build huge floating houses-on-rafts on which traders drifted down the rivers, sometimes all the way from Pittsburgh to New Orleans, but often terminating at Natchez-under-the-Hill, where they sold their rafts as house lumber, transferring their goods to real boats that conveyed them in orderly fashion to New Orleans.

'How did they get back without their rafts?' Finlay asked, and the men pointed to a surly-looking fellow who was drinking alone.

'Ask him.'

One of the men accompanied Macnab to the table where the lone man sat, and asked: 'You a Kaintuck?'

'I am.'

'Can we join you?'

'No charge for chairs, I reckon.'

The go-between explained: 'Any man who goes downriver on a raft and comes back is known as a Kaintuck. Doesn't mean he's from Kaintucky. Where you from?'

'Kaintucky.'

'Tell my friend here how you came back from Natchez.'

'Walked.'

'All the way back from Natchez?'

'Yep, and my partner, he's still walkin'. On his way to Pittsburgh.'

'Is it difficult?'

The Kaintuck launched into a vivid description of the Natchez Trace: 'Murderers, cutthroats every foot of the way, robbers, horse thieves.' He stopped abruptly and broke into a raucous laugh. 'I'm talkin' about thirty years ago. Today? Much better.'

'How many days to Natchez?'

The Kaintuck ignored this question: 'If you knowed your history, which you bein' a Scotchman you probably don't . . .'

'How do you know I'm a Scot?'

'Because I heerd you. And if'n you knowed American history, you'd know that the great Meriwether Lewis, him as went to Oregon, he was murdered comin' home on the Trace.'

'Do travelers still use it?'

'They do.'

'Is the road still open?'

'It ain't a road. I been tryin' to tell you that, but you won't listen. It's what its name says, a clear-cut trace through the wilderness.'

'But it's still open?'

'If'n it could ever be called open. Four hundred and eighty miles through swamp and forest. Never a store, never a town, a few shacks run by half-breed Indians who cut your throat when you're sleepin'.'

'Could I walk it? With a seven-year-old boy?'

'My mother walked it with two babies,' the Kaintuck said, 'down and up. But maybe you ain't the man she was.'

Other travelers who had journeyed up the Trace gave such confirming reports that Macnab had pretty well decided to follow that land route, when a chance conversation with a loquacious Pittsburgh boatman just back from Natchez raised an ugly question that cast a shadow upon the entire Texas adventure.

The conversation started favorably: 'It's grand, driftin' down the rivers, walkin' home along the Trace.'

'How many miles can you make a day?' Finlay asked during a leisurely meal at the tavern.

'Driftin' downstream, sixty miles in twenty-four hours, not allowin' time lost when hung up on sandbars, which is a lot. Walkin' back, sixteen miles a day, week after week.' Then he added something which Finlay found attractive: 'Some men can make twenty, steady, but I often like to lie under the trees . . . in daylight, so I can watch the birds and the squirrels.'

'They told me murderers prowl the Trace.'

'That ended twenty years ago. But let's be honest. I do hide my money carefully —four different spots so I can give up a small part if I meet up with a holdup man.' With a deft move of his right hand he produced an imaginary purse from his left breast. 'And I do feel safer if I travel with others through the lonely parts.'

'I wish I could have you as my partner,' Finlay said.

'I won't be walkin' the Trace no more. But if you're set on headin' for Texas, that's the cheap way to go, and you bein' a Scotchman . . .'

'We call it Scotsman.'

'Of course, when you get there, you'll be givin' up a lot more than your money.'

'What do you mean?'

The boatman looked soberly at Macnab and said: 'You're a Presbyterian? I suppose you know that before you can get land in Texas you have to swear to the Mexican officials that you're a true Catholic.'

'What?'

'And your son will have to be baptized in the Catholic faith.'

'I never heard . . .'

'My brothers and me, we was thinkin' of Texas, but we're Methodists, and when we heard about that religion business . . . no, no.'

'You give me dismal news,' said Macnab. 'I'm not sure I should risk going to Texas.'

Things were in this delicate condition when a suave and stately gentleman alighted from the Pittsburgh boat, announcing that he was Cabot Wellington from Boston, looking for a Texas traveler named Finlay Macnab. He was what was known in the trade as 'the finisher,' the relentless man who came in only after the advance men had softened up the prospect.

As soon as he saw Macnab he cried enthusiastically: 'Dear friend! I bring you your passport to riches,' and he betrayed no disappointment when Finlay drew back, refused to accept any papers, and asked bluntly: 'What's this about converting to popery?'

Grandly, and with a condescending smile, Wellington said: 'Many ask about that rumor, and there's no better way to explain than to consult with a settler who already owns an estate in Texas,' and he whistled for a raw-boned, prearranged fellow of forty, who sidled up and allowed that he owned one of the best estancias in Texas.

'What's an estancia?'

'Fancy Mexican word for farm . . . real big farm. I was born, bred a Baptist. Virginia man. So when I gets to Texas, I ain't hankerin' to turn my coat, not me. Trick's simple. Don't let no Mexican priest convert you, because if they do, it's for keeps. But they's five or six Irish priests. Yep, imported direct from Ireland, through New Orleans. They never seen Mexico City or none of that.'

'What are they doing in Texas?' Finlay asked, for he had grown suddenly afraid, knowing that there were not in this world any Catholic priests more devout and stern than the Irish. He wanted no Irish priest converting him, because that really would be forever.

'Stands to reason, the Mexican government, they cain't persuade any real Mexican priests to travel all the way to Texas. Those hanker after the fleshpots of the big city. So the oney priests they can get to work in land s'far away are Irishmen who cain't make no livin' in Ireland, and who cain't speak a word of Spanish neither, if'n you ask me.'

'Aren't they real fanatics?'

'No! No! There's this big, jolly, whiskey-guzzlin' priest called Clooney, goes about on a mule, settlement to settlement, convertin' Protestants by the hundreds, free and easy, with him knowin' it ain't serious just as well as we know it ain't.'

'Did he convert you?'

'Yep. Father Clooney's the name, and a fairer man never lived. You let him sprinkle a little holy water over you, hand in your scrip, which Mr. Wellington here will give you, and you get your league-and-a-labor.'

'Is that right?' Macnab asked.

'It is indeed,' Wellington said, and the Texas man added: 'The scrip solves ever'thin', and the day after you get your land you can revert to bein' a Baptist again. I did.'

'I'm Presbyterian.'

'My mother was a Presbyterian,' Wellington cried with real enthusiasm, and the deal was settled. Finlay Macnab and his son were entitled to twenty thousand acres of the choicest land in Texas, purchased at the ridiculous price of five cents an acre.

Otto was delighted when he learned that a firm decision had been reached. A dream long cherished was about to become reality: 'And we'll go by steamboat!' But he grew apprehensive when Finlay reviewed the perils of such a river trip: 'You know, Otto, the steamers often blow up. Pirates attack from Cave-in-Rock.' But when Otto said: 'Maybe we better walk down,' his father said: 'Robbers infest that route. Meriwether Lewis got murdered,' and the boy summarized their situation: 'Getting to Texas isn't easy.'

But now Finlay devised a stratagem which would be useful regardless of which route they adopted. They assembled with many furtive moves a pair of homespun trousers for the boy, just a little too large; same for Finlay; long lengths of cloth identical with that used in the trousers; hats for both; cloth identical with the hats; a pair of long, heavy needles, very costly; and most important of all, their total savings were converted from paper and small coins into gold.

When all these items had been smuggled into Bell's Tavern, Finlay placed his son at the door to prevent intrusion, and began sewing. In the lining of the hats, in the waists of the pants and down the seams of the legs, he sewed his new material, imbedding as he went, here and there, the gold coins he had acquired. When he finished, the Macnabs were going to be walking mints, as he demonstrated when Otto's pants and hat were finished: 'Try them on.'

Otto did not like the hat, for he had rarely worn one, and he could scarcely sit down because the coins made the pants far too stiff, but Finlay made him take the pants off, threw them on the floor, and jumped on them repeatedly: 'Now try them!' And the pants were manageable.

The Macnabs now doctored Finlay's garments until they, too, were gold-laden, and then they joined in solemn compact: 'When we reach the Trace we will never mention, not even to each other, where our gold pieces are till we get safe to Texas. Tell nobody . . . nobody.' But Otto had to break the promise immediately, for he said: 'One piece hurts my bottom,' and this, of course, had to be corrected.

They were an attractive pair of emigrants as they crossed the ferry into Kentucky and started the three-hundred-mile hike to Nashville. Finlay was thirty-seven, medium height, blue-eyed, trim of carriage and sharp of mind. He'd had a solid education at St. Andrews and a wealth of practical experience in the United States; he also had that engaging quality which would attract the eye of any unmarried woman looking for a good husband, and his easy manner acquired from working with Irishmen in the old country and with river folk in this made him an amusing addition to any group. Having outgrown those earlier acts of impulsive immaturity that had forced him to flee both Ireland and Baltimore, he now gave the appearance of a man who could work hard and earn his family a decent living, for he was very protective of his son. He was, in brief, the kind of man a nation hopes to get when it throws open its doors to immigrants, and he was typical of many who were beginning to swarm toward Texas.

His seven-year-old son was even more good-looking, with his blond hair peeping from beneath his new cap, his quick step and his thin face that looked almost sallow, for the sun seemed not to affect it. He wore heavy shoes, new homespun pants that came an inch below his knee, a thick woolen shirt and a manly kerchief about his neck. When strangers were with the pair for any length of time they were apt to remark: 'The father has a quick mind. But the lad, he's quiet, always seems to be thinking about something else.'

This was an accurate description of Otto. The confusion caused by his abrupt separation from his mother, the long walk to Cincinnati when he was first seeing the world, the loneliness at night, the fight with the bear, the constant departure of the steamboats he loved, leaving him always on the wharf, the catches of conversation about murders and explosions and sudden hangings—these unchildlike experiences, assaulting him so constantly, had aged him far beyond his years. Save only for the experiences of puberty, he was really a steely-eyed young man better prepared in some ways for the Natchez Trace than his more ebullient father.

But they were both hardened to the road by the time they completed their first two hundred and eighty miles and approached the bustling city of Nashville. There Finlay made a characteristically bold decision: 'What we'll do, Otto, is buy us as many cattle as we can handle, and we'll drove them to Natchez, put them on the boat to New Orleans, and sell them at a huge profit when we get to Texas.' Once this grandiose plan was voiced, no counsel from the experienced travelers in Nashville could dissuade him, and when stockmen pointed out that it was four hundred and eighty miles to Natchez, a right far piece for a man to drove cattle, he snapped: 'Shucks, my grandparents herded cattle clean across Scotland.' When he had left, with his thirty head of good stock, one of the sellers said: 'He'll find that Tennessee ain't Scotland.'

They would need a dog to help them, and Finlay knew they could never find one of those flawless dogs of Scotland and Ireland that could herd sheep and cattle better than a man, but they could find themselves some mongrel who would nip at the heels of strays. Since one dog would be about as good as another, Finlay left the selection to his son, and the boy identified a collie-sized female with the kind of face any boy would love. Her name was Betsy and she was owned by a family with three sons, each of whom had pets galore. When Otto asked, in his quiet voice, his blue eyes shining, what she would cost, the mother cried, almost with relief: 'Take her!' but two of the boys bellowed that she was their dog, whereupon their mother said: 'All right. Five cents.' And for this amount the deal was concluded.

Betsy had a reddish coat, a pointed nose and a set of the swiftest legs in Tennessee, but she also had a devious, calculating mind and was prone to stop and study whenever a command was given, judging whether Finlay really meant what he was saying. If she detected even the slightest hesitation, she ignored him and went her way, but if he shouted 'Damnit, Betsy!' she leaped into action. She was, in certain important ways, brighter than either of the Macnabs and she intended to train them, rather than the other way around.

The one weakness in her plan was that she quickly grew to love Otto, for he would play with her, test her running, wrestle with her, and keep her close to him when they slept on the ground at night. He also fed her, meagerly at times, but no matter how hungry she became between the food stands run by the half-breed Indians or between the deer shot by Finlay, she always sensed that she was getting her fair share of the food; if her stomach was growling with emptiness, so was Otto's.

With their cattle they could make only eight or nine miles a day, but at least they did not have to worry about pasture for their herd, for the Trace provided ample grass. Slowly, slowly they edged their way toward Texas.

Some eighty miles into the Trace they came upon the first of the notable stands, those extremely rude taverns which sometimes had food and sometimes did not, depending on whether the surrounding Indians had brought in their crops. This one was the infamous Grinder's that the Kaintuck in Cincinnati had warned about, a rough cabinlike affair containing two rooms, in one of which travelers could sleep on the floor, and a spacious porch covered by a sloping roof, where overflow travelers also slept on bare boards.

This time the stand had food, and when the broth and meat and potatoes had passed around, the men began to talk of Meriwether Lewis' tragic death twenty years earlier in 1809. 'Mark my words,' a Tennessee man said when the owners of the stand were out of the room, 'someone in this house shot him in the back, and I have a mind who done it.' He looked ominously at the door.

'You seem to forget,' another expert said, 'that he was killed not inside the stand, but outside,' and this evoked such heated discussion that the owners were summoned: 'Was Lewis killed in here or out there?'

'Out there,' a woman said, irritated by the constant bickering over this ancient crime. 'You know that my uncle was tried in court, all legal like, and not a word was proved agin' him. Clean as a baby's breath.'

When the owners were back at work in their part of the house, one man said firmly: 'My uncle knowed the coroner, and the coroner said: "Meriwether Lewis was killed inside the house, because the back of his head was blowed off and his throat was cut." '

Young Otto was repelled by this talk of murder, rejecting it as one more aspect of the rowdy life he did not wish to lead, and he was about to go outside and play with Betsy when the innkeeper said sternly: 'Time for bed!' But when Otto started to call Betsy inside to sleep with him, one of the men growled: 'We don't allow no damned fleabags in here,' so Otto and Betsy, curled together, slept on the porch.

In the morning they had covered about a quarter of a mile when Otto let out a yell. Still unaccustomed to wearing a hat, he had left his at Grinder's, in the sleeping room, with that passel of dangerous men, so without waiting for his father, he and Betsy dashed back and burst into the stand: 'Forgot my hat.' It was on the floor beside a Virginia man, and when Otto reached for it, the man lifted it and found it suspiciously heavy. Hefting it quietly in his left hand so that others could not see, he guessed the cause of its weight.

He made no comment, but before turning the hat over to Otto he accompanied the boy to the porch, where he said in very low tones: 'Excellent idea, but you would be prudent if you kept it close to you.' And he bowed as if delivering a legal opinion to a fellow citizen.

It was not easy walking the Trace. When rains persisted, freshets formed, and what had been easily negotiable gullies became roaring torrents. Then the travelers would have to camp for three or four idle days until the rains and the rivers subsided. Six men might be waiting on the south bank, heading for Nashville, and three on the north, destined for Natchez, and they would call back and forth, but they could not cross. Each year some impatient souls would try, and their bodies would be found far downstream, if found at all.

Now, in the late summer of 1829, the Macnabs with their dog Betsy and their thirty cows were pinned down on the Natchez Trace by a rampaging stream, and it was in this frustrating but not dangerous position that they met their second Kaintuck. He was a huge man, well over six feet, with bright red hair and massive shoulders; he was traveling alone and seemed indifferent to danger, for even though it must have been obvious that he was coming home carrying the profit from his trip, bandits had learned not to molest the Kaintucks, who observed one governing rule: 'If'n he makes one suspicious move, shoot him.'

This Kaintuck, bearded, scowling and irritable, was on his way north to pick up another boat in Cincinnati or Pittsburgh, and the impassable flood infuriated him.

'What the hell you doin' with them cattle?' were the first words he hurled across the treacherous stream.

'Taking them to Texas,' Finlay shouted back.

'You're a goddamned fool to try it.' That ended that conversation, for Finlay had no desire to defend his operation to a stranger. But as night was settling, the Kaintuck bellowed: 'What's the name of your dog, son?'

'Betsy.'

'That's a damned good name and she looks to be a damned good dog.'

'She is. She helps us.'

'I'll wager you need her, with all them cows.'

'We couldn't move without her.'

'I'll bet you're a big help, too.'

'I try to be.'

That was the beginning of Otto Macnab's fascination with the Kaintuck. During the two tedious days that followed, with the Macnabs only about eighteen feet from the huge man, Otto and he conversed on many subjects.

'Study this stream, son. Looks like a man could jump acrost it, and they say they's a man in Natchez that could. Big nigger with legs like oak trees. But don't never try it, son. Because one slip and they pick your bones up ten miles downstream.'

'Where do you live?' Otto's high voice shouted across the leaping wavelets.

'Goddamnedest place you ever seen. A real hog wallow.'

'Why are you going there?'

'Because it's home.'

'That sounds dumb.'

'It is dumb, but it's home.'

'How's your fire?'

'A fire's always in trouble. With wet sticks, particular.'

'Ours is all right.'

'That's because you ain't dumb, and I am.'

The two talked as if they were equals, which in a way they were, for the big man had ended his education at the level Otto was beginning his, and the more they talked the more they liked each other. The Kaintuck shouted that he'd had a wife, and a pretty good one, but she had died in childbirth: 'You know what that means, son?'

Otto may have been wise beyond his years, but there were certain important things he did not know, and now he faced one of them. Biting his lip and staring at the Kaintuck, he said: 'I think so.'

'Well, ask your father.'

'You tell me.'

'That ain't my prerogative.'

'What's a prerogative?'

'Right, son. Some things is right, some ain't. Ask your father.'

When Otto did he received a totally evasive answer, and it occurred to him that the Kaintuck would not have answered that way, but he sensed that he was caught in a mystery that was not going to be unraveled there by the pounding flood.

In late afternoon of the third day it became apparent that the flood was going to subside during the night and that passage would then be possible, but before it got dark the Kaintuck launched one more conversation.

'What's your name, mister?'

'Macnab, Finlay—and the boy's Otto.'

'That's Scottish, no?'

'You're the first person I've met who didn't call me Scotch.' No comment. 'What's your name?'

'Zave.'

'Zave!' Otto cried. 'What kind of name is that?'

'Best in the world. Named after one of the great saints. Francis Xavier.'

A hush fell over the subsiding stream, and after a long while Macnab asked: 'Is it that you're papist?'

'Aye, but I never force it.'

Macnab said no more. He felt uncomfortable sharing the wilderness with a papist, the more so because when he reached Texas there was bound to be unpleasantness over the matter of forced conversion, fraudulent though Father Clooney's were said to be. He had seen enough of the Protestantism-papism fight in Ireland and he wished for none in the forests of Mississippi.

But as the darkness lowered and shadows crept from the trees like black panthers come to steal the cattle, the Kaintuck spoke again: 'Macnab, you need help with them cattle.' No comment. 'Else you'll never get them to Natchez.' No comment. 'And I was wonderin' if maybe when the creek lowers . . . and we cross . . .'

'What?' It was a child's voice, trembling with excitement.

'I was wonderin' if maybe we could form partners.'

'Oh, Poppa!' The boy gave a wild cry of delight and started to dance about, then grasped his father's hands: 'Oh, it would be so . . .' The boy could not frame his thoughts, and added lamely: 'It would be so welcome.'

'How about it, Macnab?'

'Poppa, Poppa, yes!' For three wet days Otto had watched the big man across the swollen stream and each new thing he saw increased his attachment to the wild Kaintuck. He was strong. He had violent manners when necessary. He could laugh and make jokes at himself. And obviously he had grown to like Otto.

'Where you really from, Zave?' The voice was adult and suspicious.

'Like I said, small town in Kaintucky. Piss-poor place.'

'You mind to settle in Texas?'

'From what you and the boy said, might as well.'

A world of meaning was carried in this brief, elliptical sentence: the conclusions of a man without a home, without prospects, without any visible or sensible direction in his life. If what Macnab said about the glories of Texas and the twenty thousand acres of choice land was true, what better?

Now, across the muddy waters, the Kaintuck pleaded: 'I ain't got no home, really. I ain't got nothin' much but down the river, up the river, and if you really got all that land, I could be mighty useful.' No comment. 'Besides, Mr. Macnab, you ain't goin' to get them cattle to Natchez with just the boy to help.'

'Please, Poppa, please.'

'What's your full name, Zave?'

'Francis Xavier Campbell.'

Good God! In the middle of the Mississippi wilderness a traitorous Campbell from the Moor of Rannoch had tracked down a Macnab of Glen Lyon, and as in the ancient days, plotted his murder. 'Campbell is a forbidden name,' Finlay Macnab cried in the darkness. 'Ever since Glencoe.'

'I know Glencoe,' the voice from the other side said, 'but that was a long time ago. I am Campbell from Hopkinsville, not from Glencoe, and I seek to join with you.'

'Please!' came the boy's voice, but in the night Finlay warned his son about the infamous behavior of the Campbells at Glencoe: 'I can hear my grandfather's voice: "Wherever, whenever you meet a Campbell, expect treachery." Across that stream waits a Campbell.' And through the long dark hours Finlay kept watch on his ancestral enemy, as if the dreadful crime at Glencoe had marked with blood-guilt every Campbell who would come along thereafter.

At dawn, as Finlay expected, big Zave Campbell gathered his muddy possessions, stepped down into the receding stream, and came directly toward the two Macnabs. Finlay, preparing to fight if necessary, shouted: 'Come no more!'

But Otto, seeing in Zave a needed companion, cried: 'We want your help!' and in that fragile moment he settled the argument, for he ran and leaped into Campbell's arms.

'Come with us, Zave!' he cried, and from then on, it was four who went down the Trace: Finlay Macnab in command; Otto watching and listening; Zave Campbell, with a home at last; and the dog Betsy, terrified of the big man's commands. Under his tutelage she became twice the shepherd's companion she had been before, for when he told her to 'Git!' she got.

From their meeting at the flood they faced two hundred miles to Natchez, and often as they walked—ten miles a day now—Zave complained: 'Hell, I walked up this whole distance and now I'm walkin' down.'

'You asked to come,' Finlay growled, and each day during the first ten he kept close watch on Campbell, waiting for the sign that would betray the intended treachery. As the eleventh day waned he began to perspire so heavily that Otto asked: 'Are you sick, Poppa?' and he replied: 'I sure am. Don't you remember that it was on the eleventh night at Glencoe that the Campbells cut the throats of the Macdonalds?' Otto said: 'Last time you told me they shot them,' and Finlay snapped: 'What difference?'

When the sun set, Finlay refused to go to sleep, satisfied that once he closed his eyes this Campbell would cut his throat; instead, he sat against a tree, rifle across his knees, and when Otto rolled over at midnight and opened his eyes, there his father waited. They both looked a few feet away to where Zave snored easily, and when the boy arose at dawn nothing had changed.

Campbell was never told of the night-long vigil, but on the twelfth day Finlay astonished everyone by blurting out: 'Zave, nobody herds cattle better than you. When we reach Texas and get our land, you can have your share. You earned it.'

'You can build your barn right next to ours,' Otto said.

'You any idea how big twenty thousand acres is, son?' With a twig as chalk and a sandy bank as blackboard, Zave lined it out: 'Six hundred forty acres to a square mile. Six-forty into twenty thousand, that's thirty-five, thirty-six more or less square miles. That means six miles to a side. So my barn ain't goin' to be very close to your barn.'

That day he showed Otto just how far six miles was going to be: 'Remember this little stream, way back here. I'll reckon the miles as we drive the cattle, but you keep in mind how far away this stream is,' and as they walked off the miles the boy gained his first sense of how vast things in Texas were going to be. He had thought of his future home as a kind of farm; the way Zave explained it, the place would be an empire.

Zave then took in hand Otto's real education: 'I'm surprised you cain't shoot proper. I was your age, I could hit me a sparrow.' Using his own long rifle, he taught the boy the tricks of hunting, especially the art of rapid loading: 'Cain't never tell when that second shot, fired prompt, is goin' to turn the trick.' He drilled Otto in firing accurately, then reloading at finger-numbing speed: 'You got to do it in rhythm, like a dance. And always in the same order. Prop your gun. Right hand, grab your powder horn and pour in just enough. Right hand again, grab the wadding. Left hand, take the ramrod from its place, jam it down the muzzle, tamp down the wadding. Left hand again, ball from the pouch, slide it in. Right hand, take the percussion cap and fix it. Both hands, fire!'

When Otto began dropping birds and squirrels out of trees and reloading instantly for the next shot, Zave was ecstatic: 'Macnab! I think we got us a real man on our hands.'

The hunting experience that Otto would remember longest, however, came early one morning when he was following a squirrel as it leaped through the trees. From the north came a soft whirring sound which increased until it was a dull persistent thunder, and when he looked up he saw coming toward him more birds than he had ever imagined; the sky was dark with them, and as they came in always-increasing numbers, the morning sun was blanketed and a kind of twilight fell over the earth. All morning they came, a flock so great it must have covered entire counties and even large parts of states, an incredible flight of birds.

'Passenger pigeons,' Zave said. 'Always have flown that way, always will.' Once when the birds were low overhead he fired a musket at them, and they flew in such packed formation that he brought down eleven, and the eating was good.

On they went, two Macnabs, a Campbell and a dog, droving cattle through lonely and forlorn land as their ancestors had done for centuries in the Highlands of Scotland, and at last they arrived in Natchez, that French-Spanish-English-American town of great beauty perched high on its hill above the Mississippi, with its squalid row of half a dozen mean streets down on the flats, where the great boats docked, where the saloons never closed, where boatmen from Kentucky and Tennessee lost in an hour what they had slaved four months to earn.

As they drove their cattle along the main streets, lined with expensive and glamorous houses, Otto knew instinctively that he and his companions were not intended to stop there; threatening stares of passers-by in costly clothes told him that, but he was not prepared for what he found when Finlay and Zave herded their cattle down the steep streets leading to the waterfront. Now they passed into an entirely different world—of sweating black porters, shouting women, steamboats with their engines banked being warped into position, side by side, and bands of musicians playing music endlessly. Natchez-under-the-Hill was its own town of several thousand, and here the commerce of the great river basins—Ohio, Missouri, Mississippi—came temporarily to rest in huge warehouses that groaned with the produce of America.

It was an exciting place, a steaming hodge-podge of black and white, of Virginian and New Yorker, of buyer and seller, of slave and free, and many a man who now owned one of the big white-pillared houses on the hill, with many servants proclaiming his wealth, had started buying fish and timber on the wharfs.

But it was also a frightening place, with knives flashing in the dark, and Zave Campbell showed young Otto the spot where one of the greatest knife fighters of them all, Jim Bowie of Tennessee, had demonstrated his ferocious skill. 'Bowie had this fierce knife and he allowed hisse'f to be tied to a log, and his enemy, he was lashed down too, and there they fought it out, slashin' and duckin', and Bowie cut his man to shreds.'

'What did he do then?'

'He asked his brother Rezin to make him an even bigger knife. Foot and a half long, with a heavy guard protectin' the handle from the blade.'

'Why did he do that?'

'He said: "When you're strapped to a log, you cain't have a knife that's too long." '

'Can I see him? Where is he now?'

'Who knows? They run him out of Tennessee.'

When it came time to arrange for the cattle to move south toward New Orleans, Macnab discovered two painful truths: the cost of taking them by steamboat was prohibitive, and he had wasted his energies bringing them down from Nashville. 'Man,' he was told, 'we find all the cattle we need in New Orleans. They bring 'em in from everywhere.' And when Finlay pointed out that he intended to take them on to Texas, the speaker guffawed: 'Hector, come here and tell the man!'

Hector was a dumpy fellow in his forties. He had been to Texas and proposed to return as soon as the two boilers for his sawmill reached Natchez from Pittsburgh, where they had been bolted together and caulked. 'Cattle to Texas?' he said. 'That's the craziest thing I ever heerd of. Cattle run free all over Texas, millions of 'em. I hire two Mexicans to keep the damned things off'n my place.'

'Are you telling the truth?'

'Come here, Buster.' The sawmill man called everyone Buster, and when he had Finlay seated on one of the pilings of a wharf he explained: 'Cattle been breedin' free in Texas since the Creation, or as some say, since the Spaniards arrove. Cattle everywhere. Big . . . huge horns . . . best eatin' beef God ever made, and, Buster, strike me dead if they ain't all free. You just go out with your lasso . . .'

'What's a lasso?'

'Mexican-style rope. You form it in a loop, and you won't believe me when I tell you what a tricky hand can do with that loop.'

'It's hard to believe what you say.'

'Texas is different, Buster, and you got to accept it on faith. If you carry them cattle on to Texas, all you can do is give 'em away. You sure as hell cain't sell 'em.'

'What should I do?'

'I'd sell 'em right here. As beef.'

'They won't bring what I paid for them in Nashville.' He spat. 'And all that trouble on the Trace.'

The sawmill man clapped him on the shoulder: 'Buster, sometimes plans go sour. They promised me, solemn, that my boilers would be here six months ago. I'm still waitin' and I'm still payin' for my room, such as it is.'

Macnab and Campbell spent five days trying to reach the best deal on the cattle, and Otto was surprised one afternoon to hear them telling a prospective customer that they had thirty-three head to sell, for he knew that his father had left Nashville with thirty and had sold two to stands along the Trace that needed beef. There should be twenty-eight for sale, but what he did not know was that it was physically and morally impossible for a Macnab or a Campbell to pass through territory containing cattle without enlarging his herd. By old established practices, they had acquired an additional five head.

In the end they had to sell at a severe loss, but the transaction was not without its benefits, because the buyer was a man who ran a repair shop for steamboats, a kind of inland ships' chandlery, and when through casual conversation he discovered how experienced Finlay was in such matters, he pressed him to accept a job serving the big riverboats. At first Finlay demurred, so the man said: 'Help me and I'll double the price I offered for your beef.'

This was too gratifying for a trader like Macnab to refuse, for as he explained to Campbell: 'We make a neat profit on the animals, and we can save money for our start in Texas.' He went back to the man and said: 'I'll take the job, but you must employ my friend Campbell, too. He's a mighty worker.'

'I've seen Campbell on other trips. He eats big and works little.' He would not hire the big Kaintuck, but Macnab did find Zave a job sweeping out a saloon, and when the three settled in to Natchez-under-the-Hill as if it had always been their home, Texas grew farther away.

The only problem was Otto. He was eight now, not much taller than before, and the long tradition of the Macnabs required him to get started on his education, but schools were not a major feature of Under-the-Hill. There were some on the upper level, but it was difficult to get to them, and when Finlay inquired, he was told quite bluntly: 'We do not look kindly upon boys from Under.'

There was, however, a woman on the lower level, now married to a roustabout, who had once taught school in the rowdy town of Paducah when it was still called Pekin, and she said that she could teach Otto reading, writing and numbers up to the rule of three. She was a mournful lady, spending much of each class telling the boy of her more fortunate days in Memphis, where her father sold furniture and coffins, but she developed a real liking for the lad and gave him a rather better education than he might have received in the more fashionable classrooms of the upper level.

It was curious, Otto thought, that the two towns were so separate; a person could live his entire life in one, it seemed, without ever venturing into the other. Under-the-Hill was the bigger, the more flourishing and also much the wilder, but just as he had discovered on the long walk through Maryland that civilization could consist of a cabin in the wilderness throwing light and comfort into the darkness, so now he knew where the good life lay in Natchez: it thrived in those big, clean, white houses atop the hill, and whenever they had the chance, he and Zave would climb the steep streets and walk aimlessly beneath the arching trees, looking at the mansions.

'You ain't to think, son, that everybody in there is happy,' Zave cautioned, and he showed Otto two especially fine houses from which a boy and a girl, desperately and hopelessly in love, had come to Under-the-Hill to commit suicide. And he also knew which big one had contained the man who had run away to Pittsburgh, abandoning his wife and two daughters.

'My father ran—'

'Don't tell me about it!' Campbell thundered, and Otto pondered these complexities.

The year 1830 passed, with Finlay earning substantial wages on the waterfront and with Zave Campbell promoted to bartender, where he could steal from both his boss and his patrons. The trio was prospering financially, but Otto was not advancing in much else, for he had mastered about as much learning as the Paducah woman could dispense and was beginning to lose interest. Also, he was reaching the age when circumstances might throw him in with the rowdy urchins who pestered ship captains when their boats were tied up, and Otto himself worried about this, because everything he had so far observed inclined him toward an orderly life away from the excesses of Under-the-Hill. In that whirlpool even children witnessed murders and shanghaiings and young women committing suicide and endless brawls, and he had no taste for such a life. At age nine he had become more than cautious; he was a little Scots-German conservative set so firmly in his ways that they would probably last a lifetime.

One aspect of life Under-the-Hill he could not adjust to: the presence of so many women. It occurred to him as he looked back upon his travels that he and Finlay, and even Campbell, had always moved where there were no women; on the trails, along the waterfront, in the stands of the Trace, it had been a man's world. Even in settled Cincinnati when they talked with people who had been in Texas, they had met only one woman, the Arkansas lady who had fled.

But now they were surrounded by young women, and he perceived that even tough men like his father and Zave sometimes wanted to be with them, those very pretty girls with only first names, and although he did not understand fully, he knew it must be all right. What irritated him, though, was that the girls sometimes showed as much interest in him as they did in Zave and his father, pampering him and petting him and offering to cut his hair. They were, he realized, doing this so as to impress Finlay and Zave that they were the motherly type, and he grew quite sick of the attention.

But his irritation was forgotten whenever Zave and one of the young women from the saloon took him down to the waterfront, with rifles to shoot at objects floating down the Mississippi. Then he liked it if Zave's girl cheered when he hit a bottle and Zave did not, or when with two quick shots made possible by adroit reloading he shattered two bottles.

'You're a little sharpshooter,' a girl said one day as she kissed him, and this he did not protest.

That night he was startled when he overheard his father proposing to a new arrival from Pennsylvania that the man purchase his Texas scrip: 'Partner, I'll sell you this for half what I paid, and you can see the figures right here. Twenty thousand acres, one thousand good American dollars.' The newcomer said he would think it over, carefully, for his heart was set on Texas, and he visualized the twenty thousand acres in terms of the ultra-rich farmland of Lancaster County. He might never find such a bargain again.

Otto was distraught by his father's proposal, and he discussed it with both his teacher and Zave, and they, too, were appalled. The Paducah woman went boldly to Macnab and said: 'You have a treasure in your son Otto. Don't waste him in this sewer.'

'You're doing well here. I'm doing well.'

'I have no choice. You do.'

'A hundred men have started Under-the-Hill and moved up. And I'm to be the hundred and first. You watch.'

'And what in hell will you have if you do move up? Take your kid to Texas and make him a man. And take that worthless Campbell with you.'

Zave was even more insistent: 'Finlay, I'm workin' here only to save money to get to Texas. This is the cesspool of the world. I just been waitin' for you to say the word.'

'You've got a good job, Zave. I got a good job.'

'And Otto, he's got nothin'. He should be on a horse, on open land . . . and so should you and me.'

One night, after work, Finlay broached the subject with his son. They were living in one room over Zave's saloon, where the accumulation of eighteen rootless months lay scattered about. 'I think, Otto, that in another year we'll have enough money to buy a house on top. A hardware store, or maybe a general one like we had in Baltimore, with a good German bakery.'

'People on top ain't always happy,' Otto said. 'Sometimes they do terrible things.'

'Where'd you hear that?'

'Zave told me. He showed me where.'

'What would you like to do?'

Almost defensively the boy drew Betsy to him, cradling her head in his lap, for he was afraid to expose his true longings, but under his father's pressuring he blurted out like the little boy he still was: 'I'd like to get aboard one of those steamboats, and stay aboard when the whistle blows, and just sail and sail, and then maybe have a horse on a great big farm where me and Betsy can run forever.'

Next morning the man from Pennsylvania came to Macnab's shop and said he'd take the scrip, but Finlay said quietly: 'Yesterday it was for sale. Today it ain't. My son wants it.'

He never looked back. After giving his employer notice and receiving from him an unexpected bonus, he told Campbell to quit his job at the saloon, paid the teacher more than she expected, and bought three passages on the New Orleans steamer *Clara Murphy,* which would be putting in to Natchez on Thursday morning, 25 August 1831, on its way south from St. Louis.

Otto was elated that his long-delayed dream of steaming down the river was at last coming true, and while Finlay and Campbell slept amidst the deck cargo, he and Betsy walked back and forth, surveying the mystery of this great river. It was a trip into wonderland, and he never tired of watching strange happenings along the shore: slaves shifting bales of cotton, mules dragging a damaged boat ashore, freshly cut timbers piled sky-high. That morning, still unwilling to sleep lest he miss some dramatic scene, he imagined himself as captain maneuvering the *Clara Murphy* past treacherous sandbars, docking her at a plantation wharf where white women carrying umbrellas to protect them from the sun strolled aboard. Twice he chanted with the sweating black crew as they worked the boat, and he tried to hide his pleasure when they called him 'our little riverman.' He was prepared, at the end of that first glorious day, to be a Mississippi man for the remainder of his life.

On this trip he saw the richness of Louisiana, for it seemed that all the wealth of the state was crowded along the shores of the river, and he perceived that families acquired fine homes with vast lawns only when they owned many slaves. Not once on this long, revealing trip did it occur to him that the slaves might have rights of their own or that their condition in 1831 could be temporary. They were black, different in all respects, and obligated to serve their masters.

New Orleans was totally different from Cincinnati and Natchez. It exuded both prosperity and pleasure and had a relaxed spirit the other towns lacked. It was obviously very old, with strong French and Spanish accents bespeaking earlier settlers, and the mighty levees, raised high to keep the Mississippi out of the streets and homes, awed and impressed Otto. Also, there was a bustle about the city which delighted the boy, and he perceived that whereas the waterfront of Natchez had been unhealthy and unclean, that of New Orleans was vibrant and almost self-policing, as if the excesses tolerated in Under-the-Hill would be forbidden here.

And there was burgeoning commercial activity. In one afternoon of casual exploration among the shippers his father was offered two jobs, but Finlay had learned from his Natchez experience not to take them lest he become entangled permanently in something he intended to engage in only temporarily. 'Very well,' one trader with a French name said expansively. 'You're the boss. But when you get to Texas and start your plantation, remember me. Louis Ferry, New Orleans. I'll buy your mules, your cotton, your timber.'

'Do all those come from Texas?'

'Look at my yards. I get three parts from Louisiana, seven parts from Texas.'

'How do I get my produce here?'

'Ships run all the time, but they're expensive. Best way is with mules, herd them up and drove them in. Takes time but it costs nothing.'

'You keep speaking about mules. Don't you accept horses?'

'Rich people buy horses, now and then. U. S. Army buys mules all the time.'

He wrote out his name and address for Macnab, and added: 'I've got a better idea. Put together a big herd of mules, bring them in for a good profit, and then stay with me as my manager of the Texas trade.'

'Where would I find the money to get the mules?'

Ferry broke into laughter: 'Man, in Texas the horses run wild. Mustangs they call them. Thousands, thousands—you just go out and rope them and they're yours.'

'Yes, but where do I get the mules?'

'Man, you buy yourself a strong jackass, throw him in with the mares, and let him work himself to death.'

'What happens to the male horses?'

'You drive them to New Orleans. I can always use a few.' When Finlay looked dubious, Ferry cried: 'You ever see a Texas mustang? I got a yard full of them and wish I had a hundred more.' He led Macnab to a corral, where for the first time Finlay saw the powerful little horses of the Texas range, much smaller than he had expected, much finer-looking than he had supposed a small horse could be.

'They run wild?' He studied them carefully, exercising his eye trained among the great horses of Ireland, then said: 'They told me in Natchez that cattle run wild too.'

Ferry clapped him vigorously on the shoulder: 'In Texas everything runs wild. You just reach out and grab.'

'Why aren't you in Texas?'

'Because it's a wilderness. Not a decent place to eat in the whole damned province. And besides, it's a Mexican wilderness, and who wants to live in a country that can't govern itself?'

'Some Americans seem to like it.'

'Right! Right! And if I was that kind of American, I might like it too.'

'What kind of American are you speaking of?'

'An American like you. Energy, courage, stars in your eyes . . . and willingness to live alone. Because, man, Texas is empty. Just wild cattle and untamed horses.'

As he said this, the young man who had brought the mustangs to New Orleans appeared in the corral, and as soon as Otto saw him, he was captivated, for the herdsman was the first Mexican he had met. He was in his mid-twenties, whip-thin, dark-skinned, and clad in the distinctive uniform of the range: tight blue pants marked by a tiny white stripe, bandanna, big hat, boots and spurs. To Otto he looked the way a Texan should.

'Show them how you ride,' Ferry ordered, and with just a slight flare of resentment at being spoken to as if he were a peasant, the young man flicked the brim of his hat almost insolently, but then smiled warmly at Otto: 'Is the young man good with the horse?'

'I can ride,' Otto said, and the young Mexican whistled to one of his assistants: 'Manuel, tráenos dos caballos buenos!'

From a hitching rail near the corral, Manuel untied two horses already saddled, and deftly the young man lifted himself onto the larger one, indicating that Otto should mount his, which the boy did rather clumsily.

The Mexican then began to canter about the stable area, shouting to Otto: 'Follow me!' and a delightful comedy ensued, for the Mexican rode with skill, swinging and swaying with the motion of his horse like a practiced professional, while the boy tried energetically to keep up, slipping and sliding and nearly falling from his mount. But he did hold on, grabbing his horse's mane when necessary.

Ferry, Finlay and Campbell applauded the exhibition, whereupon the Mexican rider broke loose from Otto's comical trailing to perform a series of beautiful feats, ending with a full gallop at Campbell, bringing his steed to a halt a few inches from the Kaintuck's toes.

'The boy could learn to ride,' he said as he dismounted, and when Otto came up awkwardly, the Mexican helped him dismount and asked: 'Son, you want to ride back to Texas with me? And help me bring another remuda up for Don Louis?'

'Oh!' Otto cried with enthusiasm. 'That would be wonderful!'

'Who is this young horseman?' the senior Macnab asked, and as the rider continued talking with Otto, Ferry said: 'Young Mexican from Victoria. South Texas. Absolutely trustworthy. What he says he'll do he does.'

'He brought you all these animals?'

'He did.'

'Where did he get them?'

'In this business you never ask.'

'What's your name, young fellow?' Macnab asked.

'Garza,' the rider said, smiling. 'Benito Garza.' He pronounced each syllable carefully, drawing it out in the Mexican way: 'Beh-nee-to Gar-tsah,' with exaggerated accent on the *nee* and *Gar*. Having introduced himself verbally, he did so symbolically with another flick of his finger against the brim of his big hat, and with that, he disappeared into the stables.

At the inn where they were staying prior to arranging passage to their new lands, the Macnabs and Campbell met two authentic residents of Texas, well-educated plantation owners who had come to New Orleans to arrange for the sale of their products on a regular basis. After they had reached an understanding with Louis Ferry, whom they lauded as the best man in the business, they chatted about aspects of their new home:

'We have great men in Texas, equal of any in Massachusetts or Virginia. We plan to erect a notable state with all the advantages of South Carolina or Georgia. There's a spaciousness to our view. We can see clear to the Pacific Ocean. And a nobility to our minds, because we're determined to build a new society . . .

'Everything is of a vast dimension and we need men with vast potential to help us achieve what we've planned. Weaklings will be erased, by the climate and the distance if by nothing else, but the strong will find themselves growing even stronger. Any young man of promise who doesn't catch the first boat to Texas is an idiot . . .'

When Finlay raised several questions about things that disturbed him, the two men laughed them off: 'The Frenchman said the food was inedible? He's right. Abominable. But it can only get better. The Arkansas woman fled because of loneliness? She was surely right. My nearest neighbor is forty miles away, and I don't want him any closer because then he'd be on my land.'

But when Finlay voiced serious doubts about the instability of the Mexican government, he noticed that the men became evasive, and he was about to find out whether they favored the ultimate incorporation of Texas into the American Union when the men changed the subject dramatically. The leader, spreading his hands on the table, asked energetically: 'And where do you propose settling?'

'I was about to ask your advice.'

'Nacogdoches up here. Victoria down here. Both places wonderful for an energetic man, which I take you to be. But any reasonable place in between is just as good.'

'Where are you?'

'I'm down here at the mouth of the Brazos River. My brother-in-law, he's up here at Nacogdoches.'

'Where should I go?'

'Wherever the ship deposits you. Landing in Texas is not easy. Sometimes the ship can make one spot, sometimes another. How much land you taking up?'

'I've bought myself twenty thousand acres.'

One of the men whistled: 'That's a mighty spread. How'd you hook it?'

Proudly Macnab opened his papers, showing the men his authority for the occupation of twenty thousand acres, as approved by the Mexican government, in any likely area. The men studied the papers, then looked at each other and said nothing. Pushing the documents back to Macnab, they changed the subject to shipping.

'What you must do is catch a steamboat that goes to the mouth of the Mississippi. A sailing ship will be waiting there to carry you to Texas.'

'Why don't the steamboats go all the way?'

'They've tried it. Too many wrecks. It's never easy to enter Texas.'

'Where should I head for?'

'We told you. Wherever the ship lands you. It's all good.'

When Finlay was back in his room he pondered the suspicious manner in which the men had reacted to his papers, and he began to worry that his documents might be faulty, so well after midnight he ascertained where the men were sleeping and went to their room, knocking loudly until one of the men opened the door. 'I apologize, but this is terribly important to me. Is something wrong with my papers?'

'No, no! They're in good shape.' The man tried to close the door, but Finlay kept it open.

'They're not, and I saw it clearly in your eyes when you looked at them. You must tell me.'

There was no light in the room, but the man propped open the door and invited Macnab to sit on his bed while he sat on the bed of his brother-in-law. Painfully, hesitantly they told Macnab the truth: 'Your papers are a fraud. We see it all the time.'

'You mean . . .'

'No standing at all in Mexico. Land isn't given out that way. That traveler in the next room without a single sheet of paper has as good a chance as you of getting land in Texas.'

'How can such a thing be allowed?'

'Two different countries. Your fake company is in the United States. The land is in Mexico.'

'My God! A thousand dollars!' In anguish Macnab leaped from the bed.

'Completely lost,' the man said. But when Macnab groaned, the men both spoke in rushes of encouraging words.

'I didn't mean that everything is lost.'

'You can still get land, excellent land, but never twenty thousand acres.'

'You get it free . . . absolutely free.'

After this burst of warm reassurance, one of the men pressed Finlay to sit back down, then patiently helped as his brother-in-law explained the situation:

> 'You land in Texas wherever the ship drops you, and you establish contact with the Mexican officials. Being Scotch, I suppose you're Protestant, so you volunteer to convert to Catholicism. We're both Catholics,

legally, but we're really Baptists. Conversion entitles you to one thousand acres of land, maybe a little more because of your son. The big fellow with you, he can get the same.

'If you're lucky enough to be unmarried and can find a Mexican girl to marry, you could very well get yourself a league-and-a-labor, and that's a lot of land. Or you could buy land from someone like the two of us who already has his league-and-labor . . . I have three, he has two. We have none for sale, but it goes for about twenty cents an acre and it can be very good land. Maybe fifty cents for bottomland along the river, and I'd advise you to get some of that. Or you can apply to one of the great empresarios who already have legal title to enormous reaches of land, and you can get that for almost nothing, and sometimes for nothing at all, because they want settlers.

'I got mine in three different ways. Mexican government gave me some. I bought some. And Stephen Austin, as fine a man as you'll ever meet, he was so anxious to get settlers on his properties that he gave me a large plot. Originally one bit here, one bit up here and one bit way down there. But I traded even till I had them side by side, and now I have fifteen thousand acres for a little over two thousand dollars. You can do the same.'

The man on the bed asked in the darkness: 'Are you married, Macnab?' and after the slightest hesitation Finlay replied: 'No.' They were pleased at this information, for it meant that if all else failed, he could marry a Mexican woman and get a quadruple portion.

'Why do they make it so complicated?' he asked.

'With Mexicans, nothing is ever allowed to be simple.'

A rickety old steamboat carried thirty American adults, nine children and twenty-two slaves down the tortuously winding Mississippi south of New Orleans. Passengers marveled as they crept past beautiful moss-hung plantations of the lesser sort, for as a deckhand explained: 'If'n they got money, they has a plantation above New Orleans, not below.' Here the air hung heavy and insects droned in the heat as travelers prayed for some vagrant breeze to slip in from the Gulf of Mexico. Entire sections of land became swamps inhabited only by birds and alligators, swamps interminable, until at last the steamboat reached the strangest termination of any of the world's major rivers: a bewildering morass of passes seeking the Gulf, of blind alleys leading only to more swampland. Often it was impossible to determine whether the area ahead was fresh-water river, or salt-water Gulf, or firm land, or simply more weed-grown swamp.

'How can he tell his way?' Otto asked one of the deckhands.

'By smell.'

The answer was not entirely frivolous, for as the great river died, the smell of the vast, free Gulf intruded, and soon Otto himself could detect the larger body of water.

As soon as the vessel waiting in the Gulf became aware of the approaching steamer, its captain fired a small cannon to signify that all was in readiness, and Otto, seeing for the first time an ocean-going craft, shouted: 'There she is!' These last days had been a journey through a primeval wonderland, more challenging by far than that along the river to the north of New Orleans, and to see the sloop *Carthaginian* waiting motionless at the end of the passage was like seeing a light in the forest.

As they threw ropes to the steamer, sailors shouted the good news: 'We sail for Galveston!' and travelers who had hoped to make that important landing cheered. Fare to Texas would be twenty-one dollars total, five paid to the steamboat, sixteen to the sail-borne sloop. But no transfer from one craft to another was ever made easily, no matter how gentle the sea, and now when the steamboat dipped slightly, the sloop lifted, and contrariwise. Shins were barked and baggage imperiled, but finally the adults were safe aboard the vessel, the children could be handed across, and the slaves were able to follow. The returning steamboat, having picked up passengers for New Orleans, blew its whistle three times in farewell. The emigrants cheered. And the trip across the Gulf was begun, with the passengers having only the slightest comprehension of their destination.

'We're making for Galveston,' an officer explained, 'but if the weather's bad, we may have to put in at Matagorda Bay.'

Galveston was some four hundred miles, almost due west, and since there was a sharp breeze from the southeast, the ship could make four knots, or about one hundred and ten land miles a day. 'The trip won't require more than four days,' the officer assured the passengers, 'and I doubt that it will be rough.'

Otto loved the swaying of the ship, and whereas some of the passengers experienced a slight seasickness, he roamed everywhere and ate large quantities of everything. It was a holiday for him, but some of the travelers were agitated by the uncertainty of destination: 'We hoped to put in at Matagorda. Our people are there.'

'You can walk from Galveston to Matagorda,' a sailor said easily, as if the trip were a matter of hours.

'Why can't we go direct to Matagorda?'

'Because on this passage we never know. I don't even know if'n we'll be able to land in Galveston.'

'What kind of ship is this?' one man growled.

'It ain't the ship. It's Texas,' and the sailor outlined the problem:

'Texas is a great land, I'm sure. It's got ever'thin' a man might want—free land, free cattle, beautiful rivers, and mountains too, I hear, in the west. But one thing it ain't got is a safe harbor. None.

'It has fine big bays, best in the world. Galveston, Matagorda, Corpus, Laguna Madre. I been in 'em all, and they ain't none better. Only one thing wrong with 'em. No way you can get into 'em. God made Hisse'f these perfect bays, then guarded them with strings of sandbars, half-assed islands, marshes, and ever' other kind of impediment you could imagine.

'This is maybe the most dangerous coastline in the whole damned world. Look at the wrecks we'll see when we try to get into one of them bays. Wrecks everywhere. First steamboat tried it, wrecked. Next steamboat, went aground, and you'll see it rottin' there if'n we're driven to Matagorda. The coast of Texas is hell in salt water.'

The weather remained good, the sloop did make for Galveston, and the same sailor came back with one bit of comforting news: 'Maybe I overdone it. This is a mighty tough coast, as you'll see, but one worry we don't have. They ain't no beetlin' rocks stacked ashore. And they ain't none hidin' submerged to rip out your bottom. Anythin' you hit is soft sand.' But he returned a few minutes later with a correction: 'Of course, most of the wrecks you'll see did just that. They hit soft sand, held fast, and then turned over.' Otto noticed that he never said what happened to the passengers.

But as the *Carthaginian* neared Galveston toward the close of the fourth day, a strong northerly wind blew out from shore, creating such large waves that as the sun sank, the captain had to announce: 'Waves get that high, takes them days to subside.'

'Can't we push through?' asked a man whose home ashore was almost visible.

'Look at the last ship that tried,' the captain replied, and off to starboard, rocking back and forth in the grasping sands, a sailing ship of some size was slowly being broken to pieces. On her stern Otto read: SKYLARK NEW ORLEANS.

'It'll have to be Matagorda Bay,' the captain said, and only a few daring souls whose hearts had been set on Galveston demurred, for the others realized that any attempt to land there would be suicidal.

That night, as the ship made its way southwest through calmer seas to the alternate landing, Otto remained topside, running with his dog along the deserted decks, while his father and Zave Campbell remained below at their evening meal. When they were finished, the two men pushed back their plates and lingered in a corner of the cabin, piecing together a rough assessment of their fellow passengers: 'Twenty-three families, but only seven wives. What happened to the other sixteen? Did they all die?'

Not at all. The twenty-three men represented a true cross section of those coming into Texas at this time. Seven were married and with their wives along; four were legitimate widowers eager to launch new lives; three had never been married and looked forward to finding women in Texas, American or Mexican no matter. The nine wandering men like Macnab had left wives either abandoned permanently or clinging to some vague promise: 'If things work out well, I'll send for you and the kids.' Few were likely to do so.

Curiously, four of these iron-souled wife-deserters had, like Macnab, brought their sons along—one man from Kentucky with two—but none had brought daughters, and few would ever see them again. These were powerful stubborn men, cutting themselves loose from society.

'On one thing I seem to have been dead wrong,' Macnab confided. 'I wrote to Austin asking if most of the newcomers were criminals escaping jail back east. From what I can judge, there isn't a criminal in the lot.'

'I wouldn't trust my money with that tall fellow from Tennessee,' Campbell said.

Macnab was correct in his guess, Campbell wrong in his. Among these men there was not one criminal, not one who had had to leave Connecticut or Kentucky under even a minor cloud. They may have been men who had failed emotionally with their wives and families, but they had not otherwise failed as citizens. The popular canard that everyone who headed for the wild freedom of Texas did so because the sheriff was in pursuit was disproved, at least by this sampling.

In fact, among the twenty-three, there were not even any who had suffered a major financial loss that might have propelled them outward from their society. Most of them had actually prospered back home, and this had enabled them to leave their abandoned wives in rather gratifying security: 'You can have the store and the fields, Emma. I'll not be needin' them.'

Macnab chuckled when he thought of his own case, and Campbell asked: 'What you laughin' about?'

'Leaving Baltimore. I didn't steal their damned cattle.'

'Nobody here said you did.'

'I just sold them. They got a fair profit.'

When Macnab thought of his wife, Berthe, and her sniveling brothers he considered himself luckier than most to have escaped, and he would never have conceded that he had in any way been forced out of Maryland: 'Tell you the truth, Zave, I left her a lot better off than when I met her. She and the girls will have no trouble.'

Campbell summarized it well: 'We ain't fleein' *from* nothin'. We're fleein' *toward* freedom.' And Macnab added: 'Those two over there, who stay together all the time. I'd say they were fleeing toward life itself.'

'They escapin' hangin'?' Zave asked, and Macnab explained: 'Their doctors warned them: "You stay in this city two more years, you'll be dead of tuberculosis. Go to Texas. Let your lungs heal themselves in that good, dry air." '

Now the two men tried to tot up the educational background of the passengers, and they found out that of the twenty-three men, twenty-one could read and write, and of these, fourteen had completed academy or high school and had some knowledge of Latin, Euclid and world history. Probing further, Macnab came up with some even more surprising information: 'Did you know, Zave, that six of those men over there have been to colleges like Yale and Transylvania? I know that those two by the door studied law, they said so, and that short fellow who talks so much has a law degree from Virginia.' What the amateur investigators could not know was that five of the immigrants had been to Europe, three of them knew the principles of banking, and one was a medical doctor with service in the United States Navy. Texas was getting prime citizens.

Two other things Macnab and Campbell could not know that autumn day in 1831: four passengers were keeping journals—two men, two women—which would in later years prove invaluable; and of the men, eighteen would soon be serving in battles of one kind or another against Mexico, and of these, seven would become senior officers.

On the most important question of all—the possibility of revolution against Mexico—the two men had no opinion whatever. Few members of this group openly espoused such action; some had vague expectations that Texas would eventually, by means not yet determined, free herself from Mexican control, but they certainly did not come expecting to incite rebellion, as would their successors in 1835 and 1836. This sample of immigrants came primarily in search of free land and a fresh beginning. For example, Macnab and Campbell entered Texas honestly, without the slightest intention of causing trouble. However, like the Quimpers before them, once they settled, they would find it impossible to accept the systems of government, law and society which their new homeland, Mexico, was painfully trying to establish.

As the two men concluded their assessment, Macnab said: 'I do believe you're the only Catholic in the group,' to which Zave replied: 'From what I hear, you'll all be joinin' me within the week. If you want land.'

There was another factor which differentiated the group, as Campbell pointed out: 'Northern, against slavery but quiet about it, maybe nine. Southern, for slavery and ready to fight if you speak against it, maybe fourteen.'

Macnab volunteered two final guesses: 'Every man who can read, save you and me, Zave, has brought his quota of books, and all but one seems to be fond of strong drink.' The abstemious one was Campbell, who explained in a loud voice: 'I used to love it too much. But once you've been a bartender, you know the dangers. And if I got started again, I'd be as bad as an Irishman.' The cabin laughed at this, for all could appreciate its relevance: of this contingent of thirty adults, all but Campbell had reached America after family affiliation with the Protestants of Northern Ireland.

They were Scots-Irish, the whole cantankerous bundle of them, with all the turbulent, wonderful capabilities that the name implied.

Following these ruminations, Macnab went on deck to be with his son as Otto peered into the darkness, hoping for a glimpse of the long sand finger which delineated Matagorda Bay. He had been there only a few moments when a commotion erupted in the cabin, and when voices rose and oaths reverberated, he hurried back to find a gentleman from Alabama shouting: 'Why can't Mexico ever do anything right? Why didn't they tell us?'

'Now, now, Templeton! The solution is an easy one.'

'Not if they propose to deprive me of my property.'

'It says that, to be sure, but . . .'

'Why weren't we told?' the Alabama man shouted, and Finlay wondered what could threaten him half as much as the danger which hung over the Macnabs: the loss of their entire investment.

'What you do, Templeton, is what we've all done.'

'But why weren't we warned?'

'In a new land, you learn one thing at a time. Now you're learning that Mexican law absolutely forbids slavery and outlaws the importation of any slave.'

'Damned good law,' a man from the North growled, but softly enough so that Templeton did not hear. That outraged gentleman asked: 'If niggers are outlawed, how are you bringing yours in?'

'By the simple tactic we all use to import our property,' the conciliator said, and he spread upon the cabin table a set of papers, carefully drawn, which both amazed and delighted the man from Alabama: 'Capital! Can I do this?'

'We've all done it,' and the Southerners had. Bowing to the irrevocable law that banned slavery throughout Mexico on pain of severe punishment—and Mexico was one of the first nations to enact such a law—the Southerners had devised a foolproof tactic, and Mr. Templeton now put it into effect. Carefully copying the documents laid before him, he penned seven forms replete with legal language, then summoned his seven slaves, but the captain of the sloop warned: 'We allow no niggers in the cabin,' so he went on deck, where he collected his slaves, handed each in turn a pen, and commanded him or her to make a mark signifying acceptance of the terms spelled out in the paper:

> Being a free man/woman, of my own free will and determination I do hereby indenture myself to Mr. Owen Templeton, formerly of Tarsus, Alabama, for a term of ninety-and-nine years, and do further promise to obey his stipulations on the terms hereby agreed to and for the wages set

between us until such time as my indenture is discharged. Obijah, male 27 years, scar on left shoulder, his mark, 16 October 1831.

Each of the Templeton slaves stepped forward and bound himself or herself for this term of ninety-nine years, the period settled upon decades earlier when a Mississippi judge handed down the opinion that if an indenture ran for more than that period, it would be unreasonable.

The passengers slept fitfully that night, and long before daybreak, Otto was back on watch. As black shaded into gray, and gray into a pale rose, the boy peered intently toward the west, and before the others were awake he started shouting: 'Land! Land!' Then everyone, free and slave alike, hurried to the railing to see their new homeland looming out of the morning mists, and they were struck silent by the sight before them.

The *Carthaginian* had made landfall opposite a finger of land no more than fifteen inches above the surface of the water and of no useful purpose whatever. There was not a single dwelling, not a tree, not a rock, not a person, not an animal. It was covered with low grass that sometimes moved softly in the breeze, but the grass, which had to fight salt air, was not nutritious, so none of the famed wild cattle of Texas roamed it. Desolate, windblown, inhospitable, the great sandbars of Texas served only to keep ships from shore and would-be settlers from their homes.

The land was flat, not piled in interesting dunes as on other shorelines of the world, and beyond it the great bays it enclosed were also flat, not etched in leaping waves, and beyond the bays, when the eye could see so far, the mainland itself was utterly flat, with never a tree or a rise or a real hill visible anywhere. It was a land of sheer emptiness and as forbidding as any which had ever rebuffed a group of incoming settlers.

'Look!' Mr. Templeton of Alabama cried. 'A bird!' And all eyes turned to watch this precious creature, this one proof that life could be sustained in Texas, as it flew from north to south along the vast sandbar. Otto, stunned by the terrible loneliness of his new home, watched the bird for a long time, and it was he who first sighted the tree.

Far down on another sandbar, its crown almost blending with the sea, rose one solitary tree. Of the millions of seeds which through the generations had fallen on this desolate spot, this one seed had attached itself to some brief accumulation of nourishing soil and had survived, withstanding wind and storm as if it wished to be a hopeful signal to those like the Macnabs and their friends who would later approach by sea. There was no entrance into the bay where the tree stood, and no passage anywhere in its vicinity, but the tree was more appreciated that morning than a lighthouse, and the immigrants watched it with relief and affection, for it was the only familiar sight to welcome them to their land of freedom.

The *Carthaginian* spent most of that day working its way through the perilous entrance to Matagorda, and as predicted, the passengers saw two more wrecks, not big schooners shattered on rocks as they would have been at Hatteras or Cape Cod, but small sailing ships first trapped in sand, then turned over on their beam ends by succeeding waves, immobilized and knocked to pieces by the sea.

In late afternoon the sloop was safely inside the reef, with passengers cheering the cleverness of their captain, but now many hours of sailing to the west still lay before them, for the bay was vast. It was next morning before land was finally reached at the new town of Linnville, where Mexican port authorities waited. Linnville consisted of three wooden shacks, hastily thrown together, with chinks big enough for a hand to reach through.

One of the houses served as a store, but its surly proprietor, an American down on his luck, could offer only strips of sun-baked beef, two flitches of bacon, some rope, some nails and a jar of sugar candies. Indeed, he was much more interested in buying things from the newcomers than in selling to them, and he had ample funds for his purchases, Spanish coins principally.

Mexican authorities occupied the other two houses, and they were even more surly than the storekeeper. A Mexican law passed the previous year had banned all immigration from the United States, for the danger of unlimited influx was appreciated. But because of his enthusiastic adherence to Mexico, Stephen Austin had been exempted; he was permitted to bring in a few selected settlers, so grudgingly the customs officers had admitted the white arrivals but turned away the blacks. Then agitated Southerners cried: 'They're not slaves! They're free men, indentured for a few years.' And when Stephen Austin himself supported this interpretation, they were accepted.

Each newcomer was asked if he had been born a Catholic, and since the greater part had reached America via Northern Ireland, only Zave Campbell could claim right of entry, which was quickly promised: 'The alcalde in Victoria will give you papers.' The Protestants must report to the same official: 'He'll arrange for the Catholic padres to supervise your conversions.'

When Finlay handed these Linnville officials the beautiful sheet of embossed paper that testified to his ownership of land, they guffawed, for during the past two years they had seen many such worthless certificates: 'Nada, señor, nada.' And other Mexicans crowded about the table to laugh and assure the yanqui that his paper really was nothing: 'Es nada, señor. Es absolutamente nada.' One of the officials was about to tear it up, but Macnab rescued it, thinking to proffer it in Victoria as proof of his honest intentions.

Otto enjoyed the tedious walk to Victoria, but no one else did; he marked the soft variations in the flat wasteland: 'Look how that shrub stays protected behind the little rise of sand!' He was delighted by the way deer traveled parallel to the immigrants, always at a safe distance, and twice he saw wild horses, those small mustangs that could run with such impetuosity. On instructions from his father, he kept constant watch for that first line of trees which would mark where men could live and farm, but none appeared. 'This is awful flat,' he said. 'And so lonely. Is all of Texas . . . ?' He did not finish his question, for his father was obviously distressed by this terrible bleakness, this endless sea of softly waving grass: 'And now look at that storm!'

Big Zave, staring at the ominous black clouds sweeping in from the west, growled: 'So this is the land of milk and honey they told us about. I don't even see one bee, let alone a cow.'

'Otto!' Finlay called out. 'Cover yourself with a blanket. We're to be soaked.'

Across that endless, unrelieved grassland came a tumultuous rainstorm, immense sheets of dark and splashing water which drenched them until the two men groaned, but Otto, keeping his eyes to the ground, saw that hiding beneath the grass were hundreds upon hundreds of lovely autumn flowers: blue, white, golden yellow, fiery orange, the brightest red. 'Look!' he cried, and the men bent down to inspect the watery garden he had discovered. Soon the storm passed overhead, allowing the sun to reappear above the western horizon. When the travelers wiped the water from their faces they saw, hanging in the eastern sky, a perfect rainbow, a grand multicolored arc which they could almost reach out and touch.

'Look!' Otto cried. 'We're going to walk right into it.'

Upon a bed of flowers, with the sky ablaze about them, they walked into the Texas they had dreamed of, until even Zave was awed by the beauty: 'Maybe the Mexicans don't welcome us, Otto, but the land sure does.'

In Victoria the Macnabs learned two things: 'This town and everything as far as you can travel . . . it all belongs to the De Leóns. Spanish only spoken here. So you become full Mexican or you perish.' The other bit of knowledge disturbed Finlay equally: 'Señor Macnab, I speak little English, believe me. If you convert with our two Mexican priests . . . long walk to the mission, many times, many questions. Very severe,' and the speaker pounded his fist into his hand. Then he smiled: 'But at Quimper's Ferry . . . maybe you catch Father Clooney if he's out of jail. He make you Catholic. Very nice . . . very sweet man.'

Mexican officials quickly satisfied Macnab that his scrip was worthless, but they displayed none of the harshness he had encountered in the first office at the shore. 'Señor Macnab,' said an officer who spoke English elegantly, 'we want American settlers. That is, if you build your house at least ten leagues inland from the sea. Especially we want fine lads like your son. So you are welcome to apply in the regular fashion, but only if you've converted to our faith. Then you pay only a modest amount for your land. Stamped paper, two dollars. My commissioner's fee, seventeen dollars. The empresario's fee, about twenty-five. And the surveyor's fee, which cannot exceed one hundred and fifty dollars. We want you, but only on our terms.'

Ironically, Zave Campbell received entitlement to his land within half an hour of registering, for he had cleverly brought with him testimonials from two Catholic priests, one who had been doing missionary work among the derelicts of Under-the-Hill, one a cleric in New Orleans well regarded by the Mexican authorities. Zave did not receive a specific allocation; he would be free to choose that later, but he did now possess an impressive document which permitted him to choose his quarter-league, about a thousand acres, from whatever lands in De León's tract had not already been bespoken.

The problem now arose as to where Zave should claim his land, but Macnab prevailed upon him to delay the selection until he, Finlay, could get to Quimper's Ferry and make himself eligible through conversion; then they could choose together. Campbell, however, was hungry for his entitlement and would have designated it as soon as he could find a surveyor, except that he discovered an alluring technicality: 'Finlay, did you hear what they said at the alcalde's? I have my quarter-league, but I can have a whole league-and-a-labor if I find me a Mexican wife. Nearly five thousand acres. You go to Quimper's. I'll look around here.'

'For land?'

'No, for a wife.'

So the Macnabs, with their dog Betsy, moved northeast through land that began to look as if it might be tillable, and the more they saw of the terrain the more eager they became to get their share. Now there was a slight roll to the prairies, a differentiation between this good area and that; there were trees, too, not noble ones like those in Ohio, but real trees nevertheless. Wild horses they saw frequently, and on two occasions they spotted large herds of cattle, lean, rangy beasts with enormous horns, waiting, it seemed, for someone to claim them. It was a rich, varied Texas they saw on this trip, and no part was stranger than the bottomlands bordering some insignificant stream where towering canebrakes, a wild growth much like sugarcane but worthless, grew in such tangled profusion that earlier travelers had been required to hack tunnels through them.

To enter such a dark passageway, with the path scarcely wide enough for one to move, and to see the cane tops meeting in an archway far above the head was tedious for Finlay, delightful for Otto: 'It's a dungeon, Poppa! We're going to meet the dragon, like the King of Crete.'

Freed at last of the brakes, they intercepted the Brazos River some miles downstream from Quimper's Ferry, and even this far inland the stream gave the impression of being navigable for another hundred miles, but when Finlay looked more closely he saw it to be clogged with sunken trees and jagged stumps that prohibited vessels. Seeking always to instruct his son in the necessary arts, he asked: 'How wide is the river?' and Otto guessed: 'Maybe three hundred feet.'

'No, I mean exactly how wide,' and to the boy's delight he explained: 'All a surveyor needs is three trees, A, B and C. A is that one on the far bank which you can't get to, B is here on this bank. Now find C along there that makes a right angle with B and an angle of forty-five degrees with A.' Next he showed his son how, by folding a piece of paper, he could accurately determine each angle.

When this disposition was laid out, he revealed the secret: 'Then all you do is step off the distance from B to C on this bank, and you have the exact distance from B across the river to A.' He encouraged his son to measure the distance, and Otto said: 'Four hundred and twenty-nine feet. That's a big river.'

'And not too deep at this point.'

The essence of this vast land was beginning to seep into their souls, as it did with almost all who stayed long enough to savor it, and that night Otto reported to his father: 'When I was little I wanted to be a boatman on the Mississippi. Now I want to live in Texas.'

'So do I,' his father said, and that night they slept with deep contentment.

They were wakened in the morning by loud barking from Betsy, who was nipping at the heels of a brash young man heading upriver with two bundles slung across his back. The first contained clothing, the second the awkward tools of a blacksmith, and it seemed likely that these parcels represented a lifetime's accumulation.

He said: 'Isaac Yarrow, renegade from North Carolina, with a brief halt in Tennessee.'

When Finlay asked 'Where are you going?' the young man spat and growled: 'Got thrown out of San Felipe de Austin . . .'

'Isn't that the capital of these parts?'

'It is, and a sorrier spot God never made. Thirty-nine houses, six criminals to a house. Each house hidin' someone wanted for embezzlement, armed robbery, seduction or murder. The alcalde drifted into town smellin' distinctly of tar and feathers, and the esteemed sheriff still has four different wives in four different states, none dismissed by divorce.'

This evaluation was so contrary to the one Macnab had made in the *Carthaginian* that he had to protest: 'The immigrants we sailed with weren't like that, not at all.'

'You saw the goods. I saw the bads.'

'You're telling the truth?'

'Texas is a magnet for criminals.'

'If it's that bad, what did you have to do to get thrown out?'

Yarrow leaned against a live oak and scratched his head: 'They brought seven counts agin' me. Mostly I was too outspoken and too blasphemous.'

'Where you heading?'

'Seems like anyone with spirit who comes to Texas moves on to somewheres else. Missouri, Arkansas. Me, I'm headin' for California. Man can live decent there.'

'I thought men could live decent in Texas,' Finlay said, and Yarrow growled: 'If you want to kiss ass. I never cared for that.'

They joined forces for the short journey to Quimper's Ferry, and when they sighted the sturdy dog-run which served as inn, Yarrow grew rhapsodic: 'Now, if all people in Texas was like Mattie Quimper, this place would be a hard-workin' paradise.' When Finlay asked who Mattie was, Yarrow said: 'If she was twenty years younger, I'd marry her.'

'But what's she do?'

'She runs the ferry. She runs the inn. And she befriends people like me who've been kicked out of other places.'

As they approached the inn, Yarrow bellowed: 'Hey, Mattie!' and to the porch of the dog-run came a gray-haired woman in her forties, lean and worn from incessant labor. As she peered to see who was shouting, a young man of nineteen joined her, but remained slightly behind, as if seeking the protection of her petticoats.

'Good God, it's Isaac!' the woman called, and with a spry leap from the porch on which two travelers were asleep in their blankets, she ran to the blacksmith and kissed him. 'They tell me you've been in trouble down to San Felipe.'

'Got run out of town. They said "You've got twenty-four hours to git," and I shouted back "I'll live to see grass growin' in your goddamned streets."'

'Sshhh,' Mattie whispered. 'We got clergy inside.'

'Father Clooney?' Yarrow cried with obvious enthusiasm. 'Did he get out of jail?'

'No, sad to say,' Mattie reported. 'They sent officers from Saltillo to arrest him. Charged him with bein' too partial to the norteamericanos.'

'How long's he been in chains?'

'They didn't chain him. Not after the first month. But he's been in jail a year. Miracle he ain't dead.'

'So who is the God-shouter in there?'

'Reverend Harrison.'

Yarrow spat: 'That sanctimonious . . .'

With a quick swipe of her hand, Mattie slapped the blacksmith on the cheek: 'You shut up! Reverend Harrison has come down to see if I'll marry him.'

Yarrow caught Mattie in his arms and gave her a little waltz, feet off the ground. 'Mattie, old girl! You don't have to waste yourself on that Psalm-singer. I'll stay here and run the ferry for you.'

'Weren't you run out of the whole Austin grant?' she asked, and Yarrow replied: 'I was. But I'd stay here and protect you from Reverend Harrison.' He spoke the name with such disgust that the two Macnabs supposed the clergyman to be an ogre, but when he walked out the door onto the porch, gingerly avoiding the sleeping men, they were surprised by his commanding appearance.

'Isaac!' he said with unfeigned cordiality. 'What evil are you up to now?'

'You'll be gratified to learn that your prophecy came true. They ran me out of San Felipe.'

'High time,' Harrison said, stepping down and throwing his right arm about Yarrow in a brotherly embrace. 'We welcome you here, but we're going to watch you . . . most carefully.'

'I'm on my way to California. Just stopped off to warn Mattie Quimper not to marry you.'

Harrison laughed: 'Bad men flee to Texas. Always have. And the worst move on to California. Always will.'

Mattie, who continued her work as if the marriage under discussion involved someone fifty miles away, invited Yarrow and the Macnabs into the inn for breakfast, and when eggs, bear strips and pecans were on the table she asked Harrison if he would say grace, and the tall, forbidding man asked the others to bow their heads while he raised his face toward heaven: 'Almighty Father, watch over Thy renegade son Isaac as he heads for California. And welcome to Thy bosom the strangers who join us this day. Protect Mattie who does Thy work so endlessly, and speed the day when Thy true religion can be preached openly in these parts. Amen.'

When heads were raised, he placed his hand on young Otto's arm and said: 'They haven't told me your name.'

'Otto, and this is my father, Finlay Macnab of Baltimore.'

'Someone has taught you manners, young man.' Then he smiled at Finlay, asking: 'What brings you to these parts?' and Macnab said: 'Freedom.'

'You'll be welcomed here. What church?'

'Presbyterian. Many generations in Scotland and Ireland.'

'One of God's chosen religions,' Harrison said. 'Here we're all Methodists.'

'Not me,' Yarrow interrupted, at which Harrison warned: 'God has His eye on you, Isaac, and so do I.'

'What's this about a marriage?' the blacksmith asked, and Harrison said, blushing: 'I had not supposed that so delicate a matter would be discussed publicly,' and Yarrow replied: 'If a lovely lady like Mattie Quimper has to be protected from a lecherous old clergyman like you, Harrison, it should become public.'

'She needs a man to help her,' Harrison said with real tenderness as he watched Mattie moving about the kitchen. Smoothing down her apron, she lifted a flat metal slab from the fire and brought to the table her latest batch of salt-and-honey pecans, which she placed before Otto.

'Let 'em cool. Then eat up,' she said. She offered Finlay some and invited Yarrow to sample them, but she took pains to see that when the slab came to rest, it was before Reverend Harrison.

'Now tell me,' she said, 'what brings you to the Ferry, Mr. Macnab?'

Finlay was too embarrassed to reveal his secret, especially since a Methodist minister looked on, but Mattie could guess: 'You hoped that Father Clooney would be here, didn't you? You want to convert so you can obtain land?'

At this blunt disclosure of his plans, Finlay began to stammer, but he was saved by his son, who said openly: 'Zave Campbell, he's already Catholic, with papers from two different priests proving it, and he got his land right away. And if he can find a Mexican lady to marry, he'll get four times as much.'

To the surprise of the two Macnabs and Yarrow, but not to Mattie, for she now knew Reverend Harrison well and favorably, the austere Methodist said: 'Have no embarrassment, Macnab. It's an immoral law and to obtain your land it's quite forgivable to subvert it. Swear allegiance to the Pope but remain Presbyterian in your heart.'

'Is that your counsel?' Macnab asked, and Harrison said: 'I give it constantly. And do you know why? Because within five years at the most, Texas is going to break away from Mexico. And we can all worship as God wants us to, in His churches.'

Yarrow interrupted: 'You're convinced God is a Methodist?' and Harrison shot back: 'He certainly isn't a papist.' When Yarrow said: 'New Testament says he is,' Harrison growled: 'That's your interpretation.'

Then he changed his tenor completely: 'Isaac, return to San Felipe. Make peace with the officials. Because when war comes we'll need men like you.'

'I gave Texas its chance. And it rejected me. I'm for California.'

The newcomers spent three enjoyable days at Quimper's, talking about the future, teasing Reverend Harrison about his courtship, and stuffing themselves with Mattie's good food. Harrison was certain that revolution of some kind was inevitable; Yarrow doubted that weaklings like Stephen Austin would ever muster courage for such an act; and Finlay Macnab was startled by the frankness of the speculation: 'I thought everyone agreed that Texas was to remain Mexican. Austin said so in his letter to me,' and he produced that document.

When Yarrow finished reading it he said: 'The epistle of a weakling,' and when Harrison took the letter he said: 'He's masking his true beliefs.'

As talk turned to other matters, Yarrow asked boldly: 'Harrison, why do you insist that Mattie needs your help when she has this fine son who could run things better than you ever would?' and Harrison replied: 'She'll be in real trouble if she relies on that one.'

Yarrow and Macnab had been studying young Yancey, and the more they saw of him the more they agreed that the flabby lad needed some strong influence to force him into Texas ways. 'He's just not Texican,' Yarrow said. 'He'd get along fine in Virginia, or even better in Massachusetts, where they don't have such high standards for manliness. But in this climate I fear for him.'

What the two men disliked about Yancey was the latter's unwillingness, or inability, to take charge of the inn and the ferry. 'No woman should be doin' the work Mattie does,' Yarrow said, and one afternoon he grudgingly told Harrison: 'It could be a proper move, Reverend, if you was to marry her. How old are you?'

'I'm a year older than she is. Lost my wife to the cholera.'

'In principle I still oppose the marriage,' Yarrow said, 'but in practice . . .'

'How old are you?' Harrison asked, not belligerently, and Isaac replied: 'Very old in the ways of the world, and I can see through you. What you want is that ferry. You know it's a gold mine.'

'What I want,' Harrison said, 'is a free Texas. Stay and help us win it.'

But Yarrow, one of the best men to emigrate to Texas during these turbulent years, had seen enough of it. The good men like Austin lacked courage and the bad ones, like the fugitive murderers and embezzlers at San Felipe, lacked judgment. He could see no hope for the colony but he did foresee a kind of permanent tension between Mexico and the United States. He concluded that the best chance for a man of inventiveness and daring lay in California, so on a bright morning in January he bade the residents at Quimper's farewell, shouldered his two packs, and headed west. That afternoon, when all were still lamenting his absence, Yancey Quimper shouted from the porch where he was resting: 'Mom! Here he is!' and the Macnabs assumed it was Yarrow, changing his mind.

Instead, it was a bent old man, Father Clooney, now sixty-seven but looking much older because of his stay in the Mexican prison. 'Good God!' Mattie cried as she ran to him. 'What did they do to you?' He was limping so badly that he had to be helped by two young priests, who explained: 'The new governor pardoned him. He was supposed to find refuge in Zacatecas with the Franciscans, but he insisted on coming back to his old parish, and here he is.'

'Will you stay with him?' Mattie asked as she helped him onto the porch.

'No, we've been assigned to Nacogdoches, and in the morning we move on.'

The three clerics slept that night on the porch; Mattie offered Father Clooney a bed, but he said: 'I'll stay with me lads this last night,' and in the morning he blessed them as they started for the remotest outpost of the Mexican empire: 'You'll like it up there, lads. Good people and souls to be saved.' As they departed he stood with Mattie, watching as Finlay Macnab poled the ferry across the Brazos: 'How wonderful it must be for them, Mattie. To be young, facing a new world, and knowing there's chapels to be built and pagans to be saved.'

He was not at the inn three days—painful days of recuperation from his travail —before couples started arriving to have their informal marriages solemnized, and now Reverend Harrison felt it obligatory to withdraw. 'No need,' Father Clooney said, 'I'm sure they'd appreciate your blessing too,' but Harrison was worried more for the old man than for himself: 'You speak kindly to a Methodist, and the Mexicans'll throw you back in jail.'

'I think they'll let me run my course,' Clooney said as he wearily prepared for the weddings.

He was a tired old man now, worn out by the race of life. He had seen enough of frontier living—especially the hideous wars with Indians when each side tried to demonstrate its superior claim to savagery, and the petty rebellions, with fifteen Mexicans dead and sixteen Americans—to know that man was a frail creature who lived on this earth but briefly, and rarely well. A good horse, a reliable woman, sons to protect the old age, and enough to eat, that was the best man could hope for, and if perchance he heard far echoes of God and Jesus, never seen but surely there, so much the better. 'Life,' he told Mattie one evening, 'is a whole lot better if you have reassurances.'

He liked a good steak, cooked over embers, and he was especially fond of white bread smeared with butter, but flour was so rare in Texas that he had sometimes gone for a whole year without tasting bread: 'A hunk of meat, two Mexican flapjacks made of corn, and now and then a beer, that's my penance for having left those fine cooks in Ireland.' Having lived in four different lands—Ireland, England and Louisiana, briefly, and Mexico—it was his measured judgment that Texas cooking was the worst in the world: 'But I eat enough of it to keep me belly fat, and I do believe that when I die the table set in heaven will be a mite bit better.'

He rose at dawn on the wedding day to take breakfast with Mattie, who asked him: 'Should I marry Reverend Harrison?' and he advised her: 'If ever a woman sees a reasonably good man, take him.' She then asked if he considered Harrison a good man, and he said: 'He's a man of God, but also a man of revolution. Does one destroy the other? I don't know.' She asked if he thought the revolution which Harrison preached would materialize, and he said: 'A year of jail knocks desire for revolution out of a man.'

Then suddenly he dropped his weary head on the table, and for a moment she thought he was weeping, but when he lifted his face he was smiling: 'I'm so ashamed, Mattie. I'm covered with disgrace.'

'Why? Jail is forgivable when you go there for the reasons you did.'

'Oh, jail has nothin' to do with it. But recently I've caught myself thinkin' "I hope it all hangs together for the rest of my life, then to hell with it." What a shameful surrender.' He studied her across the rough wooden breakfast table, then confessed: 'Harrison is the voice of the future. I'm the past.' Now tears did come to his eyes, and he did not try to hide them: 'In Ireland, I wrecked me parish. Here, I converted never an Indian. In Mexico, I wound up in jail. And the years have fled so swiftly.'

Mattie rose and went about her duties, leaving him there, and after a while he went onto the porch, where he supervised the placement of the rude altar from which he would preach to the seven couples. When this was completed he returned to the doorway, looked in at Mattie, and said, his face beaming with love for the old days: 'Matt, old girl! I do wish your husband and The Kronk were here this day. I miss them.'

Marriage, to Father Clooney, remained the most sacred of rites, but when the ceremony was over he did enjoy a bit of celebration and was especially appreciative if it involved some warming spirits. That evening the dancing, the fiddle-playing and the shouting were lively, but next morning Clooney was up early, showing no signs of excessive wear.

'Now, who are the ones who seek conversion in order to grab a wee bit of land?' he asked as the day began, and when four families, including Macnab and his son, were lined up on the porch, he proceeded mechanically to make them technical Catholics. But if he took such political conversion lightly, Finlay could not, for when he stood next in line and realized that he must soon take a solemn oath abjuring John Knox's religion for which his Highland ancestors had died rather than surrender it to the Pope, his knees began to shake, his throat went dry, and a crazed look came into his eye. He recalled those great battles in Northern Ireland between the Presbyterians and the papists, the centuries of struggle of which he had been a part, and he found himself powerless to move forward.

Father Clooney had seen these symptoms before, always in people who had come to Texas via Northern Ireland, and in his compassion he made it easy for Finlay and Otto to step aside. That day the Macnabs were not converted, the shock was simply too great, but that night Clooney talked with both father and son, for he insisted that Otto be present:

'I know well the torment you feel. I've seen it before, and I respect you for your integrity. I can tell you only two things. My religion is one of the sweetest, gentlest in the world, a consolation and a redemption. I've loved it for nearly seventy years, and when I die within its embrace I shall know no fear, for God has been with me always.

'The Mexican government, in its wisdom, has said that you cannot have land unless you convert to the religion it sponsors. This is a clear law, not unreasonable, and not unfairly administered. So if you want land, you Macnabs, you must convert this day, for tomorrow I may be gone.

'Let me tell you this, my sons, to own land is a good thing, and if you find it in your hearts to join my church, you may discover, like many before you, that it's a worthy home, one which assures you much benevolence.'

The old man did not go on to finish his statement, the implied part about what would happen if the Macnabs did *not* find their new religion congenial, and he certainly did not say that so far as he was concerned, once they got their land they were free to revert to Presbyterianism, but his entire manner implied that such was his belief.

So Finlay and Otto became Catholics, trembling with fear lest they be struck dead for the blasphemy they were committing, but Father Clooney blessed them just the same and smiled at the heavy perspiration on Finlay's forehead.

That night Father Clooney slept on the porch as usual, but he was uneasy, and long after midnight he roused Finlay and sat with him by the flickering fire: 'My son, we must do something about getting you land.'

'I've converted.'

'That may not be enough. Authorities have grown suspicious of Austin. They're inspecting every grant he makes.'

'What should I do?'

'Forget Austin. Go back to Victoria and ask the De Leóns for an assignment in their grant.'

'Will they give it?'

'I know that family well. One of the best. I'll write them a letter recommending you.'

'I'd appreciate that. I'll get it in the morning.'

To Macnab's surprise, Father Clooney reached and grasped his hand as if he were responsible for his new convert's welfare: 'No, we'd better do it now.' And taking paper from the same old Bible with which he had converted the Quimpers years before, he drafted a warm note to the De Leóns, beseeching them to award land to his trusted friend Macnab. Handing Finlay the paper, he returned unsteadily to the porch.

Sometime after dawn, as was her custom, Mattie went to him with a cup of broth, but when she tried to waken him he did not respond. For several terrifying moments she kept prodding him with her foot, refusing to believe that he was dead. Then his left arm fell lifeless onto the boards of the porch and she could no longer ignore the evidence.

She did not cry out, nor did she call for help. She merely looked down at the body of a man she had first suspected, then grown to love, a faithful shepherd whose flock had been so widely scattered that he had worn himself out tending it. As if his death had also terminated a portion of her life, she gave no further thought to the proposed marriage with Reverend Harrison. After the funeral, which the Methodist conducted with a glowing tribute to his onetime adversary, she sent him north, where he married a much younger widow, who helped him fan the fires of rebellion.

Otto observed this tangled behavior of his elders—Isaac Yarrow's bitter dismissal of Texas, Reverend Harrison's erratic courtship, the willful return of Father Clooney to a parish in turmoil, the curious behavior of Yancey, ten years older than himself and therefore an adult in his eyes, and the almost inhuman drive of Mattie—without understanding many of the actions or any of their motivations. But as the Macnabs were preparing to quit the inn and move south with their letter to the De Leóns in Victoria, an event occurred which he comprehended perfectly.

From the opposite side of the Brazos, at eleven one bright morning, a loud halloo came ringing through the air, and Otto ran to see what traveler was coming south. To his delight, it was Benito Garza, the muleteer he had known in New Orleans, so without alerting Mattie he dashed to the beached ferry, jumped in and started poling across the river, shouting as he did: 'Benito! It's me! Otto Macnab!' And as he neared the far shore Garza, standing with his two helpers, recognized the boy and shouted back: 'The little horseman! Hooray!' and the two assistants added their 'Olés!'

The three traders piled into the ferry, and Otto proudly escorted them across the river and up to the inn, where he called loudly: 'Mattie! Strangers!' but when she came to the porch she deflated the boy: 'Garza! We've been friends for years.'

It was a lively reunion but also an emotional one, for after the noise and the embraces Garza almost shyly handed Mattie a present, and when she opened it to the applause of all, she found a bolt of English cloth and a simple dress made in France. They were the first such gifts she had ever received, and for a long time she was silent, then she said in a flat tone: 'You carried them a long way, Benito.'

Now everyone spoke at once, and Garza learned of Yarrow's exile, Father Clooney's death and the Macnabs' conversion. He wanted to know where Zave Campbell had located his land, and Finlay explained: 'He hasn't exactly chosen it yet, but he favors a stretch along the Guadalupe,' and Garza approved: 'Any land washed by a river is good.'

It was Otto who spoke the words that mattered: 'Fact is, he's not looking for land. He's looking for a wife.'

As Otto was talking, Benito was holding Mattie's French dress against her spare form, but the boy's words so startled him that he dropped the dress, left Mattie, and took Otto by the arm: 'What did you say?'

'He's not really looking for his land.'

'The other part. Is he looking for a wife?'

'Yes. He gets four times as much land if he finds one.'

It was then that Benito Garza's maneuvering began. Sitting at the rough table and addressing all those in the kitchen, including two travelers who were eating, he said: 'We were nine children and the family had only one ranch along the Rio Grande. No chance for me to inherit the land, so I brought my two youngest sisters with me to Victoria. I'm head of the family. With some difficulty I found the oldest one, María, a husband, José Mardones, but he didn't last long.'

'Did he run away?' Mattie asked, and he replied: 'No. He was shot. Stealing horses . . . from a norteamericano.'

Otto interrupted: 'You told me in New Orleans that horses ran free.'

'Trained horses are different,' Garza said. Then he addressed Finlay: 'So this

wonderful woman, only thirty-one, still has no husband, and if Señor Campbell
. . .'

'How about your younger sister?' Mattie asked, and he replied: 'Josefina? She's
only twenty-six. She can wait. Always get your oldest sister married first.'

This perplexed Otto: 'But if they're older than you, why don't they find their
own husbands?' and Garza replied with dignity: 'In a Mexican family it's the
father's obligation. And I am their father, so to speak.'

Now Garza became zealous for an immediate return to Victoria: 'We've got to
reach Campbell before he makes a serious mistake,' so before the Macnabs were
really ready to depart, Garza applied constant pressure for them to hurry: 'Everything is better for a norteamericano in Texas if he has a reliable Mexican wife.
Suppose he wants land? Suppose he gets into trouble with the alcalde? Or if the
priests act up?'

'He may already have found a wife.'

'I hope not! He would be throwing himself away if he didn't take María. I
promise you, Señor Macnab, this woman is exceptional. A man finds a wife like
her once in a hundred years.'

In the morning the Macnabs looked in surprise as Garza bent low over Mattie's
hands, kissing each in turn, and even Otto could see that the Mexican herdsman
loved this rough woman who ran the ferry, and they treated him with more
respect as they moved south toward Victoria. There Garza hurried ahead, shouting as he entered the town: 'Señor Campbell!' He located the big Kaintuck some
distance to the north, tenting under a big oak on the banks of the Guadalupe, and
his greeting was fervid: 'What fine land you've chosen! Have you found a wife?'

When Zave said 'No,' Garza gave an immense sigh, slumped to the earth beside
Campbell, and said softly: 'Señor, I liked you from the minute I saw you in New
Orleans. I could see then that you had character. Now let us all go back to
Victoria so that Señor Finlay can present the papers given him by Father Clooney
and claim his land.' He did not mention his sisters.

The De Leóns accepted the recommendation of the revered priest, and after
lamenting his death, they said: 'We welcome you to Victoria. Choose your land
wisely.' And it was then that Garza said almost casually: 'Since we're all here, why
don't we go see my sisters?' but he could not help adding: 'Señor Campbell, I give
you my word, you're going to like María.'

He led the way to a two-room adobe shack he had built near the central plaza,
and as he approached it he started shouting: 'María! I bring new friends!' and to
the rough wooden doorway came an ample woman with a big warm face. When
her dark eyes looked at the newcomers and her mouth broke into a smile of
welcome, Otto knew immediately that he had found a replacement for his Baltimore mother, and as the days passed in her benign presence this feeling deepened,
for María Garza Mardones was one of those women who embraced the world.

Her laugh sounded like a deep-throated bell; she was patient with the follies of men; and she adored children, chickens, colts and hard work.

The closing weeks of 1831 were memorable, because the Americans and the Garzas moved out to Campbell's land and started building a dog-run. The three men chopped trees for the timbers while the two Garza women and Otto mixed mud and straw to make adobes. Since each person worked as if the resulting cabin was to be his or her own, the floor plan could be spacious, with the open runway full eighteen feet wide, and each of the two halves larger than the ones at Quimper's Ferry.

At the end of the first week the Macnabs were surprised to see that Campbell was driving stakes to outline a third room on the north. 'What's that for?' Finlay asked, and Zave said: 'You and Otto. Till you get your own land and your own house.'

Otto, who had fallen in love with María, considered this an admirable decision, for he expected his friend Zave to marry the Mexican woman, and he was further pleased on Wednesday of the second week when Zave started driving even more stakes for a fourth room, also on the north but well separated from the one intended for the Macnabs.

'What's that one for?' Otto asked, and Zave said: 'Benito and his sister Josefina. They're to be livin' with us, too.'

'Are you marrying María?' Otto asked, and when Zave answered: 'Yep, I cain't pass over a woman who can really work,' the boy rushed to the stalwart Mexican woman and began kissing her.

So before the first room of the dog-run was even well started, Zave had planned what amounted to a frontier mansion, and that was the beginning of the good times at Zave Campbell's. What gave this particular house a touch of extra charm was its position near a solitary live oak festooned with Spanish moss, which meant that the tree provided both decoration and some protection against the sun. Also, a traditional long, low porch joined the two halves on the south side, but in this instance it also swung around to enclose the western end; at close of day the occupants could rest there and watch the sun go down.

María, once her marriage to Campbell was solemnized, showed great affection for Otto, and since she had reason to believe that she could have no children of her own, and the boy was so appreciative of anything she did for him, she considered him her son, and for his part he adopted Mexican ways, learning not only the language but also the handling of cattle. Under Benito's skilled tutelage he improved the shooting skills Zave Campbell had taught him on the Trace.

But it was in horseback riding that he appreciated Benito most, for Garza was both patient and firm in teaching him the basics, and soon he had Otto galloping at the head of the file when the Mexican hands rode forth to round up mustangs. With Benito's help he broke one for himself, a high-spirited little beast with a tawny coat and an obstinate spirit. 'What shall I call him?' he asked Benito, and that excellent horseman said: 'Chico. He'll learn he's Chico real fast.'

For a boy of ten, there was a beautiful world to be explored. It was spring, and the fields along the Guadalupe were studded with fascinating trees: the wild persimmon, the thorned huisache, the delicate pecans. There were the taller trees, too, that he had missed in those desolate flats by the sea: the post oaks, the cottonwoods, the ash, and always that persistent half tree, half shrub which fascinated him with its gnarled branches and sharp thorns, the mesquite. Sometimes as he wandered among his trees he would come upon a wild boar tusking the earth, or fawns grazing, or the silent slither of a copperhead, the noisy warning of a rattler.

Each evening, when he returned home, he found that María had prepared some new treat, for she was a most ingenious woman, capable of transforming the poorest materials into something delicious, and he grew to love the tortillas she made so patiently, kneeling before the stone metate as she beat the boiled corn into the gray-white mixture she later baked on the flat rocks.

But he liked especially the peasant dish she made with whatever bits of meat her lodgers might provide: bear, buffalo, venison, possum, goat, beef, all were alike to her. Collecting a few onions from her garden and red chili peppers that grew wild, she followed an unbroken ritual, which she explained to Otto in her flowing Spanish: 'You must have two pans. Brown the meat in this one so it looks good. In this one put a lot of bear grease, the chopped chilies, the onions and a bit of garlic if you can find it.' She was generous in the amount of grease she used, because she wanted the final dish to be golden brown in color and with lots of nourishment for her hard-working men.

When the two pans were properly heated on the coals and a rich smell was pervading the kitchen, she took from a treasured hoard imported from Monterrey or Saltillo small samples of two valuable spices, oregano and comino, and after measuring out the proper portions in a pot, she mixed in all the other ingredients with a flourish, stirred well, then placed the pot back on the coals. She would never allow any beans to be added to her dish: 'No true Mexican puts beans in chili.' The result, after hours of careful cooking, was a rich, spicy, aromatic meat dish whose principal flavor was a marvelous mix of red-hot chili and oregano.

But she never served it alone. In the evening before she made this chili con carne she threw into a pot a large helping of beans, any kind available, and these she soaked overnight. She refused ever to cook a bean until it had been soaked. 'I think God would strike me dead if I just threw beans in cold water and cooked them,' she told Otto. 'They must be soaked.' She also insisted upon sieving them three times through her fingers: 'To sort out the little rocks. Many a person has lost a tooth biting into rocks, but not in my beans.'

She rose early in the morning, simmered her soaked beans for two hours, then boiled them for two more. When they were well done, she mashed them, added a little oil and fried onions, then fried them lightly in a pan. 'Now they're ready to eat with chili,' she told Otto, but she was most careful to see that the two dishes never mixed. Each was to be respected for its own uniqueness.

With such food and affection Otto had never been happier, but one aspect of his life along the Guadalupe did cause him worry.

He was a true Macnab, descendant of a clan that had stolen cattle for hundreds of years, and he had seen how his father and his dear friend Zave had gathered strays during their trip along the Natchez Trace, but his developing sense of right and wrong had warned him that such behavior was criminal, and he was pleased when his father dropped the habit. Now he watched as Campbell instructed Benito in the tricks of bringing into his care any cattle or horses that did not have a specific home, and some that did.

Otto went to his father, pointing out that in Texas men burned marks on the flanks of their animals to prove ownership, and he had seen in Zave's fields animals with several different brands. Finlay dismissed his fears: 'All Campbells are like that.'

Worry of a more subtle kind was caused by Benito, now twenty-six, for slowly the boy of ten was beginning to realize that his Mexican friend had a violent and often vicious temper. Benito would pummel any Mexican workman who displeased him; often Otto saw that he wanted to punch Zave too, but was afraid; then his neck muscles would tremble and he would turn away and spit. In training mustangs he was needlessly cruel, and when Otto protested, he laughed: 'Horses and women need to be beaten. Then they become the best.' Otto, who had cringed when drunken men had thrashed their easy Under-the-Hill women, asked if María's Mexican husband had ever beaten her, and Benito snapped: 'Plenty, and she deserved it.'

Statements like that bewildered the boy, for he had witnessed Benito's ardor in furthering his sisters' interests, and he remembered his thoughtfulness in bringing Mattie Quimper those presents: Sometimes I don't understand him. It's like he has a dark side.

María had other concerns, for when she was satisfied that her home in the dog-run was secure, and that her norteamericano husband was a good man, she began her campaign to find equal stability for her sister Josefina. Whenever the men complimented her cooking, she told them: 'Josefina did it,' even though Otto knew she hadn't. Any fine sewing was done by Josefina, and occasionally María would say to Finlay: 'This one, she's a good girl, believe me.' When Josefina smiled, María would ask: 'See that lovely, crooked smile she has? It came from our mother, Trinidad de Saldaña, a refined lady from San Antonio.'

Despite this constant advocacy, Macnab showed no interest, until one noon, when the stew was extra good, thanks to Josefina, María said in Spanish: 'Don Finlay, did it ever occur to you that if you married Josefina, you could get a whole league-and-a-labor next to ours?' Macnab said nothing, but he did sit straighter.

'And when Xavier and I die'—she pronounced the name Hah-vee-EHR—'who would get our land but Otto?' Now Macnab was all attention. 'Don Finlay, can you imagine your son coming into possession of two leagues and more?'

On this day Finlay made no response, but often during the next month, while María continued to stress her sister's abilities, he thought of the good land along the river which Josefina, as his wife, would enable him to claim, and she became increasingly attractive. One afternoon he rode in to Victoria to talk with Martín de León, who held rights to this huge tract of land, an entitlement from the government in Mexico City in 1824, and without identifying Josefina, he asked whether a converted Catholic would also be ceded a league-and-a-labor if he married a Mexican woman.

'Of a certainty,' De León assured him in Spanish. Then De León said in good English: 'But it would be good if you would caution your friend Xavier about fooling with other people's horses. Tempers can grow very short in Tejas.'

Finlay did speak to Campbell, but not about cattle rustling. He asked: 'Zave, what would you think if I married Josefina? And claimed on the league next to yours?'

The big man rocked back and forth for some time, staring at the prairie, which could be seen from his porch: 'Your wife dead?'

'Divorced.'

'Legal?'

'Yep.'

'Marry her. Land is land.' But later, when Macnab was off tending cattle, Zave asked Otto: 'What happened to your mother in Baltimore?' and the boy replied in some confusion, for his memory of his mother was clouded: 'Things happened, and we left.'

'Was there a judge?' Zave asked.

'There was a lot of yelling,' the boy replied, and Zave said: 'I bet there was.'

The big man never mentioned the matter again, but when Finlay suggested going back to Quimper's Ferry for the wedding, Zave said: 'More better we use the priest from the mission at Goliad.'

'Why?'

'I hear the new priest serving Quimper's is very strict. Lots of questions. Maybe even letters to Baltimore.'

'You mean the priest at Goliad . . . he'd be less rigorous?'

'He's always in a hurry. Better we use him,' and Zave was so insistent that in the end he and María, Finlay and Josefina, Benito and Otto rode their horses over to Goliad, where the ceremony was performed. When the priest asked in Spanish whether any man had reasons to oppose this marriage or knew of any impediment to forbid it, both Zave and Otto looked straight ahead.

As soon as the newly married couple returned home, Finlay hurried in to

Victoria and laid claim to his league-and-a-labor. He received it promptly, with one hundred and sixty acres as a bonus for his son.

With full encouragement from María and Zave, the Macnabs delayed building their own house; they stayed on with the Campbells, adding an improvised room to match Benito's, thus increasing the value of their holdings.

Under Benito's tutelage, Zave was becoming an expert in breeding mules and herding wild long-horned cattle; María and Josefina made some of the best food in the area; Otto helped everyone; and Finlay specialized in marketing the various goods they were producing. They also offered the dog-run to the transient public as a kind of inn, one dollar a night, four dollars by the week. Guests slept in a third lean-to which Zave and Benito built, and the rambling affair became one of the better stopping places in that part of Texas, with respectable meals provided by the wives, plus occasional treats that Finlay acquired through sharp trading with ships putting into Matagorda, or from caravans of merchants hauling their goods overland from Mexican cities south of the Rio Grande.

The informal inn had both a good reputation and a bad one. Travelers said: 'No better hospitality than what these women provide at Campbell's. But Zave is exceptionally sharp. Got to keep your eye on him.' Travelers as far away as Nacogdoches and Béxar said this of the posada west of Victoria.

It was Finlay who made the proposal that since mules and cattle were prospering at the plantation, as it was called by travelers from Georgia and Alabama, why did not he and Otto, enlisting Benito as their guide and two of his relatives as helpers, take a herd to New Orleans, where Louis Ferry had promised to buy them at a good price? 'Victoria to the Sabine, maybe two hundred and fifty miles. Sabine to New Orleans, about the same,' estimated a man who had traveled it, whereupon Finlay said: 'We drove cattle lots farther than that on the Trace,' but Zave corrected him: 'Trace is four hundred and eighty. I walked every step, three round trips.'

When it was agreed that such a drive was practical, Finlay hurried down to Matagorda Bay and posted an inquiry to Mr. Ferry, and in a surprisingly short time, less than four weeks, had an answer:

> Bring all the mules and longhorns you can manage. Also some good horses. Market even better than when you were here a year ago.
>
> Louis Ferry

With this encouragement, Macnab assembled a herd of forty longhorns, thirty-one mules and two dozen mustangs broken to the saddle, and with a double supply of horses for himself and his helpers he set forth, and quickly he found himself on the famous Beef Trail.

Since those early days when Benito Garza had pioneered a trail to New Orleans for his mules, so many Texas drovers had followed in his steps that a well-defined path had taken shape. The Beef Trail flourished half a century earlier than the better-known trails like the Chisholm, which cattle followed on their way to the Kansas railheads, and in its day it provided Texas frontiersmen with a chance to earn hard cash.

Otto had been on the trail only a few days when he realized that his journey down the Natchez Trace had been, in comparison, merely a pleasant excursion. For one thing, the Texas rivers were infinitely more difficult to cross, because their banks could be steep and their currents swift after a rain. Food was scarcer and more poorly prepared, if that was possible, and above all, there was the constant threat that Indians might hear of the movement of so many horses and try to steal their share on the first moonlit night. Finally, the roads and trails in Texas were not yet as clearly marked as the Natchez Trace, which had been used by white men for a long time when the Macnabs traversed it.

But without question, the Beef Trail, rugged though it was, offered more delights to young Otto than anything in Kentucky or Tennessee. This was true wilderness, with birds and animals he had never seen before, with bayous lined by moss-covered trees, with a daring Mexican rider like Benito to search out the trail, and with always the sense of a new country to be explored in whatever direction one might care to go. Also, as Otto confided to his father at the end of a long day: 'It's a lot more fun to ride than to walk.'

Already skilled as a horseman, he now acquired from Benito those extra tricks that would make him a true expert, but Garza was powerless to make him proficient with the lariat: 'Damnit! I know you're not stupid,' he would shout in Spanish. 'You can ride. You can shoot. Surely you can learn to throw a rope.'

But Otto could not. His hands were small and his arms short, and when he tried to twirl the stiff and heavy rope about his head in great circles, he not only got it tangled but he nearly succeeded in strangling himself.

'Damnit, Otto, no! You're supposed to throw it over the mustang's neck, not your own.'

It was hopeless. Despite his sweating determination, the young Scots-Irish-German-American boy could not do what the Mexicans did so effortlessly, and sometimes he would sit astride some huge horse watching in awe as the three men competed in roping; they were superb. But if they wanted to race with Otto, they found him now able to ride as effectively as they, swaying with the horse or leaning far over the neck of his mustang until he became one with his steed, flying over the empty land.

And if the four dismounted and took their guns to hunt for food, or merely to compete at targets, young Otto proved superior. He was a superb marksman: cool, hard-eyed, even of hand and steady of wrist. 'Eres un verdadero tejano,' Benito said approvingly one day, but then he added: 'Of course, if you want to rope cattle, you must hire a real mexicano.'

One evening as he and Benito rode in, tired and dusty from chasing one of the few buffalo left in those parts, Otto washed down his horse, but then stayed with it, saying to himself: I'll never forget this day. I'll never have a friend better than Benito. Nor a mother better than María. Nor a dog better than Betsy. Where's Baltimore? It seems so far away. I'm half Texican, half Mexican. Driven by a sense of wild joy, he leaped back onto his horse and galloped across the countryside. He was an Indian chasing buffalo, a Tennesseean shooting a deer, a Mexican about to rope a longhorn. When he returned to camp he saw Garza and realized how much he owed him. Riding up to the Mexican, he dismounted, grasped his hand, and said: 'You are my friend.'

Few lads of Otto's age would understand Texas as thoroughly as he. By the time they crossed the Sabine River into Louisiana he had been pretty well across the face of settled Texas, save for the Nacogdoches quarter; he knew most of the ferries where boats could be relied upon, most of the river crossings that could be negotiated on foot. He had stopped in most of the semi-formal inns, and his knowledge of horses, cattle and the Spanish language would make him an invaluable ranch hand, or owner when he had acquired enough money to start for himself.

New Orleans had a magical effect on Finlay Macnab, for the excitement of selling his animals, the bantering of the buyers and the good fellowship of the stockyards reminded him of those faraway days at the Falkirk Tryst when he discovered the kind of person he was, and he hoped that here his son might have the same kind of awakening: 'When I wasn't much older than you I drove my grandfather's cattle to a great fair . . . and sold them, too. That was the beginning of my real life. This could be the same for you. Study New Orleans. Learn how men do things.'

Otto's instruction took a rewarding turn when Mr. Ferry, pleased by the good condition of their cattle and mules, came by their hotel to invite them to dinner at one of the fine French eating places. As an afterthought he tossed a handful of coins toward the three Mexicans: 'Get yourselves something.' Otto did not linger to see the bitterness with which Benito scorned the coins, letting them fall to the floor, or the furious manner in which he forbade his helpers to pick them up. 'Let the maids have them,' he stormed.

When Otto saw the luxurious dining room with its high ceilings and glittering lights, he said enthusiastically: 'This must be awful expensive,' and Ferry laughed: 'On the profit I'll make from your animals, I can afford it. I ship your mules to Uncle Sam's army and sell your beef to the riverboats and restaurants like this. Young man, tonight you'll feast upon one of your own longhorns.'

Otto was old enough to relish good food, and hungry enough after the frontier fare of Texas to appreciate a varied menu. In fact, he considered New Orleans to be about six levels better than Cincinnati and said so, to Mr. Ferry's approval. But as he gorged on the excellent food he could not help picturing Benito Garza eating in some grubby hole, and he winced as he recalled the niggardly manner in which Mr. Ferry had thrown the coins.

Two days later, while walking the streets, Otto came upon an auction house where consignments of slaves from Virginia and the Carolinas were being sold, and he followed the action with great interest, trying to guess which of two or three competing bidders would stay the course and win this lot or that. When he heard that one would-be purchaser intended taking his slaves, if he succeeded in buying any, to Texas, he approached the man and warned him: 'You know, mister, that slaves are not allowed in Texas.'

This news so startled both the buyer and the men near him that a vigorous discussion occurred, marked by a ridiculous lack of expert opinion, until in the end Otto had to inform the men of the situation. They refused to believe such a mere boy, but an elderly man well versed on the question came to Otto's defense and stated firmly that Mexican law forbade slavery and the importation of slaves.

'Then, by God, we'll change the law!' one hothead shouted, and this brought cheers.

'In five years Texas will be American!' More cheers.

'I'll march to Texas and so will a hundred brave lads like me,' another cried, but when this display ended, the would-be purchaser still did not know how to proceed, and Otto quietly explained ninety-nine-year indentures, and the man was delighted: 'What a thoroughly sensible solution!' And forthwith he bid high on six different lots.

Mr. Ferry introduced Macnab to the convenience of letters-of-credit and suggested that he might like to avail himself of one, but Finlay, having been burned by the skilled salesmen of the Texas Land and Improvement Company, did not propose to be hornswoggled again, and said so.

Ferry laughed at his fears but at the same time recognized his prudence: 'Goodness! I don't mean a letter-of-credit on me. I might skedaddle at any moment. No, I mean a letter on the firmest bank in the South,' and he took Finlay to the offices of the famous Louisiana and Southern States banking house, where the manager said he would be honored to accommodate any client of Mr. Ferry's.

On the spur of the moment Finlay did a most uncharacteristic thing. He was so encouraged by the success of his droving operation, and so titillated at sitting in the offices of a major bank, with every prospect of sitting there more often in the future, that he decided it would be only decent to share his good fortune with his daughters back in Baltimore, and he asked the New Orleans banker if he could convey half his funds to a bank in Baltimore for the account of the Misses Macnab.

'Easiest thing in the world, Mr. Macnab. It can be done at once.'

So it was arranged, and Macnab felt pleased with himself because of his generosity. He then asked how his and Zave's funds could best be handled: 'I'd rather not carry them on my person, seeing that pickpockets infest the steamers.'

'Easiest thing in the world,' the banker repeated. 'Leave your money on deposit with us, earn a tidy interest, and when either you or Campbell requires a load of timber for building a new house, inform me by ship mail, and your good friend Mr. Ferry will have it on board the next vessel to Galveston Bay.'

'It won't do us much good at Galveston, seeing as we live near Matagorda.' The banker chuckled and said that one of these days he must get down to Texas, for he was convinced it was bound to be a major trading center of the American Union.

'It's owned by Mexico, you know,' Macnab said.

'At the moment,' the banker said, and wherever Finlay moved in New Orleans he found this same attitude toward Texas, as if the Louisiana men sensed that their western neighbor must soon become a part of the United States.

The closing days of their visit were marred by the discovery that Benito Garza and his two relatives had quit the expedition; for three days the Macnabs tried to find them, learning only that Benito, cursing Ferry, had summoned his two cousins and ridden back to Texas. There was much castigation of the Mexicans, but when the Macnabs were alone, Otto said: 'Remember when Mr. Ferry threw the money at them? As if they weren't good enough to eat with us? I don't blame Benito for getting mad.'

When the Macnabs returned to Victoria, Finlay sought out Benito and said: 'I'm sorry for the way Mr. Ferry treated you,' and Garza snarled: 'Gringos. What can you expect?'

Since most of the Macnab horses had been taken to New Orleans, Zave had replaced them, but Otto noticed that several bore strange brands, and later two of De León's men took the boy aside and warned him: 'Your friend Señor Campbell, he better watch out. The anglos in this area are fed up with his thieving ways, and something bad will happen to him if he does not mend them.' When Otto, refusing to hear ill of his friend, protested that maybe it was Benito Garza who took horses with other brands, the men said: 'We're watching him, too.'

Otto felt it necessary to warn his father, and Finlay took it seriously, but when he confronted Zave, the big Kaintuck turned the tables by upbraiding him for not having brought home Zave's share of the profits: 'Somehow you made a deal with Ferry that does you good but not me.' When Macnab tried to explain what a deposit in a bank meant, and how it drew interest, the stubborn redhead could not follow and loudly accused his friend of chicanery.

This so irritated Macnab, who understood the facts but could not explain them over Zave's shouting, that in anger he informed Campbell that he and Otto would build their own house. 'Good riddance!' Zave yelled, but Otto cried that he would not permit this, for he had grown to love big, compassionate María and could not visualize life without her. Josefina was equally good, quite a wonderful mother, but María had come first and he saw her as the architect of his good fortunes. When he flatly refused to part from her, the shouting stopped and the breach was healed.

Thus began a perplexity which would haunt him all his life, and haunt Texas; he loved Mexicans like María and instinctively respected their values, so vastly different from his own. He saw that such Mexicans led an easy, singsong life, in harmony with the birds and the rising sun, while Texicans like his father lived a tense one in which cattle had to be counted and delivered on time. María followed the easy traditions of Catholicism, in which saints and the Virgin Mary were as real as the people who lived on the next hacienda; he would always be a Presbyterian, with that religion's harsh commands and unforgiving penalties. She sang, but he brooded; even at age eleven he brooded. To her the family was everything; to him it had proved only a shadowy remembrance. She could forgive a fellow Mexican like her brother Benito his misdemeanors; Otto could forgive no one.

And there his ambivalence deepened. He saw that American immigrants often conceded that María's way of life had commendable aspects; certainly it was more relaxed and in many ways gentler and more humane, as in its care for elderly members of a family; but often some relative like Benito performed an act which should not have been tolerated. Otto heard Mexican men accused of being shifty, unreliable, sycophantic when controlled by others, cruel when they were masters, so that what were deemed María's virtues became flaws when Benito displayed them. For example, Otto had seen Benito excuse his fellow Mexicans for the grossest misbehavior and even encourage it if it helped them gain an advantage over some anglo. Otto heard his own father charge: 'Mexican men allow themselves to be priest-ridden. They drag their church into areas where it isn't needed. Like their unstable government, Mexican men can never settle upon one course of action and follow it for a generation; even the slightest mishap diverts them. So revolution is always around the corner.' Reluctantly, the Macnabs concluded that Benito Garza, specifically, was not a very nice person, and they concluded that the chances for his living in harmony with the immigrating Americans were not good.

Otto was not yet mature enough to understand that the incoming settlers demanded that Benito behave like an American, while he and his fellow Mexicans, occupants of Texas for a century, expected the Texicans to behave like Mexicans. It was an impasse that would never be resolved, but Otto was old enough to perceive the most fundamental contradiction of all. He, like Texas itself, needed the Mexicans and often loved them, but he did not always like them.

Several months after the Macnabs returned home, a much more serious problem evolved from Finlay's impulsive generosity in the New Orleans bank, because when the Baltimore bank informed Mrs. Berthe Macnab that a substantial sum of money had been forwarded to her daughters by their father in Texas, she interpreted this as a signal of reconciliation. She was tired of living alone, and like scores of other abandoned wives in the settled states, she convinced herself that her husband in Texas needed her. With a vigor and determination that astonished her Baltimore friends, she arranged for a sea voyage to New Orleans and a Gulf trip to Victoria.

Consequently, one autumn day in 1833 a horseman rode out to the Campbell posada when the men were away, bringing news that 'A lady calling herself Mrs. Macnab, she's landed at Linnville, and she wants us to bring her here.' Very quietly Otto closed the door so that Josefina would not hear, then asked: 'What does she want?' and the messenger said: 'She told me she has come to join her husband.' When Otto said nothing, the man asked, with a jerk of his thumb toward the room in which Josefina was singing: 'And what about that one?'

Otto considered this carefully, and slowly two reactions began to form. With his real mother at hand, and not in distant Baltimore, he recovered a most positive image of her: it was daybreak and she was bringing him a bowl of hot porridge rich with butter, cream and sugar. She had been a kind mother and he remembered how he had grieved when forced to leave her. But her shadowy portrait was erased by the thought of María, the wonderful Mexican woman whom he had adopted and whom he loved so dearly and in a different way. Desperately he wanted to protect her and her sister from sorrow of any kind.

Accordingly, without saying a word to anyone, he took his horse and accompanied the messenger back to Victoria, where he intercepted his unwelcome mother at the general store, to which she had been delivered. To his amazement he found that his two sisters, striking blondes in their late teens, had accompanied her, and that disoriented him. But he barged ahead, and when his mother sought to embrace him, he held back. 'You must go home,' he said.

'This is to be our home, Otto. We were wrong when we sent you and Father away.'

'You didn't send us. We went.'

This brought sniffles, and she groped for her handkerchief, but Otto was not moved: 'You must go back, because there's no place for you here.'

'You and your father need me, Otto. The girls and I have come all this way to help.'

'Texas is a different place,' the boy said.

'I know. We were warned on the boat.'

'You won't like Texas.' His harshness now brought tears to his sisters, and when he saw these attractive girls weeping he grew ashamed of himself.

'Take them out to the farm,' one of the men in the shabby store said, and when Otto asked: 'How can I?' the man said: 'She has to know sooner or later.' Mrs.

Macnab asked: 'Know what?' and the man replied: 'Lady, you'll find out soon enough.'

The only wagon in Victoria was procured, and Otto, aware that disaster loomed, was determined to avoid involvement with these unwelcome relatives. Riding in front of the procession like a page leading ladies to a castle, he refused to talk with them, and when the entourage approached the dog-run, he rode ahead, shouting: 'Hey, Poppa!'

Finlay and Zave were home now, and when they heard Otto crying as if for help, they hurried to the spacious porch, and there they stood when Otto delivered the three women. Uncertain as to how he should explain the situation, and confused about using the word 'mother,' he said simply: 'They're here.'

Berthe Macnab burst into tears as she ran toward her husband, and the two girls stood shyly by, as embarrassed as their brother. Macnab was flabbergasted, and it was left to Campbell to extend grudging civilities: 'Madam and you gals, sit down,' and he brought forward three chairs, but he made no motion to invite them inside. However, María, hearing the commotion, came to the door, whereupon Zave said hurriedly: 'My wife, María.' There were muffled acknowledgments, with Zave whispering to his wife in Spanish: 'Dios! La esposa de Finlay,' at which María, thinking only of her sister, screamed: 'Quién es esta?' And then the morning began to fall apart, because Josefina, perplexed by the noise, hurried onto the porch, whereupon Otto ran to her, threw his arms about her, and cried: 'This is my mother now.'

It took Berthe and the girls some moments to comprehend that Josefina Garza was legally married to their father, or perhaps not so legally, because Berthe warned Macnab that she was prepared to throw him into jail, and so on. Zave did his best to placate her, pointing out that Baltimore was a long way from Texas and that oftentimes a man who was starting a new life, as many Americans in Texas were doing, broke all ties with his former life to begin afresh.

'I suppose you have a wife back . . . where?'

'Kaintucky, ma'am.'

'And is your wife waiting there for you?'

'As a matter of fact, she is.' Macnab and his son gasped, for Campbell had told them across that flooded stream on the Trace that his wife had died. Together they stared at this big fellow about whom they knew so little, and instinctively Otto went to stand with him, for if Zave was in trouble, the boy must help protect him. Then María, who knew enough English to understand that last conversation, also went to stand with him, and Campbell placed his arm about her: 'Now this one is my wife, and properly married.'

Then Josefina moved to support Finlay, and the two couples, with their mutual son Otto between them, presented a solid phalanx against the women from Baltimore; it was the emerging frontier against the established city.

'I'll have you all thrown in jail!' Berthe exploded, but Campbell told her: 'You'll have to build a big jail, considering all the men like us in Texas.'

Macnab took no part in this uproar; he had fled Berthe once and was determined not to allow her to complicate his life a second time. His attractive daughters he wished well, as proved by the fact that he had sent them half his profits, but he did not want them in Texas. He was happy with Josefina Garza, and he knew that Berthe, if confined to the house he intended building, would be able to stand the isolation and the brooding loneliness for about one week. Yet he could not even tell her to go back home, but Campbell finally did, pointing out that there was simply no place they could stay in his house and that Finlay had no house of his own, and gradually he eased the three visitors toward their wagon. When both Finlay and Otto refused to accompany them to Victoria and then down to Linnville, where they could catch the next boat back to New Orleans, Zave volunteered to go.

Humiliated, and terrified by the emptiness of Texas, the women started their retreat, while Otto, leaning against the oak tree, watched dispassionately. In confusion he stood looking at his Baltimore family, then turned on his heel and ran back to where María waited on the porch.

When the women reached Victoria, Berthe demanded to see the Catholic priest, intending to charge both Macnab and Campbell with bigamy, but there was of course no priest in attendance and Goliad was twenty-five miles away. The Mexican authorities would not concern themselves with a civil brawl, and especially not when the complainant was an anglo and the women who would be hurt were good Mexicans. In Victoria, Berthe accomplished nothing, but in one of Linnville's three houses, where they waited for the boat to New Orleans, she was approached by an American farmer who had studied the trio these last two days and who asked if he might marry the older daughter.

'I suppose you already have a wife in Kentucky,' Berthe said harshly.

'No, ma'am. I come from Mississippi, and I'm single.'

'I suppose you brought your slaves with you.'

'No, ma'am. Men like me, we can't afford slaves.' When she did not respond to his major question, he turned to the daughter and said: 'Ma'am, you're beautiful. Would you consider marryin' me?' and the women collapsed in tears.

Zave Campbell stayed with the Macnab women until the next sailing vessel arrived, and to his astonishment the ship this time was an improved steamboat that negotiated the entrance to Matagorda Bay as easily as if the pass were ten miles wide: 'Bless my sainted aunt! Civilization comes to Texas!'

But while he was celebrating in Linnville, a posse of white settlers located near Victoria visited the Campbell dog-run and demanded from Macnab a payment of nine dollars, claiming that among the horses he had driven to New Orleans were several bearing their brands, clearly placed on the flanks of the animals.

Finlay explained truthfully that the animals, cows and mules alike, had been delivered to him by Campbell and Benito Garza, and this seemed to satisfy the men, because one said: 'That's what we thought,' so after the nine dollars were handed over, they rode off, apparently content.

When Otto asked what this visit had meant, his father explained that in frontier communities where policemen and judges could not yet enforce the law, men felt they had to provide their own enforcement, serving as police and judge and sometimes executioner. He pointed out that Otto had now experienced three radically different communities: 'In Cincinnati you had judges and jails, the way things ought to be. In Under-the-Hill you had nothing, and you didn't like it. Here in Victoria we want law, but we don't know how to get it.'

'We have an alcalde.'

'Mexican law doesn't count, because the richest man can always buy the judge.'

'Will there be American law?'

'There will have to be.'

When Otto was alone, herding longhorns, he recalled the predictions of the businessmen in New Orleans; they had foreseen a day when United States law would operate in Texas, but he could not guess how this might come about.

On the day of Zave's return he told María and Josefina about his farewell to the Macnab women: 'They was weepin' and the mother said some real ugly things. She said both him and me ought to be in jail.' Pointing to Otto, he added: 'She said you would end in hell sure, associatin' with men like your daddy and me.'

On the following day, 10 November 1833, Zave rode south to intercept a caravan of merchants from beyond the Rio Grande, hoping to convince them to sell their wares to him rather than to the two storekeepers in Victoria. He told the Macnabs that he would surely be home by nightfall of the next day, but he wasn't; however, this occasioned no worry, since men on this frontier were accustomed to sleeping on the road when necessary, and their women knew it.

On the evening of the eleventh, as the Macnabs prepared for bed, they were startled by a warning cry from Josefina: 'The sky is falling!' And when they ran onto the porch they witnessed a spectacle of awesome beauty, the passage of earth through a stupendous shower of meteors.

Every year, toward the middle of November, the earth picks its way through the Leonid Meteors, with observers marveling at the lovely fireworks. Every thirty-three years, for some arcane reason, the display is so magnificent that even lay watchers record it. And through the centuries an occasional passage becomes so striking that it is judged to be unique, observers having forgotten the reports of previous such visitations. One of these miraculous passages happened over Texas in 1833, when some thirty-five thousand flaming meteors an hour were seen.

'Look!' Otto shouted. 'It's light enough to read my book!' And for two hours the family watched the spectacular display, unaware that the extraordinary illumination, which made all of southern America about as bright as day, was creating havoc for a friend.

Next morning, right before dawn, as Finlay was getting out of bed, he and Josefina heard a series of suspicious noises, then the squeaking of a door as if someone had opened it, and he was starting to investigate when a piercing scream came from some animal or human, he could not tell which. Dashing into the yard, he found Otto beneath the oak tree, holding aloft the heavy legs of Zave Campbell, who had been hanged from one of the lower branches.

'Poppa! Help!'

Before Finlay could reach the dangling man, stout María had already leaped from the porch and was helping Otto hold him aloft, but she could see that her husband's face was already growing purplish: 'Señor Finlay! Ayúdeme!'

Finlay was unable to loosen the rope that was strangling his partner, and while he was fumbling with the knot about Zave's neck, Otto ran coolly into the house, grabbed a bird gun, and took steady aim at the rope. With the explosion of the gun, Campbell fell, carrying María and Finlay with him to the ground.

Otto was first to pull apart the knot about the neck, and slowly the purple in the hanged man's face began to subside, until at last he was able to whisper: 'Thank you, son.'

That evening was long remembered as 'the night stars fell on Texas,' but in the Victoria district it was 'the night they tried to hang Zave Campbell.'

'Darned things glowed like lanterns,' he said when his windpipe healed. 'Threw a light on me just as I was herdin' the Weavers' steers.' To Otto he said sullenly: 'Don't never steal cows in Texas, boy. Down here they play by different rules.'

. . . TASK FORCE

The only time in two years we failed to produce full attendance at our Task Force meetings was at our November session in Amarillo. Ransom Rusk felt obligated to fly with a group of Texas sportsmen to their annual safari in Africa, this time to the vast Okavango Swamp in Botswana, and he apologized for deserting us: 'This junket was scheduled three years ago. Maybe I'll get me a trophy for my Africa Room. I'll leave my proxy with Lorenzo.'

I regretted his absence, for his impressive credentials and ponderous manner gave solid underpinning whenever we started questioning our visiting experts; it's extraordinary how a short question from a billionaire seems more penetrating than a long one from an assistant professor. Also, Rusk added necessary coloring

to the portrait of Texas which we hoped to present to the public, because
Quimper, dressing like a television Texan and speaking like one, often lent our
sessions an air of levity that might mislead the unwary into thinking we were a
bunch of good ol' boys. It was salutary to let them see that Rusk's more sober
competence was also part of the real Texas.

When our staff informed me that the subject for our Amarillo meeting was to
be 'Anomie in Texas' by Professor Helen Smeadon of Texas Tech in Lubbock, I
told them: 'I don't know what that word means and I'll bet none of the others do,
either.' After phone calls confirmed this, I asked the young people to formulate a
definition, which they circulated prior to the meeting:

> anomie (Fr.) or anomy (Eng.). A precise sociological term popularized
> by the French scholar Emile Durkheim. 1. Collapse of the guiding social
> structures governing a specific society. 2. State of alienation experienced
> by a class or an individual resulting from such collapse. 3. Severe
> personal disorganization resulting in antisocial behavior. [Greek
> *anomia* = lawlessness < *anomos* = lawless: *a*-without + *nomos* law.]

> Characterized by a feeling of rootlessness and a contempt for others who
> do obey the social laws. Commonly witnessed 1. in time of radical
> change; 2. during movement from one society to another; 3. as a result of
> death in one's family or divorce; 4. following severe or disorienting
> physical or mental illness. A common cause of movement to frontier
> societies or a result of such movement. Ultimate manifestation: suicide.

It looked to me as if this was going to be a handful to discuss, and as we flew low
in our approach to Amarillo, I was not at all satisfied that our meeting would be a
success. However, when I looked down at the amazingly flat terrain and the little
roads that cut across the countryside for fifty miles without taking a turn, my
mind wandered to other subjects. 'What's the weather going to be down there?' I
asked the pilot, and he turned back to tell me: 'Like those three men lost in the
Arctic. Howling wind, thermometer way down, dogs howling, and one fellow
says: "Thank God for one thing. We ain't in Amarillo on a bad day." '

I loved this lonely part of Texas, so harsh, so unrelenting, where a windmill
dominates the sky like one of the Alps in Switzerland. The Panhandle was a
powerful place to visit if distances didn't scare you, and I supported the claim of
one local resident: 'We're the hospitality capital of Texas. Weather cold, hearts
warm.'

It was so bitterly cold when we landed that my fears about the meeting revived,
but when we met Dr. Smeadon, who was waiting for us in a cozy meeting room
decorated with hot buttered rum, I concluded right away: This woman knows
what she's doing. In her forties, tallish, forthright and with a sense of humor, she

replied to my questions: 'Undergraduate work at SMU, graduate degrees at Chicago and Stanford, post-doctorate at the Sorbonne, where I specialized in the analysis of anomie with Raymond Aron.'

She barged right in: 'Anyone who seeks to get a grasp on the spiritual history of Texas is obligated to state which of the following four characterizations of our founding American immigrants he supports: "Were the newcomers (one) criminals fleeing justice, or (two) rascals fleeing the bill collector, or (three) average men who were merely restless, or (four) superior individuals tired of the evasions of society back east or overseas and lured by a vision of a better world they might achieve?" '

Rarely had I heard the options stated so clearly, and her subsequent analysis challenged us to sort out our prejudices: 'If we search the historical record, particularly the diaries, we find support for almost anything we care to believe. Who can forget the report of Víctor Ripperdá from Nacogdoches to his superiors in Mexico City in 1824:

> 'I have now served in this forsaken place for three years and in that time have watched a steady stream of Americans sneaking in to steal our frontier. If you scoured the gutters of Europe, you could not find a worse collection of undesirables and troublemakers. Half who creep across the Neutral Ground seem to be fleeing the hangman's noose for murder. The other half have stolen money from their employers. Many were outright pirates with Jean Lafitte, who now ravages the coast of Yucatán, and others fought alongside Philip Nolan when he tried to steal Tejas and was shot by our troops.

> 'The attempt by the United States to fill our countryside with its discarded criminals would be amusing were it not so dangerous. If such rabble continue to pour in, there can be only trouble.

'That's a pretty savage condemnation of our forebears, but we must temper it with the firsthand observations of the good Father Clooney of County Clare, who knew Ripperdá and who must have observed the same immigrants upon whom the Mexican official based his harsh judgments:

> 'I admit that during those rainy days when we crossed the infamous Neutral Ground, I was apprehensive about the kind of people who would be forming my massive parish, for I was forced to officiate at several hangings. But when I came to know the real settlers along the three rivers, I concluded that they provided just about the same proportion of rascals as I had found in Ireland, and rather fewer than I had

seen in New Orleans. They were a rowdy lot, but so was I when a lad, and if they liked their whiskey, so did I.

'Forgetting the occasional shooting and the few who abandoned their responsibilities, I remember them as kind-hearted, generous, quick to defend their rights, and eager to marry, respect their wives, and raise their children as Christians. I was happy to serve amongst them and have bright hopes for the land they are building.

'The judgment that the settlers were average was made rather effectively by Mattie Quimper in the brief summary she left of her days at the ferry bearing her name:

'Very few tried to use the ferry without paying, and when they did, others forced them to pay up, not me, because they said it was unfair to rob a woman. I offered bed and board to hundreds stopping at our inn, and apart from an occasional murder or a shooting after too much drink, I saw no misbehavior. If a wandering man had no money he slept free, and ate, too, but if he could afford it he paid, and few cheated me. Times were hard, but they were good, and I never saw much difference between the Mexican government and the Texican. They were both fairly decent.

'And I'm sure you remember Finlay Macnab's moving summary in which he tells of assessing his fellow ship passengers in October 1831 and found them to be stable citizens with above-average education? There were no criminals among the thirty adults and none who had been forced by the law to quit their homes back east. Remember with what respect he spoke of them and how pleased he was to be a member of such a group. He did, we must admit, point out two weaknesses: several had abandoned their families back home, and quite a few favored heavy drink. But on the whole, they justified Stephen Austin's boast in his letter to Macnab in 1829:

'I can assure you, Mr. Macnab, that the citizens of Texas are just as responsible and law-abiding as those of New Orleans or Cincinnati, and that ruffians will never be allowed in this colony.'

With that, Dr. Smeadon clasped her hands under her chin and stared at us: 'How shall we resolve these four conflicting statements?'

She spent about twenty minutes parading before us other passages from contemporary documents, some supporting the view that all Texas settlers were criminals, others depicting an orderly society in which newcomers found refuge and encouragement to rebuild their lives. At the end of her recital we were in a jumble, and Lorenzo Quimper said so: 'What do we do, toss a coin?'

'No,' Dr. Smeadon said, 'we look for a construct.'

'A what?'

'A theory which will explain the contradictions, resolve the differences.'

'That would have to be some theory! Jean Lafitte and Father Clooney in one bundle!'

'But that's exactly where they belong, where all of us belong, in one big bundle.'

She then launched into her main thesis, and as she developed it we began to acquire another vision of the Texas we loved. We neither defended it nor condemned. We merely looked at it through somewhat clearer glasses.

'The construct that clears away many of the seeming contradictions is *anomie,* and I'm pleased that members of your staff provided the definition they did. It's quite accurate. Anomie is the emotional state of mind we are apt to fall into when we are wrenched away from familiar surroundings and thrown into perplexing new ones. The two key words for me are *disorientation* at first, followed by *alienation* if it continues long enough.

'I assure you, Mr. Quimper, I have no opinion whatever as to whether our great-great-grandfathers were criminals or rowdies or gentlemen scholars. All I'm concerned with is: "How did they behave? What did they actually do?" And when I study that restricted body of information I must conclude that most of them experienced anomie.

'Stands to reason, doesn't it?' she asked. 'They were torn from settled homes. They surrendered the assured positions they had enjoyed in the pecking order. And they found themselves tossed topsy-turvy into a new environment they couldn't control.'

'Wouldn't they rejoice in their new freedom?' Quimper asked. 'I would.'

'At first you would, I'm sure. So would I. But then doubts would begin to seep in. You find that what looks like firm ground really isn't. Values begin to shift, and what was secure back east is found to be in flux. *Disorientation* is the word, and once it starts, its effect can be cumulative and catastrophic.'

When we started to argue about our susceptibility to such disorientation, Dr. Smeadon asked Quimper if he would mind being a guinea pig, and he said 'Shoot!' so she asked him to stand, and as he smiled down at us she began to dissect him: 'The attractive thing about you, Mr. Quimper, is that you wear so forthrightly the badges of your position in our Texas society. Your big hat there on the table. Your attractive bolo tie. Your neat rancher's whipcords. Your very nice boots—you make them, don't you? And your Cadillac parked in some driveway and an oil well somewhere. They define you. They give you assurance that you're part of the team, and a not inconsiderable part.' She laughed, then asked: 'You're proud of being a Texan, aren't you?' and he snapped: 'I sure am.'

Now she became serious: 'Mr. Quimper, please be seated, and I thank you for your help. But how would you feel if you were suddenly transported, let's say to New Hampshire, which is a very fine state but which respects none of your visible symbols. Its people don't cotton to Cadillacs and oil wells, and its children would laugh at you if you wore a bolo.' She moved closer to him. 'How would you react, Mr. Quimper, if all your securities were suddenly dissolved?'

She smiled at him, a generous, warm smile of encouragement. 'From what I hear, you're a strong-minded man, Mr. Quimper, and I'm sure you'd fight back. Get the confusing signals sorted out. Establish new bases for self-esteem. And fairly soon, I would suppose, you'd be back on track.'

Suddenly her manner changed completely. Very gravely she said: 'Look at the conclusion in the definition the young people gave us: The ultimate manifestation of anomie: suicide. Have you ever reflected on the large number of leading Texas citizens, in the early days, who committed suicide? Anson Jones, last-time President of the Republic of Texas, a suicide. Thomas Rusk, United States Senator from Texas and perhaps the ablest man of his time, a possible candidate for President of the United States, suicide. And what perplexes, Manuel de Mier y Terán, the ablest Mexican official ever sent north, he too committed suicide.'

'What can that possibly mean?' Miss Cobb asked, and the reply was short: 'That Texas was a fluid situation which attracted people who were prone to anomie, and that in their continuing disorganization they killed themselves.'

She proceeded with additional material which startled us: 'Look at the number of our Texas heroes who abandoned their wives back home. Sam Houston did it twice. That pretty little thing in Gallatin, Tennessee, his splendid Indian wife in Arkansas. Davy Crockett walked out the door one day without even saying goodbye, if we can believe the legend. William Travis did worse in Alabama, and I would not care to know how many others defending the Alamo had fled their wives without the formality of divorce. The Finlay Macnab who had such a favorable opinion of his fellow passengers was a standard case—left his wife and daughters in Baltimore, but brought his son with him.'

After she had poleaxed us with a score of such instances, she chuckled: 'Did you know that one of the first laws passed by the new nation of Texas in 1836 forgave bigamy if the immigrating male, like this Macnab, could claim long separation from his legal wife back east, or mail that had not been delivered, or unavoidable confusion or almost any other claim, no matter how fragile? The law assumed that a de facto divorce had occurred and that the Texas wife was legally married, with the children bearing no taint of bastardy. The law was necessary because in some areas a fourth of the husbands could have been charged with bigamy.'

After allowing this to sink in, she asked: 'What do you make of it, this irresponsible behavior, this wild resort to dueling, this sudden murder in the streets, this refusal of juries to find men guilty, and withal, this insistence that Texas was a religious state observing the highest moral principles?'

After we had paraded our ignorance and our determination to protect the reputation of our state, she said calmly: 'The best explanation, I think, is that the original situation in Texas—with the Neutral Ground more or less inviting disorganization—and the inability of the Mexican government to find consistency, and the protracted uncertainty over whether Texas would join the American Union created a fertile ground for the development of anomie. It became inescapable, a way of life whose lingering effects are with us still.'

After discussion, during which we rejected many of her ideas, she said: 'You people know your own minds, and that's good, that's Texan. But I want to crank in several additional ideas before you set yourselves in concrete. Oregon was settled at about the same time as Texas, but its citizens developed none of the Texan neuroses.'

'Ah!' Quimper cried. 'But Oregon never had the Mexican indecision. Its forerunners were decent, law-abiding Englishmen.'

'But California did have exactly the background of Texas, and it didn't develop like us.'

'False analogy,' Garza said. 'For a hundred years California experienced orderly Spanish and Mexican governments. Definitions were understood.'

'A very good point, Mr. Garza. Maybe that was the difference.'

'You're missing the real difference,' Quimper said. 'California didn't have to battle Apache and Comanche.'

'But that the two states developed quite individually, you must admit.'

'And thank God for that,' Garza said. 'Who would want to live in Los Angeles?'

'Or San Francisco?' Quimper asked. 'All those gays?'

'About the same percentage as in Texas, I would suppose,' Dr. Smeadon said.

'You say that out in Lubbock, you're gonna be fired,' Quimper warned, and she said: 'I was thinking of Houston,' at which Quimper said: 'Houston don't count.'

'My next point is that even after joining the Union, Texas continued to enjoy special freedoms denied her sister states. She had the right to separate into five states, any time she wished. Public lands, which other states had to cede to the federal government, she retained. And in many things she went her own way. I'm not sure that these were constructive experiences. I'm not sure at all.'

'What do you mean?' Quimper thundered. 'They're the backbone of this state.'

'And one of the base causes of its neuroticism.'

'Are you saying that we're a bunch of neurotics?'

'I'm certainly neurotic,' Dr. Smeadon said. 'And I've just demonstrated that you would be if you were moved to New Hampshire, and if we talked long enough, I'm fairly sure I'd find that even Miss Cobb would be—on certain tender subjects, like Texas patriotism.'

'I never voted for Lyndon Johnson,' Quimper said, 'but I had to respect him that night at the Petroleum Club in Dallas when he told us: "I love three things. God, Texas and the United States." And if there hadn't been a couple of ministers and priests in the audience, I'm sure he'd've changed the order.'

Dr. Smeadon nodded, as if she agreed. 'The lasting effect of the Texas version of anomie is that it has encouraged the state and its citizens to believe they're different. This was really the end of the road—for Spaniards, for Mexican officials and churchmen, for Americans. When you reached Nebraska in those heady years, you plunged on to Oregon. When you reached Kentucky, you forged ahead to Missouri. But when you reached Texas, you stayed put, except for the real crazies like Isaac Yarrow, who stumbled on to California.

'I like the Texas mix. The dreamers, the petty criminals. The God-driven ministers, the real estate connivers. And my heart goes out to the women like Mattie Quimper, who kept the ferries running.' She said nothing for some moments, thinking of her predecessors who lived in sod huts, and bore a dozen children, and died at thirty-nine, but did not commit suicide. 'I mourn for the strong men who were driven to self-destruction by complexities they could not understand. Texas has always been a neurotic place, a breeding ground for anomie. But it's the neuroticism of activity, of daring, and I hope it never changes, even though the cost can sometimes be so tragic.'

VI
THREE MEN,
THREE
BATTLES

THE ALAMO

COS

DUQUE

× TRAVIS

The break in the wall

TO GONZALES
71 MILES

Old Indian Quarters

× CAMPBELL
× FUQUA

Rough fence only

Cattle pens

The
Long
Barracks

Old Spanish well

New Mexican well ○

Old Indian Quarters

Old
Mission
Plaza

Roofless Chapel

CROCKETT ×

Walls still standing

Bowie in sick bed

No wall here
Palisaded

South Barracks ×

Fortified Gate

RIPPERDA

TO GOLIAD 95 MILES

MORALES

WAR FORCES MEN TO MAKE MORAL CHOICES, AND THE STRONGER THE MAN, the more difficult it can be for him to make the right choice.

Thus, when the great General Santa Anna marched north from Saltillo on the morning of 26 January 1836, determined to discipline the rebellious district of Tejas once and for all, he goaded three men to reach decisions on problems they had been contemplating for some time. Finlay Macnab and Zave Campbell, both married to cherished Mexican women, suffered immediate crises of loyalty, which each would resolve in his own arbitrary way.

Especially tormenting were the problems which perplexed Benito Garza, their unmarried brother-in-law, who faced a decision of the gravest import: To what nation do I owe my allegiance?

As a loyal Mexican he argued with himself: I love Mexico. My heart beat faster when that fine Constitution of 1824 was announced, because I saw that it made possible a free state in Tejas, one that would enjoy honest freedoms. And I was proud when Santa Anna assumed control of my country, for he promised fine changes.

But as a young man he had always been generous in welcoming American immigrants, for he recognized that vast changes were afoot and that perhaps even the basic governance of Tejas might have to be altered: I like northerners. I greeted them warmly when they arrived. I saw that we needed their vitality to fill our empty spaces, and I proved my good will by marrying my two sisters to yanquis. And when I am able to overlook the wrongs they do us mexicanos, I can imagine a new state in which we live together as equal partners. To his amazement, he was even willing to concede: If things go well, we might build in Tejas a new nation, half Texican, half mexicano.

But he never made that concession without immediately considering a major impediment: Those damned Texicans are so arrogant. Men come here from Tennessee and Kentucky, live on our land for two months, and start telling us mexicanos how to behave. Don't they know that this is our land? Has been for three hundred years. If they had decent manners, we would share our land with them.

In fairness he had to grant certain facts: Zave Campbell? No better man ever came to Tejas. Same goes for Finlay Macnab. And I'd be happy if Otto were my son. If all Texicans were like them and all mexicanos like me, we could build a tremendous state in Tejas, and it could be either a part of Mexico or a free nation of its own.

But insurmountable obstacles intruded: Campbell and Macnab are all right, and so is Mattie Quimper. But the others? Impossible. They despise our religion. They laugh at how we act. They even mock our language, imitating the way we sing the last words of a sentence as if we wanted the melody of our idea to linger in the air. What makes me bitter, they treat our women with contempt, unwilling to recognize the difference between a whore and a gentlewoman. If they insist on ridiculing everything we stand for, how can they hope to share our land with us?

Because he was an intelligent man, widely traveled, he had to admit a fact which most mexicanos living in Tejas refused to face: There seems to be an inevitability about these Texicans. They come pouring into Tejas and our mexicanos do not. In the last ten years I've seen hundreds of northerners drift in, not one mexicano and certainly never anyone from Spain. Maybe the future lies with the americanos. Maybe a new nation of some kind is inescapable.

But his accidental use of the word *americano* evoked the angriest memory of all: Those damned Texicans are such braggarts. Call themselves americanos as if they had the right to dominate both our continents. The only name they have a right to is *norteamericano,* and I will never again call them anything else.

Underlying these complaints, some of them trivial, was a deeper concern which intensified them all. Garza was a Mexican patriot who loved his beautiful, chaotic country and cherished the Spanish heritage from which his revered mother had sprung. He often thought of Mexico and Trinidad de Saldaña as one entity, an object of enormous dignity and worthy of devotion. To see this glorious world of Spain and Mexico smothered by Kentucky and Tennessee barbarism was so repugnant that he must defend the old values.

And now his conclusion: The only power that can save Tejas from being overwhelmed by the norteamericanos is Santa Anna. Forget that he destroyed the Constitution of 1824. Maybe his way of governing is best. One thing I'm sure of. He'll discipline those damned Texicans. So if he needs me, I'll have to fight on his side.

The moral and political struggle between an old Mexico and a new Tejas under a new form of government had been resolved. Benito Garza committed himself to fighting for the old, and so long as he lived he would never reconsider.

On 4 January, while Santa Anna was leading his men toward Saltillo, Benito made his final appearance in the market town of Victoria, where he talked quietly with the mexicanos he felt he could trust. Angel Guerra said frankly: 'When he tore up the Constitution of 1824 and made it impossible for us to govern ourselves . . . that day I said "To hell with Santa Anna." I'm fighting with the Texicans.' A surprising number of sensible mexicanos said the same; Santa Anna's dictatorial policies had alienated them.

But certain thoughtful men, and among them leaders of the community like

Elizondo Aldama, said: 'If the Texicans assume power, there can never be a decent role for us mexicanos. We'll always be third class, objects of contempt.'

'What are you going to do?' Garza asked guardedly.

'I'm certainly not going out to fight in Santa Anna's army, the way he treats his men, but I shall stay here within my walls and pray for his victory.' Many confided the same.

But a reassuring group took Benito aside: 'We know you're going to join Santa Anna. He'll teach those yanqui invaders. Tell him that when he finishes with Béjar and marches over here, he'll find hundreds of us eager to help.' Garza judged that the majority of the Victoria mexicanos felt that way.

He also found two young men who were burning to join the oncoming army, and to them he said solemnly: 'I'm riding to Béjar tomorrow at sunrise. Join me two miles west of the Macnab place, where the road forks.'

It was now midafternoon and Garza rode casually about Victoria, bidding farewell to a town he had grown to love. He was a striking figure, somewhat large for a mexicano, with light-brown skin, neatly trimmed mustache, dark hair across his forehead, an easy seat in his expensive saddle, and that twisted, ingratiating smile which he had inherited from his mother, the well-regarded Trinidad de Saldaña who had once ruled vast holdings along the Rio Grande. At certain turns of the rough streets he felt a pang of regret that he should be proposing to enter a war which might have disastrous consequences for Victoria and those citizens who were electing to side with the Texicans, but he knew it to be inevitable: Texicans and mexicanos cannot live side by side. As soon as he thought this he realized its impropriety: We live side by side right now, nowhere closer than in the Campbell dog-run. But we can't rule side by side. We cannot be treated justly by men who hold us in contempt. Santa Anna is right. Clean house. Shoot the tough old-timers . . . start new.

He shook his head in perplexity, for he had to appreciate the fallacy of what he had just thought. It was not the longtime Texicans who were the firebrands leading the rebellion; most of Austin's famous Old Three Hundred, the earliest anglo settlers, were content to remain mexicano citizens. It was men who had been in Tejas less than two years, less than a year, less, by God, than six weeks, who screamed for war. And now, Garza thought grimly, they're going to get it. He was prepared to annihilate all of them.

But when he reached the Campbell home and saw for the last time his three trusted friends, he had to leave the kitchen where his sisters María and Josefina were preparing supper, lest his confusion betray the harsh action he was about to take. In the darkening twilight he walked disconsolately along the banks of the Guadalupe, and under the oak tree from which Campbell had been hanged he thought of how much he loved these daring men, how he had trusted and worked with them, helping them build their homes and teaching their boy in the ways of his new land. He wondered if he should warn them of the danger that was about to engulf them, and he decided that to do so might endanger his own plans, but as they sat at supper he did suddenly blurt out: 'I think we are all in great danger. I think Santa Anna will sweep through Béjar and be here in Victoria within the month. Be careful, I beg you.'

Macnab said later: 'I guessed that night he was going to fight with Santa Anna.' When another Texican asked: 'Why didn't you stop him?' Finlay said: 'I was worried about my decision, not his.'

At dawn on 5 January, while the two mexicanos waited for Benito at the fork of the road, young Otto, who had suspected what was up, lingered far behind in the darkness to watch the three conspirators ride off. Desperately he wanted to bid his friend Godspeed but was afraid to do so. Unknown to Garza, Otto waved farewell to his Mexican friend as the sun rose over Victoria.

The three mexicanos rode speedily to Béjar, a hundred-odd miles to the northwest, where they found great confusion. Sketchy word had reached town that General Santa Anna was marching toward Tejas with an army of thousands, and Texican military men, or what passed for such, had already begun to survey the only defensible structure in Béjar, the Alamo, as the ruins of the old mission on the east side of the river were called. Since this was obviously to be the keystone of the Texican defense, Garza inspected it as carefully as he could without arousing the suspicions of the rough-clad men who patrolled it.

He saw that it was a spacious place running north and south, with sturdy adobe walls enclosing a central area large enough to house hundreds of cattle and thousands of men. Ancient buildings lined the inside of some of the walls; clearly, the place could be taken by determined assault, but if Tennessee and Kentucky men manned the walls with their powerful rifles, the cost could be sizable.

Still, Garza thought, I'd rather be outside with two thousand trying to get in than inside with a hundred and fifty trying to keep them out. He had made a cautious census of the Texicans but had arrived at a figure slightly too high; the Alamo contained only one hundred and forty-two fighting men.

At the southeast corner of the compound stood the mission church, a crumbling two-story building without a roof. Its walls were of stone and rather formidable. Anyone inside would be momentarily safe, but it could not be termed a fort and would probably play only a minor role in the siege. The ruined church was, in its way, impressive, a falling relic of those better days when Spanish friars had brought Christ and sanity to Tejas; it had been secularized in 1793, forty-three years earlier, and had from time to time been savagely abused by various army units stationed within.

One last thing Garza noticed as he completed his survey. Outside every wall of the old mission there was ample open ground, which would influence the flow of battle in two ways: the besieging army could maneuver and choose its spot for major attack; but the same open ground would enable the defenders to take unimpeded aim at any troops trying to assault the walls. Calculating the comparative advantages, Garza concluded: A determined assault will finish off the Alamo within three or four days.

Leaving the makeshift fortress on 13 January, he crossed the river, entered the town itself and checked the streets to see if any Texicans were stationed there. The Veramendi residence did contain one important Texican, Mordecai Marr, now seventy-two, but since his wife, Amalia, had converted him into a virtual mexicano, he posed no danger. At the former Saldaña house on the plaza, there were no signs of anglos. And the unfinished San Fernando Church looked down impassively on the quiet scene and tolled its bells at regular intervals.

At dusk on the same day Garza said farewell to Béjar. He rode past Rancho El Codo, once owned by the Saldañas, later by the Veramendis, now by the Marrs, and pressed on to San Juan Bautista, now called Presidio del Río Grande, from there to Monclova, and on toward Saltillo.

He did not reach this delightful little city because on the morning of 27 January 1836 he reined in his horse and stood in his stirrups to view a sight which thrilled him—marching north, raising clouds of dust, came the outriders of Santa Anna's army: Dear God, they've come to rescue us from those damned norteamericanos.

Spurring his horse, he galloped forward to meet the oncoming saviors, and when he drew within hailing distance he shouted: 'I must see General Santa Anna . . . at once.'

'Who are you?' a subaltern asked.

'A loyal mexicano, with information of great importance.'

He displayed such authority that he was led directly to the general, and saw for the first time El Salvador de México, the great Santa Anna. An imposing man of forty-one, tall, trim, dark-complexioned and with very black hair that sometimes drooped over his forehead, Santa Anna dressed himself, even on a march such as this, in uniforms of the most extravagant nature, with a flood of medals cascading down his chest. As a reward for his rape of Zacatecas, Major General Santa Anna had promoted himself to the rank of general-in-chief and taken the exalted title Benemérito en Grado Heroico, and there was gutter rumor that when he succeeded in subduing the Texicans, he was to name himself Benemérito Universal y Perpetuo.

This was the able, vainglorious, vengeful commander before whom Benito Garza bowed on the road north of Saltillo: 'Excellency, all Tejas is overjoyed to see you coming to our salvation.'

'I thank you. What is your name?'

'Benito Garza, of Victoria.'

'And how are things there?'

'The norteamericanos hold us in contempt. The mexicanos pray for your victory.'

'Their prayers will be answered,' he said, and from the resolute manner in which he spoke, Garza was convinced that they would be.

Who was this charismatic leader in whom all Mexicans seemed to place such hope? Born in 1794 in the Vera Cruz district, he had at age eighteen proved himself to be a man of extreme personal bravery, exhibited in many battles, but also one capable of adapting to almost any situation, as proved by the fact that he would ascend to the presidency of Mexico on eleven different occasions. Four times, at the height of one crisis or another, Mexico would send him into what was intended to be lifelong exile, and three times he would storm back to resume his leadership. The fourth time he tried, he failed.

There is no one in United States history remotely comparable, nor, for that matter, in any other country. He liked to call himself the Napoleon of the West, but Napoleon returned to power only once, and then for a scant hundred days; Santa Anna returned ten times.

It seemed that whenever he resumed power his actions carried special significance for Texicans, and two incidents in his remarkable career were especially relevant. In the hot summer of 1813, when he was nineteen, he had the bad luck to participate in the battle at the Medina River, which took place near San Antonio de Béjar, along the boundary between the Mexican territories of Coahuila and Tejas. Mexican dissidents aided by American adventurers had launched a minor revolution, which Spain's colonial government decided to crush with a harshness that would forever halt subversion north of the Rio Grande.

In the battle, Santa Anna helped spring a trap on the unsuspecting Americans, enabling his general to win a resounding victory, but it was what happened next that made the battle significant, for General Arredondo gave one simple order: 'Exterminate them!' A slaughter followed, with young Santa Anna participating in the execution at point-blank range of more than a hundred prisoners and the running down of many others.

He also helped cram more than two hundred captives into an improvised jail in San Antonio; by morning eighteen had suffocated. Most of the survivors were dragged into the town plaza and shot. But Arredondo's contemptuous treatment of the civilians surprised even Santa Anna. Any who were even suspected of supporting the insurgents were also summarily shot, and when the executions were completed he authorized his troops to loot and rape in the streets. To reinforce his disdain of the populace, the general ordered the leading matrons of the city to report to a detention area, where for eighteen days they were forced to do the laundry of the victorious invaders and cook their food.

This crushing victory, and Santa Anna's resulting promotion, must, however, be judged an unfortunate affair for him. The ease with which the triumph came and the harshness which followed encouraged him to believe that the way to handle insurgents was to beat them convincingly in battle, then execute the men and humiliate the women. Now, twenty-three years later, faced with another insurgency in Tejas, he was not only prepared to duplicate those punishments but also eager to do so, for he could be extremely cruel and unforgiving when he judged it necessary to be so.

Perhaps Mexico required a ruthless leader like Santa Anna, for these were turbulent years. During one period when the United States had only one President —Andrew Jackson, who helped bind his nation together—unlucky Mexico staggered through sixteen different incumbencies, the hideous penalty paid by many former Spanish colonies that seized their freedom without obtaining with it any coherent theory of responsible government.

But whenever Santa Anna resumed his leadership things seemed to be better . . . for a while; then he would do some outrageous thing and the government would collapse again. During one return to power, having taken back the presidency on a pompously announced program of reform, he assured the electorate that he was a liberal who would reform the church, discipline the army, and grant each of the constituent states a substantial degree of self-government. As we have seen, Texicans rejoiced in this promise of a constructive freedom under which they could populate and improve their frontier regions.

But in 1834 he had startled everyone, and perhaps even himself, by announcing: 'I now realize that I am really a conservative, and as such, I offer the nation a clear three-point program which will save it from its current turbulence. We must replace federalism with a supreme central government, with the individual states having few powers and no legislatures. The traditional role of the church in national affairs must be restored. And the ancient privileges by which priests and army officers were excused from the rules of common law must be restored.' Reviving the battle cry of 'Religión y Fueros' (Religion and the Rights of Priests and Army Officers), he scuttled the liberal Constitution of 1824 and converted Mexico into a conservative dictatorship—and many citizens applauded: 'At last we have a strong man in control. He should be made our leader for life.'

Now came the move which struck terror into the hearts of Texicans who had hoped for better, more orderly days. The rich silver state of Zacatecas, refusing to surrender its hard-won rights to Santa Anna's central dictatorship, launched a kind of rebellion in defense of its privileges, and this was exactly the kind of challenge Santa Anna loved, for it enabled him to don his general's bemedaled uniform, mount his white horse, and ride into battle.

Leading a large army up to the walls of Zacatecas, he then ripped a page from Napoleon's book, swung around the town, and attacked from the rear. At the same time he ordered several of his best officers to leave his ranks in apparent defection, sneak into the city, and proclaim themselves defenders of the Constitution of 1824 and mortal enemies of Santa Anna. As trained soldiers, they expected to be given command of Zacatecan troops, whom they would direct into certain slaughter when the fighting began.

On 11 May 1835, with this combination of valor and deceit, Santa Anna won a devastating victory, but it was what happened next that boded ill for Tejas, for he turned his men loose in one of the ghastly rampages of Mexican history. During the terror some two thousand five hundred women and children and men who had not participated in the battle were slain. Foreign families became special targets, with English and American husbands bayoneted and their wives stripped naked and coursed through the streets. Rape and pillage continued for two days, until the once-fair city was a burning, screaming ruin.

Zacatecas had been ravaged because it refused to change its loyalty as quickly as Santa Anna had changed his, and word went out: 'If Tejas continues to oppose the central government and tries to cling to its old constitution, it can expect like punishment.' And in the dying days of 1835, backed by an immense army, aided by good generals and strong artillery, Generalísimo Santa Anna marched north, determined to humiliate once more the recalcitrant Texicans. All who opposed him would be slain.

On 13 February 1836 this remorseless general, accompanied by a cadre of senior officers, rode ahead to the Rio Grande and were snug inside San Juan Bautista while the main body of the troops, accompanied by Benito Garza, lagged far behind, marching on foot across that exposed and dangerous wasteland between Monclova and the river. Santa Anna, always looking ahead to the next battle and disregarding the comfort of his troops, had no cause to worry about his straggling men because the day had started with the temperature near sixty and the sun so hot that many soldiers removed their jackets and marched in shirt only, and sometimes not even that.

But this was the region just south of that in which Cabeza de Vaca had experienced the dreaded blue norther, and such a storm now hit men who had never experienced the phenomenon. At its first warning blast they hastily re-donned their shirts and jackets.

Rapidly the temperature dropped to fifty, then forty, then to an appalling thirty. Men began to slow their pace, hugging themselves to keep warm, and mules started to wander in confusion. By midafternoon a wild snowstorm was sweeping across the unfettered flatlands of Tejas and northern Coahuila, and at dusk men and animals began to freeze.

All night the dreadful storm continued, throwing twelve to fourteen inches of snow upon men who had never felt its icy fingers before. They began to stumble, and many collapsed; then the snow covered them and they became inert white mounds along the route, as if in their final moments they had pulled fleecy blankets over their dying bodies.

Worst hit was a horde of pitiful Indians from Yucatán marching under the command of General Víctor de Ripperdá, governor of that tropical district and former official in charge of the frontier post at Nacogdoches. His troops, hundreds of them with no shoes, no blankets, no warm clothing of any kind, simply fell down and died. Sometimes Garza, who rode up and down the files, would find eight or nine huddled together in a hopeless mass, clutching one another for warmth; after they all perished, the covering snow formed a rounded hump, a kind of natural mausoleum. When more fortunate Indians from colder climates, those with shoes and blankets, spotted such a mound, they dug inside, stripped the dead bodies of whatever cloth remained, and wrapped their own faces against the storm.

At the rear, Garza came upon soldaderas and their children suffering terribly, but like the Yucatecs they huddled in groups, and although many died, the stronger survived. It was shocking for those soldiers who formed the rear guard to stumble upon the frozen bodies of children abandoned in the snow.

Mules, oxen and horses struggled in the blinding storm, collapsing in huge snowdrifts that quickly buried them. When the norther subsided, and the surviving men and mules were counted, General Ripperdá found that his army had suffered a tremendous loss. Santa Anna, warm inside mission walls, must have known this, but neither then nor after did he refer to it, for he realized that when many soldiers are required to march over a great distance in unfavorable weather, somebody is apt to die. That was one of the chances of war, unpleasant but acceptable.

And from the practical point of view, Ripperdá's experience in the Monclova blizzard may have been salutary, for it rid him of many largely useless Yucatecs, toughened up the line, and enabled one young lieutenant who dreamed of impending glory to assure his fellow officers: 'If we can survive that blizzard, we have little to fear from the rebels in Tejas. It'll be Zacatecas all over again.'

When Benito Garza rode north of the Rio Grande toward Tejas with Santa Anna, he had an opportunity to see why the mexicano troops, officers and enlisted men alike, loved this dynamic man. He obviously thrived on campaign conditions and could hardly wait, Benito thought, to launch the attack. 'Forward, forward!' was his constant command to himself and his troops.

The dictator was going to be forty-two years old the next day, 21 February, and he would spend it in the saddle a few miles south of his ultimate target, the Alamo. The passing years had treated him well, and he looked, if the truth were voiced—and he liked it to be voiced—a good deal like one of Napoleon's marshals, Ney or Soult, or even like the emperor himself.

On this campaign he had brought along none of his mistresses, and Garza heard him complain to General Cós: 'How can a gentleman celebrate his birthday alone?' So on Santa Anna's natal day Cós ordered salutes to be fired and a ration of wine issued for celebration. The troops were now approaching the Medina, where Santa Anna had known his first great victory, with many, many more anglo rebels in the field then than there would be now. The general wanted to leave El Camino Real briefly and veer eastward toward the old battle site, but when this was done and the steep banks of the river reached, no one could locate exactly the scene of the battle, and Santa Anna was mildly displeased.

On the day after his birthday, Santa Anna moved his troops to within sight of the tall tower of San Fernando Church, just across the river from the Alamo, and there he made camp early. Scouts rode in to inform him of conditions in the town, and everything he heard was reassuring: 'No reinforcements and none on the way. Colonel Fannin and his large detachment bottled up at Goliad and he refuses to move to Béjar. Still no more than a hundred and fifty men, but they do have some cannon. And the entire town, General, is eager to welcome you.'

'Are there any mexicanos fighting with them?' This problem of loyalty irritated him.

'Captain Juan Seguín has taken arms against you. Says he will fight for the Constitution of 1824.'

'Do any support him?'

'He led nine others into the Alamo. We have their names. Abamillo, Badillo, Espalier . . .' He continued to read from the grubby paper, nine names in all.

'They're to be hanged. Not shot. Hanged.' Even as he gave this order one of the mexicanos slipped out of the Alamo, but the other nine were determined to oppose the dictator with their lives, in defense of a new Texas which would later have little use for their kind.

Garza rode with the general as he entered the town in the lead, disregarding the possibility of isolated sniper fire from some misguided rebel. No doubt about it, this man was brave. Turning back to face Garza, he gave a short command: 'I want the flag I showed you last night to be flown immediately.' And now they reached the heart of Béjar, with Garza pointing out the church.

'Can its tower be seen at the Alamo?' the general asked.

'Unquestionably.'

'Fly the flag.'

So Benito Garza climbed the quivering tower stairs, accompanied by two dragoons, and when they reached the highest practical point he unfurled the big flag made from cloth which Santa Anna had brought north for this specific purpose.

The rude flag was very large, perhaps twelve feet long and proportionately wide, but despite its size, it carried no symbol of any kind. Its message was its color, a bold, sullen blood-red over all.

As the flag unfurled, a breeze caught it and spread it majestically in the sky. Those who saw it and understood its military meaning gasped, for this was the flag of No Surrender, No Clemency. The soldiers who fought against it knew that they must either kill or be killed, because no prisoners would be taken.

When Garza descended from the bell tower, an orderly informed him that the general wanted his assistance in translating an important document into English.

The two men went to a house located in the smaller plaza between the church and the bridge leading across the river to the Alamo. Here Santa Anna outlined the rules for this and all subsequent battles in the district of Tejas. They were, as he carefully pointed out, in strict conformance with international law and with the recently promulgated rules of the new dictatorship:

> Every Mexican who has fought with the rebels or in any way supported them is to be hanged, and I want no protracted trials. Just hang them for treason. Every American colonist who has taken arms against us, to be shot, and again, no trials. Those who supported the rebels but did not take arms, to be expelled forever from Mexican soil. All American immigrants, regardless of their sympathies, to be moved at least a hundred miles south of the Rio Grande, whether they can bring their household goods or not. Absolutely no further immigration of any kind from the American states into Tejas or any other part of Mexico. The people of Tejas to repay every peso of expense incurred on this expedition to discipline them.

> Now, this is very important and is to be stressed in any pronouncement we make. Any foreigner in Tejas who is arrested while in the possession of arms of any kind is to be judged a pirate and treated accordingly. Finally, the flag up there tells it better than I can. Once the battle begins, if the enemy has not previously surrendered, no prisoners will be taken. Make this extremely clear. No prisoners are to be taken. They are to be shot on the battlefield where we capture them.

Shortly thereafter a white flag of truce showed at the Alamo and a parley took place on the little bridge crossing the river; here the final terms were spelled out to the Americans, in their own language. But they were, as Garza noted when he delivered them, somewhat softened: 'If you surrender unconditionally, right now, lay down your arms and take a pledge never to appear in Tejas again, your lives and property will be spared.' Garza, hoping that actual battle could be avoided and the invaders peaceably expelled, prayed that the norteamericanos would accept these surprisingly generous terms, but when the emissary returned to the Alamo the answer from there was delivered in the form of a cannon shot, whose roar reverberated across the main plaza. Santa Anna had his answer.

He did not lose his temper. Coolly summoning his generals, he said: 'We'll not throw our entire force against that silly fortress. We'll save it for later punishment of the entire state.'

'How do you propose knocking them out of their position?' General Cós asked, indicating the Alamo.

'Siege. We'll strangle them, bombard them with cannon, and shoot them down when they collapse.'

'With your permission, Excellency,' General Ripperdá said. 'I had long experience with norteamericanos when I served at Nacogdoches. Those scoundrels will not collapse.'

'Your norteamericanos did not face Santa Anna.'

So the siege began, and no prisoners were to be taken alive. The customs of war as observed by civilized nations justified such terms for treasonous rebellion against a sovereign state, and that is exactly what the Texican rebels were engaged in.

The sad fracture which threatened to destroy this lovely area was reflected in the names used by its people. Mexicanos called it the town of Béjar in Tejas; Texicans, San Antonio in Texas—and between them no compromise seemed possible.

The unfurling of the great red flag produced unexpected consequences in one San Antonio household. At the northern end of Soledad Street, in the old Veramendi place, Mordecai Marr and his mexicana wife, Amalia, saw the flag lazily fluttering in the breeze and realized for the first time that this was to be a battle to the death. They had hoped that differences between the central government in Mexico and the provincial one in Tejas could be peacefully resolved, but now men had to make decisions.

This was particularly difficult for the Marrs. To begin with, they were citizens of Mexico, of that there could be no doubt. She came from the grandest family in the region, with notable ties to the Veramendis of Saltillo, and her husband had embraced Mexican citizenship back in 1792 when he married her and came into possession of the vast ranch at El Codo. Not once in succeeding years had he even contemplated trying to regain his American citizenship, and in recent years when minor troubles flared he had been a pacifying agent, assuring American newcomers that the things they disliked could be easily corrected.

But since the new year, two events had altered the family thinking. From a Zacatecan refugee connected to the Veramendis they heard harrowing reports of Santa Anna's treatment of that city, and this had made them wonder whether such a leader could retain the good will of his Tejas citizens. More confusing, they learned that inside the Alamo, among the handful of men preparing to defend it, was their respected relative Jim Bowie of Kentucky.

Back in 1831 this colorful outsider had married Ursula Veramendi, the winsome belle of the family. At first the respectable mexicano families of Saltillo and San Antonio predicted only bad consequences from such a union, but Bowie surprised them by becoming an ardent Catholic, a devoted husband and a fine father to his and Ursula's children. Even the local priest had said: 'The Jim Bowie marriage is one of the most reassuring in Tejas. Who would have expected it?'

The Marrs had deemed it imprudent to visit Jim inside the Alamo, for they certainly did not share his determination to resist Santa Anna. Also, when in 1833 the lovely Ursula and her two children died of cholera, Bowie's essential ties with the Veramendi family were broken and the Marrs had not seen him since that tragedy. 'He goes his way,' Mordecai said to the old-timers, 'and we go ours. But we respect him, always have.'

So there it stood on the afternoon when the flag signaled, and the longer Mordecai contemplated this dreadful twist of events, the more perturbed he became. He ate no supper. Pacing back and forth in the study that he had come to love as the heart of his home, he thought of the curious forces which had brought him to this unlikely spot. He did not love the United States, and he actively disliked most of the immigrants he met. Nor did he love Tejas, but he still loved the freedom, the bigness of the land he had elected for his home, and he did not want to lose that. The men in the Alamo represented a striving to keep that freedom, while the men who had unfurled the flag of death could represent only repression.

It was half after nine when he walked soberly into the big room where Amalia was busy with her needlework, and when he came upon her as she sat with the flickering light behind her lovely head, he saw her as if for the first time. How happy they had been! He'd been on the verge of marrying the Saldaña girl when Amalia Veramendi moved in to sweep him off his feet with her love, her wit, and her promises of a vast ranch if he married her. Never had he regretted the decision, although he did sometimes wonder what had happened to the Saldaña girl, whose first name he could not now remember.

'Amalia, I'm going to join Jim Bowie.'

'I will go with you.' She said this so simply, her needlework in her lap, that he was overcome by her courage, but when he started to say that if she changed her mind— 'What other choice could I have?' she interrupted, rising and kissing him. 'We've had a wonderful life, Mordecai, because we always did everything together. Let's not change now.'

They spent less than an hour getting a few things together, and it was well before midnight when they left the Veramendi home and walked quietly down dark Soledad Street to the church square. There they turned left, walked through the small area subtended by the loop in the river, and approached the little footbridge leading to the Alamo. Santa Anna's guards stopped them, of course, but when Amalia told the officer: 'I'm the Veramendi woman, my family owns that house over there,' they let her and her Mordecai pass.

Once across the bridge, the proud couple, their white hair shining in the moonlight, turned and, without provoking any action on the part of the remaining guards, walked purposefully toward the old mission. When they were in hailing distance, an American patrolling the walls shouted at them, and Mordecai called back: 'Veramendis, we come to see Jim Bowie.' They could hear conversation inside and then see the cautious opening of the gate.

Quickly they slipped through, saw the huge area inside the walls and a rather small room to the right, where Jim Bowie lay prostrate from a sudden attack of the fever. Amalia, hurrying to his cot, whispered: 'Jim, Mordecai is here. We've come to be with you.' And the sick man reached out to grasp their hands.

The Marrs found the Alamo dominated by four remarkable men. Two were wild frontier heroes: Jim Bowie, in command of the volunteers, and Davy Crockett. The other two were cool, well-educated gentlemen: Colonel William Travis, commander of the regular troops, and James Bonham, a quiet man with a personal courage matched by few and surpassed by none. The original homes of these four epitomized much of Texas history: the two frontiersmen were from Tennessee, of course, while the gentlemen were from South Carolina. On the character of these four would depend the defense of the Alamo.

Next morning, while Señora Marr comforted the despondent Bowie, her husband explored the arena in which they would do battle. The huge walled-in area astounded him: 'We could move all the people of Béjar in here and they'd fill only a corner.' But as he walked about, surveying the walls and calculating their ability to withstand Mexican cannon fire, he learned the nature of this siege, for Santa Anna's artillery began their morning bombardment. After taking refuge under a shed, Marr watched while large cannonballs came drifting in over the walls, landed in the middle of the open area, and rolled harmlessly along until they came to rest against some obstruction, hurting no one, destroying nothing.

Since the Mexican gunners seemed never to vary the position, aim or elevation of their cannon, the balls invariably landed in the same harmless spot, and when Marr realized this, he snorted: 'We can hold out a month against that stuff.'

While he was reaching this conclusion, Colonel Travis was working in a small room, as far from the barrage as possible, composing with a scratchy pen a letter that would be remembered in Texas history. Staring at the red flag, he knew that unless reinforcements arrived quickly he and his men were doomed, but instead of surrendering, he threw his gauntlet into the face of the world:

To the People of Texas and All Americans in the World—

Fellow Citizens and Compatriots:

I am besieged by a thousand or more of the Mexicans under Santa Anna . . . The enemy has demanded a surrender at discretion, otherwise, the garrison are to be put to the sword, if the fort is taken. I have answered the demand with a cannon shot, and our flag still waves proudly from

the walls. *I shall never surrender or retreat* . . . I call on you in the
name of Liberty, of patriotism and everything dear to the American
character, to come to our aid, with all dispatch . . . If this call is
neglected, I am determined to sustain myself as long as possible and die
like a soldier who never forgets what is due his honor and that of his
country.

VICTORY OR DEATH

William Barret Travis

Substantial help was available in the countryside: at Goliad, some miles to the
southeast, there was an organized branch of the army, and at Gonzales, due east, a
random collection of untrained patriots. If these forces marched swiftly to the
Alamo, it might be saved.

When Zave Campbell heard that Santa Anna was marching north with more than
two thousand troops, his first thought was a practical one: I better get some cattle
up to New Orleans. He therefore made hurried plans to get a herd together, but
he was temporarily forestalled by the sudden disappearance of Garza and by the
fact that Finlay Macnab, also apprehensive about the approach of Santa Anna,
would not allow Otto to leave home at this critical time. Despite these two
drawbacks, Zave felt that if he could but get to Gonzales and talk to the locals, he
could enlist the help he needed there. Accordingly, he scurried about, grabbing
items that would prove useful on the long drive and issuing last-minute instructions to María.

'With me gone, you can help the Macnabs, if they need it.'

'Take care of yourself, Xavier.'

In days to come he would try to recall this scene, this parting with a woman he
had grown to love late in his life, but he would be unable to do so. There was no
significant speech, no meaningful farewell and no commitment one way or another. He had left home often before, and he had never taken much account of
parting then, nor did he now.

'Goodbye, old lady. Ten cuidado.' And he was gone, thinking only briefly of
how stalwart a woman she was. He knew he'd been damned lucky to find her.
Her brother? Ah, that was another matter. With Benito and his hot temper, one
never knew. Probably heading south right now to join up with Santa Anna. Well,
that was his business and it did not affect María. In this life all men, it seemed,
had trouble with their in-laws.

With that succinct summary of his family affairs as of 12 February 1836, he
followed the Guadalupe upstream for two full days and part of a third, after
which he entered the little town of Gonzales, only to find it so involved with

plans for war that any prospect of collecting cattle vanished. One rancher who could have supplied hundreds reported: 'All my hands have quit. You ask me, they're on their way to fight for Santy Anny.'

The Gonzales men took this seriously, and for good reason. Only the previous October the Mexican government had sent soldiers to Gonzales to repossess a cannon loaned to the town; the thinking had been that with agitation spreading throughout Tejas for the establishment of a self-governing state divorced from Coahuila, it was prudent to confiscate any weapons which might be used against government troops.

To the amazement of the Mexican officers, the men of Gonzales had refused to surrender their cannon; instead, they used the thing to lob cannonballs at the troops, then unfurled an insulting flag showing a rude drawing of the cannon and the inscription, neatly lettered: COME AND TAKE IT.

The whole affair was absurd, really, because the so-called cannon was a midget affair so small that two men could drag it along, but it did throw a much larger ball than a rifle, so it was technically a cannon, and the men, exhilarated by their defeat of the Mexican army—one trooper killed—began referring to their brief skirmish as 'The Lexington of the Texican Revolution.' If Santa Anna really was on his way to Tejas, one of his first and most brutal stops would be at Gonzales.

Campbell, irritated by this interruption of his plans, moved from one former customer to another, pleading with them to assign him the cattle he needed for his drive to New Orleans, but they were preoccupied. Disgusted, he stopped on the following morning at the store of the Widow Fuqua to pass the time in idle conversation.

'How did a Jew get to a town like this?'

'We travel to all parts. Always have.'

'Where did you come from?'

'All parts.'

'You any idea how I might get my cattle together?' Mrs. Fuqua had no suggestions, for as she reminded Zave, all the Mexicans had fled.

At this moment the shopkeeper's young son, Galba, entered, and Zave asked: 'How old are you, son?' and the lad replied: 'Sixteen.'

'How'd you like to help me herd a string of cattle to New Orleans?' The prospect of such an excursion delighted the boy, small for his age but much like Otto in his apparent ability, and he responded enthusiastically: 'If Mother allows.'

When Mrs. Fuqua nodded, Zave said: 'I'll take care of your son, but first we got to gather our herd.'

'That can be done,' the boy said, and on the spot he outlined a plan whereby he and two friends, one of them a lad his own age named Johnny Gaston, could collect the longhorns as effectively as any Mexicans: 'We can ride and rope.' Permission was granted by the owners, who were glad to see their stock moved out of the way of an incoming danger, and by Tuesday, the twenty-third, it began to look as if Campbell would succeed in getting his drove on the road before the beginning of March.

But on Wednesday about noon two dusty horsemen galloped in from the west with a written plea from the American commander in the Alamo:

> The enemy in large force is in sight. We want men and provisions. Send them to us. We have 150 men and are determined to defend the Alamo to the last. Give us assistance.

Now all talk of cattle vanished. Men spoke only of what could be done to aid their imperiled fellows trapped in San Antonio, and many wild proposals involving no risk were made, but suddenly the aching truth was voiced: 'We have got to march a relief force into the Alamo.'

On Thursday the discussion resumed, and now all listened intently as the messengers honestly laid forth the situation:

> 'Santa Anna has nearly two thousand men there already, with more marching in daily. We have no more than a hundred and fifty. But think of the men we do have. Jim Bowie, Davy Crockett, this young wild man William Travis. With your help they can win.

> 'Men of Gonzales, if you do not support us now, the Alamo will fall, Santa Anna will march to your town and destroy it. Upon you depends the freedom of Texas. And you know that on the freedom of Texas depends the freedom of the United States. You must act now.'

These ringing words evoked a flurry of patriotism throughout the town, and women began assembling supplies should their men decide to march; but the decision could be reached only painfully, for the men of Gonzales were intelligent enough to know that odds against them of 2,000-to-150 were perilous. It was clearly understood that anyone who entered the Alamo within the next few days stood a very good chance of dying there, and almost no chance whatever of holding the fortress indefinitely against the overwhelming power of the enemy. On these harsh terms the debate began.

One man asked: 'Did not General Houston advise Travis to abandon the Alamo? Knock down the walls and let the Mexicans have it?'

'He did,' a messenger snapped. His knee had been badly wrenched during an intrepid scout he had made of the oncoming Mexican forces as they approached San Antonio, and he was impatient with these thoughtful, careful men: If I can risk my life on that damned horse, not a hundred yards from the whole Mexican army, why can't they see the crisis at the Alamo? Controlling his temper, he said: 'General Houston did order the place abandoned, but it is always the man on the spot who must make the final decision, and Travis, after weighing everything, decided to dig in and fight. Now you must make your decision.'

On Friday, 26 February, the men of Gonzales were beginning to think that maybe they should organize a relief party and march to the support of the men in the Alamo, and by noon the momentum to join that party became an emotional bonfire which engulfed the town. Twenty men signified their willingness, then another five, then still another five, then the richest man in town, Thomas R. Miller, whose young wife had recently run off with a more attractive fellow. By nightfall, thirty-one men had volunteered to lay down their lives, if necessary, in defense of freedom, and among them were two of the boys on whom Zave Campbell had been depending to gather his cattle: Galba Fuqua and Johnny Gaston, brother of the young girl who had run away from Miller.

Zave Campbell, idled through no fault of his own, did not jump to volunteer; this was not his war; as the husband of a wonderful Mexican woman, who became more precious the more he thought of her, he bore no general animosity toward Mexicans; and as a man who had been damn near hanged by loud-mouthed Texicans, he felt no responsibility to them. But with nothing better to do, he did watch from the sidelines as they formed in their final muster, and a more disorganized group of would-be heroes he had never seen. Short boys and gangling men, lads who had never shaved and oldsters with wandering beards, they were all dressed differently, with not a single item of true military dress in the lot. If they wore hats, they were big and floppy; their shoes were shapeless and worn; their homespun trousers were of a dozen different sizes, lengths and thicknesses. A few wore bandoleers; a few had improvised knapsacks; two had bayonets on their long rifles; but each seemed to have a long-bladed knife and three had a pair.

When the roll call was completed, the newly elected officer announced: 'We march at noon tomorrow,' and that night Zave found it difficult to sleep. He felt no urge to choose sides, but he had to respect the courage of these rude countrymen who felt obligated to defend their freedoms. So as the long night waned, he felt himself drawn ever closer to the patriots.

He spent Saturday morning watching odd corners of the town where volunteers bade farewell to their families, and as he saw these emotional scenes he became so confused that when the line formed for the march to the Alamo, he quietly joined at the rear.

In the entire history of Texas there would be none braver than these thirty-two from Gonzales, for each man in this heroic file could say to himself, between thundering heartbeats: I know I'm marching to almost certain death, and I know it's insane, but I prize freedom above life itself.

Finlay Macnab, an orderly man of forty-four, was downright disgusted at the chaos into which Tejas had fallen even before Santa Anna fired his first gun. As he explained with some bitterness to Otto: 'It's a damned disgrace. We have an army of maybe two thousand men, but our shaky government has appointed four supreme commanders. And each one holds a commission which confirms that he is superior to the other three.'

Macnab was correct. A wavering revolutionary government, unsure whether it wanted statehood within Mexico, jointure with the United States, or a free nation of its own, had appointed Sam Houston, vainglorious but demonstrably able, as commander in chief of the army on the basis of his militia rank years ago in Tennessee. But they had also designated Colonel James Fannin, a West Point man but not a graduate, as commander of the regular army contingent and subsidiary to no one. Rump forces within the government had given still another command to Dr. James Grant, born in Scotland and since 1825 owner of an enormous ranch west of Saltillo; a volatile man much hated in northern Mexico, he had served in the governing body of Coahuila-y-Tejas until Santa Anna prorogued it and now sought revenge.

The fourth contestant for top honors was an irascible Virginia-Alabama-Illinois schoolteacher and greengrocer with military delusions; at a time of crisis in 1835 he had assumed command of a privateering force that had captured the Alamo from General Cós and sent him kiting back to Mexico under pledge never to return under arms. Commander in Chief Frank W. Johnson had his own plans for subduing Mexico; in executing them with total ineptness he would lose his entire force save four, but he himself would escape and live another forty-eight years, during which he would write a five-volume history of the times he had seen and the heroisms he had performed.

There was, of course, a fifth commander, almost insanely jealous of the other four and possibly more gifted as a military leader than any of them: Colonel William Travis, who still held on to the Alamo in gross disobedience to orders from General Houston that he abandon it and blow it up.

These five warring commanders led forces totaling only two thousand troops. All Santa Anna had to do was knock them off, one by one, and this he was in the process of accomplishing.

'It's insane,' Macnab said to his son as they chopped wood on their farm along the Guadalupe. 'A man would be crazy to get himself involved in such nonsense.' Consequently, he was not moved when on 8 January, Colonel Fannin sent a horseman through the countryside with an urgent call for volunteers to help him defend the eastern lands around Victoria.

So the Macnabs refused to attend the big organizing effort at which more than a hundred late arrivals with a Georgia Battalion whooped and cheered as they joined the Fannin crusade. A lively group of Irish immigrants who had recently taken up land in the nearby Irish colonies made even more noise when they enlisted, and equally valued were four well-trained Polish engineers who reported from the scattered Polish settlers in the area. Just as their countryman Thaddeus

Kosciusko had built most of General Washington's fortifications during the Revolution, they would assume responsibility for perfecting Fannin's defenses.

Macnab, listening to reports of how successful the meeting had been, had reason to hope that in this command, at least, things would move forward intelligently, and he concluded that he and his son could leave the prosecution of this war to the enthusiasts. He was startled when he learned that this odd assortment of would-be soldiers had moved practically into his backyard, fortifying themselves noisily in the abandoned presidio at Goliad, less than thirty miles from the Macnab farm. He could no longer escape the fact that the war had encroached upon him.

Even so, he remained reluctant to associate himself with what he feared would be a disastrous experience, and he was in this confused, gloomy frame of mind when, on 18 February, a twenty-nine-year-old man of the most compelling honesty galloped unattended into nearby Goliad with urgent news. He was Lieutenant James Bonham, a lawyer from South Carolina, whose heroic longings had been ignited by reports of what the Texas patriots were attempting. Like so many others whose names would soon glorify Texas history, he had arrived only recently in the territory—less than three months before—but his cool enthusiasm was so respected that he was quickly made an officer, whereupon he volunteered for service in the Alamo. Now, as danger threatened that bastion, he had at incredible risk broken through the enemy cordon and ridden eastward for help, and the men at Goliad listened in deepening apprehension as he informed them of the facts about the Alamo:

> 'Our side has a hundred and fifty men. Santa Anna has nearly two thousand already, with more on the way. The odds sound impossible, but with the kind of heroes we have—I mean the determination, the steady fire they're capable of—I believe we can hold the fort till the rest of Texas mobilizes.
>
> 'What we need now is for every fighting man in this part of Texas to rush to the Alamo. Strengthen our perimeters! Give us help! Start to march now! The freedom of Texas and the whole United States lies in the balance! Help us!'

Colonel Fannin, listening attentively to the plea, assured Bonham that 'he would think it over,' whereupon the impetuous young lieutenant saluted, trying to hide his anger at this vacillation, and spurred his horse onward to Victoria. There he assembled the local farmers, to whom he delivered his message with such dramatic force that young Otto Macnab blurted out: 'Where are you going next?' and Bonham said without hesitation: 'Back to the Alamo.'

'Can I go with you?'

The South Carolinian looked down at the boy and said: 'Take your father to Goliad. March with Colonel Fannin and his men. They're going to reinforce us.'

'Will you go back alone?' Otto asked.

'I came alone.'

He said this so simply, so sweetly, as if he were talking to a woman about strolling through a park, that Otto was enthralled. This was the kind of man he longed to be with, and he watched with tumultuous agitation as the former lawyer turned westward toward his elected station in the Alamo. He had fought his way out of that fortress and now he was prepared to fight his way back in.

As he disappeared, Otto asked his father: 'If things are so bad, why does he go back in?' and Finlay replied: 'I doubt he considered any other possibility.'

That night neither Macnab could sleep. Otto's head was filled with images of galloping horses, challenges at dusk, guns blazing, and a lone man leaping his horse across obstacles. His father's visions were more controlled and much more sober; he saw a beleaguered Texas, chaotically led, staggering and fumbling its way toward liberty, and he saw the irresistible logic of Bonham's plea: 'Unite with us! Help us! Give us the time we need till Texas mobilizes.'

All night these words rang in his ears, growing more forceful with each reiteration, until, toward dawn, he rose and walked alone beside the river that he had grown to love. It was peaceful now, a beautiful river, home of birds and haven for thirsty animals, and it had become a real home for him. Looking up to the branches of the trees that stood along its bank, he could see debris from the last terrible flood, many feet above his head. Texas is in flood, he told himself as the sun rose, and no one can predict where the debris will finally rest.

At breakfast he told Josefina: 'Otto and I better get ready to leave.' When she asked: 'For what?' he told her in Spanish: 'We must go to Goliad.'

'To fight against my people?'

'Your people are fighting against us.'

She sat down, with her apron brought to her face as if to hide tears, and said sorrowfully: 'I think maybe so,' but what it was she truly thought, she did not confide.

She was further distressed when Otto left, obviously to say farewell to María Campbell, whom he loved first and strongest, but at noon, when the boy returned, she and Finlay had all things packed, and the two Macnabs headed southwest for the presidio at Goliad.

On leap year day, General Santa Anna's equerry came to Benito Garza and said: 'I want you to find some soldier, about thirty years old, who could look like a priest.'

'Why?'

'Do as you're told.'

So Garza wandered among the troops looking for someone who might resemble a priest if properly garbed, and by chance he came upon a real priest serving the troops, a Father Palacio, whom he took to the adjutant.

To Garza's surprise, the officer was infuriated, and although he tried to mask his rage while the priest was present, as soon as the clergyman departed he slapped Garza across the face and shouted: 'Do as you're told, damn you.' Benito was so astonished by this insulting treatment that he resumed his search in anger and finally found a rather fat fellow who looked as if he might play the drunken friar in a barracks-room comedy put on by locals.

Leading him like a child to the equerry, Garza said hopefully: 'I think this one will do,' and to his relief the officer said: 'So do I. Now find him the clothes.'

'What clothes?' Benito asked, and again the equerry started to slap him, but this time Benito grabbed the man's wrist, twisting it savagely as he whispered in a shaking voice: 'You do that again, I kill you.'

The young officer, stunned that a man he took to be a peasant should behave so, reached forward as if to strike Garza, but when he saw Benito's flaring nostrils and grim eyes, he drew back. In a chastened voice he said: 'We need some priest's clothes.' This proved a more difficult task, but after more than an hour spent searching, Benito came upon an old woman in the main plaza who said that a priest who had once boarded in her house had died. She found remnants of his habit, and when it was fitted to the fat soldier he did indeed look like a priest.

Garza knocked on the equerry's door, and when that officer saw the *soi-disant* priest he was delighted: 'Just what we need!' And he hurried both Garza and the priest down Soledad Street to the Veramendi house, where, in the old courtyard with the fountain playing, a wedding party had assembled.

Benito met the bride, a lively, attractive girl of nineteen whose mother had succeeded in protecting her from half a dozen officers who had tried to capture her: 'She marries, this one, and that's the only way.' Refusing even colonels any access to her daughter, she had proclaimed repeatedly that she and her mother before her were ladies of high quality and rigorous morals, and that she intended keeping her daughter that way. In the end, apparently, some officer had surrendered and proposed marriage, but it was clear to Garza and to the equerry at least, that the wedding was to be a cynical charade performed by a fake priest.

Benito was indignant at this, for the woman and her daughter were respectable mexicanas, and here the mexicano army was treating them with the same contempt the Texicans did. He had expected better from Santa Anna's men. The general himself had repeatedly expressed to Garza his respect for the locals, assuring him that once the norteamericanos were evicted, men like Garza would assume command and make Tejas a rich and leading province within the mexicano system. Benito thought it a good thing that Santa Anna did not know of this burlesque, for he was sure the general would have halted it.

But at this moment cheers erupted and all heads turned admiringly to greet the lucky bridegroom, who marched sedately from the interior of the palace, bestowing nods and smiles on all. It was Santa Anna himself, solidly married in Xalapa, with numerous children and with at least seven mistresses in the capital. As the tedious siege had worn on, day after day, he felt he needed amusement and had found it in the person of this lively lass who seemed to reciprocate his feelings, but her mother had imposed such a rigorous regime, never allowing her daughter a moment to herself, that in disgust Santa Anna had proposed marriage, an honorable gesture which threw the mother into paroxysms of joy.

'I could tell you were a perfect gentleman,' she assured him, and he indulged her when she wanted to make the wedding a gala affair, but he had put his foot down when she proposed to invite the entire mexicano population of Béjar to the ceremony—'To relieve the boredom of the fighting,' she had said—because he feared that some civilian would be aware that he was already married and would condemn this mock wedding as a fake.

As he stepped into the center of the crowd he bowed low before the fatuous mother, kissed her hand reverently, and said: 'This is the happiest day of my life,' and she responded: 'With me the same.'

And so the preposterous wedding party formed, there in the lovely Veramendi gardens where Jim Bowie had often sat with his beloved Ursula, and the bogus priest was moved forward, mumbling some lines and fumbling with a Bible, and the fat fellow, who really did look the part, pronounced the handsome couple man and wife. When he added: 'You may now kiss the bride,' Santa Anna swept the willing young lady into his arms and carried her into the adobe palace, where the marriage was consummated within minutes.

For many tumultuous hours the newlyweds stayed in their room, uttering squeals and chuckles that seeped out into the hallways, where the adoring mother relished each echo, and then late in the afternoon of Tuesday, 1 March, the general appeared in the garden, his uniform pressed by his new mother-in-law, to issue a rapid chain of commands.

Protected by a convoy of soldiers who could be spared from the siege, his bride was to be taken immediately south to San Luis Potosí, where she was to be given every consideration; he had reason to hope that she was pregnant, and if so, he wanted the child to be treated at least as generously as his other bastards. His mother-in-law was to be given the best house in Béjar and a pension, and to be kept as far removed from him as possible.

Now he plunged vigorously into preparations for bringing the siege to a rousing conclusion. Summoning his aides, he learned from them the gratifying news that through late arrivals his army had now grown to twenty-four hundred effectives: 'Excellent. They have a hundred and fifty. Our superiority, sixteen-to-one.'

'Excuse me, Excellency. While you were'—the colonel hesitated—'resting, about thirty additional rebels slipped into the mission. We believe they now have about a hundred and eighty.'

'Fools,' Santa Anna muttered. 'Fighting to commit suicide.' Recalculating his figures, he came up with the accurate discrepancy: 'Thirteen of us to every rebel.' It was obvious that he could charge the walls head-on if he was willing to waste the manpower.

When it became evident that the siege was not going to force the rebels to surrender in the near future, since they had all the beef they needed and more than enough water from their two wells, Santa Anna summoned General Ripperdá and said graciously: 'You were right. We'll have to storm the walls.' But before issuing the final order, which could entail the loss of perhaps a thousand of his men, he wanted to see for himself the exact state of preparation at the Alamo, so on March fourth he asked his brother-in-law General Cós and three scouts including Garza to take a long ride with him around the former mission. As they crossed the little bridge leading to the east side of the river, Benito cautioned the dictator: 'Excellency, do not ride carelessly. Remember, those men in there have what they call Kentucky rifles.'

'Every army thinks it has superior weapons.'

'But these are superior.'

'Son, I fought these rebels at Medina in 1813. They possessed nothing to fear, not even personal bravery. We fired at them and they ran.'

'Excellency, have you ever seen a Kentucky rifle in action?' When Santa Anna said 'No,' Benito told him: 'This is one. I bought it from a Kentucky man himself. How far do you think it can fire with accuracy?'

Santa Anna, always interested in firearms, said authoritatively: 'Our muskets, in good condition, ninety yards, maybe a hundred.'

'More like sixty,' Cós said.

'See that tree?' Garza asked. 'With the paper under it. Maybe some bottles. How far?'

The officers agreed that it might be as much as two hundred and fifty yards. 'Watch,' Benito said, and with careful aim he sped a bullet right into the collection of trash, throwing paper and bits of glass high in the air.

'Incredible,' Santa Anna said, drawing away from the still-distant Alamo.

'And remember, Excellency. The norteamericanos established a rule in their two wars against the British: "Always fire for the gold." '

'And what does that mean?'

'My frontier friends told me: "Never fire aimlessly. Never fire at the common soldier. Always aim at the gold decoration of the officer." Today you are wearing your gold medals, Excellency.'

Prudently, the little party moved to a distance of about three hundred yards, where, with a map, they circled the huge grounds of the Alamo, and as they rode from south to north the three scouts relayed to Santa Anna the information they had accumulated:

'The fortified main gate at the south will be impossible to breach. This long west wall is only adobe, but it's very thick. Rooms inside. You can see the patrol already on the roof. This north wall slopes at an angle and is not very stout. Difficult to climb, but our cannon could breach it, for certain.

'Here on the east, a very stout wall, don't try to force it. Those big square things are cattle pens, and the garden with one of the wells. Barracks there for the soldiers. If you try to break in here, you have to penetrate two sets of walls.

'And now the chapel of the old mission. No roof, but extremely thick walls. I doubt they will waste much time defending this, because even if we did break through, we wouldn't be anywhere. But that stretch which connects the chapel to the main south wall could prove to be their weak spot and our big opportunity.

'Look! It has no wall of any kind. Only a ditch in front, wooden palisades of a sort, mostly brush I think. It will be defended, of course, and they may put their best rifles there, but it can be breached.'

At the conclusion of this tour, which took nearly an hour, Santa Anna told Cós: 'We will attack with great force from the north and knock a hole in that exposed wall with no houses behind it. But we will also attack with maximum clamor the palisade and hope to divert their forces.'

'The church?' an officer asked, referring to the roofless chapel. 'What of that, Excellency?'

'Attack it in force, but not seriously. Just enough to keep the defenders pinned down at a meaningless spot.'

Now the deployments were made: 'We'll attack from all sides at four o'clock Sunday morning. We should have the place by sunrise.' He wheeled his beautiful horse, turned back to take one last look at the Alamo, and said: 'Remember, no prisoners.'

From the church tower the red flag of death underscored that decision.

When the Macnabs arrived at Goliad toward dusk on Saturday, 20 February, they found affairs in much greater confusion than even Finlay had anticipated. He had assumed that Colonel Fannin, in response to Lieutenant Bonham's plea, would have his men preparing to make a dash into the Alamo; instead, he learned that the two other supreme commanders, Grant the malodorous Scotsman and Johnson the wild-eyed Illinois greengrocer, had marched off on their own in the fatuous belief that with only sixty-odd untrained volunteers they could capture the important Mexican port of Matamoros near the mouth of the Rio Grande. Even their own scouts reported that General Urrea, one of the ablest Mexican leaders, had assembled more than a thousand well-armed veterans there.

'What kind of madness is that?' Finlay asked after he and his son had been assigned places to sleep inside the presidio walls.

'It gets worse,' an embittered member of the Georgia Battalion groused. 'We should be on our way to the Alamo right now. But look at him.'

And for the first time Finlay Macnab, a man whose frontier experiences had converted a somewhat aimless character into one of surprising fortitude, witnessed at close quarters the confusion and lack of decisiveness which characterized Colonel Fannin. Thirty-two years old and disappointed because of his failure to graduate from West Point with a commission in the regular United States Army, he had become a slave trader for a while, then an eager drifter looking for something to turn up. He was an adventurer, inordinately ambitious, now in Texas looking for promotion to general, and reluctant to throw his forces into the Alamo, not because of cowardice or fear of death, but rather because if he were to do so, he would lose his command and be forced to serve under the despised amateur Colonel Travis.

On his visit to Goliad, Lieutenant Bonham had pleaded with all the considerable moral force he could muster for Fannin to march to the relief of the Alamo. Fannin had given an equivocal answer: he would go, he would not go, he would consider it. Six days later, on the twenty-third, he was still weighing alternatives after Santa Anna had surrounded the Alamo, so that reinforcements would now encounter serious trouble if they tried to enter.

Macnab wondered if valiant troops, ready for battle, had ever been led by an officer so pusillanimous: I wish we could light a fire under him, to see if he'd jump. Otto, listening to the complaints of the Georgia and Irish units, decided: If either Father or Uncle Zave was leading, we'd be on our way to San Antonio now. Then, eyes blazing, he thought: And if Lieutenant Bonham had anything to do with it, we'd already be there.

Fannin allowed the most contradictory rumors to agitate his men: 'We're marching to Gonzales!' 'No, it's to Victoria to unite with reinforcements coming by sea.' 'No, that would be a retreat, and I heard Colonel Fannin swear on a stack of Bibles "I will never retreat!"' 'We march to San Antonio tomorrow to do what we can!'

The ridiculous truth was that Fannin had given each of these orders, within the space of days, and had then countermanded each one. However, on 25 February he finally made up his mind: 'Tomorrow at dawn we march to help defend the Alamo.'

On the morning of Friday the twenty-sixth, Finlay and Otto joined the three hundred and twenty soldiers from the Goliad presidio, and the hearts of all beat a little quicker at the realization that they were at last marching to the Alamo.

Colonel Fannin, astride a chestnut stallion, rode to the head of his troops, raised his sword and cried: 'On to destiny!'

But his expedition had progressed only two hundred yards when one of the major supply wagons broke down, and by the time it was repaired, other wagons that had taken the lead failed to negotiate a river crossing, so that total confusion resulted. Noon found the column stalled, and the afternoon wasted away without any significant movement. As day faded into night Macnab realized that in these fourteen hours the expeditionary force had covered less than a quarter of a mile.

At dawn on the twenty-seventh Colonel Fannin awakened to the ugly fact that he faced a seventy-mile march to the next replenishment depot, without sufficient food to sustain his troops. Having relied upon a swift dash to the first depot, he had not bothered to bring along emergency supplies. When Macnab heard that Fannin was going to ask his men to vote as to whether they wanted to move ahead to the Alamo or return to the safety of the presidio and regroup, he was outraged. 'A commander doesn't ask for a vote,' he told the Georgians and Irishmen near him. 'He senses in his gut what must be done and he does it.' But then an Irishman with a wizened, knowing face said: 'He's taking the loss of that first wagon as an omen. "Don't go on!" a little voice is surely whispering to him.'

'My God!' a Georgia man asked in disgust. 'Are we bein' led by omens?'

'In this army we are,' the Irishman said, but he was wrong, for Fannin was collecting his commissioned officers to ascertain how they interpreted not the omens but the hard facts:

> 'Gentlemen, we face a most serious situation. We have, as you well know, inadequate provisions for a long march and no reasonable means of increasing them. We have faulty transport and no way of finding better. Our artillery pieces seem too heavy to drag over riverbeds. And what seems most important to me . . . by leaving the presidio without proper garrison, we tempt the enemy to sneak in and take it. What do you recommend that we do?'

In the face of such a pessimistic review, the vote was unanimous: Return to Goliad, bolster the fortifications, and defy the enemy from inside the walls: 'The Alamo? Nothing can be done from this end to support it.'

So the expedition stumbled back to its launching spot, retreated within the safety of its walls, and began a crash program with two objectives: Build the walls so strong that they would be impregnable. Slaughter so many oxen and dry the meat so carefully that the men would never again be short of rations.

Finlay Macnab warned his son: 'When a commander loses his nerve, disasters can happen.'

'What shall we do?' Otto asked.

'Nothing.' Then, afraid that his son might be as disoriented as Fannin, he asked: 'Why? Did you want to leave?'

Otto could not explain in words, but the more he witnessed the ineptitude inside the presidio, the more he longed to serve with someone of honorable purpose like James Bonham. He was sure that Bonham would have quickly handled the perplexities that immobilized Fannin, and in the meantime he, Otto, would keep his rifle clean and await the battle he knew to be inevitable.

Just about this time an event occurred inside the Alamo which would have given Otto reassurance. James Bonham, surveying the situation with Colonel Travis and Davy Crockett, concluded that he must ride once again through the countryside in a last appeal to Fannin at Goliad and to the scattered farmers in the east for aid. Crockett, hearing his decision, said: 'You were lucky last time, threading your way out and back in. This time?'

As if he knew no care in the world, the Carolina gentleman half saluted Travis, smiled at Davy, and mounted the mare that had served him so well before. Darting suddenly from the north wall of the Alamo, he spurred his mount and galloped directly through the Mexican lines. Before the startled besiegers could prevent it, he had broken free and was on his way back to Goliad to make one final, desperate plea for help.

Like the demon rider in an ancient ballad, Bonham rode through the night, and on the twenty-eighth, reined in at the Goliad presidio, where the men cheered him lustily, for they knew what heroism his mere appearance at that spot so distant from the Alamo entailed.

Bonham's arrival did not impress Colonel Fannin, for it reopened questions long since resolved. There would be no rescue operation conducted from Goliad, and patiently he explained why: 'Distance too great, transport too chancy, cannon too heavy, food and water too uncertain.' On and on he went, reciting the best arguments in the world against any desperate lunge to the northwest, and as Bonham listened he had to concede that everything Fannin said was true, and relevant. Any cautious commander would hold back, as he was doing, but any brave commander would correct the disadvantages and forge ahead.

By the middle of the next afternoon Bonham had argued so persuasively that he was within minutes of persuading Fannin to act, when one of those freak accidents which so often determine history occurred. Bumptious Colonel Johnson, who had been trying to invade Mexico with a handful of heroes, stumbled into the presidio with a harrowing story: 'We were surrounded by Mexicans. Chopped to pieces. Only four others survived.'

'From your entire force?' Fannin asked, his hands shaking.

'And Dr. Grant, he seems to be lost.'

'My God!' Fannin cried, for this meant that the two inept leaders had lost a large part of his total force, and Bonham saw that it was futile to pressure this confused man any further. His will was gone and he had best be left alone, but when he looked at Johnson he had to think: His army lost. All but five killed. Yet he comes back alive to report. How?

Aware that he had wasted precious hours listening to such men demean themselves, Bonham saluted his unworthy superiors and told them that he must get on with his duty. 'And what is that?' Fannin asked.

'Return to the Alamo. Colonel Travis deserves a reply.'

'But the place is surrounded. You said so.'

'I got out. I'll get back in.'

'Stay here with us. Help us defend Goliad.'

Bonham looked at the two men with whom he would not care to defend anything, then at the walls they had been reinforcing. He said nothing, but thought: Fannin will pin himself into another Alamo, and three weeks from now he will be sending out cries for help.

Turning his back on the two futile commanders, confused incompetents lusting for power but incapable of the action by which it is earned, Bonham, the medieval knight resurrected for service in modern Texas, rode off toward duty. He carried with him no promises of aid, no hope for rescue, only the mournful confirmation that Texas was in mortal danger.

When Zave Campbell and the thirty-one Gonzales men broke through Mexican lines and entered the Alamo at three in the morning of Tuesday, 1 March, they found a legendary man who, even though confined to his cot, gave them hope.

He was Jim Bowie, forty-one years old and revered as the best knife-fighter on the entire frontier. He was a big red-headed man of enormous energy, and had the wishes of the men who were to do the fighting been consulted, he would have been their commander during the siege. Unluckily, on the day Santa Anna's men took their positions ringing the Alamo, Bowie, who had been ill for some time, was laid low by a raging fever somewhat like the one that had killed his wife, Ursula Veramendi, and when Zave went to report he found Bowie in bed.

'I've heard of you,' Bowie said. 'Glad to have you.'

'You look pale,' Zave said. 'Like maybe Santy Anny hit you with something.'

Bowie said wanly: 'And you look like your neck's on crooked. Like maybe somebody tried to hang you.'

'Necks don't straighten easy,' Zave confessed, and the two old frontiersmen discussed the places and people they had known, especially in and around Natchez.

'Is it true you used to rassle alligators?' Zave asked.

'Still do, if one comes after me,' Bowie said, laughing. 'Man never knows when a gator is gonna come after him.'

Zave would never see this once-powerful man standing upright, but he was impressed by the sheer sense of force that Bowie exuded, even from his cot. When the sick man learned that Campbell had also married a mexicana, he said: 'There's another fellow in here like us,' and when he sent for Mordecai Marr, these three Texicans shared memories of the joys they had known with their Mexican wives. 'The others think we married peasants,' Bowie said. 'You should've heard my wife order me about. She was twice as smart as me.'

The three men fell silent, for at the far end of the barracks in which Bowie's cot stood they saw Amalia Marr moving about, assisting the women and children who had chosen to stay in the Alamo with their men, and the graceful way she held her head, the poetry of her motion as she worked delighted them, for Bowie and Campbell could see in her a portrait of their own wives. It was then that Bowie exclaimed with deep emotion: 'Damnit, Campbell! It would have been a lot better for Texas if every unmarried man who wandered down here from Kentucky and Tennessee, or from Georgia and Alabama, for that matter . . . if he had been forced to take himself a Mexican wife. Maybe we could have bridged the gap.'

'What gap?' Zave asked.

'Americanos, mexicanos. We're bound to share this land for the next two hundred years. If we'd got started right . . .'

'They tell me that this guide Deaf Smith, best of the lot, they say he has a Mexican wife.'

'I think he does,' Bowie said. 'I wish he was in here to help us.'

'The men all feel they'd have a better chance of holdin' this place if you was leadin'.'

'Now stop that. Stop it right now. Travis will prove a damned good fighting man.'

'But the men tell me,' Marr said, 'that you were supposed to be in command.'

Jim Bowie, the most belligerent man in the Alamo, sighed: 'It hasn't been a neat affair. Seems like nothin' in Texas is ever neat. We were supposed to share a joint command, Travis in charge of the army men, me in charge of the volunteers.'

'That's what I'm sayin'. Us volunteers want to fight under your orders.'

Bowie's voice hardened with exasperation: 'How in hell can I command if I can't stand? You tell me that.' With the generosity of spirit which marked him he growled: 'I'm perfectly willing to give the leadership to Travis,' and while neither Zave nor Marr believed him, they had to respect him for his soldierly deportment.

The man all the newcomers wanted to meet was Davy Crockett, the former congressman from Tennessee. Tall, clean-shaven, and with a head somewhat larger than normal, he was a famous raconteur whose disreputable stories narrated in dialect often made him look ridiculous: 'They was me and this bear and a Injun. Now, that bear was grindin' his teeth, just waitin' to git at me. And the Injun was reachin' for his arrers to shoot one through me.'

'And what were you doin'?' someone was supposed to ask, at which Davy would reply: 'I be 'shamed to tell you, 'cept that later I had to do some washin'.'

He was irrepressible, and after conducting a survey of the situation within the Alamo, he had insisted upon defending the palisaded weak spot, where the danger would be greatest: 'I want sixteen good men here with all the rifles we can muster, and them Mexicans better beware.' When Zave saw the frailness of the palisade and the grim look of the men from Kentucky and Tennessee who would have to defend it, he whispered to Galba Fuqua: 'There's bound to be one hell of a fight here.'

Whenever Zave could not locate Galba, for whom he felt great responsibility, he would look to see where Davy Crockett was holding forth, and there the boy would be, listening intently as the wild frontiersman spun his yarns but fully aware that Crockett's mocking manner masked a character of profound determination. The boy had no way of assessing how strong a man Jim Bowie might have been if healthy, but he knew that Davy was one of the most powerful men he had ever seen: 'You killed more'n a hundred bears?'

'Most dangerous animal I ever met was that Tennessee Democrat Andrew Jackson. He'd cut a man's throat for sixpence.'

'But did you kill forty-seven bears in one month?' Galba asked.

'I sure did. Forty-seven bears, forty-six bullets.'

'How was that?'

'Two of the bears was misbehavin',' and he winked at the boy.

One morning Galba was standing guard with him atop the fort at the southwestern end of the mission. Crockett was dressed as usual—coonskin cap, deerskin jacket with Indian beads, buckskin trousers—and beside him he had two long rifles. 'You see that Mexican over there across the river?' he said to Galba. 'Tracin' marks in the dust? You see that other man behind him? As soon as I fire, slap the other gun into my hand.'

The two men were so far distant that Galba believed it impossible for Crockett to reach them, but he watched as the expert leveled his gun, firmed it against the edge of the rampart, and with breathless care pulled back his trigger finger. Poof! Not much of a crackle, for this was a good tight gun, but down went the man in front.

'Quick!' Davy whispered, as if the other man could hear, and before the latter could seek refuge, a second bullet sped across the river, dipped under the trees on the far side, and splatted into its target.

Insolently, Crockett rose from behind the protective wall, pushed back his coonskin cap, and reloaded his two rifles, daring Santa Anna's men to fire at him with their outdated smooth-bore English muskets that could not carry half that distance.

'How far was that?' Galba asked, as if the dead men had been squirrels.

Crockett said with equal indifference: 'Maybe two hundred and fifty yards,' but quickly added: 'You know, you couldn't do it at that range, not unless you could prop your gun.'

'Could I fight with you, at the palisade?'

Crockett said: 'It's gonna be easy to hold that spot, what with the men I got. A good shot like you, you're needed wherever Travis puts you.'

That night Galba Fuqua lost his heart all over again to Davy Crockett, for the famous bear hunter astounded everyone by producing a fiddle that he'd brought into the Alamo with him, and for two hours he entertained the fighters with scraping squeals of mountain music so ingratiating that even Zave Campbell danced in the moonlight.

When Colonel Travis was assigning the Gonzales men to their defensive positions, Zave volunteered for one of the more exposed locations. He chose that long western wall, knowing it would be vulnerable if the Mexican foot soldiers were brave enough to bring their scaling ladders there. To Fuqua, who volunteered to stand with him, he said: 'What we must do, Galb, is run back and forth and change our positions. Confuse 'em.'

'Will there be lots of them?'

'Lots.' And he pointed out to the boy where the danger spots would be: 'That gully gives them protection. They'll come up from there and hit us about here. We'll be waitin'. You keep your eye on those trees—not many of them, but they'll interrupt our fire. They're sure to come at us from those trees. So you're to guard this point, and never allow them to place even one ladder.'

'What am I to do?'

'The minute they place a ladder, you run there with this forked pole and push it down.'

The boy looked at the trees, saw the pitiful distance that separated them from the wall, and for the first time since he left Gonzales, realized that within a few days men were going to be killed, in great number: 'Will many be killed, Mr. Campbell?'

'Lots,' Zave said. Then, appreciating the boy's fear, he took Galba by the hand and said: 'That's what a battle is, son. The killing of men.'

'Does the red flag over there really mean no surrender?'

'It's them or us, son. Come battle day, it's purely them or us.'

At first Campbell had not liked Colonel Travis, whom he saw as an austere man with a lawyer's finicky attitude toward duty and no sense of humor: 'He talks too big, Galb.' The boy repeated what he had heard many of the men say: 'Bowie ought to be our commander,' but out of respect for the sick man's wishes Zave quieted such talk: 'Travis is our leader now. Bowie said so. And you better do what he says.'

By Wednesday, 2 March, Campbell was developing a much different opinion of Travis: 'He knows what he's doing. He knows how to defend a position. And look how he puts his finger on the weak spots.' Zave liked especially the manner in which Travis disposed his men, never carelessly, never arbitrarily, but always with an eye on firepower.

'You know, Galb, he has every weak man down there caring for the cattle and things. All the good men are up here on the ramparts.'

'You count me a good man?'

'I sure do, and so does Travis.'

But not even after Zave had granted Travis every concession did he like the man the way he admired Bowie and Crockett: 'It's the way he's always tidyin' up his clothes, Galb. When a man does that, he's apt to be prissy. Damnit, Travis ought to be commandin' a cavalry post in Carolina and attendin' afternoon teas with the ladies. He may be a fightin' man, but he sure as hell ain't a frontiersman.'

'You prefer the way Bowie dresses?'

'I sure do,' but as he said this he saw Travis standing atop the fortress corner at the north, surveying the land across which the Mexican attack would come, and his slim figure, so taut, so tense, seemed so extraordinarily military that even Zave had to confess: 'He knows what he's doing, that one.' And when Travis next inspected the rooftops, Zave saluted.

On Thursday, 3 March, at about a quarter to eleven, Colonel Travis and everyone within hearing of Galba Fuqua's voice were startled to hear the lad cry: 'Man comin' on horseback!' And when they looked toward the sun high in the sky they did indeed see a lone horseman making a wild effort to cut directly through the heart of the enemy lines.

'It's Bonham!' men began to shout. 'Go it, Bonham!'

They did more than shout. Two men limbered up a field piece and tossed cannon shells at Mexican soldiers who were trying to catch the fleeting messenger, while others grabbed their rifles to pick off individual men who sought to attack him.

'Zave!' Fuqua shouted, proudly aware that his warning cry had helped this incredibly brave rider by alerting the riflemen on the walls. 'He's going to make it!'

'Break open those gates!' Travis shouted, and men eagerly leaped to do so, just in time to bring the dodging, darting Bonham into the protection of the Alamo. Twice out to safety, twice back to his post of duty, he had ridden alone and had four times penetrated heavy enemy concentrations.

His message was brief and terrifying: 'Colonel Fannin refuses to leave Goliad. Gonzales has no more men to send us. No relief is on the way. You already have all the men you'll ever have. There'll be no more.'

Friday, 4 March, was a solemn day within the Alamo, for additional Mexican reinforcements streamed north from the Rio Grande to increase Santa Anna's superiority, so that even the most hopeful Texicans had to confront the fact that within a few hours the mighty attack would begin, and it could have only one outcome.

Each of the doomed men spent this fateful day as his personality dictated: Jim Bowie almost wept at his inability to rise from his cot and help; Davy Crockett entertained his men at the palisade with outrageous stories of his confrontations with his Tennessee constituents and especially with President Andrew Jackson, whom he despised: 'All show and bluster. Calls hisself a friend of the common man, but the only people he really befriends are the rich. If we had a real man in the White House, we'd have three thousand American troops in this building right now, and God knows how many cannon.' He refused to allow any talk of odds or dangers or the likelihood of annihilation. He was in another tight spot and he would as always do his best.

James Bonham was exhausted and reflective. He could not understand Fannin; he simply could not understand. 'Obviously,' he told Travis, 'he could have marched here fifteen days ago. I broke through yesterday and so could he, with all the men he had. I fear a great disaster is going to overtake that poor man.' He slept most of the afternoon.

Zave Campbell, as a good Scotsman, had sought out a kinsman, John McGregor, who he found had brought with him into the Alamo a set of fine bagpipes. So later in the afternoon Campbell, Fuqua and McGregor gathered in the northwest corner of the big field, and there McGregor marched back and forth as if he were in some royal castle on the Firth of Tay, piping the stirring reels and strathspeys of his youth.

Then, without announcement, he switched to a most enchanting tune, not military at all, and when Campbell said: 'I don't know that one,' the piper explained: 'We call it "The Flooers of Embry," which means "The Flowers of Edinburgh." A grand tune.' He played this sad, sweet music for some time, then once more without warning he altered his music; with head tilted back as if he were looking for omens in the sky, he offered the near-empty field one of the grand compositions of Scotland, and now Campbell knew well what it was, the great 'McCrimmon's Lament,' that historic threnody for brave men dead in battle, and as he marched back and forth, men in various parts of the Alamo seemed to sense that he was playing some notable piece of music for them, and they began to appear from odd corners.

But this haunting moment lasted only briefly, for Davy Crockett bellowed from the palisade: 'Damn that stuff! Fetch me my fiddle!' And when this was done he took it and ran the length of the field to meet with McGregor, and for about an hour as day waned the two men gave a wild and raucous concert of wailing pipes and screeching fiddle, and for a rowdy while the hundred and eighty-three men in the Alamo forgot their predicament.

Ominously, on Saturday, 5 March, the daily bombardment by the Mexicans—thirteen days of barrage without killing one Texican—ceased, and Marr predicted to those about him: 'Santa Anna's redeploying his troops. Tomorrow he'll come at us.'

Colonel Travis, reaching the same conclusion, experienced an overpowering sense of doom, and as he realistically surveyed the situation of his troops and the few women and children who had remained with them in the Alamo, he realized that to hope for any further miracles was futile. His aides reported: 'Santa Anna's army increases daily. He's moving up his big guns. The final attack cannot be delayed much longer.'

Everything Travis saw confirmed this gloom. No matter how he disposed his men along the walls, there were empty spaces which the enemy would be sure to spot. And his ammunition was limited. Unlimited was the willingness of his men to fight, but as their leader, he felt obligated to give each man one last chance to escape the certain death which faced them all. That afternoon he assembled his force near the plaza leading to the chapel, and there, with the women and children listening and even Jim Bowie on his cot, which had been hauled into the open, he told them the facts: 'The red flag still flies, and Santa Anna means it. No prisoners. His army is fifteen times ours, and he has more cannon, too. I suspect the attack will come tomorrow—that's Sunday, isn't it? I want to offer every man here one last chance to retire if he should wish to.'

What happened next would be forever debated; some, basing their accounts on those of certain women who escaped the carnage, say that Travis drew a line in the sand with the tip of his sword and indicated that those wishing to take their chances fighting beside him step over it; others laugh at the suggestion of such flamboyance but grant that he may have indicated some kind of line as he scuffed his left foot across the plaza. At any rate, he certainly warned his men that death was imminent and gave them a choice of either staying and fighting a hopeless battle with him or kiting over the wall to such escape as each man could maneuver for himself.

First over the line was white-haired Mordecai Marr, who mumbled to the two who followed: 'I'm American and Mexican, loyal to both, but it seems like the first one wins.' Jim Bowie, without question, asked that his cot be moved to where his onetime adversary was standing, and Travis welcomed him. Davy Crockett shuffled over, and of course James Bonham moved to accept the death which he had known three weeks ago to be inevitable. Zave Campbell looked down at Galba Fuqua, shrugged his shoulders, and said unheroically: 'We've come this far, Galb. Do you want to go all the way?' Without hesitation the boy took Zave's hand as they joined the patriots.

When Travis made his remarkable and moving speech, one hundred and eighty-two men and boys faced him. Of that number, all but one crossed to die with him. The one man who did not—and his reasoning for preferring shameful life to heroic death was startling to the men who heard him voice it—was Louis Rose, fifty-one years old, born in France and entitled to wear the Legion of Honor as a distinguished veteran of Napoleon's campaigns in the kingdom of Naples and in Russia. He had come to Texas as early as 1826, when he changed his first name to Moses, believing it to sound more American. At first he had served as a day laborer in Nacogdoches, then as a teamster, and finally as a self-trained butcher.

Loving the soldier's life, as soon as trouble threatened he mortgaged all his holdings and went off to join the fighting at San Antonio, where he had helped defeat General Cós in 1835.

Rose was by far the most experienced soldier in the group, and it pained Jim Bowie to see such a man reluctant to stay for the fight. Forcing himself upright in his cot, Bowie chided the Frenchman: 'You seem unwilling to die with us, Mose.'

'I came to America to live a new life, not to die needlessly,' the old campaigner said. 'Only fools and amateurs would try to defend this place.'

Davy Crockett said with a touch of levity: 'Mose, you may as well die with us, because you'll never get through them Mexican lines.'

'I speak Spanish,' Rose said, and he bundled up his clothes, climbed the wall to the very spot where Galba Fuqua would stand guard, and hesitated for a moment as if reconsidering. Looking back at his friends, he half nodded, then turned and abruptly leaped to the ground, where he quickly lost himself among the trees.

At three-thirty in the cold morning of Sunday, 6 March, Galba Fuqua reached over and nudged his friend Zave Campbell as they stood watch atop the long barracks: 'I think they're coming.'

Zave rubbed his eyes and peered into the darkness, seeing for himself that there was much movement among the trees to the west: 'I think you're right, Galb— Hey, where you goin'?'

'I gotta pee.'

'You stay here.'

'But I gotta pee.'

'So do I. When men face danger, like a fistfight or a hurricane or a battle like this . . . they often have to pee. Even the bravest. I do too. But up where I'm needed, not down there.'

So the man and the boy urinated against the adobes which they were about to defend, and as they finished, Zave said something that would encourage the boy mightily in the frenzied hours ahead: 'Galb, it's gonna be a tough fight, that's sure. If you see me showin' any signs of cowardice . . .'

'You could never be a coward, Mr. Campbell.'

'No man ever knows. So if I start to show signs, you kick me in the ankle. You don't have to say anything. Just kick me in the ankle and we'll know what it means.'

The boy considered this, then said in a trembling voice: 'I see shadows moving, Mr. Campbell.' A hush, then: 'Oh! They're coming.'

Then, in the darkness of the night, seven Mexican buglers, each marching with his own contingent, started sounding one of the most powerful calls ever heard on the world's battlefields. It was not a piercing command to charge, nor a stirring cry to enhance courage. It was the 'Degüello,' an ancient Moorish plea to an enemy to surrender. Its name meant 'The Beheading,' and once it sounded, its meaning was stark and clear: If you do not surrender immediately, we shall behead you, everyone.

Across the empty fields of Béjar it came, over the walls and into the Alamo, this wild lament, this recollection of home, of people loved, of the gentler scenes of peace. Through the vast spaces of the Alamo it echoed, and everyone who heard it understood its frightful promise that within hours everyone inside the walls would be slain.

Nine times the 'Degüello' was repeated, a terrible tattoo bringing the small, white-clad Indian troops ever closer to the walls. 'Don't waste your bullets,' Campbell told Galba. 'They'll be close soon enough.'

Santa Anna had assigned tasks skillfully: 'Cós, you command our best troops. Hit the northwest wall. General Duque, smash the northeast. That's where I'm sure we can break through. Ripperdá, you have the ones we can send forth in floods. Knock down the palisade. Morales, hit the main gate, but when they concentrate to defend it, slide off to your left. You'll find a weak spot. The rest of you, scaling ladders against that long west wall. They can't protect all of it.'

During the first minutes of battle the four generals with the important assignments made little progress, for they were attacking major positions, but the nondescript troops trying to scale the west wall became a real threat. Campbell now yelled: 'Galb, we must run back and forth, like we agreed.' And these two, with the assistance of three Tennessee men, threw down one ladder after another.

At the point of great danger, the north wall, General Cós, who had sworn in writing never to return to Tejas under arms, gained one crushing success, although at the time he did not know it: some of his men, firing a blind fusillade, luckily hit a brave Texican who was defending the northern gun batteries. This man took a shot through the head, pitching backward into the dusty yard. The dead man was Colonel William Travis, whose iron will had kept his men in the Alamo.

The grinding assault came at the palisade, where Davy Crockett had lined up his Tennessee sharpshooters, with Mordecai Marr and twelve Kentucky men in support. These tough veterans laid down a continuous rifle fire, but the pressure against them was unyielding, because General Ripperdá had an unlimited supply of barefoot Yucatán Indians whom he proposed to use as human battering rams.

When Benito Garza first heard his assignment—'You'll lead the third wave'—he found it difficult to accept, for he knew how perilous such an attack would be, but when he watched the first wave move out and get mowed down, every man, by that unrelenting fire from the palisade, he lost all fear and began to shout to the second wave: 'Take that line of sticks! Damnit, rush them!' And when this wave lost more than eighty percent of its numbers, he could hardly wait to lead his charge.

Ripperdá, cold and stiff as ever, moved always closer to the palisade, ignoring both the whistling bullets and the appalling loss of his Indians: 'Garza, you'll succeed. Drive right at the center.' And he watched with impassive approval as Benito leaped forward, bringing his horde behind him. On this bloody Sunday, Texican and Mexican alike showed what courage was.

At the west wall, Campbell mustered a brilliant defense, running back and forth, firing his four rifles with devastating effect and reloading as he ran. 'We knocked them back!' Galba Fuqua shouted to his mentor, who called back: 'Use your pole! Keep pushin' them ladders down!' And so the first hour ended with no Mexican having gained the top of the wall. It was now nearing six, and Santa Anna's bold boast to be inside the walls by sunrise had failed. Now he threw in fresh troops, who came at the weakened walls with a roar and the popping of guns. The lack of range was no longer important, for the guns were discharged at a distance of thirty feet, and often with telling effect as brave Texicans began toppling backward like their commander.

By six the remaining Texicans numbered only slightly over a hundred, and still those irrepressible Indians and mestizos came at them, little men of giant courage, for they climbed barehanded up the walls or placed their ladders and held them in the face of withering gunfire while those behind them scrambled to the top, to be greeted by swinging gun butts in the face.

But on they came, hundreds of them, thousands it seemed, and for every six of them slain, a Texican fell off the wall, a bullet through his head or a knife through his breast.

At the southern end, Colonel Morales led his troops in a vain assault on the main gate, but as the Texicans cheered his repulse, he slid easily along to the western end of that wall and surprised its defenders with a bayonet attack. The Mexicans swarmed on and gained a major advantage, for they were now inside the walls.

At almost the same moment, Generals Cós and Duque applied maximum pressure at a weak point in the north wall, and there another breach was made. Before the irresistible white-clads could storm into the central area, Benito Garza and his Yucatán troops engulfed the palisade, overrunning old Mordecai Marr, who continued trying to reload even when on his knees. Three bayonets ended his adventurous life.

At this moment Zave Campbell, still atop the roof and still pushing away ladders, uttered a terrible cry of pain, not for himself but for his much-loved companion of these past days, Galba Fuqua, who had taken a pair of bullets right through his upper and lower jaws, blowing away a part of his brave young face.

Zave saw the lad put his hand to his head, then blanch and almost faint when he found what had happened. 'Galb, go down to where the women are. Get help.' With great force he lifted the boy from the post he had defended so valiantly and dropped him to the ground, watching him as he trailed blood across the yard.

Now he fought with deadly vigor, slashing, killing. Once he waited like a cat till two men climbed the ladder at the spot left vacant by Fuqua, then dashed forth like a tiger, swinging one of his guns like a madman and crushing skulls. He was about to return to his own spot, where Mexicans were close to controlling the wall, when he saw Galba climb back onto the wall, to resume his duty. When Zave saw the bloody mass he began to vomit, and for some moments he was immobilized, whereupon the boy kicked him and moved the remnant of his face as if he were saying: 'Courage, old man! Don't play the coward now.'

With an anguished roar, speaking for them both, Zave shouted at the climbing myrmidons: 'Come ahead, you bastards,' and he saw with horror how they did come, eight of them, and how they leaped upon Galba Fuqua, and stabbed him a score of times, tossing his body like a sheaf of threshed wheat to the ground below.

Now it was Zave Campbell, with his four rifles no longer of use except as clubs, who rushed at the twenty who stormed the rooftop. Swinging and cursing and lashing out with his two knives, he held them at bay for some moments, sending three more to their deaths.

But not even he could restrain the overwhelming force of this assault, for while he was defending himself against assailants in front, three others crept up on him from behind, and one stabbed him with such terrible force that the point of the bayonet reached out four inches from his breast. He was so astonished to see it that he gasped, reached down to pull it away with his bare hand, and took nine other stabs simultaneously. Giving a wild bellow of rage, he grabbed for his tormentors, and died draped across the wall he had defended with such valor.

Not three minutes later, James Bonham, hero of heroes, tried to hold off six attackers at the mission chapel, but was overpowered. He died taking several of the enemy with him.

Now all was confusion, and by six-thirty in the morning triumphant bugle calls echoed across the big field as Santa Anna's victorious troops searched every corner of the Alamo's defenses for any remaining Texicans. Whenever they found one they obeyed their general's stern command: 'No prisoners.' Men who had fought bravely until all hope was gone endeavored to surrender, but were either gunned down or pierced by bayonets. There were no prisoners, not among the men, although Amalia Marr and the other women who were inside the walls were spared.

Jim Bowie in his cot was bayoneted.

Long after the terrible victory, when men were trying to sort out details of what had happened to the 182 Texicans, a Mexican officer claimed that the last of the famous defenders to survive was Davy Crockett: 'He hid under a pile of women's clothes and begged and pleaded and wept when we trapped him. Said he would do anything if we spared him, but we shot him in contempt.' Unlikely, that.

Who were these heroes who died defending the Alamo? From what terrain did they come and upon what traditions had they been reared to make them willing to give their lives for the freedom of a territory to which they had so recently come?

Ten were born in England, twelve in Northern Ireland, three in Scotland, two in Germany, and one each in Wales and Denmark. Those born in the United States were thirty-one from Tennessee, fourteen from Kentucky, five from Alabama, four from Mississippi, five from Georgia, thirteen from the Carolinas, eleven from Virginia, twelve from Pennsylvania, and a scattering of others from Vermont, Louisiana, Missouri, New York, New Jersey, Ohio, Massachusetts and Illinois. Of the heroic congregation, only six had been born in Texas itself. Their names: Abamillo, Badillo, Espalier, Esparza, Fuentes, Nava—Mexicans all. Juan Seguín, who was in the Alamo when the siege began, we shall see shortly.

By seven that Sunday morning the battle was over, as complete a victory as any general could have hoped for. The Tejas rebellion was crushed almost before it was fairly launched, and Santa Anna, joyous in his triumph, gave one last order: 'Burn them all.' And the pyre was lit, and all but one were burned. By special dispensation of General Cós, the body of Gregorío Esparza was released to his brother for burial.

Into an unmarked grave, unhonored and spat upon, were thrown the ashes of the Alamo heroes, but even before the acrid fumes from the fire died away, men in various parts of the world were beginning to utter the name with reverence, and anger, and hope, and determination. 'The Alamo!' screamed newspapers throughout America. 'The Alamo!' whispered men to their wives as they prepared to leave for greater battles in the future. And in the weeks ahead, when men from all parts of Texas and the United States began to muster to avenge this savagery, they voiced a threat, a blood-oath that would bind them together: 'Remember the Alamo!'

From the heroism of these ordinary men, from their unmarked grave rose an echo of immortality. By their deaths, the living were morally obligated to finish what they had begun. From their skeletons, burned to ashes, the backbone of a new nation would be formed.

Where was General Sam Houston, the hero of Texas history, when such events were taking place? As one of many would-be commanders in chief, he had tried desperately to bring order to the defense of Texas, and he had failed. 'Abandon the Alamo and blow it up,' he had counseled Travis, who had disobeyed him for his own heroic reasons. 'Abandon Goliad and blow it up,' he had ordered Colonel Fannin weeks ago, and again he had been ignored. Like Achilles before Troy, he sulked, this time among his beloved Cherokee, whom he visited to help them regularize their relations with the United States and especially with the Texas that was now arising.

If the present leaders of the emerging nation were proving themselves to be a gang of inept fools, so be it. He would do his job with the Indians and return when the real fighting men were willing to listen, to retreat in orderly fashion, to suck Santa Anna ever deeper into perilous terrain, and to save all energy for one titanic effort against the Mexicans, whose supply lines would grow longer and longer and always more difficult to defend against those backwoods tactics which had proved so disastrous to British hopes in years gone by.

Sam Houston became an American version of the Roman Fabius Maximus, derisively nicknamed *Cunctator,* the Dawdler, who in 217 B.C. avoided defeat by the Carthaginian Hannibal through a series of skillful retreats that wore down the enemy. Houston devised a masterly plan which would enable him to do the same with Santa Anna, who had a vastly superior army, good cannon, able generals, and everything in his favor except time and distance. These two lesser advantages, he thought, could defeat the Mexican dictator.

Houston was in Gonzales when he learned that the Alamo had fallen. The morning and evening guns, which had reassured distant listeners that the mission remained in Texican hands, had fallen silent, so he was not surprised when a woman Santa Anna had released for the sole purpose of spreading her tale of terror reached Gonzales with the awful news that all the Texicans, including the thirty-two from Gonzales, were dead.

Then began the great retreat, the Runaway Scrape, in which civilians fled before the onrushing Mexicans. Towns were abandoned and set to the torch by their inhabitants. Cattle were herded north and east, then left to fend for themselves at river crossings. Hamlets were left bare. Nothing seemed able to halt the victorious dictator.

To Sam Houston, retreating like the others, one thing became essential: Colonel Fannin must get his men out of that trap in Goliad. He must bring his forces north to unite with ours. The safety of all Texas depends upon his actions now.

When Finlay Macnab learned of Colonel Fannin's latest mismanagement he did not despair, though he was appalled to think that an officer with formal training could be so incompetent. Not only had Fannin ignored General Houston's urgent plea to abandon the indefensible presidio, but he was also dividing into smaller groups what few forces he did have, sending badly needed troops on a wild-goose chase to defend some willful civilians who should have left the area long before.

After heated discussion with other concerned volunteers, Macnab sought a meeting with the colonel to protest. Taking Otto along so that the boy could better understand the situation in which they were involved, he reported to the corner of the presidio grounds where Fannin had his tent. 'Sir—' he began, but he had uttered only that word when Fannin interrupted.

'Name and district?'

'Finlay Macnab, Victoria. My son, Otto.'

The colonel acknowledged the pair, then said: 'You have something to say?'

'You see, sir, we live near Victoria, and we understand that General Houston wants us to retreat—in an orderly fashion, of course—and if we go to Victoria . . .'

'We retreat nowhere,' Fannin snapped.

'But if the Alamo has already fallen . . . It was a make-believe fortress like this . . .'

Macnab had used an unfortunate word. 'Make-believe!' Fannin cried. 'Look at those walls. I've strengthened every one of them. I've had seven hundred cattle slaughtered and their meat dried in the sun. We can withstand a siege of weeks, months, till the rest of Texas mobilizes.'

'Colonel . . .'

The interview was ended. Fannin rose angrily, stalked out of his own tent, and left the Macnabs standing there.

Back in their own corner of the large compound, Finlay told his son: 'You must remember, Colonel Fannin is a West Point man. He has his own special definition of honor, of propriety. Men with their own definitions always mean trouble for other men.'

'Are we in trouble?'

'Deep. Santa Anna could be here at any minute. He's only ninety-five miles away.'

'And he could break down our walls too?'

'With enough men, he can do anything.'

'What should we do?'

'Like Houston says. Retreat now and fight later.'

Finlay delivered this prudent opinion on Tuesday, 15 March, and he was disgusted on subsequent days to see that instead of preparing for an orderly evacuation, Fannin was assigning his men tasks, adding to the fortifications and storing the dried meat of the slaughtered steers. It was as if, having the fort and the food, he felt obligated to use both, but a member of the Georgia Battalion had a simpler explanation: 'He refuses to join any movement which might mean the loss of his command. He will not serve under another man.'

The remainder of that week was spent in total confusion, then, belatedly, Fannin accepted the fact that he really must retreat; however, even then he could not act decisively. Instead of marshaling a calculated withdrawal with firm, quick decisions about what to take and what not, he vacillated miserably, telling the men first: 'We'll not try to haul those big cannon,' then snapping: 'We've got to take every one of our cannon. We can't let Santa Anna get them.'

The danger was not really from Santa Anna in the west, for he was resting with his victorious troops in Béjar, but from a much different kind of Mexican general, a soft-spoken, humanitarian professional named José de Urrea, who came thundering up from the south, sweeping before him all the American filibusters who had been harassing the Mexicans in that region. It soon became apparent that General Urrea, with a vastly superior force, could overrun Goliad at any time he wished.

'We should have left this place two weeks ago,' Macnab lamented as he watched with dismay the chaos that engulfed the men about him. 'Why doesn't someone establish order?' he asked with Scottish impatience at such sheer folly, but no one did.

At last, on Friday afternoon, 18 March, Colonel Fannin reached a decision, which he announced boldly: 'We start our withdrawal to Victoria tomorrow at dawn. Since it will be a speedy retreat, we shall not try to take our cannon with us.'

'Thank God, he's made up his mind,' Macnab told Otto, and all that day father and son moved about the presidio checking to be sure that everyone had his rifle in good condition and an adequate supply of ammunition.

'Why are you doing this?' a Georgia man asked, and Finlay replied: 'Because I don't see any of the officers doing it.'

'What do you know about military affairs?'

'Nothing. But I have common sense.'

That night he drew upon his fragmentary knowledge: 'Otto, I read once that retreat is more difficult than marching ahead. The book said you need speed and discipline.'

'Will we have them?' Otto asked, for although he was only a boy he had seen enough of the disorganization at Goliad to make him suspicious of any leadership that Colonel Fannin might provide.

'Son, at military tactics Fannin may be first-rate. It's in the management of his army . . .'

'I don't think he knows how to do anything,' Otto said, and through the night they continued to check armament.

At dawn on Saturday the two were ready to serve as scouts, leading Colonel Fannin across land they knew well, sure that by nightfall they could bring the troops to safety in Victoria, only twenty-five miles away. But as they were about to move out, Fannin decided that, after all, he had better take his cannon with him, and during the time consumed in making this radical change, for teams of oxen had to be assembled to draw the heavy pieces, he had a further idea: 'Burn all that piled-up meat. So the Mexicans can't get it.' And through the wasted morning men stacked timbers, set them ablaze, and tossed onto the resulting fire the choice meat from some seven hundred steers.

'This place never smelled so good,' an Irishman shouted, and while the soldiers waited impatiently, another Irishman started playing a mouth organ, and men danced reels.

On a day when speed was essential, for other scouts had reported Urrea on his way to Goliad, the march finally began. 'At last!' Macnab sighed as they set forth, satisfied that the men were at least well armed and prepared for battle even if overtaken from the rear, as they might well be after such a long delay.

But the farce was not over. When the troops were less than a mile from the presidio a lieutenant, checking the supply train that had been given to him to command well after the march started, found to his horror that all food supplies were gone. In their enthusiasm for destroying huge stacks of beef to prevent them from falling into enemy hands, the men had burned the entire lot. A file of three hundred and sixty men was marching into the hot empty plain east of Goliad with nothing to eat except what the occasional foot solider had sequestered in his knapsack, if he had one.

When news of this disastrous oversight spread through the ranks, a much more serious one was discovered: no one had thought to bring water, either, so that the big, patient oxen on which the movement of the cannon depended began to weaken from lack of it.

When the Macnabs heard of these incredible blunders, the sort boys would not have made when planning an overnight camping, Otto made a simple suggestion: 'Someone ought to shoot him.'

'Hush!' his father warned, clamping his hand firmly over his son's mouth. 'That's treason, and Fannin would hang you in a minute.'

When his mouth was freed, Otto said grimly: 'Fannin has rules for everyone but himself.'

Foodless, waterless, this shambles of a retreat was struggling across the plain when two rear scouts dashed up: 'General Urrea, with many men and three cannon, will overtake you before sunset.'

When Fannin heard this his face went white, and now Macnab felt that he must intervene, for it was apparent that the colonel had lost all sense of control and needed guidance: 'Sir, I know this land. My farm lies just ahead. You cannot allow yourself to be trapped in this open field. You must, you really must, turn quickly to the left and head for those trees along the river.'

'I never divide my army,' Fannin said doggedly, remembering something he had read in a military manual.

'But, sir! I know these Georgia men, these Tennessee sharpshooters. You turn them loose in those woods, with water available, they'll hold back the whole Mexican army.'

'I do not respond to panic,' Fannin said resolutely, and now, although protection was easily available after a double-time march of less than two miles toward the scrub oak, the mesquite and the river, this obstinate man insisted upon keeping his men on the route he had planned for them, a dusty, waterless path on which his oxen had begun to collapse and his soldiers to gag from thirst.

Finally, when the surviving oxen were no longer able to haul the big, useless cannon, Colonel Fannin had to order a halt. It came in one of the bleakest stretches of the route, an area which provided no protection of any kind—no trees, no water, no gully to serve as a ready-made trench, no soft soil to encourage the digging of real trenches. Fannin brought his men to rest less than a mile from all kinds of safety, and here, with no protection, he formed them into a hollow square such as the Romans had used two thousand years earlier, with wagons as occasional breastworks and the precious cannon at each corner. Meticulously, he ordered that the sides of the square run true to the compass headings, with north facing the river a short distance away, with east facing Victoria, to which they should be marching, and west facing the presidio they had recently abandoned.

It was neat, military—and fatal.

Fannin had three hundred and sixty men, Urrea well over a thousand, and as soon as the unequal battle started, it was clear that the Mexican must triumph. However, Colonel Fannin with his West Point training proved a formidable adversary, for he deployed his men well, gave them encouragement, and conducted himself like a real leader.

But because the Mexicans fought a battle of swift movement, Fannin could not bring his cannon to bear upon them, and by the time the Mexican lines had formed, the only Texicans who knew how to work the cannon were wounded and the big guns stood useless. As night fell it was obvious to the trapped men inside the Roman square that on Sunday, General Urrea could overwhelm them any time he wished.

It was a horrible night, with the wounded crying for water and the unwounded watching the encircling lights as the Mexicans moved ever closer. At three an ox that had been hit in the shoulder began bellowing so loudly that Otto went to the poor beast and shot it. Others in the doomed square, thinking that the Mexicans were upon them, began to fire wildly, but Colonel Fannin silenced them: 'Save your bullets. We'll need them tomorrow.'

By dawn on Sunday, Urrea had brought up his heavy cannon, with ample horse and oxen power to move them where they would be most effective, and now, with the norteamericanos spread neatly out before him and with not even a surface ripple on the flat to protect them, he fired at will, raking the entire camp with a deadly barrage of canister and grape. The exposed rebels, with no food or water to sustain them, had no chance of escape. Twelve hundred fresh Mexicans faced the three hundred or so exhausted survivors.

In the first three explosions of the cannon, fragments of metal ripped through the camp, killing and maiming. The next three were worse, for the Mexican gunners now had exact range, and before the next salvo could be fired, several junior officers consulted with their men and reported to Fannin: 'No hope with those cannon raking us. You must surrender.' But now the confused leader became heroic: 'Never! We'll fight to the death!' Then he lost control and watched impotently as his officers raised the white flag.

To Macnab's relief, the Mexicans responded quickly with a white flag of their own, signifying that a truce existed, and shortly thereafter Colonel Fannin, accompanied by Finlay Macnab as his interpreter, marched erect and trim to meet Urrea. The two commanders settled upon the exact terms of surrender, and a disastrous adventure, mismanaged from the start, collapsed in a disastrous finish.

Macnab, when he reported back to the men inside the square, was quite specific as to the arrangements that had been reached:

> 'Colonel Fannin demanded that our troops receive all the honors of war. Lay down our arms, officers to keep theirs. Surrender with full right to leave the country. No executions. No reprisals.

> 'General Urrea did not exactly accept these terms, at least not in writing, but he did agree to an amiable surrender with our rights protected, and a Lieutenant Colonel Holsinger, acting for Urrea, told me personally: "Well, sir! In ten days, home and liberty." When others on Urrea's staff told us the same, and many heard the promises, we were much relieved, I can tell you.

> 'General Urrea himself was less specific about the actual terms, but he was quite eager to provide us with water and food and care for our wounded. To me he seemed both a perfect gentleman and a soldier who knew what he was doing.

> 'I did the translating up to the point where Urrea and Fannin drew apart to sign a paper of some kind. What was in it, I don't know. Formal terms and all that, but as we marched out the Mexicans saluted us and Holsinger said again: "Well, gentlemen, in ten days, liberty and home." '

Less than an hour after the surrender, the men who had marched out of the presidio only the day before now marched back in, and when the Macnabs were once more within those familiar walls, Finlay told the boy to kneel beside him: 'Almighty God, we thank Thee for having rescued us from what could have been a great tragedy. Teach us to be humble. Teach us to be grateful. From the bottom of our hearts, we thank Thee.'

He then sat Otto down beside the embers of the burned meat and lectured him on the duties of a man: 'You've seen what indecision and confusion can do. I don't charge Fannin with cowardice, because in battle you saw that he was brave. But in this life, son, you must carefully make up your mind as to the right road, and then march down it. If a wall of water forty feet high comes at you, hold your nose, kick to stay afloat, and when the water recedes, get on with your job. Promise me, Otto, that you'll be a man of determination.'

'I'll try.'

In an unusual display of emotion his father embraced him: 'I was proud of you, son, the way you helped me check the rifles the night before we started our retreat. You and I did our jobs. We did the best we could. It was the others . . .'

He would condemn no one specifically, but he sat silent for a long time trying to understand how this debacle had been permitted, but in the end he said simply: 'We were lucky to escape. Now let's get back to work.'

'Since we're so close to our farm, do you think they'll let us walk home?'

'I'm sure they will,' Finlay said, for that would be the sensible thing to do, and since he was himself a sensible man, he expected others to behave in the same way.

Benito Garza, like many historians in later years, found no fault with General Santa Anna's harsh conduct at the Alamo; a band of uninvited guests on Mexican territory had raised a rebellion, which, according to explicit Mexican law, made them pirates and subject to the death penalty. Most of the dead had been killed in combat, and those few who were shot or sabered after the end of fighting had been killed in the immediate aftermath of that battle, while tempers on both sides were still hot. There had been no atrocities. No women or children had been slain. It had been a clean fight and the mexicanos had won.

True, Garza had experienced one bad moment when on Santa Anna's orders he inspected the ruins of the Alamo to ensure that men like Travis, Crockett and Bowie were dead, for as he turned one of the bodies over with the toe of his boot, he looked down to see his brother-in-law Xavier Campbell's glassy eyes staring up at him.

'Dios mío! How did he get in here?'

No one could give him an answer, for the women who had been inside the Alamo were too frightened to speak much sense, nor would they have known his history had they been able to report.

'Men!' Garza had shouted. 'Let's bury this one.' But the scene was too confused for individualized action, and Campbell's body, like the rest, was thrown into a huge pile for burning.

Later, as Benito tried to sort things out, he concluded: 'Well, if he insisted on fighting against his own nation, he deserved what he got.' But this did not alleviate his feeling of sorrow over his sister María's loss of her second husband. Of the adult Texicans he knew, Benito had liked Campbell the best, but his conviction of superiority had led him astray, and now he, like the other arrogant intruders, was dead.

Benito had curious and sometimes conflicting reactions to the great victory at

Béjar: I'm glad that the norteamericanos received a stiff lesson. They deserved it. I want to see them kicked out of Tejas. But having thus exulted over the victory, he had a less inflammatory reaction: I could have lived with Xavier Campbell. He treated my sister with dignity. I can still live with the Macnabs. They're decent. Perhaps if we have a mexicano government with mexicanos in charge, there'll be a place for a few norteamericanos. They would be very helpful in our trade with New Orleans. Or in running stores in Victoria based on the New Orleans warehouses. Or maybe even banking in Victoria with New Orleans funds.

So from the sixth of March, when the Alamo fell, to the twenty-first, when news reached Santa Anna of the surrender of the Goliad garrison, Benito Garza luxuriated in the glow of victory, planning what he would do when this mexicano army with its three or four columns had cleared Tejas of the norteamericanos. But with the arrival of the sweating, dusty rider from Goliad, things changed dramatically, for Garza was in a house near San Fernando Church when he heard Santa Anna give the order: 'I told Urrea specifically. No prisoners. No surrender. Remind him . . . order him to shoot them all.'

Garza, as an expert on life in Tejas and a man who had educated himself by reading about Napoleon and other generals, felt obligated to remonstrate against such a brutal, such an unwarranted order, and there in command headquarters, with no one else present, a vital dialogue began:

GARZA: Excellency, may I respectfully suggest that you do not send Urrea that order.

SANTA ANNA: Why not? My decree of 30 December 1835 clearly states that any foreigner taking arms against the government of Mexico is to be treated like a pirate and shot.

GARZA: But to shoot so many . . . more than three hundred, maybe four hundred. This will be taken poorly in los Estados Unidos. It will incur lasting enmity.

SANTA ANNA (with great animation): Now, there you're wrong, Garza. Remember what happened at Tampico? Just last December? A gang of norteamericanos tried to invade, coming down from New Orleans. We defeated them and shot twenty-eight of them as pirates. Everybody warned me: 'The people of New Orleans will rise up.' Nobody made a move. They realized the dead men were pirates. They deserved to be shot, and I shot them.

GARZA: But I'm worried, Excellency, that this Alamo thing might be differently interpreted. It didn't happen in Tampico. It happened here, and norteamericanos interpret Béjar and Tejas differently from the way they do Tampico.

SANTA ANNA: Again you're wrong. Our great victory here, and Urrea's in Goliad, will show them that Tejas really is an indivisible part of Mexico. That they no longer have any interest in it. They never did.

GARZA: They think they did, and that's what counts. Look at what the messenger said about the men at Goliad who are to be shot if your order prevails. Men from Georgia. From New Orleans. And Louisville. Irishmen. Poles. This is not a collection of random volunteers, like the Alamo.

SANTA ANNA (*very persuasively, his voice low and controlled*): The more reason they must be punished, and openly. See that the order to Urrea goes out promptly.

GARZA: Excellency, I must protest. I must.

SANTA ANNA: Are you a loyal mexicano? Or a damned norteamericano?

GARZA: I hope to be your governor of Tejas one of these days.

SANTA ANNA (*laughing*): And so you shall be, or someone like you. Because from now on, Tejas is forever mexicano.

GARZA: So I speak as a future governor . . . if things go well.

SANTA ANNA: I'm sure they will. With Béjar and Goliad in our hands, with our men in control of the coast, with the norteamericanos burning down their own towns—all we have to do is pin this Sam Houston down somewhere and finish him off. Clean out Nacogdoches and never again allow a norteamericano to live west of the Sabine.

GARZA: A large order, Excellency.

SANTA ANNA: It's almost done. (*Then, snapping his fingers*): I'll make you my district governor at Nacogdoches. You can guard our frontier.

GARZA: It is Nacogdoches, Excellency, that I'm worried about. Béjar and Goliad have fallen. Suppose you overtake Houston somewhere on the banks of the Brazos and wipe him out. Don't you see that this drags you all the way to the Louisiana border, and as you approach there, it's going to be like a spring? You compress it and compress it, and always it grows more powerful until . . . poof! It blows you apart.

SANTA ANNA: What do you mean?

GARZA: I mean simply this. That you can annihilate the Alamo in fair battle, and that's acceptable. And you can defeat Fannin at Goliad, and that's acceptable. But if you shoot the Goliad prisoners, and then march north, every man in Kentucky and Tennessee and Alabama and Mississippi is going to rally to the cause, so that when you reach the Sabine you will face the whole Estados Unidos.

SANTA ANNA: If the norteamericanos give me any more trouble, I may march all the way to Washington. The execution of the prisoners, that is a risk we must take. It's a risk I'm willing to take, because I feel sure that when they see the irresistible force of our armies—and remember, Garza, I'll have eight thousand shortly and they'll have trouble mustering one thousand . . .

GARZA: Their thousand will be led by Sam Houston, and he's no Fannin.

SANTA ANNA: I know little about him. What kind of man is he?

GARZA: Most of us have never seen him.

SANTA ANNA: What have you heard?

GARZA: He's drunk most of the time, but very clear-eyed when sober. He fought with their President Jackson against the Indians, but he also loves the Indians and is just in his treatment of mexicanos. The norteamericanos I know find him unfathomable.

SANTA ANNA: Nothing but a frontier gallant.

GARZA: But if you proceed with the execution of the Goliad prisoners, Excellency, you place a terrible weapon in the hands of this Houston.

SANTA ANNA: What weapon?

GARZA: Revenge. Excellency, the norteamericanos may forget the Alamo in time. It was a fair fight and they lost. But they could never forget a massacre at Goliad. They will fight us every inch of the way. They'll cut our supply lines, and our lines will be very long.

SANTA ANNA: Damnit, you sound like a yanqui.

GARZA: I want to be governor of a state that can be governed. If we make a just settlement now, bring men like Houston into a decent companionship . . .

SANTA ANNA *(slowly and with careful reasoning):* I have them by the throat, Garza. With reinforcements arriving every day, I have a chance to wipe them out. Another Zacatecas. Another Tampico. Teach them a terrible lesson, pacify them, and go back to governing Mexico as it should be governed. *(A long pause)* So the execution of the prisoners at Goliad must be seen as part of a grand design. All pieces fall into place if you look at it that way.

GARZA *(pleading):* Excellency, there's one thing I haven't told you . . . haven't told anyone. But when you sent me into the Alamo to verify the bodies—Crockett and those—the first body I could name was that of my sister's husband, Xavier Campbell, a good Catholic from Scotland.

SANTA ANNA: Scotland, England, Ireland, Wales . . . why do men from such places come to fight against us? What business have they in Mexico? *(Then, gently):* I am sorry for your sister. I shall send her a present, give her some land when this is over.

GARZA: My point is, Excellency, that at the spot which this dead Xavier Campbell defended lay nine dead mexicanos. When you cross the Brazos you will stand face to face with a thousand Xavier Campbells.

SANTA ANNA *(as if he had not heard):* So I want you, personally, to start riding right now with my message to General Urrea. Every prisoner he has must be shot. And if you do not report to me that this has been done, you will be shot.

So early on Thursday, 24 March, Benito Garza rode hard to Goliad in the company of three soldiers guiding extra mounts; he carried an order he did not want to deliver and one which he certainly did not want to see obeyed. Knowing something of General Urrea, he hoped that this strong-minded professional would refuse to obey Santa Anna and would set the prisoners free. But when he reached the stout walls of the presidio, with its four hundred and seven norteamericano prisoners, including those taken from other areas, he found that General Urrea, anticipating such an order, had generated an excuse to go south, leaving the presidio and its prisoners in the hands of a weak Colonel José Nicolás de la Portilla.

Portilla's hands trembled when he opened the dispatch, and his face paled when he read the blunt command: 'Immediate execution of every perfidious foreigner.'

He received these cruel instructions at about seven o'clock in the evening and spent the next hours in great anguish, because Urrea on departing had given him very specific orders of quite a different character: 'Treat the prisoners with consideration, especially their leader Colonel Fannin, and protect them in every way so long as they remain in your custody.'

So there it was: 'Shoot them all' or 'Protect them until they're set free.' Through the night he juggled these orders, and toward dawn he concluded that whereas his immediate superior, General Urrea, knew what was the military thing to do under the circumstances, his ultimate superior, General Santa Anna, knew what was best for the nation and was also in position to punish any subordinate who disobeyed his written order.

About half an hour before dawn on Palm Sunday, 27 March, Colonel Portilla rose, dressed in his finest uniform, and marched to the commissary, where he summoned his junior officers and told them: 'We're to shoot them all. I said *all.*'

A great commotion engulfed the presidio, with grim-lipped captains and lieutenants running here and there, and Lieutenant Colonel Juan José Holsinger still reassuring the Texicans: 'We're marching you to the boats. Home free.' He believed what he was saying, because as a German known for his sympathies toward the prisoners, he had not been trusted with the truth.

The prisoners, delighted at the prospect of being freed, were formed into three groups, with Finlay Macnab and his fourteen-year-old son Otto among the Georgia Battalion that would march along the San Antonio River. 'Can we be allowed to drop out when we pass our home?' Macnab asked Holsinger, who replied jovially: 'Yes, yes. That's entirely reasonable.'

But just then Otto shouted: 'It's Benito!' and his cry attracted the attention of Santa Anna's messenger of death, and when Garza saw that the Macnabs, part of his family, were among the unknowing doomed, he moved away lest they detect his anguish.

'Benito!' the boy cried, and Holsinger, seeing this, turned to Garza and told him: 'Friends of yours,' so Benito had to speak with them.

'We're going home at last,' Otto cried, as he reached out to greet his friend.

'Yes,' Garza said. 'You must stay close to me as we march out.'

'I want to,' Otto said, and his father added: 'Holsinger said we could drop out when we reached our home. Will you be joining us, to help your sisters?'

'Yes. Yes.'

'Campbell was killed, wasn't he? A messenger from Gonzales said that he
. . .'

'He died.'

'Were they all killed?'

'Yes, yes,' and in shame he moved away.

Now the condemned norteamericanos were told to form three separate columns
and to move toward the main gate. They would march about half a mile, each in a
different direction, and then they would be halted, each file out of sight of the
others but not out of hearing.

They were well on their way when a male nurse ran into the large room where
about forty men wounded the week before lay on cots, Colonel Fannin among
them with a leg wound which had nearly killed him. 'Drag them all into the yard.
They're to be shot,' the nurse cried hysterically. And slowly, laboriously, the cots
were dragged into the sunlight, where the men who had been saved from death
now lay dumbly awaiting it. Colonel Fannin, from his cot, begged his men to act
bravely.

Soon Mexican soldiers began moving from cot to cot, jamming pistols against
the heads of the men and blowing their brains out. Finally only Fannin was left.

West Point to the end, he never flinched, and assuming that his captors were
gentlemen like himself, he made the kind of statement officers were supposed to
make in a situation like this: 'Sir, I give you my watch and my money, with only
two requests. Please do not shoot me in the face. Please see that I am decently
buried with the honors of war.'

When the blindfold was over his eyes the officer who had accepted the watch
asked: 'Bueno?' and Fannin replied: 'It is well placed.' He was then shot right
through the face and his body was tossed on the pile with the others to be burned,
with the charred remains left for the coyotes and the vultures.

These intimate details are known because just before the executions started, a
compassionate Mexican officer, knowing that General Urrea's wounded needed
medical care, moved quietly among the Texicans, selecting men who had proved
helpful in caring for the sick. To each he whispered: 'Move toward that corner.
Hide.' His personal courage in disobeying Santa Anna's cruel orders meant that
some two dozen Texicans survived, and it was they who in later years reported the
atrocity which was now about to unfold.

The marching columns—three hundred and seventy men in all—could not
know what had happened to the wounded prisoners, and the Georgia Battalion
containing the Macnabs was well on its way to the river, with some of the men
singing, when it was ordered to halt. At this moment Benito Garza, who was with
the troops, grabbed Otto by the left shoulder, whirled him about, pointed to the
nearby woods, and said one word: 'Run!'

The boy, bewildered, did not move, so Garza gave him a strong shove and
muttered again: 'Run!'

'My father!'

'Run!' Garza shouted, and this both spurred the boy into action and alerted a wiry Mexican lieutenant with a sword, who saw what was happening. He was about to chase after Otto, but the morning's work began, which temporarily delayed him.

When the group of some hundred and twenty prisoners halted, the Mexican soldiers wheeled about, formed two lines, enclosing the Texicans, and upon command began to shoot each prisoner in the head. But when the captives realized the terrible thing that was happening, many started to fight their captors with bare fists, so that a general melee developed, with much aimless firing.

Otto, from his place among the trees, saw men from Tennessee grab the guns of their slayers and defend themselves with the butts until some Mexican shot them through the back of the head. Other men, wounded in the first fusillades, lay helplessly on the ground, looking up as soldiers came, pointed pistols directly in their faces, and blew their heads apart. He watched with horror as his father broke loose and started to run across the fields toward where he was hiding, and Finlay might have escaped had not three officers on horseback galloped after him, stabbing him in the back with their lances and cheering as he stumbled blindly about, the lances projecting from his back. Forming a circle about him with their horses, they fired at him six times, and rode off.

Desperately Otto wanted to run out to help his father, but common sense told him that Finlay was dead, so he retreated farther into the woods, and it was good that he did, because the officer who had seen him escape now came after him on foot, armed with sword and knife and pistol, to finish him off, but the sight of this great peril gave Otto newfound strength. Grasping for anything, he wrenched loose a stout oak branch, and with a power that frightened him, stripped off the twigs. He now had a heavy weapon with which to defend himself.

The officer, seeing the boy apparently defenseless, moved easily through the woods, brandishing his sword, and when he reached Otto he gave a mighty flash with his right arm, bringing the point of the sword directly athwart Otto's neck, but the boy swerved, taking a deep cut from left ear to chin. So impassioned was he that he did not feel the cut or the flow of blood, but he fell to the ground as if mortally wounded, then jammed his oak branch between the officer's legs. With a sudden twist, he threw the fellow down, grabbed his knife as it fell loose, and with three terrible stabs he struck the man in the chest, in the gut, and deep in the neck.

He had no time to assess his victory, because two other soldiers had heard the noise of the struggle and now closed in upon him. At first, as he ran for the river, he was so protected by trees that they could not use their rifles, but when he broke for the banks they had a clear shot at him and one bullet tore into his left shoulder, but did not shatter the bone.

Disregarding this second wound as he had the first, he dashed to the edge of the steep bank—it was almost a cliff—and without thinking of hidden rocks or invisible tree stumps he leaped into the water, submerged, and swam underwater for the opposite shore.

This was a mistake, for it allowed the two soldiers to spot him when he surfaced, but before they could take proper aim, he was underwater again, swimming this time for the very bank on which they stood. When he surfaced this time, right under them, they were too surprised to shoot, so down he went again, with them firing at his wake, and when signs of blood bubbled up, they assumed that they had killed him.

He had not moved. He had stayed right below them, holding his breath until he feared his lungs might burst, and this time when he edged his nose above the water and then his eyes, he found that they had left.

He remained in the river till late afternoon, allowing the water to cleanse his two wounds, and satisfying himself with probing fingers that the damage was not too serious. He was, however, losing a lot of blood, so at about five in the afternoon he climbed out on the far bank, turned his back on the scene of the massacre, and made his way eastward toward the Guadalupe, which would lead him home.

That night, resting under a tree, his left cheek and left shoulder throbbing with pain, he lost consciousness, and lay there bleeding. Toward morning he roused himself and continued his struggle toward safety, reaching the Guadalupe about sunset. Again he fell unconscious, but when he came to he saw that the bleeding had stopped.

Before dawn he was on his way again, further weakened by a rising fever. Alternately staggering forward and falling to his knees from dizziness, he reached a point along the river from which he could see the Campbell dog-run, and the realization that he was so close to salvation overwhelmed him. All the strength left his body and he fell, face down, and even when he heard a barking and felt a warm tongue licking his face and knew it was Betsy, he could not move.

María, hearing the dog's excited barking, came to her porch. For some minutes she could not see the body lying on the ground, but when Betsy ignored her whistle, she knew that something unusual must have happened, and in this way she found her adopted son.

This was the morning of Wednesday, 30 March, and Otto remained in a feverish coma till the next Sunday. Periodically he revived enough to learn that María was aware of her husband's death in the Alamo, and he told her that his father was dead, too, at Goliad.

In one moment of lucidity he realized that Josefina was in the room, commiserating with her sister, two Mexican women bereft of their anglo husbands.

Mostly, however, he spent these feverish days under the care of stout María, and as he began to mend he felt her warmth rescuing him, her love embracing him, and once he muttered: 'You're like an angel with big hands.' She told him that she had cut the bullet from his shoulder: 'No damage. No danger.' She said that he would always have a scar across his left cheek: 'No damage, no danger.' She fed him the food she had always prepared for her ailing men—refried beans, goat meat well shredded, tortillas, goat's milk with a brown-sugar candy—and he regained his strength.

On Sunday, 10 April, exactly two weeks after his near-death at Goliad, Otto Macnab walked to his own home, fetched two of his father's older rifles, and came back to the Campbell place to pick up one of Xavier's guns and a pair of knives.

'Where are you going?' María asked, her eyes filled with tears.

'To join Sam Houston.'

'To fight against my people again?'

'We've got to settle this.'

'Settle!' María wailed. 'What can you settle? Xavier dead. Finlay dead. And God knows where my brother Benito is.'

'He's all right. He was with General Urrea.'

'He was fighting against you and Campbell?'

'He saved my life.' And then a vision of that struggle under the trees returned and a thought of striking significance revealed itself: 'María, the officer who almost killed me. He saw it was Benito who saved me. If he had lived, I know he would have reported Benito and maybe had him shot. I saw the look in his face when I started to run.'

'Where is he now? Is he a danger to my brother?'

'I killed him.'

No more was said. The two Garza women had absorbed as much anguish as anyone can accept before the mind rebels; young Otto had seen things which could drive a mind to madness. Mexicana women and American boy, the three were caught in terrible currents, frightening dislocations, and no one had the capacity or the courage to untangle them. The two women knew that they had loved their norteamericano men and they appreciated how kind, how just, how loving they had been, but these same men had taken arms against legitimate mexicano power and had paid for their error with their lives.

Otto knew beyond question that members of the Garza family had twice saved his life: once, Benito on the killing ground; and more recently, María when he was near death. He owed these wonderful people a debt he could never repay, but now he must join General Houston.

With three rifles, two knives, a pistol and a nondescript collection of clothes, he started for the decisive battle which he knew could not be avoided. Betsy insisted on following him, but when they came to the ford by which he would cross the Guadalupe he told her sternly: 'Go home.' After he waded into the water, he stopped, turned to face the obedient dog, and cried: 'Take care of María!' And for some time Betsy watched him as he marched east.

When Benito Garza rejoined General Santa Anna's staff, he was both surprised and relieved to discover how little adverse effect the Goliad massacre had had upon the reputation of the dictator. Oh, there had been some grumbling among the general population, and several of Santa Anna's European officers had confided: 'I'd not have done it that way,' but since there was no open protest, Benito supposed that the matter would soon be forgotten.

What he did not know was that American journals were already blazoning the story of the Alamo with inflammatory exhortations and that mass meetings were being convened in several states demanding military intervention on behalf of the slain heroes. Nor could he anticipate that these same journals would shortly be characterizing the Goliad massacre as 'three hundred and forty-two individual cases of unjustified murder,' which was the only appropriate way of describing it.

Garza had a remarkably clear perception of the military situation, which he discussed with General Ripperdá, in whose regiment he was again serving: 'We have about seven thousand soldiers either north of the Rio Grande or near it. General Houston can't have more than eight hundred, and I doubt he can ever get them to stay behind him very long. They come and go. I've seen them—farmers, ranchers, men with small shops.'

'But we, too, have a serious problem,' Ripperdá pointed out. 'We do have those seven thousand, but we don't seem able to gather them in one place. Urrea in Matagorda. Sesma bringing his thousand up from Thompson's Ferry. Another batch at Goliad. Right now Santa Anna has less than a thousand under his immediate command.'

'But a thousand of our troops can always defeat eight hundred of theirs.'

'Certainly,' Ripperdá agreed. 'But I'd feel safer if the margin was what it ought to be. Seven hundred of them, seven thousand of us.'

'Well, isn't that Santa Anna's job? Postpone fighting until we assemble our superiority?'

Garza was confident that the supreme commander would do just that, and now as the mexicanos left Béjar and started the long march to the east, he was gratified to see that various units were catching up, while others were sending messages that they, too, would soon report.

So although he had been repelled by Santa Anna's needless brutality at Goliad, Garza still respected his generalship, for the man had an uncanny sense of what was going to happen next and a conviction that he would be clever enough to bend this occurrence to his advantage. 'An angel hovers above my left shoulder,' the general had said once, and this was proving true, for when the army approached Gonzales with a superiority less than satisfactory—so that if a battle could not be avoided, it might be more risky than desired—they found that the Texicans had set fire to the town and abandoned it.

'See, they run away from us!' Santa Anna gloated. 'But we'll catch them.' And that night amid the smoking embers he sent a series of short, clear dispatches ordering other generals to join him for a swift crossing of the Colorado and a forced march to see if they might trap Houston before he escaped over the Brazos. Once the rebels were forced to stand and fight, Santa Anna was sure his legions would crush them totally.

'We'll hang Houston and so many of his criminal supporters that oak trees will look as if they bore fruit,' he told Garza, who, contrary to what he had argued only a few weeks before, now believed it might be possible to exterminate all the troublesome norteamericanos and establish in Tejas a true mexicano province under benign leadership from Santa Anna in Mexico City, and he continued to see himself as governor.

But as they marched out of Gonzales an old man and his wife, both mexicanos, shouted at Santa Anna astride his white horse: 'Murderer'—and the word hung ominously in the air, clouding and contaminating the high hopes with which the army moved toward battle.

When it seemed that Santa Anna, forging ahead to conquer all of rebellious Tejas, was about to trap the fleeing Houston and his entire ragtag of defenders, one of those romantic miracles occurred which still convince Texans that God is on their side. In 1830 the New York investor John Jacob Astor had authorized the building of a steamboat to be used in the fur trade on the Missouri River. Called the *Yellow Stone*, it entered service in 1831, but ill fortune seemed to haunt the vessel as it tried to dodge the sunken niggerheads of the Missouri.

After less than a year's operation on that river, the *Yellow Stone* was asked to try its luck on the Mississippi, with no better results, but in 1833 the doughty little boat steamed up the Missouri all the way to the mouth of its namesake, the Yellowstone River in far North Dakota. However, that was its last run on its intended river, for soon thereafter it turned up as a grubby freight carrier in New Orleans.

On the last day of 1835, when Santa Anna was already marching north, the *Yellow Stone* left the safety of New Orleans and chugged its way to Tejas, bringing with it the New Orleans Grays, volunteers who were eager to help the rebellious state gain its independence. Having arrived in Tejas, it remained there, and it was picking its way up the tight and shallow waters of the Brazos when Sam Houston's confused army approached, needing all the help it could get.

Miraculously—there is no other word for it—the peripatetic little boat was waiting there when Houston needed it most, and it edged its nose into the western bank so that it could transport all of Houston's men to temporary safety on the eastern shore. By the time Santa Anna reached that area, the boat was gone and Houston's army, such as it was, remained intact.

While this was happening, events of a less satisfactory nature were occurring upstream on the Brazos. Houston's spies had informed him that Víctor de Ripperdá, ablest of Santa Anna's generals, was speeding north to intercept the main Texas army from the west, and it was imperative that he be slowed down. Considering the problem with what maps he had, Houston concluded that Ripperdá would make a dash for Quimper's Ferry, hoping to find it functioning.

'That ferry must be destroyed,' Houston said, and two dozen volunteers hurried upstream, realizing that if they reached Quimper's after the Mexican troops had crossed, it was the Texicans who would probably be destroyed. The average age of the adventurers was twenty-two, their average time within the boundaries of Texas, three months and three days. They came from eleven different states and two foreign countries, and if ever a group of untrained men was willing to fight for the abstract ideal of freedom, it was this disorganized mob.

By forced marches, the contingent reached Quimper's Ferry the day before General Ripperdá's troops would begin streaming in from the south. The men ran to the riverbank, saw that the ferry was on the other shore, and sent two men swimming across to fetch it, but when Mattie Quimper saw what was afoot, she ran down from the inn to confront the men: 'It's my ferry. I know what to do with it.' The men, thinking that she was refusing to destroy it, said: 'Madam, we got orders. This ferry can't fall into the hands of the Mexicans,' and she said: 'It won't.'

With the help of the two soldiers, she poled the ferry to the opposite bank, and when the expedition gathered about her, she grabbed an ax and went back down the slope to where she had tied the crude ferry and began to chop it to pieces, thus demolishing the precious craft that had served her so long. When the watching soldiers saw what she was doing, they ran down the banks and helped her with the destruction.

Slowly the muddy waters separated the logs and turned the superstructure over: 'Better come off, ma'am. She's fallin' apart.'

The ferry did not sink in the sense of disappearing in a rush; slowly the logs settled into the mud along the bank. 'Push that stuff into midstream!' a captain called, and when this was done, railing which had once enclosed the deck remained visible, drifting slowly downstream, useful to no one.

Mattie made no comment as it disappeared; it had been a good ferry, improved and enlarged over the years, and many hundreds of travelers had blessed it. But it had to be destroyed and she expressed no sorrow at its going.

But she was now on the opposite bank of the river from her home. 'I must go back,' she told the soldiers, but when they reported this to the captain, he told her: 'Stay with us. The Mexicans will burn everything over there.' She could not accept this advice and made as if to swim back, whereupon he called to some of his men: 'Fetch the little boat and take her across.' When this was done, she stood on the bank and watched silently as the Texicans marched away, taking her son Yancey with them: I hope they know how to fight. I hope Yancey behaves well.

Left on her side of the Brazos, with all other homes abandoned, all neighbors fled, she spent a lonely night pondering what to do, and looking about her deserted inn, she had visions of those who had inhabited this refuge: her husband, Jubal, with his hunting dogs; the giant Kronk; Father Clooney; Joel Job Harrison, whom she had nearly married; the Jewish peddler who had come this way; the hungry settlers gorging on her honeyed pecans; the almost saintly Stephen Austin, so small, so determined. They had been a motley but noble group, battling the wilderness, and she could not bear to see this precious place fall into enemy hands.

Slowly, and with unflagging determination, she gathered branches of trees and shards of wood, placing them where the wind would catch at them and speed the flames she intended to ignite. When the sun was well up, and the sounds of marching enemy could be heard to the south, she went from pile to pile, lighting each with brands, and when the inn was well ablaze, with fire eating at the logs which Jubal and Father Clooney first and then The Kronk had cut so carefully, she left what had been first her cave-house and then her dog-run and watched it burn.

It was only partly consumed when the first Mexican troops arrived, followed soon by General Ripperdá and his staff. Infuriated by the sight of a lone woman burning her house to deprive them of its comforts, this officer loudly directed his men to secure the ferry that his spies had assured him would be here, and when soldiers shouted: 'Colonel, it's gone, seems to be sunk, some pieces floating in the river,' he swore and turned his horse aside to view the damage for himself.

Ripperdá, an officer who honored the great traditions of the Spanish army in which so many of his ancestors had served, was not responsible for an ugly incident that occurred at this time. Some of his soldiers, intoxicated by their victories at the Alamo and Goliad, had begun to assume that the conquest of the rest of Tejas was going to be a triumphal affair. 'One more battle, we go home!' was the cry, and now when they saw themselves frustrated by this lone woman they grew enraged, and three men rushed her.

'No!' Benito Garza shouted when he came upon the scene. 'I know her!'

Too late. Three soldiers stabbed at Mattie with their bayonets. She made no outcry. Clutching her throat as blood welled up, she tried valiantly to remain upright beside her burning home, but at last she fell, face down, upon the land she had loved so deeply.

Mattie's prayer that her son perform honorably as a member of Houston's force bore quick and reassuring results, for when Yancey, now twenty-four, found himself in the company of men his own age he pulled himself together, suppressed his childish petulance, and began acting like a solid, ordinary farmhand forced into military life. He grumbled at the long marches, groused about the miserable food, and fraternized warmly with the other soldiers. What was most surprising, in view of his poor performances in the battles against the Karankawa, he could appear quite belligerent, especially when in the presence of the younger men, and he was always prepared to advise anyone on how to conduct the war.

He was a robust young fellow, with a big confident face and a voice that soared above the babble. He was never reluctant to step forward when dangerous work had to be done, but he did tend to delay his move until someone else had been clearly nominated. He liked especially to instruct the younger troops as to how they must conduct themselves when the Mexicans struck. He had become, in short, a typical Texican patriot, with his long gun, his Bowie knife, and his determination to repel Santa Anna.

One April day, as he was explaining strategy to attentive listeners, he suddenly stopped, stared down the road, and cried: 'My God! What is it? A human porcupine?'

For up the dusty trail came a fourteen-year-old boy, blood-red scar across his left cheek, lugging a collection of weapons whose ends stuck out like the disorderly quills of a hedgehog. As the boy came closer, Yancey saw that it was his onetime friend Otto Macnab, who was not in camp ten minutes before he discovered that he was facing a new Yancey Quimper, matured and self-confident, who asked in a condescending way: 'Where do you come from, son?'

'Goliad, and I come to fight.'

'Goliad!' Yancey shouted to those behind him. 'He says he was at Goliad.'

Soon Otto was surrounded by admirers who wanted to know what had happened at the presidio, how he had got that scar across his face, and what it was like fighting the Mexican regulars.

'They know which end of a gun fires,' Otto assured them.

'How'd your father allow you to join us?'

'He was killed at Goliad. Stabbed in the back after he surrendered.' He said this so matter-of-factly, but with such terrible commitment, his blue eyes hard in the river sunlight, that the men said no more.

Later, the men who had questioned him about Goliad regathered to confirm what a sorry affair Houston's march to the east had been, and from the babble of whining voices he collected these offerings:

'Always he runs away . . .'

'He's afraid to fight. Alamo and Goliad, they terrified him.'

'He's runnin' to the north, hopin' to escape into Louisiana.'

'We could of licked Santy Anny three times over if we'd stood and fought.'

'He's a coward, and until we get rid of him, we accomplish nothin'.'

Harshest in his criticism was Quimper: 'General Houston has a Gulf of Mexico jellyfish for his backbone. Look at us, achin' for a fight. Eatin' our hearts out to revenge the Alamo and Goliad. And all he does is run away.'

'Maybe he has a plan,' Otto suggested, for from his observation of Colonel Fannin he had learned that commanders oftentimes had plans they did not confide to their troops, and sometimes those plans didn't work.

'Read this, Little Porcupine?' Quimper cried, and he grabbed from a Mississippi man standing nearby a dispatch received some days before. 'Watson here stole a copy, and it tells the whole story.' It was from the man elected president of the interim government and it did indeed lay forth the problem:

> To General Sam Houston, Sir: The enemy are laughing you to scorn. You must fight them. You must retreat no farther. The country expects you to fight. The salvation of the country depends on your doing so.
>
> David G. Burnet, President

The letter, as severe a rebuke as a field commander could have received, gave Otto a sick feeling: We're back at Goliad with a general who doesn't know what he's doing. Everything is falling apart.

But toward dusk a commotion along the river forestalled any demand for a new leader, because a gang of sweating men driving sixteen oxen appeared from the east, bellowing the information that they were bringing treasure into camp. Everyone ran to greet them, even General Houston, erect and dignified despite the pressures that assailed him.

Otto, coming slowly to the realization that he would never again see either his father or Zave Campbell, felt the need of someone older to cling to, and kept close to Quimper. Together they watched the oxen drag into camp two handsome cannon, gifts from the people of Cincinnati.

'Did you know, Yancey, I used to live in that town?' Otto said.

'You did?'

'Yep, sold pork to the riverboats.'

A soldier supervising the placement of the cannon said: 'Took three months for them to come down the Mississippi. Slipped past customs in New Orleans listed as "two pieces of hollow ware." '

'Where'd they get the name Twin Sisters?' Yancey asked, and one of the soldiers explained: 'They was christened off'n the port of Galveston by the lovely twin daughters of a doctor who came on the same boat, and they'll blow the balls off'n Santy Anny.'

The men, with so little to cheer during the past weeks, saw the cannon as proof that someone in the States cared, and they insisted that the two be fired right now, to which Houston agreed, and there in the wilderness, with no sensible target before them, the Texicans loaded both, tamped the charges, and blazed away at the tops of distant oak trees. When a scatter of leaves proved that the guns could fire effectively, the men cheered.

Some days later, while helping to drag the cannon along muddy country roads, Otto had a chance to observe how the most trivial accident could sometimes determine the course of history. At this time the sweating Texicans did not know whether they would soon head north to Nacogdoches, surrendering all of central Texas to Santa Anna's fury, or east toward the Gulf of Mexico, hoping to engage the Mexicans on some favorable battleground. General Houston refused to divulge his plans, and many thought he had none. They said: 'He's markin' time, hopin' that somethin' favorable will save us.'

Now came the first accident. One of the wheels of Otto's cannon fell deep into a muddy rut, and when Houston rode by and saw the delay he growled: 'Get some oxen and drag that thing free.'

'We have no oxen,' the captain in charge of the big guns reported, and Houston said: 'Get some.'

A detail consisting of the captain, Otto and another enlisted man went searching the countryside, and soon came upon a strong-minded, brassy-voiced farm wife named Mrs. Pamela Mann, who wore men's clothing and was armed with two large pistols.

'We must borrow four of your oxen,' the officer explained courteously.

'You cain't have 'em,' she snarled.

'We must have them.'

'You touch them oxen, I blow out the seat of your pants.'

'Mrs. Mann,' the officer said, 'the future of the Texas Republic depends upon moving our cannon to face Santa Anna, and to do that we must have your oxen.'

'To hell with the Texas Republic. What's it ever done for me?'

The officer dropped his voice and beseeched so earnestly that she had to listen, and after some moments she delivered a curious judgment: 'Tell you what, if'n your general is marchin' east with his cannon to fight Santy Anny, he cain't have my beasts. They'd get kilt. But if'n he's marchin' north to safety in Nacogdoches, he can borry 'em.'

'He's marching north!' the captain said quickly, whereupon the other enlisted man, who could be seen only by Macnab, drew his thumb across his throat, indicating that if Houston did march north, he would face rebellion.

So the four oxen were taken away and yoked to the mired cannon, but as the army resumed its forward march the vital question of where they were going was left unsettled. Desiring to be sure that the wheel on Otto's cannon had not been damaged by the hole into which it had fallen, Houston was to the rear when his lead troops approached a crossroads. If they marched to the left, they would retreat to Nacogdoches; straight ahead, they would have to encounter Santa Anna.

The men on the point, not knowing what to do, drifted into a grassy area between the two roads, intending to wait there until General Houston came up to give an order. And then the second accident took place, for at the head of the next group to arrive was a brassy young fellow from Alabama, and he cried to a farmer standing nearby: 'Which way to Harrisburg and Santy Anny?' and the farmer shouted back: 'That right-hand road will carry you to Harrisburg just as straight as a compass.'

'This way!' the Alabaman cried, and by the time General Houston reached the crossroads the forefront of the Texican army was well on its way to battle. For just a moment Houston stopped, studied the terrain, and shrugged his shoulders. Then he also took the road to Harrisburg. A decision of major consequence to Texas, and perhaps to the United States, had been reached: the Texas patriots would seek out Santa Anna and give him battle.

As Otto struggled with the cannon which had kept Houston from his position of command, Yancey Quimper drifted back and whispered: 'If us fellows in front hadn't of made the choice for him, sure as hell Old Shiftless would of skedaddled off to Nacogdoches.' But the officer who had commandeered the mules said: 'Houston always intended taking this road. We talked about it.'

Otto and his borrowed oxen had dragged the cannon less than a mile when Mrs. Mann rode furiously up to General Houston, her eyes blazing, her free hand close to the pistol on her left hip: 'General, yore men told me a damn lie. They said my oxen would be safe on the Nacogdoches road. Sir, I want 'em back.'

'You can't have them, ma'am,' Houston said. 'Our cannon need them.'

'I don't care a damn for your cannon. I want my oxen,' and she jumped down, whipped out a big knife, and began cutting loose her beasts. Houston was so astonished that he was speechless, and before he could issue any orders, she was riding off with her animals.

Otto's captain cried: 'Come with me! We'll get them back!' But when the captain and Otto overtook Mrs. Mann, she astonished them by leaping from her horse, landing on the captain's back, and thrashing him with her fists as he lay on the ground. When he called for Otto to assist, she poked a gun into the boy's face and cried: 'Make one move, son, and you ain't got no head.' Standing in the mud, she held off the captain, mounted her horse, and resumed her homeward march with her beasts.

When Otto returned to his cannon with no animals to drag it into battle, the younger soldiers taunted him: 'Skeered of a woman!' and 'You stole her oxen brave enough, but you couldn't keep 'em.' Otto said nothing, but his fists tightened and his blue eyes grew hard. If I'm ever in command of anything, he swore to himself, shameful things like this will not happen.

On the morning of Tuesday, 19 April, General Houston's Fabian tactics came to fruition, because Santa Anna, chasing him wildly, had imprudently taken his entire available force onto a boggy peninsula formed by the San Jacinto River, where he could neither retreat nor receive reinforcements except over a narrow bridge. He assumed he was safe because he could not envision Houston seeking battle there, or winning if he did.

But Houston had a daring plan. Assembling as many of his nine hundred-odd troops as he could at the bank of a bayou, he told them in fighting sentences: 'The battle we have sought is upon us. The army will cross and we will meet the enemy. Some of us may be killed, and must be killed. But, men, Remember the Alamo! The Alamo!'

Yancey, delighted with the prospect of battle at last, gripped Otto's arm and said prophetically: 'After a speech like that, Little Porcupine, our boys will take damned few prisoners.'

All that day the volunteers worked to get across the bayou and onto that stretch of land from which Santa Anna could not escape. 'How brilliant,' exulted a man from Connecticut. 'We have only nine hundred, true, but Santa Anna hasn't his seven thousand. We've tricked him into facing us with less than a thousand. By God, we have a chance of winning.'

On the afternoon of the twentieth the two armies were still moving into position, but any actual engagement seemed unlikely. A detachment of mounted Texicans did make a gallant effort to capture a Mexican cannon that had been giving them trouble, but the Mexicans anticipated the move and gave a solid account of themselves. In fact, when the main body of the Texicans withdrew, three of their horsemen were left isolated—Secretary of War Thomas Rusk, an officer and a private—and a detachment of Mexican cavalry was about to capture all three when a most unlikely hero swung into action.

Infantry Private Mirabeau Buonaparte Lamar, riding a borrowed horse, was a minor poet-politician from Georgia who had arrived in Texas only a few weeks earlier, after both the Alamo and Goliad had fallen, but he was a man of such vision, such patriotism that he almost leaped into the fight for Texas freedom. Now, with the enemy all about him, he performed heroically, and by his superb horsemanship and daring, saved both Rusk and another man. Texicans and Mexicans alike cheered as the Georgian, a rather small man, outwitted the Mexicans and brought his two charges to safety. That night many asked: 'Who is this fellow with the French names?' but he did nothing to parade his valor.

On the morning of the twenty-first, General Houston slept late, for the hardships of the march and the exacerbations of command had exhausted him. His men, disgusted by his apparent indifference, renewed talk of deposing him, and they were further distressed to hear about midmorning that General Cós had joined Santa Anna with an additional four hundred-odd fresh troops. By this lucky stroke the Mexicans restored their clear superiority, some fourteen hundred of them to about nine hundred Texicans.

Heroic veterans of the frontier appeared not to be daunted by the disproportionate numbers, but shortly after dawn a grizzled scout named Erastus Smith, deaf from birth and famed throughout Texas as Deaf Smith, a man of strong opinion who never apologized for his black brother-in-law, saw to it that no more reinforcements could reach Santa Anna. Summoning five of his fellow scouts and the boy Macnab, he crept back along the route the Texicans had taken to get onto the peninsula and chopped away the only bridge. When the timbers were down he directed Otto and one of the men to set them afire, and as the smoke rose high in the windless air he led his party safely back. Now Houston and Santa Anna were entrapped; they must fight, with the Mexicans superior in numbers, and each general knew that the resulting battle, which would start next day at dawn, would determine the future history of this part of the world.

Relishing their day of rest, the weary Texicans moved idly about their camp, testing their guns and tending their horses, but at noon General Houston surprised everyone by convening a council of war. Otto and Yancey were assigned guard duty outside the headquarters tent, and there they overheard much heated argument and the taking of votes whose purpose they could not determine, but they did hear General Houston say what others who were near the tent would testify later that he never said: 'Well, the vote is clear. No battle today.'

At this, Quimper uttered a barnyard obscenity such as the Macnabs had never used: 'Shit! When does he intend to fight?'

At that moment a captain rushed into the tent to report with such enthusiasm that Macnab and Quimper could clearly catch each word: 'General, we've consulted the companies, one by one, and they vote unanimously for battle today,' at which Houston snarled: 'All right, fight and be damned.' But again there would be witnesses who swore that it was Houston who made all the decisions, and courageously.

There was one conversation which the eavesdroppers did not hear. Juan Seguín, the mexicano who had chosen to fight on the side of the Texicans, was the only man who would experience both the Alamo and San Jacinto; he had escaped the former tragedy because Colonel Travis sent him from the mission with a plea for aid. Now, in midafternoon on the fields of San Jacinto, he was consulted by General Houston, who asked: 'Seguín, what will Santa Anna and his men be doing over there?' and Seguín replied: 'Siesta, what else?' Then Houston asked: 'If we were to attack at four this afternoon, where would the sun be?' and Seguín replied: 'Standing low in the heavens behind us and directly in their eyes.'

'Would they be confused?' Houston asked, and Seguín said: 'They'd be blinded.'

It was then that Sam Houston Cunctator ended what his subordinates had called 'his running away' and made one of the crucial decisions of Texas history: 'Find the buglers. We attack.'

The Battle of San Jacinto cannot be understood in ordinary military terms; the statistics are too incredible. However, if the fortunes of several typical participants, Mexican and Texican, are followed, rational explanation may result.

Benito Garza had greeted General Cós enthusiastically that morning when the latter arrived in camp, not with four hundred troops as expected, but with a full five hundred. Garza was somewhat disappointed to learn that they were not tested veterans from the Goliad victory but a mass of untried recruits, many of them without shoes or regular equipment.

Seeing that they were exhausted from forced marches, he suggested to Santa Anna that they be granted an immediate siesta, even though it was still morning, and this was agreed to. Said Santa Anna: 'If they sleep well today, they'll fight well tomorrow,' and Garza went off to arrange quarters for the men.

Santa Anna himself did not sleep. Taking a small dose of his favorite narcotic, opium, he called for Garza and told him: 'See if she's out there,' and Benito went to a nearby farmhouse where a beautiful young mulatto slave girl named Emily from the Morgan plantation was being kept, and she was delighted at the prospect of spending yet another siesta with the general.

Garza delivered her to Santa Anna's tent at three-fifteen, and by ten minutes of four the entertainment she had been hired to provide was well under way.

General Víctor Ripperdá, perhaps the ablest Mexican leader on the field that day, was a stiff, rigorous disciplinarian who saw no need to wear medals to display his courage. He had devoted his spare time at posts like Nacogdoches and Yucatán to the study of military principles, and one thing he had learned was that generals must anticipate the unexpected. 'One of the best ways to do this,' he had told Garza at two that afternoon, 'is to be sure you have your picket lines in place.'

To check, Ripperdá had forgone the siesta taken by others and was inspecting the entire front, gazing across the empty space toward where General Houston's troops were apparently taking their rest. He realized that when those battle-ready norteamericanos marched forth the next morning, they would be formidable: 'We'll win, of course, but it won't be easy.'

But when he reached the positions farthest forward, he was appalled to find that Santa Anna had not posted advance scouts to give warning if, for some inexplicable reason, the Texicans should decide to attack that afternoon. Such a move was unlikely, but he knew that any army within sight of the enemy ought to have its picket lines at top readiness. Santa Anna had none.

In dismay, and with some apprehension, Ripperdá moved back from where the lines should have been to consult with junior officers at the artillery batteries, and to his horror he found that none were present. Indeed, most batteries had only a scattering of untrained enlisted men who would be unable to operate the big guns if the enemy approached. When he asked where the officers were, the men said: 'Siesta.'

Now, in great agitation, he dashed toward headquarters, shouting: 'Garza! We've got to see Santa Anna! Now!'

Benito, emerging from his tent without a shirt, warned: 'You mustn't go in there, General. He's with the girl.'

'To hell with the girl!' Ripperdá shouted. 'Come along!' But just as they reached the dictator's tent they were startled by a savage interruption: cannon fire from the west. Barelegged, Santa Anna rushed out, crying: 'What's happening?' and Ripperdá told him: 'The enemy are attacking.'

Santa Anna, with Emily Morgan cowering naked behind him, looked westward, where he saw in astonishment that the Texicans, marching stolidly forward as if on parade, were within fifteen yards of his still-unformed lines. Not a shot had yet been fired except the cannonade from the two unexpected guns which the Texicans had somehow got hold of.

'Cós!' Santa Anna shouted. 'Where in hell is Cós?'

'Excellency,' a pale-faced aide cried as he dashed up, his eyes still grainy with sleep, 'run for your life. All is lost.'

Even now the Texican foot soldiers had not begun to fire, but another aide dashed up: 'Excellency! They're upon us!' And the Mexican staff officers stared in awe as the bold Texicans, led by Sam Houston astride his white horse with sword aloft, came resolutely forward, no gun firing, across that forward line where the pickets should have been. On they came, and when they were practically inside the Mexican lines, Houston lowered his sword, a military band began playing an old love song, and the slaughter began.

Grabbing his pants, Santa Anna took one terrified look at the carnage about to engulf his sleeping army, and fled.

On the Texican side the three representative participants had at one time known one another at Quimper's Ferry: Otto Macnab, Yancey Quimper and a tall, grim Old Testament prophet who marched resolutely into a battle he had long predicted.

He was Reverend Joel Job Harrison, the Methodist clergyman who had secretly served his flock against the day when righteous revolution would strike down the Mexican oppressors and allow the true faith to flourish. He advanced on the left flank, one of the oldest men in action that day and one of the fiercest. Quietly, insistently he assured the younger men around him: 'Today you're doing the work of the Lord. Let nothing stop you,' and when in dreadful silence his contingent entered the Mexican lines, it was he who uttered the first cry: 'At them!' and started his long arms flailing. He did not fire the very old gun he carried, he used it like a club, and whenever the men of this flank threatened to waver, it was he who urged them on. He was unstoppable, and his men tore completely through the Mexican lines, creating a havoc which spread to other segments.

In the center Otto Macnab had volunteered, just before the battle began, to test the open ground, nearly a mile of it, and with the aid of a young fighter from Mississippi named Martin Ascot he crept forward, and to his relief he and Martin found no scouts at all, and Martin, who had studied law before coming to Texas, whispered like a young professor: 'I do believe they've forgotten to post their forward pickets!'

So he and Otto began almost running toward the Mexican lines, and where there should have been a score of guardians they found nothing, until at last Otto stood straight up and signaled boldly that it was safe for the main line to come ahead.

With what terrible determination they came! Nobody cheered. Nobody fired his rifle. The cavalry did not engage in showy display. They just came forward, guns and knives at the ready, while a make-up band played softly a sentimental song the Texicans loved:

> Will you come to the bower I have shaded for you?
> Our bed shall be roses all spangled with dew.
> There under the bower on roses you'll lie
> With a blush on your cheek but a smile in your eye!

It was perhaps symbolic of national attitudes that Santa Anna's men had marched on the Alamo to the 'Degüello,' that song of death and hatred, while the Texicans marched to their Armageddon singing a love song. But the aftermaths of the two songs would be similar.

'Hold your fire!' officers ordered as the main army caught up with Otto and Martin, and the men obeyed. Hearts pounding, and unable to believe that the Mexicans would allow them to come so close, the avengers moved on, and at this moment Otto looked about for his friend Yancey Quimper, because he wanted to fight this battle alongside someone he could depend upon, but Quimper was not in the front line, where Otto had expected he would be. He was not in the second line, either. In fact, he trailed far behind with two men who had game legs. At the time, Otto thought little of his absence.

At four sharp the Twin Sisters fired, and one set of cannon balls ricocheted through the main Mexican cannon emplacement, knocking several men off their feet. Surging forward, Otto and Ascot, with the center of the Texican line, engulfed that position and silenced the guns.

Now Otto and his new friend Martin were only eight feet—eight actual feet— from the Mexican lines, and before them they saw chaos: men fleeing, guns cast aside, officers missing. For just a moment Otto paused in disbelief, then coldly he started firing, killing his first man with a bullet through the back. Swiftly, with practiced fingers, he reloaded and shot another. With his third bullet he hit a

Mexican in the back of the neck and did not even stop to see if the man toppled over, which he did.

Fire—reload—fire—reload—fire!

Otto was seven minutes into the enemy lines before a single bullet was fired at him, and that one so wildly aimed that it posed no threat. At the end of the tenth minute of this fantastic charge, one Texican had been killed by a stray bullet, more than three hundred Mexicans had been slain, but the real horror was yet to come.

For two good reasons Otto had not been able to locate Yancey Quimper. First, the big fellow had been assigned to the extreme right flank, where Colonel Mirabeau Lamar's cavalry were supposed to wreak havoc in Santa Anna's headquarters. Second, the horsemen performed so swiftly and valiantly that Yancey and other foot soldiers who marched in their support had difficulty keeping up. The exciting prospect of an easy victory should have stifled any fears Quimper may have suffered, but when he realized he was about to enter enemy lines, where hand-to-hand fighting was under way, he froze.

Despite every desire to move forward and acquit himself well, he could not make his feet obey; he remained rigid while others rushed past, shouting encouragement each to the other.

Finally he saw a Texican with a limp, and although the man was not seriously hurt, Yancey hurried to him, trying to convince both the man and himself: 'That's a terrible cut! Let me help!' The man wanted to break away and rejoin the battle, but Yancey held him, dragged him to the ground, and pretended to tend the wound.

When the fight for the main lines had been won, Yancey regained his courage and roared ahead to participate in the climax, but now he saw an affair that was truly horrible; he grew violently sick and had to turn away. Soon he was back on the ground, crouching, his face ashen, his voice whispering mechanically: 'Charge them, men! Go after them!'

What had sickened him might have nauseated anyone. At the far end of the McCormick farm, on whose broad fields this battle occurred, there stood a body of water called Peggy's Lake; it was actually a swamp, and to its supposed sanctuary had fled the remnants of Santa Anna's army; there, knee-deep in water, the Mexican survivors, with wild gestures, tried to surrender. But the enraged Texicans—shouting 'Remember the Alamo! Remember Goliad!'—waded into the swamp after them, and using rifle butts like clubs, began to shatter their skulls.

'Me no Alamo! Me no Goliad!' pleaded Mexicans who had participated in neither massacre, but no Texican would listen. Men sorely embittered by the earlier battles pressed on, killing any dark-skinned soldier who floundered in the swamp, but especially remorseless were the men who had lost friends or relatives at Goliad, for they were avenging angels, killing even some of the soldaderas trapped in the bog.

This battle, so crucial in history, lasted only eighteen minutes. The Texicans, marching against prepared positions, lost two men, killed; the Mexicans, more than six hundred—but each side had others who were mortally wounded.

Otto Macnab, exhausted from swinging his gun butt and wielding his knife, looked for Yancey to share in the glory, but again he could not find him—in the swamp, nor at the line of battle, nor in the Mexican camp. Yancey had assigned himself the rear-echelon job of guarding some captured stores, and there he was when Otto found him, cheering his fellowmen on, telling them how brave they were to have faced such odds.

Otto, looking about for General Houston, was told by a Kentucky man: 'Lordy, he did fight! First horse shot out from under him, I give him mine, and on he goes, right into the guns. This horse killed, too. Shot out from between his knees, his own leg all shattered, but on he goes. I like to find the son-of-a-bitch said Houston was afraid to fight.'

But Otto was near the badly wounded general when a large group of Mexican soldiers who had managed to surrender were being marched to their confinement, and Houston, seeing them through the pain which assailed him as he lay immobile, supposed them to be General Filisola bringing up a thousand reinforcements. 'All is lost! All is lost!' Houston cried. 'Have I a friend in this world? Colonel Wharton, I am wounded, I am wounded. Have I a friend in this world?'

'General,' Wharton said, 'you have many friends. What you see are our prisoners.'

When the doctors cut away Houston's right boot, blood welled over the top, and they saw for themselves how seriously he had been wounded at the start of the battle.

How had Benito Garza and his general, Víctor de Ripperdá, conducted themselves during this collapse of mexicano morale? Fighting side by side, always endeavoring to stabilize their crumbling lines, they tried vainly to rally their troops. When they saw the center about to collapse, they rushed there, much too late, and escaped death from the Texicans' relentless fire only by shifting to where Colonel Lamar's cavalry were creating havoc.

Doing whatever they could to stanch the hemorrhaging of the mexicano effort, they shouted, implored, and even shot one officer who was abandoning his post, but they accomplished nothing. Finally, when Lamar's cavalry came at them, they were parted. Garza was driven into the swamp, where he sought to surrender. Ripperdá ran to the southern perimeter, where he found protection among some trees, whence he made a courageous journey on foot to intercept General Urrea's army, which would arrive at San Jacinto eager for battle, but two days late.

In the aftermath, strange things happened. General Santa Anna, running through shoulder-high weeds attended only by an aide, came upon an abandoned shack on the McCormick plantation in which he found some old clothes that he put on over his uniform. Fearing that the presence of an obvious attendant might reveal his rank, he set out by himself to hide in bushes until daylight, when he hoped to escape across the shallow streams that enclosed the battlefield.

Otto Macnab, veteran now of the Mexican horrors at Goliad and the American retaliation at San Jacinto, tried to erase both from his mind. They had not happened. He had not participated in either; he had killed no one. At dusk, exhausted, he lay down and slept as if he were a boy back in María Campbell's dog-run.

Martin Ascot, his battlefield friend, did not sleep; seated by a fire, he produced the pen and paper he always kept with him and wrote one of the most reliable accounts of this amazing battle:

> San Jacinto River
> Republic of Texas
> 21 June 1836

Revered Father,

Yet once again do I take pen in hand, by way of writing you a few lines to inform you that with God's help I survived the mighty battle, hoping you will inform Miss Betsy Belle of same.

In my last letter I told you of the heroic but doomed stand of our men at the Alamo; by now you will also have heard from the New Orleans papers about the shameless massacre at Goliad.

You would have been ashamed, Sir, of what happened next. Our Texican army, defeated twice at the Alamo and Goliad, started a shameful retreat, allowing General Santa Anna to pillage and burn the entire countryside. One town after another went up in flames and we did nothing to stop it, until we sometimes felt that all Texas was ablaze.

I was convinced that when General Santa Anna caught up with us he was going to whip us badly. But I was wrong. With extraordinary skill General Houston led us into a spot surrounded by water, forcing General Santa Anna to engage in battle at an unpromising spot and well before the rest of the Mexican army could catch up.

Then came the immortal battle! At four o'clock in the afternoon of this day, the Mexicans were resting in their tents, convinced that we would not dare attack until the next day, if ever, for they had 1400 trained men and we had few more than 800 irregulars. But I can tell you, Sir, that we marched confidently into battle. We felt that God was on our side. We felt that terrible wrongs must be avenged. And we felt that the future history of this part of the world depended upon our behavior.

On our flank the musicians played 'Yankee Doodle,' which inspired us no end. The band had but two members, a Czech named Fred with his fife and a nigger boy named Dick with his drum. They played lustily and were very brave.

I carried that good Kentucky gun you gave me when I left, and during the sixteen minutes of battle I was able to fire it six times, for as you know, it was never easy to reload. Young Otto Macnab, who fought at my side, had lost his father at Goliad, and in his fury he was able to fire at least twenty times. Like a little machine of vengeance he stalked forward, loading and firing, and with each shot he muttered 'Remember Goliad' or 'This one for Goliad.' We were now so close to the Mexicans that we might have reached out and shaken hands with them, and when they saw us stop reloading and move forward with our rifle butts, they became terrified and started running toward a swamp at their rear.

General Houston galloped up and cried 'Do not kill any more. Take them prisoner.' But when he was gone a Methodist minister name of Harrison who was fighting in the swamp with us, a real old man, must of been near fifty, shouted to Otto and me 'Boys, you know how to take prisoners! With the butt of your gun over their heads and your knife at their throats.'

All us Texicans were now in the swamp, clubbing the Mexicans over the head and causing them to drown, hundreds of them. On the third smack I broke your fine gun, but I think I can get it fixed, so I took my hunting knife and started cutting throats. Otto would club a man, knock him sideways, and I would grab him by the hair and finish him off, and we must have handled a dozen this way, for Otto was a fierce fighter. But late in the battle when I grabbed a Mexican on my own and was about to cut his throat from behind, Otto gave a great cry 'No! No!' and when I put my knife to the man's throat, Otto clubbed me over the head with his gun.

When I revived, very sore in the head I can tell you, there was Otto standing over me with his gun. The Mexican, a young man with dark skin and a mustache, was hiding behind him. Otto told me that the Mexican was Benito Garza, and that he had saved Otto's life at Goliad. I had the strange feeling that this Garza was looking at me as if he were a rattlesnake, seething inside with hatred which must some day spit forth.

At the end of that last paragraph I fell asleep, and I'm sure you can understand why, but I awoke this morning to a magnificent piece of news. One of our men, name of Yancey Quimper, by a feat of arms which he says was extraordinary, has captured Santa Anna, and we have him now in a tent being guarded by seven. Otto and I and all the men around us wanted to kill Santa Anna, and we were downright angry when General Houston treated him like an honorable foe, giving him better food than we're getting. I was one of a committee of six who met with Houston and told him 'We want to hang that man,' but he reasoned with us and said 'Our battle is only half won. Bigger ones may lie ahead, and I plan to use Santa Anna as our principal cannon.'

My friend Otto would not accept this, and when he told General Houston what he himself had seen at Goliad and how his own father had been run down like a coyote, tears came to General Houston's eyes and with his forefinger he traced the scar on Otto's face and asked 'Did you get that at Goliad?' and Otto said 'I did, Sir, killing a man who was trying to kill me,' and Houston said 'It is your badge of honor, son, and mine will be to treat Santa Anna better than he treated us.'

Tonight I am very afraid, Sir, and I hope that you will pray for me, and for Otto and for all the brave Texicans who fought so many with so few, for if the Mexicans assemble their armies in this area, they could still overwhelm us.

It is rumored that if I survive the next great battles, I shall be entitled to many acres of the best land in Texas, and this is a country with a potential for greatness. Inform Miss Betsy Belle, if you will, that she should start now to prepare the things she will want to bring to Texas, for Otto tells me that he once traveled along some excellent land on the Brazos River and he will show me how to claim on it. If I live, Sir, I shall post haste to Mississippi and marry Miss Betsy Belle the morning I arrive, and please to inform her of same.

Your loving son in God,
Martin

P.S. Do not tell Mother or Betsy Belle about the knife work in the swamp. They might not understand.

Ascot's report of Quimper's heroism in capturing Santa Anna did not reflect the truth. On the morning after the battle, Quimper and two buddies, one a young fellow from Kentucky named Sylvester, had quit trying to capture Mexican survivors and were hunting deer for the mess. When they saw six or seven bucks suddenly take flight for no apparent cause, Sylvester, a skilled huntsman, said: 'Somethin' spooked them deer,' and when they investigated, Yancey saw a man huddling on the ground and trying to hide in some bushes, dressed in old clothes.

He was about to shoot him when Sylvester shouted: 'The battle's over, for Christ's sake. Let him live.'

'Get up, you swine!' Yancey shouted, but the quivering man remained on the ground, whimpering. The men dragged their prisoner into camp, and he would have been thrown into the ordinary compound except that sharp-eyed Yancey saw several Mexicans begin to salute.

'Stop that!' one man commanded his fellow prisoners, but it was too late.

'He's a general, by God!' Yancey called, and when the man was shoved forward the Mexicans in the compound began to kiss his hands and call him El Presidente.

'We've got Santy Anny!' Quimper shouted, and he spent the rest of that day parading about the Texican tents, announcing himself as 'the man who captured Santy Anny.'

Otto, who was near General Houston's cot when the Mexican general was brought before him, heard Santa Anna's first words: 'Congratulaciones, Mi General, ha derrotado El Napoleón del Oeste.'

'What did he say?' Houston asked.

Otto translated: ' "You have defeated the Napoleon of the West." '

'Tell him to sit down.'

Houston had more difficulty with another visitor, Mrs. Peggy McCormick, owner of the farm on which the historic battle had taken place: 'Tell me, who's going to bury all these dead bodies cluttering up my place?'

'We'll bury the Texicans,' Houston replied graciously as he adjusted his throbbing leg.

'How about those hundreds of Mexicans?'

'Why, madam, your land will be famed in history as the spot where the glorious battle was fought.'

'To the devil with your glorious victory. Take off your stinking Mexicans.'

'That's Santa Anna's problem.'

She demanded to see the general, and when he was produced she asked him in Spanish: 'And what do you intend doing about all those bodies?' and he replied: 'The fortunes of war, madam. I can do nothing.'

The true miracle of the Battle of San Jacinto transpired some days after it ended, because a greater danger persisted than the one Houston had conquered. The Mexicans had under arms in Tejas some five thousand of their best troops, led by skilled generals: Filisola the Italian, Woll the Frenchman, and Ripperdá from

Yucatán, who had joined forces with Urrea, the victor at Goliad. If they coalesced, and they were not far separated, they could drive Houston right to the borders of Louisiana, and annihilate him if they overtook him.

But now Houston's brilliance showed itself, for by the force of his remarkable personality he kept Santa Anna alive, appreciating the fact that if he allowed him to be hanged, as most of the Texicans wished, the man would become an instant martyr, a hero who had to be avenged, just as the martyrs of the Alamo and Goliad had had to be avenged. But if he could be kept alive, a prisoner in humiliating disgrace, his martyrdom would be avoided; also, he would be available to issue orders to the other generals to disband their troops and go home. As dictator of Mexico he would still command their obedience.

So with a skill that Metternich or Talleyrand would have applauded, this Tennessee cardsharp used Santa Anna the way a long-practiced fisherman uses a fly to trap a trout. He coddled him, he flattered him, he even arranged for him to be sent to Washington to interview the President of the United States, but first he obtained from him orders to his generals to go home.

Miraculously, they obeyed. This powerful army, which could have won so many battles, dislodged so many plans, supinely obeyed their imprisoned leader—when the whole tradition of war dictated that they ignore any command issued by a man in the clutches of an enemy—and took their men quietly out of Tejas, which would know that lovely Spanish designation no more. It was now Texas. By the merest thread of chance it had become Texas, and so it would remain.

Of the three men from the Victoria dog-runs, each lost his battle: Campbell in the Alamo, Macnab at Goliad, and Garza in the swamps at San Jacinto. But each contributed to the grandeur upon which the Republic of Texas was founded.

For the living, the fortunes generated by this battle were both mundane and dramatic. Yancey Quimper appropriated the title 'Hero of San Jacinto.' Peggy McCormick, in the years following the war, earned tidy sums from selling the endless battle mementos scattered across her farm, but both Pamela Mann and Juan Seguín ran into trouble.

After the war Mrs. Mann moved to the burgeoning town of Houston, where she ran the Mansion House, a disreputable hotel noted for its brawls, duels and repeated police raids, which she handled deftly with her two pistols. However, an especially blatant disregard for the law resulted in a court trial, and she received the death sentence. It was commuted because of her bold behavior during the war.

Seguín started out famously as the mayor of San Antonio, but his tenure was turbulent, and he fled to Mexico. Later he returned as a member of a Mexican invading army that captured San Antonio and held it briefly. A strong opponent to union with the United States, he did his best to make Texas once more a part of Mexico, and died, disappointed, at the age of eighty-three.

Benito Garza, languishing in a prisoner-of-war camp, had to relinquish his dream of ever becoming Gobernador de la Provincia de Tejas; he spent his idle hours brooding over his opposition to the Texicans, an obsession that would intensify and never abate. And Joel Job Harrison acquired the right to conduct Methodist services openly, which he did in wooden churches he established in various parts of the new nation.

Immortality was visited upon the least likely participant in the battle. Emily Morgan, who had diverted General Santa Anna's attention that hot afternoon just before the charge of the Texicans, became celebrated in song as 'The Yellow Rose of Texas' and few who sing it in romantic settings realize that they are serenading the memory of a mulatto slave.

Meteoric was the rise of Mirabeau Buonaparte Lamar: 25 March 1836, return to Texas; 20 April, private foot soldier; 21 April, cavalry colonel; 5 May, Secretary of War in the cabinet of President Sam Houston; 24 June, major general; 25 June, commander in chief of the entire Texas army; 5 September, vice-president of the republic. And even greater glories lay ahead.

And Otto Macnab went his quiet but very determined way.

. . . TASK FORCE

As soon as the staff announced that our December meeting would be held near Houston at the monument marking the Battle of San Jacinto, we members decided that for this important session, no outside authority would be imported. Instead, we would invite the general public to a convocation at which we five would be seated at a table with microphones. Each would offer a brief opening statement regarding the significance of the Texas revolution, after which the visitors would be invited to make such observations as they wished, or pose questions that bothered them.

We anticipated a lively meeting, with perhaps two dozen local history aficionados who would know more about San Jacinto than we did. It was our hope to make them feel that they had shared decision-making regarding their schools, but when we approached the monument—'There she stands, five hundred and seventy-one feet high, taller than the Washington one'—we found a line waiting outside and standees crowding the inside. 'What's up?' I asked a guard, and he said: 'The experts you invited are here, but so is this mob. They're waiting to see Ransom Rusk,' and when I asked why, he said: 'They've never seen a real, live billionaire,' but a woman who overheard this corrected him: 'We want to see Lorenzo Quimper and his boots. He's such a dear.'

When the last person had been wedged into the hall and loudspeakers installed for those outside, I opened the session with brief remarks, commending the condition of the monument and reminding visitors that when our meeting ended they would be served punch aboard the battleship *Texas* moored nearby: 'Unique among our great warships, the *Texas* patrolled the coastline during five major landings in World War II. Texans like to participate in major events.'

Miss Cobb started our presentation with a reminder that when Texas patriots defended their rights in 1836, they not only won their own freedom but also set in motion those currents which would, a decade later, secure liberation for New Mexico, Arizona and California: 'The geographical shape of the United States today was ensured by the heroic actions of a few Texicans who resisted General Santa Anna's brutal oppressions on this very field.'

Ransom Rusk told the audience: 'I think we must recognize that even if the Texas revolution had not occurred, states like Arizona and California might have stumbled their way into the Union, because of local conditions. In the case of Texas, it was essential that some kind of stable buffer be established between the anglo-dominated Mississippi River and the Mexican-dominated Rio Grande. During the nineteenth century we provided that buffer, and at times we seemed more like a separate nation mediating between two larger nations than a typical American state like Virginia or Ohio. And I think that Texas will always have that peculiar character. It's a part of the United States, unquestionably, but it has its own personality, something unique and wonderful, which the rest of this nation needs.'

Lorenzo Quimper, recognized by the crowd as a descendant of the Hero of San Jacinto, rather neatly down-played his ancestor's performance while at the same time implying that without the heroic Yancey, the battle would probably have been lost. Starting out with what he called 'my highfalutin Texan,' he sounded like Pericles delivering his oration on the grandeur of Athens: 'On solemn days like this, when we celebrate our great victory, we must remember the true character of the Texicans who won freedom for us. Five times they faced the Mexican army, and four times they lost by tremendous margins: Alamo, Goliad, Santa Fe and the Mier Expedition, crushing defeats which might have disheartened the bravest. But mixed in with those defeats was a resplendent victory, San Jacinto.' Here the audience broke into cheers, which encouraged Lorenzo to relax his speech a bit: 'Us Texans have always had that basic character. We can absorb one defeat after another: drought, plague, financial collapse, heartbreakin' loss in the Civil War, misbehavior of elected officials . . .' At the height of his impassioned oratory he hesitated for just a moment, half smiled, and added: 'Even losin' in football to Oklahoma!' When the crowd stamped and whistled he dropped into pure ranch-hand Texan: 'But us Texans, we always recover. Fact is, we don't never know when we're whupped, which is why we so seldom git whupped.' Il Magnifico was the hit of the show, the authentic voice of Texas.

Efraín Garza took a more sober approach: 'My ancestor fought at San Jacinto, too. In the army of Santa Anna.' Silence. 'So it is highly probable that the early Quimper faced the early Garza that day, perhaps right where we sit.' Suddenly he shot out his hand to grasp Quimper's: 'But now we're friends. We're one people.' The crowd cheered and stamped again. 'But as so often happens, the battle settled only part of the problem that had caused it in the first place. It determined, as Miss Cobb has so accurately stated, that a huge corner of Mexico would ultimately become a part of the United States.' More applause. 'But it did not decide how the new addition would be incorporated. What theory of law would prevail? How would Mexicans like my ancestors who had lived here for many generations be received in the Union? And how would their rights be preserved? Some of these questions still wait to be settled.'

These last remarks were not well received by the patriots gathered to honor the Texan victory, because every anglo in the audience, and the audience was ninety-nine percent anglo, believed that the questions Garza raised *had* been settled, so I felt it incumbent upon me as chairman to come to Garza's defense: 'We wanted a Hispanic spokesman on our Task Force, and as you can see, we got a good one.' Two people clapped. 'Every battle has aftermaths, both for the victor and for the loser. Professor Garza has identified some of those which still perplex our state, and now we will accept questions or statements from the audience.'

To my disappointment, the first man to rise was not one of the local experts; he was a belligerent rancher from South Texas, who got us off to a miserable start: 'If Professor Garza don't like how we handled affairs after San Jacinto, why don't he go back to Mexico where he come from?'

I pointed out that since Garza's family had lived in Texas for a much longer time than any other family represented this day, Texas *was* where he came from, but that did not satisfy the protester: 'If he's Mexican, he accepts the rules we lay down. San Jacinto settled that.'

Eagerly I searched the audience for a more gracious speaker, and my eye lit upon a woman who had written two small books about the San Jacinto area, and she asked: 'If Mexican troops defeated us four times and we defeated them only once, why was San Jacinto so determinative?' and Quimper had a prompt answer: 'Ma'am, quite often it depends on timin' . . . and luck. When we won at San Jacinto, Santa Anna was far from home base and gettin' worried. Psychology, ma'am, sometimes it turns the tables.'

A Houston oilman, a friend of Rusk's, had for some years supported scholars working in early Texas history, and wanted to know: 'Was this battle as important as you claim?' and Ransom responded: 'I admitted in my opening remarks that great historical currents were already under way which might have carried part of Mexico into our orbit, whether we won here at San Jacinto or not, but the magnitude of those currents and their ultimate significance were intensified by our victory. It caught the imagination of the American people. It showed a light in the darkness. It stimulated the later concept of Manifest Destiny. It made conquest to the Pacific inevitable. Important, Tom? It was far more important than I stated. It was the major gift of Texas to the United States. It awakened patriotism . . . and the idea that we Americans had a duty, a responsibility, to bring democracy to the entire continent.'

Tom persisted: 'I was taught that those things came as a result of the Mexican War in 18 and 46.'

'They did,' Rusk agreed, almost eagerly. 'But remember the irresistible sequence. The Alamo led to San Jacinto. San Jacinto led to a free republic. The free republic led to 1846. And 1846 led to the United States boundaries as we know them today. And never forget, Tom, it all started with a handful of the bravest men this land ever produced, who said at the Alamo: "We will die rather than surrender our freedom." ' He paused. 'They said it, Tom, and they did it.' The crowd roared its approval, and Rusk added: 'That may still be our major gift. Courage. Optimism.'

Another woman asked: 'Why do you men always claim it was only men who made the difference?' and Quimper replied: 'Because in battle, ma'am, it's the men who do the job,' but Miss Cobb interrupted: 'That's a cogent question, madam, and in my book our Mr. Quimper's other ancestor, Mattie Quimper, who seems to have done most of the work, who kept her family afloat when her husband was away, and who finally destroyed her ferry and burned her inn to keep them from the Mexicans, was a greater Texas hero than her son, Yancey, who captured Santa Anna when the battle had already ended.' Several women applauded, and after acknowledging their support, Miss Cobb resumed: 'Texas has always underrated its women and I suppose it always will. Therefore, we must, when it's appropriate, remind our men, as you have just done, madam, that we, too, helped build this state.'

Quimper leaped to his feet: 'Let me tell you! I'm just as proud of Mattie Quimper as I am of her heroic son Yancey.' The women applauded this generous concession.

After twenty minutes of similar statements, a thoughtful man rose and said: 'I'd like to return to that first question. "What patterns will the anglos and the Mexicans devise for sharing our state?" And I'd like you to answer, Mr. Chairman.'

I spent nearly a minute with my hands folded over my chin, for I realized that this meeting would be the first to be widely reported and I did not wish to damage our Task Force before it was well launched. I wanted to say exactly the right thing, so facing the two television cameras, I spoke carefully: 'I could well be the only person in this hall whose ancestor fought in the Alamo. Moses Barlow marched from Gonzales to die there. So I've had to contemplate your question many times, sir, and I've concluded that no heavier cloud threatens our state than our reluctance to define the future relationship between the so-called Mexican and the anglo. This uncertainty keeps us fragmented into unwarranted cells, and I see no solution to this ugly estrangement.

'This morning we've heard two conflicting views. "Critical battles settle everything" or "They settle very little." The truth is that a successful battle can sometimes establish general direction for several decades, but basic, long-term results evolve slowly . . . inevitably . . . remorselessly. San Jacinto determined that Texas would be ruled in the immediate future by anglos and not Mexicans. But the long-term relationship between the two groups is far from settled.'

'Are you saying that the Mexicans might ultimately take over . . . ?'

'Not at all. What I'm saying is that Appomattox determined that the North would establish the rules for our Union . . . for the next hundred years. The North would set the freight rates so damaging to the South. The North would determine the tariffs that made it so rich and kept the South so poor. The North would determine everything, it seemed, and would do so perpetually. But look at the situation today. Where is the power flowing? Always to the South. Where are the seats in Congress coming? To Texas and Florida. Where would you like to live if you were young and active and hopeful? Vermont? Or the Sun Belt?' The audience cheered.

'Battles can be terribly important. Thank God, we won and not Hitler. I'm glad that in the Far East we decided things, not Japan. No man on this earth ever fought a more just war than Chester Nimitz of Texas did in the Pacific in 1943.' This brought more cheers. 'But look at Europe and the Pacific today. The losers in battle are the victors in peace, while the victors seem to be losing. And that's because it is not the climactic battle but the slow, inexorable force of history that determines the future.'

We had discussed these historical truths for some time when a wiry man in his sixties rose, caught my eye, and then made a statement so startling that few who heard it could believe: 'I'm proud to be here today, in the presence of Lorenzo Quimper. My grandfather fought beside Yancey Quimper on this field in 1836.'

'Did you say your grandfather?'

'I did. I'm Norman Robbins, born 1922. My father was Sam Robbins, born in these parts in 1879. His father was Jared Robbins, born in 1820, aged sixteen at the battle.'

'That's right,' a woman who specialized in genealogies called from a back row. 'The two Robbins men married late.'

Suddenly Texas history became very real, and we looked in awe at a man whose family bridged so many great events. How young the state of Texas seemed at that moment! No one in Massachusetts had a grandfather who had fought at Concord Bridge, but Norman Robbins had heard from his father a firsthand account of the launching of Texas.

Miss Cobb snapped us out of our reveries: 'Let's go to the battleship for our punch,' and as we walked across the field we could almost hear the rifles firing, because the fighting seemed so recent.

Rusk, walking with his friend the Houston oilman, said: 'Our state contains hidden powers which manifest themselves in unexpected ways at unexpected times,' and he led us onto the *Texas*.

VII
THE
TEXIANS

THE TEXIANS

WHEN THE SOVEREIGN NATION OF TEXAS, STANDING COMPLETELY ALONE AND allied to no one, inaugurated Sam Houston as its first elected president, Otto Macnab was fourteen. Thus he and the new republic would grow up together, and the major problem of each would be the same—to find a home: Otto, one in which to attain that love and security he had sought since first seeing those lights shining across the Ohio River; Texas, a secure place within the family of nations.

It was a natural affiliation, Otto and Texas, because the two had much in common. Both were self-reliant, both tended to solve problems with the gun, both believed in simple, forward action rather than in philosophical speculation, both were suspicious of Mexicans and despised Indians, and both vaguely wanted to do the right thing. Most important, both entertained lofty aspirations they could not always voice or define. It would be a lively decade as these two matured.

The nation quickly found that conducting a successful revolution was relatively easy compared with organizing a stable society thereafter. Along a hard-drinking frontier it often seemed that the major problem was to find any official who was sober, President Houston being especially addicted to the bottle.

Nevertheless, the fledgling nation made a series of critical decisions which helped establish its permanent character. Fiercely republican and abhorring the dictatorial chaos witnessed while part of Mexico, it decreed that its president would be allowed to serve only three years and then be required to sit out a term before being eligible to run again. Clergymen were forbidden to serve in the legislature, and slavery was not only permitted but protected: 'No free Negro shall reside in Texas without consent of Congress.'

The basic attitudes of the nation could be summarized in a series of adjectives: individualistic, aggressive, volatile, rural, egalitarian insofar as white Anglo-Saxon Protestants were concerned, and often violent; but the overriding characteristic during these early years would be national poverty. Texas had the bad luck to start its history as a free nation just as financial panic paralyzed the United States and slowed down transactions in Europe. With no solid economy on which to construct a currency and minimal trade on which to levy taxes, the poverty-stricken republic stumbled along, always on the verge of bankruptcy, and since the United

States had no paper money or coinage to spare, Texas had to depend upon the most dubious banknotes issued by entities not much more solvent than it was. Currency issued by states like Mississippi and Arkansas circulated at fifty-percent discount, with only the more solid notes of New Orleans and Alabama retaining a value of a hundred cents to the dollar. Mexican money was good, but most prized of all were the notes of Great Britain and France. Even so, the rule among merchants was: 'If you take money in before eleven, pass it along to somebody else before five.'

Of course, Texas did try to float its own paper money, but the result was disastrous: issued at a hundred cents on the dollar, it was immediately discounted to eighty cents, then to sixty cents before it stabilized at about fifty cents. And that was the so-called 'solid dollar backed by collateral.'

But the nation did have one sovereign currency which kept it afloat: millions of acres of unassigned land, and it employed the most ingenious devices for turning this land into cash. It gave free acreage to anyone who had served in its armed forces. It lured residents of the United States with roseate promises. And it hired a firm of New Orleans speculators, Toby and Brother, to print and sell certificates entitling any purchaser to a spacious homestead. The history of Texas in these formative years was an account of how men without money used land to keep afloat.

In the social life of the republic there were subtle changes. People began dropping the name Texican; they became Texians. Spanish accents on some words were eliminated and names simplified, so that the old Béjar became Bexar; Bexar became San Antonio. The Río Grande lost its accent, and all other ríos lost not only their accent but also their Spanish designation; henceforth they would be rivers. The lovely word *arroyo* became *creek*. As if to symbolize the transition from Spanish lyricism to Kentucky realism, poetic family names like Treviño became Trevino for the anglos, and the music was lost.

To facilitate administration, counties had to be established, and in time almost all the heroes participating in the battles were honored by having counties named after them: Austin, Bonham, Bowie, Crockett, Fannin, Houston, Lamar, Rusk, Travis; and all but Travis also had towns named in their honor. To the delight of future schoolchildren, Deaf Smith's county would retain his full name.

The names of certain famous places also became enshrined as counties: Bexar, Goliad, Gonzales and Victoria, with San Jacinto following later. The first-named was awarded an area much larger than many European nations; from Bexar County, in decades to come, well over a hundred normal-sized counties would be carved.

By this lavish display of honors Texas served notice that it took its history seriously and sought to enshrine its nobler moments. Massachusetts and Virginia produced many national leaders, but they did not become the warp and woof of existence as did the heroes of Texas; Pennsylvania had its Valley Forge and New

York its Saratoga, but they never became a living part of their region's religion the way the Alamo did in Texas. From the start the new Texians proclaimed, and in a rather loud voice: 'Look at us. We're different.'

Among the counties formed in the first flush of victory was one named after Zave Campbell, whose exploits atop the wall were recited by both Señora Mordecai Marr and Joe, the Negro slave belonging to Colonel Travis, both of whom were spared by Santa Anna. Both told of Zave's Ajax-like defense, but the most telling testimony came from a Mexican captain, who said: 'There was this tall old man whose name was called out as I bore down upon him. "Xavier! Watch out!" someone shouted as I ran him through, and when we counted the dead bodies of our soldiers around his feet, there were nine.'

It was agreed that Xavier County should be established west of the Brazos River, but how the name should be pronounced was not so quickly settled. Older settlers who spoke Spanish wanted to call it Hah-vee-ehr, with accent on the last syllable, but newcomers promptly changed that to Ecks-ah-ver, with accent on the second. Within a few months it was agreed that the county was Za-veer, with a heavy accent on the second syllable, and so it became. Like many of the early counties, and like more than half of those that were to follow, Xavier County had no principal town; there was a miserable crossroads settlement of nine houses called Campbell, and it was designated the county seat, but it would never dominate thinking or become as important as the county it served. A settler rarely said: 'I live in Campbell.' He almost invariably said: 'I live in Xavier County.'

Young Macnab became one of the first new settlers in Xavier. Reluctant to return to Victoria and a Mexican way of life with his adopted mother and aunt, he jumped at the invitation when his companion-in-arms Martin Ascot proposed: 'Let's take our free land side by side, along that river you told me about,' and when this was agreed, the Mississippian said further: 'Otto, let's go to Galveston and meet the ship when Betsy Belle arrives!'

In his battlefield letter to his father he had promised to go to Mississippi to claim her, but the problems of land acquisition had become so demanding and in unforeseen ways so complex that he had sent her an ardent letter: 'I simply cannot leave Texas now. It would be more practical for you to come here, and we shall marry as you step off the steamer.'

So off the two friends went, down the Brazos River in a flat-bottomed scow, then up to the fledgling town of Houston, where they reported to Buffalo Bayou for a sailing ship, which carried them across the wide bay to Galveston, the principal settlement in the republic. They were standing on the improvised dock when Betsy Belle's schooner braved the treacherous sandbar that both protected Galveston's harbor and sank unwary ships that could not find the only safe passage.

As soon as Otto saw Betsy Belle in her blue hat with streamers and white dress with ruffles, he knew he was going to like her, for she looked both like a young bride and like the future mother of children. 'You're lucky!' he whispered to Ascot, and he felt even more approval when he stood beside Martin as the Galveston minister intoned the marriage ceremony. When the clergyman, a Methodist with bright eyes, told Martin: 'You may kiss the bride,' Ascot did so, then told Otto: 'You must kiss her, too,' and the fourteen-year-old boy, blushing furiously, did so.

The three partners, for so they termed themselves, spent only two nights in Galveston, for they were eager to locate and take up residence on the land the government was giving them for their service at San Jacinto. Purchasing three horses with funds from the dowry Betsy Belle had brought from Mississippi, they rode the eighty-eight miles back to Xavier County, where Otto identified the land he wanted the partnership to claim, and both he and Martin stepped off the six hundred and forty acres side by side, to which each was entitled, when across the fields, riding a very small donkey, came an old comrade who was about to save them from making a serious mistake.

It was Yancey Quimper shouting 'Wait a minute! Wait a minute!' and when he halted his donkey he gallantly raised Betsy Belle's hand to his lips: 'All Texas is honored to receive such a beauty from Alabama.'

'Mississippi,' Betsy Belle said.

'What are you men doing?'

'Locating our six-forty's,' Ascot replied.

'Six-forty's!' Quimper exploded, and before the day was out he was leading his friends to the county seat at Campbell, where his good friend Judge Phinizy, formerly of the Arkansas bench, would be certifying land entitlements.

During the trip Yancey brought his friends from San Jacinto up to date regarding his fortunes: 'Many people consider me the principal citizen of Xavier County,' but what exactly he did, the travelers could not discern. At twenty-four he was what rural people called 'a fine figure of a man,' tall, rather fleshy and pale of complexion. He seemed to lack strength, as if one or two critical bones had been omitted, but he offset this by a warm, radiant smile that he flashed at anyone he wanted to impress.

He was always dressed in accordance with another ancient truism—'clothes make the man'—and he had lately purchased a big Mexican hat with a very broad brim. It was precisely sized to match his build, so that when he came picking his way down the dusty streets in Campbell, he proclaimed himself, without speaking, to be 'our leading citizen.'

He had been raised by his Tennessee father to speak rather good English, but after the death of his parents his association with the rude soldiers of the revolution had encouraged him to acquire their informal speech habits, so that now his sentences were colorfully ungrammatical and his words those of the barnyard and ranch. But he spoke with marked effectiveness, often and loud. As a verified hero of the battle in which Texas had won her freedom, he felt himself entitled, and sometimes obligated, to express his opinion on almost everything, but he did so with such an attractive mixture of gravity and wit that he did not offend. He was, in this rural setting, a man of substance.

'For a while after Independence,' he said as they neared Campbell, 'I tried to rebuild the inn at Quimper's Ferry. Impossible to get aholt of any money. Me, a hero in battle, a man with a good reputation, unable to find a cent.'

'What happened to the inn?'

'Charred posts, stickin' out of the ground.'

'Were you able to sell the land?'

'Sell?' Quimper turned sideways on his donkey and told Betsy Belle: 'My mammy gave me one piece of solid advice: "Get aholt of land and never let it go. Burn your house, even burn your Bible, but never let nobody touch your land." '

Judge Leander Phinizy, an unkempt, bearded man with dark sunken eyes that brooded as if they had witnessed all the chicanery the world could provide, had risen to become a major luminary of the Texas bar after a rather devious start. Expelled from William and Mary College in Virginia for 'prolonged, offensive and noisy drunkenness,' he had made his way to Georgia, where such behavior was tolerated. After marrying a local girl whose parents had acreage, he utilized his earlier schooling by reading for law, but before he was accepted by the Georgia bar he became involved in a malodorous land fraud involving widows and found it expedient to take his unquestioned talents farther west. Settling ultimately in the freer air of Arkansas, he announced himself as a lawyer, and when his credentials were requested he stated simply that he had read for law in the offices of 'that notable Georgia jurist Xerxes Noltworthy.' When mail addressed to his supposed mentor produced no reply, Phinizy explained: 'Poor man shot himself. Cancer of the esophagus.'

On the Arkansas frontier he proved himself to be a good lawyer, and after notable success in helping to establish order in rough territories he was promoted to judge, but his probate of certain wills subjected him to unfortunate scrutiny, and he deemed it best to emigrate to Texas. Here at last his deportment was circumspect, and he became, as Quimper had said, 'a shining light of our judicial system.'

Judge Phinizy held court in a one-room, dirt-floored hovel whose only window was a rude hole covered by a piece of calf hide that had been hammered in bear grease until it became remarkably translucent. There was a table and an armchair for the judge, carved by himself, two rickety chairs for plaintiffs, and a large bucket into which the judge shot tobacco juice often and with enviable skill, for it stood some distance from the bench.

Phinizy conducted trials with the aid of a heavy woven-leather riding crop, which he beat furiously against his table when rendering even the simplest decision, and now, as Martin and Otto, as the principals, took the two chairs and Yancey and Betsy Belle stood by the door, Judge Phinizy lashed about with his crop and shouted: 'Goddamnit, is there no courtesy left in the world? Somebody give that beautiful example of Southern womanhood a chair,' and after this was done, the judge explained: 'For jury trials we bring in those two benches.'

Smiling at the claimants, he said: 'You're very fortunate, young men, to have Mr. Quimper here to guide you. The Republic of Texas was about to award him the customary six hundred and forty acres which all you heroes get, when he pointed out to the visiting land commissioner that he was entitled to rather more.'

He paused dramatically, and remained silent for so long that Ascot realized that a question was in order, so he asked: 'How much did he get?'

'Well, his dead father should have had a league-and-a-labor from the Mexican government, but the papers were lost in the fire. He himself was assured six hundred and forty acres because of his valiant service at San Jacinto. And under our new constitution he had head rights to his own league-and-a-labor. He gets an additional six-forty for having served six months in the army. That made a total of ten thousand four hundred and ninety acres.'

Admiringly, Martin and Otto turned to nod at Yancey, who held up his hand as if to say 'Wait!' The judge continued: 'Where Mr. Quimper showed his brilliance, he asked the commissioner and me: "Isn't the government awarding six hundred and forty acres to the heirs of anyone who died at either the Alamo or Goliad?" The commissioner said: "Yes, but your father was dead before those battles took place," and Mr. Quimper explained: "Yes, but my mother wasn't, because she died fighting off Mexican soldiers at her ferry to save General Houston's retreat." So we gave him her award, too. Total? Eleven thousand one hundred and thirty acres.'

Otto gasped, but Martin, who was fascinated by law, asked: 'And what does that mean for us?' and Judge Phinizy said: 'If Mr. Quimper is prepared to vouch for Mr. Macnab's heroism, I think something can be worked out.'

'He was more than brave,' Yancey intoned. 'Whenever I looked back, there he was, keepin' close.'

'Texas wants to reward its heroes, Mr. Macnab . . . How old are you?'

Without hesitation Otto said, 'Eighteen.'

'You'll probably get your height in your twenties. Many do.'

With Yancey providing the data, this was the settlement Judge Phinizy approved: 'Otto Macnab, hero of both Goliad and San Jacinto, twelve hundred and eighty acres for your service in the army for the duration of the war, plus six hundred and forty bonus for being at San Jacinto. Then, for your brave father, who died at Goliad, six hundred and forty acres, plus another three hundred and twenty for his service for less than three months in our army. This makes a total, I believe, of two thousand eight hundred and eighty acres. So ordered.' And with a majestic pursing of his lips he arched a magisterial spray of tobacco juice right into the bucket.

Macnab and Ascot were so appreciative of the way Quimper had doubled even Martin's entitlements—1,280 acres because of extraordinary heroism—that they entered into an agreement. 'Look,' Martin said, 'none of us have much money. Let's work together and rebuild the inn. And then we'll build a house on your land, Otto.'

At this point in the discussion Otto made a significant decision: 'I don't need a house yet.'

'Where would you stay?' Ascot asked, and Otto said: 'I could work for Yancey, maybe,' and Betsy Belle cried: 'Nonsense! You'll live with us.'

In the next weeks the four young Texians did two things: they slaved like beasts of burden to erect at the ferry a shack which could only by the most careless use of words be called an inn, and they laid off the portions of land which the nation had given each of them. Quimper took a strip on the right bank of the Brazos starting from his mother's burned inn and running south; Otto chose his adjacent to that; and Martin stepped off his touching Otto's. When the portions were surveyed and legally transferred, Ascot told his wife one night: 'Come to think of it, Yancey did all the choosing for us,' and she said with a suspicion which had started that first day when he kissed her hand: 'I'm sure he expects Otto and us to clear out some day. Then he'll have it all.'

The work of building was arduous. Not only did everyone, including Betsy Belle, sweat in the summer sun chopping trees and sawing timbers, but at night, often on empty stomachs, they slept on bare ground. Of the many different types of tools they should have had for such a task, they had only three: two axes, a pair of good saws and two hammers, but with these they built a cabin through whose sides the wind and rain would whistle, and when the boxlike structure was what Yancey called 'completed like the finest palace,' they added on the south exposure a long, low porch. Quimper's Ferry was back in business.

With the first hard-earned dollars the foursome collected, Yancey felt he had to go to the national capital, Columbia-on-the-Brazos, to buy the ropes and wires necessary for the reopening of a ferry service: 'Martin, you and Betsy Belle stay here and run the inn. Otto and me, we'll ride down and get the necessaries.'

'When do we start *our* house?'

'First things first. Let's for God's sake get some money around here.' Each of the four realized that from the amount of really strenuous work they had done, they should in an orderly society have earned large sums of cash, but since little was circulating, they ended their labors with nothing. And the first three travelers to halt at the inn before crossing on a pitiful little raft that Otto and Martin had built, had not a cent to pay for their keep. They did have a cow, so a barter was concluded.

When Ascot wanted to know why Judge Phinizy had been so cooperative,

Yancey said: 'He don't get paid, either. He's supposed to, but the government's got no money.'

'What's that have to do with it?'

'I give him things to eat. He gives me land.'

On the evening before their departure for the capital, Yancey reported on a discussion he'd had with the judge: 'He told me "That young feller Ascot, he seemed real bright," and when I told him you were, he said "Why don't he read for law?" and I asked where, and he said "I'll teach him if he drops in now and then." I asked him how much, and he said "Nothin'. I could use a cow. And Texas could use a good lawyer," and I asked "How long?" and he said "If he's as bright as you claim, he could do it in mebbe six weeks," and I said you'd do it.'

The suggestion was like a rope tossed to a foundering man, for in Mississippi, before the Texas fever caught him, Ascot had been vaguely intending to study law, and his recent strenuous experience in house building had satisfied him that he was better fitted for more cerebral labors. 'When could I start?' he asked eagerly, and Yancey said: 'Right now. He give me these books for you to begin with,' and he delivered two grease-stained books printed in London in the previous century and thumbed by young Virginians who had aspired to the courts: *Blackstone's Commentaries* and *Coke's Institutes*.

Martin, taking the books reverentially, asked: 'What about Betsy Belle?' and Yancey said: 'She can run the inn while you study and we're gone,' and in the morning Martin went to work on Judge Phinizy's lawbooks while Yancey and Otto headed south to obtain equipment for the proposed ferry.

Otto was disappointed in the capital of his new nation, for Columbia had only five houses, one of which was a store-hotel. Government occupied three of the houses: representatives in a two-story frame affair with no caulking to seal the openings; senators in a windowless shack that had been used for storing cattle foodstuffs; the president in another windowless affair of two small rooms, a smoky fireplace and an earthen floor that became a quagmire when water seeped in.

As soon as Yancey saw the presidential mansion his bile began to rise, and he experienced such nausea that he stopped a passer-by to ask: 'Is that where Sam Houston lives?' When the farmer confirmed that this was the home of the president, Quimper asked: 'Is he ever sober?' and the citizen replied: 'As a matter of strict truth, he is never sober before two in the afternoon, and since it's only half past one, you can count on it that he lies in there dead drunk.' The man said that although Houston was a famous drinker, 'best in these parts, past or present,' his average day was orderly: 'Gets drunk every night of the week at seven and raises hell till midnight. Goes to bed about one in the mornin', sleeps till noon, tries to sober up till two. You can't knock him awake when he's drunk, and if the house caught fire, we'd never get him out. That gives him about four good workin' hours each afternoon, and then he does a prodigious amount runnin' the affairs of the nation. When you catch him sober, you have yourself a very good man.'

'Can we leave our affairs in the hands of such a drunk?'

'He handled them pretty well at San Jacinto,' the farmer said, and this incited Quimper: 'He was a coward! Wanted to flee north to Nacogdoches. I led his troops to the fight with Santy Anny. When we got there, he refused to fight, but I moved among the troops and made him start the battle. I say "To hell with Sam Houston." '

'Watch out! Here he comes!' And Yancey stared across the dusty road to the 'executive mansion,' where, in midafternoon sun, the president of the new republic appeared ahead of time. Standing in the low doorway, Houston was forced to stoop while he rubbed his eyes. Then he moved out onto the road, preparing to walk the short distance to where his Congress was in session. He was very tall, very powerful in appearance, but his outrageous dress made him almost a caricature of a frontier leader.

On his head he wore a George Washington tricorn hat from whose left side projected a feather. On his feet he had moccasins made of elk hide, with Indian beads along the high tops. What served as trousers were of a very thick homespun, no buttons, no belt, simply a huge swath of cloth wrapped about his middle and fastened with a length of rope. But it was his jacket that was most spectacular, for it consisted of a Mexican serape, brightly colored and well fringed, which he swept about his left shoulder so that its far end dragged along the ground. Thus attired, and with a three-day growth of beard, he moved forward to conduct the affairs of state, but when he spotted Quimper he interrupted his unsteady progress and said, without sarcasm: 'Ah-ha! The Hero of San Jacinto!' Yancey, taken by surprise, fumbled for just a moment, then flashed his toothiest smile: 'Good afternoon, sir,' and the President of Texas lurched on, not yet fully recovered from the previous night's bout.

It was on the trip home that Otto began to suspect that whatever Yancey Quimper did had to be inspected closely, because the boy could see that the enthusiastic innkeeper was apt to prove unreliable when his own interests became paramount. From something that Yancey said—'Gettin' the ferry started is our real job'—he suspected that when the time came to help the Ascots build their house, Yancey would find other obligations to keep him employed.

Otto was wrong. As soon as Yancey reached the inn, shouting to Betsy Belle as he approached, he summoned Martin, who was reading his lawbooks, and cried: 'Look what Otto and me bought for your kitchen!' and to Otto's surprise he produced a small oaken coffee grinder made in France. When Betsy Belle embraced Otto, thanking him for the gift, Yancey winked, indicating that the boy should keep his mouth shut. And next morning it was Yancey who shouted: 'Let's go downriver and build that house.' In the days that followed he labored at least as strenuously as the other two men, and after many tedious days the Ascots had their shack.

Martin's advancement in his other field had been even more spectacular, for on the evening of his third visit to Judge Phinizy, the Arkansas jurist said: 'Martin, I'm sendin' in your papers tomorrow. You're a lawyer.'

'But, Judge . . .'

'Hell, son, you know more law'n I do right now,' and he curved yet another magnificent shot of tobacco juice into the bucket to punctuate his legal decision.

When Martin expressed his gratitude for such assistance, the judge asked for the return of Coke and Blackstone and handed him in exchange the only two books he, Phinizy, had ever purchased with his own money: *Fordyce on Pleading* and *Civil Code of Virginia:* 'I never finished either of 'em, but I have found that the more you know, the better lawyer you'll be.'

Martin's introduction to the law came in two cases involving veterans, and since he appreciated their problems, he was a sympathetic counselor, but he learned quickly that in the tumult of a Texas courtroom good intentions on the part of a man's lawyer or right on the side of a client could mean little.

In his first case he represented a likable young farmer, Axel Vexter, who had fought at San Jacinto and had, with the approval of the Texas government, selected the 640 acres allotted him. He had surveyed the land with the aid of a licensed surveyor and had started erecting a small house when another veteran claimed prior rights. He, too, said he had governmental approval and a proper survey. The case rested, obviously, on the character and witnesses of the two contestants, and with considerable effort Ascot rounded up proof incontrovertible that it was Vexter who had prior rights, but when Phinizy rendered his decision, the land went to the other man, and Vexter's certificate entitling him to 640 acres was available for use elsewhere.

The young veteran was so infuriated by this obvious perversion of justice that he cursed Phinizy in open court, and was thrown in jail for contempt. When Ascot went there to console him, Vexter cursed him too, and threw the certificate in his face. In vain did the young lawyer strive to assure the prisoner that he would soon be released and that other land just as good could be found. Vexter would not listen: 'Take the damned land as your fee. I don't want it.'

This Ascot would not do, and when he told Quimper about the affair, Yancey said: 'Martin! When you have a case before Judge Phinizy, let me know. He owes me so many favors.'

Ascot stared at the innkeeper: 'Do you know what you just said?' and Yancey replied: 'You got to accept Judge Phinizy as he is.'

But when Martin told Yancey about the certificate to land rights which Vexter had rejected, Quimper became quite excited: 'Let me see that!' and when he satisfied himself that it was a legal document assuring the holder of free land, he said: 'I need these. If you have any other clients . . .' He offered Martin ten cents an acre, $6.40, to keep as a fee for services, but Martin would not accept this: 'I want you to hand it to Vexter personally. So he'll know there can be decency in the law.'

But when the time came to count out the few coins that Betsy Belle had been collecting at the inn, Yancey could come up with only $5.10. This certificate entitled the owner to 640 acres of the choicest land in the region of the three rivers, land that would later be of enormous value, but because there was no money in circulation, it could not fetch even ten cents an acre.

'Will he accept five-ten?' Yancey asked, and Martin told him: 'He'll be glad to get anything.' So the two men went to the jail, a chicken-coop affair attached to Judge Phinizy's office, and tendered Vexter the money. When he accepted, gratified by the amount, Yancey said: 'If you know any others who want to sell their rights, send them to Quimper's Ferry.' Then he went to the front of the building and told the judge: 'Let him go. He was at San Jacinto.'

On his second big case Martin Ascot learned the extraordinary legal power of the words Yancey had spoken, for this time he was defending, before Judge Phinizy, a farmer of impeccable reputation and deportment who had been grievously defrauded by a rascal named Knobby Horsham, and the case was so transparent that Ascot felt he need not bother his friend Quimper, who appeared to have the judge's ear. Carefully prepared, Ascot appeared on the morning of the trial date only to find that Sam Houston, dressed in Indian garb topped by his serape and with clanging spurs, had asked special dispensation to serve as lawyer for the defendant, despite the fact that he was the president. Judge Phinizy granted the unusual request and the trial began.

In a masterful display, young Ascot deferred to the great Houston, at the same time proving beyond any doubt that Knobby Horsham had behaved despicably. The jury, nine farmers, obviously sided with Martin's client, for some of them had been defrauded by just such rascals as Knobby.

The case really did not need to be submitted to the jury, but Judge Phinizy, in a show of judicial impartiality, asked Sam Houston if he had any witnesses. 'Only one, your Honor.' Limping to the witness box, his right leg dragging so conspicuously that the jury had to notice, he moved close to his client and looked down upon him as a loving father might, despite the fact that the man was a proved rascal. The audience leaned forward, expecting their voluble president to unlimber a scorching oration, but he uttered only two sentences: 'Knobby, you've heard the serious charges made against you. Where were you on the afternoon of 21 April 18 and 36?'

Knobby looked up like an innocent child and whispered: 'Leadin' the front-line charge at San Jacinto.'

'The defense rests,' Houston said, limping back to his chair.

'Case dismissed,' Judge Phinizy cried.

The next months were the ones that crystallized Otto's character, for he spent them almost equally divided between two contrasting lives that attracted him almost equally. He lived in the rude shack built for the Ascots, which Betsy Belle had converted into a place of warmth and illumination. As finished by the three veterans of San Jacinto, the cabin was little more than a collection of rough-cut logs piled loosely in the form of a large kitchen, a small alcove for the Ascots and a cubbyhole for Otto, but after she finished with making it habitable, it was a snug refuge in the wilderness.

First she took Otto to the river, where they routed out long lengths of soft weeds and pailfuls of mud to caulk the crevices through which wind had been blowing and rain dripping. Then she herself took thin reedlike limbs of trees growing along the Brazos and fashioned them into chairs, four in all, which were both sturdy and comfortable. After what seemed like interminable searching, she procured two iron hooks for the fireplace and three pots to hang upon them. She smoothed out five successive layers of a claylike mud to achieve a level, largely dustless floor. And to make the kitchen seem more like a city home, she nailed to its walls two colored lithographs, one sent down the Mississippi from Cincinnati, the other up across the desert from Mexico City. The first showed Andrew Jackson astride a horse at New Orleans; the second, Santa Anna in the battle at Zacatecas. Whenever Yancey Quimper visited the kitchen, he spat at Santa Anna, whereupon Betsy Belle would bang him on the ear.

To Otto this kitchen became a university, for here the Ascots introduced him to true learning, Martin speaking of the principles of law, Betsy Belle reviewing the lessons she had mastered at a school in Mississippi. They talked of Napoleon and Charlemagne and Thomas Jefferson, and always they tried to penetrate to those motives which force men and women to behave as they do. Night after night Martin would review cases which he had tried before Judge Phinizy, with Betsy Belle analyzing why this man and that woman had behaved as they had: 'You must have seen she was lying. Surely the judge pointed this out to the jury.' And Martin would explain why it was most unlikely that the judge would have done so.

From such instruction Otto began to formulate his own interpretation of society, and the Ascots might have been surprised had he revealed it. Drawing upon what he had seen at Natchez-under-the-Hill and at Goliad, he discovered that for a man to make a mark in this world, he had better have a tough core of righteousness which he should allow nothing to scar, neither the lure of money nor the pursuit of pride. He had better identify his enemies quickly and beat them down before they had a chance to do the same to him. And it would be best if he kept quiet.

Early in their evening talks around one of Betsy Belle's homemade candles, he decided that he was not fashioned to be a scholar, because the first time Martin handed him a lawbook that explained the topic under discussion, he found that his interest quickly flagged. And whenever Betsy Belle spoke reverently of some romantic tale she had picked up from her study of history, he would dismiss it as imagination. He was a tough-minded little realist, soon to be fifteen, and he would leave the life of letters to others better qualified.

But he never dismissed the essence of what the Ascots were saying. He knew from looking into their excited faces that there was a lower order of life and a higher, and he was instinctively drawn to the latter. In every court case that Martin discussed, he found himself siding with right, and justice, and what Martin sometimes called 'the only sensible thing to do.'

These growing convictions served him in good stead when he worked with Yancey Quimper at the inn, for there he saw a completely different type of person. To begin with, Yancey himself was about as far removed from the Ascots as one could be. For example, when the Ascot cabin needed caulking, Betsy Belle tied up her skirts, went into the Brazos, and dug the clay for it; at the inn when there was work to be done, Yancey always looked about for someone else to do it. He could in a single day find a dozen things for Otto to attend.

The motivations of the inn customers were also quite different from those of the Ascots. Everyone seemed to be conniving for some advantage or trying to acquire land or belongings owned by someone else. Arguments were settled not with carefully marshaled words but with fists or a flashing Bowie knife. Otto was by no means afraid of a fight; he knew from experience that he could control adversaries much bigger than he, but he saw that to engage endlessly in brawling was not productive.

Yet he enjoyed the liveliness of the inn, and despite Quimper's obvious defects in character, he liked being with him, for something was always happening, like the time two toughs from Kentucky stopped on the far side of the Brazos and clamored loudly to be ferried across. 'Go fetch them,' Yancey said, and Otto had gone down the steep bank to where the ferry waited, its two guide ropes attached by rings to the wire that stretched to a big tree on the opposite side. With deft hands he grabbed the forward rope, allowed the current to carry him downstream till the rope was taut, and then pulled sturdily so that the ferry moved forward along the fixed wire.

'What kind of contraption is this?' one of the frontiersmen bellowed as they climbed noisily aboard, and at midstream on the return trip, the man who had spoken grabbed the rope from Otto's hands, while his partner grabbed the stern rope, and pulling in the opposite direction, nearly upset the craft.

'Stop that!' Otto shouted, recovering the rope, but he could do nothing to move the ferry because now both men heaved on the back rope. He was stronger than they and knew better what he was doing, so they did not succeed in taking the ferry away from him in their boisterous game, but they did make orderly progress impossible.

Dropping his rope, Otto whipped from his belt the pistol that Zave Campbell had taught him to use so effectively. Pointing it at the two roisterers, he said quietly: 'Drop that rope.' When they refused, he calmly put a shot between the pair and said: 'Drop it or I'm coming after you.'

The threat was so preposterous, this boy challenging two grown men, that they began to laugh, and if Otto's pistol had had the capacity of a second bullet, he would have blazed away at them. Instead, he leaped forward, knocked one sideways so that he fell into the river and flattened the other.

The pistol shot had aroused men in the inn, and they came streaming down to the bank. A good swimmer, seeing that the first Kentuckian might drown, plunged in to save him, while others waded out to bring the ferry to the bank. When the two travelers were at the bar drinking the watered stuff that Quimper sold as whiskey, one said: 'You got yourself a son who's a tiger,' and Yancey said: 'He ain't my son,' and they said: 'You better adopt him.'

Next morning Yancey tried to do just that: 'Otto, I'm makin' you an offer. You run the ferry, help around the place. I'll give you room and keep, and soon as there's any money, you'll get a share. Meantime, you got yourself a leg up in life.'

'I'll think about that,' Otto said, and he might have accepted, for he knew he needed a home somewhere, and that continued residence with the Ascots was both impractical and unfair. He might have become a river-crossing roustabout had not Martin Ascot been called to the new town of Houston on an important court case. Taking Betsy Belle with him, and inviting Otto to ride along, Martin set out for what was now the capital city of the republic. The three-day ride southeast, across the low, rolling hills between the Brazos and the Trinity, was a reminder of what the new nation might become if it ever stabilized and found enough money to operate, for the fields were rich, the trees grew in attractive clusters, and flowers bloomed everywhere. It was a rougher land, Otto thought, than the terrain he had seen in Ohio, but it was powerful, and he was proud to be a part of it.

The first night out they slept under the stars, but on the second they found a farmhouse where the wife welcomed them and the husband was eager to talk politics: 'As soon as that drunk Houston serves out his term, what we got to do is elect a real fighter like Mirabeau Lamar to the presidency.'

'Who's he want to fight?' Martin asked, and the man said: 'I've heard him twice. He wants to kick the Indians out of Texas. He wants to fight Santy Anny and whip him proper. And he wants us to take Santy Fay.'

'That would be a lot of fighting,' Ascot said, and the farmer replied: 'Us Texians can do a lot.'

The town of Houston was a revelation: first houses built in late 1836, a bustling town of 1,200 by the spring of 1837, capital of the nation in May 1837. When the

Ascot party rode in, they found movement everywhere—new stores being built at a frantic rate and eight principal streets, each eight inches deep in mud. Betsy Belle, trying to alight from her horse, felt her left foot sinking into a quagmire, and remounted.

There were no hotels yet, but local citizens, inordinately proud of their metropolis, directed the visitors to a remarkable substitute, and when they were comfortably fitted into the private home of Augustus Allen they heard an extraordinary yarn from Allen himself: 'Yep, my brother and I came down from Syracuse, New York, a few dollars in our pockets, dreams in our hearts. We bought, one way or another,' and here he shrugged his shoulders to indicate the chicaneries he and his brother had engaged in. Losing his train of thought, he asked Martin: 'Do you know how much a hundred Mexican leagues of land is?' Before Ascot could reply, he said: 'That's nearly half a million acres, and that's what we acquired.'

'You have to shoot anybody?' Betsy Belle asked, and he chuckled.

'Well, we set aside the best of our land, here beside Buffalo Bayou, with entrance forty miles out there to the Gulf, and we decided to make this the capital of Texas. Yep, we give the government all the land they needed, free. We give churches all they asked for, schools if you wanted to start one. We give away so much damned land you wouldn't believe it, and why do you suppose we done that?'

They learned from Allen's wife that her husband had been a child prodigy in mathematics and a college professor at seventeen, 'the wizard of upper New York, they called him.' And he made no apologies for what he and his brother had done in founding Houston: 'We did it to make money. We give away lots to attract attention, then sell what's left at a good profit. There's no hotel for distinguished visitors like you, so I open my house to all who come, free.' To close the gap between his prodigious learning and the local customers' lack of it, he had adopted Texas speech and sounded sometimes like an illiterate, but on their third night in Houston, the Ascots were invited to attend a session of the Philosophical Society of Texas, held of course in the parlor of Allen's house, for he was the treasurer and motivating force.

As an afterthought, Allen had said when extending the invitation: 'Bring the boy, if you wish,' and Otto found himself among the founders and philosophers of his nation. Congress was meeting in Houston that week, so many of the legislators participated in the discussion, and Otto quickly realized that these men were much like his father: serious, sometimes robust in their humor and obviously committed to finding a constructive life. After a satisfying meal cooked by Mrs. Allen, she and Betsy modestly retired, as if incapable of understanding the august subjects about to be discussed, while the men listened attentively to two essays: The Federalist Papers, Key to the American Democracy, and Fielding's *Tom Jones*: A Threat to Public Morals?

Otto could not fathom either the concepts involved in these discussions or the vigor with which they were pursued, but he was proud when Martin Ascot entered the debate with such forceful comment that in the midst of the proceedings Mirabeau Lamar, president of the society and vice-president of the nation, proposed: 'Gentlemen, our young lawyer from Xavier County has spoken much sense here tonight. I recommend that he be made our corresponding member from Xavier.' The proposal was approved by acclamation, after which Lamar reported: 'At the conclusion of our last meeting several members, including Anson Jones, Thomas Rusk and James Collinsworth, suggested that the topic then debated with such illumination be continued into this meeting, should time permit. Well, time does permit, and I would like our esteemed secretary, David Burnet, to state the question.'

Burnet, an older man who had served briefly as president of the fledgling nation during its formative period, rose, coughed, and read the title of the debate which had so exercised the members: 'Women: Why Have We Had No Female Painters or Musicians?' and when the pros and cons of this question were discussed, often with great heat, even Otto could understand the proceedings. It was conceded by both sides—anti-women, eighty-eight percent; pro-women, twelve percent—that females were flighty, inconsistent, unable to pursue a goal over any extended period and apt at any moment to fly off the handle, and that these weaknesses disqualified them for any sustained intellectual or creative work such as the composition of a Mozart symphony or the paintings of the Sistine Chapel, two examples of art with which most of the members seemed to be familiar.

But granted these deficiencies, was the female physique such that it automatically precluded greatness in the arts? The majority decided that it was. Just what these limitations were, Otto could not decipher, for when they orated on this fascinating subject, the members inclined to talk in a code that he could not penetrate. However, several speakers referred with great emotion to 'the sublime work of art which women are capable of, the birth of those children on whom the future of any society must and does rest.' Such statements were always greeted with cheers, but toward the end of the evening Martin Ascot rose and said: 'I have heard much comment about the inability of women to sustain any effort through an extended period. Anyone like me who has lived on the far frontier and seen what a wife can accomplish is astounded by her energy.'

From his seat in front, ex-President Burnet grumbled: 'Ascot, you're so young.' And the meeting ended.

Its effect on Otto was magical. Even he could see that these earnest men, stuck away on a frontier so different from either Baltimore or Cincinnati, were striving to maintain their interest in the entire world, and especially in those wellsprings of human behavior from which goodness came. He liked these men and their pompous oratory. He was proud of how a younger man like Martin fitted in. And he saw with remarkable clarity that he was intended to be a man like them, and not a man like Yancey Quimper. When he returned to Xavier County he would tell Yancey that he did not want the job at the Ferry. But what he did want, and where he would make his home, he did not know.

If Otto was confused as to where he would find his home, Texas faced an equal quandary. Shortly after the establishment of its government, a plebiscite had been taken, and the citizens produced an irrefutable plurality in favor of joining the United States immediately, and upon any reasonable terms offered, but to their chagrin, the nation to the north rejected the offer. 'We ought to march to Washington!' customers at Quimper's Ferry bellowed, and Yancey predicted: 'We'll see the day when Washington comes beggin' for us. And what will we do then?'

'Spit in her eye!' the belligerents cried, but in his kitchen Martin Ascot provided a more cautious analysis: 'This dreadful panic makes everyone afraid of making bold moves.'

'I think what people are really afraid of is another war with Mexico,' Betsy Belle said, but her husband struck the deeper chord: 'It's slavery. Those damned Northerners will never let us come in as another slave state.' And he was right, because year after year the Northern senators excoriated Texas as a nest of backwardness and slavery, and annexation seemed impossible.

Now the contest for the allegiance of Texas became an international affair, with three nations involved, and with debate in the Ascot kitchen divided three ways. Betsy Belle, who had learned French from a Louisiana slave who had reared her, hoped that France would assume the control she had tried to exercise back in the 1680s when Texas was theoretically French, and from time to time this seemed possible and even likely: 'I should love to see this vast area civilized. We have great affinity with the French.'

Her husband, now a serious student of English law, hoped that Great Britain would take control, and quickly: 'We would fit in so perfectly with English ways of justice, law and government.' He was, as a Southerner, so convinced that entry into the United States was unlikely that he actively sought union with Britain and propagandized any who would listen, especially Otto: 'Can't you see? In states like Virginia and Pennsylvania and Carolina, we were English. It would be proper for us to reunite.' He assured Otto that Texas rights would be protected and even extended in such a reunion.

Quimper's interest centered on Mexico, which was threatening to resume the war. No peace treaty between Mexico and her former colony had ever been promulgated, so that renewal of the war was a real possibility: 'What we ought to do is let those damned Mexicans make a move against us, and then march right down to Mexico City and take over the whole country. They'll never be able to govern it by themselves.' Of course, when Mexico did invade Texas and capture San Antonio, which happened twice, Quimper could not believe that his Texians had allowed this to happen, and became terrified lest Santa Anna come storming back to burn once again the Quimper inn and ferry.

Young Otto, listening to these debates, kept quiet, as usual, but his ideas on foreign affairs were beginning slowly to solidify, and had he been asked for his opinion, he would have said: 'I had enough of foreigners with those Baltimore Germans. I don't want France or England, either one. And I hate the Mexicans for what they did at the Alamo and Goliad.' What did he advocate? He told no one, but he had firm beliefs: We shouldn't march to Mexico City, like Yancey says, although we could do it easy. We should go clear to Panama, and then maybe take Canada, too. He could see no reason why all of North America should not be Texian, except that the eastern seaboard, which was already American, could stay that way. Then, if the United States should some day wish to join Texas, it would be welcome.

The internal affairs of the nation were also maturing, but not always in the direction intended. All observers agreed that Texas could never become a first-class nation unless it developed both a harbor on the Gulf for ocean-going vessels, and steamboats for transit up the three principal rivers, Trinity, Brazos, Colorado. Unfortunately, immense sandbars, tenacious and drifting, blockaded all available harbors, especially Galveston's, so that sometimes two ships out of five would not make the wharves, with lives and cargo alike being lost.

River traffic was even less successful, because here, too, forbidding sandbars menaced any ship that tried to enter from the Gulf, and those that did succeed immediately encountered snags, sunken logs and smaller sandbars, and such twists in the course that boats could negotiate the worst corners only with the help of ropes dragged along the shore by sweating passengers who debarked to do the hauling.

Occasionally, some daring vessel would make it as far upriver as Quimper's Ferry, but two that did were trapped by falling water and spent the summer there. Yet it was an unbroken act of faith, all along the rivers, that 'one of these days we'll see scheduled boats landing at that dock.' In the meantime, the loss of shipping was disastrous: *Ocean* sunk at Brazoria; *Clematis* sunk trying to get to Brazoria; *Mustang* sunk at Jones Landing; *Lady Byron* sunk near Richmond; *Creole Queen* and seven others sunk trying to get into the Brazos.

But when this doleful litany was recited at Quimper's inn, Yancey insisted, with most of the men supporting him: 'When a Texian starts to do something, he does it. We'll have steamboats up here yet.' The same prediction was made along both the Trinity and the Colorado, where losses paralleled those on the Brazos.

Education was also a function of society about which something was going to be done . . . one of these days. The nation could not afford to spend what little money it could accumulate on free schools, so there were none, but it did allocate liberal portions of the only currency it did have, land, to schools. Xavier County, for example, was awarded 17,712 of its choicest acres, but no way was found to turn this into cash, so no school was founded.

However, the county did eventually offer some education, for after the children of Xavier had gone some years without schooling, the Reverend Joel Job Harrison, tall and fiery and with a wife who could cook, appeared with handbills announcing his intention to open a school: 'First course: reading, writing, spelling, multiplication tables, $1.50 per month. Second course: arithmetic, grammar, oratory, astronomy, $2.00 a month. Third course: Latin, Greek, algebra, geography, the copperplate, $3.00 a month. Mrs. Harrison will accept a few girls and boys in her home, good table, Christian discourse.' To inquiring parents, Reverend Harrison gave these assurances: 'I am an ordained minister, Methodist faith but courteous to all. I am proficient in the subjects offered. And I can promise firm discipline, for I will brook no insolence or insubordination, since I believe I can whip all but the very biggest boys in fistfighting.' He called his one-room school, a reasonably good one, the University of Xavier.

The citizens of Texas sometimes acquired a peculiar insight into how their nation functioned. When General Felix Huston, no relation to the president, was to be replaced as commander in chief of the Texian forces by Albert Sidney Johnston, the former, refusing to cede office to the latter, warned Johnston that if he wanted the command, he would have to duel Huston for it, and when the duel took place, Huston shot Johnston in the behind and held on to his command. Said the enlisted men who witnessed the duel: 'It was a fair fight. If a man wants to lead the Texian army, he better be prepared to fight for the job.'

But always the limiting factor was this strangling lack of currency, and when the distressed nation, swamped in debt, tried to salvage itself by printing two million dollars' worth of 'red-back bills' supported by no collateral except the government's word and faith, citizens evaluated the issue realistically. On the first day it was issued, a dollar bill was worth fifty cents, a few days later, thirty cents, then ten cents and four cents, until it bottomed out at an appalling two cents.

Shocked by this experience, the government sought another solution: 'We'll encourage private firms with good reputations to issue their own currency.'

'Backed by what?' cynics asked, and the government said: 'Their goods. Their mills.'

The experiment was tried, and a relieved Texas watched as this private money system stabilized at about eighty cents on the dollar. One firm whose notes ranked even higher announced that it was backing them with 'every item of our merchandise, our steamer *Claribel,* eighteen nigger slaves and our sawmill.'

In Xavier County, Yancey Quimper planned to print five thousand dollars' worth of bills 'redeemable at the Ferry,' but since he could not specify redeemable in what, the government ordered him to desist, so Xavier continued to suffer.

However, Yancey did find a way to profit from the emergency, for he let it be known that he stood ready to exchange what little cash he had for any land certificates in the possession of San Jacinto veterans, and Otto watched as a shattered chain of young men wandered in with certificates that they sold for two and three cents an acre, and glad they were to receive even those small amounts.

When Otto learned what Yancey was doing with these papers, he was amazed. One day a European gentleman, neither French nor German but something else, stopped by the inn, behaving as if he had been there before, and he gave Yancey real money for a stack of the certificates. When he was gone, Otto asked: 'What's he do with them?' and Yancey said: 'Peddles them through Europe. Everybody wants to come to Texas.'

'Even when we have no money?' and Yancey said: 'To people who know, Texas is still heaven.'

He was right in this assessment, for despite continuous setbacks, the dogged Texians strove to forge a nation based upon distinct characteristics, and none was more basic than the Texian's ability to absorb temporary setbacks. An impartial observer from either London or Boston, evaluating the new nation during this tempestuous decade, would have predicted failure, for nothing seemed to work, but he would have underestimated the capacity of the Texian to take enormous risks, sustained by the conviction that 'sooner or later, things will work out.'

Thus the Allen brothers could speculate in Houston real estate, hoping that land which they bought at twenty cents an acre would soon be worth two hundred dollars; Reverend Joel Job Harrison could call his cabin-school a university in the honest belief that it would some day become one; and Yancey Quimper could spend his last penny on land certificates, trusting that dreamers in Europe would grab them at inflated prices. Everywhere this faith in the future prevailed.

In the midst of Otto's confusion as to his future, the Texas government circulated through the counties a document which would lead to the creation of one of the cherished symbols of Texas life. It called for volunteers to man a unique corps whose nature could best be explained by stating what it was not.

First, it was not a police force with uniforms, specified duties and restricted terrains of operation. Particularly, it would not be subject to supervision by county authorities.

Second, it was not a branch of the army with highly organized structure and national obligations. The new force would have no distinguishing uniforms, no government-issued arms, no epaulet distinctions, no medals, no drill. Rarely would it perform in battle formation and never would it parade.

Finally, it was not a secret detective agency, working under the command of any district attorney, for even though it would often perform detective functions, its allegiance was to the national government, which insulated it from petty local pressures.

What would this potentially powerful new arm of government be called? During one discussion at the ramshackle capital a proponent had finished making the point that 'the men will not be tied down to any one locality, they will range all over,' and someone suggested: 'Let's call them ranging companies.' And thus were born the famous ranging units—no set duties: 'Just range the countryside and keep order.'

The unit to be enrolled from the counties centering on Xavier would be commanded by Captain Sam Garner, distinguished veteran of San Jacinto, twenty-four years old and as tall and thin as an unclothed scarecrow. His general responsibility would be along the north shore of the Nueces River, and as soon as this was known, the toughest men flocked to his temporary headquarters in Campbell, because to serve along what was called the Nueces Strip was to serve in the wildest, most dangerous and challenging part of the new nation.

The word *Strip* was misleading, for this was not some narrow stretch of land between two settled areas. At its greatest east-to-west reach, it extended some two hundred miles; at its widest north-south, a hundred and sixty. It was best visualized as a healthy wedge of pie, the arc of crust running along the Gulf, the point far to the west along the Rio Grande. It was much larger than many European nations—Belgium, the Netherlands or Switzerland, for example—and also considerably larger than substantial American states like New Hampshire, Vermont or Maryland.

Except for a few meager towns along the north bank of the Rio Grande, it was largely unsettled insofar as permanent ranches were concerned, but it was not unoccupied. For more than a century Mexican herdsmen living south of the river had run their cattle on the Strip, and now cattlemen from the Victoria area in Texas were doing the same. An interesting rule developed: if a Mexican crossed the Rio Grande to work his cattle and picked up a few strays belonging to a Texian, he was a bandit, but any Texian who led a foraging party into Mexico to increase his herd by lifting a few hundred cattle was considered a prudent citizen.

When Texas gained its independence, delineation of the border between the two countries was imprecise, with Texas claiming that its southern border lay along the Rio Grande, and Mexico arguing that the border followed the Nueces River far to the north, which under Spanish rule certainly had formed the southern border of their Tejas. A bleak, forbidding, unpopulated no man's land existed between the two rivers, and from within it undeclared warfare developed. Mexicans prowling in the Strip would strike north across the Nueces and desolate ranches in the Victoria area; Texians would organize furtive excursions across the Rio Grande.

The Texas government, ignoring the depredations of its own citizens, deplored the behavior of the outlaw Mexicans. As a senator described the situation during an impassioned debate in Houston: 'In organizing furtive thrusts into our territory north of the Nueces, the Mexicans are without shame or honor. A secret crossing of our river, a wild dash to some unprotected Texian hacienda, gunfire, a flaming dog-run, a murdered family, and cattle stampeding as they head south become common, after which the invaders scurry to sanctuary in the Strip, from where they laugh at us derisively.' It was this kind of sortie that Captain Garner's ranging company was expected to halt. Among the first group of volunteers was Otto Macnab, age fifteen but more a man than many who stepped forward. Garner, certain the boy was grossly underage, but not knowing by exactly how much, asked: 'Son, how old are you?'

In January 1838, Otto would be sixteen, so he lied and said: 'I'll be eighteen in January.'

'Come back in January,' the lanky man said, and then he instructed the others as to the rules of the new organization: 'Provide your own good horse, a change of clothes, a rifle, a pistol and a Bowie knife.'

'What kind of clothes?'

'Whatever you have. No insignia.'

'Same with the boots?'

'Whatever you have, but they should come mostly to the knee because we'll be hitting mesquite and rattlesnakes.' Believing that he had covered everything, he started to go inside the shed that served as an office; then he stopped: 'We think you should wear a big hat. Keeps the sun out of your eyes in summer, your head warm in winter.' And studying Otto carefully, he added: 'It would make you look taller, too.'

On 2 January 1838 Otto bade the Ascots farewell, placed his two rifles across his saddle and headed south, his big hat bobbing in time with the horse's gait. Before nightfall he was sworn in, smallest man in his unit, a taut little fighting machine with no uniform and no stated commission, eager to help tame the frontiers of Texas.

During the second week in January word reached the capital that the bandit Benito Garza had invaded Texas and raided a ranch north of the Nueces River, killing two Texians. This was precisely the kind of outrage the ranging companies had been organized to punish, so the informal Xavier County unit was assembled by Captain Sam Garner, twenty-six years old, six feet two, a hundred and fifty-eight pounds, flowing mustaches, icicle-straight and icicle-cool, and a very good man at firing his rifle at full gallop. His first assistant was Otto Macnab, the young fellow of indeterminate age. He claimed he was eighteen, but looked twelve because of his beardless chin, his almost-white baby-fine hair, and his slim, muscular body. 'This Macnab,' Garner told his superiors, 'impresses me as a chilly hombre. When those blue eyes fix on you, beware!'

The company assembled in the town of Campbell, fifty-two men on their own horses and with their own guns and knives who would ride casually south 'to knock some sense into the Mexicans.' When they neared Victoria, their first important stop, Otto surprised his captain by saying: 'I want to break away. My mother lives on the Guadalupe west of town.'

'We'll all head that way,' Garner said, for he was in no hurry; he had learned that fighting could be depended upon to find him out at the appointed time, no matter where he went or what he did. So the other volunteers followed Otto as he headed for the Garza dog-runs, and all were astonished when Macnab presented to them the two widows, his stepmother Josefina and his adopted mother María, for the women were obviously Mexican.

The men appreciated the hospitality the two women extended and were favorably impressed by their well-kept homes, but what won them over completely was the discovery that María had been married to Xavier Campbell, the hero of the Alamo, after whom their county and their town had been named.

'What was he like?' they wanted to know. 'Where was the tree they hanged him from?' One man, about twenty, just sat munching tortillas and staring at María: 'Were you really married to Campbell?'

'I was,' she said as her plump body moved about the kitchen.

Macnab gave his mother a farewell embrace and then kissed María affectionately. 'That one's a good Mexican,' the staring fellow said, but when they were once more on the road south he asked Captain Garner and Macnab: 'Say, I just thought of something. Isn't this troublemaker Benito Garza—the one we're supposed to catch—isn't he from Victoria somewheres?'

'He's María's brother,' Otto said with no embarrassment.

'What will you do if we catch him?'

'Arrest him.'

'Is he really as clever as they say?'

'He can ride better than you . . . or me. He can shoot better than you . . . or me. And he probably can think better than you . . . or me.'

'Why is he raising so much hell?'

'He's a Mexican,' Otto said. 'He fought with Santa Anna.'

'Didn't we capture him at San Jacinto?'

'We did.'

'Why didn't we shoot him?'

'We don't shoot prisoners.'

At first hearing, this might seem a naïve thing for a member of a ranging company to say, because these troops had already acquired a reputation among the Mexicans of Texas as ruthless killers—los tejanos sangrientes, the bloody Texians. But upon reflection it wasn't so absurd, because as Captain Garner himself explained to one newcomer: 'We rarely take prisoners,' which meant, of course, that after a fight, there were few left to take alive.

The lethal efficiency of the ranging company was multiplied by a factor of five by a fortunate incident which occurred as the riders were approaching the Nueces

River. A supply officer from the Texas army overtook them to distribute the first official issue of weapons the men would receive, and from the first moment the rangers inspected this small piece of armament they sensed that it was going to remake Texas and the West.

It was a revolver, .34 caliber, with a short octagonal barrel of blue-gray steel and a grip that nestled in the hand. It had a revolving cylinder that enabled the user to fire five times without reloading, and was, in every respect, a masterful piece of workmanship. It was made by Sam Colt in some small town in Connecticut, and a salient feature was that any one part of a given revolver could be used interchangeably in any other gun. And for some curious reason never explained, the first users, all Texians, referred to this superlative revolver as 'a Colts'—no apostrophe, just a Colts, as in the sentence 'I whipped out my Colts and drilled him between the eyes.'

Understandably, the Colts became the preferred weapon of the ranging companies, and armed with these revolvers, Captain Garner and his men crossed the Nueces confident that they now had a real chance of cleansing the Strip of Mexicans. But when they rode to the crest of a rise so slight it would have gone unnoticed elsewhere, Otto's mind was attracted to other matters, for as he reined in his horse he stared in wonder at the vast expanse of emptiness that stretched before him—an empire off by itself, brown, sere, populated by rattlesnakes and coyotes. It was his first glimpse of the Strip, and it awed him.

It's like no other part of Texas, he said to himself. And look at that sky. Then he shook his head: I'll bet the traveler who gets lost in there stays lost . . . till the buzzards find him.

As he studied the tremendous land he observed various interesting aspects: Flat as that new billiard table Yancey Quimper put in at the Ferry. Brushland with scrub oak, no tall trees. But I'd hate to ride through that thicket without protection for my legs. Out to shreds. In these decades the land seemed almost without vegetation, for the ubiquitous mesquite had not yet taken over, but when Otto looked closer he saw the real miracle of the semi-desert as it prepared for spring: Are those flowers?

They were, a multitude of the most gorgeous tiny beauties—gold, red, blue, yellow, purple—forming a dense, matted carpet covering a million acres. It was an incredible display of nature's profligate use of color, so luxuriant and beautiful that although Otto had seen the flowers of Texas before, some of the most varied in the world, he felt he had never beheld anything like the minute blossoms of this exploding garden.

Captain Garner, seeing that his young assistant lagged, rode back and said: 'Immense, eh?' and Otto replied: 'One of those flowers would be beautiful. But a million million of them!' Garner said: 'They stretch two hundred miles,' and Otto said: 'I thought I knew Texas . . .'

'Let's get moving,' Garner said, and as they overtook the others he observed:

'Some say we should let Garza and his local Mexicans have this wilderness. Folks tell me they have a reasonable claim, but I say no. With Texas, you can never predict what value land is going to have. You bring water in here, you got yourself a gold mine.'

'And how do you bring water?'

'That's for somebody else to solve. Our problem is that bastard Garza.'

Wherever the company came upon Texian cattlemen searching for cattle in the Strip, Garner's men heard constant complaint: 'This damned Benito Garza has been raidin' and runnin' off our cattle.' And as the men rode farther south they began to come upon the ruins of isolated settlements that had been razed, leaving not a shack or a longhorn. The missing owners had been either kidnapped into Mexico or shot, and after the company had seen more such scarred remains, its members became decidedly vengeful.

'God help the Mexican I meet,' one of the men said.

One afternoon the company apprehended eight Mexican vaqueros struggling to herd a large number of unbranded cattle toward the Rio Grande, and without asking questions, the Texians initiated a gun battle in which they killed five of the Mexicans. Captain Garner, by merely looking at the bodies, declared them to have been rustlers stealing Texian cattle, but when the interrogation of the three survivors made it clear that the cattle had legally belonged to the Mexicans, who had traditionally used this range, he had to concede that his enthusiastic riders might have shot the wrong men.

'What shall we do with the others?' Otto asked, and Garner weighed this problem for some minutes: 'If we keep them prisoner, a lot of questions will be asked. If we let them go, they'll get other Mexicans excited in Matamoros.'

'Hang 'em,' a rider from Austin County suggested, and it was agreed that this was the most prudent solution, so without further discussion of the legality or propriety of such action, the three trespassers were hanged.

Their leader, before he was strung up, protested vehemently: 'But we were on Mexican soil.'

'It ain't Mexican no longer,' the rope man growled as he kicked at the horse on which the doomed man sat, hands tied behind him. With a startled leap the horse sped off, leaving the Mexican suspended.

Otto did not protest this arbitrary denial of justice, for although he was as firmly as ever dedicated to the preservation of law, he, like the rest of his company, refused to concede that the law was also intended to protect Mexicans.

In succeeding days, the ranging company similarly disciplined sixteen other Mexicans, but uncovered no trace of Benito Garza, who was known to be leading this attempt to control what he and others honestly believed to be Mexican territory. One fiery-minded Mexican shouted: 'Garza will teach you, you bastards!' That hanging did not take place because an infuriated Texian shot the man, even though his hands and legs were tied.

At the end of the tour, Captain Garner spoke encouragingly to his youngest trooper: 'Otto, how many did you get in the battles?' and the boy replied, with some pride, for he had not blazed away indiscriminately like some: 'Four.' Otto Macnab had found his occupation.

When the ranging company disbanded in Xavier, for any assignment was temporary, its members found their nation involved in a presidential election unlike any other that had ever occurred in the Americas. General Sam Houston, forbidden by the constitution from serving two terms in a row, had to relinquish the presidency in December 1838, but members of his Pro-Houston party, as it was called, were determined to elect as his successor some compliant person who would merely hold the office until Sam could reclaim it.

Party choice centered upon a distinguished fifty-year-old lawyer from Kentucky, Peter Grayson, who had served the new nation in such crucial posts as attorney general and as negotiator with the United States government in Washington. Grayson's candidacy delighted Martin Ascot, who as a fellow lawyer spoke vigorously in his behalf among the settlers.

Houston's opponents saw Grayson as a colorless functionary totally unfitted for high office, an assessment which anti-Houston partisans were not slow to point out: 'A nincompoop, as bad for Texas as Houston has been. The only man worthy to be our president is Mirabeau Buonaparte Lamar, a proven hero, a man of great intellectual brilliance, and a general who'll know how to handle Indians and Mexicans.'

The campaign had become quite heated, and because of the brilliance and roughhouse vigor with which Houston defended his tenure, his supporters assumed that his man would win.

Otto, as in the days when he had not known with whom he wished to live, was confused by the haranguing, and he confided to Betsy Belle, who was not supposed to have any opinion about the choice of who would lead her nation: 'Betsy, when I listen to Martin, I'm all for Grayson, because Sam Houston saved this nation and I like his ideas. But when I hear Yancey and those others at the inn, I'm for Lamar. I think he has the right approach to Indians and Mexicans.'

'What approach?'

'Shoot them all. No place in this nation for Indians or Mexicans.'

It seemed certain, in early July, that Grayson would win, but on 9 July 1838 the Pro-Houston party received a bitter jolt. Because Grayson was so drab, so without charm on the hustings, so miserable a speaker and so without any reputation for heroics during the great battles of the revolution—which he had side-stepped by one clever trick after another—the Houston people had thought it prudent to keep him out of the country during the critical days of the campaign. As loudmouth Yancey Quimper shouted: 'They're afeerd to let us see how dumb he is. They let Sam Houston do his dirty work for him.'

But even so, Grayson might have won had he not, while hiding out at Bean's Station in Tennessee, fallen into one of the depressions to which he was subject and shot himself through the head.

This stroke of bad luck appalled Ascot and his pro-Houston cohorts, and some wanted to thrash Yancey Quimper when the big fellow chortled throughout Xavier County: 'God's will. He wants no more of Houston or his cronies.'

After a few days of sad confusion, the Pro-Houston party came forward with a much better candidate than the late Grayson. James Collinsworth, an able lawyer from Tennessee, had served Houston in many capacities, currently as the respected chief justice of the Texas Supreme Court. He was a handsome man, a gifted speaker and an able defender of Houston's policies, for he advocated conciliation with Mexico and peace with the Cherokee. After his first successful speaking engagements, Ascot and his friends agreed: 'We got ourselves a better man. Collinsworth will be our new president.'

The chief justice had only two drawbacks. First, he was thirty-two years old, three years shy of the constitutional requirement for president. No one in the Houston camp had bothered to check, and when troublemakers like Quimper bellowed: 'Even if he wins, he cain't serve,' the Houston men replied confidently: 'We'll take care of that when we get to it.' One enthusiast told Otto: 'You see, Collinsworth is already chief justice, so when the question comes before him, he can rule in his own favor.' Otto felt instinctively that there was something wrong with this strategy, and in quest of enlightenment he consulted Ascot.

'In the English-American system,' Martin said, 'any judge must excuse himself from a case in which his own interests are involved. We call that recusation.' He spoke with such clarity and with such obvious devotion to the law that Otto returned night after night to talk with him, and Ascot's little sermons formed Otto's basic attitudes toward law and order: 'Law is one of the noblest of all human preoccupations, for it establishes agreed-upon rules and states them clearly. It protects you and me from the excesses of the mob.' He always spoke to Otto as if the boy were an audience of fifty elders, and this was admirable, since the truths he enunciated were so advanced that they stretched the boy's mind. It was then that Otto developed his conviction that the law ought to defend the weak, erect protective barriers against the mighty, and clarify obscurities and conflicts. As a man who had ridden with the local ranging company and who wanted to ride again, he saw clearly that it would be his obligation to enforce just laws and dispense honest justice, and he vowed to do so. Therefore, he noted a contradiction in what Ascot was saying.

'But if Judge Collinsworth is too young, won't Lamar's people throw him out if we do elect him?' Otto asked, and now Ascot revealed to him the other side of the law: 'One of the beauties of practical law is that it enables men and women to do the things they want to, even if the printed law says otherwise.'

'What do you mean?'

'It's the law's responsibility to find a way.'

'How?'

'To prove that things aren't always quite what they seem.'

'Could you defend Judge Collinsworth? And prove that he has a right to be president, even if he is three years shy?'

'I think I could find a way,' and Otto marveled as the young lawyer began to shift ideas this way and that. 'Yes, I'm sure I could come up with a solution.'

Judge Collinsworth's second impediment was a hilarious one: he was inclined to be drunk four days each week, so drunk that he could not even dress himself, and Yancey's unrelenting gang made a great deal of this, but the pro-Houston forces had an ingenious defense. They did not try to deny the charge; too many citizens had seen Judge Collinsworth stumbling into a tree or falling into a ditch to claim that the anti-Houston forces were defaming him. They did point out, however, that since Texas had prospered rather well under General Houston, who was drunk every morning, it was reasonable to suppose that it would do even better under Collinsworth, who would be drunk all day. As one orator shouted: 'You don't want a president who sticks his nose into everything, every day,' and this argument was so persuasive that it began to look as if the all-day-drunk Collinsworth would succeed the half-day-drunk Houston.

But one day in late July, Judge Collinsworth, while crossing Galveston Bay on a steamer, jumped from the aft end, thus becoming the second opponent of Lamar to escape an election fight by suicide.

Yancey Quimper and his associates were now convinced that God was participating in the election, since He obviously wanted Lamar to put into operation his announced platform against Indians and Mexicans, and they ridiculed the Pro-Houston party's third nominee, a roustabout boat captain from the Eastern Shore of Maryland. Robert Wilson did not have a history; he had a dossier which summarized scandalous behavior in at least seven different states. In Texas he had been a little of everything—land promoter, gambler, sawmill operator, soldier in the 1835 capture of Bexar, senator—but his behavior in the last-named job was so malodorous that he had to be expelled. Promptly reelected by a district that wanted to be represented by just this kind of man, he told his supporters: 'You have reinstalled me as a great man in spite of myself.' He offered himself to the public as 'Honest Bob Wilson, a man who is always as honest as the circumstances of a particular case and the public conditions of the country at the time allow.'

Wilson was such a pathetic candidate that even stalwarts like young Otto Macnab could not stomach him, and when the presidential vote was counted, Lamar had 6,995 to Wilson's 252. The Georgia poet was now president, by a landslide, and yet his inauguration turned out to be a sorry affair.

On 10 December 1838, Mirabeau Lamar was prepared to deliver a ringing inaugural speech outlining his plans for the next three years, and supporters like Yancey Quimper were delighted with the rumors that circulated regarding the doughty little man's plans: 'War against the Indians! War against Mexico! Occupation of Santa Fe! Texas is on the move!'

It was assumed by the Lamar men that President Houston, whose nominees had fared so badly both at their own hands and at the public's, would quietly retire from the office which he had occupied with so little distinction, but he astonished them by appearing on the platform in exactly the kind of dress George Washington had worn at his farewell, even to the powdered wig. Then, grasping the lectern with unsteady hands, he delivered a three-hour blistering defense of his conduct and a warning to his successor not to change policies in midstream. At first the audience grew impatient, then restive, and finally, so rebellious that when the tirade ended, poor Lamar folded his grandiloquent speech and passed it along to an assistant, who read it in a confused monotone.

As soon as Lamar assumed the presidency, things began to change in Texas, and fire-eaters like Yancey Quimper felt their day had come: 'No more of that Houston nonsense. Now we fight.' To hear Yancey, one would suppose that the Texians were prepared to march to Santa Fe, Mexico City and anywhere else that came to mind. They were also ready to fight the Cherokee in the east and the Comanche in the west. In fact, if one listened to Yancey, there had never been as belligerent a young nation as Texas.

Lamar himself had more sense. As a poet and a well-read Georgia gentleman, he stated frequently that his first priority was education, and he laid the foundations for the little that Texas was to do in this field, for as one of his supporters complained: 'The Texas Congress is always prepared to pay verbal tribute to education but never prepared to vote a penny toward its attainment.' This was a policy established by General Houston, who was wary of books for the general public, even though he himself treasured the few that had formed his own mind, and who absolutely despised all works of fiction, advising his friends never to bother with them. Texas would for decades speak well of education but not do much about it.

Nevertheless, Lamar kept prodding his people to establish colleges and support free public schools, and many years later, when the state felt it must do something if it wished to maintain its self-respect, it did so in conformance to the ideals promulgated by its poet-president.

Lamar also advocated homestead legislation that would enable Texians to establish their families on public lands, but his greatest contribution was in the world of the spirit, for he expanded Texians' belief that they were a special people, obligated to pursue a special mission. Standing amid the mud-and-dust of Hous-

ton at the eastern edge of his nation, he could see westward to a new capital in
Austin, to powerful future cities like Lubbock and Amarillo, to Santa Fe, which
by right belonged to Texas, and beyond to the Pacific Ocean. And when he
proposed such a vision as the guiding light of his administration, he received
enthusiastic cheers from men like Yancey Quimper, who believed that one day
New Mexico, Arizona and California must fall within the Texas orbit, as well as
most of Mexico and what would later become Oklahoma: 'And Mirabeau Lamar
is the man to see that it happens.'

But once the visionary aspects of his administration had been stated, the little
president launched what might be termed the practical obligations: kill Mexicans,
expel Indians and lure New Mexico into the Texas nation. In pursuit of the first
goal, Lamar dispatched Captain Garner's ranging company back to the Nueces
River, which they crossed on various short expeditions in hopes of catching Benito
Garza. They failed, but they did shoot up several groups of Mexicans and would
have gone after more had they not been stopped by a surprising development
which forced them to withdraw: two messengers from the north rode in to announce that Indians had attacked the republic.

The official messenger was an army officer; his guide was Yancey Quimper, big
hat down over his eyes, his voice quivering with rage: 'Them damned Cherokee
that Sam Houston said he'd pacified . . .'

'What are they up to?' Garner asked.

'Nacogdoches way . . . Uprising . . . People being kilt.'

It was always difficult to ascertain exactly what truth lay behind anything that
Quimper said, but when the officer took over, it was clear that an Indian war was
under way and that the government wanted all companies to converge on Nacogdoches for a final assault on the difficult Cherokee. With some regret, the Xavier
County men started north.

As they rode, the messenger explained the source of trouble: 'An Eastern tribe
—doesn't belong in Texas—was moved west by the United States government.
They argue that they're a nation too, with the right to make treaties same as
England or Spain.'

He said that the Cherokee were led by a notorious warrior, Chief Bowles,
known with respect as The Bowl. He was eighty years old and carried into battle a
sword given him by Sam Houston; it brought him luck, for he had never been
vanquished.

Now Quimper broke in: 'When you were away, President Lamar issued a
proper policy for handlin' Indians: "Get out of Texas or get killed." '

The officer laughed: 'He didn't say it that way. His message to Congress was
"Eviction or extermination." First we'll try to evict them.'

One of Garner's men said: 'Mexicans and Indians, you can't tell the difference.'
And this verdict represented the consensus, for Yancey Quimper said loudly: 'In
Texas they ain't no place for a Cherokee or a Mexican.'

When the riders reached Victoria, Quimper insisted that he accompany Macnab when the latter rode out to visit with Josefina and María, and although Otto took no special notice of this at first, he did later realize that his friend Yancey had a deep interest in the two league-and-a-labor plots owned by the Mexican women.

'Campbell leave any children?' he asked María, and when she said no, he wanted to know how his land was left, and she said firmly: 'It was always my land.' And when he asked: 'What happens to it when you die?' she said forthrightly: 'I have signed it to my brother, Benito.'

'Did Otto's father leave any papers . . . about the land, that is?'

'It was never his land. It was always my sister's.'

'Then it would become Otto's, wouldn't it?'

'Whenever he wants it,' Josefina said with a quiet smile at her son, 'but he told me that General Houston gave him land—up north—for fighting in the war. He said he did not need my land.'

When Otto moved aside to speak with his mother, Quimper hectored María: 'Where's your brother now?' and she replied honestly: 'I don't know. He comes, he goes,' at which Yancey said: 'I'll bet he does.' Later, Otto asked María the same question, and she gave the same answer: 'He comes, he goes.'

'Tell him to be careful,' Otto said. When the company approached Xavier County a scout rode up with devastating news: 'War up north has turned full-scale. Cherokee on the rampage, and they tell us Benito Garza's with them.'

This news infuriated Garner: 'We're down south chasing his ghost while he's up here burning our farms.' It was quite clear from what Quimper kept threatening that if Garner's men ever caught Garza, they were going to hang him within the minute, but Otto argued with them: 'That's only what they say. I know Garza, and he's not messing around with Indians.'

Nevertheless, Otto decided to stay close to Quimper when parleys with the Cherokee began to forestall precipitate action, but this wise precaution proved unnecessary, because when the troop finally reached Xavier County, Yancey discovered that he had important business that would keep him there, so Captain Garner's men rode north without him.

They had barely pitched their tents in Cherokee country when Otto was summoned to a night interrogation by the colonel in command, who asked: 'Son, have you ever heard of Julian Pedro Miracle?'

'I have not, sir.'

'Do you know that we shot him about a year ago?'

'No, sir.'

'And have you heard that we found some very incriminating papers on him? That he was attempting to incite the Cherokee to join the Mexicans? To drive us Americans out of Texas?'

'I did not hear this,' Otto said.

'Well, did you know the Manuel Flores we also killed some time ago?'

'I did not, sir.'

'Have you heard what papers we found on Flores?'

'I've heard nothing, sir.' In the tent the officer thrust a translation in English of the terribly damaging report that the dead Mexican spy Flores had written just before the start of the Cherokee uprising, and they directed his attention to one paragraph:

> I have completed plans whereby the Cherokee will launch a major harassment of the norteamericanos to coincide with the army attack of mexicano troops under Generals Filisola, Cós, Urrea and Ripperdá. At the same time our trusted revolutionary Benito Garza of Victoria will set the countryside ablaze, and we shall expel all norteamericanos and regain control of Tejas.

Otto was shaken, and in the dark silence his mind flashed pictures of the Garza he had known: the bright young fellow trying to find husbands for his sisters, the gifted teacher of riding, that moment of terrible truth when he had saved Otto's life at Goliad, and the swamp knifings at San Jacinto when Otto had reciprocated. During all the chases south of the Nueces, Otto had hoped that the Mexican government would see the wisdom of letting Texas have the disputed land. Then peace between Mexico and Texas would be possible, ensuring peace between Benito and himself. Now he saw his dream was futile.

'I am not surprised,' he told the colonel.

'Is this Garza a friend of yours?'

'My father's brother-in-law. I lived with him for three years.'

The officer in charge of the interrogation breathed deeply. 'I'm glad you admitted that, son, because we knew the answer before we asked the question.' And to Otto's amazement an orderly brought into the tent Martin Ascot, who nodded in Otto's direction and smiled in friendly fashion.

'They arrested me this afternoon.'

'You were not arrested,' the officer corrected. 'You were interrogated.'

'And I told them "Of course Macnab knows Garza" and I told them about the incident in the swamp at San Jacinto when you stopped me from killing him. You see, Otto, they had a letter . . .'

'I saw it. The one they captured when they shot . . . what was his name?'

'Flores,' the officer said. 'Manuel Flores. But that is not the letter Ascot speaks of.'

'Someone who knew you in Xavier County—didn't sign his name—sent a letter,' Ascot said, 'which charges you with complicity in this affair.'

The anonymous letter was produced; its ugly charges were ventilated; and Otto had to deny on the Bible that when he stopped at the Zave Campbell dog-run on the return from the Nueces, he had consorted with the renegade Benito Garza.

'Why did you save his life at San Jacinto? If you knew at that time that he was an enemy?' Silence. 'Well, you knew he'd joined Santa Anna, didn't you?' Silence. 'You better speak up, son. You're in trouble.'

Very quietly Martin Ascot, the young lawyer, counseled his neighbor: 'You must tell them what you told me that evening.'

Standing very straight, the youngest and shortest in the tent, Otto recounted his adventures at Goliad, his surrender, the march out from the presidio that Sunday morning, the dreadful execution of his father, his fight in the woods with the Mexican swordsman, the cut across his face, the gunfire of the two foot soldiers. At the conclusion he said: 'I stand here today only because Benito Garza, under risk to himself, helped me to escape.'

The silence in the tent was overpowering. Finally the officer in charge asked: 'Macnab, what would you do tomorrow if you encountered Benito Garza on the battlefield? These papers prove he may be there.'

'I would shoot him,' Otto said.

Next day the battle was brief, and terrible, and heartbreaking. The Cherokee Nation, which had been so pathetically abused by the American nation, brought eight hundred braves onto a rolling, wooded plain near the Neches River, where they faced nine hundred well-mounted, well-armed Texians led by men skilled in such fighting.

The Bowl, eighty years old and white-haired, friend of Sam Houston and honorable negotiator with Spain, with Mexico, with the United States government and with the emerging nation of Texas, saw through copious tears that any hope of living in peace with these harsh newcomers to his land was vain. Indian and white man could not coexist in Texas, not ever.

Dressing on the morning of 15 July 1839 in his finest elkskin robes and wrapping about his waist the golden sash General Houston had given him as proof of their perpetual friendship, he girded on the silver-handled sword which Houston had also given him, mounted his best horse, and led his men into a battle he knew he could not win.

All that day Texians and Indians blazed away at each other, and at dusk it was clear to General Johnston and Vice-President Burnet that if equal pressure was applied on the morrow, total victory must be theirs. That night the confident Texians slept well, all except Martin Ascot, who had tormenting doubts. Shaking Otto awake, he asked: 'Why can't we find some kind of arrangement to let them live off to one side?' and Otto gave the answer he had developed while chasing Mexicans along the Nueces: 'Texians and Indians . . . impossible.'

'Why?'

'Martin,' Otto said like an old campaigner to a raw recruit, 'go to sleep. We got work tomorrow.'

Next day the fighting was brief, concentrated and brutal. There was a violent chase all the way into another county, where the troops cut The Bowl off from his braves, shot him from his horse and shot him again as he lay on the ground, his white hair caked with blood, his silver-handled sword a trophy to be cheered.

Without their leader, the Cherokee were lost, and well before noon they surrendered. They asked if they could go back and gather their still-unreaped crops, for they had no food, but the victorious Texians said they should just continue north and get the hell out of Texas.

So they went, honorable wanderers who had known many homes since the white men began to press down upon them. East Texas would know its Indians no more, save for one minute enclave.

Mirabeau Lamar's imperial designs suffered humiliating defeats but also enjoyed significant triumphs, proving that although Texas was no supernation, it was more viable than its economic performance might suggest.

The history of his attempt to invade Santa Fe and bring it into the Texas orbit can be told briefly. 14 April 1840: President Lamar drafts a letter to the people of New Mexico telling them of the glories of Texas and warning them that sooner or later, they will have to join up; the letter is ignored by loyal Santa Fe citizens, who are Spanish-speaking and happy under Mexican rule. 19 June 1841: Lamar personally but not governmentally approves of a convoy of twenty-one ox wagons, with military support and a contingent of 321 eager settlers, which sets out to take over the government of New Mexico. 5 August to 17 August, same year: the expedition, having no guides who have ever been to Santa Fe, becomes hopelessly lost and sends out horsemen to see if anyone can identify anything. 12 September, same year: the would-be conquerors stagger in to a remote Mexican settlement and beg for water and help. 17 September, 1841: the entire expedition surrenders to Mexican troops without having fired a single shot or having been allowed to peddle their promises to a single resident of Santa Fe. 1 October 1841: almost all of the Texians are marched to Mexico City and on to the old fort of Perote in the jungle, where they are thrown into prison. 6 April 1842: most of the Perote prisoners are released, but with bitter memories of their mistreatment.

On the other hand, President Lamar's negotiations with powers other than Mexico and the United States progressed handsomely, and in 1839, France signed a treaty recognizing the independence of the new nation, thus assuring Texas of full international standing. England, too, made overtures, and the future looked bright. As for the United States, Lamar perceived it as the enemy and refused either to initiate or to participate in talks leading to annexation.

Regarding Mexico, he was generously prepared to offer either war or peace, but he was not prepared for what his neighbor to the south actually did. Its troops marched across the Rio Grande and captured San Antonio, but fortunately for Lamar, they withdrew of their own volition.

So Texas was not an unalloyed success, but the valor of its poet-president did encourage it to make certain sensible moves, chief of which was the incredible decision to shift the capital from Houston, on the eastern malarial fringe of the nation, into Austin, at the edge of the salubrious highlands. On the day the governmental party surveyed the site for the new capital, buffalo scampered down what was to become the main street.

The intellectual life of the new nation also flourished, thanks to men like Martin Ascot, who took seriously his duties as Xavier County's corresponding secretary of the Philosophical Society. Otto watched admiringly as his friend spent six nights in a row, hunched over the table in the kitchen, drafting by candlelight his first submission to the society, and although Otto could not know it at the time, the resonant success of this paper was to account for an experience from which Otto would profit.

Corresponding secretaries were obligated to report on the 'scientific, agricultural, historical, political, moral and geographical phenomena of their counties,' so Martin chose for his topic 'The Texas Pecan, Salvator Mundi,' and he wrote with such charm that older members said: 'There's a lad to watch!'

He extolled the pecan as a miracle food, a possible source of oil, a tree with unique capabilities and God's particular blessing on the new nation, insofar as native foods were concerned. What was remembered best was the way he harmonized scientific knowledge about its cultivation with his personal reaction to it:

> If corn is our nation's primary cereal and the pecan our finest nut, is it not appropriate that the two be blended in some perfect dish? My wife, Betsy Belle, has discovered a way of doing this in a pie which has considerable merit. Using corn flour and bear grease, she bakes a fine crust, into which she pours a cooked mixture of syrup made from the boiled stalk of the corn mixed with the finest ground corn thickening. She sprinkles the top so richly with pecan halves, lightly salted, that nothing else is visible. She then puts everything in a flat iron receptacle with a cover and bakes it for an hour until all ingredients combine in what I do believe is the most tempting pie in the world.

The country's leaders in Houston were so impressed by Martin's report, and their wives so pleased with Betsy Belle's recipe, that President Lamar gave Ascot an assignment which required work in Xavier, travel to the new capital at Austin and the delivery of papers back to Houston. Martin, who had a case scheduled before Judge Phinizy, completed the work but turned it over to Otto to deliver at government expense.

Otto rode to Austin with Martin's papers, got them signed, and was told that he could take the new stagecoach down to Houston. The firm of Starke and Burgess had been awarded the right to operate a stage between the new capital and the old, and to accomplish this, had imported coaches that had seen decades of service in Mississippi and two drivers with almost as much experience in Alabama. Otto would ride to Houston in the Thursday coach driven by Jake Hornblow, who had a wealth of beard, a brazen voice and a sulphurous vocabulary. When the six passengers were assembled, four men, two women, Jake instructed everyone where to sit, then glared at Otto and said: 'You, fetch the pole and rope.'

'Where are they?'

'Damn it to hell, if I have to tell you people everything, like you was babies, we'll never get to Houston.' Asking around the office, a one-room shack with a heavy iron safe, Otto found the gear, and when he delivered it, Jake studied him contemptuously and growled: 'I was goin' to let you work the pole, but you ain't got the weight to give it leverage.'

It was a scheduled three-day trip, and before it started, Jake assured his passengers 'If this was July or August, we'd get there in great shape,' but it was late March, in the rainy season, and when they were only a few miles out of Austin, Otto learned what the rope was for, because they came to a place where a swollen stream had overrun the road, turning it into a Texas quagmire.

'All out!' Hornblow bellowed, and when everyone was standing beside the mired coach, he threw Otto the rope and told him to take it to the far side of the huge mudhole, but as Otto started to obey, Jake cursed at him as if he were both idiotic and criminal: 'Goddamnit, you stupid horse's ass. You're supposed to tie one end to the coach.' So back Otto sloshed, with Jake heaping scorn on him as he bent down to tie the hitch: 'If you was in the rangin' company, like they say, the Indians have nothin' to worry about.'

Then, surveying the male passengers as if they were members of a chain gang, he nominated one: 'You, take the pole.' This stout lever was rested upon a pile of rocks with one end thrust under the rear of the wagon, whereupon Jake yelled at the two women passengers: 'Yes, you, goddamnit, lean on the pole with the gentleman.' The other men were expected to go into the mud up to their boot tops and push.

In this way, with the horses straining, Otto pulling, the man and the two ladies prizing the rear with their lever, the others in the mud, and Jake cursing God, the rain, the creek and his lazy companions, the coach worked its way through.

The three-day trip took six days, with the rope-and-pole trick being utilized at least four times each day. The cost was fifteen dollars per passenger, not including food, which was invariably cornbread, greasy bacon and weak coffee, three times a day. When the trip ended, Otto and the other men were so outraged by the treatment they had received from Jake Hornblow that they wanted to thrash him, but when they considered his size, they refrained.

The high regard in which Lawyer Ascot was held was further demonstrated when President Lamar appointed him to head a commission with important duties in San Antonio. He was to have in his entourage a company of Texas soldiers and Captain Garner with three members of his ranging company, now known as Texas Rangers. Ascot suggested that Macnab be one, and the party set forth in the late winter of 1840.

As they rode, Commissioner Ascot explained the purpose of the meeting: 'At last the Comanche see the folly of their ways. They want a treaty with us. They propose a wide strip where a truce will be permanently observed, so that maybe now the killings will stop.'

'What did they say about the white people they hold captive?' Otto inquired, and Ascot said: 'If a treaty can be arranged, the Comanche promise to surrender every prisoner they now hold, perhaps as many as a hundred.' This was joyous news, if true, for the idea that savages held white women and children was repellent.

Captain Garner offered verification: 'I was assured all prisoners would be released. We wouldn't talk, otherwise.'

'What are we expected to do?' Otto asked, and Garner explained: 'The army's in charge. They'll give the orders. My job is to deliver Mr. Ascot to supervise the legal arrangements.'

'But what do we do?' the two other Rangers asked, and Garner snapped: 'Obey orders.'

'Whose orders?' Otto asked, for he did not work well in a confused chain of command.

'The army's orders,' Garner said.

When they got to San Antonio and saw what a handsome town it was, so much more civilized than their frontier settlements and with buildings so far superior, they had moments of real delight. The beer was good, the Mexican dishes were new to many of the soldiers, the winter vegetables were a surprising relief from the drab food many of the men had been eating, and there was an air of levity unknown in the grimmer, less settled parts of Texas. It was as if the men had come into another country, one of ancient charm rather than new rawness.

The job of Garner's three young men was to stand watchful guard at the courthouse in which the important meetings with the Comanche were to be held, and they were attentive to the plans the army officer outlined: 'Don't frighten them when they ride in tomorrow. Try to accept them as neutrals. And for God's sake, make no move toward your guns. Just let them come at us, and pray for the best.' When there was a rumble of apprehension, Garner whispered to his men: 'If trouble starts, give 'em hell.' The Rangers nodded, indicating that they understood.

Macnab and his two companions staked out a corner of the public plaza where they could stand by next morning as the Comanche braves rode in with their prisoners. 'They say there may be as many as a hundred white women and children delivered,' Otto told the Rangers, and one asked Captain Garner if he could be detailed to help these unfortunates, who might be in pitiful condition if frontier tales could be believed, but the captain pointed to a small building in which the women of San Antonio would care for the captives.

'You stay where you're put,' Garner said with unexpected sternness, emphasizing the seriousness of this assignment.

That night an old scout who had prowled the frontier with Deaf Smith told the young army men who the Comanche were:

'They came to Texas late, maybe 1730, not much sooner. Come down acrost the prairie from Ute Country. Mountain Indians movin' onto the plains. And why? Because they got theyselves horses, that's why. Yep, when them mountain Comanche got aholt of some good Spanish horses, they went wild. Now they could ride a hundred mile for buffalo, two hundred to find and burn a Mexican rancho.

'They took no prisoners, except women and children as slaves. Well, they did keep the eight or ten strongest men alive temporary. Me and Deaf Smith had a pact. "If'n I'm wounded and cain't ride and the Comanche is comin' at me, you got to shoot me, Deaf." And he said "Same with me, Oscar."

'Well, when they hit Texas, about 1730 like I said, they like to tore this place apart. Terrified the other tribes that didn't have horses. You know how the old-timers was scairt of the Apache? The Comanche treated the Apache like they was nursin' babes, that's how they treated the Apache.

'These is the savages that now say they want a treaty with us. You know what I think? I think it's all a trap. Tomorrow in that building and out here on this square somethin' terrible's goin' to happen. With Comanche it always does.'

Apparently Captain Garner and his army superiors had the same fear, because about midnight Garner told Macnab: 'Tomorrow may be touch-and-go. If at any time I rush out that door waving this handkerchief, I want you three to dash in, right past me, guns ready. No Comanche is to escape alive . . . that is, if they start something.'

There was great excitement that Thursday morning, 19 March 1840, when from the west the awesome Comanche rode in, for they were ghostly figures from some gruesome fairy tale. Taller than the Cherokee, thinner, with hollow cheeks and deep-set eyes, they wore battle finery that made them seem even more imposing, and by some trick they kept their horses stepping nervously sideways, as if the animals, too, were aching for a fight.

But there was also the gravest disappointment, for when the troop of about sixty-five neared the entrance to the town, it was obvious that only one captive was being led in, a girl of about fifteen whom someone recognized as Matilda Lockhart, captured two years before. When people saw her pitiful condition, sobs of the most deep and painful grief welled up, and many had to look away as she rode silently past.

The Comanche were led by an elderly wizened chieftain named Muguara, veteran of a hundred raids and killings, but one now apparently desirous of peace. Looking eagerly about, like a scout on the trail, he studied each element that faced him in San Antonio as if to satisfy himself that he was not heading into an ambush, and when he felt that the meeting could proceed, he signaled his women to remain behind, guarded by most of the braves, while he, twelve others and an interpreter dismounted and marched to the council house, almost dragging the mute Lockhart girl with them.

When he brought her into the room where the negotiators waited, with Commissioner Ascot prepared to offer clemency if only peace could be established, the Texian delegation gasped and one man clutched Ascot's arm: 'Jesus Christ! Is that a human being?' It was a fair question, for when Ascot moved forward to give her comfort, the girl quivered like some tortured animal and looked at him with wild, uncomprehending eyes.

It was with difficulty that Ascot prevented a break right then, but with great fortitude and holding back his own tears, he counseled patience, reminding his negotiators that they were dealing with savages who would have to be tamed by time, and he took the Lockhart girl, who would have been an attractive young woman had she been allowed to grow up on her ranch outside of San Antonio, and delivered her to the women waiting in the adobe house where they had hoped to welcome at least a hundred more. When they saw her, they began to weep, and the Rangers outside heard their cries of rage.

'Let's go in and get them now,' one shouted, but the others calmed him, and the soldiers waited, fingering their guns.

With the dreadful evidence of the Lockhart girl removed from the council house, it was possible to start serious discussion, but first Ascot and his team had to know the whereabouts of the other prisoners. However, when they asked, Chief Muguara lacked the English words for a conciliatory answer: 'Not my prisoners. Other tribes. You pay enough, you get them.' Then he added a most unfortunate phrase: 'How you like that for an answer?'

Even Ascot, who had vowed not to be unnerved by anything the Comanche did or said, blanched: 'Interpreter, tell Chief Muguara that he and his dozen warriors will be our prisoners until he arranges for the other captives to be brought in.'

The interpreter, knowing that such an ultimatum must mean war, shouted the words in a jumble, then bolted through the door, right past Captain Garner, who stood guard, and shouted to the Indians in the plaza: 'War! War!'

Garner, recovering from the shock of having the interpreter knock him aside, waved his handkerchief, at which Macnab and half a dozen others dashed into the council hall, where a general melee had erupted. Otto arrived just in time to see one of Muguara's braves leap upon Ascot and drive a long knife into his heart. The astounded commissioner gasped, and with blood gushing from his mouth, fell dead.

This so enraged Macnab that he began firing coldly at any brave who could be separated from the white men, and the room became a miasma of gunsmoke, screams and death. Macnab and others kept firing with relentless accuracy, and within a few minutes all thirteen of the Comanche inside the hall were dead.

Outside, in obedience to army commands, the soldiers stationed about the plaza killed thirty-five more Comanche before the others fled. Six white men lay dead.

It was a ghastly affair, a ghastly mistake, and it terminated any efforts to bring about peace with the Comanche. Captain Garner and his men saddled up to join the army in pursuit of whatever Comanche tribes might be in the vicinity. They came upon campfires recently abandoned where corpses testified to the fact that the Indians, enraged by their betrayal in the council house, had savagely executed all their white prisoners.

Macnab came upon one site where the rampaging Comanche had assaulted a Texian ranch; two wagons had been placed beside a fire, their tongues projecting over the embers. To the tongues, face down, had been lashed the living bodies of the men running the ranch, and the wagons had been adjusted so that the men would slowly burn to death.

'Well,' Otto said, 'Martin met the Comanche.'

That happened in March, and for the next five months the Comanche retreated deep into the plains, tricking the Texians into believing that the massacre had been so devastating, there would be no further raids.

But two days before the August moon, one of the largest bands of Comanche ever gathered for a single raid assembled well west of San Antonio, and under the leadership of skilled chiefs, prepared to spread fire and terror across Texas. Cunningly, they slipped past military outposts, keeping well to the north of Gonzales, and fell with great fury upon the unprotected town of Victoria. They captured the entire town, burning and raping and killing. Corpses were scattered about, and more than two hundred horses were herded off. On they went, down to the little town of Linnville, where Finlay Macnab's Baltimore wife had landed with her two daughters, and here, at the edge of the sea itself, they rampaged unmolested all through the day, burning more, killing more, and stomping in fury at the

shore as certain clever townspeople took refuge in boats, standing well out into
the bay without food or shelter until the savages departed.

With these two incidents—the shooting of the Indian chieftains during a parley at which they were supposed to be protected by the white man's code of honor,
and the burning of Victoria and Linnville—the Texians spoke no more of rap-
prochement with the Comanche. War of annihilation was seen to be the only
recourse, and it would be fought with terrible intensity by both sides. In 1850 the
slaughter would be appalling; in 1864, when the whites were engaged in a great
civil war of their own, with their men assigned to distant battlefields and unable
to protect their homes, the Comanche would ride right into towns and set them
ablaze; in 1870, the same; and up to 1874 this terrible war would continue. Along
the frontier Deaf Smith's rule prevailed: 'Never let a Comanche capture you.
Better you shoot yourself in the head.'

When Otto Macnab heard of the disaster at Victoria he had to assume that his
mother's unprotected home, and his aunt María's as well, must have been assaulted, so he sought permission from Captain Garner to ride down to see if the
women had survived, and the captain said: 'Sure, but watch out for stray Comanche.'

So Otto rode south from Xavier County, and as he approached Victoria and
saw the desolation spread by the Comanche six days before, it became clear that
only a miracle could have saved the Garza women.

When he reached the Guadalupe River and started down it toward Victoria he
found only burned-out ranches: Around the next bend, I'll see it. And when he
made the turn he did. The two houses which had known so much love between
Texian and Mexican were gone. The drying corpses of the two women still lay
under the hanging oak, where they had fled to escape the lances.

I better bury them, Otto told himself matter-of-factly, but digging in this hard,
clayey soil had never been easy, and he had to be satisfied with very shallow graves
indeed. But you could call it Christian burial, he thought.

That evening he bunked in one of the houses in Victoria that the Comanche
had not burned; the man in charge told him: 'Señor got himself killed out in the
street. Señora, she's with the other family.' He said it would be all right if Otto
stayed there and he even helped prepare some beans and goat's meat, but Otto
could not sleep, and at about nine he told the man: 'I think I better go back and
say goodbye.' The man insisted upon joining him, just in case, but Otto said: 'No,
it'll be all right. They've gone.'

He rode slowly back to the ruins, giving no consideration as to what he might
do when he reached them. The Comanche moon, as it was called in these parts—
that bright full moon which encouraged the Indians to raid—was waning, but it
would remain a crescent in the sky until morning, enabling him to see once more
the landscape he had loved so much when he first came to Texas: the silent
Guadalupe, that first important stand of trees after the bleak marshes of the shore,

the gently rolling hills that gave the land variation, the oak tree from which Zave
. . . Suddenly he became aware that someone else was near the tree.

'Who goes?' he called, readying his pistols.

'Amigo' came a strong Mexican voice. 'That you, Otto?'

From behind the oak, his own pistols at the draw, came Benito Garza, who had
ridden north from the Nueces Strip to pay homage to his sisters. Standing quietly,
he pointed with a pistol to the new graves. 'You bury them?' he asked in Spanish.

'I did,' Otto said.

Slowly the two men lowered their pistols and moved closer.

'What brought you?' Garza asked, still in Spanish.

'You hear about the big fight in San Antone?'

'Those Comanche can be bastards,' Garza said, still in Spanish.

'Why are you speaking Spanish with me?'

'I don't speak English no more,' he said in English, and after that explanation
he used the language no further.

After they had found rude seats on the blackened remnants of a wall, Otto
asked: 'If you think the Comanche are such bastards, why did you work with the
Cherokee, against us?' Garza was late in replying, so Otto said: 'We found papers
on the dead spy Flores . . .'

'Is he dead?'

'On his corpse were these papers, they named you as a principal. We have
orders, I suppose you know, to shoot you on sight.'

'Are you going to try?'

'Why side with the Indians? Will you be partners with the Comanche next?'

Garza laughed, freely, easily. Punching Otto on the arm, he said: 'You try
making friends with the Comanche. Go ahead, try.'

'They sure raised hell here,' Otto said.

'What will you do with your land?' And Garza pointed west toward where the
Macnab dog-run had once stood.

'It was never our land, Benito. It always belonged to your sisters.' There was
silence for a moment, then Otto reached out with his boot and kicked at some
blackened clods: 'It was your sisters' land. And now it's yours.'

'Your government will never let me have it. Me fighting on the side of Santa
Anna.' He ignored his later conspiracy with the Indians.

'I'm sure they will,' Otto said. 'We want to forget the battles.'

'You don't want it?'

'I have no use for it. They gave me land up on the Brazos. For bein' a hero, I
guess.'

'You norteamericanos got your revenge at San Jacinto.'

'You heard, I guess, Santa Anna went free. Used our good money and rode
back to Washington in style. Talked with the American President and all that.'

'You have not heard the last of Santa Anna,' Benito predicted. 'He'll be back.'

'And you'll be with him?'

'The moment he issues his grito.'

'Who will he be fighting?'

'You bastards, who else?'

'And you'll fight with him . . . against us?'

'Certainly.'

Otto pondered this a long time, then said slowly: 'You saved my life. I saved your life. We're even, Benito. Next time we meet as enemies. Draw fast, because I'll kill you.'

Garza laughed easily: 'Little boy, I taught you all you know. I can handle you.'

'But you taught me very well, Benito. Next time . . .'

They parted. No handshake. No farewell words of the affection each felt. Over the graves of the women they had loved they parted, each believing that Mexicans and Texians could never share this land.

When Otto returned to Xavier County he was a forlorn young man, bewildered by the tragedies that had overwhelmed those he loved: good, bountiful María and Josefina, slain; Martin Ascot, most promising lawyer in the nation, killed in San Antonio; Betsy Belle and her infant child adrift.

By the time he reached Xavier he had concluded that it would be improper for him to continue living in the shed at the Ascot place, for although he was five years younger than Betsy, his continued presence could cause comment, and this he would not allow. But when he came to the shack and started to collect his few belongings, Betsy said: 'What in the world are you doing?' and when he explained, she burst into robust laughter: 'People might talk? Otto, I'm trying to run a farm. I'm trying to care for a baby. I need help. I need you.'

Sometimes when he took a side of venison in to Campbell to barter for things like flour and bacon, he was aware that the townspeople did talk in whispers, just as he had expected, but one day the schoolmaster, Reverend Harrison, stopped him as he was passing and said: 'Son, you're doing God's work in succoring the fatherless child. Take Mrs. Ascot this basket of food my wife cooked.' When Otto thanked him, he added: 'But, son, if you continue to live there, I do think you ought to marry. It's the only decent way.'

Such advice caused Otto greater confusion than any he had previously known; even the death of his father had been easier to fit into the grand scheme of things, because fathers traditionally died sooner than their sons. And right there, in that simple statement, resided the source of his confusion.

'She's so much older!' He was barely eighteen, Betsy Belle twenty-three, but she was also a mite taller and had always looked upon him as a child. She was a woman wise in the twists and turns of the world, and mature enough to be his mother, a role she had adopted from the start. How vast the difference between them seemed, not only to him but also to her.

So he continued to live in the cramped shack he and Martin had built, and sometimes in the evening after an arduous day of work, he and Betsy would sit and talk about the future, and one night she said: 'You must start looking for a wife, Otto, and I must find a father for my son.' He was staggered by this bold statement, then listened as she ticked off the local girls whom he might reasonably court. She even went so far as to invite one of them to visit, and the three spent a long Sunday afternoon getting acquainted, and it was obvious that the young woman liked Otto. The visit had one salutary outcome: Otto no longer feared that Betsy Belle might be interested in him as a husband.

The presence in Texas of a widow of good character who had a son to raise became widely known quickly, and one morning a fine-looking gentleman from Nacogdoches appeared at the Ascot cabin to introduce himself. He was from Mississippi, he was a widower, he had a farm and a daughter, and he had brought with him two extra horses in hopes that Mrs. Ascot would consider riding back with her son and her family goods. He was a pious man, a Baptist, and said: 'I'd not contemplate this, ma'am, unless we was married proper before we started,' and Betsy asked: 'How did you know about me?' and he said: 'Your father,' and he showed her a letter:

> Jared, my beloved daughter Betsy Belle is a widow in Xavier County, Texas. If your sorrow over the death of your Norma has subsided, as God always wants it to, ride down and make Betsy's acquaintance, with my blessing.

At the wedding, held in Reverend Harrison's school, Yancey Quimper served as best man, and when Joel Job asked in his resonant voice: 'Who gives this woman in marriage?' Otto said: 'I do,' and it was on his arm that Betsy Belle approached her new husband.

For some days Otto lived alone in the Ascot cabin, now shorn of its warmth and liveliness, and he spent the time brooding about the inescapable manner in which the world turns, bringing day after night and the passage of months and years. He knew almost nothing about girls or women and had been astounded when one of the Rangers on a night ride in pursuit of bandits told him that 'a woman can have babies only so long, you know, and if she misses her chances, she misses.' He had never spoken to Betsy Belle about this; indeed, he had been completely embarrassed that Sunday when she invited the girl to visit, but he now supposed that she had ridden north to Nacogdoches so soon after the death of her husband because she felt the passing of the years and the limited time she could expect on a frontier like Texas.

'And what of me?' he asked in the darkness.

He was diverted from such mournful speculation by the eruption of another presidential campaign in which the men at Quimper's Ferry were determined to prevent Sam Houston from returning to power. There was much loud talk about emasculating the old drunk, and one evening when Yancey had himself imbibed rather heavily his cronies persuaded him to pen a vitriolic attack upon Houston's morals, courage, thievery, treason and bigamy. When Houston refused even to acknowledge having read the widely publicized assault, Yancey was goaded by his friends into challenging Houston to a duel. Had he been sober, he would not have dared.

Houston handled the Quimper affair with that sense of the ridiculous which characterized so many of his actions. Informed by his partisans that Yancey, now sober, was paralyzed by the anticipation of a duel in which he was likely to be killed, Houston sent him a letter which treated him as a serious opponent. Widely circulated, its ludicrous nature not only delighted Houston's rowdy partisans but also provided serious ammunition for those sober citizens who were determined to end this murderous folly of dueling:

> My dear Yancey Quimper,
>
> I have before me your challenge to a duel. My seconds will await yours and we shall fight at the spot and time they elect. Since I am the challenged party, I shall demand horse pistols at five feet.
>
> However, I have been much challenged of late and at present have twenty-two duels scheduled ahead of yours. I calculate that I can fit you in about August of next year. Until then, I am your humble servant,
>
> Sam Houston

Allowing and even encouraging a brief spell of hilarity—'Horse pistols at five feet, they'd blow each other's guts out' and 'Who can imagine Sam Houston being anybody's humble servant?'—he put a sudden stop to it and began speaking of Quimper as if the latter were an authentic and dangerous duelist. This achieved two purposes: it brought public attention back to the absurdity of dueling, and it created the image of President Houston dealing courageously with a hazardous opponent.

He abetted the rumor: 'I'd be damned lucky to escape that duel with Quimper. He's a killer. At San Jacinto he was a savage, nothing less. Quimper would do me in.'

When Yancey heard this assessment he did not appreciate what Houston was doing; and when no one took the trouble to explain, he actually began to believe that Houston was terrified of him, and as time passed he further convinced himself that had the duel taken place, he would have dropped the big drunk. He could see Houston appearing at dawn, badly inebriated, shooting wildly, then crumpling under the devastating fire of Yancey Quimper.

Free Texas being what it was in those wild days, many citizens were tricked by Houston's game, and in time it was credibly reported that the duel had taken place, that Houston had reported drunk and had fired but missed, and that Quimper, gentleman to the end, had deliberately fired in the air rather than kill a former president of Texas. Yancey was now not only the Hero of San Jacinto but also the Man Who Shamed Sam Houston in the Duel.

With this fresh-minted glory, Yancey felt encouraged to take a step popular with Texians: he awarded himself a military rank, and since he was now famous for two different acts of gallantry, San Jacinto and the duel, he made himself a general, and as soon as he had done so, an amazing transformation occurred. He stood taller. He shaved his ineffectual mustache. He sent away to New Orleans for a uniform with a decided French swagger, and he discarded his big slouch hat in favor of a smaller one with a neat cockade. He also began pronouncing final g's as if he had been to military school, and referred often to West Point without actually claiming that he had enrolled there.

When General Quimper learned that his friend Judge Phinizy was scheduled to hold sessions in Victoria County, he left the inn, explaining: 'I have some legal work to clean up.' By paying assiduous attention to all property law passed by the Texas Congress, he had learned that the ten thousand acres of choice land along the Guadalupe River—called the Wharloopey by many Texians—once owned by the dead Garza women was in jeopardy, because their brother Benito, who should have inherited it, had proclaimed himself to be an armed enemy of the nation, and had thus forfeited any right to own land in it.

The case that General Quimper brought in the Victoria court was so complicated and long-drawn that Judge Phinizy had no chance of unraveling it, but when the court was not in session Yancey explained the complexities to him. He also attended court in his new general's uniform, which lent dignity to his claims, and when he encountered any members of the huge Garza clan who were defending their shadowy rights against him, he was immaculately courteous, as if his only interest in the suit was to see justice done and the land distributed equitably.

In a series of decisions so perverse that no sensible man could have explained them, and certainly not Judge Phinizy, who handed them down, General Quimper achieved ownership of all the Garza lands, and then, as a result of additional suits equally intricate, he was awarded a further twenty-two thousand acres, the courts invariably transferring title from indistinct Mexican owners to this very real Hero of the Republic who obviously knew Texas land law better than the judges and certainly better than the original owners.

Thousands of acres which had once been owned by Trinidad de Saldaña were now passing quietly into the hands of enterprising Texians like General Quimper, until in the end more than two million of the best Nueces acres would be so 'verified,' as the Texian judges explained, or 'stolen,' as the owners complained.

The lands did not always pass quietly. When Benito Garza heard of the theft of his acres by Quimper, he led a daylight raid boldly into the outskirts of Victoria, where with the help of sixteen dispossessed men like himself he gunned down a Texian who could be considered a sheriff, so once again the ranging company had to be sent to the Nueces.

When Otto returned, with three more Mexican bandits to his record, he sat alone in the Ascot kitchen, staring at the wall. At any sound he whipped about, hoping it was Betsy Belle returning with her child, and after several such incidents he realized that it was the baby he really missed. How proud he had been to serve as its father when it cried for attention. A wolf howled, and he leaped in frustration: God, I've got to do something.

Thousands of miles from the new nation, in one of the many German principalities, historical events were painfully forging a solution to Otto's problems. The Margravate of Grenzler was in trouble. Not only did economic crisis grip the Rhineland, but a frightening surplus of population inhibited the normal functioning of society. Young people could find no homes and older ones no employment; Germany itself remained divided because no central power had yet arisen strong enough to force consolidation. There was talk that perhaps the sturdy kingdom of Prussia might provide leadership, but only the sanguine could hope for this, because each petty ruler like the posturing Margrave of Grenzler held jealously to his ancestral rights, refusing to accept leadership from anyone more powerful or more intelligent.

In the old days—the 1100s, for example—Grenzler had played such an honorable role in defense of the area, standing like an impregnable rock at the confluence of rivers down which invaders from the east must come if they sought to attack established centers like Cologne and Nuremberg, that its stubborn ruler was given the title Margrave, and although justification for continuance of this august honor had long since vanished, descendants of those ancient heroes clung to it.

On a spring day in 1842, Ludwig Allerkamp, forty years old and the father of four, prepared to leave his bookbinding shop at Burgstrasse 16 in the capital town of Grenz for an interview he dreaded. As if to exacerbate his anxiety, his wife came to the door to remind him of his duties: 'Keep in mind, Ludwig. One, two, three,' and to illustrate her points she ticked off the numbers on her fingers, which she folded back into her palm as she counted.

Ludwig was extremely fond of his wife, Thekla, and he did not interpret her reminders as heckling. No, she was simply bringing to his attention once more the perilous condition into which the Allerkamp family had fallen, so as he strode along the principal street of the town toward the rude castle at the far end where the Margrave himself lived, he lined his two children before him and kept his eye on them, using them to tick off his duties the way his wife had dropped her fingers.

One, he told himself as he looked at his son Theo, aged twenty, I must insist that he have the right to marry. Two, my daughter—this was Franziska, aged thirteen—must be allowed entry to the school. That took care of his children; he himself was the third obligation: I must have more salary for tending the castle library. I really must. Good God, we're near to starving.

He was not exaggerating. Across the German states and especially in the cold northern areas, a series of unprecedented winters had produced successive crop failures, making food so scarce and costly that families were fortunate if they ate two meals a day, because sometimes they ate none. It seemed as if the entire system had broken down; farmers could not produce enough, and what little food they did bring into town, they could not sell because people had no money. A tedious barter system had developed, much as the peasantry had operated four hundred years earlier, and there was constant grumbling.

'We must be very polite to everyone,' he warned his children. 'Not only to the Margrave but also to the Gräfin, and especially to the bailiff, for who knows, he may be in a position to influence decisions.' He spoke with almost a classical ring to his voice, for he had attended two universities, Jena and Breslau, as had his father and grandfather before him. He had hoped to attain a professorship and was more than qualified, but the present depression had begun just as he finished his studies, so no positions were available. At first he had tried teaching in the town school, but the pay was so miserable that no man could even dream of getting married.

About this time he met Thekla during a walking tour through the countryside west of the capital, and once he saw this woodland sprite, blond and lively and with a voice like a woodthrush, he knew that they must marry and earn their living as they could. Never had either of them regretted this hasty decision; despite privations, they had enjoyed a good and loving life, and on the meager salary he earned as a bookbinder, plus what he had picked up from doing casual jobs, they had raised their three boys and then grave, beautiful Franziska. It had been worth the struggle, more than worth it, for both husband and wife felt blessed a hundred times, but now they were close to starvation.

As he approached the castle, a stubby stone building whose outer walls dated back to the 1300s, he took a deep breath, surveyed his children's dress, and tugged at the bell cord. After a few moments a bailiff opened the big brass-studded door, and looked down his nose as the intruders entered an anteroom whose walls were made of unfinished rock and whose floor was paved with massive slabs of polished stone.

A door opened, and into the waiting room came the Gräfin, as she was called in deference to her family position before marriage. She had once been a great lady, but now her sixty-year-old face was painted like a girl's, and she wobbled as she swept forward, faced Franziska, and imperiously extended her right arm.

Franziska did not know what to do, nor did Ludwig, but after a moment of their agonizing indecision the bailiff pinched the girl painfully on the arm and whispered hoarsely so that even the Gräfin could hear: 'You're supposed to kiss the hem of her dress.' This Franziska was most eager to do, but as she bent forward the bailiff pushed her heavily on the shoulder, whispering again: 'Stupid, you must kneel,' and in his roughness he forced the child down onto the stone pavement, from where she grasped the hem of the great lady's gown and brought it to her lips, as all women in Grenzler were obligated to do when presented to this august personage.

But that was not the end of the affair, for when Ludwig saw the burly bailiff smiting his daughter, as it were, he lost his temper, slapped the man's hand away, and said impulsively: 'Do not strike my daughter.'

The Gräfin, who was embarrassed by nothing, saved the day. With a tinkling laugh that drew attractive wrinkles across her heavily powdered face, she said: 'He wasn't striking her. Simply teaching her how to respect her betters.' And she stalked off, to be seen no more.

The bailiff then led them out of the reception hall and into the throne room, a vaulted affair with rock walls and on a dais a heavy chair occupied by an imposing ruler. Margrave Hilmar of Grenzler was in his seventies, a big man with a red, puffy face, white hair and bushy muttonchop sideburns; for almost fifty years he had dominated this castle and the surrounding lands. As a youth he had been to Heidelberg, had lived for a while at the court of Bavaria, and had risen to the minor rank of colonel in the army of one petty German state or another. He enjoyed reading and had developed an affinity for the clarity of Schiller, whom he considered vastly superior to Goethe, who tried to encompass too much in his poems. He had dabbled in astronomy and had even purchased a small telescope with which he entertained his guests, for it was just powerful enough to show the moons of Jupiter, a sight which he still considered unbelievable.

He was in some ways an enlightened monarch, but his territory was so small and in recent years so poor that he could accomplish little. He believed that the stringent measures advocated by Prince Metternich had saved Europe from turmoil, and he would have been astounded had one of his subjects told him that Metternich was one of the sorriest forces ever to hit the Continent. Each year that the Austrian's reactionary policies prevailed, principalities like Grenzler fell deeper into despair. There are many things in this world worse than an orderly revolution that turns tables upside-down for a while, for in such violent periods men still eat and marry and think great thoughts and rearrange their prejudices and launch new ventures; and one of the worst alternatives is a deadly hand of repression which inhibits all forward motion and stifles all adventure. Ludwig

Allerkamp and his son were about to experience the soured and withered fruit that grew upon the tree cultivated by Metternich.

'Excellency, my son Theo comes before you seeking permission to marry.'

As Ludwig prepared to assure the Margrave that his son had found a proper girl in one of the ruler's subjects, the daughter of a well-regarded family, the Margrave raised his hand to stop discussion, and when there was silence he asked the two questions which at that time ruled Germany: 'Has he a house into which he can take his proposed bride? No? Then he cannot marry.' And when this was settled he asked: 'Has he a job which pays a living wage? No? Then certainly he cannot marry.'

Ignoring the father, the ruler turned to face the son: 'This is a harsh decision I must render, but throughout Germany the rules are the same. No house, no job, no wedding.' Before either of the Allerkamps could protest, he added, in an almost fatherly tone: 'But we can hope that as the years pass, conditions will relax. Maybe you'll find work. Maybe a house will fall vacant. People die, you know. When that happens, come back and I shall gladly grant you permission.'

Now, hurting inside, Ludwig pushed his daughter forward and said, pleadingly: 'My wife and I wish that an exception could be made for this child. She should be in school, learning her numbers and music and—'

The Margrave nipped this line of nonsense quickly: 'In this land we do not educate ordinary young women.' He would discuss the matter no further.

So Ludwig, almost crushed by now, launched his third futile plea: 'Excellency, I work long hours in your library, taking charge of accounts, seeking new works for your inspection, rebinding your most valued editions, and many other duties. I do most urgently request a larger salary from you, most urgently.'

Now the Margrave really hardened, because this was an attack on his generosity. In his own mind he had never really needed Allerkamp's assistance and had employed him in one trivial capacity or another merely because he was educated and pleasing to talk with; however, in recent months he had detected in his librarian's comments slight traces of instability.

'If you are unhappy with the terms of your employment, Allerkamp, it can be terminated.'

'Oh, no!' Ludwig cried with obvious terror. 'Oh, please, Excellency!' He groveled, and both he and his children knew he was groveling.

The Margrave seemed to enjoy it, for he pressed on: 'I can think of six young men in this town who would be most happy . . .'

'Please!' Ludwig begged, and the interview ended. But as the bailiff was leading the Allerkamps from the castle, Ludwig suddenly told his children to return home without him, ran back to the throne room, and threw himself upon the mercy of the Margrave: 'Excellency, I beg you, allow us to emigrate.'

As soon as that fearful word *emigrate* was spoken, the slouching Margrave stiffened, his hands gripped the griffin armrests, and he rose to an impressive standing position. 'Never speak to me of leaving Grenzler. We need you here.'

Ludwig, realizing that once broached, this vital subject had to be pursued logically regardless of how angry the Margrave might become, forged ahead: 'Excellency, I have four children, and only one house to leave one of them when I die. What are my other three to do if they can find nowhere to live, no place to work?'

'God will provide in His own mysterious way.'

'But if you would allow us to go to America, as you did Hugo Metzdorf . . .'

'Worst mistake I ever made. We need men like him working here.'

'But if my sons can find no work . . .'

'Allerkamp!' the old man shouted in real irritation over being goaded into revealing his true reasoning. 'Grenzler, and Germany, need your three sons. We could be at war with France tomorrow, or with Russia, or with that unreliable fellow in Vienna. We never know when we shall be attacked.'

'But if my sons can't marry, if they can't work . . .'

'They can do the noblest work allotted man, fight for their homeland.'

'Their country orders them to fight for it but will not allow them to live?'

'Talk like that will get you into grave trouble.'

'But Metzdorf writes from Texas . . .'

The mention of this short, memorable word *Texas* infuriated the Margrave, because there circulated throughout Germany in these years many enthusiastic accounts of travel in the western portions of the United States, with special emphasis on the advantages of settling in Texas. Most impressive was a book which the Margrave had acquired in 1829 for his own library: Gottfried Duden's *Report on a Journey to the Western States of North America.* Even the Margrave had been so excited by its roseate evidence and reasonable arguments that he had in his first flush of enthusiasm committed the error of allowing a dozen of his Grenzler families to emigrate, but when he realized that he was losing valuable manpower, he called a halt.

There was another impetus to emigration, perhaps the most insidious and long-lasting of all: thousands of young Germans had been beguiled in recent decades by an American book that had enjoyed not only public acceptance but also circulation among the knowing, who read it, savored it, dreamed about it, and discussed it with their friends. It was James Fenimore Cooper's *The Last of the Mohicans,* which extolled the frontier and gave a flashing, exciting portrait of life among the Indians. In a score of cities and a hundred small towns young men referred to themselves as Uncas or Leatherstocking or, especially, Hawkeye. The Cooper novels evoked a powerful dream world, but letters from Germans who were actually living in Texas made that dream such an attractive possibility that thousands of young people in the little states sought to emigrate. When denied official permission, they formed a slow, clandestine movement of escape, peopled by those whose hope of a good life in Germany had been killed by repression and hunger. Quietly, without even informing their rulers or obtaining proper certification, they began drifting toward the port cities of Bremen and Hamburg, dozens at first, then hundreds, and finally, thousands.

It was this seepage of young men who might be needed to fill uniforms that infuriated the princes, and now the Margrave thundered: 'You mentioned the Metzdorf I allowed to emigrate. Let me tell you, Allerkamp, the police are fully aware that he keeps sending seditious letters to someone here in Grenz, and they also know that the letters circulate, exciting people to go to Texas. The police keep a careful record of everyone who reads those letters, and they stand in the gateway to prison. And if you're not careful . . .' With this gratuitous advice the Margrave dismissed his librarian, and when Ludwig left the castle he carried with him the harsh realities of life in a German state, which he reviewed as he walked across the causeway over the moat: The Margrave cannot provide his men with homes or jobs, but he clings to them for manpower in case of war. How immoral.

He was pondering this irony when he passed the bookshop of his neighbor Alois Metzdorf, and since they were in related businesses, he stuck his head in the door and asked: 'What's the news?' Something in the way he did this, perhaps the obvious hesitancy of his stopping, alerted Metzdorf: 'What's the matter, Ludwig?' and although Allerkamp was still in the street, he started to talk. With confidences he would never before have shared with the bookseller, he told of his disastrous meeting with the Margrave, and when he was through, Metzdorf said: 'I have a letter you should read. It comes from my brother Hugo in Texas,' and he pulled the bookbinder into his shop, while a policeman far up the street took note of this latest visitor.

'What an exciting letter!' And when he passed it along, Allerkamp's hands almost trembled as he turned the flimsy pages covered with small, precise gothic script, and his breathing almost stopped as he focused on particular paragraphs which arrested his attention:

> No matter what they tell you, Alois, rattlesnakes leave an area which is well tended. I have not seen one in six months. And mosquitoes which are so dreadful along the shore of the sea do not molest us here . . .

> I assure you that there are a million wild horses to be caught and tamed if one has the patience, but we buy ours from Mexicans, who are superb at this skill . . .

> Melons, squash, beans, potatoes, cabbages of immense size, rutabagas, beets, celery, onions, radishes, peaches, pears and corn, we have them all in abundance. Venison, beef, mutton, pork we enjoy every week, but fish we do not have as yet . . .

We do not bother with a church or the ministrations of a clergyman because we have such strong memories of their having been the agents of the Margrave back home, but we do go to the English minister for our marriages, which should always be entered into with God's blessing. In daily life we are our own priests . . .

Land is available in vast quantities, millions of unclaimed acres. It is waiting for you when you come . . .

Night after night we go to bed exhausted from hard, manly work. Bohnert who was a poet in Grenzler builds furniture, the best in this area. Hoexter who wanted to be a professor in Germany is a farmer in Texas. Your friend Schmeltzer who trained to be an engineer is a grower of sheep and cattle, and a good one. And I who was to be a professor am a farmer of more than five hundred hectares. How the great wheel of the world changes in its revolutions.

I will tell you one thing, Old Friend. Sometimes at night my heart breaks in longing for Grenz, the good food, the singing, the winter fires, prayer in the church. And if you join us, as I pray you will, your heart will break too in its hunger for the old ways, especially in December and January when there is no snow on the ground. But there is a greater consolation. Here you will be free. No Margrave, no thundering minister, no conscripting officer from the regiment. You will be free, and, Alois, that makes all the difference . . .

Carefully Allerkamp refolded the letter and handed it back to Metzdorf: 'Powerful statement. He certainly seems to be happy in Texas.'

'Every letter, he begs me to join him. I don't think Hugo would deceive me.'

Allerkamp reached out and tapped the letter: 'So you accept what he says?'

Metzdorf looked about his shop and whispered: 'Every word. My brother would never deceive me.' Ludwig nodded, for the two men wanted to believe that a refuge like Texas existed.

'But,' Allerkamp warned, 'he says nothing reassuring about the Indians.'

'Ah!' Metzdorf cried. 'He said that in his last letter,' and he produced an earlier, well-thumbed epistle in which Hugo had said explicitly:

I know you must be apprehensive about the Red Indians. They have long since left these parts, and I myself in all this time have seen only three or four who came here to trade. They were much like the Poles we saw that day in Grenz, different in speech, different in coloring and appearance, but ordinary men otherwise. I myself have traded with them and thought nothing of it.

After studying this letter, Allerkamp started toward the door, wildly excited by the visions of Texas both epistles had reawakened, but before he could leave, Metzdorf said quietly: 'I have this new book from Paris, and I want you to read it.' And he took from a hiding place beneath his counter a small, unimpressive book which had been smuggled across many borders: *Poems* by Heinrich Heine, the Jewish exile. It was not a crime to have a book by this unpleasant man, but copies were confiscated when found and persons who had read them were noted by the police.

Allerkamp, like most Germans of his type—men who had been to university as had their fathers and grandfathers—adhered mainly to the great poetry of Goethe and Schiller, whom they revered, and few had any acquaintance with the renegade Heine, but they had heard rumors that he was an impassioned poet with much to say, so that they were naturally inquisitive as to his message. Also, the fact that he was Jewish lent his poetry an added aura of mystery, for such men knew few Jews and were alternately repelled by them and fascinated.

'Listen to what he says about us:

> 'And when I reached St. Gotthard Pass
> I could hear Germany snoring,
> Asleep down below in the loving care
> Of her thirty-six rulers.'

'Do the police know you have this book?' Allerkamp asked.

'No, no, but I want you to read it. Heine has a lot to say to us.'

'Will you try to join your brother in America?'

Metzdorf made no reply. He simply forced the book into his friend's hands and led him to the door. When Ludwig left the shop he looked up and down the main street, but the policeman was gone.

That evening Ludwig Allerkamp assembled his family and said gravely: 'Franziska, fetch the Bible.'

The quiet little girl, her two pigtails bobbing beside her ears, went to the bedroom, where she lifted the heavy brassbound Bible and carried it to her father. He opened it to Psalms, from which he read regularly to his brood, and asked each member of the family to place a hand upon the sacred book. This was a curious, meaningful act, for in recent years he had grown increasingly impatient with the church, which sided always with the government and invariably against the interests of its parishioners. In fact, Ludwig Allerkamp, like most Germans who were contemplating emigration, had begun to drift away from the stern Lutheranism of his youth, for he found the church repressive and unresponsive. Yet still, in any moment of crisis, he turned instinctively to the Bible.

'Swear that you will repeat what we are about to say to no one, absolutely no one.'

Six right hands shared the open pages of Psalms. Six voices took the oath.

'The question before this meeting of the Allerkamp family—shall we, with or without permission, leave Germany and go to Texas?'

No one responded. Each member of the family visualized such evidence as she or he had heard and each weighed the awful consequences of the decision to be made. Thekla the mother recalled the two earlier Metzdorf letters she had read telling of life on the prairie, and all that she had heard reassured her that only in some such refuge could her four children find freedom. She was prepared to brave the dangers of the ocean crossing, the mosquitoes and the rattlesnakes, if only she and her offspring could build good new lives, and all negative considerations were abolished, even her fear of Indians. Her eldest son, Theo, who so desperately wanted to marry but who had been sentenced perhaps to perpetual bachelorhood by the stern laws of Germany, was eager to do anything to escape. He would emigrate tomorrow and would say so when invited to speak. Brother Ernst, aged eighteen, had for some years imagined himself to be Uncas, striding through primeval forests, and was most eager to undertake such adventure. Brother Emil, sixteen, was prepared to go anywhere, and the more Indians, pirates and gold-seekers en route the better.

That left Father Ludwig and Franziska, and their preferences were more tentative than those of their kinfolk. Ludwig loved Germany and even though prevented from entering his chosen profession of teaching in some university, he felt a burning desire to stay and witness the unfolding of German history. He felt his homeland to be on the verge of great accomplishments; perhaps a unification of the hundred petty states, perhaps a release from the strictures of Metternich's oppression, perhaps a bursting forth of the German spirit into brave new worlds of industrial expansion and revitalized universities. He was extremely optimistic where Germany was concerned and foresaw the gradual disappearance of anachronisms like the old Margrave. But he was also cruelly aware that his family must somehow survive the period of transition, and he saw no likelihood of accomplishing this under current circumstances. His persistent fear was that Germany would engage in a revolution which would accomplish nothing but which would surely engulf his three sons, for they were lads of strong opinion and firm character, not likely to remain aloof from such vibrant movement. Hugo Metzdorf's most recent letter from Texas strengthened his resolve to seek refuge there immediately.

Up to now, Franziska had rarely participated in family discussions of any gravity, for she was a carefully nurtured girl who had been taught to sit properly, never intrude on a conversation, and respect the instructions of anyone older than herself. But she had a most lively imagination and a sharp perception of what was occurring about her, and her family would have been surprised at the accuracy with which she assessed their motives and anticipated their actions. Encouraged by her brother Ernst, who wanted to roam with Uncas, she had read *The Last of the Mohicans* and seen pretty quickly that it was largely romantic nonsense; also, several reports in the German press, inspired by rulers who were determined to keep their subjects at home, had told of great dust storms, hurricanes, Indian attacks and the prevalence of rattlesnakes in Texas. Unlike her brothers, she had read books sponsored by the rulers and written by Germans who had emigrated to Texas, only to return home on the first available ship:

> Texas is a dreadful place. The food is inedible. The houses have no windows. Paved floors do not exist. A strange disease they call El Vomito kills people within a week of landing. Indians and rattlesnakes prowl behind the barn, if a man is lucky enough to have a barn. Do not come to Texas. I tried it and lasted only one week. How passionately I kissed the deck of the good German vessel that carried me back to Bremen.

She was therefore not at all eager to leap into such an adventure, but when she remembered how her brother Theo had sagged when the Margrave said 'You may not marry,' she could look ahead to the mournful day when it was she standing before the ruler seeking permission to marry some young man of Grenz, only to hear the harsh words 'You may not,' and she knew that her only salvation was emigration to some free land like Texas.

She also recalled how her plea for an education had been denied, and she became angry: 'We should go,' and when her small voice uttered these words a flood of comment was loosened, and the Allerkamp family, aware of all the terrors mental and physical which threatened, decided that as soon as the opportunity presented itself they would quietly slip away from the beloved Margravate of Grenzler, with or without legal permission, and make their way through whatever dangers to the wharf at Bremen, where they would offer themselves as emigrants to a better land.

When the unanimous decision was reached, Ludwig asked them to place their hands on the Bible again: 'On our solemn oath we speak to no one.' And when this was agreed, he told his children: 'I want you to study these poems of Heine again. He's a Jew, and his work is outlawed, but he speaks like a golden trumpet,' and before passing along the book he read from it:

> 'Time passes on but that château
> That old château with its high steeple
> It never fades out of my mind
> Filled as it was with stupid people.

'That's what we're exchanging, the stupid château for the free forest.'

'Will you be a bookbinder there?' Franziska asked, and her father said: 'No. They'll have no need of bookbinders in the forest.'

'What will you do?' the girl asked, and before her father could respond, Ernst-Uncas cried: 'He'll shoot deer and make moccasins.'

'We'll certainly have a farm,' Ludwig said. 'But I'll find other work, too.'

'What kind of work?' Franziska asked, and he replied: 'We'll have to see.'

They all agreed later: 'It was a miracle.' And in a way it was a twofold miracle, because the very next day a wanderer from the north came to town and passed along the main street, stopping everyone and asking: 'Do you wish to buy paper which entitles you to free land in Texas?'

In various ways a large supply of scrip issued by the Republic of Texas had found its way to Germany, and each certificate entitled the purchaser to acres of land without further payment. Half the paper for sale consisted of legal documents circulated by Toby and Brother of New Orleans to encourage immigration, and this carried certain complexities regarding surveying and court procedures, but the other half were bounty warrants issued to veterans of the war, and this gave immediate title to three hundred and twenty acres, provided only that an official surveyor could be found to identify and map the land chosen. It was supposed that the surveyor would receive for his services one-third of the land so identified, unless the holder of the scrip wished to pay a fee in cash.

Ludwig Allerkamp, a cautious man, suspected chicanery in such an offering and would have nothing to do with the paper, regardless of which form it took. Some did buy, however, for modest sums, and it was here that the second miracle occurred, because the mayor of the town bought six certificates—four Toby, two soldier bounties—for a modest sum, only to find that the police were taking down the names of all holders: 'Nothing illegal, Mayor, but the Margrave wants to know who's been dabbling with the idea of emigration.'

'Not me!' the mayor lied. 'I have no papers of any kind.' And to make this assurance viable he quickly hurried to the bookshop of Alois Metzdorf, known to be an agitator, to whom he confided in a jumble of whispers: 'These papers . . . the police inspectors . . . In my position as mayor, you know, there's nothing wrong, you understand . . . but in my responsible position as mayor . . . Here, you take them, they can do you no harm.'

As soon as the mayor left, Metzdorf slipped out the back door and ran through alleys to the home of Allerkamp: 'Ludwig, it's providential! I know you want to go to Texas, and someone I can't name just gave me six certificates for land there. I can't emigrate yet, but . . .'

The conspirators stood silent, and slowly Metzdorf pushed the sacred papers into his friend's hands. No one spoke, and then in a rush of gratitude Allerkamp embraced his friend: 'Alois, I'll hold the best fields for you . . . till you come.'

In this way the lands of Axel Vexter, veteran of San Jacinto, found an owner.

To help the Allerkamps make decisions, Alois Metzdorf loaned them *A Practical Guide to a Wealthy Life in America,* in which sixteen German families advised newcomers as to how they could strike their fortune in the New World. It advised travelers as to what they must take for areas such as Pennsylvania, 'the most hospitable of the States and the most like Germany'; Missouri, 'the State with the most attractive free land and the greatest opportunity for getting rich'; and Texas, 'the most exciting land, an independent nation now but likely to become a part of the United States.'

'We shall need tools, and medicines, and all the clothes we can carry,' Ludwig said after studying the recommendations.

'Books?' Thekla asked, and here her husband had to make painful choices: 'Our Bible, Goethe, Schiller, the book on agriculture.' By curious choice, upon which the family would often comment in later years, he added: 'It'll be a practical land. I'll take along my two mathematics books.' These would prove to be more useful, ultimately, than all the others, but it would be the books of poetry that would echo most strongly and persistently, for they represented the soul of the Germany they were leaving.

When the secret packing was completed and hidden away so that guests could not see, the Allerkamps invited into their home for the last time the members of a singing group with whom they had known so much enjoyment, and when the various families gathered that last Sunday afternoon, the four strong-voiced Allerkamp men led the others in songs that had echoed through the town of Grenz for centuries. Ludwig had a strong baritone and Theo had a clear, ringing, high-voiced tenor, with the two younger boys filling in nicely; others of the group had fine voices too, and the air was rich with music. But Franziska saw that as her mother played the accompaniments, tears filled her eyes, and the child knew that she was saying farewell to this splendid piano over which both mother and daughter had studied so diligently. No more would this instrument guide them in song, and the realization that a glorious part of her life was ending was almost too painful to bear.

They sang till midnight, and in some mysterious way, without a word having been spoken, it became apparent to many of the older people that a requiem was being sung. Some profound change was under way; someone was departing; some new force was arriving; some secret aspect of Germany was being modified; but if certain canny men suspected what Allerkamp was up to, they did not reveal it.

Accepting what money they could get from a surreptitious sale of their possessions, they slipped out of town before dawn one Wednesday morning and slowly made their way toward the port of Bremerhaven, negotiating one passport and customs barrier after another. They moved from one petty kingdom to the next, where the rulers of each tried to prevent the entry of refugees from other principalities, lest they become squatters and a financial drain, but Ludwig, by means of cajolery, lies and even small bribes, maneuvered his caravan across half of Germany, coming at last to the busy city of Bremen, some distance from the harbor from which the ships sailed. Here he reported to the offices of the Atlantic and Caribbean Lines, which owned two sailing vessels plying to Texas, the *Poseidon* and the *Sea Nymph*. Captain Langbein, in command of the latter, assured the Allerkamps that they had chosen wisely and that he would personally oversee their pleasant trip across the Atlantic. Since his ship would not be departing for nine days, he directed the family to lodgings utilized by his firm and then extended them the courtesy of his home, where Frau Langbein proved to be a gracious, motherly lady and a superb cook.

'The captain wants me to serve you the best food,' she explained, 'so that you'll get homesick and sail back to Germany some day with him. That way he earns double fares.' She said that she had sailed once with him to Galveston: 'I was seasick, but it passes quickly. I loved the voyage, and would go tomorrow if he'd allow me.'

As guests of the Langbeins the Allerkamps attended two operas in Bremen, Mozart's *Figaros Hochzeit* and Weber's *Der Freischütz,* and the emigrants showed such appreciation of the robust singing that Captain Langbein volunteered advice: 'Take plenty of music with you. It tames the wilderness.'

'We'll have no piano,' Thekla explained, but he was insistent: 'There will be many pianos in Texas. You'll find one. And then you'll be sorry you didn't bring music for it.' This posed a problem, for the family had only the most meager funds, with not a pfennig to spare for luxuries, but as they prowled the back streets, seeking bargains, Thekla came upon used scores of Beethoven and Schubert and a collection of Mozart piano sonatas, and they were so reasonable that she cried: 'I cannot cross the ocean without them.' But when Ludwig approached the owner, even the reduced price was forbidding, and he was about to lead his family from the shop when to his amazement Franziska intruded: 'Sir, we are sailing to a far land and we must have the music.'

The man stooped till his face was level with hers, and asked: 'But can you play Mozart?' and she went stiffly to a piano, adjusted the stool, and began to play with youthful skill the Mozart sonata in C major—known as the 'Easy Sonata'—with such grace that he cried: 'Buy the Beethoven and Schubert, and I'll give your little princess the Mozart.'

Next day the Allerkamps sailed for Texas.

It was not till the rickety, swaying *Sea Nymph* reached midocean that Franziska Allerkamp felt well enough to make her first entry in the diary she had acquired in Bremerhaven:

> *Monday 31 October.* This ship is a leaky tub. It is tossed about by every wave. There's not enough water and the food is horrible.
>
> To save his leaky ship, Captain Langbein had all men passengers operate the pumps twenty-four hours a day.
>
> I have thrown up so much that I can no longer be sick. How pitiful man is upon an ocean like this.

Despite the inconveniences of shipboard life, Franziska found ways to care for her appearance, combing and braiding her hair each morning and doing everything possible to present the picture of a well-bred German lass. Her neatness was remarked by many, and several older women, when they were well enough to move about, congratulated Thekla on her daughter's cleanliness: 'And charm, too. She's a fine child.' Since Franziska secretly coveted such approbation, she took extra pains, and inevitably some of the young men began to pay attention, but her mother, obsessed with creating in Franziska a model German girl who could sew, play the piano, cook, and observe what Thekla called 'the niceties,' quickly disciplined the would-be suitors: 'No, she cannot sing with you. And she certainly can't walk the lower decks, either.'

> *Wednesday 9 November.* Grandmother taught me always to be neat and Grandfather warned me many times: 'You must smile at young men, to show them respect and make them feel important, but you must never flirt.' I don't think I would care to marry before twenty-one, because the village girls who did so and who then came in to Grenz were never happy. I could tell from looking at their long faces that they yearned to join our dances in the town square, but with babes at the knee they could not.

Obedient to her mother's standards, she had stopped being a young girl and had already become a poised little woman. As she moved about the upper decks she avoided conversation, preferring to listen to others, but on the rare occasions when she did speak she could be quite firm. Sometimes when she eavesdropped, which was not very ladylike, she picked up bits of information that confused her:

> *Saturday 10 December.* Mother and Father did not think I was listening, but I heard the elders discussing Captain Langbein, whom I like very much. A man who lives in Texas but had business in Germany told them

that Captain Langbein has a wife in Texas, as well as the one in Bremen whom I met and liked so much.

I am worried about this and would like to ask Mother whether it could be true, for if it is, Captain Langbein must be a very bad man, which I find hard to believe.

Two days later, as they were approaching Cuba, a storm more violent than any they had known in the European seas overtook them from the east, throwing their pitiful craft about as if it were a cork adrift in a whirlpool. Nearly everyone was wretchedly sick and often too weak to stagger from the cabins, but Franziska, one of the few able to stand, volunteered to clean up the smelly messes.

She had no inclination to feel sorry for herself because Captain Langbein, in obvious distress, called for all men to return to the pumps, and for three perilous days, 21 December through the night of 23 December, she knew that all four of her family's menfolk were toiling in the bowels of the ship, straining at the powerful German pumps, but almost to no avail, for an incredible amount of water continued to stream in through the many cracks, and toward midnight on the twenty-third, Ludwig staggered topside to speak with his wife: 'Thekla, if anything happens, look first for Franziska. The boys and I will have done all we could.'

At about four that morning the frail ship plowed headlong into a huge series of waves which swept a sailor and two passengers overboard. Their screams were heard briefly, then only the howling of the terrible wind. Thekla, in the cabin, was sure the ship must come apart under the dreadful strain, and so did her husband at the pumps. But these towering breakers marked the end of the violence, and by sunrise on 24 December the Caribbean had begun to subside, so that when Christmas Eve approached, a weak sun actually appeared through the clouds.

> *Sunday 25 December 1842.* We had a quiet Christmas. Father took me down into the ship, and when I saw the holes through which the sea came at us, I wondered why we did not sink. I was not afraid during the storm, because I kept busy helping the women with children, but to-night I am terribly afraid. I know this ship cannot last much longer, and I think Father knows it too. And from the look on Captain Langbein's face, he knows it better than any of us.
>
> I no longer care if he has two wives. He was very brave during the storm, always taking the wheel when the waves were worst. When I marry I would want my husband to be much like Captain Langbein, but I would not be happy if he took another wife, too.

When the limping *Sea Nymph,* her backbone almost shattered by the storms, staggered into Matagorda Bay, all hands cheered. But the sudden onset of a howling wind from across the bay prevented them from landing that day:

> *Monday 2 January 1843.* After breakfast this morning we finally landed, and it was lucky that we did, for although we got quite dampened by the heavy spray, no great damage was done. But when almost everyone was ashore, and I was looking inland to see our new home, one of the young men who had been nice to me cried in a loud voice 'Jesus Christ!' And all of us turned to look back at the sea, where our *Sea Nymph* rolled quietly over and sank.
>
> Captain Langbein swam ashore, and when he joined us he said 'For the past two weeks I thought we'd probably sink.' And I asked him what others were afraid to ask. 'Did you think so during the bad storm?' And he said 'I expected to go down any minute, little girl.'
>
> This afternoon some of the women told Mother 'The sinking of that ship was God's curse on the Captain for having two wives,' and I thought about this for a long time. Suppose the ship had sunk six days ago, with all of us passengers lost. Would that still have been God's way to punish one immoral Captain? What about us? I think the ship sank because the company took too great a risk in sending out such a rotten crate.

When the six Allerkamps stood with their luggage on the shore of Matagorda Bay, they had no specific idea of where they would sleep that night, or where they would travel in the days ahead, or where they would locate the land on which they would build their permanent home. If ever the word *immigrant* meant *one who comes into a new country,* it applied to the members of this family.

A man who built handcarts with solid wooden wheels approached Ludwig: 'You'll have to have one. Three dollars.'

'Have you ever heard of Hugo Metzdorf?'

'All the Germans have. You can trust him. Lives at a place called Hardwork,' and in the sand the wagonbuilder showed them in general how to find their way first to Victoria, forty miles to the west, and from there to Hardwork, ninety miles to the north.

'Everyone,' Ludwig cried, assembling his family and pointing to the sand, 'memorize this map.' And with no aid but that, the Allerkamps loaded their handcart, tied a rope to the front, put Theo at the handles, and set out, with Ludwig hauling on the rope and leading the way.

It was simpler than it sounded, because even in the earlier days when Otto Macnab and his father traversed this route, there was a kind of path to Victoria;

now it was a dusty road. From there, another rough-and-ready trail led north, so there was little chance of getting lost. But to walk a hundred and thirty miles with a handcart and sleep on the bare ground in January was not easy. However, in due course the pilgrims reached a slight rise, and there they looked down upon a sight that warmed them. It was a replica of a German village, complete with rough stone houses, a central square, and prosperous fields that stretched out to thick woodland.

'It was worth it!' Ludwig cried as he started down the slope, and Franziska asked: 'Is this where we'll take our land?' and her father said: 'We'll find even better.'

Until they located the land they wanted, they would stop temporarily at Hardwork, but they were surprised to find that earlier German arrivals already owned the locations in town and that in the surrounding countryside, for many miles in every direction, the attractive rolling land was also taken. 'I thought,' Theo said, 'that everything was free.'

It wasn't. Hugo Metzdorf, the acknowledged leader of the community, explained that there were millions of acres to which the Allerkamp certificates could be applied, but they were always 'out there,' meaning to the west. The newcomers were assured, however, that their papers were authentic: 'None better than these four sold by Toby and Brother in New Orleans, and of course your two military ones are best of all.'

Metzdorf, who had done a good deal of land selection, ticked off the situation, indicating each paper as he did, and in the end he whistled: 'Three thousand acres in all! You must have paid a pretty pfennig for these!' When Ludwig nodded, Hugo asked: 'You bring much money with you? No? Well, neither did any of us.' He flexed his right arm: 'That's what does it in Texas.'

He advised the Allerkamps to spend their first two years in Hardwork: 'Fine German woman here lost her husband a year ago. She'll rent you a room. Later on, build yourself a shack, not a house like mine. Then look around you, visit other towns, get yourself a horse and ride west, and wherever you go, study the land.'

'What do we do when we find it?'

'Now you have to have some money, because you must get a surveyor. He lines it out proper and files his papers with the government, and then you get title. But you have to pay the surveyor.'

'If we have no money?'

'Customary rate, he takes one-third of the land.' When Ludwig whistled, Metzdorf said: 'I know it sounds high. In your case, a thousand acres, and at eight cents an acre, that's eighty dollars American, and who in Texas has eighty dollars?'

The widowed woman was actually eager to have the Allerkamps share her half-empty house and to sell them a small plot of land, and in a shorter time than even

Metzdorf, an energetic man, could have anticipated, they were at work building not a shack, as he had prudently advised, but a real house—a kitchen and alcoves for beds—and in doing so, they repeated the heroic steps by which all parts of Texas would be settled: sunrise to sunset, work; Sunday, prayers; clothes and furniture made by hand; fields cleared by chopping and plowed by foot-shovels; food, an endless repetition of corn bread, bacon and coffee. But when a family had two energetic elders and four stalwart young people, the outcome was apt to be startling, and in the case of the Allerkamps, it was doubly so. By the end of the second month they had the corner posts of their home in place and all members of the family were learning English from a book they had purchased in Bremen.

Much sooner than they expected they were brought into full citizenship, for in early March a man came to their house riding one horse and leading another. He was a smallish fellow, and he brought a surprising invitation: 'Name's Otto Macnab, Texas Ranger. Trouble along the Nueces River, and Captain Garner of this county would like to have one of your boys join him in an expedition.'

'Is it that we are obliged to?' Ludwig asked on behalf of his three sons.

'Not an order, but if you're going to live in Texas . . .'

'We have only the guns we need for food. No horse.'

'Captain Garner figured that. He sends this horse. Guns?' He slapped the space behind his saddle, and the Allerkamps saw three rifles, plus the two pistols protruding from Otto's belt.

'Can you speak the truth?' the father asked, and before he could continue, Otto said: 'No, you don't have to come, but this is how we protect places like yours.'

'Against maybe who?'

'Mexicans, Indians . . .'

As soon as he heard the word *Indians,* Ernst Allerkamp, the middle boy reared on James Fenimore Cooper, stepped forward: 'I will go,' and it was agreed.

When Otto turned to untie the trailing horse and hand over one of the guns, he became aware of a girl hiding in the shadows, and his eyes wandered from the men and focused on her. She was a small girl, fourteen or fifteen, with flaxen braids and a shyness which manifested itself in the curious way she stood, half withdrawn from the scene, half participating. He could not bring his eyes back to the men and paid little attention to what they were saying about the Indian war; he was riveted by the girl and drank in every aspect of her attractive appearance: her white stockings, her homemade shoes, her dress with that flowery bit about the hem, her belt encompassing her narrow waist, the way her blouse was beginning to protrude, but most of all, her placid face framed by the two braids of golden hair. It was an image, emerging from shadows, that would live with him forever.

For her part, the girl saw a young man not much older than herself, towheaded, blue-eyed, clean-faced, pistols in his belt, homespun clothes and very dusty, heavy leather boots square as a box, never a smile, leading a horse by a bridle that hung carelessly from his left arm, a young man who spoke in a low voice and who stared at her as if he had never seen a girl before. From her place in the shadows she could imagine him astride his horse, riding through rolling woodlands that seemed to stretch endlessly west and south. He was capable, of that she felt sure, and she supposed that he could use his pistols and the rifles that projected from his saddlebag. He was the new man, the man of Texas, and she was fascinated by him, but as a well-bred daughter of a conservative German family, she kept to the shadows.

Neither the young man nor the girl smiled during that first meeting, nor did they speak, nor did they reveal by any gesture other than those endless glances the impression that each had made on the other, but all during his three-month fight in the Nueces Strip the man could think of little else when he rode silently or slept fitfully. And during those same long days the girl saw horsemen galloping across battlefields, or resting beside rivers, or splashing through fords, and invariably this quiet young fellow with the blue eyes and sand-colored hair was in the lead.

When Ernst Allerkamp returned to Hardwork he found his community in an uproar, because a recent immigrant named Pankratz, from the area near Munich, had arrived in town with his wife and two children, had studied the local economy with more than usual intelligence, and had decided that he could make a real profit on his investment if he bought himself a slave. In a town well to the north he found a strong young black man, and the cost was so minimal that he bought the slave's wife as well. With them he would grow cotton, for which there was a permanent demand in the markets at New Orleans.

But when Pankratz brought his two slaves to Hardwork the older residents objected not only strenuously but bitterly, with Hugo Metzdorf and Ludwig Allerkamp stating flatly that slavery was not a condition that the freedom-seeking Germans could tolerate. The Allerkamp boys supported their father, and began circulating among the people in town and those on nearby farms, arguing against the introduction of slavery into the community.

'But it's legal!' Pankratz said with stubborn force. 'It's one of the reasons why Texians fought against Santa Anna. He threatened to take away their slaves.'

'It may be legal,' Ludwig conceded, 'but it is not what Germans who flee tyranny should allow in their new villages.'

Pankratz, believing himself immune to such pressure, housed his slaves in a rude shack behind his well-built dog-run, and proceeded to use them, fourteen hours a day, in the planting of a cotton crop.

'You cannot keep human beings in such a hovel,' Hugo Metzdorf protested formally, but Pankratz pointed out that many German settlers, when they first arrived in Texas, had lived in worse.

'Yes,' Metzdorf granted. 'We did. But we did it voluntarily and with the knowledge that we would soon have better, if we applied ourselves. You intend to keep
your slaves—'

'Don't tell me what I intend!'

Pankratz was an able man who believed that southern Germans were better
educated and more civilized than men like Metzdorf and the Allerkamps, who
had come from a ridiculous place like Grenzler, and he rejected their censure,
insisting that since the Texas constitution protected slavery, he had every right to
utilize his two blacks as he saw fit, so long as he did not punish them in uncivilized ways.

He did, of course, punish them. When they lingered in their work he found it
productive to lash them with a leather strap attached to a stout oak handle, not
savagely or in any brutish manner, but enough to make them realize that if they
abused the freedoms he allowed them, sterner punishment would follow.

When Ludwig first saw his neighbor lash the woman slave across her back and
her thinly clad buttocks, he was outraged and went directly to Metzdorf as head of
the community. They discussed the matter, with great fury at first and later with
controlled bitterness, and the outcome was that one morning when Pankratz had
his two slaves in his far fields cultivating the land prior to planting, Ludwig, aided
by his Ranger son Ernst, went quietly to the Pankratz place and dismantled the
slave shack, hiding its valuable timbers in half a dozen different spots well removed from the farm.

When Pankratz was summoned from the fields by his wife, who had watched
the destruction from her kitchen, he stormed about the village threatening lawsuits and bodily damage to his enemies, but when he saw that the entire community was opposed to his remaining there with his slaves, he put a loud curse upon
the place, sold his land at a loss to Yancey Quimper and moved to Victoria, where
several families owned slaves.

When the ugly affair ended, Ludwig told his children: 'You do not flee from an
evil, and then introduce that same evil in your new home.'

The Allerkamps were constantly aware that the land they now had was not to
be their permanent home; they had those four precious documents which entitled
them to free land in Texas and they intended identifying their homestead and
moving to it as soon as practical. But now they entered upon the heartbreak of
Texas land ownership: the acres were theirs, no doubt about it, but to secure them,
one had to locate a surveyor. Also, the land system was Spanish in origin, using
strange units of measurement and customs not known in Grenzler, so that no man
merely trained in trigonometry could presume to set himself up as a surveyor; he
had first to master the tradition of varas, cordeles and leagues. So a man like
Allerkamp might have entitlement to three thousand acres, but five or six years
could elapse before he located his land or came into possession of it.

'I am consumed with anger over this system,' Ludwig cried one day, for he saw time wasting, with no permanent house built and his family still not established on their own land. Meanwhile he must earn a living and see to it that his three sons earned theirs. Theo wanted a job that paid a good salary so that he could send money back to Grenzler for the ocean crossing of the young woman he had not been allowed to marry.

'I liked that area on Matagorda Bay, where the *Sea Nymph* landed us,' he told the family as they discussed their problems. 'I asked the men there and they said: "This place has got to become a major seaport. We need young men to help build it." I'm going to try.'

The family could not give him money for his venture, but they did share generously their tools and clothing, and there were tears of regret and apprehension as they bade him farewell at the start of his long walk back to that remembered spot in the Matagorda region; soon it would acquire jetties and wharves and storage warehouses and the melodious name of Indianola. Theo Allerkamp would be well regarded by the German ship captains who put in to Indianola, and by the immigrants they deposited there, for he was a man of integrity, and also a man unusually gifted with a high tenor voice, which he would display effectively in the local singing societies. In quicker time than he now expected, he would be able to send for his bride.

Ernst Allerkamp found his occupation in a curious way. When he helped tear down the Pankratz slave quarters his job was to rip off the shabby roof, and during his trip on the *Sea Nymph* he had worked the pumps so diligently that he had become distressed by any structure that leaked. 'What a miserable roof this must have been,' he told his father, who replied: 'No house can be better than its roof. Thatch on German farms. Tiles in German towns. In Texas, they seem to use cypress shingles. Properly cut and nailed, they could be best of all.'

So Ernst had started studying roofs, and although there were few in Hardwork of thatch, for this part of Texas did not produce the necessary low shrubs, there were some houses whose owners tried to utilize sod roofing; it was too heavy and too subject to moisture penetration. He saw only one house that had half-moon tiles for its roof, and he was most favorably impressed, but these had been hauled north years ago from Saltillo and could not be duplicated in Hardwork.

Some roofs, like that on the slave hut, were disgraceful and almost a waste of time; the best they did was to keep out the sun during the blazing summers. To rain they were small impediment. So the more he studied, the more satisfied he became that his father was right, and he told his family: 'I think I could earn a good living from cypress shakes.' When he explained how simple the required tools were and how easily he could master their use, the Allerkamps agreed that he should make the effort. With saw, froe and mallet to flake off the shingles, he moved about the countryside, searching for cypress trees of proper size and testing junipers also, and as he went he stopped in villages and at crossroads to assure the settlers that he could provide them with the best roofs they had ever known.

The more Ernst worked with his shingles, the more clear it became to his father that what the various German settlements really needed was a sawmill. Always a reflective man, he mused: Civilization in a frontier like this is chronicled twice. The date of the first gristmill, so that the people in the houses can eat. The date of the first sawmill, so that proper houses can be built. But to have a sawmill required the importation of expensive equipment from centers like Cincinnati or New Orleans, and then the diversion of some stream or river to provide the waterpower to turn the great wheels that ran the heavy saws.

The Allerkamps had no money for machinery, but as the months passed they were acquiring a reputation for working hard and honoring their promises, so when in the middle of the first year Ludwig came forward with a proposal, his neighbors listened: 'Our family has no money, but we do have men who can work. If you others band together, send a deposit to Cincinnati, and buy the saws and wheel, my boys and I will dig the millrace and build the housing.'

It was a deal, and while the heavy equipment made its way slowly down the Mississippi, the Allerkamps dug the footing for the sawmill building, erected the stone walls, and set the pits in which the great saws would move slowly up and down, producing the planks with which this section of Texas would be built. When the housing was finished, they turned to the laborious task of digging the millrace along which the water from the nearby stream would run on its way to turning the big wheel that would move the saws.

It was work of such strenuous effort that once Emil joked: 'I wish we had those slaves,' and this callous remark caused his father to assemble his family on Sunday for a sharp lesson in civilization: 'It's only natural for someone doing hard work, like digging a millrace, to wish that he could have slaves to do it while he rested. You spoke sense, Emil, when you said that, but we find in history that if a man does the work himself, he gets treble benefits from it. He does it better. He does it quicker. And in doing it, he amasses capital which enables him to finance additional tasks. We learn by doing.'

The Allerkamp women never idled while their men labored; Thekla and Franziska made all the clothes worn by the family, and although they purchased a little cloth, releasing their hoarded money in a most miserly way, for the most part, they spun cotton and wove their own. Depending on the time of year, they always had something to sell to strangers: extra cloth, eggs, deer and bear meat; they also sewed the ubiquitous sunbonnets that became the mark of the Texas woman, and it seemed to Ludwig that half the women in the area wore sunbonnets made by his wife and daughter.

Ernst had been home several weeks following his duty along the Nueces before Franziska found a way to ask about Otto Macnab without using his name or betraying her interest in him: 'Did you fight alone, Ernst?'

'No, we fought as a company. Captain Garner.'

'Did you pair off, each caring for the other?'

Since Ernst had been striving to forget some of the things he had seen, he found this questioning distressful. Reluctantly he replied: 'If a man fell, we all looked after him.'

'Did your company do well? I mean, were all the men responsible?'

'Dirty work, but we were powerful.'

'Did you have a special companion?'

'No.'

'Did the Rangers from Xavier County perform well?' She used a classical kind of speech, learned from her memorization of Schiller and Goethe, and tried to speak in complete sentences.

'We did. That short fellow you met, Otto Macnab . . .'

The magical name had been spoken, and without changing her expression in any way, with her face still turned to the spinning wheel where the cotton transformed itself into thread, she asked: 'Was he brave?'

'Well now . . .' He was still reluctant to speak.

'What?' she asked softly.

'Brave he was. Blue eyes hard as flint.'

'He sounds very brave.'

'He was. But . . .'

'What?'

Memory of a confusing incident came flooding back, and now he wanted to speak: 'We were patrolling north of the Nueces where the Mexican bandits had been raiding, and we came upon a white woman whose husband had been slain. I think she was out of her mind. Anyway, we left one of the men to take her to Victoria while we rode on. At a gallop we overtook three Mexican men. I thought they were farmers, maybe. They didn't look criminal. But this Otto Macnab rode right up to them and started firing.'

He stopped, and after a while his sister asked very carefully: 'You mean, the three Mexicans had no guns?'

He shook his head and could say no more, leaving his sister with the lonely problem of sorting out what had happened and what it signified.

When the Hardwork sawmill came into operation, civilization in Xavier County took a giant leap forward, because now the heads of families could drive their oxcarts to the mill, load up with beautifully sawn timbers—two hundred produced in the time it took two men to saw one in a hand pit—and build houses of real substance. Some of the most beautiful farmhouses in this part of Texas were built with that first flood of Hardwork timber. The German carpenters did not like the rather sprawled-out and formless dog-run of the Georgia and Carolina settlers; they preferred the compact, well-designed two-story house, with cedar or cypress shingles, neat board siding, stone fireplace and chimney at each end, and a trim small porch to provide protection against rain and sun.

Earlier settlers who had lived in Texas for some years warned the Germans: 'Without the dog-run to provide ventilation, you're going to be very hot in summer,' but the stubborn Germans replied: 'We can stand a little heat in exchange for a beautiful house.' Of course, when the summer of 1844 produced a chain of forty days when the thermometer hovered above the hundred-degree mark, the Germans in their tight, compact houses did suffer, but they made no complaint; they simply lay in bed almost nude, sweated inordinately, and rose in the morning gasping for the fresh air which circulated so easily through the dog-runs. Summer in Texas, they were discovering, could be a blast straight out of hell, untempered by any passage over snowy mountains or cooling oceans. Said one old-timer: 'Come July, the devil stokes his furnaces real high, opens the draft, sends the flames to Texas so he can set up headquarters here in August and September.'

During this time of intense heat the Germans did have a respite which they enjoyed immensely, for a messenger rode in from the new settlement at a place called Lion Creek with news that there was to be an informal two-day Sängerfest to which all Germans living nearby were invited.

Any German Sängerfest, even a limited one like this, was a glorious affair, with almost every man in the community participating, as soloists if their voices were exceptional, as part of the humming chorus if obviously inadequate, and as an honorable part of the singing group if average. No women were allowed to join in the singing, of course, nor were they permitted to give the talks on such subjects as 'The Historical Plays of Friedrich Schiller' or 'The Metaphysics of Goethe.' But they did provide the food, and that most abundantly, and the younger unmarried women were the principal reason why many of the men attended, for finding a bride in German Texas was a grievous problem for which there seemed to be no solution, other than sending to Germany for one, as Theo down in the Matagorda area had done.

Of a hundred typical German men, at least ninety-seven, and perhaps even ninety-nine, would marry German women: 'It keeps the bloodlines clean. It keeps out the lesser strains.' It was therefore inevitable that when an industrious, attractive girl like Franziska appeared at a Sängerfest, her dress beautifully embroidered by her own hand, her hair in two neat braids with flowers plaited into the ends, she must attract attention and proposals from the hungry young men. Her father treated each approach with dignity, telling the swain that Franziska was too young to be thinking of such things, but his wife gave the young fellows hope that these conditions might change within the year. Franziska herself said nothing, did nothing. She had not at this time ever been kissed by a man, not even by her father or her brothers, and she felt no desire to be kissed by anyone at the festival.

But if she had never been kissed, and in this respect she resembled many reserved German girls of that time, she did experience a rich emotional life, as revealed in her diary:

> I shall hide this book even more carefully after today, because I must confide to it a thrilling event in my life. I do believe I have fallen in love. Since I cannot discuss this with anyone, I cannot be sure, but there is a young man, from Ireland I think, who once stopped by our house and who has all the qualities I would seek in a husband. He is handsome, though smaller than my brothers, and he has the frankest blue eyes. Ernst assures me that he is brave in battle with brigands, and I learned from Herr Metzdorf that he owns a substantial property. When shall I meet him? And what shall I say to him when we do meet? These questions are important, because I do honestly believe that one day I shall marry him, even if he is a Catholic. What an amazing thing to write!

Her behavior was not exceptional in these years, for the diaries of various German girls would reveal instances in which young women attended Sängerfests year after year, always knowing which of the young men there they would ultimately marry, but never would the two young people speak. They would look, and remember, and fifty years later they would confess: 'I knew I loved him' or perhaps 'I loved her from that first moment.' Germans could bide their time.

The Sängerfest this year provided two grand days of German singing, German poetry and German food, and not even the heavy rains that came at the close of the second day diminished the ardor of these good people who were keeping alive the traditions of the homeland which had treated them so badly but which still commanded their memories. Indeed, the rain became so heavy that most of the visitors from Hardwork had to lay over an extra day, and when they did set forth for home they found that what had been little streams during the trip to Lion Creek were now surging torrents, so they were forced to waste a fourth day till the floods subsided.

As they neared their house in Hardwork, Hugo Metzdorf, his face ashen, came to greet them, and without speaking, thrust into Ludwig's hand a letter just received from Grenzler. When Ludwig finished reading, he passed it dumbly to his wife, who studied it, then grasped Metzdorf's hand and uttered a low sigh: 'Ach, mein Gott!'

The letter said that the secret police had arrested Alois Metzdorf, charged him with treason and thrown him in jail, where he had hanged himself.

Unable to speak to either Metzdorf or his wife, Ludwig walked unsteadily to a rock, sat down and covered his face, overwhelmed by the tragedy. Alois, the dreamer, the one who had really wanted to come to Texas, the man who had given him the certificates. Ludwig had shaken hands with him on the pledge:

'Alois, I'll hold the best fields for you . . . till you come.' He retched, for a horrible suspicion assailed him: 'Alois Metzdorf would never commit suicide. Visions of freedom kept that man alive. My God! They hanged him in his cell.'

His hands fell to his lap, and when Thekla whispered: 'Ludwig, we must go,' he was unable to move. Stricken by grief over the death of his old friend, he could only sit there and mumble acid verses of Heine. In the depth of his despair, and in his sorrow for the German people, he understood as fully as any man might the meaning of emigration, its terrors, its relief, and the wonder of finding after long struggle a new life in a new land. Had he been invited at that moment to occupy a castle in the Margravate or any other German principality, he would have refused. He was in Texas and he loved every rolling hill, every relentless heat-filled day.

In a rush of enthusiasm like none he had known before, he decided that the Allerkamps must immediately utilize their certificates, and with the aid of a surveyor, stake out their own farm. To their relief, a man said to be an expert in such matters arrived at this crucial time to inform them that he knew a surveyor who would locate land for them if their papers were in order. When the certificates were presented, he said: 'Everything fine. Your land is on the way.'

When they met the surveyor, a thin small man from Alabama who chewed grass stems, he laid the situation honestly before them: 'We find the land together. We mark it off together. I build three-foot piles of earth and rock at each corner, and then you stand in the middle and dance up and down, shout to the four winds, and fire a gun two or three times to inform the world that this is now your land. For my fee I get one-third, so since you have certificates for six parcels, I'll just take these two and you have yourself two thousand acres, more or less.'

It seemed so simple, with the surveyor assuring them there would be no other costs, that the Allerkamps in family session agreed, and Ludwig said when the deal was closed: 'We'll have our own land. We'll work for ourselves.' They further agreed that they would apply the four certificates they still retained to some choice land in the northern part of Xavier County, not on the Brazos, for that was all taken, but not too far inland. Franziska was quietly excited when she realized that the land her father was speaking of would place her close to where Otto Macnab had his property; they had not yet spoken, but she was decidedly interested in being near him.

Unfortunately, the Alabama surveyor was a scoundrel. Immediately after obtaining possession of the Allerkamp entitlement of a thousand acres, he sold it to another man and was never seen again in that part of Texas. When Ludwig and his son Ernst tried to recover their certificate, the buyer went before Judge Phinizy and proved that he had obtained it not from the Alabama surveyor, because had he received stolen goods he would have to return them, but as a finder's fee from Allerkamp direct, in which case the land pertaining to the certificate was certainly his.

When Ludwig heard this decision, typical of hundreds then being handed down by the Texas courts against immigrants and Mexicans, he was so outraged that he could not for several days even discuss his indignation with his family, but when his fury subsided he assembled them: 'There is much wrong with Texas. The way they treat Indians, the way they own slaves, the way they allow a man like that to steal from everyone. But there is also much that is right; our neighbors represent that goodness. They're still willing to provide us food for the next six months while I study and find our land. I'm going to be a surveyor, and an honest one.'

With that firm decision as a rocklike base, he took out his trigonometry book, associated himself with a man from Mississippi who had mastered Spanish land law, and began the laborious study of varas, cordeles, labors and leagues. 'A vara,' he told his family, 'is exactly thirty-three point thirty-three inches, which means that it's just short of a yard. Texas system, seventeen hundred and sixty yards to the mile. Spanish system, nineteen hundred and one varas to the mile.' He purchased a surveyor's chain of twenty varas and accompanied his tutor on various jobs, during which he learned the rudiments of his new trade. He found that he liked the rough life of tramping across open land; he learned how to shake brush and low shrubs with a warning stick to scare away rattlesnakes; and he enjoyed the closing ceremonies when the new owner stood in the middle of his selection and jumped in the air and shouted to the four winds and fired his gun. At such moments he felt that he had accomplished something: he had helped a man to be free.

On one prolonged survey he was led to a river far to the west, the Pedernales it was called, the River of Flints, and he vowed that when he had his own credentials as a surveyor, he would return to the Pedernales and stake out his claim on the two thousand acres to which he was entitled, paying himself the surveying fee, and then buy as much more as he could afford. He said nothing of this to the man from Mississippi, lest he spread the news that his German helper had found a paradise among the rolling hills and green forests of the west.

For a long period Captain Garner's company of Rangers received no call to duty, because with the Cherokee expelled and the Comanche pushed back from Austin, the only recurring trouble spot was along the Nueces River, and this contested region fell strangely inactive.

'What's your friend Garza doing down there?' Garner asked Otto when they met in Campbell.

'Up to no good, you can be sure of that.'

'Government wants me to make a scout. But it has funds for only three Rangers.'

'I'll go without pay. I go crazy just sitting around.'

'Would you ride down and see if that Allerkamp fellow cares to come along?'

With an enthusiasm which almost betrayed his real purpose, Otto cried: 'Hey, I'd like to do that,' and it was in this way that he saw Franziska for the second time. As before, he remained on his horse, instructing Ernst as to where they would meet, and as he had hoped, the Allerkamp girl stood by the door, watching him intently. She was now a petite, handsome sixteen-year-old young miss whose flaxen hair was wound about her head. Again, neither she nor Otto spoke, but she believed that he was somewhat taller than before and he saw her as infinitely more beautiful.

When Mrs. Allerkamp came to the door to ask in heavily broken English: 'Is it that you would like maybe some drink?' he blushed painfully and allowed as how he wouldn't.

On the way home he rode in great perplexity, for if he had shied away from Betsy Belle Ascot because she was so distressingly much older than he, all of five years, he was now ashamed of himself for being interested so achingly in a child who was obviously years younger than himself. Desperately he had wanted to accept Mrs. Allerkamp's invitation and to sit in the kitchen, perhaps with the daughter, whose name he did not even know, but he had been afraid. However, when Ernst joined Captain Garner for the scout, Otto did contrive a tortuous way of discovering his sister's name.

'Franziska,' Ernst said, and there the conversation ended.

At the Nueces they did not find Benito Garza, and for a reason that would have astonished them. Now thirty-nine years old and, like Otto, still unmarried, Garza was far south of the Rio Grande astride a stolen horse and leading two others acquired in the same way. He wore a big, drooping mustache, which had become his trademark: no waxed points, no fanciness, just an ominous growth of hair which gave his face its sinister look.

He rode in bitterness, a man whose world had fallen apart. It galled him to think that because he fought to retain the Nueces Strip for Mexico, he was characterized a bandit and that notices were plastered along the Nueces River:

$300 DEAD OR ALIVE

THE NOTORIOUS BANDIT

BENITO GARCIA

'They can't even get my name right,' he grumbled as he continued down the dusty road. He thought of himself as a patriot, never a bandit. When he raided in the Nueces Strip, using ugly tactics in doing so, he saw himself, and justifiably so, as a defender of his land, land which his family had occupied long before even the first dozen anglo families had filtered in to Tejas. In recent months he had even revived his vanished dream of becoming Gobernador de la Provincia de Tejas, and he knew that to achieve it he must, as before, depend upon Santa Anna.

When he came in sight of Mexico City his heart quickened, for here he was to meet his hero, the general, and learn from him when the reconquest and punishment of Tejas was to begin.

But when he entered the capital and reported to military headquarters he learned that Santa Anna, now dictator with powers unprecedented, had as so often before left the government in the hands of others while he loafed on his beloved ranch near Xalapa, and Garza showed his disappointment. 'Damnit,' he complained to headquarters, 'I've ridden all the way from Tejas to learn how my volunteers can serve when the new war begins, and I find the commander in chief idling on his ranch.'

A very young colonel, Ignacio Bustamante, related in some way to the politician who served as nominal president in Santa Anna's absence, took him in charge: 'Never speak badly of our president. He has ten thousand ears.'

'I fought for him. I revere him.'

'That's good, because he wants to see you . . . at his hacienda.'

As the two officers rode east past the great volcanoes, Bustamante brought Garza up to date on the doings of their general: 'I suppose you know that a long time ago some high-spirited young Mexican officers stole a few pastries from the shop of a French baker, and when the French ambassador was unable to collect damages for his countryman, France imposed a blockade. Yes, a real war with ships bombarding Vera Cruz.

'Well, you know Santa Anna. Let an enemy touch his beloved Vera Cruz, and he's off like a lion. As the French landed, he leaped on his white horse and dashed into town to defend it. As usual, he behaved heroically and had the great good luck to be hit by a French cannonball, which so damaged his left leg that it had to be amputated. Yes, our noble warrior now has only one leg.'

'How does he get about?' Benito asked, and the colonel explained: 'He has four wooden legs that he carries with him in a leather case, one for dress, one for everyday wear, one for battle, and I've been told what the fourth is for but I forget. Each different, each made of different materials. The one for evening wear is very light, made of cork.'

'You said he was lucky to have been hit by the French cannonball? I don't think losing a leg is luck, even if you have four replacements.'

'Oh! You miss the meaning! You'll not listen to our general speak four sentences in a public oration, and he makes them constantly, without hearing an account of how he lost his leg in the service of his nation. He has fifteen clever ways of casually referring to it. Heroic: "I galloped into the very mouth of the French cannon and lost my leg in doing so." Self-pity, with tears: "In a moment of great danger I surrendered my leg to the glory of my country." Challenging: "Do you think that a man who has lost his leg defending his country is afraid of a threat like that?" His missing leg is his passport to glory.'

When they rode past the grim prison at Perote, where various Texian adventurers still languished in dark cells, Colonel Bustamante began pointing at choice fields and saying repeatedly: 'Santa Anna has acquired this ranch' or 'Santa Anna had this owner shot as a traitor and now the ranch is his.' The dictator owned nearly half a million acres on which roamed more than forty thousand cattle, all obtained at no cost, and Garza, proud of his hero's accomplishments, failed to realize that Santa Anna's stealing of land from peasants was precisely the same as the anglos' stealing land from mexicanos in the Nueces Strip. Nor could he know that the total corruption made popular by Santa Anna was going to become a way of life in Mexico, contaminating government for the next century and a half.

Garza was astonished when he met his hero, for Santa Anna was extremely thin, his face poetically gaunt, his heavy head of hair beginning to show gray. He limped pitifully as he came forward to greet his Alamo lieutenant: 'I lost a leg, you know, defending our nation at Vera Cruz.' He was wearing his country-landowner leg, and before Garza could reply, he reached out, clasped him by the shoulder, and said with unfeigned enthusiasm: 'In honor of the great days, my Gobernador de Tejas, let us see the cocks fight,' and he led the way, now springing along, with no perceptible difficulty, to the small circular building in which he conducted his famous cockfights.

He had invited some sportsmen up from Vera Cruz, each with three or four champion birds, and for three loud and dusty hours the great dictator indulged himself with one of the things in life he prized most, the slash-and-flash of the cockfight when two noble birds, trained to the last degree and fitted with three-inch scimitar blades, fought to the death.

Next morning Santa Anna revealed why he had asked Garza to make the long ride to Manga de Clavo, and to Benito's surprise, it did not concern the invasion of Tejas or even the guerrilla warfare there; it was an imperial concern which no visitor could have anticipated: 'My dear and trusted friend, I seek a guard of honor for a deed of honor. In response to demands from the people of Mexico, and also its religious leaders, I have consented with some reluctance, for I am essentially a modest man, to have my left leg disinterred, borne to the capital, and buried in a pantheon reserved for heroes.'

'Your leg?' Benito asked.

'Why not?' Santa Anna snapped. 'It gave itself in service to our nation, did it not? What leg has ever meant so much to a nation? Does it not deserve the treatment we give other heroes?'

'It certainly does,' Benito said hurriedly, and he was present when the leg was dug up, placed upon an ornate catafalque, and started on its triumphal journey to the capital.

He and seven other lieutenants, men who had proved their worth in battle, were issued special green-and-gold uniforms and horses with silver-encrusted saddles, and they led the procession, clearing the way through villages where entire populations turned out to honor the great man's leg as it made its way slowly past Perote prison, into Puebla, and beneath the noble volcanoes.

Garza and Bustamante rode ahead into the capital, to alert the city that the leg was coming and to ensure that multitudes lined the avenues when it arrived. Thousands turned out, and at the splendid cathedral in the center of town more than fifty priests of various ranks, including a number of bishops, waited to place the leg in a position of honor below the altar. Here legions of the faithful could come and kneel and say brief prayers.

Two days later, with Santa Anna himself in attendance, entire regiments of cavalry in resplendent uniform, young cadets from the military academy at Chapultepec, a solemn procession of priests and religious dignitaries, the entire civilian cabinet and most of the diplomatic corps marched to the beat of seven military bands, leaving the center of the city and progressing to the historic cemetery of Santa Paula, where a cenotaph had been erected to the dictator's leg.

Prayers were said. Chants were sung. Rifles fired. Santa Anna wept. The multitudes cheered. And soldiers such as Benito Garza stood stiffly at attention while flags were draped over the coffin and the leg was lowered into its new and stately grave.

Garza was still in the capital when a vast revulsion against the pomposity of Santa Anna surfaced, and he watched in horror as a mob tore down a gilded statue of the dictator in the center of the city, rampaged through the streets, and cheered when a crazy-eyed leader shouted: 'Let's get that goddamned leg!' From a safe distance Garza followed the frenzied rabble as it broke down the gates of Santa Paula, destroyed the cenotaph honoring the leg, dug up the bones, and dragged them ignominiously through the very streets where they had a short time before been paraded with such majesty. He was aghast when the bones were separated, some going to one part of the city, some to another, and all of them ending in rubbish piles.

Through back streets he made his way to the palace from which the dictator had ruled with such unchallenged authority, and there he found him packing his wooden legs in their case as he prepared for flight. When Garza informed him of events at the cemetery, the great man sat heavily upon a trunk packed with silver objects and sniffled: 'My leg! The symbol of my honor! They dragged it through the streets!' Then, pulling himself up, he hobbled off to what appeared to be a lifelong exile.

As he disappeared in the dusk, Garza swore an oath: I shall drive every norteamericano out of the Strip. I shall ride and burn and kill, because that land is Mexico's, and I shall hold it until General Santa Anna marches back with a great army to reconquer it. He had to realize, of course, that his one-legged hero was nine parts charlatan, but this deficiency was offset by the fact that it was only Santa Anna who stood any chance of defeating the Texians, and he dreamed of the day when fighting would resume.

By the spring of 1845 the varied assignments given the self-taught surveyor, Ludwig Allerkamp, had enabled him to know more of Texas than most of its other citizens, and since he had an innate curiosity and a love of nature acquired from his ramblings in the woodlands of Germany, he perceived relationships which others did not. He saw, for example, that this central part of Texas consisted of five clearly defined strips, each a minor nation of its own.

Along the Gulf, where his son Theo and his wife now had their store, Texas was a swampy flatland inhabited by mosquitoes of enormous size and birds of great beauty. Summers were intolerably hot and damp, but the remainder of the year could be dazzling in its movement of wildlife and the brilliance of its long sunsets. People brave enough to live here tended to love the loneliness, the vast expanses of marshland and the interplay of sea and shore.

Inland came the treeless flats, enormous stretches of prairie populated by wild horses and unbranded cattle. Low shrubs dominated the sandy soil and a thousand acres represented a small field, indistinguishable from a hundred others reaching farther than the eye could see. This was going to be excellent land, Ludwig believed, for the raising of cattle, and whenever he surveyed a segment he assured the new owners: 'Your land will be of great value one day.'

He appreciated most the third strip, the one in which he lived, that mysterious area in which the land began to form small hillocks, the streams wandered easily down twisting valleys and, most precious of all, trees began to appear, cedars, cypresses and four different kinds of oaks, including a small-leafed variety covered with some dead-looking substance of crepuscular character. When he asked about the sickness which attacked these small-leafed trees, he was told: 'Those are live oaks, and that's Spanish moss.' Very quickly the family came to revere the live oak as one of the great boons in Texas.

When the new capital at Austin had to be surveyed, Allerkamp had an opportunity to see at close hand the fourth strip, one of the marvels of Texas, a sudden uprising of cliffs and rocky prominences called the Balcones, which stretched north to south for over a hundred miles, delineating the end of the prairies and the beginning of the hill country. Here trees began to show in great variety, flat plains disappeared, and rivers ran through gorges. The Balcones had no great depth; east to west they were rarely more than half a mile wide, but they formed a remarkable feature which could not be missed. As Ludwig told his family when he returned from his assignment: 'It's as if nature wanted to give a signal: "Here begins a new world!" And she laid down this barrier of great rocks and hills.' He told them: 'Austin will become the most beautiful city in Texas because it lies right on the Balcones, land goes up and down, up and down.'

Now the government assigned him the task of inspecting the fifth and most noble strip, those marvelous, quiet lands which lay to the west of the Balcones. With his two sons, Ernst, home from his service with the Rangers, and Emil, he set out to explore the very best part of Texas, the hill country.

As soon as the three Allerkamps left the capital city they found themselves surrounded by low, wooded hills of the most enchanting variety, graced by exquisite valleys hiding streamlets. The scene changed constantly as they moved westward, now opening out into vistas, now closing in so that they could see only short distances ahead. 'These aren't even what they'd call hills in Switzerland,' Ludwig told his sons. 'Around Munich they'd not be dignified with names, but after the flatlands they seem like mountains. In years to come, I'm sure that people who live back there in the flatlands will rush to these hills for the summer breezes,' and the boys could see a score of places they wished the Allerkamps owned for just such relief when the hot winds arrived in July.

Such speculation about possible homesites was not idle, for the Allerkamps still owned four certificates authorizing them to claim free land. The catch, of course, was that it had to be legally surveyed, but since Ludwig was now an authorized surveyor, he could pretty much select exactly what he wanted in this fairyland so rich in hills and tumbling streams.

It was in this frame of mind that the Allerkamp men came one afternoon upon the Pedernales River, which Ludwig had discovered the year before. In those days he had deemed the river remote, but now it seemed to run only a short distance from the capital, and he and his sons began to speculate on its virtues, and after they had surveyed it for about thirty miles, they stopped at a point where a nameless little creek wandered in to join the Pedernales from the north, and without any discussion they agreed that this was the land they had been seeking since fleeing Germany.

Very quietly Ludwig told his sons: 'Let's lay out an area of ten thousand acres.'

'Our scrip allows only two thousand.'

'We'll pay for the extra.'

'How?'

Ludwig stood silent for a moment, his face in the wind. 'I've been saving,' he said, and in the deep lines of his face his sons could see the endless labor and the deprivation he had suffered to earn his family their land.

'Start stacking rocks at our corners,' he said, and when their new farm was delineated the three men stood in the center, fired their guns, threw rocks and twigs into the air, jumped up and down as custom required, and then yelled at the top of their voices: 'It's ours! It's ours!'

Back in Hardwork, Ludwig reported to his women: 'Our farm will have the big Pedernales running along the south for about six miles, and halfway along comes this beautiful little creek from the north . . . you couldn't call it anything bigger. One stretch of river cuts through a gorge, real cliffs north and south, and everywhere trees, trees, trees.'

'Is it like Germany?' Thekla asked, and her husband replied: 'Well, almost. The trees are farther apart. The land is rougher. The banks of the river are cluttered with debris from floods. And it might be difficult to build only with stone. You could never claim it was Germany, but it will be very congenial.'

'Will there be fields for us to grow crops?' practical-minded Thekla asked, and when the men assured her that with minimum effort large meadows could be cleared for crops, she said: 'It doesn't sound like Germany, but I'm ready.'

This finicky evaluation of their new home distressed Emil: 'I saw deer and rabbits and skunks and so many different birds, I lost count. We have turkeys in the woods and fish in the river, and I'm sure the soil can grow pears and peaches. Father has claimed a paradise for us, and as soon as the papers are cleared in Austin we ought to sell this place and move immediately.' He caught his mother by the hands and danced with her: 'For the hills are beautiful, Mother! They are beautiful.'

When they contacted Yancey Quimper at the county seat they found him most eager to buy their property in Hardwork, and he also offered, in an embarrassing confrontation with the two Allerkamp seniors, to take their daughter Franziska off their hands. The Allerkamp men, who had begun to worry about the future of their unmarried girl, considered his proposal seriously, for as Ludwig pointed out: 'He is well-to-do. He's respected by Xavier County as the Hero of San Jacinto, and he's certainly no coward, for he forced General Houston to back down from a duel. Of course, he's not a German, but . . .'

Mrs. Allerkamp said nothing, but her sons, eager to see their sister married—and to almost anyone—threw reasons at her: 'He's a patriot. He has that profitable ferry. He's strong in debate. And he's . . . well . . . presentable.' When the barrage was at its most intense, Mrs. Allerkamp stared at her daughter, aware that this marriage would be highly improper.

Franziska, taking strength from that silent stare, said no. She gave no reason. Drawing her arms close to her body as if protecting herself from an alien world, she shook her head, uttering only one word: 'No.' She did not say it with any undue emphasis or animosity; she simply rejected her fifth serious suitor and went about her work. She was now an expert spinner and a good weaver; she could sew clothes out of the cloth she made and form rough shoes out of the cowhides her brothers provided. She could also embroider seats for chairs and sew patterns on the dresses she made for herself and her mother. Best of all, she was an excellent cook, specializing in heavy meat dishes for the men and cookies for all festive occasions. These she liked to decorate with colored jellies and thumbprint designs, spending hours of an afternoon to make them works of art as well as delights to the taste. She had prevailed upon her brothers to carve a set of hollowed-out stars and crescents and ovals and zigzags out of oak, and with these she cut her cookies, so that when at last she brought a platter of them to the table, they shone with color and danced in lovely forms and patterns. And she always held the platter on the palms of her hands, as if she were a young goddess of the hearth, presenting her offerings to some pagan statue.

Yancey Quimper took his rejection with good spirit, half relieved that he had escaped the bondage that marriage often became in a frontier community. His failure to catch Franziska did not influence his business judgment, and he offered the Allerkamps just enough to encourage them to sell but not so much that he stood to lose. It was a good clean deal, and when it was concluded, with the two Allerkamp women weeping to think that they had lost a home in which they had known stern obligation but also much happiness, Quimper said: 'I'd like to take possession as soon as possible. I have a buyer in mind.'

So in June of 1845 the five Allerkamps loaded all their goods on two ox wagons and set out for the hill country. When they reached Austin they heard exciting news: 'A group of more than a hundred German immigrants stayed in the settlement at Neu Braunfels. But they wanted their own land. They're planning to move into that area you surveyed. Near the Pedernales.'

Many parts of the hill country, that precious segment of Texas, would be German. Its public schools, among the first in Texas, would use German, and the songs sung by the men's choruses at its great festivals would be German, and fathers would teach their daughters the poetry of their homeland, as Ludwig Allerkamp had taught his Franziska the delicate words that summarized their new life:

> In that exquisite month of May
> When all the buds were breaking,
> I felt within my bosom
> New life and love awaking.

So the German families from Neu Braunfels established the new town of Fredericksburg, which they named after a Prussian prince, and in quick order they built a struggling community in which English was almost never heard. In time it would become a superior town, with stores, watchmen and a good lodging place run by the Nimitz family; at first there was only one meeting house, but it was unique. Octagonal, it was affectionately called 'The Coffee Grinder,' and was shared amicably by all denominations.

The Allerkamps were delighted to have Fredericksburg only six miles from their farm, and even before the town was well started, Ludwig rode in to talk with the elders, purchasing from them a quarter-acre near the Nimitz farm. When the Fredericksburg people asked: 'Are you going to sell your place out in the country?' he replied: 'Not at all. In here we'll have a resting place for the women,' and that is what it became, a tiny house with only one room and a row of beds. Now the Allerkamp women could come to town on Saturday in the family wagon, while the men rode in on horseback early Sunday.

In this way the Allerkamps obtained two homes, one in the country, one in town, while Otto Macnab still had none. In fact, he was about to surrender the homestead he did have, for with the Ascots gone, his only remaining companion was Yancey Quimper, and the more he inspected that man's shady dealings the more convinced he became that Yancey was the kind of devious person with whom he did not care to associate: Life in Xavier County is finished for me. I better get going.

One morning he rode up to the Ferry and surprised Yancey: 'You want to buy my land?' Quimper made no false show of saying 'Otto, you mustn't leave!' Instead, he jumped at the offer, and men lounging at the bar who overheard the transaction said: 'Otto's bein' smart. He cain't farm it hisself and he ain't got no wife to tend it in his absence, so hell, he might as well pass it on to someone as'll care for it.' Quimper, aware of the young bachelor's determination to be gone from these parts, drove a hard bargain and got the spread for sixteen cents an acre, and before the week passed he had sold it to immigrants from Alabama for a dollar-ten.

When Otto learned of the outrageous profit Quimper made, he merely shrugged, for he had lost interest in the land. Rootless, he drifted about the county seat, accepting the hospitality of Reverend Harrison at the school, but when Captain Garner rode in one morning with the news that Company M was being reactivated, Otto quickly volunteered, for he wanted something tangible to do. It was as if he realized that his destiny was not a settled home but the wild, roving life of a Ranger.

During the time when Otto was stumbling about, trying to find a home, the young nation of Texas was doing the same: it was bankrupt, it owed tremendous debts; in Mexico, General Santa Anna, magically restored to power yet again, refused to acknowledge that Texas had ever separated from Mexico, and there was violent talk about launching a real war to recover the lost province; and from Europe, France and England continued their seductive games.

Relations with the United States were as confused as ever, for when Texas had wanted annexation, the States had refused to accept her; and recently, when a worried United States invited her southern neighbor to join lest some other nation snatch her, Texas said no. Something had to be done or the fledgling nation might collapse.

At this juncture a small-town lawyer from the hills of Tennessee, a modest man without cant or pretension, stumbled his way into the White House as America's first 'dark horse,' to the amazement of men much better qualified, such as Daniel Webster, John Calhoun, Henry Clay and Thomas Hart Benton. Future historians and men of prudent judgment when assessing the American Presidents would judge this modest but strong-willed man to have been one of our very ablest holders of that office, perhaps Number Six or Seven, behind such unchallenged giants as Washington, Jefferson, Jackson, Lincoln, and especially Roosevelt—Republican partisans nominating the first of that name; Democrats, the second.

It was said of James K. Polk: 'He entered the White House determined to serve one term and accomplish two goals. Having attained these aims, he retired as he promised he would. No President can perform more capably.'

Polk's two aims were simply stated: he wanted to bring Texas into the Union, regardless of the slavery issue or the feelings of Mexico; and he thirsted to extend American territorial sovereignty to the Pacific Ocean, even if that necessitated seizing vast portions of Mexico. To the pursuit of these aims and against venomous opposition, he dedicated his energies and his life itself, for soon after attaining them he died. Quiet, retiring in manner, he was remarkably daring, risking possible war with European powers as he hacked his way to the Pacific and provoking actual war with Mexico when he proclaimed that the Nueces Strip belonged to the new state of Texas, with the Rio Grande as its southern boundary.

He would bring into the United States more new territory than any other President, including even Thomas Jefferson with his extraordinary Louisiana Purchase. He was the personification of Manifest Destiny, and when he left the White House the outlines of the continental United States would be set, geographically and emotionally. Every nation, in time of great decision, should have in command a man of common sense like James K. Polk, for such men strengthen the character of a country.

When Polk won the 1844 presidential election on a program of annexation, the outgoing President, in obedience to the will of the nation, rushed through a joint resolution, offering Texas immediate annexation. But now Texas, certainly the sliest potential state ever to dicker with Congress on terms of entry, delayed acceptance of the belated invitation until Washington approved the draft constitution under which the new state would be governed. It was a document which reflected accurately the beliefs and prejudices of the Texians: no bank could be incorporated, never, under any circumstances; married women enjoyed full property rights; no clergyman, regardless of his church affiliation, could ever serve in the legislature. Two provisions enshrined principles to which Texians were committed: on the side of freedom, the governor would serve for only two years and not for more than four out of every six years; on the side of bondage, slavery was enthusiastically permitted. State Senator Yancey Quimper, campaigning for the constitution, shouted that it made Texas a nation within a nation, and when the vote was counted, it stood 4,000 in favor to 200 against.

And then the Texians demonstrated what a canny lot of horse traders they were. They wheedled the American Congress into awarding entry terms more favorable than those enjoyed by any other state, including two unique provisions: Texas and not the federal government would own all public lands, and the state would retain forever the right to divide into five smaller states if that proved attractive, each one to have two senators and a proportionate number of representatives.

But Congress, liberal in all else, issued a stern ultimatum on timing: Texas must accept this final offer before midnight, 29 December 1845, or annexation was killed. This did not faze the Texians, who waited till the last practical moment, the twenty-ninth, before voting acceptance, after which Senator Quimper roared: 'Texas will now lead the United States to greatness.'

Ceremonial transfer of power did not occur until 19 February 1846, when a soldier started to lower the flag as President Anson Jones uttered these words: 'The final act in this great drama is now performed. The Republic of Texas is no more.'

As the beautiful Lone Star fluttered downward, it was caught in the arms of Senator Quimper, who pressed it to his lips while tears streamed from his eyes. The free nation of Texas was no more, but the resonance from its brief, bankrupt, chaotic and often glorious existence would echo in Texas hearts forever.

. . . TASK FORCE

As I was certifying our year-end expense accounts I uncovered a fascinating bit of trivia. Quimper's legal name was not Lorenzo, but Lawrence, and when I asked about this, he volunteered a revealing explanation: 'It happened one morning like a bolt of lightning. I was a sophomore at UT, forty-five pounds overweight, bad complexion, making no time with the coeds and accomplishing zilch in general. I stared at the mirror and said: "Son, you are not a Lawrence. You're more like a Lorenzo." '

'Where'd you get that name?' I asked, and he said without hesitation: 'Heard it in a movie.'

'About the Medici?'

'Knew nothing about them. This was a thriller and Lorenzo was the villain. Played by Basil Rathbone, I think. Very slim, good at dueling, dynamite with the ladies. That's how I fancied myself.'

'Where did Il Magnifico come from?'

'Girl named Mildred Jones. Freshman history major. Nuts about Italy. She gave me the name. And do you know what? I lost forty pounds. My face cleared up. I became manager of the football team. My entire life salvaged.'

'What happened to Mildred Jones?' I asked, and he said: 'Never married. Teaches history at San Marcos. Each Valentine's Day, I send her two pounds of Godiva chocolates.'

For our February meeting in Abilene, intellectual and religious capital of West

Texas, the two young men on our staff, abetted by Rusk and Quimper, said: 'We've had enough outside professors to address us. We want to hear at least once from a real Texan.'

I had no idea what they were talking about, and was further confused when they explained: 'We want to invite this professor from Tulane in New Orleans.'

'But you just said you were fed up with outside professors,' but when they told me his name I had to admit that he was about the finest example of 'a real Texan' extant.

Diamond Jim Braden was a wiry, tense thirty-eight-year-old folk hero from Waco, and his name was doubly identified with Texas virtue. That is to say, he was a former football player. His father, also known as Diamond Jim, had played on those immortal Waco teams of the 1920s when scores were apt to be Waco 119– Opponents 0.

The first Diamond Jim, much larger than his son, had been a legendary halfback, scoring so many touchdowns that the record books exulted. Volunteering quickly in World War II, he had risen to captain and had led his company through the roughest fighting in Italy, had been repeatedly decorated, and had died just as his battalion was preparing to capture Rome. 'He behaved,' as a Waco editorial said, 'the way we expect our football heroes to behave.'

Now, there is nothing in Texas to which a man can aspire that is held in more reverence than skilled performance on the football field, especially a high school field, and Diamond Jim II, born in 1945 as a happy result of the compassionate leave granted soldiers with older wives, was reared on one simple truth: 'Your father was the best halfback this town ever produced, and he proved it against the Germans.' The second Diamond Jim might have been smaller than his illustrious father, but he had equal grit and determination, if that was possible. He, too, played halfback at Waco High, but fell short of equaling his father's scoring records because competition among the high schools had been equalized. However, he was All-State and he did win a scholarship to the University of Texas, where under Darrell Royal, patron saint of Texas football, he won All-Conference honors and nomination by quite a few national selectors as All-American.

By such performance he had assured his future; insurance companies, banks, oil prospecting consortiums and a score of other businesses sought his services. Because nothing opened the doors of Texas business more effectively than for an older man to be able to say: 'And this is our new star, Diamond Jim Braden, who scored those three touchdowns against Oklahoma.' The young man was required to know nothing about insurance, banking or oil; he did have to know how to dress, how to smile, and how to marry some extremely pretty and wealthy young woman from Dallas, Houston or Midland.

Diamond Jim, however, followed a more individual route, ignoring established precedents except for wanting a beautiful cheerleader as his wife. Selecting early and with great determination a most attractive English major at the university, he had entered the long and tedious course leading to a professorship, which, with the help of his wife, who took a teaching job in Austin, he attained.

As a lad playing football he had been fascinated by the various parts of Texas to which his team traveled, and by the time he was a senior he was a confirmed geographer, even buying with his own funds books on the subject. He grew to love the dramatic manner in which the regions of Texas changed, and once when his team played a title game in Amarillo, he sought permission to stay behind and spend three days exploring the great empty flatness of West Texas, responding to its messages as if he had been afoot in some celebrated area of geographic greatness like the Swiss Alps. As early as age eighteen he could read the messages of the land, and they thrilled him.

At the university, after his athletic advisers had arranged what they called 'a pushover schedule,' he astonished them by enrolling for a geography major. Taking the toughest courses available, he drew down straight A's and started compiling a notebook of hand-drawn analyses of Texas land types. His coaches, after their initial shock, supposed that their boy was training to go into the oil business, and with the prudence that marked the behavior of Texas coaches, they arranged for several legendary oilmen to make him offers of employment after graduation.

To their further consternation, he announced that he really wasn't interested in oil. He wanted to be a geographer, and at this critical point two vitally important things happened that altered his life: he had the great good luck to run into Regent Lorenzo Quimper, who said: 'Jim, if you really want to be a geographer, great. We can buy all the oilmen we want from the University of Oklahoma. But if it is geography, be the best. Take your graduate work at this top school in Worcester, Massachusetts. Clark University. They've forgotten more geography up there than anyone down here in Texas ever knew.'

When it was revealed that Diamond Jim lacked the funds to enter such a school, Quimper mysteriously provided a fellowship that enabled the football hero not only to study at Clark but to travel widely on field trips and explorations. There was no discussion as to repayment of the fund, only the admonition: 'If you're gonna do it, son, do it Texas style.'

Jim's second experience was one which comes to many young people. He read a book that was so strikingly different from anything he had ever read before that it expanded his horizons. *Imperial Texas* had been written by D.W. Meinig, a cultural geographer from Syracuse University, a far distance from Texas, but it was so ingenious in its observations and provocative in its generalizations that from the moment Jim put it down, he knew he wanted to be such a geographer, showing the citizens of his state the subtle ways in which their land determined how they acted and governed themselves.

With his Ph.D. from Clark, Diamond Jim landed an instructorship at Lyndon Johnson's old school, Southwest Texas State at San Marcos. From there he was promoted to an assistant professorship at TCU in Fort Worth, and he was obviously headed for a tenured professorship when he abruptly quit his job, took a lesser one in New Mexico, then one in Oklahoma, and finally a full professorship at Tulane, in New Orleans.

'What the hell are you doin', son?' Quimper asked during one vacation. 'Hopscotchin' about like a giddy girl?'

'I'm trying to learn the borderlands of Texas. When I've learned something, I'll hit you for a job at Austin.'

'I'll be your blockin' back,' Quimper assured him, and it was this remarkable scholar that Rusk and Quimper had invited to address us at Abilene.

Braden's thesis was simple and provocative: 'I have worked in Old Mexico, New Mexico, Oklahoma and Louisiana, trying to identify the factors which those areas share with Texas, and I must confess that I find very few. Texas is unique beyond what even the most ardent Lone Star patriot realizes, and the difference lies in the marvelous challenge of our land. New Mexico has primarily an arid, beautiful wasteland, but so does Texas. The difference is that we have five or six other terrains to augment our wastelands. Oklahoma has striking plains, and so does Texas, but we also have a wild variation to supplement them. Louisiana has a charming Old South terrain, but so does Confederate Texas in the Jefferson area, plus so much more.

'If a settler didn't cotton to one type of Texas land, he could move to some other that suited him better, and his options were almost unlimited. That's fundamental to an understanding of the Texas mind. The land was worthy of being loved. And both Texas women and Texas men grew to love it.'

At this point in his talk he quit his posture of lecturer and sat on the edge of a desk, legs dangling, cowboy boots showing: 'I think your committee is aware that any Texas man who makes it big in anything, first thing he wants is a ranch. If he's an oilman from Houston, he finds his ranch in the hill country back of Austin. If he's from Dallas, he finds it out toward Abilene. And if he's from Abilene, he wants his out toward the Pecos River. And when he finds his Shangri-La, he tends it as lovingly as if it were his mistress.'

Abruptly he pointed at Quimper: 'How many ranches do you have?' and Quimper said quietly but with obvious pride: 'Nine.' He then asked Rusk, who answered: 'Seven.' He was about to continue his interpretation of Texas geography when Miss Cobb said almost petulantly: 'Ask me,' and when he did, she said: 'Three.' Again he was about to proceed, when Professor Garza asked: 'And how about my family? Originally some forty thousand acres along the Rio Grande, and I still have a very small ranch down there, like you say.' Now Braden smiled at Quimper and confessed: 'I have my own little ranch. Near Hardwork, the old German settlement. Mr. Quimper made me buy it with my first savings.'

I felt naked. I was the only one in that room without a ranch, but when they teased me about this, as if I were somehow disloyal, I defended myself: 'I've been working outside the state for some years, and I'm not a millionaire.' This did not satisfy Quimper and Rusk, who said that if I was really a Texan at heart, I'd own some small piece of the countryside, no matter where in the world I worked.

Without further interruption, Diamond Jim shot generalizations at us, which our staff recorded as follows: 'Basic to an understanding of how a Texan feels about his land is the fact that for a ten-year period, 1836 to 1845, the Texians had been in command of a free, sovereign republic, and this generated such deep-rooted characteristics that all who subsequently came to live within the boundaries were subtly modified. To be a Texian implied something quite different from what was indicated when a man said "I'm a New Yorker" or "I'm a Georgian."

'Intensely varied, cruelly harsh, the land of Texas formed a little continent of its own, won by bloody courage, subdued by stubbornness, and maintained by an almost vicious protection of ownership. Men felt about the land of Texas differently from the way men of Massachusetts felt about their land; Texians devised new laws to protect their holdings, harsh customs to ensure that each family's land remained its own. I suppose you know that the homestead of a Texas man cannot be stolen from him in a bankruptcy proceeding brought by some bank.

'Newcomers from states where hunting is popular, like Michigan or Pennsylvania, experience shock when they move to Texas. It comes on the opening day of deer season, for in their home states they are accustomed to hunting pretty much where they wish, and vast areas of state-owned forest are open to them, but in all of Texas there is no acre of land on which an uninvited hunter can trespass in order to shoot a deer. Land privately owned is sacrosanct. Indeed, in Texas the verb *to trespass* is identical with the verb *to commit suicide,* for it is tacitly understood that any red-blooded Texan is entitled to shoot the trespasser.

'On his piece of land the early Texian demanded freedom. He wanted no regular army to dictate his behavior; he called his Rangers to arms only infrequently, and even then for brief and limited periods; he was never overawed by judges; and he allowed no central bank which might dictate economic policies. He was willing to act in concert with neighbors if an enemy threatened, but as soon as the danger abated he insisted upon returning to civilian life so that he could resume fighting with his neighbors. Of all the groups which would constitute the final United States, none would surpass the Texan in his devotion to freedom.'

Before sharing with us his next thesis he smiled, for he realized that he was treading where mythology and custom meet, and he wanted to exaggerate to score a point: 'The Texan sanctified his freedom behind a score of unique traditions. Any man whose wife's affections had been tampered with was free to shoot the other man, to the applause of the jury, impounded not to try him but to proclaim his innocence. And of course, any good-looking woman was free to shoot any man at any time if only her lawyer could prove that love and honor were tangentially involved. Intrusion by the federal, state or county government into a family's basic freedoms was intolerable.

'Of course, this absolute freedom did not apply to blacks, Indians or Mexicans.

Unlike the other Southern states, Texas did not provide a cadre of philosophers who agonized over this basic contradiction of freedom for everyone like me, slavery or extermination for anyone different. It was a way of life approved by ninety-seven percent at least of the anglo population, and as such, it would be preserved and augmented. In time labor unions, liberal newspaper editors and free-speaking college professors would be as outlawed as the Cherokee, the Mexican, the black slave imported from Alabama or the Comanche.

'Texas has been from the start and will always remain a frontier. It was a distant frontier for the kings of Spain ruling from Madrid; it was a shadowy frontier for Napoleon ruling from Paris; and it was always a most remote frontier for Mexican presidents and dictators attempting to rule from Mexico City. When Mirabeau Lamar had the courage to establish the national capital in Austin, it was on the frontier. When Sam Houston first came to Nacogdoches, the wild frontier lay only a few miles to the west; thirty-nine fortieths of future Texas was then a forbidden wilderness. During most of Texas history a wild frontier was always at hand, and not until 1905 or thereabouts could even half the state be classified as "settled." As late as the 1970s it would sometimes seem as if the frontier ran down the middle of Main Street in Dallas or Houston, and if you want to see the frontier still in existence in the 1980s, go to the little Rio Grande town of Polk in West Texas, where it glares across the river at the lawless Mexican town of Carlota.

'This frontier spirit engrained in Texas a spirit of adventure, a willingness to face whatever challenge came along. It encouraged the young people of Texas to be insolent, daring, self-assured and competent. It led to the imaginative utilization of natural resources and the speedy building of free-wheeling communities of unique and robust charm. The meanest family, the poorest boy in school could persuade himself that life was still dominated by the frontier, and that the qualities which had ensured success there were still honored. Texas was the permanent last frontier.

'The penalty for the perpetuation of this legend was a general lawlessness. Fistfights, duels, murders and countywide insurrections became shockingly common, and when the lynching of black men had begun to fade elsewhere, it still flourished as a form of community entertainment in Texas. Texas cities became murder capitals of the nation and therefore the world, but no one complained excessively and anyone misguided enough to preach that guns should be controlled could never hope to become an elected official. Texas would always remain one of the most violent of the American states and would violently defend its right to behave pretty much as it damn well wished.

'Texans will always be inordinately proud of their history, cognizant of the ways in which it differed from the history of the rest of the states, passionately devoted to the stories of the Alamo and San Jacinto while endeavoring to forget how they had messed up Goliad and the Santa Fe expedition.'

At this point Braden stepped down from the desk and went back to his podium: 'I studied Texas history in Grade Three, again in Grade Seven, took a special course in high school, an advanced course in college, and a regional course in graduate school. I can't tell you much about unimportant countries like Greece, France and ancient Persia, but I sure as hell can tell you about McLennan County, Texas.'

He told us that Texans revered their ancestors as only the citizens of Virginia and South Carolina could, but Texans did it with a fierceness that would have caused the other two states to be considered pusillanimous. Perhaps it was this constant living within the living past that made Texans different; certainly it made them more patriotic, so that no one could imagine a citizen of Iowa feeling about his state the way a loyal Texan felt about his.

'Despite their appalling record against Mexican armies—five losses, one win— the Texan citizen still believes he is invincible and that one good Texan can whip ten Mexicans, five Japanese, four Indians or three Germans, and they have never been loath to put this theory to the test. In later years it seemed as if Texans were running the entire American military machine, and rarely to its disadvantage. Texans boasted, but they also produced.

'Out of this heady mélange of patriotism, chauvinism and love of land evolved a way of life that Texans cherished and defended, but it produced constant contradictions. Women would spend vast amounts of money to dress better than those of Boston or Philadelphia, but their men would prefer the rough yet independent dress of the frontier. Sam Houston—congressman, governor, senator, president— established the pattern: boots, rough Mexican-style trousers, a wildly colored and embroidered shirt, a Napoleonic jacket, an immense flopping hat, all topped by a huge Mexican serape. Today the wealthy give mammoth parties at which a whole steer is barbecued, and in the early days solitary wanderers into the wilderness, which seemed always to be two miles to the west, knew that they could halt at the meanest shack and be offered bread and maybe some cheese. Titles and prerogatives meant little; courage and robust fellowship, everything.

'Very quickly Texas became a bastion of free economic activity. Speculate on the land. Risk driving seven hundred head of cattle to New Orleans or to the new railhead in Kansas. Take a chance on a wagon convoy of goods across the desert to Chihuahua. Drive the iron spikes of your railroad three hundred miles across the empty plains to El Paso. Fight the bankers. Fight the government, whether in Austin or Washington. Keep out the agitators and the labor leaders and the radicals. Protest like hell against any kind of taxation at all. And any frontier town of six hundred that did not have two or three millionaires wasn't really trying.

'In the arts the new state was unlucky. Because in its first stages it had been of Spanish heritage, it did not have among its original settlers a cadre of men and women accustomed to writing freely; it could not therefore duplicate settlements like Boston, Philadelphia, Williamsburg and Charleston, in which a predominantly English population already trained in a free English culture produced newspapers, books, impressive schools and thriving colleges. Also, Texans were so busy trying to tame their frontier that they had little time for culture, and their refusal to support education vigorously, as states like Massachusetts and Ohio did, meant that they lacked a constant infusion of fresh intellectual ideas.

'So, at the end of the nineteenth century and the beginning of the twentieth, when indigenous forms of Texas culture should have been emerging, as such forms did in the rest of America, both the foundation and the desire were lacking, and a notable Texan culture composed of songs and paintings and plays and operas and epic poetry and delightful stories did not come forth.

'But the impulses for great art, if they are legitimate, never die, and in those fallow years Texas was accumulating a legend which will surely explode into expressive statement later on. I'm confident that we'll enjoy a vigorous renaissance about 1995, because legendary storytellers like Esteban the Moor, Yancey Quimper and Panther Komax keep the legends, the icons and the images burnished until the dreaming artists of a later day mature and take them in hand.

'Texans of the republic found it easy to transfer their loyalties to the United States, which was no surprise, seeing that the vast majority of them had lived much longer in states like Tennessee and Alabama than in Texas. Later, Texans never forgot that they had once operated a free nation of their own, and a surprising number felt that if ever things went wrong in the United States as a whole, they could secede and revert to their own nationhood. In fact, one of the permanent weaknesses of Texas has been one which has not been acknowledged until recently: Texans, even today, look back to the decade of 1836 to 1845 when their ancestors enjoyed national status as "the great old days." As Americans, they feel that they are the elite among nations; as Texans, they know they are the elite among Americans.

'In the summer of 1846 a New Orleans newspaperman, endeavoring to evaluate the characteristics of the new state which now abutted Louisiana's western border, wrote:

> 'Louisiana and Texas are sisters, and have always been. At many times their heritage was identical, and far more of the supplies that Texas relied upon reached her via New Orleans than through Galveston. Today, the two states should be identical in the manner of Alabama and Mississippi.
>
> 'But Louisiana and Texas are not alike and never shall be. An immense gulf has been dug at the Sabine River, separating Texas not only from Louisiana but from all the other states of the Southern Tier, and it can never be bridged. What does the gulf consist of? The great Spanish missions, for one thing. Texas had them. We didn't. The Alamo and San

Jacinto separate us, too, because Texas went through those dramatic experiences and we didn't.

'But at its widest extent, and deepest, the chasm consists of something much simpler. For the last ten years Texas has been a free nation. Louisiana never was. And the experience of such freedom, once enjoyed, seeps into a people's soul, never to be eradicated.'

VIII
THE
RANGER

(NEW MEXICO)

El Paso

Dallas

Trinity River

Pecos River

Chihuahua

Fredericksburg
Austin
Guadalupe River
Colorado River
Houston

San Antonio

Rio Grande

San Juan Bautista
Nueces River
Frio River
Goliad
Victoria

NUECES STRIP

Laredo

Corpus Christi

GENERAL TAYLOR

Monclova

Mier
Camargo
Brownsville
Bravo
Reynosa
Palo Alto
Resaca de la Palma

Torreón

Monterrey
Saltillo
Buena Vista

Linares
Granada
Otto
Macnab
San Fernando
Matamoros
Bagdad

M E X I C O

GULF
OF
MEXICO

Zacatecas

GENERAL SANTA ANNA

San Luis Potosí
Tampico

Compostela

GENERAL SCOTT

Guadalajara

THE MEXICAN WAR
1846-1848

Mexico City
Perote
Xalapa
Puebla
Avila
Vera Cruz

0   MILES   200

IT WAS AN INTERLUDE, A TRAGICOMIC INTERRUPTION WHICH FEW IN TEXAS sought but which most later accepted as a turning point in their history. At a time when the newly approved state should have been paying attention to the building of governmental process and the sorting out of priorities, it found itself enmeshed in the Mexican War of 1846–1848, a minor affair militarily, a major event diplomatically.

Internally the effect on Texas was minimal; two battles and a disastrous cavalry encounter were fought on its soil, and its men invaded a foreign country, where they gained attention because of their bravery and lack of discipline. More important, men from the other twenty-eight states—Iowa becoming the twenty-ninth in 1846—served in Texas and sent home harrowing stories of 'bleak empty spaces, drought, Mexicans and rattlesnakes.' Of maximum importance, national newspapers sent to the war reporters, sketchers and a remarkable man named Harry Saxon, who brought with him an unprecedented amount of gear to report upon Texas and the war. Their stories and pictures circulated around the world to launch the legend of Texas.

The American army was not in Texas by accident, nor was it there in response to any specific threat by the Mexican government. Instead, there had been a gradual worsening of relations between the two countries and some curious actions on the part of each. President-elect Polk, having been a prime force in bringing Texas into the Union, was determined to add New Mexico and upper California, so as to round out the continental reach of the United States, and since Mexico was either uninterested in developing these areas, or incapable of doing so, he supposed that the Mexicans might be willing to sell them for a decent price in order to be shed of responsibility. He was aware, of course, that the sudden acquisition of so much new land would force the American government to decide once and for all whether the resulting new states should be slave or free, and that would ignite dormant antipathies between South and North, but on that thorny question he was willing to postpone decision.

Even before Polk had been inaugurated in 1845, the kettle of war was bubbling. The United States Congress authorized annexation; Mexico, feeling insulted, terminated diplomatic relations; and the new President initiated a pair of daring moves. First he ordered a sizable army unit to Corpus Christi on the northern border of the Nueces Strip, and warned its commander to be prepared to strike if events required. Next he dispatched a personal emissary, John Slidell, to Mexico with an offer to buy New Mexico for $5,000,000, California for $25,000,000, and to pay up to $40,000,000 for a more complete package. When the Mexicans rebuffed Slidell for having offended their national honor, Polk saw that the two nations were on what he believed to be an unavoidable collision course. Forthwith he began to prepare for the war which he knew, and even hoped, must come.

In command of the eager troops at Corpus Christi was a crusty general, known for his courage, his stubbornness and his lack of education, who had been sent into Texas with orders to protect the American frontier but not to invade Mexico unless hostile action made this inescapable. Zachary Taylor was an almost perfect choice for the job; his frontier manner made him congenial to the Texans and his dogged, no-frills approach to battle made him an effective opponent to the flamboyant Mexicans. He did, however, face a difficult diplomatic problem: Where was the Texas frontier he was supposed to protect?

When France controlled the Mississippi, Spain had been agitated over the border between Spanish Tejas and French Louisiana, and after Mexico won her independence she, too, kept careful watch along that border. But neither Spain nor Mexico cared much what the border between Tejas and its neighboring districts to the south was; it was assumed that this inconsequential delineation ran along the Medina and Nueces rivers. So when Tejas broke away in 1836, officials in Mexico honestly believed that these rivers still marked the boundary between new Texas and old Coahuila and Tamaulipas, and that the infamous Nueces Strip was Mexican. But the nation of Texas, and now the United States, had always argued that the boundary lay south at the Rio Grande, but neither had much reliable documentation to prove this. Now, in 1845, the Nueces Strip was as much an area of contention as it had always been.

The site of the troop concentration had not been chosen at random. The village of Corpus Christi with its two hundred citizens lay where the Nueces River entered the Gulf of Mexico, and this put it at the northeastern edge of the Nueces Strip. From here the army would stand in readiness for a leap into Mexico proper whenever events warranted. The soldiers at Corpus came from all parts of the Union and represented the emerging mix of national origins—24 percent Scots-Irish, 10 percent German, 6 percent English, 3 percent Scots direct, 4 percent other foreign-born, and 53 percent native-born—nicely balanced between infantry, cavalry and artillery, with emphasis on the latter.

When President Polk learned that John Slidell's offer to buy most of northern Mexico had been rejected, he judged that relations between the two countries had deteriorated so noticeably that he had better move General Taylor and his army closer to Mexico, so in late March 1846, Taylor leapfrogged clear across the Nueces Strip and assumed a position near the mouth of the Rio Grande. He did this knowing that such an invasion of territory claimed by Mexico must provoke reaction, and he was prepared for war, as was President Polk in Washington. If the truth were known, both the general and the President hoped for war.

Old Rough-and-Ready Taylor may have been as slow-witted as his junior officers sometimes thought, and the depths of his ignorance and fumbling were widely known, but when an enemy took a defined position on terrain that had been scouted, Taylor, sixty-two years old and wheezing, knew what to do. The first order he had issued upon leaving Corpus Christi endeared him to his subordinates: 'When we have marched three miles into the desert, I want every camp follower who has attached herself or himself to my army kicked the hell out. If they won't go back to Corpus on their own, put them in irons and march them off with bayonets at their backsides.' And in one grand sweep the hundreds of prostitutes, pimps, gamblers, whiskey peddlers, thieves and petty traders were booted out. Among these disreputables was a large, pompous gentleman who had been making a small fortune by selling a fantastic variety of things to Taylor's army: whiskey, tobacco, socks, hard candy, cigars, big hats to replace the inadequate type provided by the commissary and, some said, the favors of Mexican girls who seemed always to be available wherever he located. As soon as the order went out to rid the army of such trash, a rigidly proper West Pointer from South Carolina, Lieutenant Colonel Persifer Cobb, took it upon himself to arrest this man, whose operations he had monitored and whose behavior he deplored. But once he had the unsavory fellow corralled, Cobb found himself involved in a political scandal.

'I am a state senator of Texas,' the prisoner bellowed, 'and a general in the militia!' When Cobb questioned other prisoners, they confirmed the claims: 'He's Senator Yancey Quimper, Hero of San Jacinto, and you're in trouble, Colonel, because he has connections.'

'Damn Texas,' Cobb muttered under his breath. 'Where else would you find a general running a whorehouse?' But when Quimper kept demanding that he be taken to General Taylor, and threatening to have Cobb cashiered from the army 'because of my powerful associations in Washington,' Cobb had to protect himself, and shortly Yancey Quimper was standing before General Taylor.

'Are you indeed a senator?' Taylor asked, and when Quimper replied: 'In charge of military affairs,' Taylor asked: 'And what in hell were you doing among the rabble of my army?' and the senator explained: 'Looking after my land interests here.'

This lie was so offensive to Cobb that without having been invited to speak, he blurted out: 'He was running a cheap store, a liquor bar, and worse,' at which Quimper drew himself to attention: 'I was a general in the Texas army, and I demand an apology.'

For one sickening moment Persifer Cobb feared that General Quimper intended joining the Texan volunteers, and his face drained of blood, but General Taylor, a rough old customer who could at times be magnificent, said: 'Get the hell out of here. I suspect you're a fraud.' And Senator-General Yancey Quimper retreated, muttering threats he knew he could not fulfill.

South of the Rio Grande there was a Mexican who had spent a dozen years also longing for such a war, but who now, when it was about to erupt, had ambivalent feelings arising from an event he could never have anticipated. Benito Garza, aged forty, had fallen in love.

When it became apparent that Mexico, in protection of its honor, must oppose any yanqui intrusion into the Nueces Strip, irrevocably the territory of Mexico, Garza had ridden north to assist General Mariano Arista in his defense of Mexican integrity. He was now serving Arista as a superior scout well informed about the area under contention, and in this capacity he was willing to lay down his life.

However, when he moved with Arista to Matamoros, where the Rio Grande enters the Gulf, he found attached to the command a purveyor of salted beef, one José López, who had an attractive daughter bearing a name highly favored by Spanish mothers of a religious bent: María de la Luz, Blessed Mary of the Holy Lights, which children traditionally abbreviated to Lucha. Lucha López was nineteen when Garza met her, a tall, slim young woman of curious beauty and dominant will. Her beauty was unusual in that her features were by no means perfect or strikingly regular; rather, they were strong, powerfully molded, with high cheekbones indicating a pronounced Indian origin. Her hair, which she wore in a long braid, was jet-black, which accentuated her black and piercing eyes.

When Garza first saw her delivering a basket lunch to her father, who had been negotiating with General Arista over the price of beef, he noticed that her dark eyes carried a clear sense of sadness, and he asked her father: 'Why is your daughter so mournful?' and he replied: 'The man she was to marry was killed on the other side of the river, where he kept his cattle.'

'Who killed him?' Benito asked, and the meat-dealer said: 'Tejas Rangers.' He pronounced the hated word in the manner common along the river, *Rinches*.

'When he was on his own soil!'

'Next they'll be shooting us in Matamoros.'

In his long years in the saddle Benito had seen many attractive girls and had idly courted some of them, but his manner of life had prevented him from seriously contemplating marriage. At first when he met this impressive young woman he shied away, because he knew that wars and incursions and revolutions would deter him from being a good husband or even a reasonable one.

But Lucha López was not an easy woman to dismiss, and during a six-week interval before open warfare began, he courted her, at first tentatively, then with growing ardor. Once as he left her reluctantly, he thought: She weaves a web about me, as a spider traps a fly. And I like being trapped.

Their cautious relationship did not follow customary patterns, for on those occasions when they managed to escape her dueña they often discussed military matters. 'Is it true,' she asked one afternoon, 'that General Taylor has ten thousand troops?'

'I've been north twice to see, and I doubt he has ten thousand. But many . . . many.'

'Then war is inevitable?'

'Surely.'

'Will it involve Matamoros?'

'I don't see how you can escape.'

'Can we win?'

Since Benito had been pondering this difficult question for some months, he should have been able to respond quickly, but he did not. Very carefully he said: 'If we had not driven Santa Anna into exile, if he were here instead of languishing in Cuba, we'd have a splendid chance of recapturing Tejas.'

'Is Santa Anna so good a general?'

'He's wonderful at collecting a rabble of men and forging them into a grand army. If only we had him now . . .'

'Father thinks highly of General Arista.'

'And so do I. He'll give a good account of himself . . .' His voice trailed off.

'But he's no Santa Anna?'

'In all the world there's only one Santa Anna. And he wastes away in Cuba.'

'You will fight the norteamericanos?'

'Until I die.'

She kissed him fervently: 'Benito, I feel the same way. "The Colossus of the North" someone called them the other day. They press down upon us. We can never live with them . . . never.'

'How did your man die?'

'They came upon him, gathering his cattle. He had taken them across the river in April, as always, and they hanged him in July. No questions, no charges. He was mexicano, and that was enough to hang him.'

The hatred in her voice echoed Garza's own, and in this mutual rage against an oppressor their love deepened. But still Benito shied away from any commitment, when to his astonishment Lucha said: 'In this great battle . . . it will last our lifetimes, Benito, I want to share it with you. Marriage, home, a garden in peace, we'll not know them. They're concerns for people like my mother . . .'

He placed his fingers across her lips: 'It would have to be marriage, Lucha. I've seen how the norteamericanos ridicule us because of some of our women . . . the soldaderas they don't marry. With a respectable woman like you, it must be marriage.'

'I am not a respectable woman,' Lucha said harshly. 'I'm a woman of the new Mexico, the Mexico that's going to be free.'

'And I'm a man of the new Mexico too, the Mexico that's going to demand respect among nations. We marry, or we part now.'

Lucha's parents, prominent citizens of Matamoros with their own good home and land in the country on which López had raised most of the cattle whose meat he sold, strongly opposed the match, for as López pointed out: 'He's forty years old. He could be your father,' and as Señora López warned: 'He's a bandit, a good one, I'll admit, and on our side, but a roving bandit nevertheless. What kind of home life could you expect?'

'What kind of home life will you expect, if the Rinches keep coming over the Rio Grande?' she asked.

When her parents realized that she was stubbornly prepared to accompany Garza, married or not, they were appalled, and now they became strong advocates of immediate marriage, though not necessarily with Garza: 'A girl as pretty as you, you could have any man you wanted. How about that major on General Arista's staff? He keeps making eyes at you.'

'Aren't a major and a bandit pretty much alike?'

'That I wouldn't know,' Señora López granted, 'but this I do know. A soldadera who follows the troops is no better than a puta.'

The impasse among the four troubled Mexicans was resolved in a bizarre way. Within the body of patriotic Mexicans prepared to make extreme sacrifices for their country was a renegade priest, born in Spain, who was known only as Padre Jesús. For some years, in moral desperation and with incredible courage, he had fought for Mexican freedom, a gaunt, determined man, a natural-born ascetic, who wore clerical garb and who opposed corruption and injustice wherever he found them, in the church, in politics, in the army or in the general society.

Padre Jesús no longer bothered to report his comings and goings to his conservative religious superiors, and now, with a threat of war menacing the northern boundaries of his adopted nation, he had come without authorization to the Rio Grande to do what he could to help, and the troops had a deep affection for his efforts.

When Padre Jesús heard of the conflicts within the López family he proposed a simple solution: 'Señor López, you have a daughter who is a gem of purest category. You are correct in wanting to see her safely married to a safe man. But she is like me, a child of the revolution that must sweep Mexico. It is proper for her to marry Benito Garza, for he is the new Mexican, the honorable man. They will never have a home like yours, a garden and six children. But they will live in the heart of the real Mexico, as I do. Let them marry.'

When the elder Lópezes refused to accept this advice, Benito and Lucha faced a dilemma, for ancient Spanish custom, now hardened into a law which Mexico honored, held a female to be her father's ward until the age of twenty-five, and without his consent she could not marry; if she did, the marriage could be annulled or she could be disowned. And when Lucha pleaded for her parents to relent, they cited this law and their opposition stiffened.

But if Padre Jesús was correct in proclaiming Benito a new Mexican, he could have continued that 'I, Jesús, am the new Catholic priest,' for when he learned that Lucha's parents were obdurate, he broke the deadlock simply: 'Come with me to the rallying field,' and here, where irregulars like himself had gathered, a confused rabble of adventurers and patriots prepared to support the formal army when hostilities began, he married this ill-matched pair: the groom, more than twice the age of the bride and a son of revolution and disarray; the bride, a daughter of middle-class respectability who should have married a rich land-owner.

Just as the impromptu ceremony concluded, a messenger splashed across the Rio Grande: 'Norteamericano soldiers! Not ten miles from the river!' At this exciting news the new husband kissed his wife, then rode hard to General Arista's headquarters, where a team of skilled frontier fighters was assembling. 'Let me ride with them as scout,' Garza pleaded, and the request was granted, for among the troops, regular or irregular, no one was better at operating in the chaparral of the Nueces Strip.

'We must be very quiet, very wily,' he warned the regular cavalry as they crossed the river. 'If, as they say, the norteamericanos have Rinches as their scouts . . . they will be watchful.'

The oncoming Americans, more than sixty in noisy number, did not have Rangers as scouts, but they were led by two able captains, one a West Point graduate. However, the captains were not cautious men, for their big horses raised clouds of dust and their men engaged in careless chatter, which betrayed their advance.

Garza, slipping silently ahead of the Mexican force, watched the approach of the norteamericanos in disbelief: Where do they think they're going? Why don't they have any scouts out ahead? And after a long inspection: Good God! They don't have any Rinches, none at all!

Unable to believe that the enemy were behaving so unprofessionally, he trailed them for more than half an hour, expecting that at any moment some knowing scout, perhaps even Otto Macnab, would come upon him suddenly from the rear, but in time he satisfied himself that his first impressions were correct: No scouts. No Rinches.

As silently as a rattlesnake slipping through the grass, Garza made his dusty way back to the Mexican cavalry and helped its commander set a trap for the unsuspecting norteamericanos, who were now less than two miles from the river. Placing riders at various points, the Mexican leader kept his formidable lancers, those daring fighters with steel-tipped poles as sharp as needles, in reserve, and in this disposition his men awaited the bumbling arrival of the enemy.

Garza, well forward of the secluded Mexicans, was accompanied by ten of the best and most daring irregulars, who moved their horses about so that the norteamericanos must detect them, and when this happened, there was a flurry of shots and much galloping, but Benito and his men knew how to avoid that first fierce charge. With great skill they rode this way and that, confusing the norteamericanos and leading them into the well-laid trap.

The battle was harsh and brief. Just as the American cavalry was about to overtake Garza, who fled in apparent terror, he flashed a signal, whereupon General Arista's best lancers swung into action, and before the hard-riding dragoons from Pennsylvania, Ohio and Missouri knew what was happening, they were surrounded and captured, all sixty-three of them.

By lucky accident, sixteen of the intruders were killed or badly wounded; by design, one of the wounded was set free to inform General Taylor of the humiliating loss. He was outraged that troops of his could be so inefficient in the field, but pleased that at last the Mexicans had come across the Rio Grande and actually killed American troops. To President Polk he was able to send the message that those who sought war with Mexico had awaited: 'Today Mexican troops have invaded American soil and killed American troops. Hostilities may now be considered as commenced.' The war with Mexico had begun.

Taylor's army had three weaknesses, and he was now painfully aware of them: his horses, though big and sturdy, were not accustomed to operations in an extreme southern climate like the Strip's; he had few scouts experienced in such terrain; but most important of all, his enlisted men were an untested collection whose officers could only speculate on 'how they will perform in battle.' Therefore, when the state of Texas offered to provide a group of Rangers well versed in chaparral fighting, he faced a dilemma: as a strict disciplinarian, he did not relish accepting a group of unruly Texans into his orderly ranks, but as a general responsible for the safety of a large army in a strange land, he knew he must have sharp eyes out front, and these he lacked. With great reluctance and after a painful delay, he grudgingly announced: 'We must have reliable scouts. We'll take the Texans.'

However, West Point men like Lieutenant Colonel Cobb warned of the dangers: 'The Texans may be fine horsemen, but the word you just used doesn't apply to them.'

'What word?' Taylor growled.

'Reliable.'

'They won their independence, didn't they?'

'On their peculiar terms.'

'Damned effective terms they were,' Old Rough-and-Ready snapped. 'Kill Mexicans.' Then he added, in gentler tones: 'Before we took them into the Union they had half the nations of Europe invitin' them to join their empires, didn't they?'

'Granted, but now we're talking about bringing them into the regular army, and frankly, sir, I don't think they'd fit.'

'Why not? If we swear them in and place reliable officers over them, like yourself, Cobb, they'll do fine.'

'But their clothes! They're a rabble.'

'Cobb, haven't you noticed? I often go without a military uniform.'

'Please, sir! Don't encourage the Texans. They think they're still a free nation. They're dickering with us on the terms under which they will provide us with men.'

'They're what?'

'The state government wants to negotiate.'

'What in hell do you mean?' Taylor thundered, and Cobb explained: 'It says it may be willing to let you have two full regiments, but only on its own conditions.' He summarized the limiting conditions under which all volunteers joined the regular army, plus a few galling things which Texas had added: 'Variable terms of enlistment. Their own rate of pay. It's just as if Prussia were offering us units, on Prussian terms.'

'We'll have none of that!'

'Then you'll have no Texans.'

'You mean that at the end of three months, maybe, they could go home?'

'They'd insist upon it. That's the way they've always served.'

A colonel from Mississippi explained: 'They're farmers. They like to get back home to tend the crops. Of course, they'll come back to the army when the crops are in . . . if they feel like it.'

Cobb added: 'Nor do they wish to wear our uniform. Or use our horses. Or use our rifles. Each Texan feels he knows more about fighting than any man from New York possibly could, and he insists upon doing it his way, dressed in whatever makes him feel comfortable.'

Taylor grew impatient with the wrangling: 'Don't you suppose I know they'll be troublesome?' For some minutes, which he would in months to come remember ruefully, he toyed with the idea of rejecting them as ungovernable, but in the end he growled: 'We'll take the two regiments,' and then he added words which Cobb would also remember with bitterness: 'And since you seem to know so much about them, Persifer, you can serve as my liaison.'

It was under these slippery conditions that thirty-six Rangers of Captain Garner's Company M joined General Taylor's army of regulars, and their arrival caused Persifer Cobb only grief.

In these years the United States Army roster listed many soldiers bearing the unusual first name of Persifor, also spelled Persifer, and what accounted for its sudden popularity, or even its genesis, no one could say, but there was General

Persifor Smith and Colonel Persifer Carrick and a smattering of Major Persifors This and Captain Persifers That. Ordinary privates bearing the name have not been recorded.

The Persifer Cobb serving under General Taylor came from a noble cotton plantation which comprised most of Edisto Island off the coast of South Carolina. He had been a tense, proper young gentleman of twenty when his father announced: 'Any self-respecting Southern family ought to have a son in the army. Persifer, off to West Point!' In that austere environment he had conducted himself honorably, and upon graduation into the regular service he strove to exemplify in thought and action the best of Southern tradition. He spoke with an excessive drawl and defended in both mess and field the highest traditions of Southern chivalry. But now, on the dusty fields of Texas, he was not a happy man.

The first source of his discomfort was that irritating adjective which preceded his rank. He was a colonel, one of the most proper in the national force, but he was not yet a full colonel; he was only a lieutenant colonel, rightfully convinced that he merited higher rank. The special nature of his displeasure manifested itself in his first letter home to his younger brother, who was overseeing the Edisto plantation during the colonel's absence:

> Rio Grande
> 30 April

> Dear Brother Somerset:

> General Taylor and his troops are encamped at a new fort on the north bank of this river opposite Matamoros, and we would be well prepared to meet the Mexicans had we not been joined recently by a civilian muster out of Texas, and a more disgraceful, unruly and downright criminal element I have rarely seen. They call themselves Texas Rangers, although I am informed that not more than ten percent have previously served in that informal service. They wear no uniform, no badges of distinction, so that we regular army men cannot separate a captain from a private, and discipline they know not.

> General Taylor has made no secret of the fact that he did not want any Texas volunteers, but Texas, as you know, is now a state, having been an independent republic, and since its citizens, having once been members of a free nation, carry an exalted opinion of their own importance, local politicians forced their native sons upon us.

> Well, the Texas Rangers are among us, and their presence must give the Mexican generals hope, for a more worthless collection of men one rarely sees. What purely galls us regular army men who have slaved in the colors for years to gain our promotions is that when the Texans come

slouching into camp, they, like all volunteers, immediately hold an election, an *election,* mind you, to choose their company officers, and yesterday a Texan with never a day at military school rode into our camp announcing that the state of Texas had appointed him full colonel, and now he brazens his way about camp superior to me. I, a graduate of West Point with twelve years of arduous service behind me in all military specialties and all geographical areas, must take orders from a man who last week was herding cattle and has never heard of Hannibal or Marshal Ney.

I was requested by General Taylor, and of course accepted, to take under my charge the Company M of Rangers who are to serve as my scouts, and it will suffice to describe three of them to you. Captain Garner—*captain,* mind you, who was never lieutenant, just mysteriously captain —is enormously tall, enormously thin, with great flowing mustaches and a leather belt six inches wide. He wears whatever comes to hand, including a jacket which once served the Mexican army, for he says he took it from an officer he shot along the Rio Grande. Taciturn, mean-spirited, grimly silent when reproved, he stalks about like an avenging angel, taking orders from no one and always wanting to lead his men off to some foray under his own direction. In our regular army he would not last through sunset of the first day.

His chosen assistant, a lieutenant perhaps, but without rank, for the Rangers care little about such distinctions, is a slight young man of no more than twenty, although he claims twenty-six. I know him only as Otto, but he is unforgettable: small, not more than a hundred and forty, wiry, blond, silent, and with the brightest blue eyes. He never smiles, just looks right through you, and the other men consider him the best Ranger of the lot. What makes him stand out more than anything else is that he wears a garment they call in these parts a duster, a very light coat of linen and cotton which reaches from neck to boot top with only three buttons to fasten it en route. Otto's is a pale white in color and is supposed to keep the dust off during long rides, but when he walks about our camp the duster makes him look like a little lost ghost, for his small feet seem scarcely to move under it as he steps. On his first day in camp I told him, rather sternly: 'We do not wear clothes like that in this camp,' and he replied: 'I do,' and off he waddled, looking so much like a duck that I had no further desire to discipline him.

The third Ranger is like no one you have ever encountered on Edisto. He calls himself Panther Komax, because of the panther-pelt hat he wears with the tail hanging over his left ear, and where he comes from no one can tell me, least of all he. When I asked, he said: 'People get finicky if I bust another man over the head with an ax handle and run off with his horse and his wife.' He would put the horse first. He mentions Georgia, Massachusetts and Missouri without actually claiming to have lived in any of them. I think of him mostly as hair, for he has a huge head of it, coal-black, which he grows long, tying it matted behind his ears with a deerskin thong. He wears a beard which almost hides his face, has heavy, menacing eyebrows and long black hairs growing out of the backs of his hands. He is over six feet tall, heavyset, and with the meanest look in his eye I have ever seen. It is appropriate that he should call himself Panther, because he really is an animal. He carries an enormously heavy rifle and a knife with a twelve-inch blade. The other Rangers tell me he was a member of that ridiculous Mier Expedition of 1842, when a rabble of Texans invaded Mexico, thinking they could defeat the entire Mexican army. Outnumbered ten to one, they were tricked into surrendering, and the disaster would have been long forgotten except that the Mexican general, Santa Anna, about whom I wrote you when we were in camp in Mississippi, ordered one Texas prisoner in every ten shot, and the decimation was to be determined by drawing beans from a clay pot. White bean, you lived. Black bean, you were shot on the spot. I asked Panther Komax if he had drawn a bean, and he said: 'Yep, white.' I then asked him if he had served time in Perote Prison, an infamous place somewhere deep in Mexico, and he said: 'Yep, killed two guards and escaped.' He is a frightening man, capable of anything, and when I asked him why he wanted to go back into Mexico with us, he said: 'They is certain individuals down there as I would like to meet again.'

These are the men, the untrained ruffians, who are to be my scouts. I have not the slightest hope of disciplining them or converting them into regular army members. I do not look forward to leading such riffraff into Mexico, but just before starting this letter I saw my three chosen Rangers coming at me from a distance, lanky Captain Garner on the left, big, burly Panther Komax on the right, and little-boy Otto in his long, flapping duster in the middle, a head or more shorter than his companions, and as I watched them come at me I thought: God preserve the officer who attempts to lead those fellows, and God preserve doubly any Mexicans they meet, for I have learned an interesting fact from my orderly: 'This kid Otto, his father and uncle was killed by Mexicans, his mother and aunt by the Comanche. He's afraid of nothin'. Just starts comin' at you and never stops.'

I am not happy in Texas and shall feel greatly relieved when we finally cross into Mexico.

Your brother,
Persifer

With his reconnaissance and cavalry problems solved, General Taylor was able to deploy his inferior number of troops into excellent arrangement, especially his heavy guns, and at Palo Alto on 8 May 1846 and Resaca de la Palma on the following day, gained crushing victories which sent the Mexicans fleeing in disarray back across the Rio Grande. Persifer Cobb, who was cited in dispatches for his personal bravery, gave most of the credit to his infamous Texans:

Somerset, there can be no glory like the smoke of battle on a hard-won field. General Arista, seeking to cut our supply lines, brought his troops deep into the Nueces Strip, where in a two-day battle involving thousands we taught him a lesson. I was commended for turning the enemy's right flank in a hot and dusty business. Rarely have I known a day of such blazing sun and such constant sweat. It was no parade exercise, and had not our artillery provided a stout performance, we might have lost.

The Mexicans fought with a valor we had not expected, but what amazed me was the skill of my Texans, for I believe that they can, at full gallop, deliver a greater concentration of fire than any other troops in world. An officer on our staff who knows cavalry history told me: 'I would choose these men above Rupert's Cavaliers, or the best Cossacks, or the Turkish Mamelukes or even the Moss Troopers who used to surge out of the bogs of Scotland to ravage the English towns.'

At the height of the battle yesterday I understood what he meant, for I was riding with this boy Otto at my side, his white duster flying behind, and he was so skilled with his various arms that after we had routed the Mexican cavalry I talked with him. His name is Macnab, which means that he comes of good stock, which counts for something, I think. When we started our run at the enemy he had two rifles, two pistols, two daggers and two revolving pistols of a new make. He told me they were called Colts, of the Texas design, made in Paterson, New Jersey, and he showed me how they came completely apart into three separate pieces: barrel, a revolving cylinder containing five bullets, and stock.

This young fellow could fire ten shots with his two Colts while I fired one with my old-fashioned pistol, and he was so dexterous that he could reload without dismounting and then fire ten more times. When you have twenty such men at your elbow, you can turn any Mexican attack.

Tonight I am not displeased with my Texans, except that when you see twenty of them dashing ahead, each on his own, each wearing his own outrageous interpretation of a military uniform, you do wish that they'd had some proper training.

Postscriptum: Macnab, the little killer, just came to me with an astonishing request. He wants to quit the army temporarily, and for what reason do you suppose? To get married! Yes, he told me shyly that he had known his intended for some years, a fine German lass. 'And has she accepted your proposal?' I asked, and he surprised me by saying: 'I haven't spoken to her yet.' I asked if it wasn't risky, riding so far to court a lady when the outcome was uncertain, and he astounded me by confessing: 'I mean, we have never spoken.' 'Not one word?' I asked, and he said: 'Not one.' I asked: 'Then how do you know she'll say yes?' and he replied: 'I know,' but he did not explain how he knew.

Before he left camp I asked if I could rely upon his returning to duty, and he said rather grimly: 'I have several scores to settle with Mexico. I'll be back.' Strange thing, Somerset, I already miss him, for I have found him to be a man I want at my side when the fighting begins.

One afternoon when the Allerkamps returned from a visit to Fredericksburg, Emil said a surprising thing: 'They told me that one of the Rangers on leave from chasing Mexicans with General Taylor has taken a room at the Nimitz place.'

Mrs. Allerkamp happened to be looking at Franziska when this was said, and she noticed that her daughter stiffened, hands pressed close against her dress, and when Ludwig asked: 'What young man?' and Emil said: 'His name is Macnab,' Mrs. Allerkamp saw that Franziska blushed furiously, even though, to her mother's knowledge, she had never even spoken to the young man.

The name Macnab caused Ernst, the now-and-then Ranger, to say: 'What a wonderful fighter he is! Nothing scares him!' Now Ludwig spotted his daughter's extremely flushed face and asked her sternly: 'Franza, what's the matter?'

Sitting very straight, her little body drawn tightly together as if facing an assault, her hands in her lap, Franziska said softly: 'He has come to marry me.'

Her statement created an uproar: 'You've never met the man!' 'How do you know what he's here for?' 'Who ever heard of such an idea?'

But now the great force of character which had been building in this quiet young woman—product of her bravery during the ocean crossing, of her ceaseless work around the farm, of her unwavering love for a young man to whom she had never spoken—manifested itself, and she fended off her entire family: 'He's come to marry me, and I shall marry him.'

This was a challenge which her father could not ignore: 'Have you and he had some arrangement?'

She blushed even more at the suggestion, set her jaw more firmly, and said: 'No. How could we?'

'Then it's true? You've never spoken to him?'

'Never.'

'Then how can you say such a thing? That he's come to marry you?'

'I know and he knows.' She was so resolute that her father gave up, but now her mother took over.

'Isn't he Catholic?'

'He is,' Ernst interrupted. 'But I think he did it only to get land.'

'He's Irish, isn't he?' Thekla asked.

'Yes, but I don't think all Irish have to be Catholic.'

'I think they do,' Mrs. Allerkamp said, and she looked fiercely at her wayward daughter.

Ludwig was not satisfied: 'You still say he's come here to marry you?'

'Yes.'

'But how can you possibly know that?'

Now Emil interrupted: 'I heard that someone had taken papers on the land just west of ours.'

'Where did you hear that?' Ludwig snapped. This conversation was becoming too involved for his fatherly tastes.

'Someone, I don't remember who, said that papers from the land office in Austin had been forwarded.'

'Do you think it could have been this Macnab?'

Emil broke in again: 'He'd be a good man to have on our frontier against the Comanche. He knows how to handle them.'

Such talk disturbed Ernst and irritated Ludwig, who rose from the table, stalked out of the kitchen, saddled his horse, and rode in to town, for he was not a man to delay unpleasant obligations.

When he reached the wide and dusty main street of Fredericksburg, he reined in at the Nimitz place, where the family was building an extension to their small house in order to open a formal inn for the convenience of the travelers who would soon be coming this way. There he asked: 'Have you a lodger named Macnab?' Without waiting for permission, Allerkamp strode to the door, pushed it open, and stood face-to-face with Otto Macnab.

'Are you Macnab?'

'The same.'

'You the one who rode with Ernst in the Nueces Strip?'

'The same.'

'And you've been with General Taylor at the big battles?'

'I have.'

With both men still standing, Ludwig asked: 'Have you come to marry my daughter?'

Otto had not intended that his proposal be broached in this abrupt manner; he had been in the vicinity three days, scouting his newly acquired land, satisfying himself that it abutted the Allerkamp acres, and learning to his relief that Franziska was not already married. With his courage increasing daily, he had decided that tomorrow he would let Ernst know he was in the vicinity and perhaps in a day or so he could meet Franziska herself. Speaking to her parents could come the following week. But here stood her father, far ahead of schedule.

'Will you sit down, sir?'

'I will,' Ludwig said fiercely. 'Now tell me, how did you get to know my daughter?'

'I saw her . . . twice . . . when I came to fetch Ernst.'

'What kind of secrets did you have with her?'

'None. We never spoke.'

'And just looking . . . ?'

'Yes, just from looking, and from what Ernst told me.'

'Did he discuss his sister?'

'Never. But he told me of your family, and I decided . . .'

Otto could not continue. Either Mr. Allerkamp understood what impels a young man to sell his land and travel so far into a wilderness, or he did not, and if he had forgotten what tremendous pressures of emotion and longing and desire a mere glimpse of a beautiful girl could arouse, there was no sense in talking. Nor could Otto speak of the nights along the Ohio River when he first became aware of what a home was, nor of his intense sense of tragedy when Martin Ascot was killed during the murder of the Comanche, leaving pretty Betsy Belle a widow, nor of the fact, to put it simply, that he was in love and had been for a long time.

Abruptly, Ludwig asked: 'Are you Catholic?'

Firmly, Otto answered: 'I had to be, for my father to get us land.'

'Are you a Catholic now?'

'Who knows?'

'Well, shouldn't all Irishmen be Catholic?'

'I'm not Irish.'

Allerkamp was startled: 'What are you?'

'Scots. My father moved to Ireland years ago, then left.'

'You're a Scotchman?'

'We call it Scotsman. And my mother was German.'

Allerkamp gasped, looked at the young man sitting opposite him, and asked in a low voice: 'What did you just say?'

'I said we call it Scotsman, not Scotchman.'

'I mean the next part.'

'Oh, my mother was German. From Baltimore.'

'What was her name?'

'Berthe.'

'I mean her last name.'

'I don't know. I never knew.'

This Allerkamp could not believe—to have had a German mother and to have forgotten her name, the name that entitled you to membership in the greatest of all races! 'You forgot? You forgot your mother's German name?'

'I never knew it.'

For a moment the two sat facing each other, then Allerkamp rose with a cry of joy and embraced his newfound friend, his son-in-law to be: 'You're German! How wonderful!'

Otto, who had never up to now considered his German ancestry an asset, was not allowed to remain indifferent, because Allerkamp grasped him by the shoulders, gave him a second embrace, and cried: 'Come! We must tell her at once.'

He dragged Otto out of the boardinghouse, obviously intending to ride the six miles out to the farm.

'It's almost dark,' the young man protested, but Ludwig dismissed this sensible objection: 'If she's waited this long for you, she deserves to know.' When Otto said nothing, Allerkamp went on: 'We found her four good husbands—five, counting Quimper—but she'd have none of them.' He said no more as they mounted their horses, then added: 'We could never understand why she refused. She never mentioned your name until tonight. When Emil told us that you were at the Nimitz house.'

'What did she say?' Otto asked as they rode.

'She said "He's come to marry me." She must have known all along.'

The two men followed a rough road out of town, and as the stars appeared, always brighter as if to encourage them, each knew a great joy: Allerkamp realizing that his child had come safe to harbor with a trustworthy German; Macnab accepting the miracle that his strange courtship had come to such splendid fruition.

At eight the moon appeared, waning, but still strong enough to lighten the way, so that the happy travelers rode through the best of Texas in the best of conditions. In the tall branches of one tree a brood of turkeys conversed briefly as they passed, as if they were gossiping about the strange events of this long day, and a coyote moved furtively along with them for a short distance, then cut sharply to the west in search of prey.

They moved through gently rolling hills, with trees sparsely distributed marking the watered valleys. Live oak, post oak, ash and hickory showed their rounded forms against the sky, with cedars standing darker in the background. 'It's not like a proper German forest,' Allerkamp said, 'but it will do.'

'What's different?' Otto asked, and the surveyor, who had mastered all the nuances of his new land, explained: 'There we had real trees. One after another, all joined together. Here each tree stands apart . . . jealous of its allotted space.' After reflecting on this for some minutes, he snapped his fingers and said: 'Maybe that's the difference, son. In Germany we were like the trees, all forced to live together wherever the Margrave said. In Texas each of us stands stubbornly apart, each man on his own land.' As they made their way toward the Pedernales, Allerkamp continued his reflections: 'Not a day passes, son, but that I think of Germany—the wine, the singing, the walks in the forest, the peasant food I knew so well, the good talk with Metzdorf at his shop. I long for those things so desperately, my heart could break.' He turned in his saddle to face Otto: 'You know what I don't long for? The tyranny. The false preaching of the churchmen. The horrible day when the Margrave told my son Theo he couldn't marry.'

The passionate remembrance of that day which had so altered his life brought tears to his eyes, and after a moment of silence he offered Otto remarkable advice: 'When we get to our home, if suddenly I should cry out "Macnab, you can't have her. You can't marry," kick my backside, grab her, and go where you will—but find freedom.' He was trembling; he allowed his horse to move away from Otto's; then from the darkness that rose up between them he said: 'Freedom is everything. Freedom is the salt of life that makes hard work palatable. Freedom is the only basis for a home, and marriage, and children.'

In some dim way Otto had already discovered the truth of what Allerkamp was saying. He had sensed it when his father railed so bitterly against the ineptitude of Colonel Fannin: 'Damnit, son. If a group of men are fighting for their freedom, they ought to do certain things, instantly, without thinking.' He had perceived it also when his detachment started marching head-on into the Mexican lines at San Jacinto. No sensible men would perform such an extraordinary act unless impelled by a lust for freedom, a determination to be free. And he glimpsed the universal truth of this when he saw the new Allerkamp farm along the Pedernales, for no family would have the courage to move so far from settled areas unless it longed for the freedom which space assured.

'There it is!' Allerkamp said as he pointed to the solid house he and his sons had built. And with a sharp goading of his horse, he rode into the yard before the entrance, shouting: 'Here he comes! Tell Franza that here he comes!'

When the men entered the warm kitchen they found Thekla Allerkamp and her two sons sitting there. Franziska was not visible, for she had gone early to bed, and her absence caused Otto to feel a stab of disappointment. Ludwig, sensing this, shouted: 'Franza! Out of bed! He's come to claim you!'

As Mrs. Allerkamp disappeared quietly into the smaller of the two bedrooms, Otto was left standing awkwardly in the middle of the room, twenty-four years old, blond hair, blue eyes, short, less than a hundred and fifty pounds, hands close to his sides and extremely nervous. 'He came, just as she said,' Ludwig told his sons, and he was about to say more when Thekla reappeared, leading her sleepy-eyed daughter into the bright light of the kitchen.

For a protracted moment the two young people stood there, each looking with delight at the other, but the spell was broken when Ludwig shouted with joy that could not be misunderstood: 'And he's German!'

When questions were asked, with the two lovers still gazing at each other, Ludwig explained his marvelous news: 'He's not Irish at all. And he's not Catholic, not really. He's a good German. His mother was from Germany, from Baltimore.' Mrs. Allerkamp and her sons breathed with relief at this extraordinary news. In order to find Franziska a long-overdue husband, they had been willing to have their unsullied German line diminished by the admission of a non-German man, even a Catholic, and to find that he was of their stock was a reassurance which they had not expected. The bloodlines would remain clean; the admission of lesser strains would be avoided; a good thing was being done and a faulty one had not happened. Otto Macnab was to their satisfaction German, and all was well with the world.

'Kiss her, you dummy!' Ernst cried, pushing his fellow Ranger forward.

'You may kiss her!' Ludwig shouted.

And the first word Otto and Franziska shared was a kiss.

After his resounding victories at Palo Alto and Resaca de la Palma, General Taylor could well have thundered across the Rio Grande and chased the demoralized Mexicans all the way to some logical stopping point like San Luis Potosí far to the south, but he was an extremely cautious man who could not visualize penetrating so far into enemy territory without his supply lines in good order. He dawdled away the months of May, June, July and much of August before making a move against the northern Mexico fortress city of Monterrey, and when he finally did start, he had no clear idea of what route to follow.

In his confusion he called upon Captain Garner to take sixteen of his Rangers and a unit of dragoons to explore the long southern route via Linares while regular army scouting parties surveyed the more direct but potentially dangerous route along the Rio Grande. Garner elected to take with him his usual companions: Panther Komax, who had proved himself a terror during the two big battles, and Otto Macnab, now back from Fredericksburg, whom Garner called 'my artillery on the right.'

The Rangers headed due south to explore the possibility of a route through the small town of San Fernando, and since it formed an important launch point for a dash westward to Linares, they anticipated a difficult fight. But when they approached San Fernando, with Macnab and Komax slipping ahead as scouts, they found the place undefended, so the dragoons placed their Negro cook at the head of the column, where, on a fiddle he had brought with him from Alabama, he played a screechy 'Yankee Doodle' while the surprised victors marched into the empty town.

In their attack on the next little town, Granada, the Rangers behaved differently, leaving the regular troops ashen-faced. The unimportant little town lay to the west, toward Linares, and was defended by a ragtag rearguard of the regular Mexican army. When these troops satisfied themselves that the norteamericanos seriously outnumbered and outgunned them, they fired a few shots and withdrew, but a handful of village youths decided to protect their settlement.

From atop the roofs of houses they sniped at the invaders, and by ill luck, killed a Ranger named Corley who rode with a good friend named Lucas. When Lucas saw his companion fall from this casual fire, he dashed into the village and began shooting at anyone or anything he saw. His fire was so intense that other Rangers believed him to be in peril, so in they dashed, Komax and Macnab among them, and now the firing became so furious that houses were pocked with bullet holes.

Soon Captain Garner and his men were in the heart of the village, where the killing became so general that a regular from Illinois listened in a state of shock: 'What in hell are they doing in there?'

He could not know that Otto Macnab had been at the massacre at Goliad, or that Panther Komax had one evening been forced at gunpoint to pick a bean from a clay pot and then watch as his friends who picked black were shot, or that Ranger Lucas had just lost his best friend, or that Ranger Tumlinson had seen his father's ranch near the Strip burned to nothing and his father slain by bandits who called themselves Mexican patriots. The Illinois man could not conceive of the general hatred with which most of the Rangers viewed all Mexicans, nor appreciate why, now that sniper fire had endangered them, they wanted to punish the little town for every accumulated wrong they thought they had suffered: substantial ones like real murders and burnings, imaginary ones like whispered tales of Mexican barbarities.

When Lieutenant Colonel Cobb read reports of the incident at Granada, he was so shaken by the brutal behavior of his Texans that he conducted personal interviews with all regulars who had information about the slaughter, and when he was satisfied that the evidence was accurate, he marched in to General Taylor's tent and demanded that the Rangers be dismissed from the army and sent home.

'That I cannot do,' Taylor said flatly.

'They will destroy your army, sir.'

'How?'

'By their senseless slaughter of Mexicans. They'll ignite the whole countryside against you.'

'That's a risk I must take. I need them as my eyes and ears.'

'You know that they take no prisoners?'

'Santa Anna took none of them prisoner.'

'Are we to descend to Santa Anna's level?'

'Texans are different. They were their own nation. They have their own rules. But remind them that this time they aren't fighting Santa Anna.'

'Respectfully, sir, I see only tragedy ahead. Send them home. Now!'

General Taylor, always mindful of difficult tasks to come, refused, and a month later even Cobb was quite satisfied to have the Texans on the scene, for when the army reached Monterrey everyone saw that the capture of this sizable city, with its numerous forts, gun emplacements and interlocking alleyways that armed civilians could defend, was not going to be easy. East of the city the ground was relatively flat, but it too was guarded by numerous forts, each with its own heavy artillery; and west of the city, on the important road to Saltillo, rose two small mountains, not unduly large but high enough and protected by slopes that looked impossible to scale.

The mountain on the south flank of the road was Federación, topped by a substantial fort; the one to the north was Independencia, topped by a massive, stout-walled, dilapidated building called the Bishop's Palace. To capture Monterrey, these two peaks must be taken; if they were left in Mexican hands, enemy artillery would make retention of the city impossible.

The Texas Rangers, supported by a much larger cadre of the best regular army troops under General Worth, were assigned to take the two mountains while Taylor took the city itself, and on the night of 19 September amid a downpour the Texans moved in a wide circle to the north, coming down to the Saltillo road, where on the next day they captured that highway. Now all they had to do was climb two mountains in the face of heavy enemy fire and capture a fort on one of them, a stout-walled, defended palace on the other.

On 22 September, a rainy Monday morning, General Worth decided to make the attempt on Federación and its fort. His men spent the first six hours gaining, with much difficulty, positions from which to launch the charge up the final slopes, and at noon all was ready. 'We go,' Captain Garner called with no discernible emotion.

Up the formidable steeps the Texans went, and whenever they were pinned down by enemy fire, the regular troops, just as brave, surged forward in their sector, but as the miserably hot afternoon unfolded, the wiry Texans had one advantage: they were accustomed to the oppressive heat and the rivers of sweat that poured down their faces.

'Give 'em hell,' Garner called quietly, and on his Rangers went.

Incredibly, they gained the crest of the mountain and diverted so many defenders that the panting regulars soon took their sector too. Without cheers or battle cries, the regular officer in charge simply pointed at the waiting fort, and like an army of remorseless ants attacking a parcel of food, they started across the top of the mountain and literally overwhelmed the fort, not by sheer numbers, but by the terrible firepower and irresistible force they represented.

At three that hot, wet afternoon Federación and its fort were in their hands, but before the Texans could congratulate themselves, Garner pointed north across the chasm that separated them from Independencia and said: 'Tomorrow we take that.'

Without adequate food and with no tents or protection from the intermittent rains, the Rangers passed a short, fitful night, during which Lucas, who had led the slaughter at Granada, asked Otto Macnab: 'Do you think we can climb that one? It looks steeper.'

'We'll see.'

'That stone building. Much stouter than the fort.'

'We'll find out.'

'Were you afraid, today? I mean, you're so much younger than me.' When Otto made no reply, Lucas confessed: 'I was scared real bad.'

'Only natural.'

'Tomorrow, can I fight alongside you? I never seen a man fire as fast as you can.'

'I always fight with Panther Komax.'

'I know. But can I sort of trail along?'

'Nobody stopping you.'

At three in morning, when the rains ceased, the Rangers launched their attack on Independencia, but now the rocky slopes were so steep and slick that it seemed absolutely impossible that they could be scaled. 'Christ, this can't be done,' but then came the quiet voice of Garner, that indomitable man who found handholds where none existed: 'A little more,' and up the struggling men went.

This time they left the regular troops well behind, but close to the top their sector became so steep that each man had to fend for himself, and the regulars moved well ahead over their easier terrain. At this perilous point, with Mexican riflemen shooting down from the rim of their protected hilltop, Otto found himself with Lucas, who was on the verge of exhaustion.

'Breathe deep,' Otto said, and extending his right leg so that Lucas could grasp it, he pulled the near-fainting man up to the next level. There they rested, unable to catch any breath, but soon Otto pointed to a declivity in the rocks and said: 'Looks easy,' and he led Lucas up a steep incline and onto the crest of the hill.

There a wild fight was in progress, with the regular troops giving an exceptionally strong account of themselves and driving the enemy always backward toward the security of the Bishop's Palace. But now Garner, seeing an advantage while the Mexicans were engaged with the regular troops, gave a wild shout, no longer muted, and rallied his Texans, who with a mighty surge drove at the palace gates. The fighting was intense and terrifying, but with the horrendous firepower of their repeater Colts, the Texans simply shot the Mexican defenders out of their positions.

'Otto!' came a fierce cry from Panther Komax, and together the two men dashed at the gate, blasting a score of Mexicans and forcing their way into the interior. In doing so, they had moved far ahead of their companions, but their experience as Rangers made them confident that others would soon crowd in to support them. Within minutes Garner and six or eight of his best men had joined them inside the walls.

The killing was short and sharp, for the Mexicans had no response to the deadly fire of the Colts. How many died was not immediately determined, but when the fight was almost over, a brave Mexican who had holed himself into a position from which there was no escape fired resolutely at the Texans, and put his last bullet through the guts of Ranger Lucas, who died in prolonged agony.

Macnab, seeing him fall, wheeled about, spotted the trapped Mexican and blasted him with his revolver.

The guardian hills were taken and the fall of Monterrey was assured. The pathway to Saltillo lay open and the culminating battle of the north now became inevitable, for a Mexican adversary much more powerful and competent than pusillanimous General Arista was preparing an army at San Luis Potosí, an army so huge that it might well drive the norteamericanos from the soil of Mexico forever.

Although President Polk and General Taylor started this war, it was Benito Garza who started the fighting with his bold foray across the Rio Grande. But he did not participate in the disaster at Monterrey, where a fortified city protected by superior numbers failed to defend itself. As recognized leader of the irregular forces in the north, he had been summoned south, where he would participate in a bewildering series of events that would alter the progress of the war.

In Havana the exiled dictator Santa Anna, who faced immediate death if he returned to Mexico, had been having clandestine discussions with American officials during which the invasion of Mexico was discussed in candid and sometimes shocking terms. The wily general pointed out that a bumbling old fool like Zachary Taylor was never going to march all the way to Mexico City. 'Frankly,' Santa Anna told his listeners, 'he's incompetent,' and he proceeded to analyze with remarkable insight the other weaknesses of the American position: 'Should you try to land at Vera Cruz and force your way onto the central plateau, all Mexico will rise against you and cut your supply lines, and no army can sustain an invasion over that distance without adequate supplies.'

When the American strategists argued that their troops could live off the land, Santa Anna replied: 'Never! A million patriots will destroy them in the night.'

His arguments were so seductive that President Polk, hoping that a bold move would solve the strategic impasse, launched one of the most extraordinary diplomatic maneuvers in history. 'What we must do,' Polk told his advisers, 'is test this Santa Anna to determine how reliable he will be . . . how far we can trust him, that is. Then use him to our advantage.'

'Risky,' an army man warned. 'He's a sly fox.'

'We're just as sly,' Polk assured him, a boast that each man would often remember in later years.

New negotiators sailed to Havana, where they talked frankly with Santa Anna, receiving from him a brazen proposal: 'There's only one sure way to end this war. Have your fleet deposit me at Vera Cruz with half a million dollars, in gold. I will then act as your agent and terminate this unfortunate affair on terms favorable to you and acceptable to Mexico.'

'But will Mexico accept you?'

'When I set foot in Vera Cruz . . . I lost my leg in that city, you must remember. The people of Vera Cruz venerate me. I can handle this in a week.'

The American representatives were not fools, and before accepting such a proposal, they investigated it from all angles, but when they talked with silver-tongued Santa Anna, who knew English well enough to smother them with glibness at any difficult juncture, they convinced themselves that here was a noble patriot who wished only to end a disagreeable war on terms favorable to both sides.

A remarkable agreement was drawn up, initialed by everyone: Santa Anna would be given a huge sum in gold, with more to come when the peace treaty was signed; a boat of British registry would be provided at the port of Havana; and Commodore David Conner, commanding the United States Caribbean fleet, would be issued presidential orders directing him to assure Santa Anna's ship safe passage through the American blockade and into the port of Vera Cruz. If necessary, Commodore Conner could sink any Mexican vessels that tried to prevent the return of the hero to his native soil.

At this point Benito Garza received cryptic instructions forwarded secretly from Cuba: 'Report immediately to Vera Cruz and prepare a spectacular reception for a secret arrival.' He was not pleased with these orders, but he was prepared to report where his country needed him.

So Benito dropped other responsibilities, including his often-interrupted honeymoon, rode south along back roads where norteamericano patrols would not stumble upon him, reached Potosí, and hurried on to Vera Cruz, where secretly he organized a rabble for one of those demonstrations that flourished regularly in Mexico. He had not the slightest intimation of what was afoot, but he supposed that some general opposed to the present inept government of the country was going to make a pronouncement with a fresh new plan—fifty-third since 1821, counting those which flourished for a single heady afternoon—for saving the country. On the reasonable grounds that anything would be better than what Mexico now had, he supposed that he would support the new grito.

How astonished he was on the morning of 16 August 1846 when the latest hero prepared to save the country arrived not from some inland barracks but from the little British steamer *Arab,* delivered into the harbor by the American fleet itself! Even at that dramatic moment Benito did not guess the identity of the savior, and then to his great joy he saw General Santa Anna, Benemérito de la Patria, come stumping down the gangplank on his best ceremonial leg. Garza needed no prodding to start his wild cheering, but to his dismay hardly anyone watching this charade bothered to join him, and the resuscitated dictator marched into his domain in near-silence. Seven or eight men, led by Garza, shouted: 'Santa Anna! Santa Anna!' but older men and wiser asked quietly: 'What can he be up to this time?'

Soon all knew that Antonio López de Santa Anna was once again Mexico's El Supremo, with powers doubling any he had enjoyed before, and it was rumored that he himself would assume command of all armed forces, north or south. But whether he would fight, as some said, or sell out to the norteamericanos, as others predicted, no one knew.

When Benito and a score of trusted lieutenants met with Santa Anna that night, they asked bluntly: 'Excellency, what are your plans?' and he replied: 'Only one. Crush General Taylor at Saltillo. Drive General Scott back into the sea if he tries to land here in Vera Cruz.'

When the applause ended, Garza asked: 'When do we march north?' and his hero replied: 'When my nation calls me. And she will call.'

President Polk had by this rash action placed on Mexican soil the one leader who had a chance to defeat America's grandiose plans, and what was more astonishing, Polk had also provided the American dollars which could help Santa Anna turn the trick.

When word reached General Taylor that Santa Anna had returned to Mexico as supreme dictator and was assembling a massive army to bring north, the old man faced a series of difficult decisions. It had become apparent to President Polk, a Democrat and a wily one, that General Taylor, a Whig and a blunt one, was receiving in the press a flood of adulation as reward for his victories at Palo Alto, Resaca and Monterrey. With the shrewd insight which characterized Tennessee politicians like Andrew Jackson and Sam Houston, Polk foresaw that Taylor was going to use his military popularity to win the presidency in 1848, and this had to be forestalled, because Polk considered that the general would be a hopeless President.

Making a move that was both politically and militarily astute, Polk forbade Taylor to leave Monterrey lest he become trapped in the vast desert area separating Saltillo and San Luis Potosí. When Taylor's officers received the orders, they immediately spotted the error: 'My God! This keeps us from chasing the defeated Mexicans into Saltillo and crushing them there.'

Persifer Cobb fired off a bitter letter to his brother:

The only good news I can report is that during this enforced idleness we have had the good sense to send all the Texans home. Yes, they're all gone, and I'm a free man at last, one who can sleep well at night. Did you know that at the height of our effort one Texas company of foot soldiers demurred at fighting as infantry, saying that every decent Texan was entitled to his horse? Well, they took a vote. Yes, Somerset, on the eve of battle they took a vote whether to fight or not and it was 318 to 224 in favor of quitting. So they just quit. Can you imagine Hannibal, as he faced the Alps, allowing his soldiers to take a vote as to whether they wished to scale those snowy heights? That clinched matters with General Taylor, who summoned me and said: 'I want no more of your Texans. Send them home.' I wanted to remind him that they were not *my* Texans, but instead I saluted and informed Captain Garner: 'Your Rangers are dismissed. Take them home.' And what do you suppose he did? Stared at me with those icy eyes and said: 'We voted last night to quit when our second three-month enlistments were up. You're not *sending* us home. We're *going* home.' As we watched them ride off, one of my officers muttered: 'I pray that all decent Mexicans are safe in their beds,' because as I've told you, the Texans shoot at anything that moves and take no prisoners.

When one Mexican general surrendered at Monterrey he insisted upon an unusual paragraph in the papers of the agreement: 'I must be accompanied from the city by a strong escort of regular army officers lest I fall into the hands of your Texans.' I led him forth assisted by eleven well-armed officers who had orders to shoot to kill if the Texans tried to attack.

I was sorry, in a way, to lose Otto Macnab, not because I like him, for he is a steely-eyed killer, but because I wanted to understand how a man so young could have developed so forceful a character. Judging his entire performance with me, I found him an abler tactician than Captain Garner and certainly a more controlled fighter than Panther Komax. But I simply could not understand his savagery. During the incident in Granada, I'm told, it was he who reloaded his four pistols twice, meaning that he may have killed a great many Mexicans, none of them well armed. When I asked him about this, he said nothing.

Rumor insists that General Taylor will ignore orders and march directly to Saltillo, daring Santa Anna to challenge him. I hope he does, but when I discussed the possibility with his assistants they alarmed me by saying: 'If he does, he'll need your Texans again. He despises them, but he knows he can't move without their scouting.' My God! They may come back!

Otto Macnab, mustered out at Monterrey on 29 September 1846, rode with Garner and Panther to Laredo, then on to San Antonio, where the other two cut east to Xavier County. 'Give them my best,' Otto said in farewell.

From San Antonio he headed north toward the German settlement at Fredericksburg, and as he rode down the side of a hill he saw in the distance the outlines of the rude wooden house that, in his absence, the Allerkamp men had erected for their sister. It was such a surprising object of civilization that those sentiments which had so deeply affected him when he saw the light gleaming from the cabin surged back, causing him to halt his horse while he gazed at this symbol of what was good in life. The powerful difference was that this was *his* home, *his* light in the wilderness, and he was so overcome by this powerful sensation of love and things civilized that he spurred his horse and raced down the rest of the hill, shouting at the top of his voice: 'Franziska! Franziska!' And when at last he saw her come to the door, wiping her hands on her apron, he thought to himself: This is what we fought for.

He spent most of these days of autumnal peace by working slavishly to improve his home. And when the Allerkamps went in to Fredericksburg on Saturdays he spent much of his time playing with the neighbors' children and teaching them games, or serving as their four-legged horse, down on his knees, while they galloped about the grass, lashing at his flanks with little twigs. Franziska, watching with pleasure as he gamboled with the children, wished that she could add to his pleasure by informing him that she was pregnant, but for the present this was not to be.

He had once told her, during their long talks when they were getting to know each other after their unusual marriage, that he had been driven to acquire the land at Fredericksburg not only because of his intense love for her, but also because he had so treasured those evenings spent talking with Martin Ascot and Betsy Belle that he had become determined to have a home of his own, 'where people could stop by and talk about what was happening.'

They did not as yet actually have such a home, on their own land, that is, because it had been deemed prudent, in view of Otto's absences as a Ranger, for everyone to delay building a Macnab house on the Macnab holdings. But during this unexpected reprieve from battle they began collecting the field stones and slabs of limestone from which a true Macnab home could one day be built.

If the Germans had the materials, the manpower and the determination to build Otto and Franziska a house, what deterred them? The Comanche. As soon as the Indians learned that the Texans were embroiled in a war with Mexico, with most white fighting men engaged below the Rio Grande, they moved daringly closer to all white settlements, so that there was a constant fear of new massacres, kidnappings and burnings. 'It would be unthinkable to leave our daughter alone on a farm two or three miles away from our protection,' Ludwig explained to Otto when the latter wanted to start building his own home. 'The Comanche are becoming bold and terrible.'

The Germans had acquired extra rifles and were teaching Thekla and Franziska to reload and fire the weapons, and no Allerkamp man ever worked alone in a field. He either worked with another man, or perched his woman on a stump to guard him with a loaded rifle while he labored.

'Ernst is different,' Franziska explained to her husband one night soon after his return as they lay on their straw-mattress bed. 'We didn't want to worry you, but he actually goes out among the Comanche.'

'What?' Otto sat bolt upright.

'Yes, he knows their language now. He talks with them.'

'Why?'

'He's trying to persuade them to make a lasting peace treaty with us Germans. He tells them we're different. That we can be trusted.'

'Good God! Doesn't he know what happened at the San Antonio council house . . . the massacre?'

'He tells them that was not our fault. That with us Germans it could never happen.'

'But what about Victoria?' In his confusion, Otto rose from bed and stomped about the little room. 'The Comanche are our enemy. You didn't see my mother . . . my aunt. Franza, it was horrible.'

'Ernst says it needn't be that way any longer. Not here. Not with us Germans.'

'I better talk with Ernst,' and despite her protests and the lateness of the hour, he strode over to the other house and roused his brother-in-law, the one who called himself Uncas.

'I know all about the massacres, Otto, and I know how much you loved your two Mexican women. The Comanche are terrible, but the time comes when peace must be reached.'

'With the Comanche, never.'

'What's going on there?' Ludwig's deep voice called, and when the two young men explained they were arguing about the Comanche, he growled: 'Argue outside and let honest people sleep.'

Wrapping themselves in blankets, they went out into the October stillness, and when Ernst saw the huge golden disk of the full moon he said: 'Comanche moon, that's what they call it. It's on bright nights like this they make their attacks,' and the two men looked into the shadows, half expecting to see the savages preparing for an assault on the Allerkamp place.

'Do you honestly think that peace . . . ?' Before Otto could finish his question, Ernst gripped his arm and said: 'I know that peace is possible with anyone

. . . anyone. When your battles down there end, won't you have to arrange peace with the Mexicans? Of course. And we must arrange peace with the Comanche.'

In the days that followed, Franziska told her husband about an astonishing frontier drama centering upon a German immigrant whom Otto did not know. Ottfried Hans, Freiherr von Meusebach, was one of those admirable, inquisitive young noblemen whom the European countries occasionally produced. Born in a German duchy, educated in various German universities, he spoke five languages and seemed destined to follow his brother as a major diplomat, when he was dispatched to Texas to bolster the sagging German settlements in the area north of San Antonio. Instantly charmed by the democratic freedoms of his new country, he surrendered the honorific Freiherr, took an American name, and performed notably as John O. Meusebach.

As soon as he had arrived he was visited by Ernst Allerkamp, who assured him: 'I have worked with the Comanche for two years. I know their language. I think I know their hearts. And they have told me: "Peace is possible. But only with you Germans." ' Meusebach, listening carefully, said: 'Let us talk further about this,' and when the two men found themselves in harmony on all points, they issued a simple statement: 'We think a lasting treaty of peace with the Comanche is possible.'

Frenzied discussion had followed, Franziska told Otto, with old-time Kentucky settlers warning Meusebach: 'You wasn't here when President Lamar laid down the basic rule for handlin' Indians in Texas. "Eviction or extermination!" Ain't no way white men can live aside Indians, because they ain't human like us.'

'How did Ernst take that?' Otto asked, and she replied: 'Shouted in a public meeting "Peace is possible!" and he volunteered to lead a party out to the Comanche, if anyone was brave enough to follow.'

'Anyone volunteer?'

'Meusebach.'

'The German nobleman?' and Franza said: 'Yes.'

So that was the way things stood at year's end: two young men ready for great adventure, Ernst among the Comanche, Otto back in Mexico if the army called.

The Meusebach expedition into the heart of the Comanchería assembled its gear in mid-January 1847, and when Otto realized that these men really were going to plunge into enemy territory, where the risk of death by torture was great, he insisted upon going along with his multiple weapons, but Ernst said: 'No, this is a peaceful mission,' and Meusebach agreed.

Otto, disgusted by this non-military attempt, warned: 'You'll die staked out before a fire, but don't call for the Rangers. It'll be too late.'

He was considering whether he should, to protect these headstrong Germans, gather a few men like himself and ride discreetly behind the would-be peacemakers, when he heard Franziska call from her kitchen door the single word 'Liebchen.' Their affinity through the years of their extraordinary courtship and in the early months of their marriage had become so intuitive that whenever Franza uttered the word *Liebchen* in a certain inflection, her husband knew that she was about to say something of importance.

'What?' he asked, turning his whole attention to her.

She blushed, hesitated, then said in a low voice: 'I'm to have a baby.' She said no more, and he refrained from jumping in the air or embracing her fervently; instead, he bowed to her and she to him, for they were people of silent moments deeply cherished.

But the moment of reverence was broken by the arrival of Panther Komax, who bellowed as he approached the cabin: 'Macnab! General Taylor needs us at Saltillo! Garner's taking down his best men from Company M.'

When the bearlike man saw Franziska, he whisked her up in his arms, threw her in the air, and shouted: 'How did you ever catch this one, Little Nubbin?'

'Put her down!' Otto yelled, and when he saw her safely on the ground he whispered to Komax: 'She's going to have a baby.'

Panther stepped back, surveyed the couple, and clucked his tongue: 'Fräulein Macnab, you are beautiful! Simply beautiful!' And he gave her a great hairy kiss which practically covered her face. He was the second man to have kissed her, and she was astonished at his boldness.

'Yes,' he snorted as the Allerkamp women fed him gargantuan quantities of food, 'messengers came north with news that Old Rough-and-Ready was bulldogging his way into the heart of Mexico. Without scouts. With disaster every time he moved. After six or seven routs of his dragoons—' Here he leaped to his feet and galloped about the place, imitating the American cavalry on their big horses riding fat and dumb right into Mexican ambushes. 'Hell, he knowed he needed us to do his dirty work.'

'Can't you stay the night?' Thekla asked, and he said: 'Nope, we got to join up with Garner and the others at Laredo.'

So packing was done hastily, but when Franziska went out to put Otto's gear on his waiting horse, she saw his saddle blanket and uttered a cry: 'There's blood on your saddle.' And when Panther went to scratch the discoloration, he confirmed: 'Yep. It's blood.'

'Otto, were you wounded?' Franza asked, her face even paler than before, but Panther dissipated her fears: 'Your little man never gets wounded. He wounds other people,' and the two Rangers explained how they had captured those two little mountains at Monterrey, Federación and Independencia, and how on the latter hill, when they attacked the Bishop's Palace, Ranger Lucas had been killed.

'Me and your husband carried his body down and tied it to Otto's saddle,' Panther said, and when he saw Franziska blanch, he added: 'Hell, ma'am, him and me's been in a dozen fights like that. We never get hurt.'

This mention of death, something the families of Rangers rarely discussed, for they appreciated the perils of their men's rough occupation, spurred Franziska to reveal something she had intended never to tell her husband. Now, taking his hand and leading him away from Panther, she whispered: 'While you were in Mexico, your friend Yancey Quimper rode into Fredericksburg, seeking to buy land, or open a store, or anything. Nobody trusted him, so he left. But he stopped by here and asked me many questions, and . . . Otto, he wanted to know . . . if you got killed in the war . . . if he could come speak with me . . . and . . .'

She hesitated, for she knew that if she revealed the remainder of that incredible visit, Otto might go storming out and kill Quimper, but the realization of death compelled her to speak: 'He tried to kiss me. I pushed him away and told him to begone. He stood in the doorway and said: "Remember, Franziska, I wanted to marry you before Otto ever saw you. If anything happens . . ." '

Otto said nothing, hands at his side, linen duster about his feet, but his wife added: 'He wants you dead, Otto. Please, please take care of yourself.'

'Time to go!' Komax warned, and the two Rangers, taking extra horses with them and Otto's arsenal of guns, headed south and overtook Garner and the rest of the company at Laredo. From there they splashed across the shallow Rio Grande and started the dangerous passage to Saltillo, where General Taylor would be encamped awaiting the arrival of Santa Anna with the main Mexican army.

'Any danger of Mexican raiding parties?' Otto asked, and Garner replied: 'There's always danger as long as Benito Garza is alive, and especially when Taylor's army hasn't been keeping scouts on the perimeters.'

Each day Otto served with this gangling man he respected his abilities more; Garner was certainly not a compelling figure, and he lacked the fiery oratory of a dashing leader, but in all he did he was completely sensible, a man who seemed to anticipate the flow of battle with an acute awareness of where he and his troops could be used with maximum effect. Panther once said: 'Twenty of us Rangers with Garner at our head is equal to forty. Outen him, we're just twenty.'

Garner demonstrated his professionalism shortly after his contingent completed its furtive crossing of the northern desert on 4 February 1847 and reported to Lieutenant Colonel Cobb, who, as before, would serve as their superior. The fastidious South Carolinian, watching them straggle in, a disjointed file with men and horses in every conceivable condition, winced at the ugly prospect of dealing with them through another campaign, but he did take Captain Garner in to see General Taylor, who proved to be as gruff as ever: 'Bad situation. We know Santa Anna's coming north. But where and when and how many? That we don't know.'

'And it's our job to find out?' Garner asked without bravado.

'That's why I sent for you.' The general hesitated, then decided to be frank: 'I was damned glad to see you go, Garner. Never seen a rowdier group of soldiers. Can't you instill any discipline?' Before the lanky captain could respond, Taylor added: 'And I'm damned glad to have you back.' He wanted to shake Garner's hand or even embrace him in a soldierly way, but instead he said gruffly: 'Everything hangs on the next few days. Find out what they're up to.'

Garner decided to take eight Rangers with him on a protracted scout of the southern approaches to Saltillo, and as his men gathered in that beautiful cathedral square where the Frenchman René-Claude d'Ambreuze had courted Trinidad de Saldaña, he knew their task was a dangerous one, for if discovered on this foray, they might have to fight large forces of Mexican lancers. But the Rangers were skilled in clandestine operations, and if a solitary Ranger was suddenly cut off from his fellows, he would know that he must proceed alone; he could be counted upon to sneak his way back to headquarters with a reliable report of how things stood in the areas he had seen. And if only that one Ranger survived to deliver essential information regarding the forthcoming battle, the scout would be judged a success.

When Garner's men left Saltillo they entered almost immediately upon a terrain that seemed as if it had been carved out of rock by the god of battles for some special Armageddon. It was a narrow defile, lined on the east by mountains so high they could not be scaled; their lower reaches, however, provided a sloping field across which cavalry could charge. The west flank consisted of a deep gully backed by lower hills; here cavalry could not function but foot soldiers could. General Taylor, marching south into the defile, would have to smash head-on into General Santa Anna marching north, and the outcome would depend upon how skillfully each general utilized the sloping hills to the east and those gaping gullies to the west.

'This ain't gonna be easy,' Panther told Otto as they studied the brutal terrain. When Otto made no reply, for none would have been relevant, Panther added: 'But I guess you fight your battles where they happen,' and again Otto said nothing, for he was studying those ominous slopes to the east, wondering how his Rangers would utilize them if an attack by Santa Anna's lancers suddenly developed.

On 20 February 1847, Garner and his men reconnoitered the oncoming Mexican army, and as brave as the Rangers were, they were shaken when they got to the crest of a hill and saw the endless manpower that Santa Anna was bringing north. Panther called back to those still climbing below: 'Damned lines go on forever.'

'Can you spot the camp they'll be using tonight?' Cobb asked, cupping his hands to muffle his voice.

'Off to one side,' Komax replied, lowering his voice too. And then he tossed in a typical Ranger addition: 'We can reach it tonight.'

When the huge fellow clambered down, Garner asked: 'Panther, can you and three men ride ahead and create a diversion? Allow them to chase you back this way without getting caught?'

'Don't mind if I do get caught. We can handle them . . .'

'Panther, you're not to get caught. You're to tease them on. Because me and Macnab, we're gonna go right into the heart of their camp, and we want them to be chasing you, not us.'

Otto displayed not the slightest emotion. He dismounted, took off his white duster, folded it meticulously, and handed it for safekeeping to one of the two Rangers who would not be involved in either foray. This done, he hitched up his trousers, felt for his two Colts, stowed his two old pistols in his saddle, and climbed back on his horse. Together with Garner he started the perilous, tortuous advance to the Mexican lines.

They rode through the scattered advance posts, boldly keeping to their horses. Disguised as Mexicans, with Garner wearing a colorful serape, they rode straight into a position at which they could dismount, tethered their horses, and moved cautiously about, noting strengths and dispositions.

For a day, twenty-six hours, they remained inside enemy lines, one sleeping while the other watched, and in the early part of the night when the Mexicans were careless and talkative, they crept very close to the tents, and it was in the moon-cast shadow of one of these that Macnab saw a Mexican officer bending over to tighten the guy ropes. As he did so, Otto realized that it was Benito Garza, not fifteen yards away.

'Captain,' he whispered. 'That's Garza, I'm sure. I'm going in and kill him.' Garner restrained him: 'Any noise would be fatal.'

'But he's the brains in the Strip.'

'I know who he is,' Garner snapped, 'and I know that any motion now . . .'

Now Macnab experienced agonies of indecision: there was Garza, an enemy he was obligated to kill, almost within touching distance; behind was the American army needing information. It was Garner who solved this dilemma: 'If he's that important to you, Otto, break in and shoot him. You'll not get out alive, but . . . Give me fifteen minutes lead, and I'll be safe.'

'It is that important,' Macnab said.

'So be it,' Garner said, but before he could return to his tethered horse, someone else left the tent to catch a breath of clean night air, and the watchers saw that it was a woman, a young woman of great charm and obvious breeding. She was, it seemed likely, the wife of some officer, and her presence deterred Macnab's plan of bursting in with pistols blazing. Garner grasped him by the arm, as if to pull him away, but then Garza reappeared, and placed his arm about the woman's waist, and kissed her.

Who could the woman be? She seemed no more than twenty, and Garza must be at least forty, but that they were in love there could be no doubt, none whatever.

'Has he a wife?' Garner asked.

'Who knows?' Otto replied, and quietly the two Rangers retreated.

They slept about a hundred yards from their horses, Garner spreading his serape on the ground for both of them, and when the sun was well up, they mounted their steeds, walked them quietly north, saluted sentries as if on an inspection tour, and when they saw a break in the lines, galloped like terrified ghosts, neither shouting nor looking back at the men who were firing the bullets that whistled past their heads.

When they reported to General Taylor, he was awed by their adventure and dismayed by the estimates they gave of Santa Anna's strength. 'We must draw back,' he said. 'If we stay, we're trapped.' He thanked Garner for his daring and turned to do the same for Macnab, but the little Ranger was gone.

'Where is he?' Taylor asked, and Garner pointed to where Otto was retrieving his duster from its custodian. Shaking it out and slapping away any dust, he slipped it about his shoulders and considered himself ready for the impending battle.

Benito Garza, commanding General Santa Anna's scouts, was not informed of the infiltration of the mexicano lines by American spies; the sentries who had fired at Garner and Macnab were afraid to report the sortie lest they be shot for having allowed it to happen.

He remained in his tent with his wife, Lucha López, and with the regular army officers with whom he worked. This was 21 February 1847, a cold, damp day, and because the two armies had moved so near to each other, it was obvious that battle could not be avoided, with visible advantage to the mexicanos. Garza was especially hopeful: 'This time, Lucha, we annihilate them.' He spent the morning making arrangements for her to move far to the rear, to be with the other women who had accompanied their men, but at noon he was alerted by reports from his scouts: 'General Taylor is retreating.'

Kissing Lucha, he rode out to check this surprising development and found that the news was accurate: the Americans were withdrawing, and rather precipitately, but he was not deceived by their tactic: 'They're seeking more favorable ground, and they're right.'

Nevertheless he had reason to be hopeful about this battle, for Santa Anna, blustering across Mexico, a wooden leg in one stirrup, had performed his customary miracle of assembling a huge number of men and forging them into a respectable army. He had at his disposal, of course, a reliable cadre of young, able and dedicated officers like Benito Garza, none better in all the armies of the world, and on them he relied to stiffen the ranks. He was also supported by a fierce patriotism which invariably rallied whenever Spanish, or French, or especially American enemies threatened. But most important, he still retained that tremendous charisma which designated him a true romantic hero and which bound men like Garza to him with unbreakable bonds.

Santa Anna in the saddle again! A thrill ran through the nation. Santa Anna was in command of the army again! Men marched with more vigor, lancers rode with more élan. Santa Anna was heading back to avenge his unlucky defeat at San Jacinto, to repeat his earlier triumphs at the Alamo and Goliad. Tejas would be regained. New Mexico and California would be saved. As the sun set almost every man in the mexicano army believed that on the morrow Santa Anna would celebrate his birthday with another stupendous victory.

He almost did. In fact, he should have, not on the twenty-second, which was more or less a stalemate, with the Americans suffering major casualties and a loss of valuable position, but on the twenty-third, when the three-to-one Mexican superiority in numbers and mobility began to tell.

About midmorning the attack along the foothills of the eastern mountains, the attack which Garner and his men had known to be inevitable, began, with a furious charge by several companies of elite lancers supported by rapid-firing dragoons. Ashen-faced, General Taylor observed: 'They're turning our left flank!' Perceiving that if they did, the superb Mexican cavalry would chop up his rear echelons and throw the entire American army into rout, he called for all available men to stanch the blood being let by the lancers, and under his stalwart leadership, a few cavalry and many foot soldiers assembled to halt the surging Mexican horsemen.

Old Rough-and-Ready may have been slow-witted, but he was no fool. Never first-rate in overall strategy, when engaged in a specific battle, he knew where to throw his strength at critical moments, and now he dug in, a stubborn man fighting his last encounter.

With appalling power and skill the Mexicans hammered at his left flank, but like a wounded bear Taylor growled and gathered power and fought back. At the critical moment, when the battle seemed lost, he called upon a Mississippi gentleman whom he had once despised to save the day. Twelve years before, Colonel Jefferson Davis, then age twenty-seven, had eloped with Taylor's daughter Sarah, an act that still rankled the general. But now Taylor had to swallow his pride and call upon Davis and his Mississippi Rifles to hold off Santa Anna's rampaging cavalry, and with support from the Texas Rangers, Davis led his troops in a gallant charge.

The Rangers were led by Persifer Cobb, braver almost than they, who relished the chance to gallop his horse right at the Mexican lancers and test his skill against theirs. Cobb was supported, he was relieved to note, by Garner and Komax on his left and Otto Macnab on his right, the latter firing his pistols like a little arsenal. Together they simply rode down the Mexicans, who had smaller steeds and inferior firepower.

'Watch the lances!' Cobb shouted as he knocked down a lancer about to pierce Macnab, who raised his Colts in a salute as he roared past in pursuit of his own targets.

When General Taylor saw that the day had been saved, he had the grace to say to his son-in-law: 'Colonel Davis, my daughter was a better judge of men than I was.' But none of the Americans believed this battle to have been a victory, not by any means. Losses were great. Valuable positions had once more been wrested away by superior Mexican numbers and performance. Indeed, as night fell General Taylor had to consider the likelihood that on the morrow he was doomed to suffer a crushing defeat, and with this mournful prospect staring at him, he assembled his officers.

'Can we hold them if they make a dawn attack?' he asked.

'Our men and horses are exhausted.'

'But can they make one last effort?'

'They can always make an effort. But . . .'

Throughout the night the discussions continued, and at one o'clock or thereabouts Taylor suggested that his best Texas scouts be sent out to bring news of exactly when the Mexicans would begin their major attack. Lieutenant Colonel Cobb thought the general had tears in his eyes as he said: 'Give us what help you can, Persifer. I knew your uncle Leander. Good man. Good man with horses, that one.'

Despite Captain Garner's urgent suggestion that Cobb remain safe with General Taylor, the South Carolinian insisted upon sharing the scout with his Texans, and they went alarmingly deep into enemy territory. Two o'clock, and only sporadic signs of enemy action. Three o'clock, and still darkest winter night, with Mexican troops huddling to keep warm. Four o'clock, and only that ominous silence. Five o'clock, and just a faint show of light from a campfire visible here and there.

At six, when dawn would betray their presence, the Rangers were in maximum danger, and Cobb, aware of this, cautioned additional care, but Panther Komax ignored his warnings, rose boldly in his saddle, stared ahead in disbelief, and shouted: 'Jesus Christ!'

When the others rode up, several of them repeated Panther's cry: 'Jesus Christ!'

On the evening after the great battle at Buena Vista, when the Mexicans had stood within six inches or six minutes of an astounding victory, General Santa Anna had convened a meeting of *his* officers, and such is the strangeness of battle that approximately identical questions were being asked.

'Can we crush them in the morning?' the one-legged Napoleon asked.

'Our lancers, all our cavalry, they did what they could this afternoon.'

'Can they repeat?'

Silence. No one dared tell the dictator of Mexico, the commander in chief, the Benemérito de la Patria, El Supremo, that something was impossible, but it was clear even to him that the mexicano cavalry had shot its bolt. It had been a gallant bolt, one of the best, but it was finished.

'The infantry?'

More silence. No other infantry in the world suffered the disadvantages that were the common lot of the peasants who formed the bulk of any Santa Anna army. Conscripted at gunpoint, they marched barefoot, clad only in thin cotton shirts even in the dead of winter—like now. And they bled and shivered and died of dysentery, for their army provided no field hospitals to accompany them and no medicines to soften the dreadful fevers they contracted. Despite these deprivations and the lack of food, they were obedient and brave, and when they started running at an enemy line they usually breached it. Such soldiers had defeated Spaniards, Frenchmen, Americans and other Mexicans, and if ordered on the morrow to attack the weakened American lines, they would do so, until their bodies piled higher than a small tree.

But their officers stood silent, for they knew that because of supply problems, those faithful soldiers shivering in the wintry blast had eaten nothing for nearly thirty hours. They would obey orders and start toward the norteamericano lines tomorrow, that was certain, but they might well collapse before they got there, and not necessarily from enemy gunfire.

To the surprise of everyone in his tent, Santa Anna changed the course of his discussion and said most abruptly: 'We had a great victory today, did we not?'

'Yes, General.'

'And we overran six or seven headquarters positions, did we not?'

'We did.'

'Did we capture many enemy flags?'

'We did. Cortés alone has seven. I saw them.'

'Let Cortés speak for himself.' The gallant lancer was sent for, and Santa Anna asked: 'Did you capture enemy flags?'

'Yes, General, seven.'

'Any other trophies?'

'Many. Many.'

Santa Anna now turned to the one man he knew he could trust in any adversity, a man who had always given straight answers: 'Garza, can we defeat them tomorrow?'

'Unquestionably.'

'Why do you say that, when these others . . .'

'Because I know what's going on over there.' He pointed north, toward Saltillo and the American lines: 'They're holding a meeting like this, and they know they've been defeated.'

'Will they retreat, do you think?'

Now Garza had to pause, for in his careful study of the norteamericanos he had perceived that Zachary Taylor was not the clever kind of general who saw things in big design. He was a man who took a position and held on to it until he was knocked off. 'Retreat?' Garza said slowly. 'Maybe not, but . . .'

Santa Anna had heard enough. On the very threshold of a victory which would have enshrined him in the bosom of Mexico forever, he gave his order: 'Immediately, we march back to Potosí.'

'Excellency!' Garza protested, but the fatal die had been cast.

'Strike camp. Abandon everything not instantly needed, and march. Before dawn.'

When Garza dashed to the tent where his wife was sleeping, he wakened her roughly: 'It's ended, Lucha. Back to Potosí.'

'Oh, no!' she cried, for she saw in the resumed battle a chance of victory for her beliefs.

'It's the end for Santa Anna,' Garza said with great sadness, and when his wife, packing furiously, asked what he meant, he explained prophetically: 'Another norteamericano army will land at Vera Cruz. They'll march to Puebla and surround Mexico City. Defeat, defeat. They'll depose Santa Anna, and then they'll go home, thinking it's all over.' He interrupted Lucha's packing and took her by the hands: 'But for us it will never be over. If they want to steal that land south of the Nueces, they better be prepared to pay in blood.'

It was this flight south at dawn that had so astonished Panther Komax and his fellow Rangers.

On the day that General Taylor realized he had won the battle at Buena Vista—if one did not inspect the facts too closely—he agreed to let the Texans disband and go home. He explained to Garner that although he appreciated their contributions, 'none more valiant,' he could not endanger the security of his army by allowing them to harass guiltless Mexican citizens and expose the regular army to guerrilla action in retaliation: 'You must leave at once, and try not to arouse the countryside by thoughtless killings as you go.'

In the morning Taylor said goodbye to the Rangers: 'I thank you for your gallant efforts. But before you depart, I want you to hear the summary prepared by Colonel Cobb,' whereupon the South Carolinian, in his trimmest uniform, stepped forward to read a report he had compiled:

> 'While it is conceded by all that the Texas Rangers have performed satisfactorily all military tasks assigned them, there have unfortunately been certain deficiencies in discipline, the consequences of which I shall now summarize.
>
> 'General riots, pitting volunteers against regulars, five. Ordinary courts-martial, one hundred and nineteen. General courts-martial, eleven. Murders, four. Murders of Mexican citizens, eighty-four. Attempted

murder, eleven. Insubordination and mutinous acts, sixty-one. Cowardice in the face of the enemy, nine.' (At this, several Rangers cried 'No!
No!'—but the charges continued.) 'Desertion, seventeen. Discharged by
the commanding general because of general worthlessness, nineteen.
Discharged because of suspicion of insanity, no other charge appearing
to be reasonable, eleven.

'The Ranger known as Panther Komax, who started the riot last night
which caused at least six hundred dollars' worth of damage to government property, and who told a superior to go to hell, was subjected last
night to a legally convened court-martial whose judgment is hereby
delivered: "The Texas Ranger Leroy Komax, known as Panther, shall
receive a dishonorable discharge and shall hear 'The Rogue's March.' " '

Panther stood rigid, but many Rangers, including Captain Garner, shouted 'No!
No!'—for there was no greater disgrace in the armed services than for a man to
stand at his final attention as the band started to sound the miserable notes of 'The
Rogue's March,' and then to march goosestepping out of the company while some
stout sergeant jerked high the seat of his pants.

Four burly sergeants surrounded Panther and brought him to face the band,
which launched immediately into that doleful, insulting lament for things gone
wrong. As soon as the first notes sounded, a fifth sergeant, bigger than the others,
grabbed Panther by the seat and started marching him off the parade ground;
never again could such a disgraced man serve with the regular army, and Panther
should have gone in silence, accepting his punishment, but at the edge of the field
as he was about to be shoved off, he turned and challenged the army of northern
Mexico: 'Give me six good Rangers and we'll knock the shit outa your whole
force.'

When he was removed, Persifer Cobb returned stiffly to the reading of the
citation:

'Acts of bravery, unnumbered. Devotion to duty, unparalleled. Patriotism, unquestioned.' (He paused.) 'Rangers of Texas, you are unforgettable.'

With that, both he and General Taylor snapped to attention and saluted.

Often during these hectic days of the Mexican War, Otto worried about what was
happening to Ernst Allerkamp on his foray into the Comanchería, and on the way
back to Texas he told Komax, who seemed undisturbed by his rude dismissal from
military service: 'I'll bet those men who went out among the Indians had it a lot

rougher than we did,' and as soon as he reached his home and satisfied himself that Franziska was in good health, he asked: 'And what happened to Ernst?'

In response she rang the bell which the Allerkamp women used for signaling their men—two short, two long for Ernst—and in a moment he came from the fields, delighted to see his brother-in-law. In self-effacing words he summarized a remarkable event:

> 'Three days after you left for Mexico, Herr Meusebach started his expedition for the Comanchería, and I was able to lead him to the principal chiefs. I translated, you know, and we conducted long talks, for the Indians like to go over everything many times.
>
> 'But during hours when I wasn't working I made friends with a young Comanche warrior. Blond hair, pale complexion, he was surely a white man. At first he would explain nothing, but when I gave him tobacco he wanted to talk. "My name is Thomas Lyons. I lived near Austin. The Comanche came to our farm and murdered my parents. Took me away with them. I like being an Indian and do not care to go back to Austin, where my brother lives."
>
> 'I could understand this; as a boy I wanted to be an Indian. But what shocked me was the answer I got when I asked: "Who is this little Mexican boy who follows you about?" And Thomas Lyons said: "I captured him during one of our raids on the Rio Grande." And when I suggested that I take the boy with me and return him to his parents, Lyons asked: "Why?" '

Ernst fell silent, still disturbed by the fact that Indians, too, had slaves, and after a while Otto asked: 'What happened with the Comanche?' and Ernst explained how Meusebach, with skill and patience, had engineered a compassionate treaty which was to be ratified in Fredericksburg within two weeks.

Otto was alarmed: 'Ernst! The Comanche never honor a treaty!' and in the days that followed, while Ernst rode out to lead the great chiefs of that tribe in for the signing, Otto moved through Fredericksburg, repeating his softly stated warning: 'I'm a Ranger. I've fought Indians and Mexicans alike. They're both no good. No place in Texas for either of them.'

For three days, as Ernst and the chieftains approached from the west, Otto strove to discredit the treaty, and he might have continued had not Franziska intervened: 'Otto, there's a new day. New rules. Ernst is right. It's time for peace.'

Macnab was so startled to hear a woman oppose him, a dutiful German housewife, that he stood agape. He looked at her, small, tense, her hair in braids as if she were still a young girl, and to his own amazement he dropped the argument. Taking her in his arms, he whispered: 'I came home to build us a real house. Our home. If Ernst's treaty makes it possible, I'm all for it.' He kissed her twice, then added: 'But when those Indians come into our town, I'm going to be watching. Very careful.'

On a lovely May morning the Comanche arrived, fearful Indians on sleek ponies. Remembering well the tragedy their brothers had encountered during such a meeting in San Antonio, they insisted upon a safeguard, which Ernst interpreted: 'They will lay down their weapons, all of them, even their daggers, in the middle of the roadway if we Germans would do the same.' Meusebach pleaded with the townsmen to accept these terms, and when, against Otto's advice, the pile was made, two Indian braves and Macnab were assigned to watch it.

Otto had wanted to be inside the hotel to safeguard the meeting, but Meusebach had outsmarted him, so there he sat in the warm May sunlight, guarding the weapons and noticing where his Colts five-shooters lay in case he had to grab them in a hurry. He noticed also that the two braves were marking the location of their weapons in case of crisis: he judged that he could outgrab and outshoot them. Next he studied how, having gunned down the two guardians, he could whip about and aim his fire at the entrance to the Nimitz House to shoot the parleying chiefs if they attempted to join the fray.

But the tragedy of San Antonio was not repeated, because John Meusebach, supported by Ernst Allerkamp, had convinced both the Comanche and the Germans that this little paradise set down among the hills, this land of tumbling fields and flowing streams, this Eden of bluebonnets and Indian paintbrush was indeed different, and that amidst the gunfire that echoed across Texas, here stood a refuge of sanity.

The treaty was agreed upon. Braves and Germans recovered their weapons. Macnab, as he picked up his revolvers, muttered to himself: 'Be on watch when the next Comanche moon rides the sky.' He wanted peace as much as anyone in Fredericksburg, but he would continue to prepare for war.

At Easter, as he had predicted, the Comanche came sneaking back, and on a night as calm and lovely as the hill country had known, they crept toward the sleeping town.

Otto Macnab, always on guard, saw them first, terrifying figures on the silvery horizon, and running for his guns he shouted: 'Franza! Quick! Bring the extra powder!' But Ernst stopped him, pointing to the surrounding hills—and there in the brightness of the Easter moon the Indians had lighted signal fires, scores of them on all perimeters, signaling the Germans that in these valleys at least peace prevailed, now and in the future.

Otto was amazed. With Franza beside him, he laid down his guns to watch the fires, but Ernst did not look. Uncas had lowered his head, and he was weeping.

When General Zachary Taylor failed to crush the Mexican army in his questionable victory at Buena Vista, General Winfield Scott was given the job of disembarking at Vera Cruz and finishing the job in the vicinity of Mexico City, but with an army of only ten thousand American troops to subdue millions of Mexicans on their home ground, he was forced to take draconian steps. When guerrillas struck at his supply lines, secretly at night and outside the rules of what he called 'organized warfare,' he issued a startling set of orders, summarized in these words:

> No quarter will be extended to murderers, robbers or any man out of uniform who attacks our convoys. They are equally dangerous to Mexicans, foreigners and American troops, and they shall be exterminated.

> But you are to observe certain rules. Your prisoners are not to be put to death without due solemnity. That is, there shall be no killing of prisoners. What you must do is arrest them, hold them momentarily as prisoners, convene a hearing, sentence them on the spot, and then shoot them.

Therefore, the Americans who had protested so vigorously the savage actions of General Santa Anna at the Alamo and Goliad were now going to operate under almost the same rules.

Scott's second action was perhaps the more significant, for in order to have at his command men prepared to act with such severity, he asked the army to call back into service as many Texas Rangers as possible, and in compliance with this summons, Captain Sam Garner, in retirement on his farm, agreed to reassemble his Company M, if he could have with him Otto Macnab and Panther Komax.

Garner had no trouble signing up the Panther: 'I'd rather fight greasers than eat!' But after the captain had spent two days with the Macnabs, he knew that Otto was completely absorbed in his son Hamish and not at all disposed to return to Mexico: 'Look, I got me a son. I want to stay here and help Franziska with the place. You know, Captain Garner, it really is something for a man to have a son. Can you imagine a tiny little hand like that . . . he can't even keep it straight . . . holding a Colts one of these days?'

Garner was finding it difficult to believe that Otto, deadliest of his Rangers, could be so domesticated, so on the third day at breakfast he turned to Mrs. Macnab: 'Franza, I want to take your man with me again,' and she agreed: 'I think he's ready to go now. Be careful. All of you.'

When the company assembled, Otto was surprised to see Panther in the ranks: 'How can you go back after they gave you that "Rogue's March" in Saltillo?' The big man brushed aside such apprehension: 'That was up north. Scott's down south.' And when Otto reminded him that armies keep records, he said: 'They do, that they do. Come peace, they don't want bastards like me. But come war, and Scott has plenty of that, they're glad to have us.'

'Aren't you afraid your record will follow you?' Otto asked, and Panther replied: 'And when Scott sees it, he's gonna shout: "That's just the son-of-a-bitch I want." He may even make me an officer.'

When their warship delivered them to the steaming port of Vera Cruz, the Rangers lining the rail of the tender that brought them ashore let out a wild yell of joy, for awaiting them stood the austere, primly dressed figure of their old commander, Persifer Cobb, breveted to full colonel for his bravery. 'We're back!' Komax shouted exuberantly, and when the South Carolinian realized that this incorrigible was being returned to his command, he blanched. 'Oh, no!' he cried to no one. 'That I will not tolerate!' But when the reunion was completed, Colonel Cobb outlined the Rangers' new mission.

'We're trying to do what no major army in recent history has ever attempted, so far as I know. With only a handful of men, cut off from reinforcements, we're trying to conquer and pacify an entire nation. We're Hernando Cortés in the nineteenth century, and we're in just as much danger.'

He traced the perilous route to the capital: 'Guerrilleros molest every column we send over these hills. Our job is to stop them. To exterminate them. Without quarter.'

Stern disciplinarian that he was, Persifer Cobb took pride in being as strict with himself as with his underlings, so he firmed his jaw and tried once more to bring some sort of order to the Texans. But he failed. Despite orders, the Rangers drank whatever water they pleased, and soon they were stricken with violent cases of dysentery, which immobilized them for about a week; they were too sick to stand, let alone march. And even when the tougher men like Macnab and Komax revived, they found that their captain remained terribly sick, not only with dysentery but also with the more threatening El Vomito.

Practiced hands advised Colonel Cobb to send Garner back to a homeward-bound ship, but the fighting Ranger would not allow this, so on a litter he made the painful progress to the upland town of Jalapa. In that beautiful spot, where the rigors of Vera Cruz vanished amid flowers, beautiful homes and literally acres of fresh fruit and fields full of cattle, Garner recovered, and it was believed later that had he been in full health and therefore better able to command his men, the tragedy at Avila might not have happened, but Colonel Cobb did not agree: 'All Texans are murderers whenever a Mexican is involved, and had Captain Garner been his usual self, I'm sure he would have led the disgraceful affair.'

La Desolación de Avila they called it in the steamy rain forests leading to the altiplano, and it was the result of the daring action of the guerrilla leader Benito Garza, who waited in the jungle until Captain Garner's detachment was well strung out, then struck with fury at the vulnerable midpoint. The sudden attack caught the still-weakened Garner unawares, and before his startled men could protect him, he was impaled by three swords. Summoning all his frail strength, he straightened in the saddle, tried to catch up with his men, then toppled forward over his horse's neck.

His men, seeing him fall, lashed out at any Mexican they could find, and in their blind rage came upon the innocent village of Avila, in which one of Garza's men had taken refuge.

Galloping into the central plaza, they began shooting any Mexicans they saw, whereupon the guerrilla took aim and struck the man riding next to Komax square in the forehead, dropping him like a bird; he did not bleed profusely, but the bullet hole was so conspicuous on his fever-blanched skin that every Ranger who leaped over his dead body could see it.

No person inside the sniper's hiding place survived the Rangers' revenge, not even the three children. Methodically the Texans then swept through the half-dozen adobes that lined the square, and by evil luck Komax and Macnab found themselves dashing from the last house directly at the open door of the village church. Without stopping, they burst into the church, killed three old men who had taken refuge there, and proceeded to wreck the place, scattering holy implements here and there in the roadway outside. As they withdrew, they killed six cows in a final surge of fury.

When a great outcry rose from Avila and surrounding towns, with the bishop himself protesting, Colonel Cobb summoned his offending Rangers.

'We were fired on by irregulars,' Komax explained.

'Is that true, Macnab?' Cobb asked.

'From the house with the brown door.'

'Were guerrillas found inside? When you finished, that is?'

'There were,' Macnab said.

'What about the church?' Cobb asked. 'The desecration of the church?'

'Three guerrillas ran in there,' Komax said.

'Did you see them run in?' Cobb asked Macnab.

'I did.'

'And what did you do?' Cobb asked.

'I stood guard in the street. I figured Panther and his men, they could handle it.'

'Did you see the guerrillas? You, yourself?'

'Twice. When they ran in. When they were dead.'

Colonel Cobb turned to the bishop and the other protesters: 'Gentlemen, I'm sure you have copies of General Scott's orders concerning the suppression of guerrillas. They're to be eliminated, for your safety as well as ours.'

'But the children . . .' the bishop pleaded.

'Our men cannot check in advance, at peril to their lives.'

'And the church? The holy vestments, the altar?'

'Major Wells will give you a signed statement attesting to the fact that known guerrillas unfortunately ran into the church, and that in pursuit, some minor damage proved unavoidable. There will be compensation.'

Some time later, after the dead Ranger was buried, and the graves of the villagers decked with flowers and the church restored, Cobb asked Komax and Macnab: 'Were there guerrillas in the church?'

'There could of been,' said Panther.

Riding with the Rangers was a civilian from New York named Harry Saxon, twenty-two years old, red-headed and encumbered by an extraordinary amount of gear which he protected with a horse pistol. At first Cobb's men thought he must be a medical man, but when Saxon ignored the fallen and trembled whenever he saw blood, they knew that guess was wrong. Finally Komax, catching the newcomer staring at him offensively, roared: 'Son, who in hell are you?'

'Harry Saxon, *New York Dispatch.*'

'Newspaperman?'

'Yep.'

'And what is all that stuff?'

'I'm a photographer.'

'And what in hell is that?'

Patting his gear, he explained: 'I make pictures. They're called daguerreotypes.'

These words were new to the Rangers, who crowded about to see the miracle of photography. Unwittingly, Harry Saxon occupied a unique place in world military history: he was taking the first-ever photographs of an army engaged in battle, and it was the photograph he took this sunny afternoon, with the desolated buildings of Avila in the background, which made him famous and which would last as long as men cherished visual records of their exploits.

This daguerreotype, remarkably clear and evocative, showed the ruined church, a tethered donkey and, in the foreground, two savage, scowling Texas Rangers: a towering Panther Komax, bearded, unkempt, with his coonskin over his left ear; and a small, smooth-faced Otto Macnab, linen duster covering his toes and a hardened stare which warned: 'Don't touch me!' It was a summarizing picture of the newly fledged Texas state at war, seeking revenge for past insults, and to look at its subjects was to share their seething rage.

But it was Saxon's written account of how the victorious Texans entered Mexico City in their crusade of pacification that was of the greater significance to the new state. Unfamiliar with the insolent behavior of Rangers, he could not comprehend what he had witnessed, and when wood-engravers in New York translated his word-pictures into newspaper illustrations, citizens across the nation asked, also in disbelief: 'My God, is that Texas? Have we taken men like that into our Union?'

Hearing that the Texans were about to approach the capital, I left Mexico City and rode east toward the little village of Avila, hoping to intercept them as they came up out of the jungle. I arrived on a fateful morning and had breakfast with their captain, Sam Garner, a scarecrow, gaunt from prolonged dysentery, who told me: 'We teach them that you can't stop a man who knows he's right and keeps coming, especially if he has two Colts .44 and you don't.' An hour later weakened Captain Garner was killed by a Mexican guerrilla.

Deprived of their captain, the Rangers were in an ugly mood when we entered Mexico City this morning, but no one could have guessed how they would express their rage. At the outskirts of the capital a big, hairy Ranger called Panther Komax shouted in a loud voice: 'Men, let's remind these b————s who's in charge.'

I supposed they were going to gallop in, firing their Colts, but no, they had a true Texan gesture up their sleeves, one that I could never have imagined. What they did was clothe themselves in their most outrageous garments, no two alike, fluff out their beards, stow their Colts so they were always visible, don their big hats, and then take every imaginable position astride their horses, some riding fallen forward as if asleep, others facing sideways and ignoring their horses as they glared at the Mexicans crowding the sides of the streets. Eight or nine, including Panther with red flowers in his hair, sat backwards, facing the tails of their horses and looking very serious, as if that was the way they always rode.

No Ranger spoke. They just came into the city, announcing with their brazen behavior that they were now in Mexico City and that the town was under their control. Los tejanos sangrientes, the local people who have heard of their exploits call them, and one incident during the entry gave support to this name. A daring pickpocket, believing backward-riding Panther to be asleep, which he feigned to be, deftly reached up and filched the colorful handkerchief that some Rangers wear about their necks. Without making any protest, or even moving unusually, Panther unlimbered his Colts, shot the thief in the back, rode over, leaned way down, recovered his neckerchief, retied it about his throat, and rode on. Believe me, the streets cleared. The Texans were in town.

Colonel Cobb did not write his brother about the dreadful incident of 13 February 1848, nor did Harry Saxon report it to New York, for it was too disgraceful to record; indeed, it was later characterized as one of the least explicable of American military exploits. On that afternoon a gang of knife-wielding thieves caught a Ranger named Adam Allsens alone in an unsavory corner of the city. He apparently did nothing to provoke them, and even when they began to assault him he allowed them to have his neckerchief and his hat, for he realized that he could not fight his way clear from so large a mob. Encouraged by their initial success, they began to stab at him so viciously that he fell to the street, almost dead.

When Otto Macnab and two others came to his rescue, they found him in pitiful shape, one deep cut across his chest having exposed his heart, which beat visibly while they carried his failing body to headquarters. Eighteen or nineteen Rangers watched him die; they actually saw his heart begin to falter and then stop. At supper that night Macnab had to leave the table.

Toward ten the next night, when the streets of the capital were crowded, Panther Komax began quietly circulating among the Rangers, and with no one speaking or making any kind of commitment, men like Macnab, acting individually, started leaving the mess hall. A short time later, Harry Saxon entered the hall and asked: 'Where's everyone?' but no one offered a sensible answer. He therefore reported to Colonel Cobb: 'I think something's amiss. Your men were extremely silent at supper.'

'They feel the loss of Allsens,' Cobb said, offering Saxon both a cigar and a shot of whiskey. The two men were talking amiably about the favorable terms of the peace treaty when Saxon thought he heard distant gunfire.

'Could that be any of your men firing?'

'Certainly not,' Cobb said warily. 'They would not be firing at night.'

At about eleven the firing increased in volume and sound, and now Saxon cried: 'That could come only from Colts!' but Cobb assured him: 'It's that company of Horse Marines, practicing.'

'Why would they practice at night?'

'You never know.'

But now the firing drew so close that any military man would have to know it came from repeating revolvers, and both Cobb and Saxon ran out into the night, but at this point the shooting had stopped.

At breakfast no Ranger said anything about the night firing, but at about midmorning Harry Saxon visited the Mexican police, who showed him the wooden litters on which it was their custom to collect dead bodies found in alleyways at dawn, and on a dozen of them were piled some fifty corpses. When Saxon inquired what had happened, an officer explained: 'The Rangers took their revenge,' and fifty-three bodies were counted out for him—pimps, pickpockets, paid murderers, scoundrels, plain citizens, all shot at random—and some had apparently taken three or four shots right in the face, for the big Colts bullets had blown their heads apart.

All day Saxon tried to piece together what had happened, but no one would tell him that a band of some dozen Rangers, led by Panther Komax, had roamed quietly through the back alleyways of the city, through the slums and the red-light districts, and had carefully executed anyone who even looked as if he might have wielded a knife on Adam Allsens.

In the late afternoon Saxon went to the morgue, where he saw an additional eighty dead Mexicans, and he noticed that in the capital the Rangers were molested no more.

Photographer Harry Saxon took two more daguerreotypes of historic interest. One showed three fighting men, unposed and beautifully positioned against the background of Popocatépetl: Colonel Cobb—stiff, proper in his most imposing uniform—talking with Komax and Macnab, who were dressed like a pair of complete degenerates.

The other picture was more carefully posed, for it had been taken only after sustained negotiation. It depicted the leadership of the Mexican side, General Antonio López de Santa Anna in full regalia with at least eight big medals, accompanied by his guerrilla leader Benito Garza, jungle-thin and glaring behind his huge mustaches. The text that Saxon submitted to accompany his two splendid pictures explained how they were related and summarized the ending of this strange war:

> Your correspondent was privileged to participate in the final stages of the Mexican War. Hearing that General Santa Anna, a major cause of the war and a principal agent of its loss, was being sent into exile in disgrace, I dogged the Mexican headquarters for an opportunity to capture a picture of this colorful man.
>
> Returning to the Texas Rangers, whom I had accompanied in their campaign against the guerrillas, I found their leader and two of their most colorful members in deep conversation, and I took a chance that they would remain relatively stationary and allow me to use my camera. They did, but at the same time they talked loud enough for me to hear their conversation, which I report faithfully:
>
> COBB: 'It's true. Santa Anna passes through our lines tomorrow at eight.'
>
> KOMAX: 'Let's shoot him.'
>
> COBB: 'None of that! He has a safe-conduct from General Scott.'
>
> KOMAX: 'Santy Anny is a butcher. Let's give him a taste of butcherin'.'

COBB: 'Macnab, can you reason with this wild man?'

KOMAX: 'You ain't never drawed a bean outen a clay pot. You ain't never seen your father speared down in cold blood, while he was a honorable prisoner.'

COBB: 'Gentlemen of Texas, we've been through a great deal together . . .'

KOMAX: 'You had me given "The Rogue's March." '

COBB: 'And I'd do it again tomorrow, but here in the south I've learned what a heroic group of men you are. I have never served with better. I would ride anywhere on earth, up to the face of any cannon . . .' (At this point his voice broke and for almost a minute he stared at the ground.) 'Men, do not sully a splendid reputation. If you assault your defeated enemy . . .' (His voice broke again and, angry at himself, he spoke rapidly.) 'Hell, he's your prisoner. He's unarmed. Do you want to be regarded by all the civilized world as lacking in honor? What are you, anyway, a bunch of miserable bastards? Do you really want to befoul the fair name of Texas? Do you want to stand in shame before the world?'

KOMAX: 'We'll think about that.'

Unable to extract a promise, Cobb drew himself to full height, saluted, and left his men for what I believe was the last time. His final words to Macnab and Komax which I heard as he passed me were: 'Don't be a pair of Texas sons-a-bitches.' He left us, head high, eyes straight ahead, his beautiful uniform without one misplaced seam.

It was a bright morning when General Antonio López de Santa Anna prepared to ride through the gauntlet of American soldiers.

In the open carriage, pulled by four horses and managed by two drivers fore and two uniformed outriders standing aft, the newly wedded general and his child bride would ride, accompanied by Benito Garza and Lucha López. As Garza stepped into the carriage he blurted out: 'Excellency, the heart of Mexico goes with you into exile.'

Hands clasped about his bejeweled sword to mask their trembling, Santa Anna gave the order 'Forward!'—then stared straight ahead. Silently he passed between the double file of Rangers standing less than five feet from him on each side. He glanced at none of them, because he knew that they had sworn to kill him and he could not guess at what signal they would strike.

Each Ranger looked hard at him, each conveyed the bitterness of this extraordinary moment, but none looked with more strangled emotions than their liaison-colonel, Persifer Cobb: God, let this moment pass. Let them keep their big mouths shut.

Otto Macnab stared at Santa Anna as if to engrave the Mexican's features on his memory, then, turning his head, stiffened with shock when he saw who was sitting opposite the general. It was Benito Garza, and for a long moment the two old friends, the two perpetual adversaries, looked into each other's eyes—Garza's ebony-black, Macnab's cerulean-blue—and the respect, the hatred and the confusion glowed. Neither man made a gesture of recognition. For some reason the carriage hesitated, and the moment of meeting was agonizingly prolonged.

Then the carriage moved forward again. Each man kept his head turned toward the other until dust intervened. The war had ended.

It was a perplexing war, which few had welcomed except President Polk and the expansionists, and its significance is revealed only when viewed from three aspects.

First, it was an inescapable prolongation of the 1836 Texas revolution. Since Mexican leadership had never accepted the loss of territory resulting from that struggle, and since Mexico had as many superpatriots as Texas, it was inevitable that continued attempts would be made to recapture the lost province. Arrival of United States power put a stop to such plotting.

Second, the war was an application of the new slogan of Manifest Destiny. American patriots had looked at the map and proclaimed almost automatically: 'We must control this continent from the Atlantic to the Pacific.' Texas dreamers could cry: 'We must have everything down to the Isthmus of Panama,' and frenzied New Englanders could and did shout for the annexation of Canada, even launching abortive military campaigns to achieve that worthy purpose. The successful outcome of the Mexican War meant that the Pacific coast was secured, and a good thing, in terms of geography at least, was accomplished.

Third, the war had a powerful psychological effect on the new state of Texas. It was exerted not on Texas itself, for the war really had only a limited influence internally: it was fought primarily by men and officers from the twenty-seven other states in the Union and it served as a training ground for the greater War Between the States of 1861–1865, which lurched ever closer. The names of the younger officers who had fought under Taylor and Scott sound like a roll call to military greatness: Robert E. Lee, Ulysses S. Grant, Braxton Bragg, George Gordon Meade, Albert Sidney Johnston, Jubal Early, William Tecumseh Sherman, P.G.T. Beauregard, Joseph E. Johnston, James Longstreet, George B. McClellan, and the two popular heroes Stonewall Jackson and Fighting Joe Hooker.

It also strengthened the American propensity for electing military heroes to the presidency, four of the American officers in this war attaining that high office—Taylor, Grant, Jefferson Davis, Franklin Pierce—with three others, Scott, Frémont and McClellan, trying. Three Mexican officers also attained the presidency of their nation, including the ineffable Santa Anna, who would be summoned back from exile to lead his country once more.

If the war had little effect in Texas in tangible terms, how was its significance for the state manifested? Thanks to the newspaper stories of reporters like Harry Saxon and the brilliantly colored lithographs of Currier and Ives, the rest of the nation acquired a romantic and often favorable view of their new state. The Texas Ranger became a legendary figure, composed partly of Panther Komax and his undisciplined ways, partly of Otto Macnab and his merciless efficiency. A deluge of lurid penny-thrillers recounted the adventures of Davy Crockett, Jim Bowie and the Texas Rangers. Tall stories were told about life in Texas decades before most people had heard the word *cowboy* or ever a steer was driven north.

Of course, not every soldier who served in Texas returned home singing its praises. One Pennsylvania volunteer said: 'If I was ordered back to Texas, I'd cut my throat.' A general said later: 'If I owned Hell and Texas, I would rent out Texas and live in Hell.' Perhaps Colonel Persifer Cobb of Edisto Island, South Carolina, said it with deepest feeling: 'I am often haunted by nightmares. I'm back in Texas trying to discipline thirty-six Rangers.'

The war left one indelible heritage: it intensified the animosity that already existed between Texans and Mexicans. The savage behavior of the Rangers in both the Monterrey area and Mexico City established them nationally as los tejanos sangrientes, and along the Rio Grande as los Rinches.

War often produces unexpected transformations of social life, and this one gave America and Texas each an unusual boon. During negotiations with Santa Anna, that wily gentleman told a group of American businessmen: 'When I was on duty in Yucatán, I came upon a product which I am sure will make one of you rich. It was called chicle.' And thus chewing gum was introduced into the States. Texas received a gift almost as far-reaching, for in one of Harry Saxon's finest daguerreotypes, he caught the birth of a legend. Panther Komax, hairy as ever, is shown with a barefoot Mexican peon kneeling at his feet. The accompanying story read:

> I must confess that I posed this picture the morning after the event occurred. When Colonel Cobb and I went out on the night of the great killings in Mexico City we were so late that we discovered nothing, so we retired to quarters, but shortly thereafter I returned to the streets, suspecting that something of moment was occurring, and I came upon the tail end of the slaughter. Komax and his partner Otto Macnab had been shooting anyone in sight, but they ran out of ammunition. Seeing this disreputable peon who looked as if he might have been one of the murderers of Allsens, Macnab was preparing to cut the man's throat

when the latter broke loose, fell to the ground, and began grabbing at Komax's boot.

From prolonged use, the boot was in sad repair, and this the groveling man indicated, tugging at it and informing us in some way that he, the peon, was a bootmaker, and that given the proper tools, he could mend that boot. Macnab, who spoke excellent Spanish, put away his knife and interrogated the man. Yes, he carried the universal name Juan Hernández. Yes, he was a bootmaker and a good one. Yes, he could either mend Komax's boot or make him one much better.

Komax, catching the drift, raised the man to his feet and asked, through Macnab: 'Can you make a boot as good as this?' and Hernández broke into nervous laughter: 'If I made a boot that bad, my mother would beat me.' In this way, on a night of carnage and at the very point of death, my company of Texas Rangers acquired a bootmaker who now marches with us, tending our shoes.

When the Rangers left their transport at Indianola, that thriving harbor on Matagorda Bay, Otto stayed three days with his brother-in-law, Theo Allerkamp; then, on a horse provided by Theo, he started on the long ride to Fredericksburg.

His spirits rose as he neared Austin, where he spent two days verifying title to his acreage at Fredericksburg. With reassuring documents in his pocket he started westward, and for the first time in his life took time to appreciate the miracle of a luxuriant Texas spring, not the ordinary blossoming of trees at Victoria, or the sparse flowers along the Brazos, or that wilderness of minute flowerlets in the Nueces desert, but the unbelievable expanse of two distinct flowers, one a rich blue, the other a reddish gold. Sometimes they covered entire fields: And not little fields, either. Look at them! How many acres?

He was staring at a spread of flowers along the banks of the Colorado River, so many and in such dazzling array that they almost blinded him. Here rose the wonderful bluebonnets of Texas, each stem ending in a sturdy pyramid of delightful blue flowers. Intermixed with them was the only other flower that could make the blue stand out, the Indian paintbrush in burnt orange. Blue and red-orange, what a surprising combination, made even more vibrant by the fact that both flowers bore at their apex a fleck of white, so that the field pulsated with beauty. So vast it was in extent that Otto could scarcely believe that so many flowers, each its own masterpiece, could combine to create a picture of such harmony. 'Red, white and blue,' he murmured. 'What a flag.'

But then he reached the spot where the Pedernales River joined the Colorado, and now he knew he was approaching his destination, and as he climbed a slight rise he was confronted by a field not of forty acres or of eighty, but of limitless extent, and it was solid bluebonnet and paintbrush, a benediction of nature so prodigal that he could only halt and gaze. Then slowly he turned his horse and rode toward home.

Benito Garza also went home, but to a tormented scene. Exhausted from long days of guerrilla warfare, he left Vera Cruz with his wife and three commandeered horses as weary of battle as their riders. Painfully the couple made their way through the jungle and up to the altiplano, where they witnessed the desolation of Avila and the other ruins wrought by the war.

They felt a bleeding sorrow for their country, for wherever they looked they saw the costs of defeat: the punished villages in which they had sometimes hidden; the horribly wounded men striving to master new crutches; children with distended bellies; the ugly penalties paid by those who had obeyed the rash decrees of Santa Anna.

During the first eighteen days of this bleak pilgrimage Benito refused to place the blame upon his hero: 'No! Don't say that, Lucha. Santa Anna had a fine plan, but it fell astray.'

'His plans always fell astray.'

'He'll come back, I promise you. He'll land at Vera Cruz, just as before, except that this time . . .'

At the start of the third week, when the Garzas learned from friends in Mexico City how tremendous the loss of territory was to be—more than half the country turned over to the norteamericanos—he began to admit that his hero had made fearful errors: 'He could have engineered it better. Lose Tejas, yes. But never should he have given up so much more.'

When they reached San Luis Potosí they heard a constant wail of grief, and now the recriminations against Santa Anna became vociferous, for this region contained many who had fought at Buena Vista, and who knew that Santa Anna had fled the battlefield when victory was at hand. As Lucha said: 'That last night María and I crept out on scout while you were meeting with Santa Anna. Secretly, along the shoulder of the hill, we could see that the yanquis were retreating in disarray. But when we returned we were not allowed to report. Women were not welcomed in that tent.'

How tragic the defeat was! The litany of lost lands carried its own sorrow, never to be erased from the mexicano soul: 'Tejas, Nuevo México, Arizona, California, qué lástima, qué dolor!' The names formed a rosary of despair, the heart of Mexico torn away and bleeding.

As the Garzas approached the Rio Grande before turning east toward Matamoros, they paused to look across the river into the still-contested Nueces Strip, and resting in their saddles, they reached brutal conclusions: 'Santa Anna failed us. In the present leadership there is no hope. Mexico will never know peace, and there is no chance of turning back the norteamericanos.' But in the depth of their despair they saw a chance for personal salvation, and Benito, his mustaches dark in the blazing sunlight, phrased their oath: 'The yanquis who try to steal that Strip from us, they'll never know a night of security. Their cattle will never graze in peace. By God, Lucha, they'll pay a terrible price for their arrogance. Promise me you'll never surrender.'

'I promise.'

. . . TASK FORCE

I believe that all of us, older members and youthful staff alike, looked forward with greater eagerness to our April meeting than to any before. It was to be held in Alpine, an authentic frontier town of some six thousand population situated in the heart of rugged ranch country in West Texas. To the south, along the Rio Grande, lies remote Big Bend National Park with its peaks and canyons, an overgrazed semi-desert in 1944, when it was taken into the park system, but now a miraculously recovered primitive wilderness. To the north, rising as if to protect it, are the Guadalupes, tallest mountains in Texas, and Fort Davis, best restored of the old Texas battle stations.

Alpine stands at an altitude of 4,485 feet, blizzardlike in winter, ninety degrees in summer, and its charm lies in its successful preservation of old-time ways. It serves as the seat of Brewster County, an almost unpopulated area about the size of Rhode Island and Connecticut combined, and is surrounded by ranches of staggering size.

'Out here, ma'am,' said the tour driver, 'we never state the size in acres. It's sections. The Baker Ranch you're asking about, it has fifty-five sections, that's better'n thirty-five thousand acres. Middlin' size, I'd say, because it takes a hundred and fifty acres of that barren land to feed one unit . . . A unit, ma'am, is a cow and a calf, with hopefully another calf on the way. So the Bakers, they cain't run but two hundred-odd cows on their ranch, and that's why we classify it middlin'.'

Ransom Rusk had provided the planes to fly us to Alpine, and as we drove from the little airport we saw two signs which prepared us for what was to be one of our best sessions:

REAL OIL PAINTINGS
$3.50 AND UP

THIS MOTEL IS RUN
BY HONEST NATIVE-BORN TEXANS

Our meetings were to be held at Sul Ross University, a handsome collection of red-brick buildings perched on the side of a hill, and there a real surprise awaited us, for we were met by a short, white-haired, sparkling-eyed man in his sixties whose face positively glowed with enthusiasm: 'I'm Professor Mark Berninghaus, Texas history, and we'll pile right into these two ranch wagons.' He would drive the lead car, he said, which the Task Force members would share. Then he introduced us to a young man of imposing build wearing a big Stetson: 'This is Texas Ranger Cletus Macnab, and if you know your frontier history, you'll remember that one of his ancestors was the legendary Ranger Otto Macnab. And another was the equally famous Oscar Macnab, also a Ranger.'

Macnab, a handsome young fellow in a pearl-gray whipcord suit, bowed to us but did not remove his hat. To the girl from SMU who had arranged this session he said: 'Staff'll ride with me,' and to the rest of us he said: 'I've provided maps of the region we'll be traveling,' and with that, we headed south along Route 69 to the twin border towns of Polk on the American side and Carlota on the Mexican. It was a journey of eighty miles through absolutely empty land—not even a filling station—but one which, under the loving tutelage of Professor Berninghaus, provided us with an intimate glimpse of a Texas that few visitors ever get to see.

'I want you to notice the vegetation, and how it changes as we drop down to the Rio Grande, two thousand feet lower in elevation.' Then he began an instruction which was shared by intercom with the staff in the following car: 'Look at the bleakness of land, only one shrub to an area the size of a football field.' When we studied the barren earth we saw at first only a reddish, rocky soil, but as our eyes grew accustomed to the vast empty space and the arching blue sky, cloudless and perfect, we began to see lone bushlike plants clinging to the arid earth. They were dark green and had many narrow leaves that branched out like untended hair, forming beautiful globes: 'Sotol, one of the major plants of our barren plains. Remember how green it is, because later I'll provide you with a surprise.'

Imperceptibly the landscape changed—worsened, in my opinion—until we were in the heart of a real desert, but not the sandy kind featured in Grade B movies: 'We call this the Chihuahuan Desert, eight hundred miles, maybe, north and south, two hundred east to west. And here we have one of its characteristic plants.' He pointed to a remarkable growth, a tall, reedy plant composed of forty or fifty slender whips, each bearing at its tip a cluster of brilliant red flowerlets. The ocotillo, which looked as if it had been thrown together helter-skelter, was appropriate to its bleak surroundings, for only a plant so thin, so conservative of water, could have survived here.

'Look!' Miss Cobb cried as we descended into a protected valley. 'What can that be?' It was an imposing plant of the desert, a low-growing cluster of heavy brownish leaves, quite undistinguished, except that from its middle rose a thick stem high in the air, topped by clusters of beautiful gold-white flowers that seemed to fill the blue sky.

'A special yucca,' Berninghaus said over his intercom. 'But hold your applause till we climb out of this depression. Because then you're going to see what many never see. A forest of yucca . . . many species . . . beautiful.'

I think we watched with a sense of disbelief, for we could not associate this tremendous desert with beauty as we were accustomed to know it, but as we reached the crest of a small rise we saw spreading off to our right a vision of Texas that would never be erased; it was so different, so grandiose that it seemed to represent the state in its original form before intrusions like Houston and Dallas.

It was a small forest of three kinds of yucca: the noble ones we'd already seen, a more beautiful version called Spanish Dagger, and a veritable tree with sturdy jagged trunk, a cluster of leaves well above the ground, and a glorious collection of white flowers rising high into the air. The sight was so compelling that several of us in the lead car said: 'Let's stop!' And when we looked back we saw that Ranger Macnab had already done so in order that his young passengers might see these splendid plants.

They had a strange effect on me. I compared them to the delicate garden flowers I'd known when a student in England, and with the carefully cultivated flowers in Geneva. Obviously they were flowers, but big and brutal and self-protective against the rainless wind. Compared to the pansy or the tulip, they were gross; one handful of their heavy blooms at the end of a stalk seemed larger than a garden of English flowers or a bed of Boston blooms. They were frightening in the awkwardness of their limbs, unkempt in the way their trunks shed, and when Miss Cobb insisted upon leaving our ranch wagon to inspect one of the nearer yuccas, she quickly returned, for a rattlesnake lay coiled at its base.

How beautiful they were, those yuccas of the Chihuahuan Desert, how Texan. As we moved past their tremendous forms we carried with us a new understanding of the West, that bleak and barren land which offered so many hidden rewards.

But now we were descending to regions with a much different vegetation, and Berninghaus assured us: 'Flowers that look like flowers. See down there.'

He was pointing to one of the strangest flowers I had ever seen or, rather, to a cluster of some hundred individual flowers congregated into a round cactuslike globe more than four feet in diameter. When I looked closely I saw that each plant forming the globe had powerful thorns that interlocked with those of other plants to make the globe impenetrable. These proved that the thing was a cactus, but the blizzard of delicate purple flowers proved that it was also a luxuriant bouquet. However, the real surprise was to come: 'In the autumn each of these flowers produces a spiny fruit, brilliant red in color. When you peel away the skin you find a delicious treat. Tastes like strawberries.'

'What's it called?' one of the students in the rear asked, and Berninghaus said: 'Strawberry cactus.'

And then, at the lower levels, we came upon the plant that affected me most deeply; I saw it first alongside the road, a low gray woody bush with tiny five-thorned leaves. I took it for a weed, but Berninghaus said: 'Let's stop and inspect it.' He broke off a branch to show that the interior wood was one of the most vivid yellows in nature: 'The Indians prized it for coloring their blankets,' and I supposed that this completed the story, but he continued: 'It's one of our best shrubs, quite precious, really.'

'What's it called?' I asked, and he said: 'Cenizo, but some spell it with a final *a*. Its more effective name, Barometer Bush.'

'Why?'

'If we pass a spot that's had some recent rain, you'll see why,' and before long we came to such a place, and there a stretch of cenizo had burst into soft, gentle gray-purple flowers. They were like miniature lilacs beside some Illinois farmhouse, or dusty asters in a Pennsylvania field; they spoke of home and evening firesides. As I looked down at them, imagining how joyously they must have been greeted by Indians who sought their brilliant dye, I felt as if Texas had somehow reached out to embrace me, to protect me from the barrenness of this western land, and I could understand how Berninghaus had come here fresh from his doctorate at Chicago and decided after one week that this would be his home for life. We would have known only half of Texas had we missed Alpine.

Just as I was beginning to feel sentimental about the plant, Berninghaus threw in one of those obiter dicta which can make travel with a scholar so rewarding: 'This is the flower, of course, which made Zane Grey immortal. But imagine how flat his title would have sounded had he called the plant by its proper Spanish name, *Riders of the Purple Cenizo.*'

Now the talk turned to what Texans seemed to like best—numbers of staggering dimension: 'We're threading along the great Ramsdale Ranch, six hundred thousand acres.' Or, 'Over there, reaching twenty miles, is the Falstaff Ranch, nearly as big as Rhode Island and filled with deer and javelinas and mountain lions.' But when I asked who owned these ranches, I was invariably told: 'Fellow from Houston who struck it big in oil,' and I began to realize that no matter how far one traveled from the oil fields of Texas, the pervasive power of petroleum remained.

When we stopped for cold drinks at Polk, the forlorn American settlement, Ranger Macnab informed us: 'We'll cross into Carlota so you can see what a Mexican border town can sometimes be, but I must in fairness warn you that there'll be other settlements of larger size which are much better. This one is pathetic.'

When we saw it, we agreed. Four times as large as Polk, it was a hundred times more desolate. It was as if the centuries had hesitated, waiting for some revolutionary invasion to burn down the walls. The fabulous wealth of Mexico had not penetrated here, and the streets were mean and forbidding. Adobe houses crumbled and open sewers went untended. Stores were adorned with broken bottles and old cars rusted at the crossroads. The railway station had lost its tiles and the policemen guarding it wore outmoded and tattered uniforms.

Carlota, named in honor of a European empress who had gone mad as her husband tried to govern Mexico, wasted in the blazing sunlight, and we were content to go back across the bridge to Polk. At first sight we had not rated the American town favorably, but now it seemed a beacon of civilization. Ransom Rusk, who had shown in previous meetings that he disapproved of Mexican ways and also of Mexicans living in Texas, said as we left Carlota: 'Now I can understand why they want to slip into the United States. I would if I had to live over there.'

Our two ranch wagons now headed northwest along the Rio Grande, passing an adobe fort long vacated and the dusty town of Presidio, famed for its appalling summer temperatures. Television viewers grew familiar with the refrain: 'Hottest spot in the nation today, Presidio, Texas, 114 degrees Fahrenheit.'

Then we passed through empty land leading to nowhere, and when we paused to drink from our thermos I asked: 'Where are we going now?' the staff members smiled, and Berninghaus said: 'We've a few more surprises for you.'

I could not imagine what this forbidding land could hold as a surprise, but at the end of the paved road, in what must have been one of the loneliest and gloomiest sections of Texas, we came upon a minute village, Ruidosa, with six houses and a crumbling low Spanish mission, the Sacred Heart, built like a fort and now moldering in the desert sun. When I saw it I said over the intercom: 'At our first meeting the governor said we were to probe into every nook and cranny of the state. This is one of the crannies.'

It still retained its roof, though probably not for much longer, and its façade was sturdy, with a wooden entrance that must often have been barricaded when the Apache attacked. It was an honorable relic, testifying to the courage of the missionaries who had stubbornly tried to pacify this part of Texas.

For me the most rewarding segment of the trip now began, for our cars skirted the mission ruins to pick up a trail which appeared on none of our maps. It wound its way due north for eighteen miles along the Rio Grande, so that whenever we looked to our left we saw the mountains of Mexico. Over the intercom we heard our young woman from SMU ask Ranger Macnab: 'Tell us the truth. Does this trail lead anywhere, or is this a kidnapping?' and he replied: 'We're heading for the end of the world.'

When we stopped we found ourselves in the adobe village of Candelaria, where the pretensions of Texas and the United States ended, for this was one of the loneliest and most inaccessible settlements along the southern border, with people living much as they had in the previous century.

But to me it was compelling, a view of Texas that few ever saw, and my heart beat faster when Berninghaus said: 'Imagine, an international border, and from here, for more than a hundred miles, nothing.' But what delighted our staff was the fact that when we strolled down to the Rio Grande, that river with the magical name, it was so narrow and shallow that a tattered rope-and-wire suspension bridge sufficed to cross it. And as we looked, a pantalooned workman from Mexico carrying a battered gasoline tin with handles came across its swaying planks to purchase some commodity in Candelaria.

'Behold the commerce of great empires!' Berninghaus cried, and we stood silent, confused by the hugeness of Texas and the meanness of its historic river. I think we were all gratified when Berninghaus explained the anomaly: 'We Americans in New Mexico and Texas take so much water out of the Rio Grande for irrigation that if this little stream were allowed to run toward the Gulf in this condition, it would simply disappear. But at a spot near Presidio, a large Mexican river joins up, the Río Conchos. So the fabled Río Grande, which we admire so much downstream, should more accurately be called the Conchos. It's mostly Mexican.'

Then came a clatter from the town, and he said: 'I think they've arrived,' and when we returned to our cars we found that students from Sul Ross had brought a picnic lunch for us and had spread it on blankets under a tree.

'There will be no speeches,' Berninghaus assured us. 'I wanted you to imagine yourselves as Spanish immigrants coming here to settle, four hundred years ago. I wanted you to see the great empty Texas that they saw.'

On the trip back, following an unmarked trail through mountains and canyons, I noticed that Berninghaus maintained a sharp lookout, and finally he announced: 'If I remember correctly, it's in the next valley that our little cheerleaders climb the hillside,' and when we reached the crest from which we could look across to the opposite hill we saw a bewitching sight, for the entire hill from creek to crest was covered with something I could not identify.

'Look at them, the golden leaves at the bottom, the beautiful green at the top. And tell me what they are if they aren't a gaggle of girl cheerleaders in the stadium on a bright autumn day.'

From a distance, that's what they were, a host of girls in the green-and-gold of their team, scattered at random over a sloping field of some fifty acres, as jaunty a performance as nature provided.

'What are they?' one of the students asked, and Berninghaus said: 'Sotols. Dead leaves golden at the foot, new leaves green at the top. I feel better about life whenever I enter this valley.'

So for sixty miles along a forsaken road we picked our way toward Marfa, one of the choice cattle towns of the West, with a flawless courthouse. There we turned east, and when we reached the outskirts of Alpine, to which most of us now wanted to move, we saw our third sign:

U.N. OUT OF U.S.

U.S. OUT OF TEXAS

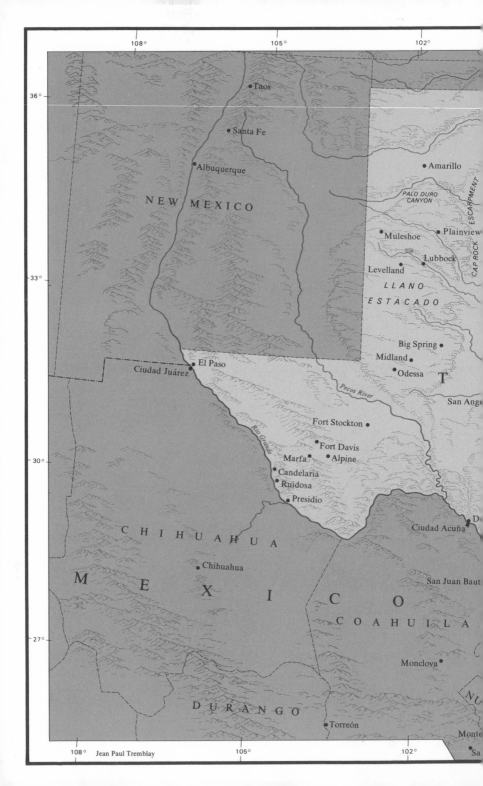

listening to the nighttime noises, the hum of passing
Derby Street traffic, the distant low moan of an offshore
buoy and—something else. It was the *click* of a lighter,
followed by the tiny, round red glow of a cigarette.
Another silhouette took shape. A tall man, facing in
my direction, was leaning against the driver's-side door
of my car.

I spun around and sprinted for the sidewalk, hoping
that the front-door code hadn't changed since I'd
stopped working there. Once safely inside, I'd call Pete
or a cab or my aunt to come and get me. I wasn't about
to chance another bad experience beside that seawall.

Footsteps pounded behind me.

"Lee! Hey, Lee Barrett. Is that you?" The voice was
familiar. I stopped running.

"Scott?"

He reached my side and flicked the cigarette away.
"Did I scare you? I'm sorry."

My near panic turned to anger. "Of course you scared
me, you big jerk! Standing there in the dark, leaning
on my car, watching me. Don't you ever even *touch* that
car again! Are you crazy? What the hell are you trying
to do?"

He grasped my elbow. "I'm really sorry."

I pulled my arm away and pushed my hand hard
against his chest. "Get away from me, Scott. What do you
want anyway?" I wasn't even trying to control my temper.
I hadn't been this angry in years. If we'd been a little
closer to the seawall, I would have shoved the SOB overboard.

"Jeez, Lee. I said I was sorry. I just need to talk to you
about something."

I was about to tell him to use the telephone, when I realized that maybe he was going to tell me something Pete might need to know, so I took a deep breath and tried to think calm thoughts. "Okay. What's so important that you have to scare me half to death?" We approached the front of the building. "Shall we go inside and you can tell me whatever it is?"

"No. Not in there. Everybody is too damned nosy. Anyway, none of them even know that Eric was staying at my place. Want to go over to the Pig's Eye and have a beer with me?"

Of all the things in the world that I didn't want to do just then, having a beer with Scott Palmer topped the list.

"Sure," I said, pasting on a big, fake smile. "Why not?"

CHAPTER 20

"Hi, Lee. Back again so soon? Hi, Scotty." The bartender welcomed us.

Scott led the way to two stools at the empty far end of the curved bar. "You still drink light beer?" he asked.

"I'll just have a Pepsi, thanks." I looked at my watch. "Can we make this quick? It's pretty late."

He ordered our drinks, then waited until they were served, and the bartender had moved away, before he spoke again. This time it was in a quiet, un-newscaster-like monotone. "When the police came over to my place to pick up Eric's things, I told them that I'd given them everything he'd left there. It wasn't a lot. Mostly clothes and shampoo and deodorant, stuff like that, and some Salem souvenirs he'd bought to take back to Illinois He took his laptop and his camera with him when he went out that night." He looked up from his beer. "Your friend Pete said those weren't in the rental car. I think they thought I kept them."

"Did you?" I asked, hoping I wasn't going to hear a confession.

"Of course not." He scowled. "What kind of person do you think I am?"

I let that question go unanswered.

"I did keep one little thing of his. I let them search my apartment, you know. It was in my bookcase, but Eric's name wasn't even on it, so they probably wouldn't have noticed it anyway. Honest to God, Lee. I didn't think it was important."

"If you brought me here to ask what you should do, you already know the answer. Give whatever it is to the police."

"I can't. It's gone."

"What do you mean?"

He put his glass down and put both hands on the edge of the bar. He didn't look at me and his voice was so low I had to lean toward him to hear. "When Chief Whaley handed out those pictures this morning, I damn near keeled over. It was him. The bearded guy. I think he grabbed Eric's notebook."

"Wait a minute. You've lost me."

He exhaled loudly, as though he'd been holding his breath for a long time. "I thought it was his address book, you know? I mean, it had names and numbers in it. Eric knew all the heavy hitters, the important people back in Illinois. I figured these were the kinds of contacts I'd need when . . . if I decided to go back there." He shrugged. "I'm not getting anywhere here. Covering high-school football games and supermarket openings. Crap! And chintzy pay to boot."

"Tell me about the man, Scott."

"He must have known about the notebook. A little

leather book, kind of beat-up, with a leather tie holding it closed."

"Go on."

"I figured it wouldn't do any harm to keep it, you know? I mean, Eric was a friend of mine. If I'd asked to see it, he probably would have handed it right over. That's what I figured. Before I left for work, I took it out of the bookcase. Put it on the front seat next to me. I thought I'd check on those addresses, call some of the phone numbers, you know? Maybe see what else was in there that I could use." He took a long swallow of beer.

"The man, Scott. What about the man?"

"I drove to the station the same as I always do. Parked where I always park. I got out of the car, picked up the notebook and stuck it in my pocket. I started for the back door of the station and this big guy—guy with a beard— bumped right into me. Knocked me over. He's a really big guy."

"Did you get hurt? What did you do?"

"It was no big deal. I just lost my balance is all. Anyway, he helped me up, tried to brush off my jacket. Said he was sorry, over and over. Hard to understand. Had a real thick accent."

I saw where he was going with this. "He picked your pocket?"

He looked down, embarrassed. "Yeah. I didn't realize it was gone until after I'd done the noon news. You know what I think that book really is? I think it might be some kind of a codebook. I'm thinking that if this creep had Eric's computer, he needed that book to figure out what was on it. That's what I'm thinking." He gave a kind of self-satisfied nod and took another long swig of his beer. "What do you think?"

"You were robbed, Scott. Didn't you call the police?"

"Couldn't. They'd know I was—what do you call it? Withholding evidence in a murder case. And another thing, Lee. There was something familiar about the guy. Like maybe I'd seen him, or at least seen a picture of him a long time ago. Now I don't know what to do."

"Yes, you do." I said it as gently as I could, remembering the Barbara Walters technique. "You know exactly what to do. Would you like me to call Pete, ask him to come here so you can tell him all about it now?"

He put his elbows on the bar, holding his head in his hands. "Shit! I don't know. I guess so. Yeah. Go ahead. Call him. Let's get it over with."

Pete answered on the first ring. "Hi, babe. Just dropped the boys off. Took 'em out for pizza after practice. My sister gave me hell for keeping them out so late. What's up?"

I explained what was going on as briefly, and considering the state of mind of the man sitting next to me, as impartially as I could. "He'd like to talk it over with you now, Pete, if you could come down here."

"Okay. On my way."

Pete must have realized that I wasn't really as calm as I'd tried to sound on the phone. Less than ten minutes had passed when I saw the Crown Vic round the corner. Pete appeared in the doorway, wearing his red-white-and-blue Police Athletic League T-shirt and hurried across the room to where Scott and I sat. He gave me a fast peck on the cheek and took the stool next to Scott and ordered a Coke. Scott was on his third beer by then, while I sipped on my second Pepsi.

Pete gave the slight motion of his head, which I'd learned meant that I should leave them alone for a while. I took the not-unwelcome hint. "Time for a powder room break," I said, "excuse me, please." I headed for the ladies' room. I dillydallied around in there for as long as seemed plausible, then peeked around the corner to see what was going on at the far end of the bar. The two men still appeared to be in deep conversation, and Pete was scribbling in his notebook. The TV was tuned to River's show and several bar patrons had gathered in front of the set. I joined them, pretending interest in *The Ship of Monsters*, which involved some women space explorers in skimpy uniforms who were busy gathering male specimens from each planet they visited. There was a singing cowboy too, and a cow named Lollabrigida. I realized that I needed to get back to Pete and Scott, whether they wanted me to or not, when the plot began to make sense.

By then, Pete had put his notebook away, and Scott was concentrating on his cell, so it seemed like a good moment to rejoin them. This time I took the seat next to Pete, glad of his comforting presence. There was an awkward moment of silence among the three of us. I broke it by stating the obvious. "Getting late, you guys."

Scott put his phone into his pocket and stood up. "Yeah, well, I guess I'll go back over to the station and help Marty put *Tarot Time* to bed. Thanks for listening to me, Lee." He held out his hand to Pete. "Guess I'll be seeing you tomorrow, right, Detective?" The two shook hands and Scott put a few bills on the counter, waved to the bartender and headed out the door onto Derby Street.

I watched him leave, then turned to Pete. "How'd that go? Did he tell you about the notebook? And the man with the beard?"

"He did. What about you? Are you okay? I was worried when you called. You sounded nervous. Scared, almost."

"I was a little scared, but mostly ticked off once I found out it was him." I told him how Scott had frightened me, leaning on my car in that dark lot. "I couldn't see who it was, lurking there, watching me."

"What a moron. No wonder you were scared. What did you do?"

"Turned around and ran."

"Good girl. But you got us some useful information. Scott's coming down to headquarters in the morning to make a statement, and to file a belated robbery report. You'd make a good cop, you know."

"I think you've mentioned that before. No thanks. But, seriously, are you going to charge Scott with anything? He said he was worried about being accused of withholding evidence."

Pete shrugged. "Well, there is that little detail, isn't there?"

"He told you all about that codebook, didn't he?"

"I guess so. It's hard to say whether Palmer tells *all* about anything."

"Did he tell you that he felt as though he'd seen that bearded man somewhere before? A long time ago?"

He frowned. "No, but I'll talk to him about that tomorrow for sure."

"It sure would be helpful, though, if we could find that book, wouldn't it?"

Pete smiled, and put his arm around my shoulders. "If *we* could find it?"

"Oh, you know what I mean."

"I'm afraid I do. You can't be running around playing girl detective on this one, Lee. I'm serious. There's a killer out there. Leave the detecting to the professionals, okay?"

"Okay, but, Pete, Aunt Ibby's the one who needs a lecture on minding her own business. She's found a kindred spirit in your blond person of interest, Karl Smith."

"What do you mean? A kindred spirit?"

"They're both writing cookbooks and she wants him to help cater a charity high tea at the library next month."

"I'll talk to her. Come on." He stood and motioned for the bartender. "Where's your car?"

"In the station parking lot. Down by the water."

He paid the tab and steered me toward the door. "I'll drive you over there, then follow you home." We were both quiet on the short ride to where I'd parked. Pete pulled up beside the Corvette and asked for my keys. "Wait here a minute," he said, climbed out and opened the door of the convertible. Poking his head inside, he inspected the interior. What was he looking for? He was worried about something. Worried about me? A murky sea fog had moved in, hovering over the shadowy expanse of the near-empty parking lot. I shivered.

"Okay. Let's go home," he said, taking my hand as I got out of his car and started toward mine. "Your hands are freezing. Still a little shook-up?"

"I'm fine," I lied. I pulled out of the lot, checking my rearview mirror every minute or so, just to be sure he was still there. I put the 'Vette into the garage, next to the Buick, and Pete parked in the driveway.

We walked together to the back door. "Would you feel better if I stayed here with you tonight?" he whispered.

"I would," I said, and I certainly did.

CHAPTER 21

I awoke to the sound of the cat door opening. I pulled on a terry cloth robe and tiptoed into the kitchen, closing the bedroom door behind me. Cuckoo announced six-thirty. O'Ryan sat in front of the spot where I usually placed his breakfast bowl, looking up at me expectantly. "Okay, okay. It's coming. Don't rush me." I poured his salmon-flavored kitty kibble into a blue Willow-pattern bowl and placed it in front of him. "There, Your Majesty. *Bon appétit.*" He hunched down in the happy way he does when dining, and I opened the refrigerator, hoping to find inspiration there for breakfast for Pete and me.

A pound of bacon and a half-dozen eggs. *So far, so good.* Cinnamon raisin bread for toast. *Excellent.* Butter and about ten of those little restaurant jelly packages. *Perfect.* With coffee and hazelnut creamer, breakfast was good to go. I put a couple of place mats on the table, set out plates, silverware and coffee mugs and put the egg carton on the counter—because Aunt Ibby says eggs are better for frying when they're at room temperature.

I padded down the hall to the bathroom, showered,

washed hair and brushed teeth—getting back to the kitchen just as Cuckoo began her seven a.m. proclamation. O'Ryan, having finished his meal, sat on the windowsill, grooming his whiskers. I knew that Pete didn't have to go to work until afternoon. I decided to wake him, if the clock hadn't done so already. Maybe he'd be ready for breakfast—or whatever.

He was wide-awake and smiling. After some mutually enjoyable kissing and cuddling, he pointed to the mirror at the foot of the bed. "What's the cat doing up there?"

In the mirror, angled so it reflected part of the kitchen counter, we saw O'Ryan batting at the egg carton. He'd worked the cover open and had managed to push one egg out onto the smooth granite surface.

"Stop that, you naughty boy!" I bolted from the bed and dashed from the room. Too late. With one more tap of his big paw, the cat rolled that egg over the edge, with the expected result. It hurtled downward, liberally splattering egg goo onto the tile floor and wooden cabinet. Without a backward look the culprit leaped from the countertop and darted out through the cat door. No point in chasing him. I knew he could be down the stairs and out the back door, or even hiding under Aunt Ibby's bed, in less than a minute.

"What the heck was that all about?" I muttered as I grabbed a roll of paper towels and prepared to mop up the mess. "What's with all the knocking things onto the floor?"

Pete took the towel roll from me and wiped up the sticky residue. "Cat getting clumsy, or did he do that on purpose?"

"If it was an ordinary cat, I'd think he was just being

playful," I said. "But in O'Ryan's case, no. He probably did it on purpose. But why?" I poured water into the coffeemaker.

"Did you say he's been knocking other things onto the floor too?"

I told him about the pencil sharpeners.

Pete measured out the coffee and put it into the basket. "The Statue of Liberty and a skier, huh?"

"Yes. Aunt Ibby and I thought Lady Liberty could be about the Novikovas coming to America. The skier pencil sharpener was a souvenir from Colorado. That's where they lived when they first arrived here."

Pete's cop face replaced his happy face. "Then you think the egg probably means something too. Something about the Novikovas?"

"Who knows?" I tried to smile, to shrug it all away. "Maybe it's just some silly cat game, after all, and maybe my aunt and I have wild imaginations." I put the frying pan onto the stove and arranged the bacon strips. "Eggs over easy?"

Pete couldn't resist. "I think that's what the cat said when he rolled the egg off the counter."

"Very funny." I pushed the bacon around in the pan with a spatula while it cooked, and I thought about the Novikovas and eggs. "Seriously, the only egg I can think of that might have anything to do with all this is that carved one Mrs. McKenna has. I took a couple of pictures of it. Maybe we should look at them after breakfast."

"Might as well. Maybe the cat is onto something."

"I just wish Scott hadn't lost that notebook of Dillon's. That's probably where the important answers are."

"Wait a sec. He did remember a few things." He disappeared into the bedroom and came back, carrying his own notebook. He flipped through the pages. "See what you think about this. Palmer told me that what made him believe that it was an address book was the fact that he saw several pages of names and addresses and phone numbers. Some of the addresses were circled."

"Circles," I said. "This whole thing goes around in circles. Aunt Ibby says it reminds her of a merry-go-round, where none of the horses ever catch up with the one up ahead."

"She's probably right. Nothing solid enough yet to bring to the chief."

The very thought of what Chief Whaley's reaction would be to a murder investigation involving a cat, some painted wooden eggs, a couple of old pencil sharpeners and a bunch of worthless stuff in trash bags made me muffle a laugh.

"I learned one thing the chief might be interested in though," I said. "I think I know why those people in Connecticut thought there was witchcraft involved in the baker's murder. It has something to do with a mythical Russian witch named Baba Yaga."

"A witch?"

"River told me. It's because of the pointed metal things on the garrote. Baba Yaga, the witch, has pointed teeth just like that."

"Great. Now if I tell Chief about that, he'll be having me check all our files for criminals with metal teeth."

"Stasia has some gold teeth," I said. "Does that count?"

"Don't worry about her. And, no, her gold teeth don't count."

I put the bacon and the eggs—perfectly done, if I do say so myself—onto Pete's plate and my own. The toast popped up, nicely brown, and Pete poured the coffee. We sat down to eat our breakfasts. The conversation then turned to more normal topics, like Aunt Ibby's plan to help Karl Smith with his book. Not that assisting a sort of shady character with a recipe index was actually a normal thing to do, but compared to dismembered horses, bubblegum-popping fortune-tellers and dead bakers, it seemed positively ordinary.

"My aunt says she's going to meet with Chef Karl in the library. You suppose that's okay?"

Pete had put his notebook aside. "Seems like a safe-enough place to meet. You said something about him helping with some kind of tea party though? What does that involve?"

"That's a library event too. She wants him to cater it. Prepare some Russian pastries."

"She's been on a kind of Russian kick ever since she bought that silver teapot thing, hasn't she?"

"We both have," I admitted. "Did Scott mention whether any of those names he saw in Dillon's book happened to be Russian?"

"He didn't remember any of them. At least that's what he said."

"He told me that at first he thought the names might be some of Eric Dillon's contacts back in Illinois. Names he could use in case he went back there to work."

Cop face back in place. "Palmer's planning to leave town?"

"I don't think so. He's just kind of dissatisfied with his situation at WICH-TV. Too much work. Not enough chance for advancement. The usual complaints."

"Uh-huh." Cop voice was back too.

"Something wrong? About Scott I mean."

"Not really. Tell me some more about your aunt's tea party."

"It's a fund-raiser for the bookmobile. She's even got her old friend Nigel flying over from London with fresh British treats from Harrods. The pastries from Chef Karl bring the Russian touch. She's going to use some of the carved Russian toys in the decorations, and as soon as I get dressed, I'm going to print out those pictures of the McKenna egg. Blow them up so we can see the details. Might be a clue there. Why are you smiling?"

"Can't help it. You. Always looking for clues. You think like a detective. Or maybe a mystery writer."

I couldn't hide my own smile. He was right. And maybe O'Ryan was right too. Somehow the carved eggs had something to do with all this—the storage locker, the murdered man, the toys, maybe even the witch with pointed teeth.

Breakfast over, Pete headed for the shower and I got dressed. I'd meant what I'd said about taking a close look at those egg photos. I also planned to find out who Nikita Novikova's five friends were. By the time Pete returned to the kitchen, I'd pulled up the photos of the nested eggs.

"Look," I said. "Six little eggs in a row." I zoomed in on one of them. "This one has a number three worked into the design. See it? Right next to that little flower." I pointed. "Did the circles Scott saw on those pages have numbers?"

He pulled his notebook from his pocket. "Bingo. Some of them were numbered. He remembered that part."

"Scott probably thought the higher numbers meant

the most important TV contacts," I said. "But what do you think they really mean?"

He shrugged. "Beats me. But don't worry. If it's important, we'll figure it out."

"*We?*"

"*We*—the police department. Not *we*—you and me."

"Maybe it'll be you, me and a certain nosy yellow cat."

I knew that Pete had a hard time adjusting to the idea that O'Ryan wasn't an ordinary cat, and probably an even harder time adjusting to the idea that I'm not exactly an ordinary person. I switched subjects.

"Aunt Ibby thinks they may need extra security at the library for the tea party. Would you want to do it?"

"No kidding? Why? That teapot can't be worth a lot, can it?"

"No. It's because of Mrs. Abney-Babcock's china. Priceless antiques. If somebody stole the set, I guess the library insurance wouldn't be enough to cover the loss."

"What if somebody drops a teacup?"

"Big bucks."

"I could work security for it, I guess, but I'll have my tea in a paper cup, thanks."

Pete left for work at noon and I headed downstairs. Aunt Ibby has apps for all kinds of historical documents and I thought that would be a good place to begin my search for Nikita Novikova's five long-lost friends. At the same time I could see if that naughty cat was still hiding after his egg-tossing adventure.

My aunt was anxious to join me in the hunt for Grandpa Nick's missing friends, and assured me that O'Ryan was happily napping on her bed, and had not molested any of her breakfast eggs. And so began the search for arrivals of Russian immigrants at Ellis Island in 1915. I had two names to start with. Novikova, of course, and on a strong hunch—the Connecticut baker's name, Alex Chopiak.

Having a reference librarian in the family is a great advantage in this sort of search, but that doesn't mean it's easy! Thanks to my tech-savvy aunt's ability, to say nothing of her vast circle of knowledgeable Facebook friends, and her full-boat membership in Ancestry.com—it took us only six hours to find the name of the ship, the names of passengers, the town and country of origin of each person aboard, names of other family members, the port of origin and the occupation of each one. Who knew we could find all that while sitting in Aunt Ibby's office, nibbling on her first attempt at *chernika tartaletki*?

But find it we did.

The printer cranked out page after page of information. Novikova, the carpenter, and Chopiak, the baker, were on that ship and had each given the same Russian town of origin: Tsarskoe Selo. A quick Google search placed it as a few miles from St. Petersburg. There were four more men from Tsarskoe Selo aboard with their families: Pasternak, a horse trainer, Krupkin, a butler, Orlov, a valet, and Yakovlev, a doctor.

"Sounds as though some important somebody in Tsarskoe Selo was sending some of their household staff to America," Aunt Ibby said. "And who among Russia's rich and famous lived in Tsarskoe Selo in 1915?"

I knew the answer to that one. "Czar Nicholas II. Both Grandpa Nick and the baker from Connecticut claimed to work in his palace, and I'll bet the other four did too."

"I believe the czar and his family planned to escape to America." Her tone was firm. "I believe he sent some staff ahead. And knowing a little of the Romanoff history, and knowing that Eric Dillon was a treasure hunter, I'll just bet that each of them was carrying something of value. Something the czar could reclaim later. There's still five hundred tons of Russian gold missing, you know—supposed to be on a sunken ship somewhere. I think that family was feathering nests all over the world in anticipation of escaping before the revolution. Mark my words, those six families were hiding something valuable."

I remembered what Pete had said: *"Something worth killing over."*

CHAPTER 22

"Okay," I said. "So we've got the six of them and their families landing on Ellis Island in 1915. Where'd they all go from there? We know that there were Novikovas someplace in Colorado because Stasia visited from there when she was a child, and the baker wound up in Connecticut. Eric Dillon must have figured out where they all went. But how?"

"Probably the 1920 United States Census," my aunt said. "We can figure it out too. But we'll save that for another day. I'm tired."

I could have kept going, but I knew things would move faster and more accurately under my aunt's supervision. Reluctantly, I stacked the printed pages carefully, along with a few handwritten notes and put it all in a folder.

"We're off to a good start, don't you think?" I said.

"Very good," she agreed.

"Do you have any idea what the six of them could be carrying—smuggling—that would be valuable? Gold maybe?"

"A large amount of gold would be heavy. The czar sent that away on trains or ships, I'm sure. It would be too easily noticed in luggage. No, it's something fairly small. Something a wood-carver could hide in a toolbox, or a doctor might conceal in a medical bag." She paused. "Something one could hide inside a Mickey Mouse toy—or in a carousel horse."

"I guess we know now that's two places where whatever it is surely isn't."

"Could be jewelry of some sort, I suppose." Aunt Ibby turned off the computer and then stood. "They say there were millions of dollars' worth of diamonds and rubies and emeralds sewn into the czar's children's clothing when they tried to escape on that last, sad night before the revolution."

I followed her into the living room and thought about the poor murdered children. "Anastasia too," I said.

"Of course Anastasia too. That reminds me. I want to show you something." She sat on the couch and reached for a slim red-covered book on the coffee table. "Here. Sit by me." She patted the seat beside her and handed me the book. A pretty child smiled shyly from the cover. *Anastasia's Album* was the title. "See? They've gathered together some of her letters, drawings and photos and made it into sort of an album. Look carefully at the cover. Anything look familiar?"

The girl was posed sitting on a carpet, her lace-trimmed dress neatly arranged, curls spilling over her shoulder.

"No. Should it?"

"Took me a while to figure it out too. It's the dress."

She flipped through the pages. "Not just that one. This one. And this. I recognized most of them."

"The doll clothes," I said. "They're copies of Anastasia's own dresses."

"Meticulous copies," she said. "I wouldn't be surprised if the same person who made some of the child's dresses, made the doll dresses too."

"Lydia Novikova?"

"Might very well be. I've found a few other books showing the dresses too. Apparently, Anastasia and her sisters were the Princess Dianas of their day. Everyone was interested in where they went and what they wore. Here." She pulled a small case from behind the couch. "See if you think I'm right." Carefully unwrapping blue tissue paper, she held up a small pale blue silk dress, while at the same time, displaying a page in the red book. "Of course the photos are all in black and white, but I'll bet anything the dress Anastasia is wearing in that picture is blue."

"I'm sure you're right," I said, reaching out to touch gently the intricate hand stitching, the tiny pearl buttons on the doll dress. "This makes me think that maybe Lydia was just as important a member of the czar's household staff as her wood-carver husband."

"Wouldn't that be something interesting to pursue?" My aunt sounded thoughtful, and I could almost hear those librarian wheels turning in her head. "Lydia, the seamstress, hmmm?"

"Do you remember, though, that Stasia said her grandmother lapsed into some kind of dementia? Didn't know where she'd put things. Stasia seemed quite upset about it."

"Yes. So sad. Even so, we may be able to figure out a few things. Perhaps I'll call on the McKennas again. Bring them some cookies or a cake. Just a neighborly visit, you understand."

"I understand perfectly," I said, watching as my aunt wrapped the delicate silk dress in its blue tissue paper and replaced it in the case. "How many of those little dresses are there?"

"A dozen. All perfectly preserved too. As good as new. I wonder where the doll is."

"Probably somewhere in Russia or else destroyed in the revolution. It must have been Anastasia's own doll, don't you think?"

"Maybe. Maybe not. When I go to visit the McKennas, do you want to come with me this time?"

"Wouldn't miss it for anything," I said. "What kind of cookies?"

"Snickerdoodles, I think," she said. "Everybody likes them, and carrying cookies to a neighbor couldn't possibly be considered meddling, now could it?"

"I'm sure it couldn't," I said with a straight face.

We began our census checking right after breakfast the following morning. We sat at Aunt Ibby's round kitchen table, each with a laptop and a full cup of coffee. We divided the list. Three names each. Figuring out exactly where in this vast country six individual Russian immigrant families lived over a century ago seems as though it should be difficult, time-consuming and tedious. Thanks to the Internet and Ancestry.com it was none of those. Fill out a form with names and dates, and up comes the information, along with a view of the original handwritten census record. Amazing.

Pasternak, the horse trainer, had gone to Louisville, Kentucky. A logical choice. Krupkin and Orlov, the butler and the valet, had each chosen Los Angeles. Doctor Yakovlev had found work in Boston. In 1920, Chopiak, the baker, had lived in the same city where he'd died, New Haven, Connecticut. Nikita Novikova and his family had settled in Burlington, Colorado, where Grandpa Nick was listed as an "amusement park worker," and Lydia was a "seamstress." They had a young son named Nikita Junior.

"Nikita Junior must have grown up to be Stasia's father," I told my aunt, "and listen to what became of Krupkin, the butler," I said. "He's listed as a motion picture actor in Los Angeles, California. Do you suppose he got a job playing a butler in the silent movies?"

"I wouldn't be one bit surprised," she said. "Doctor Yakovlev is listed as a laboratory worker. I wonder if he was eventually able to work as a doctor in America. Later we can look them all up again in the 1930 census and see what became of them." She smiled. "This is fun, isn't it?"

"It really is. You have Orlov, the valet, on your list. What happened to him?"

"He was listed as an actor too, same as Krupkin." She closed her laptop. "Well, that takes care of the first five years our Russian friends spent here. Time for me to start making cookies."

While she bustled around the kitchen, measuring and mixing, I Googled Colorado amusement parks. Up came the name of a park in Denver where, from

1905 until 1927, there'd been a stationary carousel featuring carved horses, all "standers" like my horse. In 1928, that old carousel was sold and delivered to an amusement park in the city of Burlington. So Grandpa Nick, "amusement park worker," would have had an opportunity to display his carving skill by repairing and maintaining those carousel horses. That made me smile. I was beginning to feel as though I knew the old man. I searched further and found that the old carousel had once again been restored and was open to the public right there in Burlington, Colorado.

"I'll bet Grandpa Nick would have been proud to know that horses he worked on are still carrying kids around." I remembered how I'd loved the merry-go-round at the Salem Willows. My horse must have been one he made for the Salem carousel.

"I heard that Macy's Department Store in New York City bought the old Willows merry-go-round," my aunt said, reading my thoughts as she sometimes does. "I wonder how your horse got left behind."

"Colleen said her grandfather still had some work to do on it. He said someday he'd put it back where it belonged."

"Quite likely when he learned it was going to be part of Macy's Christmas display, he gave up on that idea." It wasn't long before the smell of cookies baking wafted through the air. Aunt Ibby placed a couple of wire racks onto the table.

"Are we just going to go over there and barge in with a plate of cookies?" I asked. "Won't that seem odd?"

My aunt made a "tsk-tsk" sound. "Certainly not. I thought I'd raised you better than to even think we'd ever be so impolite. I phoned Mrs. McKenna yesterday. Thanked her for being so kind to you and Pete and asked if we might call on her at . . . ." She paused and glanced at the clock. ". . . at two o'clock this afternoon."

"'Call on her.'" I laughed. "That sounds so Victorian."

"I know. It is. Nobody knows how to refuse when you say it that way." The oven timer dinged and she put the pan of perfectly browned treats across the racks to cool. "Try it sometime. You'll see. Now scoot along upstairs and put on a calling-on-the-neighbors outfit while I find a nice, little basket for the Snickerdoodles."

I did as she asked, retaining jeans but exchanging my NASCAR T-shirt for a plain white blouse, which seemed suitable for the occasion. As I walked back through the living room, I saw O'Ryan sitting in the zebra print chair, his back to me, pointedly ignoring the teddy bear pencil sharpener on the floor. I shook my head, picked up poor Teddy and put him back on the shelf. "Now you think this is just a game, don't you? A cute, little, harmless bronzed teddy bear has nothing to do with anything. Stop it! Do you hear me?" Big, innocent golden eyes looked my way for an instant, then closed as the cat assumed a Sphinx-like position. "You big fake," I said. "Try to behave yourself while I'm gone."

At five minutes before two, appropriately dressed, Aunt Ibby and I started around the block to Williams Street, arriving at the McKennas' front door, the basket of still-warm cookies safely tucked beneath a red-and-white-checked napkin, at precisely two o'clock. Colleen McKenna answered about a second after I pushed the doorbell. She must have been standing in the front hall waiting for us.

"Come in, come in." Colleen was all smiles. "Glad to see you again, Lee. And I know you're Ms. Russell. You don't remember me, but I used to see you in the library all the time back when I was in college."

Aunt Ibby squinted up her eyes for a moment, then widened them. "Of course. You were studying early-childhood development. Planning a teaching career, right?" She handed the basket to the woman. "We thought you might enjoy some cookies."

"Thank you so much." Colleen looked both pleased and amazed by my aunt's accurate memory. I was pretty impressed by it myself. "That's right. I taught kindergarten for quite a while, then I got married and the boys came along." She shrugged. "But enough about me. I know you're both interested in this old house. Mother thought Miss Russell might like to see the egg that the old man carved, and I have something special to show you too. We were both so happy to get your call."

We followed her down a long, narrow hall wallpapered in a brown-and-white pastoral toile pattern, with framed photos in even rows.

"This has been a day full of surprises for us," Colleen continued. "My mother's in the kitchen." She turned a corner into a bright yellow room, where two women sat at a long maple harvest table, where the carved nested eggs were lined up in a neat row. "You won't believe who arrived about an hour ago."

Mrs. McKenna stood facing us with a broad, welcoming grin. The other woman remained seated, and turned slowly in our direction. She wore what would certainly pass as proper calling-on-the-neighbors attire, with her orange hair neatly twisted into a bun. She smiled.

Just behind where the woman sat in that pleasant room, there was a glass-fronted china cabinet. Without warning came the pinpoints of light, the swirl of color. This vision was no harmless teddy bear. Instead, a real bear, black and fierce, mouth open, teeth bared, glared at me over Stasia Novikova's shoulder.

CHAPTER 23

I blinked and the thing was gone. Only Stasia and the glass-fronted cabinet were there. No scary bear.

"Hello, Lee," Stasia said. "You look surprised to see me."

I was damned sure I looked surprised. This so-called gift of mine has never been a welcome one, and compared to other visions I've seen since I'd discovered that I was a scryer, that bear was, by far, the most terrifying.

Mrs. McKenna saved me from having to answer right away. She moved forward quickly, extending her hand to my aunt. "You're Miss Russell! Lennie was so excited about meeting you the other day. And, of course, we've met Lee and her handsome gentleman friend. Do I smell cookies? You shouldn't have. Colleen, put the cookies on a plate. Come and sit down, everybody. Look. Our old friend Stasia has come by to visit. Her grandfather used to live in this very house. Stasia, did you say you know Lee?" The woman barely paused for breath. "We haven't seen Stasia for years. So many years. Stasia and Colleen were best friends when they were children. Miss Russell, this is Stasia Novikova, and I guess you've met my daughter, Colleen. Can I offer you some tea?"

Her breathless monologue gave me time to recover from the nightmare image I'd just seen reflected in the cabinet glass. I managed a polite response, shook hands with Mrs. McKenna and Stasia, then sat beside Colleen. As her mother poured tea, I listened as my aunt steered the conversation back to Stasia's grandfather.

"How very interesting. Colleen and Stasia must share so many lovely childhood memories of this house and especially of Mr. Novikova—such a talented gentleman." She pointed to the row of graduated eggs. "Like these. Thanks to a lucky bid at a storage locker auction, Lee and I have a few examples of his handiwork too."

"I saw you at that locker sale," Stasia said in a matter-of-fact tone.

We all turned toward her, perhaps expecting her to say something else about it. But she didn't. It was one of those moments when everyone has stopped speaking. Awkward silence. Colleen grabbed the cookie plate and passed it to me. "These look delicious."

"My aunt is a wonderful cook. She's writing a cookbook."

That somehow got the conversation going once more. "No kidding. What kind of cookbook?"

Aunt Ibby gave a quick rundown of the history of the Tabitha Trumbull recipe collection. "So you see," she summed up, "family history, family keepsakes, can sometimes be brought together—sometimes in book form, sometimes as a collection of objects—which may interest present generations and generations yet to be born.

This lovely carved egg, for instance." She touched the smallest egg gently.

"I get it." Mrs. McKenna reached for her third cookie. "You've put together Tabitha Trumbull's recipes so that not only the people in her family can enjoy them, but so can hundreds of other people. And"—she held up one finger—"if we can put together all we know about Grandpa Nick . . . Mr. Novikova and the things he made, like my beautiful egg and the matryoshka dolls, it could be interesting to all kinds of people."

"That's why it's so great that you happened to come here today, Stasia." Colleen reached across the table and clasped her old friend's hand. Stasia smiled briefly. "You can fill in the blanks, and maybe if Miss Russell writes it all down, someday you'll be in a book too!"

Stasia shook her head. "I don't want to be in a book. I just want to know what became of all my grandmother's things. She gave me the doll, but she couldn't remember where she'd put the clothes."

I heard my aunt's sharp intake of breath. I thought she was about to speak, to tell Stasia not to worry, that she had the clothes and they were safe. But Stasia hadn't finished. "By then, she thought *I* was Anastasia. I mean, my name *is* Anastasia, but she thought I was the real one. The Grand Duchess Anastasia. Imagine that! Me! Crazy, old Stasia. A grand duchess. That's why my grandmother gave me the doll. Anastasia, the real one, was supposed to get it back when she escaped to America."

My aunt gave me what I think of as her ah-ha look. Maybe our story about the czar planning an escape from Russia wasn't so far-fetched, after all.

"Those poor children." Mrs. McKenna looked genuinely sad. "Never got away at all. But it was nice, Stasia, that Lydia believed Anastasia had escaped. It must have given her great comfort to give you that doll."

"Maybe." Stasia spoke sharply then. "Lee, I know you got that dumb, old horse. That's how I knew it was the right locker."

"I did keep the horse," I said, "but you probably saw what happened to it if you've been watching the news. It's in pieces and I don't even know what they were looking for in it."

"They wasted their time anyway, didn't they?" Stasia smiled. "It was empty, wasn't it? Darned horse was empty, after all. Everybody got fooled."

Stasia reached into a side pocket of the gray silk dress and pulled out the now-familiar wrapped oblong. She popped the gum into her mouth and chewed thoughtfully for a moment, then blew a large pink bubble. She leaned back in the chair, inhaling the thing. "Stupid horse."

"Your grandfather carved it, Stasia." My aunt spoke softly. "That makes it special, doesn't it?"

"I guess so. I was sorry when he died. My parents came for the funeral, and to take me home. They didn't want to leave me with my grandmother. Right after he died, she got kind of . . ." She shrugged. "You know."

"She didn't live very long after that," Mrs. McKenna said. "She was a little confused is all. She wasn't crazy or anything, Stasia. She used to talk about you all the time. She called you by your given name. Anastasia. Thought the world of you. Then after she passed, your father came back here again and went through all their stuff with a fine-tooth comb, I swear. He took a few things and I guess he gave the rest of it to St. Vladimir's. At least that's what he told us when he sold us this house. The whole upstairs and the basement were clean as a whistle when we passed papers on the place."

"I know. I remember." Stasia's eyes grew misty.

"Why didn't you write to me anymore? And when you came back to Salem, why didn't you call me?" Colleen looked about to cry too. "And why did you really come here today? After all this time?"

"I came to warn you." Stasia wiped her eyes with the back of her hand. "Boris Medvedev is here. I saw his picture on TV. If he knows about this house, he may come here. See, he thought there was something in the horse too. He might think you have what he's looking for."

"What is it?" I asked, wanting to shake her. "What is he looking for?"

"I don't know." She looked into my eyes. "They never told me."

CHAPTER 24

Aunt Ibby was instantly busy on her smartphone. She didn't even try to hide it under the table. "Boris Medvedev," she said. "A professional wrestler in the late 1950s. Is that the Boris you're talking about, Stasia?"

"Yes. That's him. An old friend of the family. My dad liked wrestling." She laughed, but it was the kind of snorting laugh that wasn't one bit funny. "He looked a lot different in that picture on TV. The beard and the wrinkles. He was good-looking when he was young. He's really old now. But that's him."

"Medvedev," I said aloud. I remembered that Chef Karl had said he didn't know Boris's last name, and I thought about what Scott had said about the bearded man looking familiar. Scott had been a young sports reporter back then. Makes sense he would know something about professional wrestlers. It only took a couple of seconds for me to text Pete.

It wasn't a long message. I texted **Boris Medvedev wrestler** and returned to the conversation. "I don't think these people need to worry about the bearded man,

Stasia. It's been so many years since your grandparents lived here, I doubt very much that he'd expect to find anything of value." I mentally crossed my fingers and vowed to ask Pete to ask for an extra patrol car to keep an eye on the McKennas, just in case. "We were talking about your grandmother? Lydia?"

"Hope you're right about that," Colleen said. "Sure wouldn't want to run into him. But look, I brought my tablecloth with me. Thought you might like to see it. It's really beautiful work." She opened a canvas bag and brought out a large tissue-wrapped square.

The tablecloth was a big one. Heavy too. We each automatically moved our teacups out of the way as she spread it, partially unfolded, on the tabletop. Colorful embroidery covered most of the surface. This wasn't the typical decorated-around-the-border, preprinted needle-work project.

"What an amazing piece of work!" my aunt exclaimed. "Look at the detail. Flowers and birds and buildings."

"When my boys were little, I taught them their al-phabet and simple numbers from it," Colleen pointed to capital letters in seemingly random arrangements, and fancifully formed numerals here and there among the flowers and birds and animals. "Lydia gave it to me because I was a kindergarten teacher. She knew I'd appreciate it."

"We were lucky that she gave us the things she did," Mrs. McKenna offered. "Otherwise, I guess all these beautiful handmade treasures would have gone to St. Vladimir's and wound up in that abandoned storage locker."

"I've been going to all the locker auctions around

here for over a year," Stasia said. "I knew Grandpa Nick's things had to turn up eventually."

"How'd you know that?" I asked.

"When I came back to Salem, I began looking for my doll clothes. I went to see the priest at St. Vladimir's. He's young. Didn't know my grandfather. He said that Grandpa's stuff had been stored in the church basement for ages, but after the old priest retired, it all got sent to a storage locker. He didn't know exactly where." Stasia chewed her gum thoughtfully for a moment. "I have a friend who does the bookkeeping at St. Vladimir's. She told me that somebody had agreed to pay the locker rental, so it was off their books. That would have been my dad. After I heard that he'd died, I figured the time would be up sometime this year."

"I wonder if that old priest is still living," my aunt said. "I remember him. Father Richard. I guess your grandparents went to his church?"

"Sure. There's a big Russian community here in Salem. Most of them go to St. Vladimir's. Grandpa Nick and Father Richard used to play chess together right in this house. I'm pretty sure he's still living. It would've been a big deal at church if he'd died."

"We went to the tearoom next to the church the other day," I said. "Seems to be a popular place. Wonderful pastries. We'll be going back for a full meal soon."

"Have the *blinchik*." Mrs. McKenna rubbed her hands together. "Duck with pomegranate. To die for."

"The *latkes* are my favorite," said Colleen.

"Mine too." Stasia smiled at her old friend.

"Do you know Chef Karl?" my aunt asked of no one in particular.

All three women nodded. "Everybody likes Karl," Mrs. McKenna said. "That restaurant was a big flop until he took over. Watery borscht. Canned strawberries in the Romanoff. Disgusting."

"Karl made the place a success." Colleen began to fold her tablecloth. "The Rotary Club even eats there every month."

"I'm thinking of asking him to cater an event at the library with me. Just the pastries and maybe that delicious tea they serve." Aunt Ibby reluctantly let go of the corner of Colleen's tablecloth. "Thank you for showing this to us, Colleen. Could I snap a photo of it?"

If she hadn't asked, I would have. I'd recognized the same little flower with a 3 woven through it that I could see on the wooden eggs. Colleen stood and held the cloth with outstretched arms so that most of the embroidery was visible. My aunt took several pictures, then Colleen resumed her careful folding. Stasia reached out and touched the soft linen fabric just before Colleen wrapped it, once again in tissue, and slipped it back into her bag.

"You be sure to let us know when that library thing is happening, won't you?" Mrs. McKenna smiled. "I'd go anywhere for Karl's Russian tea cakes. They just melt in your mouth."

"I'll be sure we include them. Thank you so much for welcoming us to your home. It's been such a pleasure meeting all of you." Aunt Ibby stood and I took the cue. Time to leave. Whether it was a matter of proper etiquette, or whether she had some other reason to leave with questions still unanswered, I couldn't tell. I stood and shook hands with the three women, promising to stay in touch—and meaning it sincerely.

Colleen escorted us down the long hall, past the gallery of photos. I paused to look at them. They ranged from recent shots of Kevin and Colin to some 1960s-looking wedding portraits and some old black-and-white photos. "What an interesting display. It's like a family history on the wall."

"Thank you for noticing, Lee. Not just our family. There are a few that the Novikovas gave to Mother, so it's more like a 'house history.' There's Grandpa Nick and Lydia sitting on the back porch with me when I was little." She pointed at a faded black-and-white photo. "You'll be interested in this one. It shows Grandpa Nick carving your horse." I peered at the picture. The lines of my horse were recognizable, even the little rose—but there was no paint on him at all. The man posing with the horse held a small chisel in one hand and a long knife in the other.

"Thanks for pointing it out. May I take a picture of it?"

Colleen gave permission, then led us to the front door and stood in the doorway, waving as we headed down Williams Street. Stasia stayed behind, and I was pleased by that. The two friends had been estranged for far too many years, no matter what the reason. I hoped they'd resume the childhood relationship.

"What did you think about all that?" Aunt Ibby asked as we approached Washington Square. "Were you as surprised as I was to see Stasia Novikova there? Such a well-dressed and well-spoken Stasia at that."

"I was surprised to hear her say that we're probably right about the czar plotting an escape to America, but

I was mostly surprised that she knows the mysterious Boris. I texted Pete about it."

"Good. Do you think that Boris person would be apt to bother the McKennas?"

"I kind of doubt it. It's been such a long time since the Novikovas moved out of the house, but I'm going to tell Pete what Stasia said about him. Aren't you going to tell her that you have the doll clothes she's looking for?"

"Yes. In good time. The tablecloth is magnificent, don't you think?"

"Absolutely. I'm really glad you took those photos."

"Any special reason?"

I told her about the number 3 and the flower I'd seen on the carved egg. "The same pattern is on the tablecloth. I think it might be important—I just can't figure out how. There are so many things I can't figure out lately."

"Is something wrong, dear? You sound anxious."

"You know how I've told you that the visions come suddenly sometimes—at the darnedest times and in the darnedest places. I hate it when they just pop in and out like that. I thought maybe if I learned to call them up, it would keep them from surprising me—scaring me."

"Of course. Do you mean you've seen something . . . recently?"

"Very recently. It was while we were sitting at Mrs. McKenna's table. In the glass-fronted china cabinet, right behind Stasia."

"Oh, my dear! You've certainly learned to control your emotions awfully well. You must have been frightened, but you didn't show it at all."

"Stasia noticed, but she took it as my surprise at

seeing her there. But it wasn't her." I closed my eyes, seeing again the bear's terrible head, the hideous teeth. "It was a bear. A big, mean black bear. Want to take a guess as to what that's supposed to mean? I sure don't have a clue."

She stopped walking and grasped my arm tightly. "Medvedev," she said. "Medvedev."

"Boris Medvedev? What about him?"

"His name. *Medvedev* means 'bear' in Russian."

CHAPTER 25

By the time we'd reached home, I'd elaborated a little about the image of the bear I'd seen. I gave her the whole yellow-teeth, saliva-dripping jaws, furious-eyed beast description. We were in the front hall when Pete texted me back: Thx, LvU

The message quickly erased the slobbering bear/beast image from my mind, but not Aunt Ibby's. "Maralee, how absolutely terrifying for you." She grasped my arm. "I'm so sorry that you're burdened with this . . . this thing you have. You must be so frightened. What can we do?"

I patted her hand. "The images are always metaphorical. I'm not going to be eaten by a bear. It was just giving me the man's name. Medvedev. Bear. It's going to be okay. Pete's on it. Don't worry."

I hoped we really didn't have to worry. That bear may have been a metaphor, but it was definitely not a nice bear.

"If you say so." She didn't sound convinced. "It was

interesting meeting Stasia today. She didn't look or sound at all crazy."

"I know. She's a puzzle, all right. I think maybe it's a charade, a disguise. Can't imagine why though."

"That tablecloth is a marvel, isn't it? Looks like a museum piece. Maybe I should be more careful with my quilt."

"You'll have to talk the cat out of sleeping on it."

"I know. He loves it." The cat in question met us at the back door. I headed up to my place with O'Ryan bounding ahead.

It was Chinese-food night for me and Pete—his turn to pick it up. I could hardly wait for him to arrive—mostly because I love him, of course, but partly because I wanted to hear what he'd been able to learn about Boris Medvedev. I was pretty sure he'd share some more information about this case with me. After all, I was the one who'd come up with the last name! I hadn't said anything to Aunt Ibby about it, but I was suspicious that her new friend Chef Karl wasn't being exactly forthcoming about his connection to the bearded, old wrestler. His explanation about how he happened to be out collecting other people's trash in the middle of the night didn't make much sense to me, and I was confident the police would want to take another look at his flimsy excuse.

Pete arrived, bearing a shopping bag filled with those enticing, slant-sided, wire-handled boxes with the picture of a pagoda on the front, along with fortune cookies and two pairs of chopsticks. "I was hungry," he said, grinning. "Besides, there was a special on the crab Rangoon." He put the bag on the counter and pulled me close for a long kiss—one that was certain to delay dinner.

Oh, well, that's what microwaves are for.

Pete had made a delicious selection of Asian goodies and reheating didn't hurt them one bit. We sat at the Lucite table, with O'Ryan lurking below, hoping for a stray shrimp or morsel of chicken to be dropped his way. Pete thanked me again for giving him Medvedev's name.

"Guy's got a record from Miami to Moscow. How did you find out that he was an old-time wrestler? He doesn't look much like he did when he was young. Did somebody you know recognize him? Scott Palmer, maybe?" He frowned. "If it was him, he should have called us first."

"No. Not Scott. I'm sure he would have called you. It was Stasia." I told him about our visit with the McKennas, and how Stasia had surprised everybody by showing up. "She was quite talkative, and, Pete, she's not as nutty as everyone thinks. In fact, I doubt that she's crazy at all."

"Tell me what she said. Do you think she knows something about Dillon's murder? I hate to bring her in for questioning. Every time we talk to her, she stares into space, blows bubbles and babbles nonsense. You think it's an act?"

"I do. It's as if she's hiding behind a mask, covering up the real Stasia. I didn't catch any connection to the murder, but she knows Medvedev. Apparently, she's known him since she was a child. The reason she went to the McKennas' today was to warn them about him. She thinks he may come looking for something hidden in their house. Do you think you could ask for an extra patrol around Williams Street until you find him?"

"Maybe. I'll check into it. What's he looking for?"

"She doesn't know. But she knows now that whatever it is wasn't inside my horse. Seemed surprised by that—and even a bit annoyed."

"No kidding. I guess Eric Dillon didn't know it was empty either, and whoever broke into Paul's place sure thought there was something in it."

"Guess they were all wrong. Aunt Ibby and I have a kind of theory about the treasures Dillon might have been tracking," I said, thinking of our hours of careful study on the six Russian friends and their journey to America. "Want to hear it?"

His smile was just short of condescending. "Sure, Nancy. Tell me about it."

I was a little ticked off by his attitude and changed my mind about sharing what we'd learned. The information would keep and maybe it wasn't even important anyway. "On second thought our theory isn't quite ready for prime time. I think we need a little more research. I'll tell you about it later."

"As long as it's just research, librarian stuff, nothing you can get hurt doing."

"Just 'librarian stuff,'" I agreed.

"You two be careful. We're talking about murder here. We found that stolen van, you know, wiped clean and burned. Hardly anything left of it." He wore his cop face for a second, then smiled and handed me a fortune cookie and took one for himself. We always open them together. Mine said, *Prepare for the unexpected*. Pete's was *Take a break and enjoy your life.*

"I'm already enjoying my life," he said, giving me one of those heart-melting smiles that made me forget I'd been annoyed with him a few seconds earlier. "But I don't think taking a break is anywhere in my near future. What about you? Prepared for the 'unexpected'?"

"I doubt it. Who is? But I guess I should tell you I . . . um . . . saw something 'unexpected' today."

"A vision? What was it?"

I told him about the bear I'd seen in the glass behind Stasia. "I had no idea what it could mean, but Aunt Ibby figured it out right away. *Medvedev* means 'bear' in Russian. But what was an old wrestler looking for in our trash? And what about Karl Smith? I don't think it's possible that he doesn't know who Boris really is." O'Ryan had hopped from under the table, up into my lap when I started to describe the bear. "Yes, O'Ryan. I know. You were right about the bear."

Pete raised an eyebrow. "The cat knew about the bear?"

"There was a teddy bear pencil sharpener on the floor this morning."

"That cat! Anyway, we ran a quick check on Medvedev as soon as I got your message. He came here from Russia, was billed as 'the Russian Bear' and was pretty popular on the wrestling circuit back in the seventies. Bad guy, of course. Chief saw him wrestle once at the old Salem Arena. He says the ref had to stop the match because of the illegal choke hold Boris had on some poor guy.

Anyway, he eventually killed somebody in the ring, and that was the end of his career in the States."

"He killed somebody in a wrestling match?"

"Sure did. After that, it looks like he went back to Russia. We understand that he still had some KGB connections there." He shrugged. "Maybe he still does. Anyway, he showed up in California a couple of years ago—joined up with the Russian Mafia. They call it *Bratva*—'brotherhood.' Medvedev is what they call a 'fixer.' If there's enough money involved, he'll get you whatever you want. No rough stuff out there though. Did a little time for trying to buy a submarine for a drug dealer. But at least now we have some fairly recent mug shots. That should help someone ID him."

"How about Karl Smith? What's up with him?"

"No record we can find, and Smith's sticking to his story that he doesn't know Boris's last name."

"You believe him?"

He shrugged and reached for another fortune cookie. "It's not my job to believe him or disbelieve him—or Palmer or this Boris guy when we catch him. I just take their statements. Try to get the facts."

I took that as a signal that he wasn't going to discuss police business any further. It was okay. I was surprised he'd shared as much as he had. I guessed it was because of the Russian Bear lead I'd given him. I still had a lot of questions about Karl Smith though. If my aunt was actually going to collaborate with him on the cookbook and the library tea, I thought we needed to know a lot more than that Chef Karl's Russian tea cakes would melt in your mouth.

"I think I'll check with Paul tomorrow and see how he's coming along with the restoration," I said.

"I stopped by the shop this morning," Pete said. "The forensics team finished with their work on the murder site, so things are back to normal over there."

I decided to push my luck. "Did they find anything useful?"

"Nothing they didn't get on the first day. Dillon's camera minus the memory card and the vomit sample."

"Vomit?"

"Oops. Sorry. You still eating?"

"No. It's just I didn't know about that. The paper didn't say anything about it."

"I shouldn't have mentioned it. Forget it."

"Was it his? Eric Dillon's? From being choked like that?"

"No. Forget it." This time the "forget it" was in a tone of voice that convinced me I wasn't going to get any more information about the crime scene. Time for a subject change.

"I can hardly wait to see my horse looking like he did when he was new," I said. "You won't be able to call him Old Paint anymore."

"I know. I bet the old man would have been happy about it being restored."

"I saw a photo of my horse today without any paint at all on him. Mr. McKenna told Aunt Ibby that Nikita said the horse used to be on a merry-go-round and he was going to fix it up someday and put it back where it belonged."

"I remember. But did anyone explain just *where* that might be?"

"No. Sorry. It might have been made for the Willows carousel. Why? Is it important?"

"I don't know. Maybe. Didn't your aunt say that the bearded man she saw in the library was looking for information on old amusement parks? Places where merry-go-rounds belong?"

"You're right. She did. Want to go downstairs and talk to her about it?"

"It's not too late, is it?" As if in answer to his question, Cuckoo announced nine o'clock.

"Still early," I said. "I'll call her."

Aunt Ibby said she'd love to see us both, and if we had any Chinese food left over, she wouldn't mind having a taste. Pete grabbed his pen and notebook while I arranged a plate, from chicken fried rice to crab Rangoon, bagged a few fortune cookies, and we, with O'Ryan following, headed down the front staircase.

Aunt Ibby is always happy to be consulted on just about any topic—maybe from long years as a reference librarian. Between bites of egg roll she recounted her front-gate conversation with Mr. McKenna. "I'm sure he'll be happy to talk about the experience with you, Pete."

Pete scribbled in his notebook. "You told Lee about seeing a man who might have been this Boris Medvedev in the library once. Could you tell me about that?"

"I'm sure now that it was the same man, and I wish I'd paid more attention, or been more observant, but"— she spread her hands apart—"the request wasn't a bit out of the ordinary. The only reason I remember him was the bushy beard."

I thought of how she'd remembered Colleen

McKenna's college major. "Aunt Ibby's memory is very accurate," I told Pete. "Even if a lot of time has passed."

He nodded. "I know. Go on, Miss Russell."

"It's just as she told you. The man asked for information and pictures of vintage amusement parks. He mentioned Salem Willows in particular. I showed him what we had, which, considering that the place is right here in Salem, was less than I would have hoped." She paused for a sip of tea. "We've corrected that oversight since. But at the time, all I could offer was the suggestion that he go to the Essex Institute. They have such a wealth of local historical material. I suspect that he went there, but you'd have to check with them."

"We did," he said. "We had no dates to go by and no last name. Though they do keep records of people who consult things in the archives there, it seemed like a wild-goose chase. Now that we have recent photos of Medvedev and his full name, maybe we'll have better luck finding out just what he was looking for."

My aunt looked back and forth between Pete and me. "Did Maralee tell you anything about what she saw this afternoon? When we were at the McKennas'?"

"The bear? Yes, she did." He looked uncomfortable.

"It was just a metaphor," I said. "A way of giving me the man's name. And it worked just fine. Nothing to worry about."

"I'm sure we don't have to worry about bears wandering around in Salem, but, Miss Russell, Lee tells me you've found a cookbook buddy. That right?"

"Oh, yes. Chef Karl. Such a talented man. We're going to meet at the library tomorrow to work on his index. A cookbook index can be quite a chore, you know." She sighed briefly, then brightened. "I hope to convince him to cater the tea. Authentic Russian pastries will add just the perfect touch to the toys and my samovar."

"You two did pretty well on that auction, after all, didn't you?" Pete tucked his notebook into his pocket. "When I came over to help you carry it all home, it didn't look like much of a bargain."

"We got some nice items—it's true." Aunt Ibby lifted a forkful of moo goo gai pan. "I think if I'd known we'd be wrapped up in a murder mystery, I would have chosen something else to do that day, wouldn't you, Maralee?"

I thought about the dead man with the line of blood on his throat, the stolen trash, the hideous bear and even the mutilated Mickey Mouse. My "Oh, yes" was heartfelt.

"Pete, I don't know whether this is important or not," my aunt said, "but we found out why Stasia was looking for doll clothes when she followed us to Goodwill."

Out came the notebook again. "Why was that?"

She explained about Anastasia's dresses and how she thought Lydia Novikova's handiwork could be just as important as her husband's carvings. "Lee's probably told you, we've really been diving into the research lately. Stasia apparently has a doll her grandmother gave to her. It may very well have once belonged to the real Anastasia. Stasia is looking for the dresses that fit it. I want to give them to her, but I'm torn because they really belong in a museum, along with the doll."

"I wonder if it would be a good idea to display Stasia's

doll with the clothes and the pictures of Anastasia at the library tea," I said. "We could advertise it. Something that rare might attract more people for your fundraiser."

"You're right." My aunt beamed. "What a good idea, Maralee."

Pete's expression grew serious. "It might even attract Boris Medvedev. I'll definitely work security for your tea party."

Pete and I returned to my apartment, loaded the dishwasher and mixed together everything that was left of our Chinese feast—except for the cookies—and stuck it into one of the containers. "Take it with you for your lunch tomorrow," I said.

"Thanks. I will. I like it all mushed up like that."

"I know you do."

He put the carton into the refrigerator. "I hope I didn't upset your aunt by saying Medvedev might show up at the library. Probably never will happen, but I want to be there, especially if he's still on the loose by then. And listen, you girls did a good job with your research. Figuring out what Stasia was looking for was pretty smart."

With our research? He must have thought I was talking about the doll dresses when I'd started to tell him about the Russian men. I tried again. "Oh, that," I said. "Thanks. But there's one more thing I need to tell you."

"I know. You're worried about that bear."

He was dead right about that. I was very worried about that bear, no matter what kind of brave face I'd been putting on.

"Uh-huh," I said. "It was . . . disturbing."

He put a finger against my lips. "How about I stay here tonight . . . to protect you from lions and tigers and bears?"

My research story could wait until tomorrow.

CHAPTER 26

We didn't have to worry about Boris Medvedev's whereabouts for long. He was picked up later that same night at a bar in Gloucester. Somebody recognized him from the mug shot they'd shown on the eleven o'clock news. However, since he was just a "person of interest," and because he denied taking the notebook after "accidentally" bumping into Scott in the station parking lot, they had to let him go after a few hours. No cause to arrest him for anything, even though Pete and I and Aunt Ibby weren't the only ones who thought he had something to do with Eric Dillon's murder. But he got a lawyer right away, and made a big scene at the police station, yelling in Russian and stomping around as though he was still in the wrestling ring. Some of the older guys at the station remembered him and even asked for autographs.

Medvedev seemed to enjoy the attention. He didn't try to hide, just strolled around as though he owned the city. According to the *Salem News,* people all over town were asking him to pose with them for selfies, and he even had the nerve to go to Sunday services at St. Vladimir's. It turned out that he'd followed Aunt Ibby's suggestion and checked with the Essex Institute about vintage amusement parks, but nobody there remembered anything out of the ordinary about his request.

I did a little checking into Chef Karl Smith's background on my own. I didn't have to work very hard at it. His Facebook page told me about his days at a highly rated New England culinary college and his participation in an international baking and pastry program. He'd worked at some famous hotels and he'd even had a local TV cooking show in Boston for a while. The Russian Tea Experience next door to St. Vladimir's was the first restaurant he'd owned outright, and from all outward signs and a slew of Yelp reviews, it was a smashing success. Nothing sinister there at all. I talked with Aunt Ibby about what I'd learned.

"I hope you don't mind that I've been checking up on him," I told her. "It's not that I don't trust your judgment, but I worry about you, you know. Same as I know you do about me."

"Don't mind a bit, child," she said. "As a matter of fact, I checked up on him too. Got the same reports you did. *And* one more thing."

"What was that?"

"He's part of the church's outreach program for ex-offenders. They provide programs to help people who've been in prison find jobs and homes and hope for the future. I think maybe the Medvedev man has been in prison and that's how Karl knows him."

I remembered what Pete had told me. "He was in prison in California. Something about money laundering."

"You see? Karl is just a good, helpful person. You don't need to worry about me one bit. Now tell me what Pete thought of our theory about the six Russian men carrying treasure to America for the czar. I hope he didn't think we were meddling in police business."

"I never got around to telling him," I admitted. "I started to, a couple of times, then somehow the subject got changed. We're going to a movie tonight. I'll tell him all about it then."

"Good. I'll be interested in what he thinks. Want to work on it some more? See whatever became of the horse trainer and the doctor and the others?"

"I'd like to," I said. "They've all become quite real to me."

We began with Pasternak. "Look at this," my aunt said. "He certainly did well here in a short time. When he arrived in 1915, he was a horse trainer, but he was a stable owner in 1920. Quite a leap, I should say."

I typed his full name into my own laptop. He even had a page on Wikipedia. Turned out that Mr. Pasternak rose from horse trainer to the owner of one of Kentucky's most prestigious training facilities in just three years. He'd been written up quite extensively in newspapers and magazines of the early twentieth century. "In 1918, he bought the stable where he'd been employed as a groom," I said. "What do you think of that?"

"The revolution was going on in Russia by then," Aunt Ibby said. "The czar was killed in 1918."

"Makes you wonder if he might have had something worth a lot of money, doesn't it?" I asked. "This is getting exciting. Let's see if any of the others came into sudden fortunes."

"You try the doctor," she said. "I'll see what I can find out about the butler."

Dr. Peter Yakovlev had done well in America too. He had worked as a laboratory technician at Massachusetts General Hospital, at least until 1920. But the census listed him in 1930 as an oncologist at the same hospital. By 1940, he wasn't listed. I checked Boston newspapers for his name, thinking I'd find his obituary, but instead found another surprise. He'd been reported as a missing person in 1932. I wondered if they'd ever found him.

Aunt Ibby had checked on both Krupkin, the butler, and Orlov, the valet. Turns out they'd both worked as extras at Paramount Pictures during the silent-movie era. Then, in 1929, they'd bought a Beverly Hills mansion together and were noted for their lavish parties. Orlov had died of natural causes in 1969 and Krupkin had passed away a year later.

"What do you think?" she asked. "Some sort of hanky-panky there? I don't think movie extras made a great deal of money back then. At least, not 'Beverly Hills mansion'–type money."

"It's all pretty fishy, isn't it? The baker was murdered. The doctor disappeared. The horse trainer, the valet, and the butler all came up with sudden wealth, and now somebody is seriously interested in Nikita Novikova's belongings."

"Can't be all coincidental, can it?"

"River doesn't believe in coincidences," I said, "and in this case I don't either. Is there some way to dig deeper into this? To find out how three immigrants got so rich so fast? I know America is a land of opportunity, but unless they all won the lottery, this is unbelievable."

"I'm thinking that once they found that the czar and his family were dead, there was no point in waiting for him to collect whatever it was that they were holding for him. They probably sold it. That would account for the sudden wealth." She turned her computer off. "Except that maybe the baker held on to whatever it was and someone took it away from him."

"And maybe they lost track of the wood-carver," I said. "I hate to think of what may have become of the doctor. It wasn't until 2007 that they found the bodies of Anastasia and her little brother. Maybe the baker, the doctor and the Novikovas thought those two kids had escaped to America, and kept their promise to the czar."

Aunt Ibby smiled. "I'll check the microfilm of the 1930s Boston papers and see if your doctor ever turned up, as soon as I get a chance. But don't forget, we're just speculating about them making a promise to the czar, remember?"

"You're right." I shook my head and closed my laptop. "All this stuff sounds like some kind of crazy fairy tale. I'm beginning to mix up what's real and what's imaginary."

"I don't wonder," she said. "Between your frightening

visions and your poor horse getting dissected, no wonder you're a little confused."

"Just the same, I need to tell Pete about Grandpa Nick's five friends. He doesn't believe in coincidence either. I'm going to call him and then I have to call Paul Carbone to ask how the repair is coming along. I'm sure I didn't imagine the horse dissection."

"Good idea. I'm going to call Karl and see if he's willing to cater the library tea. If he isn't, I'll have to make other arrangements."

"Maybe after your friend Nigel picks up the scones and biscuits at Harrods he can hop on over to Moscow and grab some tea cakes," I teased.

"Don't think he wouldn't, if I asked nicely." She winked.

"I don't doubt it at all," I said, and I didn't. I was pretty sure Chef Karl was a gone goose too. I returned to my place to make the calls to Pete and the repair shop. Pete first. He answered right away.

"Got a minute?" I asked, even though I was sure what I had to say would take more than a minute. "I think Aunt Ibby and I may have discovered something important."

"About Eric Dillon?"

"About what Eric Dillon was looking for."

"Can it wait until tonight? I'm on my way into the interrogation room. Have to have a chat with your aunt's new cookbook friend."

Why not? It's waited about a century already.

"Okay," I said. "See you around eight?"

"Eight o'clock. See ya."

Suddenly what he had just said registered. "Wait a minute. What was that about Chef Karl?"

Too late.

Click.

He was gone.

I hurried back downstairs to warn Aunt Ibby that her cookbook friend might be in trouble.

CHAPTER 27

I reported to Aunt Ibby what Pete had said and she set out for the Russian Tea Experience to see what she could learn from the staff—and "to be there when poor Karl returns." I noodled around online for a little while, hoping to dig up some more information on the six friends, but found nothing new. My aunt was gone; Pete was working; River was asleep; Paul Carbone's phone sent me to voice mail.

Stasia! The thought came like a bolt of late-summer lightning. I tossed on a jacket and ran down the stairs, grabbing a Red Sox cap from the hall tree for protection against pigeon poop, hoping that she'd be on her accustomed bench.

She was there. No stylish midi or silver belt today. She wore one of her shapeless bright print muumuus, the orange hair in disarray. Pigeons were clustered around the bench, cooing and squabbling over bits of bread. No palm-reading customers were nearby, although a small crowd of kids had gathered, watching from a respectful distance as she blew one gigantic pink bubble after another.

I shooed a couple of birds out of the way and sat beside her. "Hi, Stasia. Can we talk?"

She inhaled a bubble, held out one hand, palm up. "For ten dollars I can look into your future."

I opened my wallet. "May I ask questions?"

"Twenty dollars," she said, not moving her hand or changing her expression.

I handed her two tens. "I was surprised that you were at the McKennas'. I'll bet Colleen was glad to see you after such a long time." She stuffed the bills into her pocket and motioned for me to show her my hand. I offered my right hand, as I had before. She studied my hand and traced a line with her forefinger.

She looked up and her smile seemed genuine. "I was glad to see her too. And to be back in my grandparents' house."

"Good memories?"

She nodded and returned her attention to my open palm. "You want to ask a question?"

"Yes," I said, hoping that her answers weren't going to cost twenty dollars apiece, and wishing I'd brought more money. "You said that Boris Medvedev was 'an old friend of the family,' but you obviously didn't mean it. Was your grandfather afraid of him?"

"I'm not sure if my grandfather ever even saw him. He showed up one day at our place in Colorado. He wanted to know what had become of Grandpa Nick's belongings . . . especially that horse." She dropped my hand and leaned closer, speaking softly. "Boris Medvedev was a KGB agent back then. Maybe he still is. I think my father was afraid of him."

"He told Medvedev that the horse was in the storage locker?"

"Daddy didn't know exactly where it was. He'd asked the church to store his father's stuff. Couldn't bear to sell it or throw it away, you know, and he figured he'd get a truck and go back to Salem and get it all someday. Anyway, St. Vlad's had all the boxes in their basement. Then one day they called and said they needed the space. So he sent money every few years to pay in advance for storage. So he told Medvedev the truth. That it was stored somewhere around Salem. He died a while back and I came back to Salem. I was pretty sure the storage rent money was due to run out sometime this year."

"I suppose Medvedev figured it out too."

"My grandfather always told everyone that the horse was a 'secret keeper.' I guess that's why some people thought there was something inside it."

"Mr. McKenna told us about that. But you just wanted the clothes for your doll. That's why you were following the storage locker auctions."

"Exactly. I'm still looking for them."

"Don't give up on that," I said. "My aunt may have some good news about the dresses for you."

Her expression brightened and she took my hand again. "Really? Does she know where they are? All I've ever wanted from my grandparents was the doll clothes, and, oh, there was an old cuckoo clock I liked too."

"I definitely know where the cuckoo clock is," I told her. "It's in my kitchen and it still works perfectly. I'll be happy to give it to you. My boyfriend doesn't like it at all."

"Really? He doesn't like it?" She shook her head, looking genuinely surprised, and began tracing the lines of my hand again. "Did I tell you last time that you have an optimistic outlook and a good sense of humor?"

"No, but that's good, isn't it?"

"In your case? It's a very good thing you have them, because you seem to need both. Often."

I thought about that. She was right. I decided to push my luck—and my twenty dollars—by asking another question. "You told me once that your grandfather had the same five friends his whole life. Did you ever meet any of them?"

"I think so. Some of them. I was very young." She leaned back on the bench, a faraway look crossing her face. "I was visiting here for the summer. Two or three old men and they all spoke Russian. Grandpa and the men sat at the dining-room table, drinking something. Vodka, I suppose. Grandmother and I sat quietly in the corner of the room in our rocking chairs. My chair was a miniature of hers. We rocked, and they talked. I was cutting out Barbie paper dolls. She was doing needlework, some sort of patchwork. Bright colors, different patterns." She looked down at her dress. "That's why I like bright colors, I suppose."

"Could you understand what they were saying? The men and your grandfather? What they were talking about?"

She closed her eyes. "They talked about America. The places where they lived and about their friends who had died."

"You mean they talked about their houses?"

Her eyes flew open. "No. Their states. Their cities. Where they lived. That's enough for now. Here comes one of my regular customers. Shoo now." She flapped her hands at me as though I was one of the pigeons.

Obediently, I stood. "I'll come back again soon," I told her. "We'll talk about the doll dresses and the cuckoo clock."

"All right. Fine. Good-bye." The blank look was back. She nodded toward the woman approaching the bench. "Read your palm, ma'am? Tell your future?"

I'd learned a few new things. I didn't know where they fit in, but I was anxious to get them onto the growing pile of index cards. I hurried home. Aunt Ibby wasn't back yet, so the cat and I had the whole place to ourselves. I checked the living-room floor for wayward pencil sharpeners right away. Nothing out of place. I wasn't sure whether to be pleased or disappointed. Maybe I was actually looking forward to finding the little bronzed clues.

I'd just assembled my index cards on the kitchen counter when Paul Carbone called back. "Hello, Lee. I'm just putting a few finishing touches on your carousel horse. I think you'll be happy with his new look."

"I'm sure I will. I'm excited. When can we have the unveiling?"

"The paint should be dry by tomorrow afternoon, I should think. I'm applying a little extra gold leaf to the mane right now. Want to call me in the morning and we'll set up a time?"

"I will, Paul. I'll talk to Pete this evening and see if we

can borrow the truck again. I don't think the horse will fit in the front seat of my two-seater."

"Probably not, but he'd look pretty there! Call me tomorrow and let me know when you'll be here. Business has picked up lately."

That surprised me. "That's good. I was afraid the publicity might scare customers away."

"I thought that too. At first it brought out the lookie-loos. You know, the nosy ones who slow down at accident scenes, like to see where deaths have happened. But enough of them were interested in my work to keep me busy for quite a while." He chuckled. "Of course I was working on your horse in the front of the shop. That attracted attention, all right. He's a beauty."

We said our good-byes and I'd barely had time to begin making notes about my conversation with Stasia when Aunt Ibby tapped on my kitchen door. "Are you busy, Maralee? May I come in?"

"Of course." I called, hurrying to let her in. O'Ryan beat me to it. He streaked out the cat door into the hall before I could turn the knob, then escorted her into the kitchen as though the whole thing had been his idea. "Come right on in, both of you," I said.

Barely acknowledging the cat, she sat on the stool I'd just vacated. "I'm concerned about Karl," she said. "Chef Karl from the Russian Tea Experience." O'Ryan hopped up onto the stool beside her and I stood facing them from across the counter.

"Yes, I know who you mean. What's wrong? Did you find out what the police wanted to talk to him about?"

"It was all about his friend Boris. They'd questioned

him before about how he'd helped the man collect other people's trash from the curb."

"They didn't believe the 'hoarder' story, I suppose. Nothing strange about that. I don't believe it either." I looked at her closely. "Do you?"

"Not really," she admitted. "But Karl was really quite distressed."

"They haven't accused him of anything, have they?"

Her "no" was hesitant. "Not exactly. But they asked him not to leave town. And they asked his permission to take his fingerprints and to stick one of those swab things in his mouth. That sounds like the things they do on those TV crime shows, doesn't it?"

I had to admit that it did. "Did he agree to the prints and the swab?"

"Oh, yes. He has nothing to hide, you know."

"Did he give you any explanation of what he and Boris were looking for in our trash? The Novikovas' trash, really."

"He thinks Boris was looking for something in particular, but he doesn't know enough Russian to understand what it is. Just that whatever it is, it's small enough to hide inside a wedding cake. Of course Karl could only understand the words connected to food."

"Makes sense," I said.

"*Svadeebniy tort*," she pronounced slowly. "'Wedding cake.' At least that's what it sounded like to me. Anyway, Karl says that Boris conveyed to him that they were looking for something small enough to fit inside a wedding cake."

"'Inside a wedding cake,'" I repeated her words. "Like a big papier-mâché wedding cake in Connecticut?"

"That's what I'm thinking."

"And he's looking for something that would fit inside such a cake. Or a Mickey Mouse," I said. "Or a wooden horse."

"Or practically anything in the whole darned locker." She reached out and touched the index cards I'd spread across the granite top. "Getting anywhere with these?"

"I just had another little talk with Stasia. I was about to make some new notes when you knocked."

"Sorry I interrupted." She patted her knees, signaling O'Ryan that it was okay to move over to her lap. "Come. Sit. Tell me about Stasia while you fill out your cards." I resumed my seat at the counter, picked up the pen and a fresh card and wrote, *Boris knows about the wedding cake.*

"Stasia speaks Russian too, you know," I told my aunt. "She told me about a conversation she overheard when she was a little girl. A conversation between her grandfather and some of his friends." I paused, and made a note of what Stasia had told me.

Aunt Ibby looked at the card. "Was Lydia part of the conversation?"

"No. Stasia said that she and Lydia sat in rocking chairs. Stasia played with paper dolls. Lydia worked on a patchwork quilt."

We looked at one another.

"A patchwork quilt?" My aunt stood, dislodging the cat, who ran for the living room. "Maybe we should take a closer look at mine."

I put down my pen. "Maybe. But a seamstress with Lydia's talent probably made dozens of quilts, don't you think?"

She started for the kitchen door. "Sure. But we only have the one. Let's go downstairs and examine the evidence!"

I smiled at her excitement. "Okay," I said, following behind her. Just as she stepped out into the hall, I heard a soft *plunk* from the direction of my living room, followed by the creak of the cat door. "Uh-oh. Sounds like O'Ryan is playing with the pencil sharpeners again. Go on down. I'll meet you in your room in a minute."

I was right. The cat had once again invaded my collection. My favorites among the bronzed figures were the ones with moving parts. The little wheel was still spinning when I bent to pick up the tiny sewing machine. I carried it with me as I headed downstairs to my aunt's bedroom.

CHAPTER 28

Aunt Ibby was on her knees beside the queen-sized bed. She held a large magnifying glass—one of the Sherlock Holmes variety. She looked up at me, the glass still in place, displaying one enormous green eye when I entered through the open bedroom door. The cat crouched in the center of the quilt, whiskers twitching, attention fixed intently on my aunt. "I think I have some of the pattern figured out, Maralee," she said, lowering the glass, returning her eye to its normal size. "This is not your everyday crazy quilt."

I sat on the edge of the bed. "What do you mean? Look, it's pretty clear that O'Ryan agrees that sewing has something to do with our mystery. This was on my living-room floor." The cat glanced in my direction, leaned over and gave my elbow a lick and returned to his crouch.

My aunt put the magnifying glass on the nearby bed-side table, reached over and patted his head. "He's probably right. I haven't actually figured out what Lydia was trying to tell us, but some of these scraps are less random than others, if you know what I mean."

"I don't," I admitted, peering more closely at the dizzying juxtaposition of squares and triangles, oblongs and diamonds, many with their own designs of polka dots, stripes, florals and patterns with the occasional splash of bright, solid color. Some of the pieces had bits of embroidery highlighting the designs. "Just looking at it gives me vertigo."

"Here's what I mean," she said, tapping the quilt in the spot she'd been inspecting. "See this oblong piece? Notice anything different about it?"

"It's a nice, neat oblong, with pictures of bunnies on it. Oh, I see what you mean. It has a lot of embroidery on top of the bunnies. Not just a few lines around the edges."

"Right. And look here." She walked around to the other side of the bed. "It's another oblong, but this one has a small notch at the top and a ragged edge at the bottom. And some more heavy embroidery."

I moved to where she stood, inspecting the patch she touched. The fabric had a red background with white dots. She was right. There were embroidered symbols among the dots. "Look at this," I said. "That looks like the number three. Just like the one on Mrs. McKenna's egg, and Colleen's tablecloth." I hurried around the bed to take another look at the oblong piece with the bunnies on it. "And here's another number. It's a six. See it? The numbers must mean something," I said, "but what?"

She shrugged. "Beats me. I think it has something to do with the six men you saw coming to America. Between us, I'm sure we'll figure it out. I'm going to examine every inch of this quilt, see what else I can find. Now tell me what else Stasia said."

I wasn't as confident as she was about us being able to figure out the crazy quilt, but didn't say so. "Stasia said that the old men were drinking vodka and talking about where they lived in America, and she talked about how the grandfather's things wound up in our storage locker."

"Interesting. What else?"

I told her what Stasia had said about Boris Medvedev coming to their house, asking her father what he'd done with his parents' belongings, especially the horse. "She said her father was afraid of Medvedev, because of his old KGB connections."

"No wonder. What did he tell the man?"

"Pretty much what she told us when we were at the McKennas'. I guess he didn't think there was anything special about the horse."

"Eric Dillon must have thought there was something in it."

"I know. The horse is still a keeper of secrets, even after all these years, isn't it?"

"I wish we could find out what Eric Dillon had learned. It has to be about treasure, because that's what he always wrote about." I stood and smoothed the quilt. "And speaking of secrets, I wonder if Scott Palmer is still holding back whatever it was Dillon told him in confidence."

"Why don't you just ask him?" my aunt said. "He doesn't seem to mind consulting you on every little thing."

"You're right," I said. "He's invited me to come over

to the station. I think I'll take him up on it. I'd like to know if he's remembered where he'd seen Medvedev before too."

"You do that. Don't be shy about asking for what you want."

I checked my watch. "He should be between newscasts about now. I'm going to run upstairs and call him—invite myself over for a little visit to WICH-TV."

That's exactly what I did. I tried out Aunt Ibby's trick. "Scott," I said, "would it be all right if I call on you this afternoon?" He seemed pleased to hear from me. I knew he thought I'd called because of his irresistible charm. We made a date for three that afternoon. "That'll give you time to connect with the old gang," he said, "then we can duck across the street to the Pig's Eye for some private time."

"Wonderful," I said. "It'll be great to see everybody—even Mr. Doan."

"Sure. Same old, same old. Things don't change much around here."

When Cuckoo announced two-thirty, I was ready to leave. New jeans, boots with heels high enough to make me taller than Scott, white cashmere sweater and my black leather NASCAR jacket. Light makeup and I was good to go.

I wheeled into my old parking space at quarter to three, and arrived at the WICH-TV receptionist's desk with time to spare.

"Lee Barrett! Where have you been?" Rhonda was clearly happy to see me. She practically flew around the curved desk and enveloped me in a gardenia-scented hug. "You look fabulous! Do you still like teaching? How's that hunky detective? We all miss you around here."

I returned the hug, realizing as I glanced over her shoulder at the purple-and-chrome décor of the place, that I missed all of them too. Bruce Doan, the station manager, emerged from his office and greeted me with a hearty handshake, saying, "Don't be such a stranger, Barrett. Drop in anytime."

"Okay if I go down to the studio and see Marty?" I asked. Marty McCarthy had been camera operator on my ill-fated *Nightshades* show, and we'd shared some good times. Some pretty frightening ones too. I looked forward to seeing her again.

"Sure thing. You know the way." He retreated to his office. Rhonda waited until he'd closed his door before putting a hand-lettered BACK IN FIVE MINUTES sign on the desk and grabbing my hand. "Come on. I'll go down there with you."

Rhonda led the way past the glass-enclosed news-room, through the scarred metal doors to the long, black-walled studio. We chattered all the way, catching each other up on our lives. Rhonda enthused about a new boyfriend, a planned cruise to Mexico and an online course she was taking on understanding invest-ments. Rhonda is a never-ending source of surprises. Plus she knows everybody's business at WICH-TV.

"You got a date with Scotty, huh?" she asked as we approached the sports desk. "He told me you were coming over today. He's around here somewhere. He's been kinda moody lately. What's up with that?"

"I don't really know," I told her, more or less honestly. "I think his friend dying like that probably affected him quite a bit."

"Yeah. That's probably it. Nice guy, Eric."

"You met him?"

"Sure. We went out for drinks a couple of times while he was here."

I'd thought of Rhonda when I was giving myself that crash course in interviewing before I talked to Stasia the first time. Rhonda is a natural interviewer. The pretty brunette has a way of making people tell her things they probably regret later, and I don't think she even knows she's doing it. I wondered what Eric Dillon might have told her over drinks. I intended to find out.

"Hey, there's Marty!" Rhonda called. "Marty, look who's here!" The gray-haired woman's head popped up from behind a display of back-to-school items. "Stop working for a minute. Lee's here!"

My old friend hurried down the aisle to greet me. Never as effusive as Rhonda, her welcoming hand clasp and "Glad to see ya, kid" was sincere.

"Ready to come back to the old grind? Be a television star again?" she said. "We like River, of course, but I kinda miss you around here in the middle of the night."

"Thanks, I miss you guys too, but I've already got a pretty nice day job."

"Aw, come on. You can handle both." Scott Palmer came up from behind me and threw an arm around my shoulders. Startled, I pulled away.

"You've got to stop sneaking up on me like that, Scott." I smiled, but I meant it.

"Sorry," he said. "Well, if you girls are through visiting, I'm going to take this gorgeous woman away."

"Don't go far," Rhonda warned. "You know Doan is apt to start yelling for you any minute."

"No worries. We'll be right across the street. Bye."

The bar was nearly empty and Scott and I sat in a narrow booth at the rear of the room. "Pepsi for you?" he said. I nodded. He ordered the same. "Okay," he said. "I'm sure you're not here just for the pleasure of my company. What's up?"

"It's about your friend Eric Dillon."

He looked surprised. "Eric? What about him?"

"You mentioned that he'd told you a secret. Something you shouldn't talk about until after the book was published."

"That's true. So you want to know what he told me?"

"Yes."

"Why?"

"Well, somehow my aunt and I are involved in whatever Eric was researching. We know the storage locker we bought is central to everything. Eric was aware of it and now he's dead. We're not after whatever treasure he was tracking down. But if we're in danger, we need to learn everything we can about whatever it is. Will you help me?"

He gave me one of his long, silent, eye-to-eye looks. If I'd just met him, it might have seemed sexy, but it's just a thing he does. I think it gives him time to think of what he's going to say next. I waited.

"Okay," he said. "I'm going to tell you what I know.

It's not much." He frowned. "But if what I tell you means you find a treasure chest or pirate gold or something, you have to split with me. Right?"

I thought he was kidding. He wasn't. He stuck out his right hand. "Shake on it?"

I shook his hand. "Deal," I said.

"Fifty-fifty?"

"Sure. Why not? I don't think we're going to find any treasure."

"Eric thought he was going to. But I got the impression he didn't think it was here."

"Here, as in inside my horse?"

"No. Here, as in anywhere in Salem."

"Do you know what he was doing outside Paul Carbone's shop that night?"

He looked down at the table, making a pattern of wet circles with the bottom of his glass. He spoke so softly I had to lean forward to hear him. "'I'll be right back,' that's what Eric told me. 'Just need to make a quick trip to get a couple of pictures. Comparison shots.'" Scott looked up. This time the long look was sincere. "I never saw him again. I keep thinking about that. Comparison shots of what? That stupid, old horse? I should have asked him. I didn't, because he said he'd be right back."

"I know. His laptop was missing from the car too. But you still had his notebook."

"Yeah. For all the good that did. Addresses, scribbled pictures. Nothing that made sense."

"Scribbled pictures? Of what?"

"Just doodles. Numbers. Flowers. You know. Doodles."

Numbers and flowers made a little bit of sense to me. There were numbers and flowers on Colleen's

CHAPTER 29

While I sat in my kitchen, attempting to sort through thoughts, index cards and creepy visions, downstairs in the Winter Street house, plans for the high tea were in full swing. Aunt Ibby had invited her friend, and prominent Salem socialite, Louisa Abney-Babcock for an evening "brainstorming" session. Plans called for my aunt's New Scotland Yard gentleman friend, Nigel, to participate via speakerphone from London, and she'd also asked Chef Karl to sit in and give his input on recipes, both British and Russian. I'd been summoned too, to offer suggestions about publicity.

I joined the three at my aunt's dining-room table. The silver samovar once again served as centerpiece. It was flanked by a place setting of Louisa's delicate, heirloom Canton blue-and-white pieces. I avoided looking at the samovar, commented on the beauty of the china and focused on what was obviously Karl Smith's contribution to the conference. A gorgeous display of pastries was artfully arranged on Grandmother Forbes's silver platter.

"Come and join us, Maralee," my aunt said. "You know

my good friend Louisa, and this is Karl Smith, the famous chef from the Russian Tea Experience."

"Hardly famous, Ibby," Smith protested with a smile. "How do you do, Maralee?"

So person-of-interest Smith is on a first-name basis with my aunt.

"Call me Lee," I said. "How do you do?"

Louisa patted the chair next to her. "Sit by me, dear. What do you think about our fund-raiser? I think Ibby's idea is marvelous."

O'Ryan had quietly followed me into the room. He hopped up onto a Hepplewhite side chair next to the fireplace and sat facing the chef, focusing those golden eyes on the man with the kind of riveting stare he usually reserved for mice and birds. Not even the ringing of the house phone, which Aunt Ibby had placed on the table, diverted the cat's attention.

"Oh, that will be Nigel!" she exclaimed, clearly pleased. "He's always so prompt."

I'd never met Nigel St. John, but I'd seen photos. He looked to me a bit like Sean Connery, with black-rimmed glasses and a tweed jacket, very British. I'd always imagined that his voice would be on the deep side, with the kind of clipped English accent you hear on the PBS mystery channels. I wasn't disappointed. He was perfect.

"I've made arrangements to pick up our order at Harrods at four a.m., our time," he said. "They don't open to the public until ten, but"—a modest laugh—"the Yard has its privileges and, of course, the cooks there work all night anyway." He rattled off a list of possible pastry choices he might bring with him on the morning of the tea party.

"Perhaps your guests would enjoy the salted caramel biscuits," he said, "a favorite of mine. The demerara shortbread is popular here, and the almond loaf cake travels well. Cocoa cream pastries are a bit flaky, but if I hand carry the lot, I'm sure they'll be fine. Of course, dearest Ibby, I'll bring your favorite Highland whiskey cake."

Was my aunt blushing? I thought so. "Those sound perfect, Nigel," she said, "and it's so kind of you to do this for us. The bookmobile is such a worthy cause."

"Nonsense. It's my great pleasure. I say, another visit to Salem will be a welcome change. Weather's dreary here."

Another visit to Salem? What have I been missing?

Karl Smith spoke up. "Chef Karl here. It all sounds good, except maybe the salted caramel biscuits. Perhaps an assortment of their sweet biscuits to complement the citrus tea?"

"Done," said Nigel. "Mrs. Abney-Babcock, any suggestions?"

"The menu sounds delightful," Louisa said, "but if it isn't too much trouble, could you pick up a teensy tin of their rum and raisin fudge for me?"

"No problem at all, dear lady. Happy to oblige. Are you there too, Maralee? Or do you prefer Lee?"

"Either one is fine, sir," I said. "I'm here."

"Do you happen to be acquainted with Chief Tom Whaley of the Salem Police Department?"

"Yes. I know him." This was a surprise. "Why do you ask?"

"Your name was mentioned. I'm doing a bit of international inquiry for him. Plan to see him while I'm in the city."

Big surprise. Why had Chief Whaley, who decidedly isn't one of my fans, mentioned my name in connection with an international inquiry to New Scotland Yard? And how did he know Nigel? Pete had to be the connection there. I'd be sure to ask him about it tonight.

My aunt and Nigel discussed plane schedules and pickup times at Logan Airport; Chef Karl asked a few more culinary questions; Louisa enthused about shopping at Harrods and asked Nigel if he'd seen Will and Kate's newest baby. Turns out, he'd been to the christening! I was impressed. After the phone call ended, it was my turn to propose the various ideas I'd come up with for publicizing the event. The three agreed with everything I mentioned. I asked for permission to photograph the place setting, clicked off a couple of shots with my phone, and assured Louisa that I'd already arranged for security.

I excused myself and called, "Come on, big boy. Let's go upstairs" to O'Ryan, who hadn't stopped staring at Karl. I could see that the man was uncomfortably aware of the attention. I didn't blame him. The cat obediently jumped down from the chair and trotted behind me without a backward glance.

I had a lot to tell Pete when he arrived at eight o'clock. We'd planned to catch a movie and a couple of burgers, but decided to settle for Netflix, Hamburger Helper and conversation at my place. So much had happened that day that I hardly knew where to begin. I was dying to know how my name had turned up at New Scotland Yard, but maybe the things I'd learned on my visit to the station were priority. The Helper du jour was simmering and we hadn't turned on the TV. Pete sliced rye bread while I chopped tomatoes and celery for salad. O'Ryan apparently didn't find the menu interesting and left via the kitchen cat door.

The first thing I told him about was the strange shapes and numbers we'd found on Aunt Ibby's quilt. "We haven't figured out what they mean yet, but we thought you should know about it, since the quilt was in the locker and somebody seems to be awfully interested in something else that was in there."

"Hmmm." He stopped slicing bread for a few seconds. "That is interesting. Let me know if you two come up with anything. What else is new?"

"I went to see Scott Palmer at WICH-TV today," I said, "and he told me a few things you might want to hear about."

"How'd you happen to go see him?" Pete didn't look happy.

"He'd invited me to come down and see the old gang," I said, "so I thought I'd try to find out what secret Eric had told him."

"And?"

"And I did."

The scowl disappeared. "No kidding? What did he say?"

"It doesn't make a lot of sense." I repeated what Scott had said, as closely as I could remember it, from "six, six, six" to the part about *"Cherchez la femme."*

"Make any sense to you?" I asked.

"Not a lot. Never sure about anything that guy says."

I gave him a playful poke in the arm. "Hey, what happened to 'it's not my job to believe him or disbelieve him.'"

He put down the bread knife and pulled me close.

"You're right. I guess where Palmer's concerned, maybe I'm not completely objective."

"And why is that?"

His jawline tightened. "I can't be objective about anything that concerns you. Especially good-looking ex-boyfriends."

I put down my tomato-chopping knife and took his face in both hands. "Listen to me. You have nothing to worry about in that department. *Nothing*. And, anyway, he's not half as good-looking as you are." I gave him a long, wholehearted, wickedly suggestive kiss, which I was sure convinced him of my devotion. It also delayed dinner for a while.

I had so many things to tell Pete that we never did get around to watching a movie. Pete stayed busy scribbling in his own notebook as I tried to remember everything that had happened since I'd talked with him last.

"When you talked to Scott, did he tell you that Eric went out that night to take pictures?" I asked.

"Yes, he did. But the memory card is still missing, along with the laptop."

"I suppose his whole book manuscript is in that laptop. Whoever took it probably wouldn't know his password though. So they'll still be looking for—whatever it is they're looking for. Hey, did you know about the necklace of bear's teeth that Boris used to wear when he was wrestling?" I asked.

"Real bear's teeth? No, I didn't. Did Palmer tell you that?"

"Um-hum. He said he remembered it from an old

publicity poster they had in the sports department at the Illinois station. Are you thinking what I'm thinking?"

He nodded and kept writing. "The garrote with the pointed triangles."

"Can't be a coincidence."

"Nope. Maybe Palmer will be helpful, after all."

"Could be," I said. "Now I have a question for you. We had a meeting downstairs tonight about the charity tea party. Aunt Ibby's New Scotland Yard friend, Nigel, was on the phone with us and said that Chief Whaley called him and mentioned my name. I guess you have something to do with that."

"Nigel St. John," he repeated, pronouncing it as "Saint John."

"Sin Jin," I corrected. "Nigel pronounces it as Sin Jin."

He raised an eyebrow and went on. "Chief wants some background information on our friend Boris. I told him a long time ago that you and your aunt had a friend in New Scotland Yard. He figured they probably have better access to foreign records than we do." He smiled. "I gave him the name, even though I pronounced it wrong."

"Did he find anything?"

"Not sure. But he thanked me for the tip. Anything else to tell me?"

I closed my eyes, running over the conversation with Scott in my mind. "Eric said he was going to take comparison pictures."

"Compared to what?"

I shrugged. "Don't know. Oh, and one more thing. About the meeting tonight—Chef Karl Smith was there."

"Boris's pal?"

"Yes. He's going to prepare the Russian goodies for the tea."

Pete didn't look happy. "I'm not crazy about him being in this house. There's something I wasn't going to mention, but since you and your aunt have involved yourselves . . ."

"What is it?"

"When we brought Medvedev in for questioning, he gave the same address as Karl Smith's."

"They live together?"

"Apparently. Of course they'd already admitted they were friends, so maybe it doesn't mean anything. I just don't like it."

"I know, but Aunt Ibby is stubborn. She seems to think Karl is okay. He brought samples."

"She's probably right. I worry about you two. Just be careful," he said, then paused. "What kind of samples?"

"I have a plateful in the refrigerator. Coffee?"

Smiling, he headed for the bedroom while I started the Mr. Coffee. I heard the secret cubby panel where Pete secures his gun open and close. "Guess I'll stay over, just to be sure you're safe," he said as he came back to the kitchen. "Did he bring any of those powdered-sugar things?"

CHAPTER 30

It seemed to be my week for renewing acquaintances. Not long after Pete left for work, my boss at the Tabby, Rupert Pennington, called and asked me to stop by the school for an "informal tour of the new sound studio." I looked forward to seeing the changes that had been made over the summer. School would start in a couple of weeks and we'd been anticipating the new addition for months. I asked if I could bring Aunt Ibby along and the suggestion was welcomed with undisguised enthusiasm. Mr. Pennington and my aunt have an on-again, off-again relationship, and I was pretty sure they'd both be happy to see one another. I was glad to have an opportunity to check out my classroom area, to make sure everything was shipshape for the start of the new school year.

It was another cool but glorious almost-autumn day, so Aunt Ibby and I decided to walk to the school. Salem is a good city for walking when the weather is fine. Pleasant, tree-shaded pedestrian malls provided contrast to narrow, cobblestoned streets and wide, modern highways.

"Look, Maralee." My aunt pointed to a group of people gathered across the street from the Tabby. "They're all taking pictures of the statue of Samantha." She indicated the life-sized statue of Samantha Stephens of *Bewitched* fame, which occupies a prominent spot in the center of the city. "It's nice that she's still so popular after all these years."

I agreed. "Samantha made witches cool. No wonder Salem loves her." It was, however, an unusually large crowd of photographers for so late in the tourist season. I took a closer look. "Uh-oh," I said, tugging on my aunt's arm. "It's not all about Samantha. Look at who's posing right in front of her."

"It's that man. The bear man," she said. "What on God's green earth is he doing there?"

"Let's go," I said, pulling her toward the glass doors of the school. "I'd rather look at Boris Medvedev from inside the building. The paper said he's enjoying the publicity he's had lately. He's trying to remind people of what a big deal he was in the wrestling world years ago."

"A brand-new fifteen minutes of fame for him, I suppose," she said as the door of the school closed behind us. "Look, there's Rupert." She hurried across the gleaming expanse of hardwood floor to the base of the broad, curving staircase, where Mr. Pennington stood, arms extended.

"Ibby, my dear! How wonderful to see you on this lovely day." He nodded in my direction. "Ms. Barrett, thank you for coming, and for bringing your delightful aunt."

The two exchanged a fast hug with over-the-shoulder air kisses, and then the three of us proceeded to the newly refurbished entrance to the downstairs studio. The once-unadorned entry to the old store's basement now featured white-painted Doric columns flanking double glass doors. The overhead sign read: THE JONATHAN WILSON STUDIO. It had been named for the late city councilor.

"After you, dear ladies," Mr. Pennington stood to one side and my aunt stepped onto a broad carpeted landing. "I'm sure you'll find the area much changed from the last time you saw it. Behold!" He gestured dramatically with both arms to the room below. Mr. Pennington was once a Shakespearean actor and hasn't forgotten it, or allowed anyone else to forget it either. I hesitated before following my aunt. My memory of that basement was the stuff of nightmares. I peered over her shoulder and realized immediately that the entire place had been completely transformed, without the slightest hint of the dark and terrifying place it had once been. So it was with a sense of grateful relief that I grasped the smooth wooden railing and walked down the stairway.

The tour of the new facility took nearly an hour. Mr. Pennington described in detail each piece of state-of-the-art sound and lighting equipment. It was impressive and he was justifiably proud of all of it. "And you, Ms. Barrett, with your class project on Salem history last year, can take a great deal of credit for this amazing transformation," he said as we returned to the school lobby. "Without the generous government grant your class earned, none of this would have been possible."

I mumbled something modest, but I really was proud of my part in this much-needed addition to the school. "I hope this year's class will be able to do something just as helpful," I told him.

My aunt and I expressed our thanks for the tour and our admiration for the project as a whole. I excused myself for a few minutes so that I could run up to the mezzanine floor and take a look at my classroom area, where the old store's shoe department had once been. Some of the old décor had been retained. A vintage cutout sign featuring Buster Brown and his dog, Tige, shared space with a row of textbooks. A green screen, along with an enormous new TV monitor, dwarfed a neon wall piece advertising Poll-Parrot shoes, and the original Thonet bentwood chairs merged nicely with starkly modern student workstations.

"I'm really looking forward to opening day," I told Mr. Pennington when I returned to the main floor. "Everything looks fine. The students are going to be excited to be here, I'm sure." I moved to one side and looked out the big show window, giving the director and my aunt a bit of privacy for their good-byes. The crowd we'd noticed earlier had diminished, and I was relieved to see that the bearded man was no longer posing in front of beautiful bronzed Elizabeth Montgomery.

That sense of relief didn't last long. Boris Medvedev, still smiling, now stood on the curb just outside of the Tabitha Trumbull Academy of the Arts. Seeing him at such close range allowed me to realize how very tall, how very powerfully built, the man was, and this time the smile was directed at me. My first instinct was to turn away, to close my eyes, to hide, figuratively, under the covers from the bogeyman. But I didn't. I returned the stare, but not the smile.

As I watched, he slowly lifted a huge right hand to his throat, resting beefy fingers on a gold-chain necklace. He pulled it away from his black shirt collar and, still smiling, revealed the neatly spaced row of yellowed, pointed teeth.

I took an involuntary step back. "Aunt Ibby!" The words came out in a harsh whisper. "It's him."

"What? Who? Are you all right?" She grasped my hand.

"Ms. Barrett, you've gone quite pale," Mr. Pennington said. "I'll fetch a bottle of water." He hurried away in the direction of the cafeteria.

I clung tightly to my aunt's hand, too tightly for her comfort probably, and pointed to the window. "He's looking right at me."

She looked where I pointed, then back at me. Her voice was gentle. "Who's looking at you, dear heart? Who do you see?"

I blinked, then shielded my eyes with my free hand. There was no tall, frightening, smiling man on the Tabby's sidewalk—just the normal, late-afternoon parade of mothers pushing strollers, laughing teenagers enjoying the last days of summer vacation, dog walkers—not a bogeyman in sight.

"I saw . . . I thought I saw Boris Medvedev. He was right there. Standing on the curb." I turned away from the window. "He showed me the necklace—the necklace with real bear's teeth on it. And he smiled." I hadn't yet let go of her hand. "It was a terrible smile."

Mr. Pennington rushed across the main floor with the promised bottle of water. "Here you are. Perhaps you should sit down. Ibby says you walked here. Shall I call a cab for you?"

"No need for that," I said, my heart still pounding and my voice still not sounding quite right.

"Yes, Rupert. Please do call a cab for us." My aunt's tone didn't invite argument.

Aunt Ibby and I waited in one of several informal furniture groupings situated at the edges of the main floor. Comfortable leather chairs surrounded a low table. The attractive spaces, designed for small groups of students, were another new addition to the Tabby. I sipped cold water gratefully and felt my body returning to its normal rhythms.

"Feeling better?" she asked.

"Much. Sorry for all the drama, but he really frightened me." I looked toward the front window again. "I don't see how he disappeared so fast though. You didn't see him?"

She shook her head. "Maralee, I looked as soon as you spoke. There was no one there. Have you considered the possibility that this was one of your . . . visions?"

I hadn't. There had been no twinkling lights. No swirling colors. No warning. I didn't answer her question. Couldn't. The vision—if that's what it was—had been so clearly defined, so solid, that it was difficult for me to believe that it wasn't real.

The taxi pulled up in front of the building. Mr. Pennington accompanied us to the waiting vehicle, handing

me into the backseat as though I was made of glass.
Then he ran around to the other side to hold the door
for Aunt Ibby. "Be well, Ms. Barrett," he said. "Ibby, I'll
telephone you tomorrow to firm up our arrangement
for Friday evening."

"I'll look forward to it, Rupert," she said, and we sped
away toward Winter Street. It was a quiet ride. I didn't
want to discuss the possible vision in front of the driver,
and at that point I didn't know what to think or say
about it anyway. I was relieved and happy when my aunt
and I together climbed the front steps to the safety and
comfort of home. O'Ryan, as usual, waited just inside
the front door to deliver his enthusiastic welcome.

"Coffee?" she said as soon as we'd hung up our
jackets.

"Of course." I followed her to the kitchen.

She began the soothing, familiar coffee making
ritual. Cold water. Paper filter. Three measures of freshly
ground beans. "Want to tell me about it?" She pushed a
button and the heartening scent began to fill the room.
Tight muscles relaxed as my aunt bustled about her
kitchen, selecting my favorite mug, selecting a big round
cookie from the old cookie jar. *There's no place like home*,
I thought. *There's no place like home.*

"Yes, I do." I closed my eyes, concentrating on the
memory, and haltingly told her how the man had suddenly appeared on the curb in front of the window
where I stood looking out. "I hadn't realized how big
he is—how threatening he is—until I saw him close up
like that."

"You said something about bear's teeth."

I told her about the wrestler's necklace of teeth,

and how Pete and I agreed that it was too similar to the garrote with its pointed triangles to be a coincidence. "He pulled that necklace out of his shirt. Pointed at it. He wanted me to see it."

"Do you still think that what you saw was real, not a vision, a reflection in the glass?"

"I don't know," I admitted. "It seemed so real. But if it was him, how did he disappear like that? He was there one second and gone the next. If it was a vision, why didn't I get any warning? The lights. The swirling colors."

She poured our coffees. "It seems to me, Maralee, that this 'gift' of yours is evolving as time passes. At first you only saw things in shiny black surfaces, remember?"

I nodded. "Yes. Then it was mirrors. Then silver."

"The one you saw at the McKennas'. The terrible bear. That was in the glass front of a cabinet. Plain glass. Like the window of the school."

She was right. I didn't know whether to be relieved or more frightened. If it was a vision, then Boris Medvedev had not actually sought me out, had not shown me the garrotelike necklace. But if I'd really seen him there on the Tabby's sidewalk, if he'd really been there, smiling his evil smile, deliberately trying to frighten me, what would his next move be? If the image of the old wrestler was a product of my scrying ability, and not an actual threat, I needed to figure out what the vision was trying to tell me. I felt much better after my talk with my aunt, and as O'Ryan and I made our way up the front stairs to my apartment, I thought about who would be the best person to help me decipher it. I dialed River's number the minute I stepped into my own kitchen.

"Sure, I can come over. Another vision, huh? I'll read the cards while you tell me about it, then maybe we can figure out what it means." I could tell that River was excited by the prospect of understanding the significance of what I'd seen, no matter how scary it was.

It didn't take long for her to arrive. I'd become so accustomed lately to River wearing her glitzy *Tarot Time* regalia that seeing her at my living-room door, sans makeup, in sweats and sneakers, with her long, black hair in a ponytail, made me smile. "Wow. You look like a cute twelve-year-old."

"I know. I'm on my way to the gym. When I'm being the real me, like now, sometimes I feel as if I'm in disguise. I know I can walk right past people who watch me on TV and they never connect me with sexpot late-show River."

"Wouldn't sexpot late-show River be the disguise then?"

She put the ever-present deck of tarot cards on the coffee table, along with a paperback copy of *A Dream Dictionary for Dummies,* and sat in the zebra print wing chair. O'Ryan hopped up into her lap. He loves River. "Maybe. Sometimes I even mix the two of me up."

"That must be how Stasia Novikova feels," I said, sitting on the couch. "Part smart, articulate woman, who speaks at least two languages, and part monosyllabic, crazy bubblegum lady with a pigeon on her head."

River cocked her head to one side. "She's a puzzle, all right. I didn't know about the languages."

"Russian," I said.

"Makes sense. Now let me do the cards, and you can tell me about the new vision." She patted the yellow cover of the dream book. "I guess visions are sort of like dreams, so we might find something useful in here."

When I began to talk, the words just bubbled out. It was such a relief to have a nonjudgmental friend, like River, who really listened. The *slap-slap* of the cards on the table, the rumbling purring of the cat, one "coo-coo" marking the half hour provided background for the one-sided conversation. I started by describing the two visions involving the bear. "They were both in plain glass," I told her. "Does that mean anything?" I didn't wait for an answer, rushing on to explain the yellow bear teeth and the garrotes that had killed Eric Dillon and the Connecticut baker. "The baker was one of six men who came here from Russia in 1915. Did I tell you about them before?" Again, I rambled on, not expecting a reply. "Aunt Ibby has a crazy quilt Stasia's grandmother made. It has symbols and shapes we think mean something. But what?"

I jabbered about Karl Smith and Nigel and Mrs. Abney-Babcock's china. I talked about Mrs. McKenna's carved egg, with the numbers on it, about Colleen's tablecloth and about Eric Dillon's notebook. Finally, out of breath and out of words, I exhaled, closed my eyes and leaned back against the couch cushions. "Did you get all that?"

"Hmmm? Oh, sure. Of course." She flipped a card

over. "Reversed Two of Pentacles. You're trying to handle two situations at once."

I opened my eyes. "Only two?"

"Two major ones. You could find some answers in news and messages in writing."

"News, as in WICH-TV? Writing, as in the missing notebook?"

"Maybe." She turned another card. "Look. The Page of Swords. Know any diplomats? Someone in government service?"

"That would be Nigel, I suppose. What about him?"

"He has a message from far away."

"Did I tell you Chief Whaley contacted him? Mentioned my name too."

"You didn't. But that's interesting. Is Nigel a spy or something?"

That made me laugh. "Not that I know of."

Another card turned faceup. O'Ryan sat up on River's lap, leaned forward and sniffed at the colorful picture of a woman with a tame bird on her hand. "The Nine of Pentacles," River said. "O'Ryan seems interested."

"If the bird is a pigeon, that's probably Stasia," I said. "What does it mean?"

"It's reversed. It can mean danger from thieves or a canceled project. Not a good card, Lee. Be careful. Sometimes it means an unfaithful friend."

The cards made a now-familiar pattern as River put them, one by one, on the tabletop. She mentioned several things that had appeared in earlier readings: intuition, imagination, secrets, latent psychic powers, risk taking.

"Pete's card hasn't shown up yet. I'm kind of used

to his card being close to mine," I said. I was halfway kidding, but the Knight of Swords almost always turned up when River read me. So did Moon Mother, which we took to mean Aunt Ibby. They were both my protectors. I watched for them all the way to the end of the reading. This time neither one made an appearance.

"No protectors this time?" I asked. "So am I facing the damned bear all alone?"

"Maybe the bear isn't as bad as he looks," she said, reaching for the dream book. "If he's a dream bear, there may be an explanation for why he's appearing to you."

"Twice," I said.

"Twice," she repeated, opening the book to the *B*'s. "Here we go. Let's see if this makes any sense. 'Bears are symbols of the cycle of life. You may be particularly introspective at this time.'" She looked up. "Ring any bells?"

I shook my head.

"Okay. How about this one? 'To dream you are being chased or attacked by a bear can mean you are in a threatening situation, facing some overwhelming obstacle.'"

"Great. I don't think I like that one."

"Me either. The last one says the bear might be a mother figure, trying to encourage you to explore the world."

"This bear is definitely not a fuzzy pink Care Bear. I'm afraid the threatening-situation bear might be the closest thing to the vision."

"Sorry," she said.

"Me too. Well, it is what it is. Thanks for coming and thanks for listening."

She stood, gently dislodging the cat, and gave me a hug. "I'm not always right, you know. And I'm sure the dream book for dummies isn't either. You'll be fine. When I leave here, I'll do a spell for protection of this house and all who dwell within. You burn red candles and ask your aunt and Pete to do the same. Okay?"

I promised to do as she asked and opened the door for her. She turned and gestured toward the bay window. "You're still planning to put the horse and plants over there, aren't you?"

"Yes. And I think I'll have my horse back tomorrow. I can hardly wait to see what he looks like with his new paint job."

"It'll be perfect feng shui. I'll help you pick the right plants. Let me know when you're ready to do the arrangement."

"I'll walk downstairs with you. I want to check in with Aunt Ibby. Maybe she's figured out what the weird-shaped pieces in the quilt mean."

"If it's a crazy quilt, aren't they all weird shapes?"

"Some of these are crazier than others. Thanks again for coming over and listening to me. And for the reading."

"My pleasure," she said. "Even if it wasn't what you wanted to hear."

I waved good-bye as she walked down the path to her car. As I watched, she turned, facing the house, raised her arms and bowed her head. The promised spell, I guessed. Relocking the back entrance, I knocked on

Aunt Ibby's kitchen door. "It's me," I called. "Got a minute?"

The door popped open immediately. "Come in. It's so exciting! I've discovered the secret of the old quilt."

That made me smile. "Sounds like the title of a Nancy Drew mystery."

CHAPTER 31

The quilt had been moved from Aunt Ibby's bedroom and was now spread across the dining-room table. "I could hardly wait to show you," she said. "I know what the odd-shaped quilt pieces are. They're states! Look. Here's Connecticut. Here's Massachusetts. There's Colorado." She hurried around to the other side of the table. "California over here. And Kentucky." Her smile was triumphant. "Five different states."

"There should be six," I said. "Shouldn't there? For the six friends?"

"Ha! That's what I thought at first. But don't forget the valet and the butler were both in California!"

I took a closer look at the California patch. "That's so obviously California," I said. "How did we miss it in the first place?"

"I know. Kentucky, with all those wavy edges, is pretty obvious too." She pointed at it. "And look at Cape Cod sticking out of Massachusetts! We should have noticed that one right away. Like anything else, once you figure out what you're looking for, it's easy."

"Hidden in plain sight," I said. "Very clever, isn't it? The mixed-up fabrics, and all the patterns and colors and shapes, remind me of *Where's Waldo?*"

"Exactly. And you see how random patches here and there have bits of embroidery on them? Little outlines of the images on the fabric? Flowers and animals and stars and such?"

"Sure. That's one of the things that makes the whole thing so beautiful."

"The embroidered motifs on the state-shaped pieces are different from the others. Look again."

It took me a moment to locate Connecticut because it's so symmetrical. But once I found it, I saw what she meant. There was the number 3 I'd noticed before. It was twined around something that looked like a spoon. There was also a tiny, three-tiered cake, perfect down to the cherry on top. "The baker," I said. "The poor, murdered baker."

Kentucky had number 4 and a horseshoe. The horse trainer, of course. California had numbers 1 and 2. It took a moment to figure out the meaning of the needlework motifs—two pairs of white gloves. "Get it?" Aunt Ibby asked. "The white gloves? They stand for the valet and the butler. I'm quite sure that back in 1915 servants wore white gloves. And look. There's a little teakettle on a tray, just in case we didn't get the glove clue."

"Embroidery for Dummies," I muttered.

"What?"

"Nothing. It just reminded me of a book I saw today.

Now, what's that black blob on Massachusetts, with the five on it?"

She handed me the Sherlock Holmes magnifying glass. "I've been trying to figure that out. Take a peek through this. See what you think it is."

The thing lost its blobby look when it came into sharp focus. "It's a doctor's bag," I said. "Number five is the doctor."

"So number six must be in Colorado, where the Novikovas lived before they came to Salem."

The Colorado patch was a nice, neat oblong. Nothing to distinguish it from other oblong patches, except for the extra embroidery. The picture Lydia had chosen for Colorado was a saddle with a rose and number 6 on it. "There it is. My horse has a saddle and a carved rose. All six of the friends accounted for. But what does it mean, besides telling us where they all settled? We already knew that. If the six numbers are connected to treasure, where is it? What is it? We know there was nothing in the horse."

"We need to look closer. What else is on the state patches that isn't on the others?" Aunt Ibby asked, picking up the magnifying glass and walking around the edges of the table. She peered at Kentucky. "It's such intricate, beautiful needlework. Here's a little flower, and a tiny bug. The other things are just lovely delicate shapes, like this little rainbow-colored oval."

I looked up from the Massachusetts patch. "Hey, there's one of those rainbow ovals here too. See it, just under that green frog?"

A quick check of the other four numbers revealed that identical, colorful ovals decorated each one. "What if they're not just ovals," my aunt said, looking up from Connecticut with the magnifying glass still in front of her eye. "What if they're eggs?"

We spoke the magic word in unison.

"Fabergé."

A quick glance passed between us and together we dashed for Aunt Ibby's office and that amazing font of knowledge—the Internet.

"The missing Fabergé eggs!" My aunt's fingers flew across the keyboard. "How many of them are there anyway?"

"Not many." I remembered reading the occasional newspaper article about the fabulous jeweled eggs Peter Carl Fabergé and his company had created for the Russian czars.

She answered her own question. "There were around fifty of what they call 'the Imperial eggs' to start with," she said. "There are apparently seven still missing."

"We might know what became of six of them," I said. "Czar Nicholas II could have sent them to America with six trusted servants."

"Eric Dillon must have figured it out. He must have known what's become of those eggs. That's what the new treasure book was going to be about."

"Scott said there were numbers and doodles in the notebook. I'll bet some of those numbers would match up with the designs on the quilt."

"That wouldn't surprise me," she said. "But I'll just bet Dillon was as cryptic in his notebook as Lydia was with the designs on the quilt. Scott couldn't figure out what it was all about, could he?"

"He *says* not. And, anyway, he says Boris stole the book from him before he had a chance to really look through it."

"You sound hesitant. Don't you believe him?"

"With Scott, that's hard to say."

"You know, I've been thinking about Grandpa Nick," she said. "And about the people who knew him. Tomorrow I'm going to talk with one of his old friends. Someone he trusted—and now that I think about it—if we're right about this—someone who might possibly know about the eggs."

"You are? Who is that?"

"Father Richard, the old priest from St. Vladimir's. I called the church and found out he's in a nursing home in Danvers—well and happy and would be glad to see me. I'm going tomorrow afternoon. I think I'll bring him a gift of one of the carved chess sets we found in the toy box. Want to come with me?"

"I'd love to, but tomorrow afternoon Pete and I are going to pick up my horse from Paul. It's the only time we can borrow the truck, and, well, I just can't wait to see the finished product. I'll tell Pete about our Fabergé egg theory too, but I'm thinking he probably won't buy it."

"He should. It's a pretty good theory. Well researched."

"Maybe." I was doubtful. "Think about it. It starts with me seeing a vision in a mirror. Then you and I make up a story about a long-dead czar trusting a half-dozen household servants with some kind of treasure. A neighbor shows us a carved Easter egg. We see some embroidered ovals on an old quilt and decide we've discovered a lost fortune that experts have spent a century looking for. I'm not even sure *I* buy it."

"I do." Confident smile. "You'll see."

I didn't see my aunt the next morning. She left a message on my phone saying she'd be at the library firming up plans for the tea and that she'd leave from there to visit Father Richard. There was no mention of eggs, fried, fictional or Fabergé.

I lit a red candle, per River's instructions, and browsed through the Dumas book in an attempt to see if the adventures of the detective Monsieur Jackal related in any way to our mixed-up mystery, or at least to see why Eric Dillon had used the phrase *"Cherchez la femme."* It wasn't much help. In the book Jackal tries to solve a cold case involving three people: an artist, a writer and a doctor. The detective decides to "look for the woman." Okay, so we had an artist, Nikita Novikova, a writer, Eric Dillon, and a doctor, Yakovlev—who disappeared from Boston. A big, crazy coincidence. Or not? Was the murdered writer looking for a woman? Who?

I tossed the book aside and removed the index cards from the bureau. I reshuffled and separated cards relating to women from the others. Which women knew the artist? Stasia, Lydia, Colleen and her mother. Which knew the doctor? Lydia certainly did. And who knew Eric Dillon? That eliminated Lydia. He'd probably talked to Stasia. She was easy enough to find on the Salem Common. He could have spoken to Mrs. McKenna or Colleen when he'd posed for a photo in front of their house. Clearly, I needed to conduct some more interviews.

Cuckoo said it was noon. I didn't expect Pete until two o'clock, so I had plenty of time for a trip to the Common. I blew out the candle, hoping it had burned long enough to do its cleansing magic, pulled on a warm jacket, put a few ten-dollar bills in my jeans pocket, then stepped outside. Walking along Winter Street, I could see across Washington Square. Stasia was sitting in her usual spot, but she wasn't alone. I recognized the man right away. It was Karl Smith.

I hesitated. The two appeared to be in deep conversation, the neat blond head and the wild-haired orange one close together. Should I interrupt? Why not? It was a public park in the middle of the city in the middle of the day. I quickened my step and crossed the street onto the path leading to what I'd come to think of as "Stasia's bench."

The pigeons scattered in a flutter of wings as I approached and the two looked up. Chef Karl spoke first. "Ms. Barrett, good afternoon. Do you know my friend Stasia?"

"Hello, Mr. Smith. How are you, Stasia?" The woman didn't answer, but moved over to make room for me beside her. I took the proffered seat between the two. Awkward.

"Stasia sometimes acts as translator for me," Karl said, hastily tucking a sheaf of papers into his jacket pocket. "My Russian recipes are authentic and being unable to read the language is inconvenient." He stood. "I won't take any more of your valuable time, Stasia. I'll see you later. Good-bye, Ms. Barrett. Do give my regards to your aunt."

He left us, walking with such quick steps that he was out of sight within less than a minute. "You want another reading so soon?" She reached for my hand.

"Not today." I pulled a ten from my jeans. "I wonder if I could ask you a couple of questions. About your grandparents."

She waved the bill away. "Are you interested in my family because of your horse?"

"In a way," I said, "Did the writer, Mr. Dillon, talk to you about your family?"

She looked away. "The man who died? Yes. I didn't tell him much though. He was looking for . . . something."

"Do you know what it was? What he was looking for?"

An annoyed shaking of her head. "I told you before. I don't know. They never told me. But he knew what it was. He just didn't know where it was." She laughed. "He wrote down everything I said in his little brown book. He said he was a treasure hunter."

"He wrote books about people who found treasures," I said. "I guess the stories were treasures to him. Did he tell you any of his stories?"

"Oh, yes. He was a good storyteller. There was one about a man in Florida who found a whole lot of gold in a ship that was underwater, and another one about a man right here in Massachusetts who bought an old house and found out someone had used paintings by a famous folk artist to make the walls. He knew about that horse you bought, did you know that?"

"Yes." I nodded. "We figured that out."

"He told me a joke about it."

"He did? A joke?"

"Yep. He laughed out loud. Sitting right there, where you're sitting. Laughed so hard he scared my pigeons."

"What was the joke?"

"He said he'd come all the way across the country to bet on the wrong horse."

CHAPTER 32

As I walked along the path leading to Washington Square, I stepped on a piece of paper. I've been conscientious about picking up litter since I was little, thanks to my aunt's rules on the matter, so I automatically picked it up. It looked to me like a lined page torn from a pad or a notebook. The lettering on it was foreign, and I realized right away that it must be one of Karl Smith's Russian recipes. I turned back toward Stasia's bench, but she was already looking into the palm of a new customer. *I'll ask Aunt Ibby to return it to him,* I thought, folding the paper carefully and putting it into my pocket. I continued on my way to Winter Street, still thinking about Eric Dillon's "joke," and didn't even notice Donnie's truck until Pete beeped the horn. He rolled down his window. "Ready to go pick up Old Paint?"

"I'll meet you out front in a couple of minutes," I said. "Have to run upstairs and get my checkbook."

He gave a thumbs-up and pulled ahead of me. By the time I'd reached the house, he'd already parked at the curb, climbed out of the truck and was sitting on the top step. "I'll come up with you," he said. "Look. O'Ryan's expecting us." The cat's pink nose was pressed against the side windowpane.

I unlocked the front door. "Did I tell you O'Ryan tossed a little sewing machine on the rug?" We climbed the two flights to my apartment and stepped into the kitchen.

"No. Why? Is a cat playing with a sewing machine supposed to mean something?"

I realized as soon as I mentioned the sewing machine how nutty our patchwork quilt and Fabergé egg theory would sound to Pete—and even worse, how it would sound to Chief Whaley.

"No. Of course not. Just another silly cat trick." I tried for a fast change of subject. "Wait here a sec while I grab my checkbook and let's go get my fine steed."

He raised one eyebrow in the way he does when I'm not making much sense, but he didn't comment. I ducked into the bedroom, changed my jacket and picked up the checkbook. Within a few minutes we were on our way to Paul Carbone's shop. Even though I wasn't ready to talk eggs and embroidery with Pete, I thought he might want to know what Stasia had said about her conversation with Eric Dillon.

"The wrong horse, huh?" Pete frowned. "She didn't tell us that when we talked to her."

"I guess she just thought of it because of the way I asked the question," I said. "I've been practicing interviewing techniques."

"For your online criminology course?"

"No. For the course I'll be teaching at the Tabby in a

couple of weeks. I have to stay a little bit ahead of my students."

"I don't know if it's about interviewing techniques—though I'm sure yours is great." He reached over and squeezed my hand. "Getting a straight answer from Stasia is a hit-or-miss proposition. For that matter your friend Palmer is the same way."

I nodded. "I know what you mean. It's not as though they're deliberately lying. It's more as if they're leaving a few little things out. Scott's always been like that." I thought about it for a minute. "But didn't he say that Eric told him he was going to take a 'comparison shot'? That kind of fits in with the 'wrong horse' joke, doesn't it?"

"Sure does. Sounds like we're dealing with more than one horse here, doesn't it?"

"A whole herd of them?"

He rolled his eyes. "Let's hope not. It's one horse at a time for right now, and that's Old Paint."

The rest of the ride to Paul's shop was quiet. That's one of the things I love about being with Pete. We can lapse into periods of silence without one of us saying, "What's wrong?"

We parked the truck close to the doorway, where a smiling Paul greeted us. "I could hardly wait for you two to get here. You're going to be surprised, happily, I think."

He was right. I was. My horse stood in the middle of the shop floor, straining at the halter, mane wind-whipped, right hoof raised. He looked beautiful, and very different from what I'd expected. No longer a pale palomino, he was a rich honey color. The once-brown streaked mane was pure white, made richer with bright gold-leaf highlights. The chipped pink rose was whole again, a brilliant scarlet, and the saddle and halter of polished black dazzled with multicolored jewels.

"What? How . . . ?" The transformation was amazing. "He looks like a different horse altogether."

"I know he does." There was pride in Paul's voice. "When I began to sand him down, I found layer after layer of paint. So I took it down to the original colors— the colors the craftsman who created him chose in the first place. This, I believe, is how he looked when he graced some late 1800s carousel."

"Late 1800s?" The date confused me. "No. It can't be that old. Nikita Novikova carved it, and he didn't arrive in America until 1915. Didn't work in the amusement park until around the 1920s."

Paul smiled an indulgent smile. "My dear, I know wood and I know paint. I've chipped away about thirty layers of old park paint. This charming animal is well over a century old. More like a hundred and fifty."

If Paul was right, and I was pretty darned sure he was, then Grandpa Nick didn't carve this horse, after all. I said so out loud.

"Maybe he didn't," Paul said gently. "But it's a treasure anyway. Are you disappointed?"

"No. How could I be? He's beyond beautiful. Thank you so much, Paul. May we take him home now?"

I wrote a check, protesting that the amount he asked was too low for the work he'd done, and Pete and I loaded Old Paint into the back of the truck, securing him with bungee cords from every possible direction. I'd given up on finding a new name, especially since we'd learned how extremely old his paint had actually been. I thought about that.

"It doesn't make sense, does it?"

He knew what I was talking about. "It doesn't. But Paul knows his business. If he says the horse is over a hundred years old, I have to believe him."

"Grandpa Nick called the horse a 'secret keeper.'"

Pete just nodded and grew quiet again. On the way home I checked the rearview mirror about every ten seconds, just to be sure Old Paint was still there. We stopped at the Northeast Nursery, where I selected plants and a variety of colorful pots for his bay window setting. I hoped my choice of greenery would meet with River's approval.

Pete and I maneuvered the horse up the two flights of stairs, through the kitchen and down the hall to the designated spot in the window. Aunt Ibby had returned from her visit with Father Richard and she joined us for uncounted repeat trips, up and back, carrying pots and plants. Finally we all stood back to admire the result. It was everything I'd expected and more.

"Magnificent," breathed my aunt. "Paul certainly works restoration magic, doesn't he? You say the horse is twice as old as we thought?"

"That's right. Doesn't quite add up, does it?"

"No, it doesn't at all," she said. "Especially since we've seen a twentieth-century photograph of Mr. Novikova carving this very animal."

That got Pete's attention. Mine too. I'd forgotten about the McKennas' photo gallery. "A picture?" Pete asked. "Where did you see that?"

"It's in the McKennas' house," I said. "Front hall."

"I mentioned the horse to Father Richard today, and he said he remembered seeing it at the Novikovas'," my aunt said. "He and Nick often played chess together, you know. He was very pleased with the chess set I gave him, but says he has no one to play with anymore. Made me sorry I've never learned the game myself. I told him exactly what we knew so far. Didn't think it would do any harm. I thought Father might be able to fill in some of the blanks for us. He told me that Nick mostly talked about the old days at Tsarskoe Selo and about his friends.

"One interesting thing he told me though." She held up one finger. "He said he and Nick used to bet on their chess games—but only pennies. Father said that Nick had often told him he could have been a rich man if he hadn't been so set on keeping promises."

"That is interesting," I said, thinking of how some of his friends had become wealthy. As she spoke, a couple of my index-card thoughts tumbled into place. "Eric Dillon told Scott he wanted a comparison picture," I said, "and Stasia said he'd joked about betting on the wrong horse."

Pete summed it up. "There are two horses."

"Gotta be," I said. "But where is the other one?"

"More important," my aunt said, "what's inside the other one?"

CHAPTER 33

It seemed like a good time for us to share our Fabergé egg theory with Pete, no matter how far-out it might sound. We started at the beginning and told him, in tag team fashion, everything we'd discovered and intuited, while Pete listened, not taking notes. Just listening.

"So you think this czar gave a half-dozen ordinary guys who worked for him these valuable egg things to take to America, and planned to collect them later when he and his family escaped from Russia?"

"Right," I said.

"Not out of character at all," my aunt added. "Nicholas II shipped literal trainloads of gold out of the country too. The revolutionists confiscated some of his treasure, but much of it's never been found—including at least six Fabergé eggs worth millions."

Pete was quiet for a moment. "You two think some of these guys sold their eggs and some of them held on to them."

"We do," I said. "We think Eric Dillon had the same

idea. We think he'd probably already figured out what happened to five of them. He was looking for the sixth egg. Here in Salem. But he was wrong."

"He was trying to sneak a quick picture of Old Paint so he could get out of town to look for the twin before anyone else did. That's when he got killed," Pete said, almost to himself.

From the kitchen came Cuckoo's announcement that it was three thirty. Aunt Ibby stood, brushing a bit of potting soil from her skirt. "Oh, dear. Karl is coming over at four. He has some new cookie samples for me to consider. I'd best be getting downstairs. Your horse is wonderful, dear. Pete, do think about what we've said. I'll go down the back stairs." She pulled open the living-room door. O'Ryan darted out ahead of her. "Why don't you both come down and join us? We value your input, and I know you'll enjoy sampling the goodies."

Pete stood and politely agreed to think about eggs. I couldn't tell whether he was serious or not. "I'm not crazy about that Karl character hanging around here," he said after she'd left. "Let's take her up on that invitation. Kind of keep an eye on things."

"Okay. I forgot to tell her I have one of Karl's recipes. He dropped it on the Common. He might need it."

He smiled. "I wonder if he's bringing over any more of those powdered-sugar things. Want to tell me some more about what you two have been up to while you weren't meddling in police work?"

"Okay. I've wanted to talk to you about it, but some of it sounds kind of nutty. Come on out to the kitchen. I'll show you my collection of index cards."

For the next half hour we sat at the kitchen table as

Pete pored over my cards, asking a question once in a while, and occasionally copying a few words into his own notebook. He stacked them together in one pile, and pushed them toward me. "Did I ever tell you—"

"That I'd make a good cop?" I smiled. "Yes, you have, and I still don't want the job, thank you," I said. "But tell me, what do *you* think? About the six friends? About the eggs?"

"Well, it's better than anything I've come up with. I'll run it by the chief as soon as I can figure out how to do it without mentioning the embroidered quilt, the palm-reading bubblegum lady, the bear in the store window and the pointy-teethed witch."

"I'm glad I told you," I said. "I don't like keeping anything from you."

"I don't like keeping things from you either," he said, "but sometimes I have to." He stood and came around to my side of the table.

"I understand." I stood facing him.

"But you don't like it."

"Not one darned bit."

He pulled me close and kissed the top of my head. "Deal with it. Let's go downstairs and get some of those cookies."

Cuckoo announced four o'clock. Pete watched the clock bird as she popped back and forth on her little wooden perch. "Do you know how often I've been tempted to shoot that thing?"

"I forgot to tell you. I've promised to give her to Stasia."

"Best news I've heard all day."

"I'll go get that recipe for Karl." I went to the bedroom

and removed the folded sheet from my jacket pocket. "Karl doesn't read Russian, so he has Stasia translate the recipes into English for him." I opened the paper and smoothed it out.

"Where did you say you got this?" He moved closer, squinting at it.

"At the Common. Karl had a bunch of them for Stasia to translate. He must have dropped this one when he left. I picked it up off the ground."

"Hmmm. Maybe I can arrest the chef for littering. Can't seem to pin anything else on him . . . or his big, bearded friend." He reached for the paper. "Mind if I look at this?"

I handed it to him. He turned it over. "Wait a minute. This is supposed to be a Russian recipe?"

"Right. Stasia translates the Russian into English for him."

"So the original recipe, or whatever it is, would be centered on the page, and the corrections or translation would be the handwriting between the lines or in the margins."

"Sure." This seemed pretty basic to me, so I wondered why he was confused.

"Did you read this?"

"Nope. Not interested. I can't read Russian and I don't cook."

He put the paper on the table. "What does this look like to you?"

It took about half a second to see what was wrong. The writing in the center definitely was English and the writing in the margins and between the lines definitely was not.

"She's translating English to Russian for him," I said. "How can that be? He doesn't understand Russian."

"So he says." Pete picked the paper up again, holding it carefully by one edge. "And this isn't a recipe."

"What is it?"

"Looks like some names and telephone numbers. I think it's a page from Eric Dillon's missing notebook, with the English names translated into Russian. See? Eva is Eba, and Anna is Ahha. Got a plastic bag?"

"There are some over there in the cabinet." I pointed. "Take your pick. Sandwich, quart, gallon, freezer—I have all kinds. All sizes."

Pete stood with the cabinet door open, debating bag choices. He held up a quart-sized, sealable clear bag. "This looks about right." He slipped the page into it. "Perfect fit."

"Are you going to ask Karl about it tonight?"

He put his finger to his lips. "I think we'll let it stay lost for a little while longer. Let's just keep quiet about this until I do a little checking. As far as the law is concerned, it's just a stray piece of litter you picked up from the Salem Common."

He was right, of course.

"So we just go down to Aunt Ibby's and eat cookies and be polite?"

"Eat cookies, be polite and listen."

"That's pretty much what Barbara Walters says."

He raised one eyebrow, but didn't ask what the hell Barbara Walters had to do with anything. He put the bagged letter on top of the refrigerator. "Where the cat can't get it," he said. "Let's go downstairs."

The meeting was in Aunt Ibby's kitchen this time. Mrs. Abney-Babcock wasn't there and there was no representative of New Scotland Yard on speakerphone, so the atmosphere was a little less formal than the previous planning event had been. My aunt had made coffee and once again a silver platter of beautiful pastries held center stage. O'Ryan was curled up, sound asleep, on the seat of one of the captain's chairs.

"I'm so glad you could join us," my aunt said. "I guess you all know each other."

Karl looked uncomfortable. I couldn't blame him. The last time he'd seen Pete, he'd been getting fingerprinted and having a swab stuck into his mouth. I knew what that was like. It had happened to me the first day I'd met Pete.

But Pete smiled, shook Karl's hand, sipped on his coffee and reached for one of the little powdered-sugar things. And listened.

With the library high tea just days away, it was crunch time and even my usually unflappable aunt appeared a bit unsettled. There were several yellow lined legal pads and a copper mug full of sharp pencils in front of her. She passed a pad and pencil to each of us. "This is a last-minute brainstorming session," she said, "to be sure we've thought of everything we can do to make this fund-raiser a success."

"Shall we just toss ideas around," I asked, "or make notes first and talk later?"

"Ideas," she said. "Let's first see if we agree on the menu." She passed a sheet of copy paper to each of us. "I've noted the pastries we've approved so far. Of course we're trusting Nigel with the Harrods selection. What we need to do with Karl's offerings"—she smiled in the chef's direction—"is narrow the field down to the very best ones."

"Why narrow it down?" Pete asked. "They're all good."

"Thank you, Detective." The chef sounded pleased by the compliment. "But some are better than others. May I select those I feel would make the best impression?"

"Please do," my aunt said. "You are certainly the best judge of that."

Karl picked up his pencil and began to write rapidly on his pad.

"How about security?" She looked at Pete. "I understand that you'll be there?"

"All arranged," he said. "I'll do the inside duty, but if you want an officer to direct the traffic out front, you'll need to call the department. Can you get some volunteers to take care of the parking?"

"I've done so and I believe Mrs. Abney-Babcock's insurance company has arranged for some sort of private security for her china."

"With all that, plus Scotland Yard on duty," I said. "The library will be the safest place in town."

"Agreed," my aunt said. "Now there's one more thing I want to discuss with you all. There is a possibility that a doll that once belonged to the Grand Duchess Anastasia, with a complete wardrobe of handmade dresses, might be available for display." She looked at me. "If we can arrange it, do you think it would attract more of a crowd than just tea and cakes and matryoshkas?"

Karl put down his pencil. "You know where such a doll is?"

O'Ryan sat up, stretched and raced for the front hall.

"Somebody must be coming," I said. "Are we expecting anyone?"

"If I'm right, that might be Anastasia's doll now." My aunt clasped her hands together and stood up, just as the doorbell chimed "The Impossible Dream."

"Pete, would you answer the door?"

Pete followed the cat while Aunt Ibby opened a nearby cabinet. She lifted out a clear plastic box and placed it on the table. Tissue-wrapped parcels were visible inside. She winked in my direction. "After I met with Father Richard, I stopped at the Common and had a talk with Stasia. I think she's here with her doll."

Of course she was right. Pete escorted the woman into the kitchen. If he was surprised to see Stasia there, he didn't show it. O'Ryan resumed his place on the captain's chair and sat up straight, once again turning that golden-eyed stare on Karl Smith. I'd expected the doll to be kept in a box of some kind, but it was wrapped in a pink blanket and Stasia held it against her shoulder as one would carry an infant. She approached the table and reached a tentative hand toward the plastic box. "My dresses?" Her voice was a whisper. Then louder: "They're really the ones my grandmother sewed for her? For Anastasia?"

"I'm sure they are. Come and sit by me, Stasia. Will you tell us about your doll?"

She did as my aunt asked. Sitting down, she removed the pink blanket, revealing the doll's sweet porcelain features, strawberry blond hair and blue glass eyes. It was dressed in a white chemise. Lace-trimmed pantalets peeked from beneath, and tiny white kid boots, slightly yellowed with age, covered porcelain feet. I knew the doll had to be over a century old, but it looked almost new.

My aunt echoed my thought. "She looks like new, Stasia."

"I've taken good care of her. May I see the clothes?"

"Of course. Here they are. All yours." She pushed the box closer.

One by one, Stasia lifted the dresses from the box and held them in front of her doll. "My grandmother told me when she gave me the doll that I could have the clothes too, but she'd forgotten where she'd put them." She pressed a pale yellow long-sleeved dress to her cheek, stroking the soft fabric lovingly. "She was quite crazy by then. She even thought she might have put them into the refrigerator." She laughed and picked up another dress. "She told me they might be with the eggs. Silly me, I really looked there." Another laugh. "Now here they are after all these years. How can I thank you?" She carefully rewrapped each dress in tissue and put it back into the box.

Pete, Aunt Ibby and I looked at one another. Karl Smith's eyes narrowed and he leaned forward. His voice was harsh. "Your grandmother said that? They might be with the eggs? Are you sure?"

Stasia held her doll closer. "What do you care, Karl? It's none of your business. I told you, she was crazy. Who would put these beautiful things in the refrigerator? She only gave me the doll because she thought I was the real Anastasia."

The chef's eyes shifted rapidly from left to right, then focused on the doll. With a much softer tone, he apologized. "I'm sorry, Stasia. It was just such an odd thing for your grandmother to say." A nervous laugh. "The refrigerator indeed!"

"Well, then." My aunt broke an awkward silence. "May we have your permission to display the doll in the library? It would just be for the one evening. A few hours at the most. Before you arrived, we were discussing the extraordinary security that will be in place. As my niece said, the library will be the safest place in town."

Stasia agreed to the arrangement, but declined to comment on my aunt's suggestion that the best and safest place for the doll and her wardrobe would be in a museum setting. I promised to prepare a new press release and some more ads featuring the doll.

"I can probably get a few spots on WICH-TV. I'll need a couple of pictures of her," I said. "My camera is upstairs. Let's go up and dress her in something pretty. Come on, Stasia."

I picked up the box of dresses and Stasia wrapped the doll in the pink blanket. "We'll be right back," I said. "Don't eat all the goodies while we're gone." With O'Ryan following, we climbed the front staircase to the third floor.

I'm convinced that grown-up women don't ever lose their love of playing dolls. At least I was sure I hadn't. We brought the doll—Stasia said her name was Tatiana—into my room and spread the twelve tissue-wrapped parcels on the bed. "I've waited a very long time for this," Stasia said, carefully unwrapping the blue lace dress with the pearl buttons.

"I know. We have a book with a photo of Anastasia wearing a dress exactly like that one."

"My grandmother told me that the dresses were just like the ones she'd made for Anastasia back in the old country. So it's true?"

"We think so. I'm sure my aunt will show you the book. Shall we dress her in the blue dress then?"

"Yes. I think my grandmother would like that. She used to make clothes for me too, you know."

"How nice. I'll bet they were beautiful."

"They were. But of course mine didn't have jewels sewed inside them."

"Jewels?"

"Yes. She told me that long ago the czar had told her to make special underwear for all of his children. Underwear with jewels sewed inside. She said she thought it was for them to wear in case they had to escape someday." Stasia carefully pulled Tatiana's arms through the sleeves of the blue dress.

"I've read about that," I said. "So Lydia sewed those clothes?"

"That's what she said." She secured tiny pearl buttons, then held the doll up for my inspection. "There now. She looks perfect, doesn't she?"

"Perfect," I said. Tatiana looked absolutely museum-worthy and I hoped that Stasia would agree to my aunt's idea of permanently housing her in a secure environment. "Let's go back downstairs and pose her on one of my aunt's antique chairs."

As I spoke, Cuckoo chirped out the half-hour mark and Stasia turned toward the sound. "That's it. It's the same clock, isn't it?"

"Yes. Come on out to the kitchen and see for yourself."

"You said I could have it . . . the clock?" She sounded doubtful.

"Of course you may. You have your hands full right now, with Tatiana and the box of clothes. But I'll take it down from the wall and get it to you tomorrow. How's that?"

"Can I just look at it for a minute? So many memories. It used to be in my grandmother's room. She loved the sound, even when she was old and confused."

There were tears in her eyes. I almost wanted to hug her, to comfort her, but I knew she'd be embarrassed. Stasia stood in front of the clock, smiling a little. "It's nice to see it again," she said, and carrying the doll cradled in one arm and the plastic box under the other, followed me downstairs.

Back in Aunt Ibby's living room, I decided that the Victorian armchair, with soft gold-colored velvet upholstery, would be a good backdrop for Tatiana. I snapped several pictures, pausing while Stasia fussed over the doll's hair and dress and boots between shots, just like a proud mother making her little girl look "just so" for the annual picture with Santa.

It was touching in a sad sort of way. "Want a shot of you holding her?" I asked. She covered her face with one hand. "No. I don't like having my picture taken.

Sometimes on the Common the doggoned tourists walk right up and take my picture, like I'm one of the statues, like Roger Conant or Nathaniel Hawthorne or Samantha Stephens. Without even asking. I stick my tongue out or cross my eyes, just to mess them up." She dropped her hand and crossed her eyes and we both laughed. She patted the doll's hair. "Well, just one picture. But promise you won't show it to anyone but me."

CHAPTER 34

With the Russian pastry menu decided upon, content and placement of last-minute press releases discussed and security measures in place, Aunt Ibby collected our yellow pads and returned the pencils to the copper mug. "Thanks, everybody, for coming, and for all your help. Karl, I'll meet you tomorrow noon at the restaurant and we can go over the table of contents for your book. Stasia, you didn't ride your scooter here, did you? Do you need a ride home?"

The woman pulled a piece of bubblegum from her pocket, unwrapped it and popped it into her mouth. I realized that she'd forgone chewing for the entire evening. It must have been like a smoker going without a cigarette. "Would you call a cab for me?" she asked, crumbling the gum wrapper into a tiny ball, once again arranging the blanket-wrapped doll against her shoulder, and putting the plastic box under her arm.

"Nonsense," my aunt said. "We all have automobiles. One of us will drive you home; Karl has his nice Jeep and of course Lee has that pretty blue convertible." But her expectant look was leveled in Pete's direction. "We want to be sure you and Tatiana get home *safely*."

Pete looked at his watch. "I have to return Donnie's truck in about an hour and I don't have to check in at the station until seven. I can drop you off, if you don't mind riding in a truck. You still living in the same place?"

How come he knows where Stasia lives?

"Sure. Thanks." She turned to face Aunt Ibby. "Thank you for the dresses. Let me know when you want me to bring Tatiana to the library."

"Of course, dear. Give me your phone number."

"Don't have a phone. I'll be on my bench most days."

"Oh. Well. That's fine." I knew that my aunt, who is so connected to the rest of the world by every possible means—cell phone, home phone, cloud, e-mail, Facebook, LinkedIn, Twitter, Instagram, Meetup—was struggling to process the fact that some people, by choice, avoid all of those things.

Karl Smith was the first to leave, the almost-full tray of goodies still on the kitchen table. I knew Pete would be happy about that. "Breakfast tomorrow morning?" he whispered when I walked to the door with him and Stasia.

"Yes," I said, "as long as it's not apricot torte and Russian tea cakes."

"Killjoy," he said. "See you around six?"

"I'll be here."

I closed the door and returned to the kitchen, where my efficient aunt had already cleared the table. "I've put the leftover pastries in a tin," she said. "I thought Pete might like to take them to the station to share with the others."

"Good idea. Now let's look up that amusement park in Colorado where Grandpa Nick used to work. That's where the twin horse has to be, right?"

"Already checked. The carousel is still there. They treat it like a museum piece. Only let the kids ride horses on special holidays and such. I was dying to tell Pete, but I didn't want to say anything in front of the others. Come on into my office." She led the way. "I'll show you the park, but there weren't any close-up photos of the carousel."

"I'm having breakfast with Pete at six in the morning. This will keep until then. Do you suppose the gazillion-dollar egg is really still inside the other horse?"

"Could be. If all the park has done over the years is sand and touch up the paint from time to time, there'd be no need to take it apart. That's all Paul was going to do to yours before it got dismembered." She sat at her desk and turned on the computer. I pulled up a chair beside her.

"If Pete—and the chief—believe our story, someone in Colorado will have to get a search warrant for the carousel, I suppose. What do you think they'll do to the horse?"

"I'm not sure, but if it was up to me, I'd X-ray him," she said. "Then, if it's in there, they'll have to take him apart, I guess."

"Do you think we'll ever get to see it? The egg, I mean. I've never seen one, have you?"

"Once. It was at the Metropolitan Museum of Art in New York. Fabulous." She tapped the screen, enlarging the picture. "There. That's the entrance to the park. You can see the carousel, but not close enough to really see the individual animals."

"I wonder if Mr. Dillon had seen the first five eggs. He told Scott this would be a six-chapter book, so I'm guessing there's a good story about each egg."

"I'll bet there is. And whoever stole his laptop might know by now where each of those eggs is."

"If they have the password, or have figured out how to hack into it." The idea of someone stealing the man's book after taking his life made me angry. "I wonder if he'd had a chance to write about the two horses before . . . you know."

"I think he may have. What was it he told Stasia? He'd driven all the way across the country to bet on the wrong horse?"

"I think so too," I said. "How does this sound? Eric Dillon knew that Nikita Novikova had one of the eggs and that he worked on carousel horses at a park in Colorado. He learned that Grandpa Nick had moved to Salem and that he had a carved horse with him. It's only logical to think that *if* he'd hidden an egg, and *if* he'd taken that egg with him when he moved, it would be in *that* horse."

My aunt picked up the story. "But Nikita didn't do what was logical. Maybe the egg didn't fit safely inside the old horse. Maybe it would have rattled around, gotten damaged. So instead of repairing it, refinishing it, he carved a new one with a hollow spot inside that was just the right shape. It was an exact duplicate, as though he had chipped all the old paint away and re-painted it, just as Paul has done to yours."

"Lydia still believed that Grand Duchess Anastasia would someday come for her egg," I said, getting excited about the plot we were building. "Maybe they knew someone was trying to collect all the eggs. Maybe they thought the egg would be safer if it was far away from them. So they made sure that the new horse was in a protected place, took the other one with them and moved far away—to Salem." I had another thought. "That picture of Grandpa Nick with a horse . . . it was taken in Colorado!"

"Yes!" Aunt Ibby was excited too. "Nikita and Lydia probably knew that the valet and the butler and the horse trainer had sold their eggs. Then later, when they heard about what had happened to their friends— the baker and the doctor—they were sure they'd done the right thing. Lydia had put the approximate locations of each egg on her quilt. They'd done all they could to save Anastasia's treasure."

"But Nikita died," I said, "and Lydia lost her memory. Poor Anastasia was dead, after all, and no one figured out the horse's secret until Eric Dillon decided to write a book about the lost eggs."

We grew quiet for a long moment and just looked at each other. O'Ryan hopped up onto the desk and sat in front of the monitor, looking back and forth, first at me and then at my aunt.

"Mrrrup?" he said. It sounded like a question.

"O'Ryan wants to know the end of the story," my aunt said.

"So do I."

* * *

In the morning, by the time Cuckoo told me it was six o'clock, I was already awake, out of bed and halfway through a pot of coffee. O'Ryan, sprawled out along the kitchen windowsill, listened for the sunrise sounds of birds while I paced up and down the hall between the kitchen and the living room, listening for the sound of Pete's key in the door.

"Wow! Look at you—all bright, shining and alert." He pulled me close for a hug, then stepped back, his hands on my shoulders. "Jacket on, purse in hand, ready to roll. Anxious to see me or just hungry?"

"Both, I guess. Come on. I have so much to tell you."

"Since just last night? I saw you"—he looked at his watch—"twelve hours ago."

"I know. A lot has happened." I tapped my forehead. "In here."

"Uh-oh." He frowned and followed me out the door and down the staircase. "You haven't been seeing things, have you?"

"No. No visions. But I think Aunt Ibby and I have figured out just what Eric Dillon was looking for. I want to tell you the story the way we think it all happened."

I barely remember the ride to the restaurant, or even what I ordered that morning, I was so focused on making sure that Pete understood exactly what my aunt and I believed was true, and exactly why we were so sure about it.

I talked all the way through breakfast, stopping only when Pete asked a question. When I'd finished, I leaned back in the booth, took a deep breath, a hefty swallow of coffee and watched his face. "What do you think? Was

Eric Dillon right? Are we? Is the sixth egg riding around on an old carousel in Colorado?"

"You've given this a lot of thought. A lot of research." One elbow on the table, his chin on his fist, his expression was serious—not cop face serious, but thoughtful, concentrating serious. It's a look I love, one that can always easily sidetrack my own concentration.

Stay focused!

I rattled the spoon in my coffee cup. "So, tell me. What do you think?"

"I think you and your aunt, and maybe even your sharpener-snitching cat, are good detectives. You and the department have each come to some of the same conclusions about this case. Including Colorado. Maybe even about a cold case in the Boston area."

"Doctor Yakovlev? You know what became of him?"

"Possibly. When they did some work enlarging Logan Airport about twenty years ago, they found a skeleton, the remains of a leather medical bag beside it. The case has been reopened."

"It's him," I said, knowing I was right. "Any pointed metal teeth there too?"

"I can't tell you everything. It's an open case."

"I understand." I began to count on my fingers. "So the baker in Connecticut was murdered. The doctor in Boston was murdered. . . ."

"Possibly."

"So the doctor in Boston was murdered—*possibly*. Eric Dillon was murdered, certainly. But who's doing the killing? The murders are the same, yet different, just as Eric Dillon said. They're too many years apart for one person to have done it, aren't they?"

"You're right about that." He spread his hands apart. "We're working on it. And your friend Nigel St. John"— he pronounced the name correctly and smiled—"has given us some useful information from over there." He gestured toward what may or may not have been Europe. "He and Chief Whaley have a meeting scheduled as soon as he gets here next week." Another smile. "After the party, of course."

"That reminds me. Aunt Ibby packed up all the left-over Russian goodies for you."

"Great. I'll take them to the station this afternoon. She's getting pretty tight with that chef, isn't she? What do you think of him?"

"I don't know," I admitted. "I go back and forth about that. One minute I think he's all he claims to be—an almost-famous chef running a supergood restaurant and trying to write a cookbook. Then, every once in a while, I get a different feeling. Like what's up between him and Boris Medvedev? That can't be good. And Stasia? The Russian-English translation thing. And last night, he seemed to pick up on her eggs-in-the-refrigerator reference. Did you catch that?"

"I did, but only because you'd just told me your idea about the Fabergé eggs. Might be something. Might be nothing."

"I know. I wish I could see things as analytically as you do. I get an idea and I just want to run with it. Even if it takes me up a dead-end alley." We left the cozy warmth of the restaurant, stepped out into the early-morning chill of the oncoming fall and started for home.

Pete came upstairs with me to pick up the promised box of goodies and also to retrieve the plastic bagged notebook page. "Might be something. Might be nothing."

"It's something," I said. "You'll see."

He cocked his head to one side. "Maybe." A quick kiss and he headed down the stairs, then looked back. "I get off early today. Want to do something around five?"

"Sure. Call me."

O'Ryan hadn't left his windowsill perch. When I sat in the chair nearest the window, he twisted his head around without moving the rest of his body in that way cats can do and we can't. He fixed the golden eyes on me, much the way he had stared so relentlessly at Karl Smith.

"So, cat," I said, "what did you think of the great story Aunt Ibby and I made up about the dead baker and the missing doctor and the carousel horse and the quilt"— I dropped my voice to the spooky near-whisper I used to use on *Nightshades* to introduce the horror movies— "and all those murders?"

O'Ryan stood and stretched, gave me an un-catlike up-and-down look, jumped to the floor and headed to the bedroom. He glanced back over his shoulder.

"Meh," he said quite plainly.

"'Meh'?" I said. "What do you mean, 'meh'? It's a good story."

"Meh," he said again, and hopped up onto the bed, facing the damned mirror.

CHAPTER 35

"Okay. I guess I'd rather face whatever it is here than
have it pop up in a random store window or somebody
else's kitchen cabinet." I lay down on my tummy next to
the cat and looked into the mirror. From this angle I
could see O'Ryan's windowsill and part of the Lucite
table. "Okay, mirror. What've you got?"

The sparkling lights and swirling colors began right
away and lasted a little longer than usual. *They're really
kind of pretty, in a strange sort of way,* I thought. Soon
enough, that happy thought went away as something
else began to take shape.

At first it was just a scene. A place. There was something vaguely familiar about it, but I didn't recognize it
right away. There were people walking around among
some of the buildings, but I didn't know who they were.
Their clothing was odd. Old-fashioned. Then I saw the
carousel and remembered where I'd seen this place
before. It was the amusement park we'd looked up
online the night before—the one in Colorado.

The same, only different.

Last night we'd seen it the way it looks now. The mirror showed me the way it had looked a long time ago. I seemed to be moving closer to the carousel. I saw my horse then. He looked just as he did in my living room—honey brown, the white mane, gold-tinged, wind-whipped. I smiled. Then the animal just behind him began to move. It wasn't at all like the other beautiful carved horses and tigers and dragons going around and around in that magical circle.

It was a bear—the same bear I'd seen in the McKennas' kitchen cabinet—and it looked very real. Long claws reached for the horse. My horse. The thing opened huge jaws displaying sharp, triangular teeth. It lunged for the horse. A thin red line of blood spread on the honey-brown throat and spattered onto the pure white mane.

Enough. No more.

When I opened my eyes again, the bear was gone. The merry-go-round turned slowly. A little girl rode on the honey-colored horse, her hand on the carved scarlet rose, the pearl buttons on her blue dress catching the light as she spun around and around. The picture froze that way for a moment before it began to fade away. I felt O'Ryan's rough tongue on my face; his warm, soft fur was against my neck as he licked tears from my cheek.

I picked the cat up and carried him back into the kitchen. He didn't squirm or try to jump out of my arms. Sometimes he doesn't feel like being held, but this time he seemed comfortable with it. I sat, holding him, in the Lucite chair closest to the window and together we looked out into our pretty backyard, where there were no bears. I wondered what Aunt Ibby or River or Pete might make of the vision.

I decided I'd keep this one to myself. At least for now.

I stayed busy for the rest of the morning, e-mailing pictures and new press releases about the Library Bookmobile Benefit High Tea to all the area papers. I used many adjectives extolling the deliciousness of the pastries and the rarity of the Canton china teacups, along with special mention of a doll named Tatiana that may have once belonged to Grand Duchess Anastasia. I used Aunt Ibby's state-of-the-art, professional-quality color printer and made a few eight-by-tens of the doll pictures for WICH-TV. I remembered that Marty liked to use photos or sometimes even greeting cards in the opening shots for various programs. She'd zoom in on the picture, superimposing credits or titles. I was sure she'd love Tatiana and that the tea would get some extra on-air exposure. I made just one print of the Stasia and Tatiana photo.

It was around noon when I put the photos for Marty and the one for Stasia into separate envelopes and left for the station. Aunt Ibby had gone dress shopping for something to wear on Friday evening when she and Mr. Pennington planned to attend a performance of *West Side Story* at the North Shore Music Theatre. This time I didn't park by the seawall. I used one of the VISITOR spaces near the street and went in through the front door. The brass-doored vintage elevator growled its slowpoke way up to the second-floor reception area, in all its purple-and-turquoise splendor.

Rhonda looked up from a copy of *People* and smiled broadly when she saw me. "Nice surprise! You here to see Scotty again?"

"Nope. Here on business. I need to get some free ad time for the library's latest fund-raiser. Mr. Doan around?"

"Yeah, but you know how he feels about freebies. Even for you."

"He'll have to like this one. Mrs. Doan is on the library board and she's already RSVP'd for the two of them."

I was right. The station manager agreed to air a few spots, using my copy and photos, then summarily shooed me away. "I know you're busy, so I'll let you go now. Drop in anytime. Bye."

"That was fast." Rhonda raised a penciled eyebrow. "Did he throw you out?"

"He did, but he said okay first. That gives me time to visit with you. Got a minute?"

Smiling, she put down her magazine. "Sure. What do you want to know?"

That surprised me. "Am I that obvious?"

"Come on. Everybody knows I'm the eyes and ears around here. Everything comes by this desk"—she tapped her headset—"or through this phone. I never signed a confidentiality contract. I love to talk. What'll it be? Mrs. Doan's boob job? Wanda's weekend in Vegas with the married science teacher? What?"

"You've got me," I said, laughing. "But it's about you."

"Me? Nothing interesting ever happens to me."

"You told me last time I was here that you'd spent some time with Eric Dillon."

"Oh, that poor guy." Her shoulders slumped and a look of genuine sadness crossed her pretty face. "He was so sweet. So smart too. I really liked him. Everybody at the station did."

"You said you'd dated him a few times?"

A shrug of one shoulder. "Couple of times. Drinks. Dinner. You know. Casual stuff. Nothing heavy."

"But you talked? Swapped stories?"

"Oh, sure. He told me about his home in Illinois, and how he got into the broadcast business—how he met Scotty—that kind of thing."

"Didn't he talk about his books at all? How he did his research?"

She leaned forward, eyes sparkling with interest. "That was the best part. I could have listened to him talk about those books all night. What an interesting life he had . . . until, you know—he got killed."

"I know. What a shame. Did he tell you anything at all about the new book?"

"Quite a lot, actually," she said. "I'm glad you asked. Nobody around here is much interested in that part—the research it took to write all those books. Did you know he learned to dive on undersea wrecks to do the Florida book? Explored old gold mines for the California one? Even went inside the pyramids in Egypt. He had adventures all over the world." She looked around the room and dropped her voice. "He'd been working on the new one, the one he didn't get to finish, for years. It was going to be different from the others—the best one of all, he said. A real mystery book—and at the end, all the treasures would still be lost—except one. He was worried about finishing the last chapter though. Something about finding the treasure before it disappeared, like all the rest of them."

Five treasures are still missing. We're pretty sure we know where the sixth one is. Who else knows?

"Did he tell you what the treasure was?"

"Not exactly."

"What do you mean?"

"The last time I saw him, he said that with any luck at all he'd be the one to find the golden goose. So I guess the treasure is something gold. He didn't have much luck though, did he?"

That goose laid golden eggs.

"No, he didn't. You never heard from him again?"

"I didn't. He took my number and I hoped he'd call me again, but he never did."

I thought about the piece of notepaper Karl Smith had dropped. It had women's names and numbers on it. "Did he write your name in a brown notebook?"

"No. He put it into his phone." She laughed. "He said the only phone numbers he wrote down anymore were the ones he used for passwords on the Internet."

I was confused. "Passwords?"

"Yes. He used names of old girlfriends and their phone numbers for passwords. I told you he was smart. He figured no hacker would ever break a silly code like that. Listen, you want to go down to the studio and say hi to Marty?"

My mind was busy processing the information she'd given me, absorbing Eric's revelation about the golden goose and Rhonda's offhand comment about passwords. "Marty? Oh, yes. I do want to see her." I waved the envelope containing the photos of Tatiana. "I have some photos for her to use as bumper shots."

"I'll go down with you. It's time for a break anyway." She fished the hand-lettered BACK IN FIVE sign from her desk drawer and led the way to the downstairs studio.

It took a moment for my eyes to become accustomed to the darkness. The long room with its black painted walls had sets for the station's various shows in neat cubicles, along both sidewalls. Only one of the areas, the kitchen set up for the *Cooking with Wanda the Weathergirl Show,* was lit. The gray-haired camerawoman was busily sweeping the 1950s-style, random-brick linoleum floor.

"Marty, look," Rhonda called. "You have company."

I wasn't surprised to see the station's top camera operator doing the cleaning lady's job. Marty loves to stay busy and Mr. Doan likes his help to wear as many hats as possible.

That's why Scott thinks about leaving WICH-TV. He's field reporter, newsman and high-school sports commentator. All for one salary.

Marty got to her feet, washed her hands and rushed down the center aisle to meet us. "Barrett! Great to see you again." Her handshake was firm, and her smile genuine. "What's up?"

I put the envelope on top of Wanda's freezer and pulled out the photos. "This doll is going to be on display at the library fund-raiser. I thought maybe you could use it as a bumper shot, with maybe a line or two of copy."

She inspected the picture. "Nice shot. Cute doll. Yours?"

"I wish. No, she may have belonged to Grand Duchess Anastasia, the czar's youngest daughter."

"Really? Does she have a name?"

"Tatiana."

"Oh, that's nice," Rhonda said. "Anastasia named the doll after one of her older sisters."

Marty and I both looked at the receptionist. "How'd you know that?" Marty asked.

Rhonda shrugged. "One of my degrees is in world history. Well, my five minutes is up. Gotta get back to work."

Rhonda is a never-ending source of surprises.

I was anxious to get home to tell my aunt about the golden-goose remark and I knew Pete would be interested in Eric Dillon's password trick. I pulled into our garage and was glad to see that the Buick was already there. I let myself into the back hall and knocked on Aunt Ibby's kitchen door. "It's open," she said. "Come on in. I just this minute got here myself."

"How'd the shopping go?" I asked as I stepped inside. "Did you find something you like?"

"I certainly did, dear. I bought two outfits. One for the theater with Rupert, and one for the high tea with Nigel. I feel like quite the social butterfly."

"Good for you. Got a few minutes? I went down to the TV station this afternoon and learned a couple of things."

"Come and sit. O'Ryan and I were just having a little afternoon snack." The cat's red bowl was filled with the different-colored, dry cat food that's shaped like little steaks and cheeses and drumsticks and fish—as though cats knew what the shapes meant. So silly. My aunt's snack was a sensible grilled cheese. "Want one?" she asked.

"Of course I do," I said. "It's one of my favorite childhood comfort foods."

"I know," she said, buttering both sides of the sandwich and flipping it into the old black iron skillet. "Tell me what you've learned. More about our case?"

"It's not *our* case," I scolded. "At least don't let Pete hear you say that." I took one bite of the perfectly golden melted cheese in the middle of the sandwich and heard Aunt Ibby's phone ring.

"Now who could that be?" she wondered aloud. "Hello?" There was a long pause and she covered the mouthpiece with one hand. "It's Nigel," she whispered. "Calling from London."

I hoped all was well in the United Kingdom and that Nigel would be arriving in Boston on schedule. Aunt Ibby doesn't like changes in plans, and, besides, she was counting on those fresh Harrods pastries. I listened to her end of the conversation and tried to figure out what was going on. I could tell that O'Ryan was listening too. He'd stopped eating in the middle of a pink fish, with his ears straight up, tail switching.

Other than the occasional "Oh, my goodness" and "Doesn't that beat all," she didn't contribute much to the transatlantic conversation. She ended by saying, "One of us will pick you up at Logan Airport early on Saturday afternoon. Ta-ta!"

I was sure the scone-and-biscuit department was accounted for, but what else was going on? "What's up?" I asked. "Is Nigel all right?"

She wasn't smiling. "Yes. He's fine. He'll be here, as planned. But he's concerned about us. About what we've been doing, you and I."

"'What we've been doing'?"

"The case. All of it. I've been e-mailing him bits and pieces of what we've learned so far. You knew he'd been in contact with Chief Whaley about an international matter?"

"Yes, of course. I talked to Pete about it."

"He didn't tell me a lot. I suppose he couldn't, but he's been looking into this Boris person's activities over there for the chief and he's learned some disturbing things. He called to warn us to be cautious." She looked down at her plate. "He said for us to stop meddling in police business. He was quite stern about it. Medvedev isn't that man's real name, and he's very, very dangerous." She repeated it. "That's what Nigel said. 'Very, very dangerous.'"

CHAPTER 36

I was pretty certain that Pete must know whatever it was that Nigel was hinting about. More than hinting. Was Boris wanted for something? I doubted that, or certainly the Salem police could have found out about it and arrested him by now. If he wasn't Boris Medvedev, who was he? Maybe he'd taken the Russian word for bear for his wrestling image. A stage name. That made sense. So did the bear's teeth necklace. The image of the ravening bear on the merry-go-round, attacking the helpless, little stationary horse, resurfaced in my mind.

"What do you think we should do about it?" Aunt Ibby's voice interrupted the unpleasant thought.

"Do about it? There's nothing much we can do, except take Nigel's advice, I suppose. It's the same as Pete's. Stop meddling in police business."

"You're right. Want a soda with your sandwich?"

"Yes, please. In the can is okay."

We sat in silence, sipping Mountain Dew, and then we both spoke at once.

"But if it wasn't for us . . . ," my aunt said.

"We're the ones who . . ." I waved my hand in the air.

"We were on the right track with this, from the very beginning," she declared, wearing her wise-old-owl face. "From the minute I recognized the McKennas' house on Eric Dillon's Facebook page."

"From the time we bought the storage locker, really," I put in, "and Eric Dillon followed you home."

"Can't very well stop now," she said. "We'll just be very cautious. Tell me what you learned at the television station. Did you talk to Scott Palmer again?"

"No. This time it was Rhonda. Seems she dated Mr. Dillon a couple of times."

"Rhonda. That girl is a lot smarter than she looks, you know. What did she have to say?"

I told her first about the golden-goose remark. "He had to be talking about the goose that laid the golden eggs," I said.

"Had to be," she agreed. "Everything points to the eggs. I'm sure we're right."

"There's more. I never told you about the notebook page I found on the ground on the Common. I think it came from the missing notebook, and I'm pretty sure Karl Smith dropped it there. Pete asked me to be quiet about it until he could do some checking."

She frowned. "Do you think it would be proper for you to tell me about it now?"

"Yes. Now I *know* it's from the notebook, and I know what it means. I haven't had a chance to talk to Pete about it yet."

I explained about Stasia translating recipes from Russian to English for Karl.

"That sounds reasonable," she said.

I knew she didn't want to hear anything bad about her new friend, so I tried to phrase things carefully. "Pete noticed right away that this particular page didn't look like a recipe. It was a list of women's names and what looked like telephone numbers."

"That doesn't sound like anything sinister," she said. "Are you sure Karl dropped it?"

"No. I can't be positive about that," I admitted. "As Pete said, it could have just been a piece of litter lying on the ground."

"Go on. What about it?"

"We realized that on this page the translation was from English to Russian, not the other way around."

"Maybe Stasia translates for other people, as well as for Karl." She sounded hopeful.

"That could be, except for what Rhonda told me."

"Which was?"

"Eric Dillon used old girlfriends' first names and telephone numbers for all of his passwords."

"What a remarkably good idea. Anyone who found it would think it was just what it looked like."

"It stands to reason that the password to the missing laptop is on that list."

"And the missing manuscript of the new book is on the laptop."

I nodded. "I'm thinking that manuscript holds the solution to the whole mystery of the missing eggs."

Her smile was wry. "The mystery of the missing eggs. Another Nancy Drew title. And sad to say, it looks as though Karl is deeply involved in the whole mess, doesn't it? He was at the storage locker auction. He helped Boris to take our trash, and he may have the stolen notebook—pages from it anyway."

"I'm afraid so."

"When you tell Pete what Rhonda said about the girls' names and numbers being passwords, he'll connect it to the page from the Dillon notebook. Maybe he'll put Karl in jail!"

"Remember, there's no proof that Karl dropped it," I said, knowing that it was a pretty safe bet that he had.

"You're right. Let's not borrow trouble. We need to stay busy. Not in a meddlesome way, of course."

"At least not in an *obviously* meddlesome way," I said. "Any suggestions?"

"Let's look up Fabergé eggs again. See if we've missed anything there."

We picked up what was left of our sandwiches and sodas and once again headed for her office. She's much faster on the keyboard than I am; so, as usual, I pulled up a chair beside her and watched as photos of Imperial eggs, one after another, appeared on the screen.

"Look at this one, Maralee," she said. "Here's an article about the most recent find. A Midwestern scrap metal dealer bought it at a flea market. He was going to melt it down for the gold. Turned out to be the third Imperial egg Fabergé made, and it was sold in 2011 to a private collector for thirty-three million dollars."

"Thirty-three million dollars! Imagine finding a treasure like that at a rummage sale."

"Or at a storage locker sale." She winked. "It could happen. Maybe we should get on that auctioneer's list and go to them regularly."

"No thanks," I said. "One was enough for me."

We spent nearly an hour learning about the eggs—they weren't very big, only about three or four inches tall—small enough to fit easily inside a doctor's bag or a papier-mâché wedding cake or a wooden horse. "Look at that one," I said, pointing. "It has a little cuckoo clock on the top."

That 1900 Cockerel Egg reminded me of my promise to give Cuckoo to Stasia, so I excused myself from our cautious meddling session, went upstairs and by quarter to five the cuckoo clock was carefully wrapped and boxed and ready to be delivered to Stasia. Cuckoo had been replaced on my wall by a vintage Kit-Cat clock I'd been saving for years. I knew Pete wouldn't like googly eyes and wagging tail as much as I did, but at least this one didn't talk.

"Do you notice anything missing?" I asked him just as soon as he stepped into the kitchen, followed by O'Ryan, who'd been waiting for him at the door as usual.

He spotted it right away. "That smart-ass little noise-maker is gone. Good riddance. The funny-looking black cat doesn't meow on the hour or anything, does it?"

I assured him that Kit-Cat was silent, except for a friendly ticking sound when it rolled its eyes and wagged its tail, and told him I had the other clock ready to give to Stasia. "She doesn't have a phone, so I suppose I'll just drop it off to her at the bench on the Common someday." I watched his face. "Since you know where she lives, maybe we could take it over there tonight. I know she's anxious to get it."

"Sure. She lives over near my sister's place. Can't miss it. A small pink one-bedroom place."

"I've seen that cute, little house a hundred times," I said. "It looks like one of those 'tiny houses' on the TV show. I never made the connection."

"I hadn't either," he said, "until you told me about the pink scooter. I saw it parked in front of the house one day and there was Stasia sitting on her front steps."

"What are we doing tonight anyway? You didn't tell me, so I didn't know exactly what I should wear." I looked from my navy capris and white camp shirt to his jeans and Boston Strong sweatshirt.

"You're perfect," he said. "Just put on a jacket. We're going to the Salem Willows amusement park. The traditional end-of-summer date."

I put my arms around his waist and reached up for a kiss. "What a good idea. We haven't done that for ages."

Maybe a couple of hours of bumper cars, pinball machines and saltwater taffy will clear away thoughts of unwelcome visions and the very, very dangerous Boris Medvedev. I know I need to tell Pete about the golden goose and Eric Dillon's password codes. That stuff can wait. I need a little bit of normalcy just now. Later. I'll do it later.

I grabbed my jacket. Pete picked up the package with the clock in it, and after stopping to admire Old Paint in his lush, new green surroundings, we headed for the Willows.

The first thing we did was ride the merry-go-round. The original carved animals from the old structure are gone, but the sturdy replicas are clean and colorful. As the carousel picked up speed and my dappled horse rode up and down on his pole, I felt as carefree as I had when I rode the original version of the horse when I was a child.

Pete and I strolled the park, eating chop suey sandwiches and homemade ice cream, playing foosball (he beat me) and pinball (I beat him). We found a vacant bench under a white willow tree and I told him what Rhonda had told me about the passwords and the golden goose.

"That pretty much nails it, doesn't it?" he said. "The page came from Dillon's notebook and Smith was the one who dropped it."

"Afraid so. Aunt Ibby is hoping it's not true. She had a phone call from Nigel this afternoon. She's been e-mailing him about the research she and I have been doing."

"Chief Whaley had a call from him too." He took my hand. "Nigel is worried about you and Miss Russell."

"Yes. He told Aunt Ibby we need to be cautious and to stop messing with police business."

"Excellent advice. Come on. Your hands are cold and it's getting dark. Let's go deliver that clock to Stasia."

"Are you going to tell me what Nigel said to Chief Whaley? Why is he so worried about my aunt and me?"

"No. Not yet. We're checking on it."

"That's what you say about everything."

"That's what I do about everything." He pulled me to my feet. "Come on. Let's get rid of that damned clock before you change your mind about it."

CHAPTER 37

Even in the dark the pink house stood out among its gray and white and tan neighbors. The pink scooter was locked to a chain-link fence and a small sign proclaimed: PALM READER—WALK-INS WELCOME.

Pete parked the Crown Vic in front of the open gate and together we approached a narrow porch. I didn't see any lights on inside. "Maybe she's not here."

"It's still early. She's probably watching TV with the lights out."

Pete carried the clock and I knocked on the door, painted a brighter pink than the rest of the house. "Stasia? It's Lee Barrett. I've brought your clock."

The door opened a crack, and a bright brown eye peeked out. "Lee? I'm busy. I have a . . . a client. Just leave it on the steps, okay? Thank you." The door shut abruptly. Pete and I looked at each other. I backed away and headed for the car.

"Wait a minute." Pete handed me the clock package and knocked much louder and harder than I had. "Stasia? It's Pete Mondello. Are you all right?"

There was no reply for a long moment; then an overhead light clicked on and the pink door swung open. "Sure. Sure. I'm fine." She stepped out onto the porch, pulling the door closed behind her, and reached for the clock. "This it? Wow. Thanks, Lee. Thanks for coming over, Pete. Well, gotta go." She stood there, clutching the package against her chest. The blank look I'd seen before came over her features. We'd been dismissed.

I stepped down into the yard and started toward the gate. "Good-bye, Stasia," I said. Pete waited there, facing her. Again he asked, "Are you all right?" She didn't answer or make a move to go into the house.

I climbed onto the step and tugged on Pete's sleeve. "It's okay. She does that sometimes when she doesn't want to talk anymore. I've seen it before. She just . . . shuts down."

"Okay." He took my elbow with one hand, texted on his phone with the other and steered me toward his car. "I'm dropping you off at my sister Marie's," he said. "It's right around the corner. She'll take you home. I'm going back to keep an eye on Stasia's house."

"What's wrong?" I didn't expect an answer and didn't get one. He barely slowed down in front of the neat white ranch house. Donnie stood in the driveway, waiting for me. Pete stopped the car. "I'll call you later," he said, and that was that.

Marie drove me home, as promised. (Yes, Pete's sister and brother-in-law are named Donnie and Marie.) I didn't get much information from her either. "He doesn't tell me anything," she said. "That's how cops are. Our dad was the same way. You'll get used to it." She smiled. "He knows what he's doing. Don't worry."

When we pulled up in front of the Winter Street house, I invited her in to see Old Paint. She said she needed to get back to pick the boys up from a friend's birthday party. "Don't worry," she repeated as I got out of the car.

So I finished my day with more questions than I'd started: What did Nigel and Chief Whaley know about Boris Medvedev that they weren't telling us? Why was Pete staking out Stasia's house?

By eleven o'clock I still hadn't heard from Pete. I was tempted to call, but knew better. O'Ryan and I sat in the kitchen, listening to the wind whistling outside. "Getting cold," I said to the cat.

"Mmrup," he agreed, and moved away from the windowsill onto my lap. I patted his fuzzy head, and looked around the warm, cozy room. My phone was on the table in front of me. Silent. "Where *is* he?" I asked the cat. "Why hasn't he called? He must know I'm worried." O'Ryan nuzzled closer to my hand and delivered a comforting lick just as the phone buzzed.

"It's me, babe," Pete said. "You must have been worried."

"I was just telling O'Ryan that," I said, relief flooding over me.

"I'm on my way over to your place now. Okay?"

O'Ryan and I waited in the living room for the sound of Pete's key in the lock. O'Ryan gave him a purring reception, with much ankle rubbing and a happy "mmrup," while I hugged him close and murmured silly love words.

"What a reception," he said, "I should stay out late more often."

"I wish you wouldn't."

"Please don't worry." He returned my hug and added a long, sweet kiss. "I know what I'm doing."

"So I've heard. Come on out to the kitchen. Coffee's hot. Can you tell me what's going on with Stasia?"

"Yes. There are definitely some things you need to know."

So with a northeast wind whipping at the trees outside, a mug full of hot coffee, a warm cat on my lap and the man I loved across the table, I listened.

"After I dropped you off, I went back to Stasia's street. I parked a little way off, in the shadow of one of the big chestnut trees, and shut off the engine.

"What were you expecting to see?"

He smiled. "I wasn't sure. Just had a hunch that something was wrong in that house."

"Was there?"

"Wrong? I don't know. But surprising, definitely."

"What happened?"

"So there I was, hiding under that old tree, freezing my butt off, when a car pulls up right in front of Stasia's house. Green Jeep Grand Cherokee."

"Not Karl Smith!"

"Ran the plate to be sure. Karl Smith. He didn't get out. Sat there with the motor running for a good ten minutes. Then the porch light flashes once and goes off." He leaned toward me, eyes fixed on mine. "The door opens and I see someone come onto the porch. It's Stasia. She comes out and puts something in the backseat of the Jeep. She goes back to the porch and a tall guy comes out. They get in a big clinch, and then she goes in the house. The guy walks across the sidewalk to the Jeep. It's dark. I can't make out who it is. Just that he's big."

I realized I was holding my breath.

Pete leaned back in his chair and took a mouthful of coffee. "Then the door of the Jeep opened and the interior light went on. There he was in plain sight. Boris Medvedev. He put some kind of a briefcase into the backseat, then went back into the house again."

It took a minute for all that to digest. Medvedev? In Stasia's house? "She was afraid of him," I said. "She said her father was afraid of him too. Why would he be in her house?"

Pete shook his head. "She didn't look afraid of him tonight on her porch. What I saw was definitely a more-than-friendly hug. Anyway, he came back out after a while, carrying a suitcase, climbed into the front seat of the Jeep and off they went."

"Did you follow them?" I wanted to know. "Where did they go?"

"To the Beverly Airport," he said, and drank some more coffee. The busy city-owned airport in nearby Beverly is home to lots of small private planes—some used for business, some for pleasure, some for both. Aunt Ibby and I traveled from there once on a friend's private jet when the Patriots played the Packers in New Orleans.

"They flew somewhere?"

"Medvedev did. Private plane. I took the numbers and relayed them to the station. They're running a check on it now. Smith took off and came back to Salem. I called you and came here. That's all."

"*That's all?* Are you going to arrest somebody? *Anybody?*"

"We'll bring Smith in for questioning again, but he doesn't have to talk to us if he doesn't want to. It's not against the law to drive a friend to the airport, any more than it's against the law to help that friend look through other people's trash." He ran his hand through his hair. "I'd like to interrogate the whole bunch of them, including Stasia, but that's not the way it works."

"You keep telling me I'd make a good cop," I said. "I wouldn't be able to be patient like you are. I'd go over there and pound on Stasia's door and make her tell me what she's doing, messing around with a creep like Medvedev. I'd make that chef admit whatever's going on with the phony recipe translations. I'd throw that evil Russian Bear into a cell and lock him up until he admitted to murder."

"Whoa! Wait a minute. Nobody said anything about Medvedev being a murderer—I mean outside of the ring. What brought that on? Have you been seeing things again?"

I hadn't meant to tell him about the bear on the merry-go-round, but I did. "I know Medvedev is a killer," I said. "I saw him—I mean the bear that I know *is* him—I saw him attack the horse that has the sixth egg inside. He made a red line on the horse's throat with his teeth. It's the horse on the merry-go-round in Colorado." I covered my face with my hands, not wanting to see the scene in my mind again. "It was just like the line on Dillon's throat."

"And that somehow proves he killed Dillon?"

"It does to me," I said, "but I know it's nothing you can take to the chief. Nothing at all."

"I'm sorry. I know Medvedev could be a killer. He's done it before, in the ring. But as you just said, I've got nothing. His record is clean since he got out of jail. Hell, I can't even get a warrant to X-ray that horse, and I'm pretty sure you're right about that too." He walked around the table and knelt beside my chair. "I need evidence. Something real."

I didn't have an answer for that. The things Aunt Ibby and I had thought of as evidence—embroidery, eggs, six long-ago friends, bear's teeth—weren't *real*. As evidence they weren't even circumstantial. They're only made-up stories.

I tried to think of something positive to say—to lighten the gloomy mood. "The plans for the tea are moving along nicely," I said. "Aunt Ibby is so excited about it. Lots of reservations so far, and I guess the food is going to be spectacular. Only one more day to go before Saturday. We're going tomorrow morning to pick up a couple of pastry carts from Karl and get the preliminary stuff set up at the library."

Pete stood up. "Tomorrow's Friday? Wow. Time flies. I have a Friday appointment with the fire marshal at eight a.m. to check things out at the library. Maybe I'll see you there."

"Wouldn't be surprised. We're planning to be there at seven. Aunt Ibby has the key."

"I'd better get going then," he said. "We both have early days coming up."

I kissed him good night at the door. As he turned to leave, I said, "Pete, do you have any red candles?"

A puzzled look. "Yeah. Marie gave me a strawberry one for my bathroom. Why?"

"Just light it once in a while, okay? For protection."

He smiled. "River?"

"Uh-huh."

"Call me crazy," he said, "but I'll do it."

CHAPTER 38

My aunt backed the Buick out of the garage at six forty-five the next morning. In the interests of time, and with her abject apology, we had a drive-through breakfast. I'd never told her, but during all the growing-up years of homemade, hot, healthy breakfasts, the occasional perfectly round yellow eggy thing on an English muffin and a cardboard sleeve of greasy home fries had been singular treats.

I told my aunt about the peculiar goings-on at Stasia's house the night before.

"Good heavens. You mean she's involved with the Medvedev person? That can't be good. I had the impression that she was afraid of him."

"I did too. And now he's gone who-knows-where in a private plane."

"Good riddance, I say. I hope he's gone for good. Perhaps he was just saying good-bye. You said she knew him as a child. And as we know, Karl is a friend of his."

"I hope it's something that simple," I said. "It's too

early for Stasia to be on her bench, but I really need to get in touch with her today to pick up Tatiana."

"You're right. I'd like to get the doll settled in the display case this afternoon. Stasia'll probably be along later. Don't worry. I know she's excited about displaying her after all these years."

At precisely seven o'clock we passed between the Ionic pillars in front of the main library and she inserted her key into the lock, pressed her employee number into a keypad, and an access number into another. A buzzer sounded and we went inside.

"I love the smell of this place," I said.

She took a deep breath. "Books," she said. "Books and magazines. Paper and ink. You love the printed word. Kindles and Nooks have their place, but they don't have that smell."

A couple of men from the Friends of the Library volunteers showed up a few minutes after we got there and were assigned to move tables and chairs onto the main floor to conform to the neatly drawn layout my aunt had prepared. Earlier in the week the rental company had dropped off cartons of snowy-white tablecloths, silverware and extra teacups and plates for those not fortunate enough, or important enough, to rate the expensive Canton china setups.

By the time Pete and Fire Marshal Jim Lynch arrived at eight, the library was buzzing with activity. Pete got right to work inspecting the security alarm system, the video cameras—both visible and hidden—and the door and window locks. He walked up and down each aisle, checked the stacks, the basement, the employees' break room. The fire marshal examined the sprinkler system, the fire extinguishers, the exits, and probably every single electrical outlet in the building. As I'd observed before, Salem's main library would undoubtedly be the safest place in the city—maybe the whole state—on Saturday.

By eight-thirty in the morning, the regular staff had arrived and early patrons began to drift in. After some minor confusion and questions about the roped-off tea party area, things seemed to be moving along to Aunt Ibby's satisfaction. "Let's go along to the tearoom now, Maralee," she said. "We'll be able to fit one of the carts into the Buick, and Karl will follow along with the other in his Jeep."

We climbed into the Buick and fastened our seat belts. I waited expectantly for my aunt to start the engine, but instead there was a long pause. "Maralee," she said, "I've been thinking."

I knew that tone of voice, and sighed. "Okay. Spill it. Whatever it is, I'm guessing it's trouble."

"Not really." She started the Buick and we rolled smoothly onto Essex Street—heading the wrong way. "It's still early. We know Boris is far away. Karl has been at the shop for hours. Let's drive past that house Boris and Karl are sharing. Just take a little look around. Hmmm?"

"We don't even know where it is," I protested, then caught her sly smile. "Or do we?"

"I was curious, you know? I had Karl's address from a sweet thank-you note he'd sent me. It's not too far from here. Look"—she pointed to the backseat—"I have Karl's cookie tray. If anyone says anything about us being there, I'll just say we're returning his nice tray."

"Well . . . maybe."

"Goody." She smiled. "Here we are." We'd pulled up into the gravel driveway of a medium-sized white saltbox house. "Hurry up. We don't have all day." She reached into the backseat, retrieved the silver tray and headed for the front porch.

I tagged along behind her. "What are we going to do? Peek in windows? What?"

"I have it all figured out." She whispered, even though there was no one around to hear. "I'll stand here and pretend to ring the doorbell. You go out back and look around. In the windows or whatever." Broad wink. "Maybe you'll see a way to get inside. If I see anyone coming, I'll really ring the doorbell and you just scoot over to the next street, and I'll pick you up there. Simple."

"*Simple* is right," I said. "You and I are *simple* to even think about doing this."

"As long as we're already here," she said in a most reasonable tone, "what harm can it do?"

So we did it, of course. Getting inside was easy. New Englanders are notorious for leaving doors unlocked. Probably even more common than the old key-under-the-flowerpot trick. The back door opened with the tiniest push. There were tall hedges all around the yard. Sure that no one could see me, I slipped inside. I was in a kitchen. Looked kind of small for a chef's place, neat and tidy, with nothing on the counter except a toaster and a telephone. The OLD MESSAGE light on the phone blinked invitingly. I pointed a tentative finger and pushed. An accented voice spoke.

"Karl. This message is for Boris. He's not answering

his phone. This is Dimitri. Tell him, the gardeners have planted the seeds. The harvest begins on Saturday afternoon at four o'clock."

As I stood there, frozen, trying to make sense of what I'd heard, the doorbell buzzed and buzzed again. Aunt Ibby was sending the get-out-of-there-fast signal. Before I could turn away from the counter, I saw the swirling colors on the side of the chrome toaster. The little girl in a blue dress rode on a wooden horse. The bear was close behind her.

I ran out the door, across the yard, through the hedges onto a side street. With my heart pounding, I tried to look nonchalant as the Buick came into sight.

"Come on. Get in," she said, holding the door open for me.

"What happened?" I said. "Why did you ring the doorbell?"

"A police car went by, with lights flashing. False alarm, I guess. Sorry."

"Any problems?" she asked.

"Piece of cake," I lied.

"Did you learn anything?"

"I don't know," I admitted. "I'll tell you later. And please don't have any more great ideas today."

We pulled into the tearoom's parking lot just as another car pulled out of the space closest to the front door. "What good luck," my aunt said as she backed into the slot. "Everything is falling into place so nicely." She picked up Karl's tray once again and we were barely inside the restaurant when the police car—red, white

and blue lights flashing—came to a stop in the driveway.
Pete and a uniformed officer got out, and, almost at a
dead run, entered the building, showed badges to the
flustered hostess and pushed through the louvered
kitchen door.

The typical background sounds of a lunch crowd, the
hum of conversation, the clinking of spoons on cups,
stopped instantly. The room was silent. Then from the
kitchen came a chilling wail.

"*Noooo!* Please, no!"

Amidst the silence the louvered door swung open
again. Pete led the handcuffed man past astonished
diners. As they passed us, we could hear the officer's low
monotone. "'You have the right to remain silent. . . .'"

Tears streamed from Karl Smith's pale blue eyes. "I
didn't kill him. It wasn't me. I swear." Catching sight of
us standing there, he called out, "Ibby, I'm so sorry! I've
spoiled your party. I'm sorry. I'm sorry."

"'If you cannot afford an attorney, one will be appointed for you. . . .'"

Pete acknowledged our presence with a curt nod. He
held the door open for the other two men, opened the
rear door of the cruiser and, with his hand on Karl's
head, guided him into the backseat. With police car
sirens blaring, they were gone.

We looked at each other. "What are we going to do
now?" I whispered.

Aunt Ibby signaled the hostess. "The best thing to do
at a time like this," she said as we followed the still-
shaken woman to a table for two, "is to have a nice cup
of tea and think things out."

She was right, of course. We sipped Darjeeling tea and

nibbled thin sandwiches of smoked salmon, with chive cream cheese and cucumbers, and thought things out.

"Obviously, our friend Karl is in serious trouble," she said. "Whether he is or is not guilty of a crime—and I believe he is not—we cannot count on his help for our party, can we?"

"We cannot." I agreed. "And I doubt that the cooks here can handle a special order like ours, considering that they won't know if they even have jobs. Is there another place where we can get Russian pastries by tomorrow afternoon? Boston, maybe?"

"Nonsense. I have several of his very best recipes," she said. "We'll need to use both ovens, yours and mine. We can prepare all we'll need."

"You're welcome to the oven, but as you know, I'm lacking in the cooking-skills department."

"Don't worry. You'll be fine. Now about the pastry carts, I'm quite sure Karl has left word that we're to borrow them."

"We'll have to make two trips," I said. "We'll take one cart now and drop it off at the library. Then we'll go home and you pick up my car and get started on shopping for baking supplies. I'll take the Buick and get the other cart and try to round up Stasia."

I hadn't yet told her what I'd heard—and seen—on our recent housebreaking adventure, but decided it could wait until we'd implemented the current plans. First the hostess recruited one of the cooks to help us put the cart in the Buick and we dropped it off at the library before continuing to Winter Street. On the way past the Common I looked for Stasia on her bench, but it was empty except for a couple of pigeons. I reluctantly handed my aunt the keys to the 'Vette—I don't really like anyone else to drive it—and slid behind the wheel of the Buick.

The second cart transfer went just as smoothly as the first. Things were humming along at the library, and colorful, oversized posters of the proposed new bookmobile were already in place.

I headed back to the Common, hoping to see the familiar orange hair and bright dress in the usual spot. No such luck. I drove all the way around the square surrounding the park, just in case she'd decided to try a different spot for palmistry. No Stasia.

I wished I could talk to Pete about what to do next—especially about what in the world was going on with Karl—but I knew that he was much too busy. I hadn't figured out how to tell him about the message on Karl's phone yet. I was pretty sure it might be important. But I knew I'd have to tell him how I'd gotten the information, and I was not looking forward to that conversation.

I'll just take a ride over to her house, I thought. *If her scooter's out front, there'd be no harm in knocking on the door. We do need that doll.*

So that's what I did. I parked right in front of the gate, where the pink scooter was chained to the fence, and walked up onto the narrow porch. I knocked on the door. Waited. Knocked again, louder. "Stasia," I called, my face close to the door. "You okay?" All was quiet.

Maybe she's in a back bedroom. Maybe's she's sick. I started around the side of the building. I tried to look into the windows, but the tinted glass was backed by heavy draperies. There was a back door and it, too, was pink. I knocked. Nothing. I stood there, thinking of my next option when I heard a soft "meow." I looked around and saw a small gray cat, daintily walking along the fence. She stopped and hopped down onto the top of an over-flowing trash can. "Meow," she said again.

The cat began to dig at the newspapers and aluminum cans piled in the can. As I watched, a tiny paw flipped something brown onto the ground. Litter-conscious me hurried across the sparse lawn and picked it up. I recognized it immediately.

Poor little Cuckoo. She was missing a foot and her head looked crooked, but it was my cuckoo. The cat jumped down to the ground, and I hastily brushed papers, sardine cans and rags aside, revealing the ruined clock. Springs and wheels and broken numbers, the pendulum smashed and even the sweet carved doors had been broken in half. I knew without doubt that it was beyond repair, even with skill like Paul Carbone's. Sadly, I covered those remains with a tattered dish towel and slipped what was left of the bird into my pocket.

The gray cat, with a look of what I could have sworn was sympathy, walked slowly away. "Little cat," I called softly, "did O'Ryan send you?"

She looked at me again. "Meh," she said.

I climbed into the Buick and drove home without the doll, without Stasia and without any explanation of what was going on around me. I pulled my aunt's car into the garage, noting that the Stingray had made it safely home too. I admit I took a quick turn around it—just to be sure all was well with that shimmering Laguna Blue finish—then hurried to the house.

As soon as I opened the door, I could hear Aunt Ibby humming in the kitchen. That meant that despite the morning's drama, she was happily involved in food preparation. "Did you get everything you need?" I asked.

"I did," she said. "Have you heard anything about poor Karl? Did you deliver the second cart? How does the library look? Did you see Stasia?"

"No, yes, fine, and no," I told her. "I even went to her house. Couldn't find her anywhere. What shall we do about the doll?"

"Why, Tatiana and her wardrobe are here. The whole package was on the front steps when I got home. I thought you'd carelessly dropped it off there. I was going to scold you for it."

"Not me. I'd never do that. But the main thing is, the doll and dresses are safely here." I was relieved and annoyed at the same time. "I suppose Stasia dropped them off. Have *you* heard anything about Karl? I had the radio on in the car and I didn't hear a word about it."

"No. I'd hoped you might have heard something from Pete."

"Not yet. Is your date with Mr. Pennington still on?"

"Dear Rupert. He's so understanding. I explained what was happening and begged off. He's going to call me later.

"What can I do?"

"Food prep, my dear. It will be a good experience for you. Some of the pastry recipes call for the dough to be mixed in a food processor and then chilled overnight. All you need to do is follow the directions."

I didn't believe for a minute that I was in for a "good experience," but I was willing to try my best—for Aunt Ibby and the bookmobile. Personally, I would have loaded those trays up with goodies from the closest Italian bakery and plenty of chocolate. Who would know the difference?

I carried the food-processing thing up to my own kitchen, along with a sheet of instructions, a bag full of ingredients and a recipe. I put on one of Aunt Ibby's aprons (the one with the words *Cat Mom*), then sat down on a tall stool to figure it all out. Eye-glazing bewilderment was quickly followed by panicked uncertainty. I put the instruction sheet aside and stared at the phone. *Call me. Pete.*

It rang.

"Pete? What's going on? There's nothing on the news yet. Is Karl really under arrest?"

"He sure is. Murder one. Sorry you and Miss Russell had to see all that. I know she likes the guy."

"Can't you tell me anything at all about what's going on? Karl's been arrested and Stasia is missing, and somebody smashed the cuckoo clock, and . . ."

"What did you say about Stasia? She's missing?"

"Yes. I went over there, and . . ."

"What do you mean you went over there? You promised to stay out of all this." Cop voice, big-time.

"I had to get the doll for the library."

"Oh, Lee. What am I going to do with you? Stay put. I'll be out of here in a few minutes. I'm coming over. I'll tell you what I can. It'll be on the five o'clock news anyway. This place is crawling with press."

By the time O'Ryan ran for the door, signaling Pete's arrival, I had the processor instructions pretty well figured out. It wasn't much different from reading a motor manual. I'd located the electric shock warning signal, the vertically projecting motor shaft, the circuit breaker and the feed blade. I'd even identified the dough blade I'd be using tonight.

Piece of cake. Or, in this case, piece of torte. Of course I hadn't read the recipe yet.

I'd expected Pete to come in the back way and use his key, but I heard his footsteps outside the kitchen door and realized that he must have stopped downstairs to see Aunt Ibby first. He and O'Ryan came in together. O'Ryan headed for his food bowl while Pete gave me a quick kiss, tossed his jacket on the back of a chair and took the stool beside me. "What's up with the apron? Looks good on you. Very domestic."

"It's all an act," I said. "Please tell me what's going on. I'm totally confused."

He glanced at the blank screen of the TV. "News'll be on in about ten minutes," he said, "and you can see it in living color. But here's what we've got. Smith's DNA came back a match with the vomit specimen from the Dillon murder location. That puts him at the crime scene. It's enough for an arrest."

"He says he's innocent. That he didn't kill anybody. We heard him say so."

Pete shrugged and raised an eyebrow. "They all say that. He lawyered up right away. High-priced top attorney. He'll be defended well. But, Lee, it doesn't look good for him."

"You talked to Aunt Ibby?"

"I did, and she looked as close to tears as I've ever seen her. I tried to talk her out of this cooking project, but she says she needs to keep her mind off Karl." He looked at the bags of flour and sugar lined up on the counter. "She's got you involved too, I see."

"Afraid so."

"Okay. Now tell me what makes you think Stasia is missing? You say you went to her house?" The look was disapproving. Very disapproving.

"I did. Had to. She was supposed to bring the doll back—for the display at the library, you know? I looked for her at the usual place—even looked in different parts of the Common. No luck. I knew you had your hands full . . . so . . ." I put down the feed blade and spread my hands apart. "Anyway, it was broad daylight in a perfectly safe neighborhood. Your own sister lives there."

He wasn't buying it. "First of all, there's no such thing as a perfectly safe neighborhood, including this one, which you of all people should know. So go on. What happened at Stasia's house?"

I told him about knocking on the door, walking around, peeking in windows and getting no response. He just nodded. "All this creeping around where you have no business being was just about getting that doll back, I suppose." His cop voice's tone was classic disapproval.

"It really was. And the weird thing is, she'd already brought the doll back anyway. Aunt Ibby found it on the front steps this morning."

"Seems like a careless way to handle a valuable antique. Go on."

He sat up straight when I got to the part about the smashed cuckoo clock. "What?"

"Smithereens," I said. "Total loss. Wait a minute. I'll show you." I went into the bedroom and retrieved the remains of poor Cuckoo from my pocket. I laid it on the counter. "There. Pitiful, isn't it?"

He poked the little brown thing with a tentative finger. "Why would she do this? You said she particularly wanted the clock. It was smashed so badly it couldn't be repaired?"

"Like somebody took a sledgehammer to the poor thing."

"Wait a minute. Why were you looking into Stasia's trash barrel in the first place?"

I'd avoided mentioning the small gray cat so far. What could I say? That I'd met a friend of O'Ryan's who'd pointed it out?

"There was this cat digging around in the trash. I suppose she was looking for something to eat. She knocked a broken part of the clock onto the ground. That's all."

"Strange," he said.

O'Ryan looked up from his bowl and said, "Meh."

I took a deep breath. "Pete," I said, "there's something I need to tell you, and I don't want to tell you right now how I know about it. Is that okay?"

"Another vision, I suppose," he said. "Shoot."

Good. He's going to blame the visions. "It's just kind of a little message," I said. "I have no idea what it means if anything."

"Go ahead." He sounded impatient. I didn't blame him.

"It's for Boris, I think. Here it is. 'The gardeners have planted the seeds. The harvest begins on Saturday afternoon at four o'clock.' Does it mean anything?"

"Maybe," he said. "Maybe it does. Don't worry about it—and thanks for telling me."

CHAPTER 39

Pete was right about the TV news having the story about Karl's arrest for the murder of Eric Dillon. We both went downstairs so that we could be with Aunt Ibby while she watched her friend, cuffed and orange jump-suited, standing before a judge. I noticed that she'd closed her eyes through most of it.

Scott Palmer did the standup afterward from in front of the county courthouse. "Local restauranteur Karl Smith is currently housed in the county jail," he said in the breathless voice he used for such occasions—not at all like the jock voice he used for the high-school foot-ball games or the uptown, phony, big-network voice he used for the rip-and-read national news stories that came over the wire. "Smith is the owner-manager of Salem's popular Russian Tea Experience. He was ar-rested this morning at that location. We have several cell phone videos of the actual arrest taken by patrons of the restaurant at noon today."

I hadn't thought about that. Should have known there'd be the ever-present amateur videographers around. There were at least three videos—each one worse and sadder than the one before. There was even a close-up of Karl with tears rolling down his cheeks. In another we saw Aunt Ibby and me in the background and heard the officer reciting the Miranda rights as Karl stumbled out the door of his restaurant—possibly for the last time.

"I know he's your friend, Miss Russell," Pete said. "I'm sorry about all this. He has an excellent lawyer and he'll get a fair trial, I promise you. But please be prepared for the worst. There's evidence that positively places him at the crime scene."

"Ha!" Aunt Ibby said. "At the scene isn't the same thing as committing the crime, is it?"

"You're right," Pete said. "But for now, it's all we've got. If Karl and his lawyer can prove he didn't do it, you can be sure we'll find out who did."

"I'll hold you to your word on that. For now, I have a tea party to run. Cookies to bake. A doll to dress." She pulled the apron off and hung it on its hook behind the pantry door. "Maralee, the library will be closing soon. I'm going to take Tatiana and dash over there to meet Rupert."

Pete looked at me. "Who's Tatiana?"

"Stasia's doll. Rhonda says she named it after the grand duchess's sister."

He nodded as though he understood what I was talking about. "Right. Rhonda and the grand duchess. Okay. Let's go upstairs and play with the food processor."

O'Ryan followed us back to my kitchen, where I inserted the dough blade into the mixer, put my largest green Pyrex bowl on the counter, while Pete read the recipe to me aloud. It took us over an hour. Most of the granite countertop was dusted with flour and I had a generous smudge of butter on my nose, but we'd produced three bowls of perfectly processed dough—each in a different flavor. Sparkling in their plastic wrap covers, they looked quite pretty on the refrigerator shelf. I was proud of myself. Aunt Ibby was right. All in all, it had been a good experience for me—though not one I intended to repeat any time soon.

It was still early, and Pete and I were in the process of discussing what else we might do with the rest of our evening when my phone buzzed. Caller ID identified my aunt.

"Maralee, I just opened Tatiana's box and there's something quite disturbing in it."

"What's wrong?"

"There's a note from Stasia. She's gone away to join her husband."

"I don't understand. Stasia isn't married. What does the note say?"

"Is Pete still there?" she asked. "Maybe you two ought to come over here and look at this."

Pete had moved close enough to me to overhear part of the conversation. He motioned for me to hand him the cell. "We'll be right there, Miss Russell," he told my aunt. "Don't touch anything else in that box." He handed back my phone. "Come on."

I washed my hands and grabbed my jacket. I'd deal with the mess in the kitchen later. Pete was already on his way downstairs and O'Ryan had returned to his windowsill perch.

When we got to the library, the brown packing box

containing Tatiana and her wardrobe was on one of the pastry carts. The glass door of the display case was open, a blowup copy of the photo of the grand duchess wearing the blue dress from the *Anastasia's Album* book posted on the background.

"I haven't touched anything but the note," she said, waving a piece of lined paper. "Here it is."

Pete reached for the note and, holding it by the edges, read it aloud.

> *Dear Miss Russell and Lee,*
>   *Here's Tatiana. I can't take her with me and I know you'll find a safe place for her. My husband has come for me and we are going home to Russia. Don't worry about me. We have more money than you've ever dreamed of and will live in a great house where no one will find us. My husband broke the clock. I'm sorry. Sometimes he has a bad temper.*
>   *Stasia Novikova Ivanov*

"Ivanov! My God," Pete said. "She's married to Boris Medvedev."

"Medvedev is really Ivanov?" my aunt asked.

"Your friend St. John gave us that information last week," Pete said. "Boris took Medvedev as his professional wrestling name. We didn't know about the wife though. We traced the private jet, so we know exactly where Medvedev went last night. She's probably gone to meet him. I'd better get back to the station and follow through on this. I don't like it one damned bit." He put the note on top of the doll and picked up the box. "Sorry.

I'm going to have to ask your permission to take"—he looked down at the doll—"Tatiana here with me."

"Of course if you must. But please be careful with her." My aunt gave a long sigh.

"They must have figured out how to hack into Dillon's laptop," I said. "The location of the other horse . . . the one with the egg in it—it must be in his manuscript."

"She's gone to meet him in Colorado," my aunt said. "Are we right?"

But Pete was already on his way out the door. "See that Lee gets home, will you?"

We finished setting up a table with a map of Russia on an easel, along with the carved matryoshkas and the chess pieces, and we closed the display cabinet, sans Tatiana. I rode back to Winter Street with Aunt Ibby.

"Rupert is going to pick me up shortly, dear, if you don't mind. It's still early enough for us to go to dinner. It'll help to get my mind off Karl. I do hope he isn't involved in any of Boris's shenanigans."

"I hope not," I said, but I said it without much hope. After all, Karl Smith was the one who'd driven Boris Medvedev—or Ivanov—to the getaway plane.

I'd barely climbed the stairs to my apartment when my phone buzzed. It was Pete.

"Sorry to race off like that, but we have to move fast on this. You don't happen to have a recent picture of Stasia, do you? I'm on my way to Logan Airport. Guessing she's gone to Colorado. Got to see if Homeland Security there can tell us what flight she was on. They track everything and everybody."

"I do. I'll send it to your phone right now. I hope you can stop her before they do anything . . . foolish."

"I hope so. Love you. Bye."

I had to break my promise to Stasia, but I sent Pete the photo of her with Tatiana. It was a beautiful picture. I hoped she'd get to see it someday. I loaded the dishwasher and swept the kitchen floor. The little brown bird was still on the counter, slightly dusted with cinnamon. I couldn't bring myself to throw her away, so I tucked her into one of the secret compartments in my bureau. She was in there, next to a lucky quarter Pete gave me once, and a white satin-covered button from an old wedding dress. I save the darnedest things. I polished the countertop and re-read the directions to the food processor, trying to take my mind off everything that was going on. Maybe it would be fun to try the other blades someday.

It was after eleven when O'Ryan and I went to bed. I hadn't heard Aunt Ibby come in yet, but she and Mr. Pennington often stayed out quite late. I turned on the news, wondering if there'd be anything new on Karl Smith's arrest. It was pretty much the same as the earlier broadcast, with the addition of some interviews with some of the Russian Tea Experience staff who all spoke highly of their employer—and publicly worried about their jobs.

I usually manage to stay awake long enough to catch the beginning of River's show, but I felt myself dozing off when her theme music, *Danse macabre, Opus 40*, began. I noticed that Marty had used my doll photo, with a caption announcing the Library Bookmobile Benefit High Tea, in the bumper. I smiled in the darkness as I clicked the TV off. "Good night, cat," I said, "and thanks for sending your little gray friend to see me today."

"Meh," he said, which I took as an acknowledgment that I was right.

O'Ryan wasn't as ready for sleep as I was and he made that clear by nibbling on my ear. I pushed him away. "Go to sleep, fur ball," I said, "or go back in the kitchen and look out the window."

He obeyed that time. I watched in the tilted mirror as he stalked across the room and hopped up onto the windowsill. He didn't stretch out and gaze at the moon though. He sat there on the sill and meowed. Loudly.

I pulled a pillow over my head, but it didn't drown out the increasingly piteous wails coming from the kitchen. I began to feel guilty. Suppose he was in pain? Maybe he had a splinter in his paw or a toothache. I climbed out of bed, put the kitchen light on and sat in the chair beside the cat. I stroked his back, then scratched beneath his chin—two activities he likes very much. The meows immediately changed to purrs.

"Okay, now that you've got me wide-awake," I said as he leaned into the stroking hand, "what do you want?"

He moved from the windowsill to my lap, and from there to the floor. He started across the room toward the hall. He looked back at me in a way that clearly meant to follow him.

"All right. Here I come." I padded along behind him, thinking it was a good thing nobody could see me— playing follow the leader with a cat in the middle of the night. He led me to the living room and stood immobile in the middle of the room, facing the horse.

The room was dark, but there was enough light from streetlights and a brilliant half-moon to give a luminous glow to the horse's white mane and the polished leaves of philodendron and bird's-nest fern.

"Lovely," I said. "Thanks for sharing this with me. Can I go back to bed now?"

He didn't move, but fixed those golden eyes on a spot above the horse. It was, of course, just a spot on plain, old, ordinary window glass. I followed his gaze. The pinpoints of light and the swirling colors began.

I saw a room, one I was sure I'd never seen before. It was an ordinary living room—a couch with throw pillows, two chairs, a coffee table, with a bowl of candy on it. There was a large suitcase next to the door. The view shifted, exactly the way a TV camera pans around a set. Close-up of the throw pillows. Both pink. Close-up of the candy bowl. Not candy, but wrapped oblongs of bubblegum.

Stasia's house!

There was a swirl of colors and I saw another room. A bedroom this time. A small night-light glowed pink. There was a figure on the bed.

Is it Stasia? I have to get closer.

In an instant it was as though I was hovering over her. It was Stasia—blood streaming from a cut on her forehead, eyes swollen shut, mouth covered with gray tape. Her legs were bound together with that same gray tape, arms behind her back.

Is she alive?

A tiny flicker of the bruised eyelids answered my unspoken question. The scene began to fade.

Don't go away! What am I supposed to do?

I was looking at plain window glass in my own dark living room. *Is this vision real? River says they can show the past, the present or the future. Which is this? Dear God, what if it's the present?*

I had to make a fast decision. Aunt Ibby wasn't home. Pete was on his way to Boston. River was on live TV. Even Nigel was probably on a plane. No one to call—no one to help me decide. I couldn't call 911. What would I say? I have visions and I think there's a woman tied up in her house across town? I had to find out if what I saw in the window was happening now, or like so many other visions, something that happened in the past.

I dressed and grabbed my purse, phone, flashlight and keys. Telling myself I was crazy, all the way down the stairs, I broke into a dead run to the garage, backed my car out and took off.

CHAPTER 40

Stasia's street was deadly quiet. No traffic, very few lights. I parked in front of the house and walked up to the porch. It was so quiet my footsteps on the wooden floorboards sounded like firecrackers. I knocked, much as I had earlier that same day, and called, "Stasia?" There was no reply. Had I really expected one? I walked all the way around the house again, deliberately not looking at the trash can. I knocked on the back door and thought I heard something. A moan? A cry? Or just the wind?

I returned to the front of the house with a feeling of panic beginning to build. I wasn't sure I should break into the house, not sure I'd even know how. A gentle "meow" sounded from behind me and I stopped to pat the gray cat.

"I'm glad to see you," I said. "Do you know how to get in here?"

I'm turning into a crazy, old cat lady—talking to every cat I see.

The cat turned abruptly away from me and walked

to a flowerpot on the top step, where a scraggly pink geranium leaned to one side. The small gray paw snaked out, scratching at the saucer beneath the clay pot. It took about two seconds to figure out what she was showing me. The old key-under-the-flowerpot trick. Everybody does it. I used to hide one under a bird-of-paradise on my patio in Florida. I moved the pot, picked up the key and opened Stasia's pink front door.

It's not breaking and entering if you have a key, is it?

Closing the door behind me, I switched on the flashlight. I was in the right place. The couch, the pink pillows, it was all the same as the room in my vision. I heard a sound from the next room and this time I was sure it was a moan.

Stasia was on the bed, just as I'd seen her. Her mouth was covered with tape; blood streaked her forehead, matting the orange hair. Her arms and legs were tightly bound with tape.

"Stasia," I whispered her name; then again, more loudly. "Stasia! It's me. Lee." The eyes opened in the battered face and she moaned again. I peeled the tape back from her mouth as gently as I could, knowing it must hurt. Her lips were swollen, one gold tooth broken. I hit 911 on my phone and, at the same time, tried to free her arms. "You're going to be okay," I said, over and over again. "You're going to be okay."

I gave the 911 operator the address and told her we needed an ambulance and the police. "They're on the way," she said. "Are you safe where you are?"

I hadn't thought about that. Suppose whoever did

this to Stasia came back? "I don't know," I said. "Please tell them to hurry."

"On the way," she said. "I'll stay on the line with you."

I turned Stasia onto her side and worked one of her arms free. The pink chenille bedspread was soiled where'd she'd been lying. "My God, Stasia, how long have you been here like this? Who did this to you?"

Her voice was a cracked whisper. "My husband. Boris. He . . . he hit me." Tears mixed with the blood on her face. "I didn't know. I thought we were going away together. All these years. All these plans."

I heard sirens and saw the flashing lights. "Thank God, they're here, Operator. Thank you." I hung up, ran to open the front door and hit Pete's number.

"Pete. I'm at Stasia's. She's here. She's hurt. She never went to the airport. Boris beat her, Pete. She's been right here since Thursday night."

"Are you all right?"

"Yes. I'm fine. The police and the ambulance are here now. Come as soon as you can. Will you call Aunt Ibby for me and tell her what's going on—and that I'm okay?"

I hung up and led the men with a stretcher to Stasia's room.

Everything moved quickly after that. Stasia was wheeled into the waiting ambulance. They let me ride with her, holding her hand as one EMT monitored her blood pressure and another administered oxygen. With the police car leading the way, we headed for the Salem Hospital emergency room.

"Did Karl bring Tatiana to you?" She strained to get the words through swollen lips.

Karl?

"Yes, Stasia. Tatiana is fine. We have her."

"Good." She tried to smile. "We were going to Russia, Lee. To live like the czars, he said." Tears, mixed with the drying blood on her cheek, stained the white sheet. "He lied. Always lied. Now he's gone to get it. The last one."

"Where is it, Stasia? Where did he go?"

No reply. The ambulance rolled to a stop and everything moved quickly, efficiently. Stasia disappeared on a rolling gurney through automatic doors.

"May I come with her? She's very frightened."

"The police will want to talk to you, miss. Just go to the waiting room."

There were about a dozen people in the large, bleak room. Some of them looked as though they'd been waiting for a long time. Curious stares followed me as a uniformed officer motioned me to the far end of the room.

"Sit down, miss. I'll be recording your statement. What's your name?"

Name, address, occupation—these are easy. How am I going to explain why I was there? A cat sent me, and another cat showed me how to get in?

"Why were you there?"

"I was very worried about her. She's involved in an event at the library tomorrow—today. I couldn't get in touch with her. So I went to her house."

True.

"Was the door unlocked?"

"No. She kept the key under a flowerpot."

True.

He shook his head. "Wish people wouldn't do that. Okay. Was she able to tell you anything? Who did this to her?"

"She said it was her husband."

Another headshake, but no comment. "You know him?"

"I've never met him."

True. Pete, hurry up and help me out here.

Aunt Ibby and Pete arrived at the same time. Pete had called her on his way back to Salem. My aunt swooped into the room, rushing past interested onlookers to embrace me. "Excuse me, George," she said to the officer. "This is my niece."

"Miss Russell." He tipped his hat, then turned to Pete. "Detective, this lady discovered the victim. She called 911."

"It's okay," Pete said. "I know her. I'll take over here. Chief Whaley's been informed."

Pete turned to me. He didn't look pleased. Extreme cop face in place. "What were you thinking, going over there alone in the middle of the night? I guess you know the chief isn't happy about this."

"I . . . I knew something was wrong. You were gone. Aunt Ibby wasn't home. Stasia needed help. Right away."

His expression softened. "You 'saw' something."

"I did." I looked around the room at questioning faces. "I can't talk about it here."

"I know. You two go along home and I'll come by when I finish up here."

My aunt took my hand. "Come along, Maralee. Dear

Rupert has gone to stay with your car to be sure it doesn't come to any harm. I'll drive you there. Then we'll go home and wait for Pete."

There's something so comforting about having someone in control, someone who knows how to take charge in a bad situation. I'm blessed to have Aunt Ibby.

At her direction Mr. Pennington, indeed, had gone to stand guard over my precious car. When we arrived, there he stood in the middle of the street, smiling, directing traffic around it—with dramatic Shakespearean bows and flourishes. Then, with Aunt Ibby's Buick, Mr. Pennington's Lincoln, and my Corvette, we formed a convoy of sorts and headed back to Winter Street.

Once at home, my aunt sent me upstairs to retrieve the three chilled bowls of cookie dough and handed out aprons. Within fifteen minutes, she'd organized the three of us into an assembly line of cookie makers. (Never mind that I had visions of Lucy and Ethel at that point.)

By the time Pete arrived, both ovens were producing perfectly browned circles, braids and mounds. Cooling racks, upstairs and down, held hundreds of examples of authentic-looking tearoom treats and the whole house smelled wonderful. At any other time this might have been fun, but the sad and strange events of that long day cast a pall of gloom over it all.

I was still watching over the oven in my kitchen, setting the timer with each batch. Pete came upstairs to help me, leaving my aunt and Mr. Pennington to finish their cooking and to tend to the packaging of the cooled finished products.

"Is Stasia going to be all right?"

"Her injuries looked a lot worse than they are," he said. "Once they got her cleaned up, it wasn't so bad. She'll be hurting for a while. Her nose is broken and one arm is sprained, but she'll be okay. Physically, at least."

"And otherwise?"

"We don't know yet how much she's involved with the husband's criminal operations."

"Some pretty bad stuff?"

"New Scotland Yard sent us some transcripts of his connections over there in the old KGB and in that 'brotherhood' he's part of. Back when Boris's wrestling career was winding down, he was getting well known in some circles as a 'fixer.' His underground contacts came in handy and there were plenty of people wanting things fixed. Boris was big enough, and mean enough, to do absolutely anything for enough money. Old Boris was the kind of 'fixer' who gets phony documents for terrorists, and acquires plastic explosives for people who want to blow up planes. There's also a matter of priceless artwork stolen from various museums around the globe. He may be involved with that too."

"I can't imagine how Stasia got tangled up with such a person."

He hesitated and I wondered how much of this he could share with me.

"Pete," I said, "you know Aunt Ibby and I are mixed up in this whole mess. Have been ever since the beginning, when we bought the storage locker."

"I know that," he said. "You've both been a big help—even though you were meddling in things you shouldn't have been. The truth is, if you hadn't rushed out in the middle of the night and found Stasia . . . I hate to think of what could have happened." He brushed baking powder from my cheek with gentle fingers. "You're the hero of it all, you know."

"What do you mean?"

"Saving Stasia just when you did prevented Boris from taking some innocent lives. And that vision you had? About the gardeners and the harvest? That gave us the location of what came close to being a disaster."

I guess I'll have to tell him eventually that it wasn't exactly a vision . . . more like a B and E.

"You and your aunt will never get credit for all you did to solve this mess. I guess you know by now that the successful police work doesn't always make the papers. You read more about the failures."

"I see," I said, although I really didn't.

He took my hand. "I can tell you this much. Stasia will probably tell you herself anyway. She met him when she was fifteen," he said. "Medvedev was a big star. Her dad was a fan. She thought she was in love."

"That happens."

"He seduced her. Her parents found out and disowned her. When she turned sixteen, he took her with him to Russia and married her there, under his real name—Ivanov. That's when she stopped writing to her friend Colleen."

I nodded, finally understanding. "She couldn't let anyone know what her husband was doing. So young to be mixed up in such a mess. Poor Stasia." I thought of the way she could shut down—go blank sometimes. Self-protection, I guess. "Do you know how Boris was able to open Dillon's manuscript without the password page from the notebook?" I wondered. "I know those English-to-Russian pages were for him, not Karl."

"Stasia said she helped him with that. She remembered that the missing page had American girls' names on it, with seven digit numbers. Boris's old KGB hacking experts broke that code in a day."

"So Dillon had finished the book? The answers were all in there?"

"All of it. Homeland Security has a transcript. Dillon found out that the first three eggs had been sold to an anonymous collector in Russia way back in the twenties or thirties—someone very high up in government. I don't know who. That's classified. When they learned that the doctor had an egg, they tried to buy that one too. He refused, so . . ." He made a slashing motion across his throat. "We figure some long-ago hired hand killed him and took it."

"What about the baker in Connecticut in the seventies? His egg was in the wedding cake."

"The same family in Russia was still collecting the czar's treasures. They wanted more of the lost eggs. Boris landed the contract and delivered one of them. He killed the baker." He looked around the kitchen. "Do I smell cookies burning?"

That was the end of that conversation. I rescued the cookies and put them on a cooling rack. Pete made coffee and we ate the ones that were a little bit burned, just like Lucy and Ethel.

By the time all of the cookies and tortes and tea cakes

were packed and refrigerated, the sun was up and the day of the Library Bookmobile Benefit High Tea was upon us. Pete made a quick run to the police station to pick up Tatiana, whose dresses all had to be carefully ironed again, after being examined for clues or contraband and found free of both. Aunt Ibby and I drove doll and dresses to the library in order to complete the planned doll display, and to supervise the unpacking, unfolding and precise placement of tablecloths and napkins. Fresh-flower arrangements had been delivered and pronounced perfect.

Mrs. Abney-Babcock, accompanied by a very large security guard and two white-gloved women, proceeded to unpack and put in place the cups, saucers and cake plates from the much-praised and promoted set of her great-grandmother's wedding china, to be enjoyed by the event's biggest donors. Library volunteers arranged the plain white, but serviceable, rented china to be used by the rest of the guests, while I positioned the colorful matryoshkas and chess pieces on the table where Aunt Ibby would preside over the samovar, the silver trays, sugar bowl and cream pitcher. Mr. Pennington had been pressed into service to pick Nigel up at Logan Airport at noon.

From all of our outward appearances, no one would guess that none of us had slept, or that Pete, via phone, Internet and wire service was coordinating a nationwide search for Boris Medvedev.

CHAPTER 41

I sat beside Aunt Ibby as she proudly dispensed fragrant citrus Russian tea from the beautifully molded spigot on the side of the silver samovar. "It looks as though it's a smashing success, don't you think, Maralee?" she whispered.

"Sure does," I agreed as I manipulated the sugar tongs, asking, "One lump or two?" to guests who passed by, carefully holding the precious blue-and-white cups. "Everyone seems to love the food. The press is interviewing people all over the place, and Tatiana is the star of the show. And look. All of the McKenna family is here."

"I saw them," Aunt Ibby said. "They're all so pleased to see Grandpa Nick's toys on display. The mayor could hardly believe that we had real English pastries, delivered fresh from Harrods this very morning. And I doubt that anyone but an expert could tell the difference between Karl's Russian treats and ours." We'd bowed to the constraints of time when it came to the requisite tiny sandwiches and had found a local caterer, who'd done a super last-minute job on the dainty tidbits.

"It's just too bad that Karl and Stasia couldn't be here to enjoy it."

She nodded sad agreement. "I know. I wish things had turned out differently for both of them."

When Mrs. Abney-Babcock took her turn to relieve me at the sugar bowl, I joined Pete and Nigel next to the front door. "Jolly good show, Lee," Nigel said. "Ibby knows how to throw a party, doesn't she?"

"You've been a wonderful help, Nigel," I said. "Traveling all this way, just to deliver pastries."

"Not *just to deliver pastries,* my dear. Your lovely aunt is reason enough for a man to make a transatlantic trip."

That made me blush. It's hard to think about a maiden aunt in her sixties who's apparently still "got it."

"Well, anyway," I said, "the mayor is very impressed. She says there's no mistaking Harrods demerara shortbread."

"You've been a big help to the department too, sir," Pete said. "The information you gave us helped a lot to get Lee, here, out of the doghouse with Chief Whaley, for snooping around where she didn't belong."

"Glad to help out, old man," Nigel said. "Thwarting a terrorist attack on an innocent amusement park before afternoon tea is no small feat."

He must have known by my expression that I had no idea what he was talking about. "Oh, dear, have I let the cat out of the bag? So sorry." He didn't look sorry at all, and I could have sworn he winked at me when he said it.

"Want to catch me up on things?" I asked Pete. "This sounds like something that will be in the newspapers soon enough."

"It might not," Pete said. "The ones we stop don't make news. The successful ones get all the press."

"Don't you think I deserve to know?"

"I do." His expression was serious. "If it wasn't for you getting involved, we would have been too late."

Nigel gave a slight bow. "Handed you a bit of a sticky wicket, have I? I'll just join the ladies at the tea table whilst you two youngsters sort it out. Ta-ta."

He glanced at Nigel's departing back. "Okay. Here it is. Between Stasia's being ticked off about the beating she took—and even more furious because he called her 'old' and 'fat' and said he had a younger bride in Russia ready to share his millions—and to top it off, he'd already smashed her cuckoo clock—and Karl Smith's spilling everything he knew, we were able to move on this before it turned to a real tragedy."

I gasped. "You're talking about a *real* attack. On the park with the old carousel."

"Right. He'd already had some of his goons disguised as gardeners plant bombs all around the perimeter of the park. It was your vision that tipped us off to the gardeners. When he got there early this morning, he phoned in the threat. Again, because of your tip, we knew he had the whole operation planned for four o'clock, Colorado time. As soon as the dogs started sniffing out the explosives, they'd planned to detonate a couple of them. In the confusion Boris and one of his badass friends from the brotherhood would saw the horse apart, grab the egg and join the crowd running from the park. As soon as they were out, they'd blow up the carousel, destroying the evidence, head for the airport and be home free."

"But you stopped them in time. Nobody got killed."

"Everybody's okay. He shouldn't have let Stasia in on the plan, but he figured as his wife she'd never have to testify against him. Like the man said, *'Cherchez la femme.'*"

"What about Karl? How in the world did he get involved in such a mess?"

"Smith was in some kind of church outreach program, teaching ex-prisoners how to get jobs in the outside world. He was teaching Boris how to cook." Pete, ever the cop, surveyed the room as he spoke. "Smith wanted to buy that restaurant, but had no money. Boris had contacts for big money—at really high interest. When Smith couldn't pay, he got roped into the trash-picking run and then the break-in at Paul's."

"I hope you're not going to tell me that Karl killed Eric Dillon."

He smiled and took my hand. "No, that was Boris. When Karl saw the body, he got sick."

Another question bothered me. "How did Boris know Eric Dillon was onto what they were doing?"

"Funny thing about that," Pete said. "According to Stasia, he didn't. He spotted Dillon outside the window. Killed him just so he wouldn't identify him and Smith. Took the laptop and destroyed the memory card, but he didn't know about the treasure books until it was in the papers." Pete shook his head. "Bad luck. Boris thought the egg was in your horse. So did Stasia. Dillon had already figured out that it wasn't. We think he just wanted a picture so he could easily pick out the twin horse back in Colorado. He'd already bought a plane ticket to Denver for the next morning."

"So Boris killed Dillon with the same kind of garrote

he'd used on the baker. Gruesome thing," I said. "I guess he thought it looked like bear's teeth."

Pete laughed. "Stasia says he was really mad when everyone blamed that old witch, Baba Yaga. He'd intended for them to blame a bear." He suddenly dropped my hand. "Oops. Excuse me, babe, I think I just saw a guy slipping one of those blue-and-white dishes into his pocket. Gotta go."

I watched as Pete approached a well-dressed, but red-faced, man and diplomatically retrieved the "accidentally" pocketed dish. I smiled and remembered that we'd planned extra security to make the library the safest place in Salem because we'd halfway expected a visit from a murderer—not a light-fingered, white-collar saucer snitcher.

Sipping tea from a plain white cup, I thought about that peaceful picture of the amusement park, where there certainly would have been families and kids. I knew there were lots of details to clear up among Pete and me and Aunt Ibby about this case.

Yes, I was calling it a *case*—just as though I was a real girl detective. I knew, too, that most of it would never be in the papers, and that we'd all keep what we knew among us three.

I was perfectly content to replay his words quietly in my mind— *"If it wasn't for you getting involved, we would have been too late."*

EPILOGUE

Eventually I did get most of the story. Pete told me all that he could without violating police department rules, Homeland Security mandates or New Scotland Yard confidences. The Colorado police apprehended Boris at the park before he'd had a chance to blow anything up, and Stasia was happy to testify against him. It seems there was more than one wife waiting in the wings. There were several Mrs. Ivanovs, each involved in one or another of his illicit schemes. Each of them, like Stasia, had expected to live a life of luxury in a Russian mansion with her multimillionaire husband, and each was willing to talk. Boris will live out his days in a maximum-security prison, guilty of the murders of Eric Dillon and Alex Chopiak, the baker, with even more trials pending. Dillon's stolen laptop is now in the hands of his publisher, so soon readers will know the whole story of the missing eggs.

Stasia's orange-haired, oddball Salem character persona was, as I'd suspected, an act. She was there simply to locate the locker. Boris knew that she'd recognize her grandparents' belongings, and that no one would ever peg the local crazy lady as part of an international crime ring. She didn't go to jail because she was helpful to the authorities, both here and overseas. On probation, she stayed in Salem and is often seen feeding the pigeons on the Common. She returned her hair to its natural salt-and-pepper gray, but was never able to kick her bubblegum habit. Tatiana went on a tour of American museums and arrangements have been made for her to visit Russia too.

Karl Smith now works in the kitchen of the county's newest correctional facility, and will be there for some time to come. St. Vladimir's is keeping the Russian Tea Experience open, using Karl's recipes and making enough money to show a little profit for the church. The library high tea put the bookmobile fund over the top and soon kids all over Salem will have the reading adventures Aunt Ibby has long envisioned for them. The Fabergé egg, valued at fifty million dollars, was safely nestled right where Grandpa Nick had hidden it so many years ago—inside my horse's twin. It was carefully extracted from the horse and it now belongs to the people in Colorado who'd had the foresight to preserve the precious, old carousel for the enjoyment of generations of kids.

Nigel St. John extended his stay in Salem for an extra week and has invited Aunt Ibby to spend next New Year's Eve with him in London. I've learned to make Russian tea cakes—those little powdered-sugar things—for Pete, who's been quite understanding about my interfering in his investigation. In fact, he thinks that if it all wasn't such a top secret international case, I'd probably get a medal.

Chief Whaley isn't buying it. Still thinks I'm a nosy pest. Maybe he's right.

I haven't seen the little gray cat again, but I have a feeling that someday I will. I told O'Ryan that, but he just said "meh" and licked my face.

From the *Tabitha Trumbull Book of
New England Cookery*
(Recipes adapted and edited by Isobel Russell)

Chocolate Chip Banana Bread

Back in the late-1800s, Captain Lorenzo Baker of Wellfleet, Massachusetts, was about to return home from a trip to Jamaica. Just before he left, he picked up a bunch of green bananas and tossed them into the cargo hold. Of course the bananas ripened nicely during the voyage home, and Wellfleet folks raved about the exotic, new fruit. Next trip out, and knowing a good thing when he tasted one, Captain Baker filled the hold with green bananas and steered straight for the Boston market. Orders poured in, and before long his voyages to the West Indies were strictly for bananas. By the last quarter of the nineteenth century, boats built especially for carrying bananas were being built; and with the advent of the railroad, people all around America could enjoy the novel delicacies.

Captain Baker, by the way, formed the Boston Fruit Company, which later became the United Fruit Company, and made himself a tidy fortune.

1¾ cups flour
2 tsp baking powder
½ tsp salt
¼ tsp baking soda
⅓ cup shortening
⅔ cup sugar
2 eggs
1 cup ripe, mashed bananas (2 to 3 bananas)
1 cup mini semisweet chocolate morsels

Sift together flour, baking powder, baking soda and salt. Beat shortening until creamy. Add sugar gradually and beat until light and fluffy. Add eggs and continue beating until well blended. Add flour mixture alternately with bananas, a small amount at a time, mixing after each addition enough to moisten dry ingredients. Stir in mini semisweet chocolate morsels. Turn into greased 9x5x3 loaf pan. Bake in 350-degree oven about 1 hour and 10 minutes or until done. Test with toothpick or cake tester after one hour.

Karl Smith's Russian Tea Cakes
(Pete's favorite)

1 cup soft butter
½ cup sifted confectioners' sugar
1 tsp vanilla
2¼ cups sifted all-purpose flour
¼ tsp salt
¾ finely chopped nuts
(More confectioners' sugar for finishing)

Mix together thoroughly the butter, confectioners' sugar and vanilla. Sift together the flour and salt and stir into the butter/sugar mixture. Add chopped nuts. Chill dough. Roll into one-inch balls and place them 2½ inches apart on an ungreased baking sheet. Bake at 400 degrees until set, but not brown—about 10 to 12 minutes. While still warm, roll in confectioners' sugar. Cool. Roll in confectioners' sugar again. Makes about 4 dozen 1½-inch cookies.

Love the Witch City Mysteries?
Keep reading for a sneak peek at

GRAVE ERRORS

Coming soon

from

Kensington Books

If you've ever been to my hometown of Salem, Massachusetts, during the month of October, you know how crazy it can be—and the closer you get to Halloween, the nuttier it becomes. The following week, though, is the exact opposite—kind of like a deflated balloon. The empty candy wrappers have been swept from the streets, the carved pumpkins have gone soft, with their jagged-toothed smiles sagging crookedly, and most of the visiting witches and witch wannabes have left town.

I'm Lee Barrett, nee Maralee Kowolski, thirty-two, red-haired and Salem born. I was orphaned early, married once and widowed young. I teach a course in television production at the Tabitha Trumbull Academy of the Arts—Salem's newest school. We call it "the Tabby." The sprawling building was once Trumbull's Department Store, back in the sixties before the shopping malls came. Tabitha Trumbull, the school's namesake, was the founder's wife.

I've worked in television, mostly in front of the camera, ever since graduating from Emerson College, but this was just my second year as a teacher. My lesson plan called for special emphasis on interview skills and investigative reporting. I'd been boning up on those topics myself, with the aid of a shelf filled with textbooks and some real-life investigation advice from my police detective boyfriend, Pete Mondello.

Early in September one of my students thought of a way to spice up the annual letdown that invariably follows Halloween and, at the same time, to fulfill our annual class assignment—producing a video involving some aspect of Salem's history. Hilda Mendez thought it might be fun to get the city involved in honoring *Dia de los Muertos,* the traditional Mexican celebration that takes place at the beginning of November.

"It's a happier holiday than Halloween," she said. "It celebrates all the cool stuff people enjoyed when they were alive—food and drinks and fancy clothes and parties. There are sugar skulls and paper skeletons and flowers at the gravesides and everybody has a good time." Hilda's enthusiasm was contagious. "Salem has such wicked cool cemeteries. Think about it! Close-ups of those really creepy headstones—the ones with the winged skeleton faces and the weird inscriptions. What great video!"

Therese Della Monica, a returning student (and a novice witch-in-training), chimed in. "I'm sure at least one of the old cemeteries is haunted. Maybe all of them!"

"I like it," I said. "Those cemeteries are historical sites for sure, and the whole celebration seems like a perfect fit for Salem. What do the rest of you think?"

I glanced around my classroom, located in what had been the mezzanine shoe department of the old

Trumbull's Department Store. Now a green screen, TV monitors, news desk and cameras—both rolling and stationary—shared space with vintage Thonet chairs, a lithographed cutout of Buster Brown and his dog, Tige, a neon macaw advertising Poll-Parrot shoes and a large half-model of a black patent-leather pump.

Two men and four women had signed up for the course. Therese was back for more behind-the-camera training, while Hilda and the others were new faces. The arts courses offered at the Tabby held attraction for people of all ages who'd always wanted to act, paint, dance, write or—as in the case of my classes—be involved in the world of television, either behind or in front of the camera.

My oldest students were a pair of identical twins, over the age of sixty-five—retired Boston police officers named Roger and Ray Temple—with aspirations of investigative reporting. The two not only dressed alike, but they often spoke in unison and/or finished each other's sentences. Quite disconcerting until you got used to it.

"Well," began Roger, "gotta go by the book here, y'know. Pull the right permits. Involve city hall."

"By the book," echoed Ray. "Can't just go around stomping through cemeteries, violating ordinances."

Shannon Dumas paused in midapplication of lip gloss. "Anybody can visit the graveyards. They even have tours you can go on." Shannon, at nineteen, was the youngest of the group and looked forward to a career as a television anchor. "Can we wear those great off-the-shoulder Mexican dresses? With all the gorgeous embroidery?"

The twins gave synchronized headshakes and arm foldings. Hilda nodded and Therese looked thoughtful.

The remaining woman in the class, Dorothy Alden, spoke softly. Too softly for the on-camera investigative-reporting role she seemed to be envisioning, but we were working on that. I leaned forward to catch her words.

"Maybe we could go on one of those tours Shannon was talking about?"

The suggestion was met with "yeah" and "good idea," and a simultaneous nod between the twins.

"I know one of the best guides," Therese said. "Want me to see if we can get a reservation for a private tour? Just us, no tourists?"

"A reservation is probably a good idea," I said. "The summer visitors have pretty much left, but the leaf-peepers are here now, and in a few weeks the Halloween mob will start showing up."

"It doesn't give us much time to plan if we're going to pull this off in November," said Hilda, "but it's not a supercomplicated event. We should be able to do it."

"We can involve the art department," Therese offered. "Maybe costumes and makeup too."

"Of course we'll need Mr. Pennington's approval," I said. "I'm sure he'll like the idea though."

Rupert Pennington was the director of the Tabby, and since last year's video project had scored the school a substantial federal grant, I was confident he'd okay the plan. Besides that, Mr. Pennington was dating my sixty-something ball-of-fire aunt, Isobel Russell. Aunt Ibby was the one who'd raised me after my parents died in a plane accident when I was five.

"How many cemeteries are there in Salem anyway?"

Shannon asked. "We ought to check them all out to be sure we pick the best one."

Hilda held up her smartphone. "There are ten," she said. "I already checked."

"We should probably narrow it down to the really old ones." Dorothy spoke a little louder this time.

Hilda nodded. "Yeah. The ones with the really creepy headstones."

"It's the Howard Street cemetery then, for sure." Therese's tone was firm. "It has the creepy headstones *and* it's definitely haunted."

"Haunted? Really?" Shannon's already-wide eyes grew even bigger.

The twins snorted in unison. "Nonsense," said Ray. "No such thing," Roger sputtered.

Therese smiled. "You'll see. Old Giles Corey is still there . . . floating around . . . touching people with his cold, dead hands." She waved her arms in the air, fixing the twins with a blue-eyed stare. "And it was the sheriff who tortured him to death. Piled rocks on the poor old man's chest until he suffocated, just because he wouldn't admit to being a witch." She dropped her voice to a whisper, still smiling. "Hey, you guys weren't sheriffs by any chance, were you?"

That brought firm headshakes of denial from the two.

Hilda snapped her fingers. "Hey! The cemetery covers the history angle and we can probably get some interviews from people who think they've been groped by a ghost."

"Then we can investigate the dumb ghost story," Ray said, "and debunk the whole thing."

Roger nodded. "That's real investigative reporting. Right, Ms. Barrett?"

"That's one way to look at it," I agreed. "It's a short ride over to Howard Street. What do you say we take a little field trip? Then we'll put together a proposal for Mr. Pennington."

The idea of a field trip, of spending time outside of a school building, is just as attractive to adult students as it is to little kids. Carpooling arrangements were hastily made. The twins would take Shannon with them in their Ford Crown Victoria, Hilda and Therese would ride in Hilda's Jeep, and Dorothy would come with me in my almost-new two-seater Stingray.

Since second-year student Therese had the most experience with camcorders, I entrusted her with one of the Tabby's new Panasonic shoulder-mounted models. "Therese, put on your director's hat. You're in charge." I could tell by her shy smile that she was pleased with the responsibility. "The rest of us can use our phones or personal cameras," I said. "This is just a preliminary exercise. A little 'show and tell' for Mr. Pennington."

In a more or less orderly fashion, we trooped from the classroom area to the mezzanine landing, where a life-sized portrait of the old store's founder, Oliver Wendell Trumbull, gazed benignly across the main floor of his once-upon-a-time retail kingdom. Together we clattered down the broad stairway, across the polished hardwood floor and through the glass doors onto Essex Street.

At the entrance to the Tabby's parking lot, we separated, each of us heading for his or her designated ride. I motioned for Dorothy to follow me to the Laguna Blue

'Vette, glad for the opportunity to spend a few one-on-one minutes with the soft-spoken young woman. She'd told us that she'd come to Salem from Alaska, but other than answering a few general questions about cold weather, northern lights, ice fishing and the presence of bears in her backyard, she'd shared very little information about herself.

"What a beautiful car." She gave the sweet curve of a rear fender a gentle pat and I noticed that her fingernails were bitten down to the quick. "Bet it's fast too," she murmured.

"Sure is," I said. "My late husband, Johnny Barrett, was a NASCAR driver. Got my love for big, speedy American cars from him."

She climbed into the passenger seat and I took my place behind the wheel.

"I'm sorry," she said, "about your husband. I know what it's like to lose someone you love."

I waited for her to continue—to tell me about her own loss. But she'd lapsed into silence, turning away from me, seemingly intent on the passing scenery. It had been three years since Johnny's death, but I still didn't like talking about it, so I could understand her not opening up. I searched for another topic as we approached the fenced-in green expanse of the Salem Common before she spoke again.

"It seems to me there ought to be sheep in there, enjoying all that nice grass."

"A few hundred years ago, I guess there were. But today the only livestock on the Common are the squirrels and, of course, dogs chasing Frisbees."

"Do you have a dog?"

"Nope. No dog. Just a big yellow cat. Do you?" I smiled, thinking of O'Ryan, the very special cat who shared the big house on Winter Street with Aunt Ibby and me. O'Ryan is far from being an ordinary housecat. He once belonged to a witch—her "familiar," some say. In Salem, a witch's familiar is to be respected—and sometimes feared.

"I have several dogs, back in Alaska," she said. "They're quite necessary for transportation."

"Transportation?" Surprise showed in my voice. "You mean like dogsleds? Mush? Like that?"

She laughed. "I guess I didn't mention that I've been living 'off the grid,' as they say, for several years."

"Wow." I was seriously impressed. "I've never met anyone who did that before. No TV? No indoor plumbing? No electricity?"

"That's about it," she said as we turned onto Howard Street and moved slowly downhill toward the cemetery. She leaned forward in her seat as staggered rows of tombstones came into view. "And as soon as I've learned what you can teach me about conducting an investigation, I'll be heading back to Alaska."

"I'll do my best," I said. "I think you'll find the course useful. Are you planning a TV-reporting career up there?"

Again, the soft laugh. "Hell no. I just think your class might save me some time in figuring out who murdered my sister."

ACKNOWLEDGMENTS

While writing the Witch City Mysteries, I think so often of my growing-up years in the magical city of Salem. Names of friends, classmates, acquaintances come popping up from the way-back machine and find their way into each manuscript. So I'd like to acknowledge some of the names, culled from memories and the rich tapestry of nationalities and cultures of the Witch City and nearby Cape Ann.

Thank you to the bearers of some of the names I've so liberally borrowed, in no particular order: Kowalski, Litka, Mondello, Della Monica, Dowgin, Russell, Murphy, McKenna, Greene, Wilkins, Whaley, Sullivan, Lalonde.

No doubt, there'll be more to come!